中英語頭韻詩の繰返し技巧と連語
Repetition and Collocation in Middle English Alliterative Verse

守屋靖代
Yasuyo Moriya

Swarte smekyd smeþes smateryd wyth smoke; dryue me to deth
wyth den of here dyntes; Swech noys on nyghtys herd men
neuer; What knauene cry & clateryng of knockes; þe cammede
kongons cryen after col col; & blowen here bellewys, þat al here
brayn brestes; huf puf seyth þat on, haf paf þat oþir; Þei spyttyn
& spraulyn & spellyn many spelles; Þei gnauen & gnacchen
þei gronys togydere; and holdyn hem hote wyth here hard hameres
of a bole hyde ben here barm fellys; here schankes ben schakeled
for þe fere flunderys; heuy hameres þei han & hard ben handled
stark strokes þei stryken on a stelyd stokke; lus bus las das.
rowtyn be rowe; Swech dolful a dreme þe deuyl it to dryue;
þe mayster longyth a lityl & lascheth a lesse; twyneth hem tweyn
and towcheth a treble; tik tak hic hac tiket taket tyk tak
lus bus lus das; swych lyf þei ledyn; Alle cloþemerys
cryst hem gyue sorwe; may no man for brenwaterys on nyght
han hys   rest:-

Much glam and gle glent vp þerinne
Aboute þe fyre vpon flet, and on fele wyse
At þe soper and after, mony aþel songez,
As coundutes of Krystmasse and carolez newe
With al þe manerly merþe þat mon may of. telle.
　　　Sir Gawain and the Green Knight ll. 1652-56

　　　　　　　　　　　　湧き出づる　　歓喜の調べ
　　　　　　　　　　　　炉辺(ろべ)の火は　赫々(あかあか)と燃え
　　　　　　　　　　　　尽きもせず　　宴(うたげ)のさざめき
　　　　　　　　　　　　歌あまた　　　聖夜を祝(ほ)ぎて
　　　　　　　　　　　　その盛り　　　言わむ術(すべ)なし
　　　　　　　　　　　　　　　　　　（translation by YM）

はじめに

　本書は、中英語頭韻詩 (Middle English Alliterative Verse) を現代言語学と伝統的書誌文献学を融合した韻律研究方法により、リズム、音韻、文体等と関連づけながら、国内及び国際学会で研究発表をすると共に、国内外の学術誌に研究論文として発表して来たデータと議論を、集大成とするには未完であるが、リサーチの枠組みとデータ集積の途中経過を公にすることでその意義を問うものである。中英語頭韻詩の韻律は複雑で、その法則がどのようなものであったか統一見解は未だ得られていないが、頭韻の制約の中で、音の繰返しの意義と、語の組み合わせ、すなわち連語 (collocation) が文芸手法として果たす役割を分析することでその複雑な韻律に共通するテンプレートと作品ごとの特徴や違いを解明できるのではないかという試みである。言葉による遊びが英詩の伝統が形成されるなかでどのようにして文芸にまで高められていったか解明を試みる端緒となるものである。

　従って本書は大きく分けて、英語における音の繰返しから始めて頭韻詩の韻律と技巧を概観し主立った作品の分析を議論する本文 (第1章〜第7章)、文献リスト、主立った9編の中英語頭韻詩の分析資料、の3つから成っている。データの収集は以下のように行った。電子テクストとして入手できるものは、コンピュータ上に移し、行ごとに音韻と文法構成の情報をインプットして第一段階のデータベースとした。電子テクストで入手できないものは、印刷されたテクストをスキャンするなどして電子化し、第一段階のデータベースに整えた。更に古英語辞書、中英

語辞書、コンコーダンス、*The Oxford English Dictionary* などを用いて頭韻やストレス位置、語順等についてマークし、定型表現が頭韻音、語順、語の組み合わせから検索できるコーパスを作成した。中英語頭韻詩において行の後半が韻律を決定する重要な働きを担うという Cable, Duggan, Oakden らの先行研究に従い、1) 全行、2) 前半行と後半行の間の構成、3) 後半行の構成、4) 後半行の連語、5) 全体の韻律の5点について主立った作品約 22,000 行について詳細なデータを得た。分析の着眼点およびその意義については第4章以下で詳しく述べる。

　中英語は現代英語へつながる過渡期の言語として重要な位置を占めるものであるが、複雑な音韻変化、語形変化の単純化、おびただしい数のロマンス語語彙の借用など言語自体複雑な様相を呈するうえ、ヨーロッパの歴史的社会的背景がさまざまに絡み、古英語より解明が難しいとされている。そのため、中英語頭韻詩の韻律研究は、古英語頭韻詩の韻律ほどには研究者の合意を見ていない。伝統的な文学研究の方式や、現代言語学のルールをあてはめて音韻論の研究方法等が用いられて来たが、近年国内外の研究者が強い関心を寄せているのが、コーパスを用いて頻度の分類から研究する方法である。先に韻律や語の組み合わせの基準を定めるのではなく、実際の現象を詳細にわたって分析し、全体の傾向から基になるテンプレートを導き出し、個々の行、また作品ごとに、忠実にルールに従うものと、そうでないものとに区別してその意義と役割を考えるアプローチである。このアプローチに従って、繰返し登場する一定の語の組み合わせに注目し、それぞれの作品の中で特定の連語が韻律とどのような関係にあるかを解明してコーパスを作成した。書き言葉を前提とした中英語頭韻詩ではあるが、声に出して読むことが依然前提とされていた当時において、繰返しを好み、さまざまな技巧を駆使して独自のリズムを生み出した頭韻詩の詩人たちは、斬新的な技巧と古くからの伝統の両方をどのように取り入れ、韻律の遵守と逸脱をどのように展開したかを解明すれば、中世英語における文芸の意義を再確認し、また英語史研究にも貢献することができると考えたからである。似通った表現を集め、音韻と統語の関係を明らかにし、個々の作品の特徴と全体に共通するテンプレートを明示することで13世紀から15世紀のあいだ

に英語文芸活動が頭韻詩において表現しようとした繰返し表現の意味と言語変化を再構築することができるであろう。

　日本における中英語頭韻詩研究は、同時代の詩人チョーサーに関する研究ほど広く知られてはいないが、多数ではないにしろ、優秀な研究者によってその意義が論じられて来た。欧米の学会では、中英語頭韻詩の研究は、英語の言語の特徴、アングロ・サクソン以来の文化を受け継ぐ表現として重要な分野と認識されており、研究者の数も多い。電子テクストやコーパスの広がりにより、日本にいながら資料の入手がたやすくなったとはいえ、現代の日本で研究する者に時として立ちはだかる時空の隔たりを乗り越えて、どのような学問的貢献が可能か、本書はひとつの試みを示唆するものでもある。データが複雑で詳細なものになり、これを引き続き利用しやすい形に整え、最終的に著書としてまとめるためには、更に時間を要する。精緻な分析を助けるデータを揃え、中英語の特徴に合わせた使い方ができるようデータベースを整えることと、それを基にこれまでの研究の集大成として中英語頭韻詩について韻律と連語の関連を解明したいと考えている。21世紀を迎え、文学、言語学、フィロロジーにおける日本人研究者の緻密な学びがこれからは世界に発信され、研究成果が世界に知られていくであろう。この研究がその流れの一部となって難解とされる中英語頭韻詩韻律の理解がさらに深まればと願う。

目　次

はじめに	3
第1章　繰返しの役割	11
第2章　英語のリズムと頭韻	17
第3章　14世紀頭韻詩の技巧	24
第4章　中英語頭韻詩における繰り返しのリズムと連語	36
第5章　*The Alliterative Morte Arthure* における名詞で終わる後半行の連語	54
第6章　*The Alliterative Morte Arthure* における韻律と連語	60
第7章　*Sir Gawain and the Green Knight* における韻律と連語	76
むすび	89
Select Bibliography	91
Notes to the Data	107
Data	113
Wynnere and Wastoure	115
(Stage One, Stage Two, Stage Three, Stage Four)	
Saint Erkenwald	144
The Parlement of the Thre Ages	150
The Siege of Jerusalem	160
Patience	178
Cleanness	186
Sir Gawain and the Green Knight	212
The Alliterative Morte Arthure	241
The Wars of Alexander	270
あとがき	299

中英語頭韻詩の繰返し技巧と連語

第1章

繰返しの役割

　英語特有のリズムは一朝一夕に出来上がったものではなく、449年のアングロ・サクソン人のブリテン島上陸を英語史の始まりとすれば、1500年の歳月の中で起こったさまざまな変化や他言語との接触を経て形成され、そして今も変化の直中にある。近年、英語音韻論の進展により、英語のリズム、特に metrical phonology, English prosody 等の分野で英語特有のリズムはどのようにして成り立っているかが明らかにされて来た。この章が目的とするところは、ゲルマン語の特徴を充分に備えていた古英語から始めて、中英語、殊に14世紀までの音韻変化を、頭韻詩の変遷を辿ることで、英語のリズムがどのように形成されたかを考察することである。具体的には、ゲルマン語が好んだ頭韻詩のリズム、語順、韻律などがどのように変化し、現代においても芸術や娯楽、広告、ジャーナリズムにおいて効果的に用いられることも考慮し、中英語頭韻詩から分かる英語特有の音の組み合わせ、繰返しについて考察する。

　英語に限らずどの言語においても、同じ音の繰返しは、強調や言葉遊び等の特別な役割を担う。ゲルマン語に属する英語においては伝統的に頭韻が用いられたが、脚韻の使用もあり、ロマンス語の影響が濃くなると脚韻は更に頻繁に使われた。頭韻は、強勢音節の頭につく同音の子音を、韻文であれば一行内で、散文であれば繰返しと認識できる句や節の範囲内で数度繰り返すことであり、脚韻は語尾の母音と子音を揃えて繰り返すことである。詩ではなくとも、この頭韻、脚韻による同一音の繰返しは英語文化に深く根づき、特別な役割を果たしている。例えば、自

然の発話ではあり得ないような例ではあるが、(1)のような文を聞いたときには誰でもが何かおもしろみを感じるであろうし、この文を口に出して言う際には、英語のリズムに忠実に発話しなければ、おもしろみが活かされない。

(1) She sells seashells down by the seashore.

この文に使われている7語中4語が /s/ 音で始まっており、*seashells, seashore* という複合語はゲルマン語のルールにより最初の音節に強勢音節を持つことから、否が応でも最初の /s/ 音が強調される。英語の自然な発話としては以下のような強勢音節の置き方が一般的であろう。

(1)' She sélls séashells dówn by the séashore.

数人が声を揃えて同一文を読み上げるときには、その言語のリズムの根幹となるルールを使わなければ揃わない、すなわち、ある言語のリズムの根幹を知るためには、数人に声を揃えて読んでもらう unled choral reading が有効であると Boomsliter et al. は述べている。Boomsliter et al. の実験では、グループで声を揃えてナーサリー・ライム、ディッケンソンの詩、テニソンの詩などを朗読させ、リズムがどのように強調されるかを観察した。声を揃えて朗読する際には、その言語特有のリズムに忠実に読み、特に英語では強勢音節の位置を強調しないと揃わないことを証明した実験である。(1) も数人で一緒に読んでもらうと頭韻と強勢音節が強調されていかにも英語らしいリズムをかもし出す。/s/ の音に影響されて、*seashells, seashore* の *-shells, -shore* にも強勢音節が置かれる可能性もある。

脚韻は、詩にも頻繁に登場するが、格言などにも使われる。

(2) Early to bed and early to rise
    Makes a man healthy wealthy and wise.

(2) の格言では、*rise* と *wise* の脚韻がまず耳に残るが、early to... という句の繰返し、*makes a man* に見られる頭韻、*healthy, wealthy* という語に見られる脚韻、そして *wealthy and wise* の /w/ による頭韻など、いくつもの繰返しによって全体が覚え易く、耳と記憶に残るような音の構成になっている。語の始めか終わりかによって頭韻、脚韻と区別されるが、表れる場所は異なっても、同一音の繰返しは、単なる意味の伝達という機能を超えて言葉が果たす特別な役割を表している。同一構造を持つように聞こえる *early to bed, early to rise* であるが、実は to の後に名詞と動詞という異なる品詞がおかれることは興味深い。言葉は単なる情報の伝達のためだけにあるのではなく、それが使われる文化を反映するものとして深く根づいているということである。頭韻や脚韻を使うことで洒落た言い回しになったり、覚え易くなったり、またおおげさな表現になったりということを使い手も聞き手も楽しむのである。人間の言語の最も重要な機能は、コミュニケーションにあると言われるが、そのコミュニケーションの内容は事実の伝達だけでなく、さまざまな広がりを見せるのであり、機能だけで考えれば一見不必要に思われる句、節の繰返しが、実はその言語のスピーチ・コミュニティにとってはアイデンティティに直結する役割を担っていると言えるだろう。頭韻や脚韻を認識し評価、享受することはその言語の根幹を知っていなければ不可能であることから、このような繰返しの機能が言語を決定する中核にあたることが分かる。

言語のリズムについて論じるとき、繰返しはどの言語にも見られる普遍的なものであるということがどちらかと言うと否定的な評価を伴って説明される。(3)に掲げる例は、全く同一の語を繰返しているために、普段使いの、または子供が使うような言い回しを多く含んでいる。洗練されていない、幼稚、素朴だと評価される例である。

(3)　yum-yum; tum-tum; cous-cous; bon-bon

このような言い方は、繰り返す必要がないと思われたり、繰返しの一部が確たる意味を持たなかったりすることから、人間の言語の原始的な

部分、動物と人間を区別する境目を反映しているということがよく言われる (Barber, p. 26-27; Sadowski, p. 38)。言語が使われ始めたときには理屈や理由よりも原始的な必要性から繰返しを用いたという説である。*mama, dada, papa* などを子供が早い時期に覚えるのは原始的な言い方であり発話し易いからであるとする。Crystal (p. 289) によれば言語起源説には、pooh-pooh theory, yo-he-ho theory 等が論じられて来たが、そのどれも言語の始まりと決定的必然性を解明するには至っていない。

しかし、同一語でなく、同じ音で始まり語尾の音が異なる組み合わせであれば、さほど野蛮ではなく、むしろ日常的に使われる言葉にも多く見られることが分かる。すなわち、全く同一のシラブルを繰り返す *yum-yum* のような reduplication は高尚とはみなされないが、(4) に掲げるような一部が異なった似通った表現は関心を惹いたりおもしろいと受けとめられる。このような例は日常語のなかに見られる頭韻による繰返しを含む表現をまとめたものであるが、*Alcoholics Anonymous* や *clean cut* は、素朴でもないしまた詩的でもない。ただ強勢音節を持つ語頭のシラブルが同一音で始まることで語頭が強調され、ゲルマン語の伝統以来語頭にアクセントを置くという英語のリズムの根幹が反映されているために注意をひく。このような繰返しは jingles (Meredith, pp. 45-47, pp. 95-98) と呼ばれ、音の繰返しが果たすことのできる機能のひとつである。

(4) Alcoholics Anonymous; American Automobile Association; best buy; clean cut; Coca-Cola; cozy corner; Donald Duck; frequent flyer; good grief; Mickey Mouse; Mighty Mouse; no nonsense; proof positive; quite a quandary; Sesame Street; sweet sixteen; University of Utah; Yale Yuppi

普段の常套句にも同様の例が見られる。似たような音、同意語を繰り返す、redundant な表現を多用するという特徴を英語は持つ。

(5) bruised and battered; fire and flood; hale and hardy; might and main;

safe and sane; tattered and torn; wear and tear

helter-skelter, hoity-toity, hurdy-gurdy, hurly-burly, hodge-podge 等 を引いて、このような繰返しは /h/ で始まる例が多いと Meredith は述べている (p. 183)。脚韻の例も枚挙に暇がないが、(6) のような例が日常語からの例として挙げられる。

(6)　helter-skelter; hodge-podge; nitty-gritty; super-duper

　英語ではないが、ラテン語の "Veni, vidi, vici."（来た、見た、勝った）も、アカデミアでよく言われる "Publish or perish."（研究成果を出版しなければ消え去るのみ）という言い方も、頭韻と脚韻の両方が巧みに使われて linguistic gew-gaws を形成しているからこそ印象に残るのであろう。
　古英語時代から音の繰返しは世俗的なものにも詩的なものにも使用された。頭韻のリズムは特に普段の言葉、土着の文化として好まれ、アングロ・サクソン人にはその分かりやすさが言葉遊びを楽しむ道具となった。言語は機能面だけでなく、言葉遊び、言葉による芸術という形で特別な役割を担っている。恣意的に選ばれた音の組み合わせというより、その言語が好む、Smith が phonaesthesia (2000, p. 95) と呼ぶ特別な音の組み合わせが存在する、ということである。Sadowski は、言語の意味を、emotive, iconic, arbitrary の三つに分類し、Smith は sound-symbolism として onomatopoeia と phonaesthesia を挙げる。これらの分類が的確か、またどちらが本質をついているかはここでは論じないが、音と意味には時によって必然的な関係があることは確かである。その最たる表れが頭韻や脚韻の頻用である。子供の歌や世俗の歌も元は原始的な成り立ちであったと言われるが、そこにも英語が好む繰返しが登場する。英語でよく引き合いに出されるナーサリー・ライムを (7) に掲げる。短い数行の間に頭韻と脚韻が繰り返され印象に残り易い言い回しになっている。

(7)　To market, to market, to buy a fat pig,
　　　Home again, home again, jiggety-jig;
　　　To market, to market, to buy a fat hog,
　　　Home again, home again, jiggety-jog.

　このように、音と意味には時によって必然的な関係があることは確かである。このような繰返しは、英語の音やリズムの成り立ちとどのように関わって、英語独特の響きを作り出すのか、次の節で考察する。

第2章

英語のリズムと頭韻

　第1章で掲げた日常語だけでなく、芸術として高められた英詩においても頭韻、脚韻は頻繁に登場する。伝統的なゲルマンの頭韻は古英語の時代から用いられて来たが、中英語に入ってからはロマンス語の影響で脚韻への傾倒が一層顕著になる。チョーサーは大陸の華々しい貴族文化を英語に巧みに取り入れ中英語の頂点となった詩人であるが、カンタベリー物語において(8)のように頭韻詩を揶揄している。

(8)　But trusteth wel, I am a Southren man,
　　　I kan nat geeste 'rum, ram, ruf,' by lettre,
　　　　　　　　　　　　　　　　　(*The Canterbury Tales* X.42f)

　自分は南の人間であるから、"rum, ram, ruf"というような野暮な頭韻を使った *geeste* (jest) など使いませんのでね、と頭韻詩を見下している。
　現代言語学の理論や分析方法が言語芸術にも用いられるようになると、普段の言語と詩の言語がどのように異なるか、またどのように似通っているかが解明されるようになった (Fabb; Freeborn 1996; Furniss and Bath: Jakobson; Jespersen; Schaefer; Smith 1999, 2000)。Minkova (2003, p. 270) の言うように、"Alliterative meter is a repetitive mode of composition utilizing reduplication of the same word-initial sounds" であり、この reduplication は普段の言葉でも言葉による遊び、洒落として使わ

れるが、前述の *Donald Duck* や *hodge-podge* という言い回しは高尚だとか芸術的だとかは思われないだろう。そうすると、頭韻詩を日常の言語や単なる繰返しと区別して芸術的と感じさせる要素は一体何か、という問いが生じる。すなわち、芸術的と感じる頭韻詩には日常の繰返しを超えるどのような要素が働いているかという問いである。英語においては頭韻が日常語のリズムを直接に表す方法として用いられたが、語頭の音の繰返しは、barbarian, illiterate, uncultured, pagan 等という言葉で表されるような根幹の土着のリズムを呼び覚ます。しかし、そのような否定的な評価にも拘わらず、Bloomfield and Dunn (pp. 1 - 6) が述べているように、頭韻は耳に心地よく記憶に残り易い。だからこそ、今日でも広告や新聞記事の見出しに頻用される。

　英語のスピーチ・リズムは、シラブル構成と、一般的に強勢音節と弱勢音節に二分されるストレスによって成り立つ。英語のいわゆる stress を、アクセントと称することがあるが、American accent, British accent というように、アクセントは方言の違いを指すこともあるため、本書ではストレスという用語を用いる。シラブルは核になる母音の前後に子音が組み合わされているが、子音の数とその組み合わせ方が複雑という特徴を持つ。以下は英語のシラブルの模式図である。

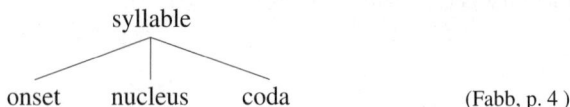

(Fabb, p. 4)

Onset, peak, coda を同レベルで扱わず、以下のような hierarchy で考える研究者もある。

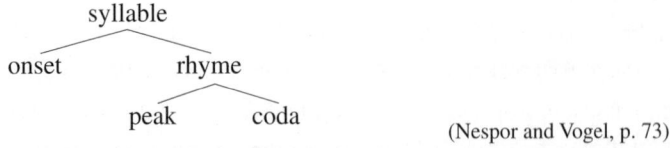

(Nespor and Vogel, p. 73)

　シラブル形成には peak とも称される nucleus が不可欠であるが、onset, coda はなくてもよい。可能な組み合わせは (9) に掲げたとおりであ

る。

(9)
	onset	peak	coda
oh	ø	oh	ø
go	g	o	ø
oat	ø	oa	t
goat	g	oa	t

このように、シラブルには nucleus となる母音の前後に子音が optional に組み合わされ、語を形成する。

(10)
peak	*a, I,* etc.
peak + coda	*us, end, east,* etc.
onset + peak	*go, three, shy, straw,* etc.
onset + peak + coda	*map, take, smart, strength,* etc.

子音は最大 onset に3つ、coda に4つが可能であり、(11) は、onset の子音数が左から1、2、3の例である。

(11)　　<u>r</u>ay　　　<u>pr</u>ay　　　<u>spr</u>ay

一方、coda は最大4つまで子音を重ねることができる。

(12)　　spa　　top　　a<u>pt</u>　　ar<u>ched</u>　　si<u>xths</u>

また、*sub<u>scr</u>ibe, con<u>str</u>uct* のように affix により中間で子音が4つ重なるということも可能である (Haugen, p. 218)。*Five-<u>sixths</u> <u>str</u>awberry pie* という句の下線部には、実際の発話では省略される音もあるが理論上は連続で7つの子音が含まれていることになる。Word boundary をまたがって子音が多数重なることも英語の大きな特徴である。

　言語の類型を考える際、主たるリズムの要素がストレスによるかシラ

ブルによるかで区別することがある。英語は stress-timing languages の代表、日本語、ヨルバ語などは、syllable-timed languages と呼ばれる。リズムの最小単位がストレスを持つシラブルによるのか、均等の長さのシラブルによるのかでリズムの根本が異なるという考え方である。(13)で示した例で、一般的なストレスの箇所に ´ を置いて示す。

(13)　páper　　　　báby　　　　　éarnest　　　péople
　　　amúse　　　　betwéen　　　 exchánge　　towárds
　　　argumentátion　methodólogy　certificáte

　強弱の位置は分かりやすいようでいて、実際の発話においては実は簡単ではない。1 音節以上の音節を持つ機能語 (into, although, many, every 等) やロマンス系の長い単語、複合語などは、前後のストレスによってストレスレベルが簡単に変化し、ストレスが失われる、あるいは弱勢音節がストレスを持つことがあるからである。すなわち英語のストレスはそのシラブルが置かれた環境により、句の hierarchy の中で前後のシラブルとの関係によりその強弱を変化させることができる。Primary stress, secondary stress という用語が用いられるのも英語のストレスが隣接するシラブルとの関係により違うレベルに動くことを反映している。機能語 (the, of 等) でない単音節の語、例えば three、map 等には、当然ストレスの場所は一箇所しかないが、二音節やそれ以上の音節の単語は、大体のストレス位置は決まっていても、環境により変化の可能性がある。例えば (14) のように、同じ thirteen という語が、後に来るシラブルのストレスにより異なるストレスの位置を示すことが知られている。

(14)　thírteen élephants　　　　thirtéen repórters

　このように、英語のストレスの位置は絶対的ではなく、前語のシラブルとの相対関係によるという特徴を持つ。強弱の繰返しをできるだけ均一に保ちたいという英語のリズムはこの相対的ストレスにより可能に

なっている。英語の stress-timing は、mobile stress により成り立っているのである。

　強弱の繰返しをできるだけ均一にしたい、ということは、強勢音節が間に弱勢音節を挟むことなく続く、あるいは弱勢音節だけが続く、ということが特別な意味や強調になるということを意味する。強勢音節だけが続き、間に弱勢音節が入らないと特別なリズムをかもし出す。(15) に掲げた人名は強勢音節のみで構成され、間に弱勢音節なしに並ぶふたつの単音節語が強調される。

(15)　　Géorge Búsh　　Tóm Crúise　　Brád Pítt　　Bíll Gátes

　一方、*Leonárdo DiCáprio, Bárack Obáma* は、*Bárack* を除いてアクセントの位置が語頭にないため、土着の感が薄い。アングロ・サクソンの土着のリズムは、ストレスがどのように配置されるかで強くなるが、アングロ・サクソン系の単語全てにアクセントを置いて強調が可能である。例えば、"We will cáll you." という文は、普通の発話では、ストレスは *call* にのみ置かれるが、(16) のポピュラーソングでは一語一語にストレスが置かれることで特異なリズムを創り出す。

(16)　　Wé wíll, wé wíll róck yóu.

　このような英語のリズムの特徴は、古英語時代から存在していた。ゲルマン詩の頭韻リズムで書かれた *Cædmon's Hymn* はその一例である。1行に4つの強勢音節が含まれ、各半行の最初のシラブルが頭韻を踏むというのが基本のルールであった。強弱のリズムを一定に保つゲルマンの伝統である。

(17)　Nū wē sculon herigean　　heonfonrīces Weard,
　　　Meotodes meahte　　　　ond his mōdgeþanc,
　　　weorc Wuldorfæder,　　　swā hē wundra gehwæs,
　　　ēce Drihten,　　　　　　　ōr onstealde.

> Hē ǣrest sceōp　　　eorðan bearnum
> heofon tō hrōfe,　　　hālig Scyppend.
> Þā middangeard　　　monncynnes Weard,
> ēce Dryhten,　　　　æfter tēode
> fīrum foldan,　　　　Frēa ælmihtig.

　古英語詩の韻律は、1行に4つの強勢音節で成り立ち、各半行の最初の強勢音節が頭韻を踏むという、純粋に accentual rhythm に基づいたものであった。この頭韻詩のリズムは、その非日常的な同一音の繰返しと強勢音節の特別な強調により闘いのシーンや英雄の活躍等ドラマチックな描写において特に効果的であった。*Cædmon's Hymn* を例に引いて古英語頭韻詩韻律を Treharne and Yu は以下のように説明している。

> . . . alliteration occurs on stressed syllables; that is, on the important and emphatic words in the verse-line. The poetry can be described as two half-lines (*a* and *b*), each linked by the alliteration which runs across the verse-line . . . the caesura in the middle represents the break between the two half-lines: the natural pause for added emphasis.

　古英語から中英語に至る時期、頭韻詩の伝統はすたれたかと思われるほど作品が少ない。しかし、14世紀になって、主にイングランド中部地方を中心に頭韻詩は新たな展開を見る。音韻変化やロマンス語の影響等で、頭韻詩のリズム自体に大きな変化が起こり、1行あたりの強勢音節数が4または5と広がった。中英語頭韻詩の枠組みは、4つの強勢音節を持つ行であれば、最初の3つが頭韻を踏み、半行の間には古英語詩ほどの明らかな区切りはない。Burrow and Turville-Petre (pp. 58-59) による説明は以下のとおりである。

> In the later fourteenth century alliterative poetry flourished in the hands of some remarkable poets of the West and North-West Midlands. They are represented . . . by William Langland, the *Gawain*-poet, and the au-

thor of *St. Erkenwald*. . . . Each line is divided into half-lines bound together by alliteration. Each half-line normally has two stressed syllables; the two stresses of the first half-line alliterate with the first stress of the second half-line, while the last stress does not alliterate. So with *a* standing for 'alliteration', the standard alliterative pattern is denoted *aa/ax*.

　古英語も中英語も、それぞれ特有の頭韻詩韻律を用いて、言葉の遊びを芸術に高めようとしたのであった。頭韻詩の持つ linguistic vigor がどのように14世紀の詩人たちにより新たな展開を見たのか、次の章から具体的な検討を始める。

第3章

14世紀頭韻詩の技巧

　14世紀に盛んに作られるようになった頭韻詩は、alliterative revival と称されるが、頭韻詩の伝統は消滅しなかったのだから、alliterative survival, renewal, reflourishing 等の呼び方も提唱されている (Bennett; Everett; Huntsuman-Mc; Lawton 1982; Moorman; Pearsall 1981; Salter)。用語は何であれ再び盛んになった背景には、古英語から中英語への変化により、古英語時代の頭韻詩とは違った韻律の仕組みが作用している。例えば、ゲルマンのルールにより語頭にあったストレスが、ロマンス語の影響で後ろへ移動したり、格変化の簡素化や代わって頻度の増した前置詞等により、英語のリズム自体変化の中にあった。更に、スカンジナビア語、ロマンス語から大量の語彙が流入し、語頭を同一子音で揃えるのに、外来語を用い、ストレスの位置を元の言語に従ったりゲルマン式に読むなどして、頭韻詩はさまざまな新しい技巧を見せるようになった。ロンドンではチョーサーを中心にロマンス詩型が流行したが、中部地方では頭韻詩が好まれたのは、頭韻詩の持つアングロ・サクソン以来の力強いリズムによるだろう。

　頭韻詩韻律と技巧については、守屋 (2006b) で説明したが、第4章以降必要な情報を含むので、そこで取り上げた以外の作品で行数の比較的多い4作品、*The Wars of Alexander (A), The Parlement of the Thre Ages (AG), The Siege of Jerusalem (J), The Alliterative Morte Arthure (MA)* から例を引きながら概略を説明する。頭韻パターンは行の後に [ ] に入れて示し、*a* は頭韻を踏む強勢音節、*x* は頭韻を踏まない強勢音節を表

第 3 章　14 世紀頭韻詩の技巧

す。(18) に掲げたものが基本例である。以降 Attridge (1982) に従い、頭韻詩韻律中で強勢音節となるシラブルを metrical beats、弱勢音節となるシラブルを metrical offbeats と称する。

(18)
A 872	*Bl*ischis vp to the *b*erne, and *br*aste out at grete.	[aaax]
AG 1	In the *m*onethe of *M*aye when *m*irthes bene fele,	[aaax]
J 1	In *T*iberyus *t*yme the *tr*ewe emperour	[aaax]
MA 196	Than *cr*anes and *c*urlues *cr*aftyly rosted,	[aaax]

頭韻は同一子音の繰返しであるが、母音同士は同一頭韻、/h/ と母音も同一頭韻とみなされる。古英語では子音群、例えば /str/ は同じ /str/ としか頭韻を踏むとみなされなかったが、中英語では、/s/ で始まればどんな子音群でも頭韻とみなされるようになった。中英語頭韻詩は 1 行に 4 つまたは 5 つの metrical beats を持つが、この 4 つまたは 5 つということがそのリズムを複雑にしている。第 1 章の終りでも例を引いたが、ナーサリー・ライム等普段の生活に密着しているものは 4 つのリズムで構成されることが多い。

(19)　　Ráin, ráin, gó awáy,
　　　　Cóme agáin anóther dáy,
　　　　Ráin, ráin, gó to Spáin.
　　　　Néver shów your fáce agáin.

4 は 2 で割れるので単純明快なリズムを創り出す。4 のリズムと 5 のリズムの違いを Attridge (1995, p. 159) は例を引いて説明している。(20) の (a) は 4 のリズム、(b) は 5 のリズムである。

(20)
(a)　　　Had I the store in younder mountain
　　　　Where gold and silver are had for counting,

>   I could not count for the thought of thee,
>   My eyes so full I could not see.
> (b)   Had I the store in the cave of younder mountain
>   Where precious gold and silver are had for counting,
>   I would not be able to count for the thought of thee,
>   My eyes so full I would scarcely be able to see.

　(20-a) には 4 × 4 構造の rhythmic swing が顕著であり、数人で声を揃えて読めばその特徴が強調される。(20-b) はひとつ metrical beat が増えたことで単純な区分ができなくなり、unled choral reading は (20-a) に比べて格段に難しくなる。5 のリズムは、今の英語のスピーチ・リズムをより忠実に反映していると Attridge は述べているが、4 のリズムより日常語に近い印象を与える。この 5 のリズムを時折使うことは、単調さを解消するという解釈も可能であろう (Kane)。この普段使いの言葉に歩み寄った韻律の枠組みの中でどのような音の繰返しが凝らされたのか、以下にその技巧を列挙する。

　まず、4つの metrical beats を持つ行は最初の3つが頭韻を踏むという (18) で見た4のリズムの基本型に加えて、5のリズムによる行の例を挙げる。5つの metrical beats がある場合、前半行 (*a*-verse) に3つという例が圧倒的であり、(21) のようにその3つが頭韻を踏む場合は特に基本型の2つの metrical beats で読むのは難しい。

(21)

A 1	When *f*olk ere *f*estid and *f*ed, *f*ayn wald thai here	[aaaax]
AG 505	And *W*awayne *w*ondres of this *w*erke, and *w*endes bylyve	
		[aaaax]
J 369	The *b*urnes *b*usken out of *b*urwe *b*ounden alle twelf	
		[aaaax]
*MA*1287	Palaisez *p*roudliche *p*yghte, that *p*alyd ware ryche,	[aaaax]

　また、(22) の例のように全ての metrical beats が頭韻を踏むことがあ

る。同一音の繰返しは日常の言い回しを超えて特異なものになっている。

(22)

A 134	Vn-*w*etandly to any *w*ee, that *w*ont in his *w*anes.	[aaaa]
AG 70	And I *sl*itte hym at the a*s*saye to *s*ee how me *s*emyde,	[aaaa]
J 598	As *h*ail froward *h*euen *h*epe ouer *o*ther	[aaaa]
MA 239	Bot the *s*oueraingne *s*othely, for *s*olauce of hym *s*eluen,	[aaaa]

古英語頭韻詩では、子音が重なるときには同一の組み合わせしか頭韻とみなされなかったが、この伝統は中英語頭韻詩にも見られないわけではない。

(23)

A 1347	A *g*rowen *g*rape of a *g*rype, a *g*rete and a rype,	[aaaax]
AG 147	Of *st*iewardes, of *st*orrours, *st*irkes to bye,	[aaax]
J 658	*Br*osten the *br*itages and the *br*ode toures	[aaax]
MA 1479	Wyth *pr*ekers the *pr*oudeste that to the *pr*esse lengez.	[aaax]

(24) に掲げるのは最初の子音が同一であれば次の子音は異なっても頭韻を踏むとされる例である。頭韻パターンとしてはこのような自由な組み合せの方が圧倒的に多い。/f/, /g/, /k/, /p/, /s/, /t/ などは次に異なる子音が来ても頭韻を踏むとみなされる。

(24)

A 334	Thus *p*assis he fra the *p*lace, to *p*roue his sleʒtis,	[aaax]
AG 372	And *Fl*orydase full *fr*eschely *f*oundes hym aftir,	[aaax]
J 244	For *c*omfort of the *cl*oth he *cr*ied wel loude	[aaax]
MA 782	He *b*altyrde, he *bl*eryde, he *br*aundyschte therafter;	[aaax]

(25) は十二使徒の名前を組み込むのに頭韻を工夫している例である。このような意味と音が巧みに組み合わさって強調される例はどの作品にも見られる。

(26)

J 141	Peter James and Jon and Jacob the ferthe	
J 142	And the fifthe of his felawys Phelip was hoten	
J 143	The sixte Symond was caled and the seueth eke	
J 144	Bertholomewe that his bone neuer breke nolde	
J 145	The eyʒt man was Mathu that is myche yloued	
J 146	Tadde and Tomas her ben ten euen	
J 147	And Andreu the elleueth that auntred hym myche	
J 148	Byfor princes to preche was Petrus brother	
J 149	The laste man was vnlele and luther of his dedis	
J 150	Judas that Jesu Crist to the Jewes solde	

同一音による頭韻が数行に亘って現れることもある。これは *The Alliterative Morte Arthure* に顕著であり、(26) の例では6行続けて /r/、2行続けて /k/、2行続けて母音、更に6行続けて /r/ による頭韻が用いられている。

(26)

MA 1665	The araye and the ryalltez of the Rounde Table	/r/
MA 1666	Es wyth rankour rehersede in rewmes full many;	/r/
MA 1667	Of oure renttez of Rome syche reuell he haldys,	/r/
MA 1668	He sall ʒife resoun full rathe, ʒif vs reghte happen,	/r/
MA 1669	That many sall repente that in his rowtte rydez,	/r/
MA 1670	For the reklesse roy so rewlez hym selfen!"	/r/
MA 1671	"A!" sais Sir Clegis than, "so me Criste helpe,	/k/
MA 1672	I knawe be thi carpyng a cowntere the semes!	/k/
MA 1673	Bot be thou auditoure or erle or Emperour thi selfen,	

			/vowels/
MA 1674	Appon Arthurez by*h*alue I *a*nswere the sone:		/vowels/
MA 1675	The *r*enke so *r*eall that *r*ewllez vs all,		/r/
MA 1676	The *r*yotous men and the *r*yche of the *R*ounde Table,		/r/
MA 1677	He has a*r*aysede his accownte and *r*edde all his *r*ollez,		/r/
MA 1678	For he wyll gyfe a *r*ekenyng that *r*ewe sall aftyre,		/r/
MA 1679	That all the *r*yche sall *r*epente that to *R*ome langez,		/r/
MA 1680	Or the *r*ereage be *r*equit of *r*entez that he claymez.		/r/

このような頭韻の使い方は、running alliteration、identical alliteration (Oakden, Schmidt) と呼ばれその使用が以前から知られている。

更に double alliteration と称される、1行が2組の頭韻を含む場合がある (Waldron 1970, p. 26)。この用語は古英語研究者間で混乱が見られ、半行内で2度頭韻が現れるものをそのように呼ぶ場合と (Bliss, p. 12; Le Page, p. 435)、1行内で2組の頭韻が現れるものを指す場合 (Kendall, p. 7; Russom 1998, p. 64-96) に使われている。(27) に二組の頭韻を含む行の例を示す。

(27)
A 1622	"*N*outhire *h*aylsid I him, ne *h*ildid him *n*outhire,	[abba]
AG 332	*A*ftir this Sir *A*lysaunder alle the *w*orlde *w*anne,	[aabb]
J 283	*Ff*resch *w*ater and *w*yn *w*ounden yn *f*aste	[abbba]
MA 3707	And all the *c*ogges *g*rete he *g*afe to his *k*nyghtes,	[abba]

頭韻は常に語頭に現れるとは限らない。(28) の a-férd, ecchékkes, vn-pérsched, ouerráne がその例である。

(28)
A 492	That all the *f*est was a-*f*erd, and othire *f*olke bathe.	[aaax]
AG 235	*C*heres thaym full *ch*efely ec*ch*ekkes to leve,	[aaax]
J 76	Vn*p*ersched *p*assed hadde the *p*eryles wer so many	[aaax]

MA 2035   And the *r*enkez oue*rr*ane all that *r*eg*n*ede in *e*rthe.   [aaax]

数は多くはないが、語の間のリエゾンにより、頭韻音が生み出されることがある。目では分かりにくいが、声に出して読むと、頭韻の繰返しで同一音の繰返しに対して敏感になっているために、この elision alliteration (Duggan and Turville-Petre, p. xix) が感じられる。(29) の例で、下線部が先行する語の最後の /n/ や /t/ の音を利用して頭韻を踏む metirical beat の部分である。

(29)

A 364   *N*owthire my*ne a*wen ne na *n*othire, god lat the *n*oȝt spare,
                                                                      [aaaxx]
A 582   And *n*orisch him as *n*amely, as he my*ne a*wyn warre,   [aaax]
A 1829   *T*akis tham with him to his *t*ent, and tham a*t e*se makis.
                                                                      [aaax]
Pe 233   Ho watz me *n*erre the*n au*nte or *n*ece: [xaaa]
G 356   Bot for as *m*uch as ȝe ar *myn em* I a*m* only to prayse,
                                                                      [aaax]
G 962   The twey*ne* y̆ȝen and the *n*ase, the *n*aked lylppez,
                                                                      [aaax]
MA 130   It is *l*efull ti*ll* v̱s his *l*ikyng till wyrche;   [aaax]

頭韻は metrical beats に加えて、metrical offbeat(s) にも現れることがある。(30) の例ではそのような頭韻もイタリックで示した。

(30)

A 1011   O*r a*ny *a*ngwische o*f a*rmes, *a*ny mare suffire.   [aaxx]
AG 577   To *h*ave *a*nd to *h*olde *i*t to *h*ym *a*nd to *h*is *a*yers.   [aaaa]
J 439   *B*y that *b*emys on the *b*urwe *b*lowen ful loude   [aaax]
MA 2258   For *f*erdnesse of oure *f*olke, by the *f*resche strandez;   [aaax]

metrical beats だけに頭韻が現れる significant alliteration に対しこのような頭韻の強調は incidental alliteration と呼ばれる (Creed, pp. 49-50)。

(30) の *J 439, MA 2258* の例は、いきなり頭韻音で始まるため metrical beat を形成すると解釈し 5 つの metrical beats を認める研究者もある。(31) の例では、行頭の、*For, Bothe, With, Bot* に metrical beat を認めるかによって 4 または 5 のリズムに解釈可能である。

(31)

A 1738   *For thou ert fere al to faynt, oure force to ministere;*
                                                        [aaax] / [aaaax]
AG 22   *Bothe my body and my bowe I buskede with leves,*
                                                        [aaax] / [aaaax]
J 631   *With wacche vmbe the walles to many wyes sorowe*
                                                        [aaax] / [aaaax]
MA 1013   *Bot thowe hafe broghte that berde, bowne the no forthire,*
                                                        [aaax] / [aaaax]

(32) は *Sir Gawain and the Green Knight* 第 1 行であるが *sithen* のストレスをどう扱うか意見が分かれる (Moriya 1996a, p. 149)。

(32)

G 1   *Sithen the sege and the assaut watz sesed at Troye,*

4 つまたは 5 つの metrical beats が問題になるケースとして、両方に読むことが可能な例がある。(33) の例は形容詞プラス名詞の組み合せが形容詞の方が頭韻を踏んでいるため形容詞に metrical beat を置き [aaax] と読むであろうか。しかし、名詞の方に metrical beat を置いて [axax] とする読み方も間違いとは言えない。更に形容詞にも名詞にも metrical beats を認めれば [aaxax] 等のように 5 のリズムで読むこともできる。

(33)

A 1169	Than *p*leynis him the *p*roud *k*yng, the *p*ete of his men,
AG 538	And *Ch*erlemayne oure *ch*efe kynge *ch*eses into the burgh,
J 138	*P*ore men and noȝt *p*rute *a*postles wer hoten
MA 806	Than *w*aknez the *w*yese *k*yng, *w*ery foretrauaillede,

他方、名詞の方が頭韻を踏むケースもある。

(34)

A 1580	And ilk *s*eg in a *s*oyte, at *s*elly him thinkis.
AG 27	With iche *f*eetur as thi *f*ote, *f*orfrayed in the greves,
J 87	To *s*ofte the grete *s*ore that *s*itteth on my cheke

The Alliterative Morte Arthure は (35) のように形容詞が頭韻を踏むことが圧倒的である。

(35)

MA 3216	Syne *g*raythe ouer the *g*rette see with *g*ud men of armes,

形容詞と名詞両方が頭韻を踏むことも多い。この場合5のリズムで読むことが自然であるかもしれない。

(36)

A 1387	*Bl*ewe *b*emys of *b*ras, *b*ernes assemblis,
AG 115	*L*onge *l*egges and *l*arge, and *l*ele for to schewe.
J 747	A *g*rete *g*irdel of *g*old with-out *g*er other
MA 1	How *g*rett *g*lorious *G*odd, thurgh *g*race of Hym seluen,

明らかに5 metrical beatsと読む行は存在するので5のリズムで読む

ことは前提とされている。

(37)
A 1　　　　 When *f*olk ere *f*estid and *f*ed, *f*ayn wald thai here
AG 608　　 And *g*raythed *G*alyan a boure to kepe hyr therin,
J 673　　　 *W*aspasian *w*endeth fram the *w*alles *w*ariande hem alle
MA 1541　 The *ch*eefe *ch*aunchelere of Rome, a *ch*eftayne full noble,

また動詞プラス名詞にもこのような現象は見られる。

(38)
A 227　　　 <u>Put</u> vp his *h*and to his *h*are, and *h*eldid it bot littill.
AG 269　　 I <u>sett</u> en*s*ample bi my*s*elfe and *s*ekis it no forthire:
J 635　　　 The *k*yng <u>co*m*aundeth</u> a *c*ry that *c*omsed was sone
MA 154　　 To <u>see</u> whatte *l*yfe that wee *l*eede in thees *l*awe *l*aundes,

このような現象、特に短い形容詞プラス名詞、短い動詞プラス名詞という語順において頭韻と metrical beat(s) の位置を決めるのに metrical subordination の関係からある程度自由な読み方ができる (Moriya 2004)。頭韻に忠実に読むか、普段の言葉のように頭韻にあまり拘らず読むか、許容範囲を設けたことも中英語頭韻詩の特徴であった。

　以上のように中英語頭韻詩の技巧はさまざまな音やシラブルの組み合わせ、語彙を駆使して、頭韻を生み出す。究極の例が (39) に掲げた *The Blacksmiths* である。鍛冶屋の騒音をわずか22行だが過剰な音の繰返し、特に子音の繰返しによって強調している。Metrical beats のみだけでなく行中で繰り返される同一子音 (母音が頭韻の場合その母音) をイタリックで示した。

(39)　　　 *Sw*arte *sm*ekyd *sm*ethes *sm*ateryd wyth *sm*oke
　　　　　 *Dr*yue me to *d*eth wyth *d*en of here *d*yntes.
　　　　　 *Sw*ech *n*oys on *n*yghtes *n*e herd men *n*euer:

What *kn*auene *cr*y and *cl*ateryng of *kn*ockes!
The *c*ammede *k*ongons *c*ryen after 'c*ol, c*ol!'
And *bl*owen here *b*elllewys, that al here *br*ayn *br*estes:
'*H*uf, puf!' seith that *o*n; '*h*af, paf!' that *o*ther.
Thei *sp*yttyn and *spr*aulyn and *sp*ellyn many *sp*elles;
Thei *gn*auen and *gn*acchen, thei *gr*onys to*g*ydere,
And *h*oldyn *h*em *h*ote wyth *h*ere *h*ard *h*amers.
Of *a* *b*ole-*h*yde *b*en *h*ere *b*arm-fellys;
Here *sch*ankes ben *sch*akeled *f*or the *f*ere-*fl*underys;
Heuy *h*amerys thei *h*an, that *h*ard ben *h*andled,
Stark *str*okes thei *str*yken on a *st*elyd *st*okke:
*L*us, bus! *l*as, *d*as! *r*owtyn be *r*owe.
Swech *d*olful a *dr*eme the *d*euyl it to*dr*yue!
The mayster *l*ongith a *l*ityl, and *l*ascheth a *l*esse,
*Tw*yneth hem *tw*eyn, and *t*owchith a *tr*eble:
*T*ik, *t*ak! *h*ic, *h*ac! *t*iket, *t*aket! *t*yk, *t*ak!
*L*us, bus! *l*us, das! swych *l*yf thei *l*edyn
Alle *cl*othemerys: *Cr*yst hem gyue sorwe!
*M*ay no *m*an for brenwaterys on nyght han hys rest!

この詩に関して Oakden は以下のように述べている。

The most remarkable feature of the metre is . . . the excessive alliteration. . . . The alliterative metre is skillfully handled, but his satire is a signpost, indicating the trend of the alliterative metre; alliteration once structural, is becoming more and more ornamental.　　(vol. 1, p. 150)

Oakden の著作は、中英語頭韻詩研究の基盤であるが、特に Metrical Survey の部分において以下のような記述が随所に見られる。

It was the desire for ornament that led these poets to overcrowd their lines with alliterating sounds, and to employ so many metrical devices. In its last stages the long line is a mere jingle of sounds. (vol. 1, p. 244)

　詩人達が頭韻技巧に懲りすぎた結果、リバイバルと称されるほど隆盛を極めた中英語頭韻詩は消滅するしかなかった、というのが Oakden の解釈である。ゲルマンのリズムとロマンスのリズムの拮抗、繰返しを好み冗長を楽しむ verbal art としての頭韻詩形式、作品ごとに複雑な頭韻技巧を駆使した高尚な芸術を生み出した中英語頭韻詩の伝統は、音の繰返しがただの jingles に終わる危険はあるが、日常の言葉を芸術に高める重要な機能をも備えていることを証明したのであった。

第4章

中英語頭韻詩における繰返しのリズムと連語

　第1～第3章で概観した英語のリズムの特徴と中英語頭韻詩の技法をふまえ、第4章から第7章では、具体的な作品の分析と、そこから得られる中英語頭韻詩の韻律と連語について考察する。資料として巻末に載せたのは、各作品の基本データであるが、Stage One から Stage Four までの段階を経て、以下の理由と経緯で作成されたものである。

　1953年 *Speculum* 誌に発表された Magoun の古英語詩における定型表現についての論文は、古英語頭韻詩に定型表現が使用されているかについて活発な議論を喚起した。1960年代から現在に至るまで Campbell, Foley, Niles, Stevick, Whitman などにより古英語詩において口承様式による定型表現 (以下 Parry-Lord の用いた用語により formulaic style あるいは formulaic expressions と呼ぶ) がどのように表れているか、様々なゲルマン詩やホメーロス詩などとの比較も含め、定型表現が定められた韻律のなかで果たす役割が明らかにされ、この50年で様々な研究成果が報告されて来た。しかし、中英語頭韻詩に関する研究は古英語定型表現に関する研究ほどの進展を見ていない。中英語頭韻詩についてのパイオニアとなったのは、Waldron が1957年 *Speculum* 誌に発表した "Oral-Formulaic Technique and Middle English Alliterative Poetry" であった。この論文を契機に、Johnson, Krishna, Ritzke-Rutherford らによる精緻な研究が発表されたが、formulae の存在が実証できそうな同一句の繰返しが多い *The Alliterative Morte Arthure* が中心であり、1999年に出版された Hartle の著作、*Hunting the Letter: Middle English Allit-*

erative Verse and the Formulaic Theory も、大半のページを割いて分析データを提供しているにも拘わらず、*Joseph of Arimathie, Death and Liffe, Saint Erkenwald, Scotish Feilde* という比較的短い4作品を分析したのみで、中英語頭韻詩全体を見通すには至っていない。中英語頭韻詩に古英語に見られるような定型表現が存在したか結論を出すには未だ解明すべき点が多々あり、個別の作品に関しての研究も偏りがあるというのが現状である。中英語頭韻詩における formulaic style についての研究がなかなか進められない原因としては、古英語詩に比べてすぐ目に付くような定型表現が頻繁に登場しないということ、formulae の定義自体がまだ定まっておらず、formulaic style という概念をあてはめること自体がさまざまな議論を呼び起こしていることがあるだろう。中英語頭韻詩にどのような繰返しの技巧が使われ、どのような効果があるかを論ずるためには系統だった分析データを多数の作品から集めることから始めなければならない。

　中英語頭韻詩には全く同一の句の繰返しはあまり登場しないが、類似した言葉使いが用いられることは多い。韻律の枠組みに従ってそれぞれの行を完成する技法として formulaic style は便利であっただろう。これまでは metrical patterns のみ研究されて来たが、韻律のみならず語順まで含めて検討し、metrical-syntactic patterns に拡大して分析することで、中英語頭韻詩の formulaic style を実証することが可能ではないか。実際に分析を始めてみると、韻律と語順の両面から分析するというのは思ったより多くの時間と細かい作業を要し、簡単には進まないことが分かったが、一方において一見ルールがあるようには思われない語句の並べ方に一定の法則があることも明らかになり、頭韻詩という制約のなかで特定の語と語が一定のつながりを持っていることを解明していけば、古英語詩の formulae とは異なる形態をとってはいるが、中英語詩にも formulae が存在することを証明できるのではないかと考えられる。ここではまず分析方法について説明し、分析の結果から想定される中英語詩全体についての formulaic expressions について検討する。

　分析をすすめる際注目したのは *b*-verse と呼ばれる後半行である。Oakden による *Alliterative Poetry in Middle English* (1930, 1935) は、中

英語頭韻詩に関する基本書であり、コーパスや IT 等により迅速かつ精緻にデータが揃う時代ではなかったため不備も見られるが、70年を経てもいくつかの重要な論点を示唆している。そのうちのひとつが、中英語頭韻詩において後半行の果たす特異な役割である。また Duggan (1986, 1988) などが指摘するように、後半行は韻律のルールが比較的遵守され、それに反することは行全体のリズムを危うくし、作品全体の価値を下げる危険を伴うことが知られている。韻律の乱れが比較的少ない *b*-verse においてどのような語と語の組み合わせや語順が用いられているかを調べれば、formulaic style といえるような系統だった枠組みが働いているかを解明できるであろう。

　b-verse の特異な役割について論じ formulaic characters に関してもかなりのページを割いて説明している Oakden であるが、実はその役割をあまり高く評価していない。韻律に従って行を完成させるとき必要に応じて用いられる tags は時として Oakden を苛立たせ、特に *The Alliterative Morte Arthure* は安易な繰返しを使い過ぎるとして、*b*-vsere における tags は empty で意味を持たないとまで言わせた (1935, p. 381)。しかし、他の箇所で Oakden は *b*-verse 独自に発達した技法として tags の果たす意義を積極的に認めてもいる。Hartle (p. 23) は Oakden を踏襲しつつ、tags を以下のように定義している。

The use of "tags" to fill out the line, while adding little or nothing to the meaning, certainly indicates that there are habitual collocations in this kind of verse which do tend to take up a particular position in the line, and thus, in a sense, are more than merely lexical "formulas." Often these "tags" are not lexically identical, but they share a basic pattern of both form and meaning, which establishes a more than casual relationship between them: the poet clearly forms one on the principle of another, as is necessary for the metrical correctness of the line.

　Hartle の説に従えば、全く同一の語句が使われることはあまりないが、行のある特定の場所で慣習のように使われる語の組み合わせ、"habitual collocations in a particular position in the ine" が韻律と同じくらい重要な役割を果たしており、それを tags と呼ぶことができる、ということになる。しかし、tags, clichés, unnecessary repetition などの用語が却ってその役割が「埋まらないときの詰め物」であるかのような印象を与えている。最近の研究者はこの点を重視し、Schaefer や Smith のように、similar collocations of words and common meaning というように、より具体的な表現を用いている。このような議論から明らかなことは、中英語頭韻詩が行の特定のポジションにおいて特定の語順を用いる傾向にあり、そこには頭韻のルールに加えて特定の collocation についてのルールが働いている、ということである。以下この collocation を連語と称することにする。

　頭韻詩は同一音の繰返しで成り立つ詩の形態である。語頭に同一音が幾度も繰り返されることは日常語ではそう頻繁に起こることではないから、この繰返しの形態は非日常的な組み合わせとして聞き手の注意を喚起し、言葉遊びとして聞き手を楽しませるということもあれば、くどい表現として敬遠されることもあり得る。即ち、Riddy の言うように、同一音の繰返しは、weight and formality を強調し、ひとつひとつの語を際立たせる効果を持つ。(40) に掲げた *Sir Gawain and the Green Knight* の冒頭14行は典型的な中英語頭韻詩のリズムの例である。各行の頭韻音を / / で示した。

(40)

G 1	Sithen the sege and the assaut watz sesed at Troye,	/s/
G 2	The borʒ brittened and brent to brondeʒ and askez,	/b/
G 3	The tulk that the trammes of tresoun ther wroʒt	/t/
G 4	Watz tried for his tricherie, the trewest on erthe:	/t/
G 5	Hit watz Ennias the athel, and his highe kynde,	/h/ and /vowels/
G 6	That sithen depreced prouinces, and patrounes bicome	/p/
G 7	Welneʒe of al the wele in the west iles.	/w/
G 8	Fro riche Romulus to Rome ricchis hym swythe,	/r/
G 9	With gret bobbaunce that burʒe he biges vpon fyrst,	/b/

G 10	And neuenes hit his aune nome, as hit now hat;	/n/
G 11	Tirius to Tuskan and teldes bigynnes,	/t/
G 12	Langaberde in Lumbardie lyftes vp homes,	/l/
G 13	And fer ouer the French flod Felix Brutus	/f/
G 14	On mony bonkkes ful brode Bretayn he settez	/b/

このような頻繁な音の繰返しは、日常の言葉では起こりにくい。第1章 (4) の例で考察したように、*Alcoholics Anonymous, Donald Duck, good grief, Mickey Mouse, sweet sixteen, Yale Yuppie* といった頭韻を踏む表現が洒落た言い回しとして印象に残るのは、そのような音の組み合わせが意図的な繰返しであるからだろう。Smith (2000, p. 96) は詩の sound symbolism に関して、onomatopoeia と phonaesthesia を挙げている。Onomatopoeia は、"the formation of a word in imitation of the sound of the thing meant" と定義され、phonaesthesia は、"a phenomenon whereby the presence of a particular phonological component seems to correspond regularly-though, disconcertingly, not consistently-to one semantic component." と定義されるが、これらの sound symbolism が語の配置とどのように関わっているかに注目する。

　頭韻は短い句においても特別な強調を伴い、まして何百行、何千行に亘って同一行内で同一音が繰り返される頭韻詩は、非日常的な言葉の組み合わせによる特殊な技巧として onomatopoetic effects を生み出す。G. Allen によれば、octosyllabic couplets に比べ、頭韻詩は、同一音の繰返しのせいで朗読する際より多くの時間を要することが知られている。声に出して読み進むほどにスピードが低下する、ということを頭韻詩を朗読する時に経験する。読み進むほどに tongue twister のようになっていく頭韻詩を recite するには相当の訓練と技巧を要する。一方でそれがある程度できるようになれば特別な技能として言葉による娯楽、芸術として享受される。

　以上のような頭韻詩の特徴と繰返しの果たす役割に注意しつつ分析した作品とその行数、略語は以下のようである。紙幅の関係上、巻末の資料に全てを含めなかったが詳細は資料についての註に示した。

Pearl (Pe)	1212 lines
Cleanness (C)	1812 lines
Patience (Pat)	531 lines
Sir Gawain and the Green Knight (G)	2020 lines
Excerpts from *The Wars of Alexander (A)*	2005 lines
Excerpts from *The Destruction of Troy (T)*	3531 lines
The Alliterative Morte Arthure (MA)	4345 lines
Excerpts from *Piers Plowman, A Text (PPA)*	1180 lines
Excerpts from *Piers Plowman, B Text (PPB)*	1030 lines
The Siege of Jerusalem (J)	1134 lines
Saint Erkenwald (E)	352 lines
Wynnere and Wastoure (W)	503 lines
The Parlement of the Thre Ages (AG)	661 lines
Dispute Between Mary and the Cross (D)	900 lines
Festivals of the Church (F)	334 lines
A Pistel of Susan (PS)	364 lines
Somer Soneday (SS)	133 lines
The Three Dead Kings (K)	143 lines
Total	22,190 lines

　以下各 Stage One から Stage Four に分けて行った分析を、異なる作品から例を引いて説明する。まず b-verse を最初の metrical beat 以下行の最後までを分離し、その韻律の構成と語の組み合わせをマークする。b-verse が冠詞、前置詞、代名詞、接続詞などの unstressed syllable(s) で始まることも多くあるが、unstressed syllable(s) がどちらの半行に属するか曖昧な行もあり、連語については b-verse 最初の metrical beat からを対象にした。先に挙げた *Sir Gawain and the Green Knight* の冒頭14行はこの段階で以下のように分離される。

G 1-b	seʒed at Troye,
G 2-b	brondeʒ and askez,
G 3-b	tresoun ther wroʒt
G 4-b	trewest on erthe:
G 5-b	highe kynde,
G 6-b	patrounes bicome
G 7-b	west iles.
G 8-b	ricchis hym swythe,
G 9-b	biges vpon fyrst,
G 10-b	now hat;
G 11-b	teldes bigynnes,
G 12-b	lyftes vp homes,
G 13-b	Felix Brutus
G 14-b	Bretayn he settez

b-verse が揃ったところで、その構成要素となる品詞と並び順を平行に並べる。使用する品詞名と、品詞の種類と略語に関しては資料の註に示したが、次のようなシンボルを各品詞に用いて分析する。

A：Adjective	G：Present Participle	P：Preposition
C：Conjunction	H：Pronoun	V：Verb
D：Determiner	I：Interjection	X：Auxiliary Verb
E：Past Participle	N：Noun	Z：Adverb

第一段階での *Sir Gawain and the Green Knight* の最初の14行の構成を以下に掲げた。b-verse の連語が、右側にその語順どおりに示されている。品詞の区別で、*at morrow, apon lofte, none nere* などのようにいくつかの語が句として副詞の役割を果たすものは語数に関係なく Z とマークした。また前置詞でない不定詞を導く *to* や否定 *not*、関係詞 *that* などの機能語などはそのまま残した。

Stage One

G 1	sesed at Troye,	E P N
G 2	brondeʒ and askez,	N C N
G 3	tresoun ther wroʒt	N Z V
G 4	trewest on erthe:	A P N
G 5	highe kynde,	A N
G 6	patrounes bicome	N V
G 7	west iles.	N N
G 8	ricchis hym swythe,	V H Z
G 9	biges vpon fyrst,	V P Z
G 10	now hat;	Z V
G 11	teldes bigynnes,	N V
G 12	lyftes vp homes,	V P N
G 13	Felix Brutus	N N
G 14	Bretayn he settez	N H V

　b-verse 最初の metrical beat の前に来る unstressed syllable、すなわち *a*-verse と *b*-verse の間の位置に置かれる語は、その品詞により、例えば前置詞、接続詞、関係詞であれば、*b*-verse 全体の果たす文法機能 (前置詞節や従属節等) が変わって来るので、unstressed syllables の有無と、あるのならその品詞もマークする。従って、基礎となるデータはひとつの作品について、

　　　　1)　行ナンバー
　　　　2)　全行
　　　　3)　*a*-verse と *b*-verse の間の語の有無とあればその品詞
　　　　4)　*b*-verse
　　　　5)　行末で最後の metrical beat を形成する語
　　　　6)　*b*-verse の連語
　　　　7)　註

の7列に分けて作成した。これを Stage One とする。註の p.112 に示したのがこの基礎データのサンプルである。

Stage Two では、*a*-verse と *b*-verse の間に何が置かれるかによって分類する。*Sir Gawain and the Green Knight* 冒頭14行では以下のような品詞が登場する。何も置かれない場合は / で示した。

Stage Two

G 1	be
G 2	P
G 3	P
G 4	D
G 5	C D
G 6	C
G 7	P D
G 8	/
G 9	H
G 10	C H
G 11	C
G 12	/
G 13	/
G 14	/

Stage Three では、*b*-verse 最初の語によって全行をアルファベット順に並べかえる。これは同一の連語が用いられていることがあるか、出来合いの語句のようなものが使用されているかを見るためである。Stage Three の例として以下に、*Sir Gawain and the Green Knight* の /r/ で始まる *b*-verse のアルファベット順リストを掲げる。Alliterative long lines と称される2020行中、83行が *b*-verse 最初の metrical beat が /r/ で始まる。

Stage Three

G 1907	rach mouthes,	N N
G 251	rad was he neuer,	A be H Z
G 1343	radly thay lance;	Z H V
G 1164	radly hem folȝes,	Z H V
G 2219	rapely a throwe.	Z Z
G 1309	rapes hym sone,	V H Z
G 2204	rawthe to here.	N to V
G 1735	rayked hir theder	V H Z
G 952	rayled ayquere,	E Z
G 745	rayled aywhere,	E Z
G 457	raynez he tornez,	N H V
G 66	reche hondeselle,	V N
G 1804	reche myȝt;	V X
G 40	rechles merthes.	A N
G 857	red golde ryngez,	A A N
G 1817	red golde werkez,	A A N
G 663	rede gowlez,	A N
G 373	redly I trowe	Z H V
G 1821	redyly he sayde,	Z H V
G 2324	redyly schal quyte,	Z X V
G 2059	redyly, if I myȝt.'	Z C H X
G 895	rehayted hym at onez,	V H Z
G 1243	reherce here	V Z
G 2246	rele as vus likez.	V C H V
G 304	reled aboute,	V Z
G 2434	remorde to myseluen	V P H self
G 1916	Renaude saule	N N
G 1728	Reniarde watz wyle.	N be A
G 2337	renk sayde:	N V
G 1911	renk seȝen.	N V
G 2206	renk, to mete	N to V

G 1134	renkkez ful mony;	N Z A
G 862	renkkez hym broʒten,	N H V
G 432	renkkez stoden,	N V
G 1570	rennez the boerne.	V D N
G 1332	rent of the hyde,	V P D N
G 1056	require yow here,	V H Z
G 1168	resayt,	N
G 2076	resayue.	V
G 392	resoun ful trwe,	N Z A
G 8	ricchis hym swythe,	V H Z
G 39	rich brether,	A N
G 2018	riche bruny;	A N
G 1744	riche wordes,	A N
G 1695	rises the sunne,	V D N
G 2198	roʒ wonez.	A N
G 2177	roʒe braunche.	A N
G 1898	roʒe greue,	A N
G 821	rod ouer the brygge.	V P D N
G 2144	rokke syde,	N N
G 2521	romaunce.	N
G 1466	ronez ful thyk,	N Z A
G 528	ros vpon fyrst,	V Z
G 2294	rotez a hundreth.	N D N
G 313	Rounde Table	A N
G 905	Rounde Table,	A N
G 2519	Rounde Table,	A N
G 538	Rounde Table.	A N
G 2458	Rounde Table;	A N
G 367	ruchched hym fayre,	V H Z
G 303	ruched in his sadel,	V P D N
G 1427	rungen aboute;	G Z
G 1698	rurde of her hornes;	N P D N

第 4 章　中英語頭韻詩における繰返しのリズムと連語　　　47

G 931	ry3t as thay schulden,	Z C H X
G 1899	ry3t at his helez.	Z P D N
G 1903	ry3t er he my3t,	Z Z H X
G 1703	ry3t fare,	A N
G 308	ry3t hym to speke:	V H to V
G 2346	ry3t I the proffered	N H H V
G 1341	ry3t to the by3t,	Z P D N
G 2162	ry3t to the dale;	Z P D N
G 2342	ry3tes alle other.	N A H
G 691	ryalme of Logres,	N P N
G 310	ryalmes so mony?	N Z A
G 1223	rych yow better,	V H Z
G 2401	ryche fest	A N
G 1827	ryche for hit semez,	A C H V
G 603	ryche golde naylez,	A A N
G 2036	ryche watz to schewe.	A be to V
G 1130	ryde alle arayde,	V Z E
G 1608	rygge after,	N Z
G 1344	rygge bonez,	N N
G 1558	ryses to the masse,	V P D N

　同じ語で始まっても b-verse 全体が同一句になっていることは少ないことが分かる。ただ、下線で示した *Round Table* という組み合わせは同じ形で使われている。次の章で詳しく分析するが、*The Alliterative Morte Arthure* では、同一の語で始まる b-verse が同一または非常に類似した語順構成になっている例が多数見られる。

　Stage Four では、基礎データを b-verse の連語によって分類する。即ち StageThree では左側の実際に用いられた語によって分析したが、Stage Four では右側の構成要素の連語によって分析を試みる。*Stage Three* から分かるように、同一語句の繰返しは作品によって頻度に違いがあるものの、全体としてさほど多くは見られない。このことは、

1000行、2000行を越える詩作において詩人たちは同一句の繰返しに安易に頼らなかったということであり、逆に頻繁に同一句を繰り返す4000行を超える *The Alliterative Morte Arthure* の特異性が際立つ。これまでの formulaic expressions についての研究は、*The Alliterative Morte Arthure* が主であり、他の作品はあまり対象にされていない (Ritzke-Rutherford)。しかし、Stage Four で得られた連語タイプを分類すると次第に何か法則が働いていることが明らかになる。取り扱った作品のうちあまり長くない作品、*Wynnere and Wastoure* (全503行) を用いてどのような連語タイプが見られるか分析を試みる。

　Wynnere and Wastoure の *b*-verse には70以上の連語タイプがあるが、主立った品詞と optional element として使われる語を (　) に入れてまとめると、最終的に5つのタイプに分けられる。1、2例しか使われない稀なパターンは除いたがその数はあまり多くない。即ち、ほとんどの *b*-verse が、optitonal elements は異なるかもしれないが、その基本構造においては5つのタイプにおさまるということである。以下の分類では、optional elements は (　) で示し、/ はその内から一つを選択することを示す。特に頻度の高いタイプに星印を付した。[　] に入れた語は、*b*-verse 内で metrical beats を占めるものであり、ふたつの [　] が metrical positions として *b*-verse を形成する。間の小さい文字で示したものは metrical offbeats としてふたつの metrical beats をつなぐ役割を果たす。

Stage Four: *b*-verse Collocation Types (*Wynnere and Wastoure*)
Type One：名詞で始まる *b*-verse

[	N	]	+			[	V	]*
[	N	]	+	(*for to*)	+	[	V	]*
[	N	]	+	(X/Z/N)	+	[	V	]
[	N	]	+	(*be*)	+	[E/A/Z/N]		
[	N	]	+			[	N	]*
[	N	]	+	(C/P)	+	[	N	]*
[	N	]	+			[	P/Z	]*

第4章　中英語頭韻詩における繰返しのリズムと連語

$$[\quad N\quad] + (Z) + [\quad A\quad]$$
$$[\quad N\quad] \quad\ \, + \quad [\ \textit{-self}\ ]$$

Type Two: 動詞で始まる *b*-verse

$$[\quad V\quad] + (D) + [\quad N\quad]*$$
$$[\quad V\quad] + P + [\quad N\quad]*$$
$$[\quad V\quad] + N + [\quad N\quad]*$$
$$[\quad V\quad] + N + [\quad V\quad]$$
$$[\quad V\quad] + N + [\quad A\quad]$$
$$[\quad V\quad] \quad\ \, + \quad [\quad X\quad]$$
$$[\quad V\quad] + (\textit{for})\,\textit{to} + [\quad V\quad]$$
$$[\quad V\quad] \quad\ \, + \quad [\quad Z\quad]*$$
$$[\quad V\quad] + A + [\quad Z\quad]$$
$$[\quad V\quad] + N + [\quad Z\quad]*$$
$$[\quad V\quad] + N+N + [\quad Z\quad]$$

Type Three: 形容詞で始まる *b*-verse

$$[\quad A\quad] \quad\ \, + \quad [\quad N\quad]*$$
$$[\quad A\quad] + P + [\quad N\quad]*$$
$$[\quad A\quad] \quad\ \, + \quad [\quad Z\quad]*$$
$$[\quad A\quad] + V + [\quad N\quad]$$
$$[\quad A\quad] + (\text{for})\,\text{to} + [\quad V\quad]$$
$$[\quad E\quad] + (Z)(A) + [\quad Z\quad]$$
$$[\quad E\quad] + (\textit{be}) + [\quad Z\quad]$$

Type Four: 副詞で始まる *b*-verse

$$[\quad Z\quad] \quad\ \, + \quad [\quad V\quad]*$$
$$[\quad Z\quad] \quad\ \, + \quad [\quad Z\quad]$$
$$[\quad Z\quad] + P + [\quad N\quad]$$
$$[\quad Z\quad] \quad\ \, + \quad [\quad A\quad]$$
$$[\quad Z\quad] + N + [\quad V\quad]$$

Type Five: 従属節、付加節となる *b*-verse
[N/V/A/ADV]　　+　(C/Q/that) +　[　S　]
　　　　　　　　　　　　　　　　　　　　　(S=Sentence)

　Type Five の例が今まで掲げたデータに僅かしか見られないので、具体例を挙げる。このタイプは、非人称動詞等により複文を形成する場合や関係節や接続詞などによって *b*-verse が従属節や別の文を含む場合である。*Wynnere and Wastoure* から例を (41) に掲げる。

(41)

W 83	knyghte that I see,
W 93	blewe als me thoghte
W 99	selly me thynke
W 101	by hym that stondeth,
W 107	stynte thay ne thynken."
W 146	say als me thynkes,
W 148	folke that he ledis.
W 186	oughte that I wene,
W 187	banere I knewe.
W 195	stynt thay ne thynken
W 201	wirche als he demeth."
W 202	renke als me thoghte,
W 218	Kythe what ye hatten,
W 327	knyghte that the folowes,
W 328	beryn that thou loveste,
W 352	take what him lykes;
W 378	laddes as tham falles;
W 382	povert that standes,
W 397	all that ther growes;
W 401	sell it ye thynken.
W 448	case as it falles,
W 502	knyghtes that me foloen,

第4章 中英語頭韻詩における繰返しのリズムと連語

　従属節を b-verse に置くことは、最後の metrical beat が頭韻の制約を受けないことからも合理的に見える。als me thynkes, as the book says のような連語は同一の構造を持つ従属節として b-verse に登場することが多い。

　このようにして Stage One から Stage Four までの分析により、いくつかの特徴が明らかになる。第一に、頻度の高い連語タイプは、最も自然にふたつの metrical beats が並ぶ、名詞プラス名詞、形容詞プラス名詞、などの組み合わせである。b-verse は a-verse に比べ metrical beats の数がふたつの場合がほとんどで、名詞、形容詞、動詞等の強勢音節位置が一定している語がふたつ並ぶことで、metircal beats の位置も安定する。現代英語では特別の場合以外使われなくなった名詞の後に形容詞が置かれる、動詞の前に目的語が置かれる、といった比較的自由な語順は、頭韻の制約を考慮しなくてはならない詩人に大いなる助けであったことは明白である。ほとんどの場合、名詞プラス動詞、名詞プラス形容詞、動詞プラス副詞といった組み合わせは、語順を変えても意味に違いは生じず、頭韻を優先して語順を入れ替えることが可能であったことが分かる。

　第2に、品詞の区別が厳密でないこと、造語の方法がさまざまに用いられることで同じ語の組み合わせであっても異なる意味を表わすことができる、という厳密でない文法カテゴリーが語の組み合わせを比較的自由にしていることが明らかである。例えば過去分詞、現在分詞は元来動詞に語尾をつけることで派生したのであるが、interesting/interested のように形容詞と分類されるものもある。形容詞と副詞の区別も -lich などが付けられて明らかな場合もあるが、同一語が形容詞と副詞両方に使われることがある。high, new, long といった語の場合、形容詞として使われているか副詞として使われているか、文脈を確かめなければ分からないことが多い。また after や beside のように、前置詞なのか副詞なのかその語だけでは分からない場合もある。Another, many, one などは元来形容詞であるが代名詞としても使われる。数を表す five や twenty、色を表す blue, silver なども形容詞として使われる場合がある。分析に際しては、これら異なる品詞として使われる可能性のある語はどの品詞

で使われているかできる限り詳細にマークした。使用したテクストには、異なる品詞の可能性を掌握し、その情報をグロッサリーにも載せている編集者とそうでない編集者とあり、後者の場合、注意して品詞を特定した。ただふたつの品詞があてはまる可能性のある場合にはどちらかを選択し、選択肢は註に列挙した。

第3点として気付くことは、行末において副詞が特別な役割を果たしていることである。先に掲げた5つのタイプのなかにも副詞で始まるものがあるが、数はそれほど多くなく、b-verse に副詞が使われる場合その副詞は行末に使われるという顕著な傾向がある。前置詞プラス名詞、前置詞プラス形容詞などが句として副詞の役割を果たす場合を含めるとその頻度はかなり高くなる。行末に副詞が来るタイプは3つに分けることができる。

b-verse が副詞で終わるタイプ

[N]	+	[Z]	ryde umbestonde;	(W 100)
			howes one lofte,	(W 150, W 314)
[V]	+	[Z]	durste never.	(W 303)
			payes all the better	(W 297, W 433)
[A]	+	[Z]	warre sone	(W 85)
			raughten so heghe	(W 42)

これらの例に見られるように、副詞で終わる b-verse が多いということは即ち副詞で終わる行が多いということであり、行末のポジションは頭韻の制約を受けないことを鑑みると、副詞を最後に置くことは韻律の点からも自由に副詞を選ぶことが可能であったことが分かる。

最後に、行末において関係節や従属節が特別な働きをすることが Type Five の例から分かる。関係節や従属節を付加することで詳しい説明や解釈を添えることができ、頭韻の制約も従属節全体には及ばず頭韻を踏む最初の metrical beat のみ注意を要したが、付加的要素を加える手法は有益な方法であっただろう。特に *hym thouȝt, me likes, als hym lykede* のような非人称動詞や、*as the storye tellis, hit semed, as the wryt*

第 4 章　中英語頭韻詩における繰返しのリズムと連語

telles などのような従属節が行末に置かれるのは顕著な特徴である。*b*-verse は異なるセンテンスレベルの導入にもよく使われるポジションであった。

　中英語頭韻詩と総称はしても個々の作品には特徴があり、*The Alliterative Morte Arthure* のように頻繁に同一句が繰り返されるものや、その逆に、一見して分かる繰返しがないものなどさまざまである。*b*-verse の構成が formulaic style と言えるような普遍性をもつかどうかは全作品の分析を済ませ全体の傾向を掌握しなくてはならない。次の節では、繰返し表現の最も頻繁な *The Alliterative Morte Arthure* の連語について考察する。

第5章

The Alliterative Morte Arthure における名詞で終わる後半行の連語

　第4章で説明した手順、Stage One, Stage Two, Stage Three, Stage Four の分析により、*The Alliterative Morte Arthure* ではどのような繰返しの技法が用いられているかを解明する。*The Alliterative Morte Arthure* は全4346行と行数が多く、その技法も複雑多岐に亘るので、まず第5章で、行が名詞で終わる場合の韻律と連語について検討し、第6章では *The Alliterative Morte Arthure* 全体の韻律と連語について考察する。

　行が名詞で終わる *The Alliterative Morte Arthure* の場合、以下の3つの特徴を持つ。

　1　連語タイプは5つあり、最も頻度の高いタイプは行末の名詞の前に名詞または形容詞が置かれる場合である。

　2　連語によって頭韻に制約が生じることはあまりないが、特定の音での頭韻としか用いられない場合もある。

　3　*b*-verse 全部が同一句の繰返しである場合、その句は formulaic expressions と考えてよいのではないか。例として *b*-verse 全体を使って繰り返される *be craftes of armes, the round table* などの句がある。

　The Alliterative Morte Arthure の行末に表れる名詞のうち、頻度の高い19の名詞について韻律と語順を分析した。19の名詞はその意味から以下の4つの種類に分けることができる。Category One は一般的な物を表す名詞、Category Two は場所を表す名詞、Category Three は人を表す名詞、Category Four は代名詞として用いられる名詞である。よく

使われるスペルを用い、変種は挙げていない。

Category 1： *armes, handes, heart, horses, stede, table, wapen, wordes*
Category 2： *erthe, land, Rome*
Category 3： *beryns, knight, kynges, lord, pople*
Category 4： *one, other, selfen*

特定の連語で用いられるかは語によって異なるが、*berynes* という語について観察すると全42例は3つのパターンに分けられることが分かる。

Collocation Types: *berynes*

(1)　P + (D) + [　A　]　+　[*berynes*]
(2)　　　(D) + [　A　]　+　[*berynes*]
(3)　　　　　[　V　] + (D) + [*berynes*]

それぞれの例を以下に掲げる。*b*-verse に付随する unstressed syllables も必要に応じて表示した。右に示したのは、特定の連語に特定の頭韻が用いられるかを調べるための、行全体の頭韻の成り立ちである。

(1)　P + (D) + [　A　] + [*berynes*]

MA 630	with ȝowre beste beryns;	b-b-b-b
MA 1012	wyth his beste berynes.	b-b-b-b
MA 1483	for all theire bale biernez.	b-b-b-b
MA 3519	with all my bolde beryns?	f-b-b-b
MA 3344	and fele of thi biernez.	f-f-f-b
MA 3772	amonge all his beryns,	m-m-m-b
MA 655	wyth semlyche berynes;	s-s-s-b
MA 3531	of selcouthe berynes;	s-s-s-b
MA 2169	in the schire byerne,	ʃ-ʃ-ʃ-ʃ-b

MA 3844	in the schire beryn,	ʃ-ʃ-ʃ-ʃ-b
MA 148	of valiante beryns,	t-v-v-b
MA 2864	of valyant biernez,	v-v-v-b
MA 3055	this valyante bierne	v-v-v-b
MA 3765	with valyant beryns.	v-v-v-b
MA 4124	with venymos beryns;	v-v-v-b
MA 1662	and att his hathell bierns,	a-a-h-b
MA 3780	of owtlawede beryns,	e-o-o-b

(2) (D) + [A] + [*berynes*]

MA 2139	thes frekk byernez,	f-f-f-b
MA 2502	theis fresclyche byernes,	f-f-f-b
MA 3371	thow freliche byerne,	f-f-f-b
MA 2910	hawtayne biernez,	h-h-h-b
MA 1814	lordly biernez.	l-l-l-b
MA 2281	thas lordlyche byernes.	l-l-l-b
MA 2541	thes lordlyche byernez,	l-l-l-b
MA 3696	lordeliche berynes;	l-l-l-b
MA 1947	trauaillede biernez;	tr-tr-tr-b
MA 2656	wirchipfull biernez,	w-w-w-b
MA 3500	that auenaunt byerne;	a-i-a-b
MA 3933	and Estriche berynes,	e-a-e-b
MA 4161	thes excellente beryns,	e-e-e-b

(3) [V] + (P) + (D) + [*berynes*]

MA 3672	killide the braynes;	k-k-k-b
MA 1391	relyede to his byerns:	r-r-r-b
MA 1752	to rescewe hys biernez."	b-k-r-r-b
MA 2022	arayes his byernez,	r-r-r-b
MA 2784	to reschewe that byerne,	r-r-r-b

第5章　*The Alliterative Morte Arthure* における名詞で終わる後半行の連語

MA 4073	arrayes his beryns,	r-r-r-b
MA 4027	and semble thi berynes,	s-s-s-b
MA 3165	he vetailles his biernez,	v-v-v-b
MA 4297	to vencows this beryns;	g-v-w-v-b
MA 3562	he wakkenysse his berynns,	w-w-w-b
MA 4285	that wanttes hir beryn;	w-w-w-b
MA 3534	owtlawede berynes.	i-o-o-b

これらのパターンは以下の2つに集約される。(　) は optional elements を、[　] は metrical beat の位置を示す。

b-verse ⟶　(P) + (D) +　[　A　]　+　[*berynes*]
b-verse ⟶　　　　　　　[　V　] + (D) + [*berynes*]

このようにして、行末によく置かれる名詞の連語をひとつひとつに関して調べ、更に19の名詞全体が *b*-verse においてどのような連語で表れるかについてまとめると、大きく分けて5つのグループに分けられる。下線を引いた最初の連語が個々の例を総括するタイプであり、[　] は metrical beat の位置を示す。

Group One: [　A　] + [　N　]

[A]	+	[*berynes*]
[A]	+	[*knyghte*]
[A]	+	[*lorde*]
[*round*]	+	[*table*]
[A]	+	[*wapens*]
[A]	+	[*horses*]
[A]	+	[*stede*]
[A]	+	[*herte*]
[A]	+	[*wordes*]

| [A |] | + | [handes |] |
| [A |] | + | [landes |] |

Group Two: [N] + P + (D) + [N]

[N	]	+ P + D +	[pople	]
[help/sake	]	+ (of) one's +	[lord	]
[presence	]	+ of +	[lord	]
[N	]	+ of +	[Rome	]
[men	]	+ of +	[armes	]
[craftes	]	+ of +	[armes	]
[N	]	+ of +	[armes	]
[N	]	+ of/with + (one's) +	[handes	]

Group Three: [N/H] + [self/one/other]

[N	]	+ H +	[self	]
[H	]	+	[self	]
[H	]	+	[one	]
[self	]	+	[one	]
[N	]	+ (and/or) +	[other	]

Group Four: [P] + (D) + [earth/hand]

[in	]	+	[erthe	]
[appon	]	+	[erthe	]
[to/on	]	+ the +	[erthe	]
[P	]	+ one's +	[herte	]

Group Five: [V] + [words]

| [V |] | + | [wordes |] |

全く同一句の繰返しが現れることは頻繁ではないが、繰返し用いられる連語が formulaic style として機能していることが明らかではないか。定型表現をホメーロス詩や古英語詩と同様同一句の繰返しとして定義すると中英語頭韻詩でそのような繰返しは僅少であり、従って中英語頭韻詩には定型表現はない、ということになってしまう。しかし、似通った語順と文法構成という枠で見れば、既成の句に頼るのではなく語は自由に選びながらある程度決まった語群、語順によって行末が統一されていたことが明らかである。

第 6 章

The Alliterative Morte Arthure における韻律と連語

　この章では、さらに *The Alliterative Morte Arthure* 全体を分析し、中英語頭韻詩において一定の語順や連語が果たす役割と韻律との関係について解明を試みる。第5章で見たように、中英語頭韻詩における定型表現について、行末で繰返し用いられる似通った表現について語彙や語順の構造から分析すれば formulaic expressions の使われ方が解明できるとの考えに基づき、行の後半 (*b*-verse) の韻律と語順を検討した結果、*b*-verse で起こり得る連語には *b*-verse 内の最初の metircal beat が置かれる語の品詞 (名詞、動詞、形容詞、副詞) によって4つ、更に、*b*-verse 全体が従属節や付加節で成り立つ場合も顕著に見られることから、これを含めて全体で5つのタイプがあることが明らかになった。*The Alliterative Morte Arthure* は、連続する複数行 (最大で11行) が同一の頭韻を持ち、全行の約4分の3が前後の行と同一の頭韻によるという特徴を持つ (Moriya 2000a) が、その他にもさまざまな繰返しの技法が用いられ、Johnson (1978), Krishna (1982), Moriya (2003), Rizke-Rutherford (1981a; 1981b) 等の先行研究においても formulaic expressions の使い方が注目されている。

　第5章で説明したように、Stage One から Stage Four に分けて分析した結果、以下のことが明らかになった。1) 大半の行は、最も自然にふたつの metrical beats が並ぶ、名詞プラス名詞、形容詞プラス名詞、などの連語によっている。2) 品詞の区別が厳密でないこと、造語の方法がさまざまに用いられるという厳密でない文法カテゴリーが語の組み合わせを比較的自由にし頭韻を揃える際の助けとなっている。3) 従属節

や付加節が行末において特別な働きをする、即ち、頭韻の制約を受けない行末にレベルが異なる節を導入することで詳しい説明や解釈を添えることができる。4)この作品に限っては、特定の語が決まり文句のようにして同一語と共に繰り返されることが多くある。

Kaneを引用して、Smithは以下のように頭韻詩の特徴を示している。

There is no formal handbook of alliterative poetry surviving from the Middle English period. . . . One key principle, however, seems to be accepted by modern scholars: it seems almost certain that, as in other kinds of poetry, a framework of modulation between norm and deviation, linked to literary salience, lies at the heart of alliterative verse-practice. This view has been argued very effectively by George Kane, who points out that a poet's success derives from the way in which 'his versification exists as part of the meaning of his poetic statements, not merely because the verse is effective in making that meaning more emphatic, clearer, more evidently interrelated, but also because it will engage the reader's auditory interest and confer the combination of physical and intellectual pleasure experienced when pattern and meaning are simultaneously apprehended.' (Smith, 2000, p. 93)

(42) に掲げた11行は *The Alliterative Morte Arthure* の冒頭部分であるが、一部定型から逸脱したものもあるが、典型的な中英語頭韻詩のリズムを呈している。Kaneのいう "physical and intellectual pleasure experienced when pattern and meaning are simultaneously apprehended" を感じさせる音の構成になっている。

(42)

MA 1	How *g*rett *g*lorious *G*odd, thurgh *g*race of Hym seluen,	/g/
MA 2	And the *p*recyous *p*rayere of Hys *p*rys Modyr,	/p/
MA 3	*Sch*elde vs fro *sch*amesdede and *s*ynfull werkes,	/s/

MA 4	And *g*yffe vs *g*race to *g*ye and *g*ouerne vs here,	/g/
MA 5	In this *w*rechyd *w*erld, thorowe *v*ertous lywynge,	/w/ and /v/
MA 6	That we may *k*ayre til Hys *c*ourte, the *k*yngdom of Hevyne,	/k/
MA 7	When oure *s*aules schall parte and *s*undyre fra the body,	/s/
MA 8	Ewyre to *b*elde and to *b*yde in *bl*ysse wyth Hym seluen;	/b/
MA 9	And *w*ysse me to *w*erpe owte som *w*orde at this tym	/w/
MA 10	That nothyre *v*oyde be ne *v*ayne, bot *w*yrchip till Hym selvyn,	/v/ and /w/
MA 11	*Pl*esande and *pr*ofitabill to the *p*opule that them heres.	/p/

頭韻は短い句においても特別な強調を伴い、まして何百行、何千行に亘って同一行内で同一音が繰り返される頭韻詩は、非日常的な言葉の組み合わせによる特殊な技巧としてオノマトペの効果を生み出す。加えてこの作品では連続する多数の行に同一の頭韻音が用いられる。(43) と (44) に掲げるのは10行と11行に亘る同一頭韻音の例である。

(43)

MA 3509	'Me awghte to *k*nowe the *K*ynge: he es my *k*ydde lorde,	/k/
MA 3510	And I *c*alde in his *c*ourte a *k*nyghte of his chambire;	/k/
MA 3511	Sir *Cr*addoke was I *c*allide in his *c*ourte riche,	/k/
MA 3512	*K*epare of *K*arlyon vndir the *K*ynge selfen:	/k/
MA 3513	Nowe am I *c*achede owtt of *k*yth with *k*are at my herte,	/k/
MA 3514	And that *c*astell es *c*awghte with vn*c*owthe ledys."	/k/
MA 3515	Than the *c*omliche *k*ynge *k*aughte hym in armes,	/k/
MA 3516	*K*este of his *k*etille-hatte and *k*yssede hym full sone,	/k/
MA 3517	Saide "Wel*c*om, sir *Cr*addoke, so *Cr*iste mott me helpe!	/k/
MA 3518	Dere *c*osyn of *k*ynde, thowe *c*oldis myn herte;	/k/

(44)

MA 2755	*Fl*orent and *Fl*oridas, with *f*yve score knyghttez,	/f/
MA 2756	*F*olowede in the *f*oreste, and on the way *f*owndys,	/f/

第 6 章　*The Alliterative Morte Arthure* における韻律と連語　　　63

MA 2757	*Fl*yngande a *f*aste trott, and on the *f*olke dryffes.	/f/
MA 2758	Than *f*elewes *f*ast to oure *f*olke wele a *f*yve hundreth	/f/
MA 2759	Of *f*reke men to the *f*yrthe, appon *f*resche horses;	/f/
MA 2760	One Sir *F*eraunt be*f*ore, apon a *f*ayre stede,	/f/
MA 2761	Was *f*osterde in *F*amacoste- the *F*ende was his *f*adyre.	/f/
MA 2762	He *fl*enges to Sir *Fl*orent, and pristly he kryes,	/f/
MA 2763	"Why *fl*ees thow, *f*alls knyghte? The *F*ende hafe thi saule!"	/f/
MA 2764	Thane sir *Fl*orent was *f*ayne and in *f*ewter castys;	/f/
MA 2765	One *F*awuell of *F*ryselande to *F*eraunt he rydys,	/f/

　行内の横の頭韻と、連続する行で繰り返される縦の頭韻が組み合わさったこの過剰な繰返しは *The Alliterative Morte Arthure* の大きな特徴であり、そのような繰返しによる音の効果は格別である。この繰返しのリズムと語の配置がどのように関わっているか、韻律と連語を分析し解明を試みる。

　まず、Stage Two で *a*-verse と *b*-verse の間に何が来るかによって分類して明らかになったのは、半行の間に来る語の種類が非常に限られているということである。*a*-verse と *b*-verse の間に置かれる metrical off-beat (s) を形成する最初の品詞とその割合は Table One のようである。前置詞で始まってその後に冠詞等が続く場合も Preposition として数え、単独の時と他の語を伴う時の合計を示した。

Table One: Categories of Metircal Offbeats Between the *a*-verse and the *b*-verse (*The Alliterative Morte Arthure*)

Preposition	25.2 %
None (/)	21.2 %
Conjunction	20.2 %
Determiner	7.9 %
that	7.6 %
Pronoun	7.3 %
Other lexical items	10.6%
Total	100.0%

　Table One から明らかなことは、前置詞または接続詞に続く *b*-verse が40% を越えており、また、unstressed syllable が存在しない (None)、すなわちいきなり metrical beat で *b*-verse が始まる行も20% を越えるということである。指示代名詞でない関係詞としての *that*、代名詞、または決定詞 (Determiner) で始まる *b*-verse も多く、この６種類が全体の９割を占める。このことは、前半行と後半行の間で前置詞、接続詞、または何もない場合にはポーズが置かれるという予測が成り立つことであり、半行の境目 (caesura) が特定の品詞あるいはポーズによって示されていることになる。*b*-verse の始まりの品詞ごとに１例づつ以下に示す。

Preposition に導かれる *b*-verse
MA 831　　And thise that saillez ouer the see, <u>with</u> thy sekyre knyghtez."

***a*-verse との間に metirical offbeat のない *b*-verse**
MA 1045　　He lay lenand on <u>lang, lugand</u> vnfaire,

Conjunction に導かれる *b*-verse
MA 145　　Off dukes and duspers <u>and</u> doctours noble,

第6章 *The Alliterative Morte Arthure* における韻律と連語

Determiner に導かれる *b*-verse
MA 3104   Gosse in by Goddarde, <u>the</u> garett he wynnys,

that に導かれる *b*-verse
MA 3301   The fayreste of fegure <u>that</u> fourmede was euer:

Pronoun に導かれる *b*-verse
MA 4180   To encowntere the Kyng <u>he</u> castes hym sone.

　Stage Three で *b*-verse 最初の語によって全部をアルファベット順に並べかえるのは、同一の語句が用いられていることがあるか、出来合いの語句のようなものが *b*-verse 全体をユニットとして使用されているかどうかを見るためである。*The Alliterative Morte Arthure* では特定の句が高い頻度で登場する。*b*-verse には metrical beats ふたつが入ることから、stressed syllables を持つ語ふたつが少なくとも存在するというのが一般的であるが、最初の語が同じでもふたつめの語は異なる場合と、最初の語と2ばんめの語が同一の場合がある。最初の語とふたつめの語両方が同じであるというのは、代名詞や冠詞など付随するものに違いはあるかもしれないが、全くまたはほぼ同一句で *b*-verse が占められることであり、そのような例が多ければ formula と考えられる。以下のような一定の表現が定型句のように *b*-verse において繰り返されるのは、他の中英語頭韻詩と比べた *The Alliterative Morte Arthure* の大きな特徴である。

areste founden	areste halden	Arthur hymseluen
austeryn knyghtez	austeryn wordes	bachelors noble
baners noble	baners displayed	Bedwere the ryche
beste beryns	beste knyghttez	beste lykez
blithe stremes	brande ryche	broghte owtte of lyue
carpes thes wordez	castez in fewtire	certayne knyghttez
certayne lordez	cheualrous knyghtez	cheualrye noble

clene iren	clene syluere	clenlyche arrayede
clergye and other	comforthe hym seluen	coroun langez
craftez of armes	crewel wordez	Criste helpe
curtays and noble	dukes and erles	Emperour of Rome
faire marches	faire stedes	fay leuede
ferse men of armes	formede was euere	fraiste when the likes
fresche strandez	fyftene wynter	galyarde knyghttez
gentill knyghttez	harageous knyghttez	honourable kyngez
kyng seluen	kythe ryche	other ynowe
prelates and other	presence of lordys	price knyghttez
process of tyme	Rome lengez	Round Table
ryche stedez	ryotous knyghttez	salte strandez
say what H likes	sekyre knyghttez	senatours many
sere halfes	seuen wyntteres	sextene kyngez
solace H seluen	werlde ryche	(H=Pronoun)

このように、特定の名詞が全く同一の形容詞を伴う例も多くあるが、他方、似たような形容詞との組み合わせもよく見られる。特定の決まった句ではなく、異なる語を組み合わせながら繰返しの印象を与える例として、*strandez* (streams) という名詞がどのような形容詞と *b*-verse において登場するか、(45) に示す。

(45)
- MA 883   That enclosez the clyfe with the <u>clere strandez</u>;
- MA 1998   The Kyng casts to kepe þe thaa <u>clere strandes</u>;
- MA 2373   One the coste of Costantyne, by the <u>clere strandez</u>,
- MA 1227   The Kyng fraystez a furth ouer the <u>fresche strandez</u>,
- MA 1497   Fey on the faire felde by tha <u>fresche strandez</u>.
- MA 1535   We hafe foughten, in faithe, by ȝone <u>fresche strandez</u>,
- MA 2258   For ferdnesse of oure folke, by the <u>fresche strandez</u>;
- MA 2280   Lugez thaym luflye by tha <u>lyghte strandez</u>,

第 6 章　*The Alliterative Morte Arthure* における韻律と連語

MA 1517	O lawe in the launde than, by the <u>lythe strandez</u>,
MA 1600	That thus are lamede for my lufe be this <u>lythe strandez</u>."
MA 598	They sailede with a syde wynde oure the <u>salte strandez</u>,
MA 1337	Ensegge al tha cetese be the <u>salte strandez</u>,
MA 1422	And sett sodanly on our seggez, by the <u>salte strandez</u>;
MA 1457	Now thei semblede vnsaughte by the <u>salte strandez</u>:
MA 1573	I had leuer see hym synke on the <u>salte strandez</u>,
MA 2315	That has sauede oure lyfe by theise <u>salte strandys</u>,
MA 3789	Sodaynly in dischayte by tha <u>salte strandes</u>.
MA 3627	Thus they scheften fore schotys one thas <u>schire strandys</u>,

これらの例から *strandez* は以下の語順でよく登場することが分かる。

b-verse → (P) + (D) + [　A　] + [*strandez*]

その行の頭韻音によって *clear, fresh, bright* などの形容詞が選択されている。後述するように、この前置詞プラス形容詞プラス名詞という構造は *The Alliterative Morte Arthure* において頻繁に登場する連語タイプである。

極端な例であるが、付随する形容詞がほとんど常に同一という場合が *table* という名詞について見られる。(46) に示したのは *table* という語を *b*-verse に含む全ての用例である。

(46)

MA 17	Off the ryeall renkys of the <u>Rownnde Table</u>,
MA 53	Then rystede that ryall and helde the <u>Rounde Tabyll</u>;
MA 74	Thus on ryall araye he helde his <u>Rounde Table</u>,
MA 93	That thow bee redy at Rome with all thi <u>Rounde Table</u>,
MA 102	Thare schall thow gyffe rekkynynge for all thy <u>Round Table</u>
MA 147	Off the richeste renkys of the <u>Rounde Table</u>;
MA 173	Richely on the ryghte hannde at the <u>Rounde Table</u>,

MA 389	I sall at the reuerence of the Rounde Table,
MA 412	Wyth reuerence and ryotte of all his Rounde Table,
MA 424	By the reyuere of Reone halde my Rounde Table,
MA 524	In the moste reale place of the Rounde Table,
MA 719	Wyth a reall rowte of the Rounde Table
MA 726	Rewlys before the ryche of the Rounde Table;
MA 1429	Arestede of the richeste of the Rounde Table,
MA 1524	Ouerredyn with renkes of the Round Table.
MA 1655	His ryche retenuz here all of his Round Table,
MA 1665	The araye and the ryalltez of the Rounde Table
MA 1676	The ryotous men and the ryche of the Rounde Table,
MA 1732	Thynke on ryche renoun of the Rounde Table,
MA 1882	Thane relyez the renkez of the Rounde Table,
MA 1994	With renkkes renownnd of the Rounde Table,
MA 2135	Than the Romaynes and the rennkkez of the Rounde Table
MA 2243	To reschewe the ryche men of the Rounde Table,
MA 2278	Thane releuis the renkes of the Rounde Table
MA 2372	The roy ryalle renownde, with his Rownde Table,
MA 2402	The renke rebell has bene vnto my Rownde Table,
MA 2453	The renkez renownde of the Rounnd Table.
MA 2641	And rollede the richeste of all the Rounde Table.
MA 2790	Bot thane a renke, sir Richere of the Rounde Table,
MA 2878	As was when the ryche men of the Rownde Table
MA 2902	And thane the ryalle renkkes of the Rownde Table
MA 2912	Than the renkes renownd of the Rownd Table
MA 2919	To the ryall rowte of the Rownde Table;
MA 2988	And rydez into the rowte of the Rownde Table.
MA 3173	This roy with his ryall men of the Rownde Table,
MA 3214	Ryngne in my ryalltés and holde my Rownde Table,
MA 3526	Kaughte in all the rentis of the Rownde Tabill;
MA 3571	With renttes and reches of the Rownde Table;

第 6 章 *The Alliterative Morte Arthure* における韻律と連語

MA 3612	Than the Roye and the renkes of the <u>Rownde Table</u>
MA 3893	Of reuerence and ryotes of the <u>Rownde Table</u>,
MA 3940	And vp rypes the renkes of all the <u>Rownde Tabyll</u>;
MA 4005	Ne regne in my royaltez, ne halde my <u>Rownde Table</u>,
MA 4048	Thare durste no renke hym areste of all the <u>Rownde Table</u>,
MA 4072	Than the royall roy of the <u>Rownde Table</u>
MA 4081	The rekeneste redy men of the <u>Rownde Table</u>,
MA 4117	Redily thas rydde men of the <u>Rownde Table</u>
MA 4282	Here rystys the riche blude of the <u>Rownde Table</u>,
MA 4291	Thane relyes the renkes of all the <u>Rownde Table</u>:
MA 1331	Ne ware it for reuerence of my <u>ryche table</u>,
MA 3198	Rehetez the Romaynes at his <u>riche table</u>,
MA 3201	Reuerence the Romayns in his <u>riche table</u>.
MA 1301	Reght as they weschen and went to the table,

　最後の 4 例を除く 48 例が *Round Table* という決まり文句になっている。そして、1331, 3198, 3201 行では *rich* という語と共に使われている。頭韻について言えば、52 例中 51 例が /r/ で頭韻を踏むという顕著な特徴が見られる。第 5 章で見たように、他の名詞に関しては豊かな語彙を駆使して言い換えを試みそれに合わせた頭韻を揃える才能を発揮する詩人が *table* に関してだけは常に *round* と組み合わせている。このような決まり文句のような繰返しは他の中英語頭韻詩にはあまり見られないので、*Round Table* がそのまま繰り返されるのはこの作品の特徴である。*Sir Gawain and the Green Knight* においても例は少ないが *round table* という連語が常に用いられていることを第 4 章でも注目した。

　Stage Four で連語による分類を試みるが、第 4 章で総括したように、同一語句の繰返しは作品によって頻度に違いがあり、他の作品にはすぐに目につくほど頻繁には見られない。しかし、頻繁に同一語句や似通った連語を繰り返す *The Alliterative Morte Arthure* は、頭韻詩の枠組みをことさらに強調するものとなっている。*The Alliterative Morte Arthure* の b-verse には 70 近い語順がある。分析した中英語頭韻詩のどれもが、

大体70前後の語順を持つというのは、ひとつの特徴である。
　さらに Stage Five として、まだ全ての作品を分析してはいないが、行末の metrical beat を占める語によって全体を並べ替え、特定の単語が集中することがあるか調べることも有益である。The Alliterative Morte Arthure についてそのことを調べた結果、以下に挙げた語が行末に頻繁に登場することが分かった。30例を越えて行末に現れる語とその使用回数を示してある。因に、4346行のうち、914行が動詞、770行が形容詞または副詞、1941行が名詞または代名詞で終わり、この３つの合計は、全体の約83%にあたる。即ち、動詞で終わるもの約21%、形容詞または副詞で終わるもの約18%、名詞で終わるもの約45%という比率になる。頻度の高い語とその語で終わる行数は以下のようである

動詞：	*halden* 43; *lengede* 48; *likes* 94
形容詞または副詞：	*after* 34; *euer* 43; *littyll* 39; *neuer* 55; *noble* 50; *ryche* 66; *thareaftyre* 36
名詞または代名詞：	*armes* 81; *berynes* 43; *erthe* 64; *handes* 48; *herte* 49; *knyghtes* 209; *landes* 60; *lorde* 98; *one* 85; *other* 65; *pople* 36; *selfen* 121; *stede* 35; *Table* 52; *wapen* 37; *wordes* 72

　The Alliterative Morte Arthure に見られる連語タイプは以下のとおりである。[　]に品詞名のないものは特定の品詞に限定されないポジションである。Z は副詞、S は別のセンテンスを表す。

Table Two: *b*-verse Collocation Types　　　(*The Alliterative Morte Arthure*)

Type One:	[N]	+	[　]	35.3%
Type Two:	[V]	+	[　]	31.2%
Type Three:	[A]	+	[　]	22.8%
Type Four:	[Z]	+	[V]	7.9%
Type Five:	[　]	+	[S]	2.8%
Total				100.0%

第 6 章　*The Alliterative Morte Arthure* における韻律と連語

ほとんどの *b*-verse が、基本構造において 5 つのタイプいずれかに属する。ここでも、第 4 章で述べたのと同様の特徴が見られる。まず、頻度の高い連語タイプは、最も自然にふたつの metrical beats が並ぶ、名詞プラス名詞、形容詞プラス名詞、などの組み合せである。自由な語順が、頭韻を優先させる上で重要な役割を果たしている。しかし、その自由な語順のなかでも、*The Alliterative Morte Arthure* には特定のタイプをよく用いるという傾向が見られる。以下の組み合せがよく登場する。

[A]　　+　　　　[N]
[N]　　+　　　　[A]
[N]　+ P (D) +　[N]
[N]　　+　　　　[V]
[V]　　+　　　　[Z]
[V]　+ (D) +　　[N]
[V]　　+ H +　　[Z]
[V]　+ P (D) +　[N]

ここで特徴的なことは、名詞や動詞は複数の異なる品詞と組み合わさるが、形容詞は名詞が後ろに来るというワンパターンに集約される、ということである。語順が自由であるのだから、名詞プラス形容詞も多くていいはずだが、そのタイプは少数に留まっている。しかもこのタイプの大きな特徴は、それが前置詞に導かれるということが多いということである。(47) に典型的な例を挙げる。

(47)

MA 2　　　And the precyous prayere <u>of</u> Hys prys Modyr,
MA 5　　　In this wrechyd werld, <u>thorowe</u> vertous lywynge,
MA 13　　Off elders of alde tym and <u>of</u> theire awke dedys,
MA 17　　Off the ryeall renkys <u>of</u> the Rownnde Table,
MA 49　　Dyuysyde dowcherys and delte <u>in</u> dyuerse remmes,
MA 57　　Sweys into Swaldye <u>with</u> his snell houndes,

MA 58	For to hunt at the hartes <u>in</u> thas hye laundes,
MA 61	That Caerlyon was callid, <u>with</u> curius walles,
MA 66	Wyth dukez and duspers <u>of</u> dyuers rewmes,
MA 88	It es credens, Sir Kyng, <u>with</u> cruell wordez;
MA 93	That thow bee redy at Rome <u>with</u> all thi Rounde Table,
MA 94	Appere in his presens <u>with</u> thy price knyghtez,
MA 102	Thare schall thow gyffe rekkynyng <u>for</u> all thy Round Table
MA 115	That Iulius Cesar wan <u>with</u> his ientill knyghttes."
MA 116	The Kyng blyschit on the beryn <u>with</u> his brode eghn,
MA 118	Keste colours as Kyng, <u>with</u> crouell lates,
MA 147	Off the richeste renkys <u>of</u> the Rounde Table;
MA 148	Thus schall I take avisemente <u>of</u> valiant beryns,
MA 154	To see whatte lyfe that wee leede <u>in</u> thees lawe laundes,
MA 158	That they bee herberde in haste <u>in</u> thoos heghe chambres,
MA 167	Hastyly wyth hende men <u>within</u> thees heghe wallez;
MA 173	Richely on the ryghte hannde <u>at</u> the Round Table,
MA 185	Grett swannes full swythe <u>in</u> silueryn chargeours,

(47) は、冒頭200行からの例のみを挙げたが、b-verse が前置詞プラス形容詞プラス名詞という構造になっているものが200行中23回も登場する。作品全体では、形容詞プラス名詞のタイプのうち、その約3/4が前置詞によって導かれている。

品詞の区別が厳密でないこと、ひとつの語が複数の文法カテゴリーを持ち得ることが語の組み合わせを比較的自由にしていることも、他の作品同様 *The Alliterative Morte Arthure* においても確認される。形容詞の働きをする過去分詞、現在分詞や、形容詞と副詞の両方に使われる語等、品詞の機能が複数ある語が行末に来ることが多い。

The Alliterative Morte Arthure においても、Type Five は、b-verse 最初の語とそれに続く語の関係というよりむしろ全体がひとつの単位となっており、関係節や接続詞などによって従属節を伴う、または新たな主節を導入することにより行の前半を従属節とマークする役割を果た

第 6 章 *The Alliterative Morte Arthure* における韻律と連語

す。関係節を含む例を以下に掲げる。最初の例は、関係詞に導かれるもの、次ふたつは、接続詞に導かれるもの、そして最後の例は、非人称動詞を伴うものである。

(1) 関係詞に導かれる *b*-verse

MA 807	Takes hym two phylozophirs that folowede hym euer,
MA 3489	Onye grome vndire Gode that one this grownde walkes.
MA 1669	That *MA*ny sall repente that in his rowtte rydez,
MA 287	That thus regnez at Rome, whate ryghte that he claymes."
MA 2282	Thay kaire to the karyage and tuke whate them likes,
MA 899	In Seynt Mighell Mount, there myraclez are schewede."
MA 4268	With langoure in the launde thare he layes them togedire,

(2) 等位接続詞に導かれる *b*-verse

MA 346	Wyth full creuell knyghtez, so Cryste mot me helpe!
MA 467	"Sir," sais the Senatour, "so Crist mot me helpe,
MA 4144	Bot I forsake this gate, so me Gode helpe,
MA 371	And hafe no lettyng be lawe, bot lystynnys thise wordez:
MA 2795	Roris full ruydlye, bot rade he no more.
MA 3853	And scholde haue slottede hym in, bot no slytte happenede:

(3) 従位接続詞に導かれる *b*-verse

MA 31	Irelande vttirly, as occyane rynnys;
MA 274	Couerd it of comons, as cronicles telles.
MA 573	To Inde and to Ermonye, as Ewfrates rynnys,
MA 1251	He drawes into douce Fraunce, as Duchemen tellez,
MA 4346	Into Bretayne the Brode, as the Bruytte tellys.
MA 676	When I to contre come, if Cryste will it thole;
MA 4317	Alls becomys hym of kynde, ȝife Criste will hym thole;

MA 879	And take trewe for a tym, till it may tyde bettyr"
MA 462	Aftyr the aughtende day, when vndroun es rungen,
MA 582	To Tartary and Turky, when tythynngez es comen;
MA 1570	That towchez to the temporaltee, whills my tym lastez.
MA 398	And latte me neuere wanntte ȝow, whylls I in werlde regne;
MA 1705	Be with rebawdez rebuykyde whills I in werlde regne!"

(4) 他の文を付加する b-verse

MA 305	Counsayles Sir Arthure, and of hym besekys
MA 458	Be now lathe or lette, ryghte as the thynkes,
MA 564	And a bekyn abouen to brynne when them lykys,
MA 971	Bot thow arte fay, be my faythe, and that me forthynkkys.
MA 1154	Ouerfallen with a fende, vs es full hapnede!
MA 1684	Of syche trauaylande men trecherye me thnykes.
MA 2494	Wardayne full wyrchipfull, and so hym wele semes;
MA 2842	Bot they be fesede in faye ferly me thynkes.
MA 2861	Ȝone folk is one frountere, vnfraistede theym semes;
MA 3215	Withe the rentes of Rome, as me beste lykes;
MA 3393	And now wate thow my woo, worde as the lykes.
MA 4100	Ȝe wotte my wele and my woo- wirkkys as ȝow likys.

このような例から、b-verse における連語の中で、従属節や付加節を含むものが特別な役割を果たしていることが明らかになる。特徴的なのは、that, where, when 等に導かれる行と代名詞プラス動詞 likes で終わる行の多さである。前述のように likes という動詞は行末に全部で94回登場し、動詞の中でもその頻度は群を抜いている。また、関係詞で新たな文を付加するということは、行末において従属節が特別な働きをすること、非人称動詞でしめくくることは、syntactic hierarchy のレベルが異なる節を導入するということである。従属節または更なる主節を付加することで詳しい説明や解釈を添えることができ、頭韻の制約も従属節

全体には及ばず頭韻を踏む最初の metrical beat のみ注意を要したが、付加的要素を加えることは有益な方法であっただろう。特に *hym thouȝt, me likes, als hym lykede* のような非人称表現や、*as the storye tellis, as hit semed, as cronicles telles* などのような従属節がよく用いられている。そして、行末に来る *likes, thought, tells* 等は頭韻の制約を受けないのであるから、その行の頭韻音が何であれ使えるという特徴を持つ。中英語頭韻詩において従属節または付加説明を加える節が行の後半に現れることは、行末が頭韻を踏まないという韻律との関係が強く作用していると考えられる。

　The Alliterative Morte Arthure は、1行のなかで通常3度繰り返される頭韻音の繰返しを、さらに複数行に亘って同じ頭韻音を繰り返すという過剰な頭韻音の繰返し技法を用いることで他と比べて特殊である。さらに、*b-verse* における同じ語の繰返し、同一構造の繰返しは、繰返しの相乗効果をもたらしている。定型表現を同一句の繰返しと定義すると、中英語頭韻詩にそれを見いだすことは難しい。しかし、似通った語順と連語という枠で見れば、既成の句に頼るのではなく語は自由に選びながらある程度決まった語群によって行末が統一されていたことが明らかである。この recurrent phrases を広義に formulae と見ることで、Schumidt や Sievers が pan-Germanic と称した頭韻詩の技法が中英語頭韻詩にも継承されていると言えるだろう。既成の句に頼るかと見える時もあり、使われる語は異なっていても同じような言い回しが繰り返されると思わせる時もある。このような複雑な変化を可能にするテンプレートを解明することによって、全く同一句の繰返しではないが繰返し用いられる連語が韻律と強く結びついて formulaic style として機能していることが証明されると考える。

第7章

Sir Gawain and the Green Knight における韻律と連語

　巻末に掲げたデータを利用したもうひとつの分析として、中英語頭韻詩の主立った作品である *Sir Gawain and the Green Knight* の韻律と formulaic expressions について考察する。中英語頭韻詩において従属節または付加説明を加える節が行の後半によく用いられることから、このような節が果たす役割と韻律との関係を一定の語の組み合わせ、即ち *b*-verse における連語の観点から解明する。第4章と第6章で検討したように、*The Alliterative Morte Arthure* の *b*-verse には5つの連語タイプがあることが明らかになった。この章では、従属節または付加節等の付随的な節を含む第5ばんめのタイプが *Sir Gawain and the Green Knight* においてどのような構造になっているかを解明する。決まった言い回しは、並列されるふたつの語が頭韻を踏まない場合は特に、頭韻の制約を満たすためには行末に置かざるを得ない。すなわち、従属節や付随的な節が、頭韻の制約がない行末においてかなりの頻度で用いられ、広義の定型表現となっていると解釈できる。韻律のルールだけが大事なのではなく、規範に忠実なことと同じくらい、逸脱の限界まで挑戦することに新しい意義を求めるのが詩人の仕事であった。Smith は metrical norm/rhythmical deviation の関係を以下のように説明している。

　In discussions of medieval English verse, it is usual to emphasise the formal characteristics of the verse-form in question: the patterns of stress in relation to alliteration, for instance, or the formal patterning of rhyme. But such a restriction to surface characteristics has always seemed to me both limited and limiting. After all, the function of metre in verse has traditionally been taken as to do with the interplay of metrical norm and rhythmical deviation with the intention of making the modulation between norm and deviation salient in terms of meaning-something which poets often emphasise by accompanying their metrical choices with other stylistic effects. (2000, p. 92)

この章では *Sir Gawain and the Green Knight* において *b*-verse には norm/deviation がどのように展開するか分析し、連語タイプが韻律や頭韻の繰返しと同じくらい積極的意義を持つことを解明する。中英語頭韻詩が行の特定のポジションにおいて特定の語順を用いる傾向にあり、そこには頭韻のルールに加えて特定の連語のルールが働いていると考えられるからである。Smith (2000, p. 96) の言う sound symbolism が語の配置とどのように関わっているかに注目し、*Sir Gawain and the Green Knight* 2525行 (いわゆる the bob and the wheel 部分は除くので実際の分析を行ったのは2020行) に関するデータとそこから導き出される結果について考察する。中英語頭韻詩の韻律は、*a*-verse に2または3の metrical beats を持ち、*b*-verse に2つの metrical beats を持つ、行末の metrical beat は頭韻を踏まないが、他は原則として頭韻を踏む。これを Attridge が提唱する式で書き表すと以下のようになる。

The Metrical Rule of Middle English Alliterative Verse
Verse $\rightarrow$ (o B_0) o B_1 o B_2 o B_3 o B_4 o   [(a)aa/ax]

a-verse は3つの metrical beats を持つこともあるので、最初の *B0*は、optional と考え (　　) に入れる。B_0からB_3までは頭韻を踏み、metrical beats のあいだには unstressed syllable(s) が offbeat を形成する。*o* というシンボルで表したのは通常ゼロまたは1から3までの弱勢音節であり、行末にもこの弱勢音節が付けられることが多い。基本の頭韻パター

ンは「　」に示したようになる。

　分析はこれまで同様、Stage One で、*b*-verse を切り離す。*b*-verse の最初の metrical beat 以下行の最後までを分離し、その韻律の構成と連語タイプをマークする。Stage Two では、*a*-verse と *b*-verse の間に置かれる metrical offbeat の有無、あればその品詞構成によって分類する。Stage Three では、*b*-verse の最初の metrical beat を持つ語によって分類し、最後の Stage Four では、語の連語タイプを品詞により分類する。

　Stage Three で、*b*-verse 最初の語によって全部をアルファベット順に並べかえることで、同一の語句が用いられていることがあるか、出来合いの語句ようなものが使用されているかを見ることが出来る。同一の語で始まる *b*-verse の特徴はさまざまにあるが、そのひとつとして、*The Alliterative Morte Arthure* においても顕著に見られたように、後半行最初の metrical beat 即ち行全体でいうと三番目の metrical beat に、*knight, man, worrior* などを示す語が現れることが多くある。B3に用いられる語による分類では、*burne, freke, knyght, mon, renk, segge, wyʒe* などが頻繁に登場する。以下に掲げたのは、*Sir Gawain and the Green Knight* に見られる現代英語の *knight, man, worrior* に当たる語で始まる *b*-verse のグループである。同一の語で始まる *b*-verse が同一または非常に類似した語順構成になっている例が多いことが分かる。*knight, man, worrior* 等を示す語が *B3* の位置に置かれるこのような例は、それに続く語のアルファベット順に例を並べたので、そのグループ内で行番号順には並んでいない。語形はグロッサリーの見出し語によった。

bu(u)rn(e)

G 20	Ande quen this Bretayn watz bigged bi this <u>burn</u> rych,
G 1189	And boʒed towarde the bed; and the <u>burne</u> schamed,
G 2377	Brayde brothely the belt to the <u>burne</u> seluen:
G 1071	Bot ʒe schal be in yowre bed, <u>burne</u>, at thyn ese,
G 1616	The bores hed watz borne bifore the <u>burnes</u> seluen
G 481	Thenne thay boʒed to a borde thise <u>burnes</u> togeder,
G 1582	Syʒ hym byde at the bay, his <u>burnez</u> bysyde;

第 7 章 *Sir Gawain and the Green Knight* における韻律と連語

G 1461	Then, braynwod for bate, on <u>burnez</u> he rasez,
G 852	And there were boun at his bode <u>burnez</u> innoȝe,
G 1325	The best boȝed therto with <u>burnez</u> innoghe,
G 272	Bot if thou be so bold as alle <u>burnez</u> tellen,

frek(e)

G 651	The fyft fyue that I finde that the <u>frek</u> vsed
G 196	Such a fole vpon folde, ne <u>freke</u> that hym rydes,
G 2125	That euer ȝe fondet to fle for <u>freke</u> that I wyst."
G 1925	Fyndez fire vpon flet, the <u>freke</u> ther-byside,
G 2373	The forme worde vpon folde that the <u>freke</u> meled:
G 430	And nawther faltered ne fel the <u>freke</u> neuer the helder,
G 2274	Nawther fyked I ne flaȝe, <u>freke</u>, quen thou myntest,
G 703	And ay he frayned, as he ferde, at <u>frekez</u> that he met,
G 1374	Bifore alle the folk on the flette, <u>frekez</u> he beddez
G 1433	Thay ferden to the fyndyng, and <u>frekez</u> hem after;
G 1172	And hem tofylched, as fast as <u>frekez</u> myȝt loke,
G 537	And he made a fare on that fest for the <u>frekez</u> sake,

hathel

G 771	That holde on that on syde the <u>hathel</u> auysed,
G 655	Were harder happed on that <u>hathel</u> then on any other.
G 309	"What, is this Arthures hous," quoth the <u>hathel</u> thenne,
G 2408	And hatz hit of hendely, and the <u>hathel</u> thonkkez,
G 2056	And halden honour in her honde, the <u>hathel</u> hem ȝelde
G 949	And heȝly honowred with <u>hathelez</u> aboute.
G 1602	Heȝe halowin*G* on hiȝe with <u>hathelez</u> that myȝt;
G 1723	Here he watz halawed, when <u>hathelez</u> hym metten,
G 829	Then haylsed he ful hendly tho <u>hathelez</u> vchone,

knyȝt

G 767	A castel the comlokest that euer knyȝt aȝte,
G 2489	And thus he commes to the court, knyȝt al in sounde.
G 1366	Into the comly castel, ther the knyȝt bidez
G 1303	I schal kysse at your comaundement, as a knyȝt fallez,
G 366	Then comaunded the kynG the knyȝt for to ryse;
G 704	If thay hade herde any karp of a knyȝt grene,
G 377	Then carppez to Sir Gawan the knyȝt in the grene,
G 2111	Com ȝe there, ȝe be kylled, may the knyȝt rede,
G 1476	Ho commes to the cortyn, and at the knyȝt totes.
G 1272	For the costes that I haf knowen vpon the, knyȝt, here,
G 62	Fro the kynG watz cummen with knyȝtes into the halle,
G 473	AmonG thise kynde caroles of knyȝtez and ladyez.

kyng(e)

G 393	Clanly al the couenaunt that I the kynge asked,
G 2275	Ne kest no kauelacion in kyngez hous Arthor.
G 2340	Ne kyd bot as couenaunde at kyngez kort schaped.

lord(e)

G 1729	And ȝe he lad hem bi lagmon, the lorde and his meyny,
G 1960	Thenne loȝly his leue at the lorde fyrst
G 1634	And let lodly therat the lorde for to here.
G 316	Wyth this he laȝes so loude that the lorde greued;
G 1055	For alle the londe inwyth Logres, so me oure lorde help!
G 988	Thus wyth laȝande lotez the lorde hit tayt makez,
G 595	Lachez lufly his leue at lordez and ladyez;

mon

G 749	Thurȝ mony misy and myre, mon al hym one,
G 878	And thenne a meré mantyle watz on that mon cast

第 7 章 *Sir Gawain and the Green Knight* における韻律と連語

G 2108	Monk other masseprest, other any <u>mon</u> elles,
G 718	So mony meruayl bi mount ther the <u>mon</u> fyndez,
G 2295	Then muryly efte con he mele, the <u>mon</u> in the grene:
G 1682	For the lur may mon lach when-so <u>mon</u> lykez."
G 964	A mensk lady on molde <u>mon</u> may hir calle,
G 1656	With al the manerly merthe that <u>mon</u> may of telle,
G 834	For to mete wyth menske the <u>mon</u> on the flor;
G 2290	He myntez at hym maȝtyly, bot not the <u>mon</u> rynez,
G 2350	That other munt for the morne, <u>mon</u>, I the profered,
G 1313	And made myry al day, til the <u>mone</u> rysed,
G 1447	Mony watz the myry mouthe of <u>men</u> and of houndez
G 45	With alle the mete and the mirthe that <u>men</u> couthe avyse;
G 1915	Hit watz the myriest mute that euer <u>men</u> herde,
G 1953	Thay maden as mery as any <u>men</u> moȝten-
G 1690	After messe a morsel he and his <u>men</u> token;

renk

G 2337	And wyth a rynkande rurde he to the <u>renk</u> sayde:
G 1911	Ay rechatande aryȝt til thay the <u>renk</u> seȝen.
G 2206	Is ryched at the reuerence me, <u>renk</u>, to mete
G 1134	Arayed for the rydyng, with <u>renkkez</u> ful mony;
G 862	Ryche robes ful rad <u>renkkez</u> hym broȝten,
G 432	And runyschly he raȝt out, there as <u>renkkez</u> stoden,

segg(e)

G 115	And sithen mony siker <u>segge</u> at the sidbordez.
G 1882	And of absolucioun he on the <u>segge</u> calles;
G 1589	The swyn settez hym out on the <u>segge</u> euen,
G 848	And wel hym semed, for sothe, as the <u>segge</u> thuȝt,
G 574	Thenne set thay the sabatounz vpon the <u>segge</u> fotez,
G 893	And ay sawes so sleȝe that the <u>segge</u> lyked.

G 1091	"ȝe, sir, for sothe," sayd the segge trwe.
G 394	Saf that thou schal siker me, segge, bi thi trawthe,
G 763	NADE he sayned hymself, segge, bot thrye,
G 1438	And he vnsoundyly out soȝt seggez ouerthwert;

wyȝ(e)

G 1743	Wayuez vp a wyndow, and on the wyȝe callez,
G 945	And wener then Wenore, as the wyȝe thoȝt.
G 2321	Watz he neuer in this worlde wyȝe half so blithe-
G 2441	Wyth yow wyth worschyp- the wyȝe hit yow ȝelde
G 938	And sayde he watz the welcomest wyȝe of the worlde;
G 2074	And went on his way with his wyȝe one,
G 715	At vche warthe other water ther the wyȝe passed
G 1028	Vchon to wende on his way that watz wyȝe stronge.
G 2091	"For I haf wonnen yow hider, wyȝe, at this tyme,
G 2469	And I wol the as wel, wyȝe, bi my faythe,
G 2240	Iwysse thou art welcom, wyȝe, to my place,
G 1167	What wylde so atwaped wyȝes that schotten
G 314	Ouerwalt wyth a worde of on wyȝes speche,

前述のように中英語頭韻詩 *b*-verse はその最初に来る語の品詞によって以下のような 5 つのタイプに分けることができる。

Type 1 ： *b*-verse が名詞で始まる
Type 2 ： *b*-verse が動詞で始まる
Type 3 ： *b*-verse が形容詞で始まる
Type 4 ： *b*-verse が副詞で始まる
Type 5 ： *b*-verse が従属節、付加節を含む

以下は、*Sir Gawain and the Green Knight* における連語タイプである。今まで同様、optional elements は（　　）内に示し、/ はその内から一つ

第7章　*Sir Gawain and the Green Knight* における韻律と連語

を選択することを示す。特に頻度の高いタイプには星印を付した。

Stage Four; *b*-verse Collocation Types

(Sir Gawain and the Green Knight)

Type One: 名詞で始まる *b*-verse

```
[ N ]      +          [ N ]*
[ N ]   + C    +   [ N ]
[ N ]   + P (D) +  [ N ]*
[ N ]   + (Z)  +   [ A ]*
[ N ]   + (X)  +   [ V ]*
[ N ]   + (be) +   [ E/A ]
[ N ]   + P    +   [ V ]*
[ N ]   + (for) to + [ V ]*
[ N ]   + Z    +   [ V ]
[ N ]          +   [ Z ]*
[ N ]   + (H)  +   [ P ]
[ N ]   +          /(no B₄)
```

Type Two: 動詞で始まる *b*-verse

```
[ V ]  + (D/N/Z) +  [ N ]*
[ V ]    + P     +  [ N ]*
[ V ]    + H     +  [ P ]
[ V ]    + N     +  [ Z ]*
[ V ]  + (H/P/Z) +  [ Z ]*
[ G ]            +  [ Z ]*
[ E/G ] + (be/H) +  [ Z/V ]
[ V ]  + N/H (to) + [ V ]
[ V ]    + to +     [ V ]
[ X ]  + (P/H/Z) +  [ V ]
[ V ]            +  [ X ]
```

Type Three: 形容詞で始まる *b*-verse

[A] + (P) (D) + [N]*
[A] + A + [N]
[A] + N/H + [V/A/N/P]
[A] + N + [Z]
[A] + [Z]
[A] + *to* + [V]

Type Four: 副詞で始まる *b*-verse

[Z] + (*to*) + [V/X]*
[Z] + H + [V]*
[Z] + [Z]
[Z] + (be) + [A/E]
[Z] + P (D) + [N]

Type Five: 従属節、付加節となる *b*-verse

[N/V/A/ADV] + (C/Q/that) + [S]
(S=Sentence)

従属節または付加的な節を含む Type Five は、*Sir Gawain and the Green Knight* では次のように分類することができる。第6章で分析した *The Alliterative Morte Arthure* とは少々異なった分類になっている。

(1) 関係詞に導かれる *b*-verse

G 429　　　The blod brayd fro the body, <u>that</u> blykked on the grene;
G 1726　　And ay the titleres at his tayl, <u>that</u> tary he ne myȝt;

(2) 従属接続詞に導かれる *b*-verse

G 69	Ladies laȝed ful loude, thoȝ thay lost haden,
G 700	Ouer at the Holy Hede, til he hade eft bonk

(3) 非人称動詞で終わる *b*-verse

G 679	A lowande leder of ledez in londe hym wel semez,
G 1241	"In god fayth," quoth Gawayn, "gayn hit me thynkkez,

(4) *say*, *tell* 等により話法を導く *b*-verse

G 1208	"God moroun, Sir Gawayn," sayde that gay lady,
G 1940	"Ȝe, of the chepe no charg," quoth chefly that other,

(5) 一文を付加する *b*-verse

G 257	To wone any quyle in this won, hit watz not myn ernde;
G 2408	And hatz hit of hendely, and the hathel thonkkez,

　a-verse と *b*-verse の間にどのような語が置かれるかが重要な役割を果たしている。なぜなら、*b*-verse の前に前置詞や関係詞が来たとき、*b*-verse 全体の果たす役割が文法的に決まるからである。このように半行の間に使われる品詞によって *b*-verse が関係節、付加節になるものが Type Five であり、Type One から Type Four までのタイプとその構造が著しく異なっている。即ち、*b*-verse 最初の語とそれに続く語の関係というよりむしろ全体がひとつの単位となっており、関係節や接続詞などによって従属節を伴う、または新たな主節を導入することにより行の前半を従属節とマークする役割を果たす。*Sir Gawain and the Green Knight* における Type Five の主なパターンを以下に掲げる。関係詞などの位置によって、その後に metrical beat がいくつ置かれるかが異なるので、ふたつの metrical beats つまり *b*-verse 全体が関わるものを Type A、行末の metircal beat ひとつのみが関わるものを Type B としてまとめた。

Type Five (*Sir Gawain and the Green Knight*)

(1) 関係詞に導かれる (**Type A**)

G 528	Thenne al rypez and rotez <u>that</u> ros vpon fyrst,
G 1928	He were a bleaunt of blwe <u>that</u> bradde to the erthe,
G 152	A strayte cote ful stre3t, <u>that</u> stek on his sides,
G 1562	Swez his vncely swyn, <u>that</u> swyngez bi the bonkkez
G 406	"3if I the telle trwly, <u>quen</u> I the tape haue
G 1570	Of a rasse bi a rokk <u>ther</u> rennez the boerne.

関係詞に導かれる (**Type B**)

G 703	And ay he frayned, as he ferde, at frekez <u>that</u> he met,
G 2251	I schal gruch the no grwe for grem <u>that</u> fallez.
G 1087	As wy3 that wolde of his wyte, ne wyst <u>quat</u> he my3t.
G 1544	As I am, other euer schal, in erde <u>ther</u> I leue,

(2) 従属接続詞に導かれる (**Type A**)

G 31	I schal telle hit as-tit, <u>as</u> I in toun herde,
G 1999	The day dryuez to the derk, <u>as</u> Dry3tyn biddez;
G 69	Ladies la3ed ful loude, <u>tho3</u> thay lost haden,
G 2038	For pryde of the pendauntez, <u>tha3</u> polyst thay were,
G 1415	The douthe dressed to the wod, <u>er</u> any day sprenged,
G 2009	Deliuerly he dressed vp, <u>er</u> the day sprenged,
G 1280	Thus thay meled of muchquat <u>til</u> mydmorn paste,
G 1467	Suande this wylde swyn <u>til</u> the sunne schafted.
G 1774	And more for his meschef <u>3if</u> he schulde make synne,
G 2457	For to assay the surquidré, <u>3if</u> hit soth were
G 805	To herber in that hostel <u>whyl</u> halyday lested,
G 1235	I schal ware my whyle wel, <u>quyl</u> hit lastez,
G 1642	Of alle the couenauntes that we knyt, <u>sythen</u> I com hider,

第 7 章 *Sir Gawain and the Green Knight* における韻律と連語

G 2394	As thou hadez neuer forfeted <u>sythen</u> thou watz first borne;
G 251	And rekenly hym reuerenced, <u>for</u> rad was he neuer,
G 1266	Bot the daynté that thay delen, <u>for</u> my disert nys euen,
G 1588	That fele ferde for the freke, <u>lest</u> felle hym the worre.
G 1773	He cared for his cortaysye, <u>lest</u> crathayn he were,

従属接続詞に導かれる (**Type B**)

G 931	Rungen ful rychely, ryȝt <u>as</u> thay schulden,
G 2171	Saue, a lyttel on a launde, a lawe <u>as</u> hit were;
G 1494	If I were werned, I were wrang, iwysse, <u>ȝif</u> I profered."
G 1992	For he hade muche on the morn to mynne, <u>ȝif</u> he wolde,
G 279	"Nay, frayst I no fyȝt, in fayth I the <u>telle</u>,
G 2337	And wyth a rynkande rurde he to the renk <u>sayde</u>:

(3) 非人称動詞で終わる (**Type B**)

| G 235 | As growe grene as the gres and grener hit <u>semed</u>, |
| G 2167 | The skwez of the scowtes skayned hym <u>thoȝt</u>. |

(4) *say* や *tell* を含んで話法を導く (**Type A**)

| G 1208 | "God moroun, Sir Gawayn," <u>sayde</u> that gay lady, |
| G 1940 | "Ȝe, of the chepe no charg," <u>quoth</u> chefly that other, |

(5) 一文を付加する (**Type A**)

| G 1963 | Your honour at this hyȝe fest, <u>the hyȝe kyng yow ȝelde</u>! |
| G 2239 | "Gawayn," quoth that grene gome, "<u>God the mot loke</u>! |

以上のタイプを用例数と共に表にしたのが Table Three である。

Table Three: Words Preceding the Collocation Types Five-A and Five-B (*Sir Gawain and the Green Knight*)

	Type A	Type B	Total
that	143	45	188
as	47	16	63
other relative pronouns/adverbs	39	18	57
impersonal verbs	0	54	54
sayde/telle/quath	13	9	22
single sentence	19	0	19
bifore/er	17	0	17
if	9	5	14
though	6	0	6
for	5	0	5
whyl/quyle	2	3	5
lest/newther	4	0	4
sythen	3	0	3
Total	307	150	457

　このようにして b-verse における従属節や付加節の特別の役割が明らかになる。まず、*that, where, when* 等に導かれる節の多さである。関係詞で新たな文を付加するということは、行末において従属節が特別な働きをすること、そして時には *tell, say* 等の動詞により主節をも導入すること、そしてそれは即ち、*syntactic hierarchy* が異なる節を導入するということである。従属節または更なる主節を付加することで詳しい説明や解釈を添えることができ、頭韻の制約も従属節全体には及ばず頭韻を踏む最初の metrical beat のみ注意を払えばよい。ここでも *hym thouȝt, me likes, als hym lykede* のような impersonal expressions や、*as the storye tellis, hit semed, as the wryt telles* 等のような従属節が活用されている。このような形でテンプレートを解明することによって、全く同一句の繰返しではないが繰返し用いられる連語が formulaic style として機能していることを中英語頭韻詩全体に関して証明されるであろう。

むすび

　頭韻詩は、音の繰返しとさまざまな技巧を駆使して独自のリズムを生み出す。中英語頭韻詩の定型に近い表現と似通った連語タイプを集め、音韻と統語の関係を明らかにし、個々の作品の特徴と全体に共通するテンプレートを再構築するための基礎データが巻末の分析資料である。また、この研究に関連する文献を Select　Bibliography としてまとめた。データ資料は、最初の *Wynner and Wastour* に関しては、Stage One から Stage Four までを示し、他の作品は Stage One のデータのみを示した。それぞれのデータベースは Stage ごとに利用可能な状態でデジタル化済みである。最終的には Stage One, Stage Two, Stage Three, Stage Four のデータすべてを整えて韻律と連語の関係についてコーパスとしての利用を可能にし、以下に Turville-Petre が述べているように解明が簡単ではないが predictable とされる verbal and conceptual echoes を明らかにしたい。

The tendency of words to cluster together in this way inevitably leads to recurrent verbal and conceptual echoes between one poem and another. The structure of the alliterative line encourages the poet to build his half-lines around established collocations in a predictable way, and so in any poem many half-lines are repeated more or less exactly both within that poem and in poems by other writers. The repetition of whole lines is not so common, but it occurs especially when the poet is describing a set topic. Faced with these parallels, earlier critics assumed them to be the result of imitation or identity of authorship. However, it is rarely possible to pin down the 'source' of a collocation, and nearly always it owes its existence to an alliterative school of poetry, or more generally still to the English poetic tradition.　　　　　(1977, p.86)

　これからの課題として、他の作品の分析結果を含めることと、中英語の特徴に合わせた使い方ができるようデータを整え、最終的には、全作品を amalgamate して、韻律、実際の語、連語タイプから検索できるデータとして整える予定である。精緻な分析を助ける正確なデータを揃えた後、Duggan, Minkova, Oakden, Turville-Petre 等の先行研究において定型表現として挙げられている句や節が実際にどのように使われ、韻律との関係はどのようになっているかを検証する。そして、Turville-Petre が示唆するように、簡単には解明できないが英語の根幹に脈々と息づいている頭韻の伝統と、中世の詩人たちが目指した言葉の芸術の意義について実証的な分析を目指したい。

Select Bibliography

Primary Sources

The Alliterative Morte Arthure: A Critical Edition. Ed. Valerie Krishna. New York: B. Franklin, 1976.

Morte Arthure: A Critical Edition. Ed. Mary Hamel. New York: Garland, 1984.

Morte Arthure. Ed. Edmund Brock. EETS 8. 1961.

Cleanness. Patience, Sir Gawain and the Green Knight.
    The Poems of the Pearl Manuscript. Eds. Malcolm Andrew and Ronald Waldron. Exeter: University of Exeter, 1987.

Sir Gawain and the Green Knight. Ed. I. Gollancz, EETS 210. 1957.

The Parlement of the Thre Ages. Wynnere and Wastoure Ed. Warren Ginsberg. Kalamazoo: Medieval Institute, 1992.

The Parlement of the Thre Ages. Ed. M. Y. Offord. EETS 246. 1959.

The Siege of Jerusalem. Eds. E. Kölbing and M. Day. EETS 188. 1932.

St. Erkenwald. Ed. Turville-Petre, Thorlac. *Alliterative Poetry of the Later Middle Ages: An Anthology.* London: Routledge, 1989.

The Wars of Alexander. Eds. Hoyt Duggan and Thorlac Turville-Petre. EETS SS 10. 1989.

Wynnere and Wastoure. Ed. Stephanie Trigg. EETS 297. 1990.

Secondary Sources

Allen, G. D. "The Location of Rhythmic Stress Beats in English Speech, Parts I and II." *Language and Speech* 15 (1972): 72-100; 179-95.

Allen, G. D. "Speech Rhythm: Its Relation to Performance Universals and Articulatory Timing." *Journal of Phonetics* 3 (1975): 75-86.

Allen, Rosamund. "Performance and Structure in *The Alliterative Morte Arthure.*" *New Perspectives on Middle English Texts: A Festschrift for R. A. Waldron.* Eds. S.

Powell and J. Smith. Cambridge: D. S. Brewer, 2000. 17-29.
Amodio, Mark C., and Sarah G. Miller, eds. *Oral Poetics in Middle English Poetry*. New York: Garland, 1994.
Andrew, Malcolm, and Ronald Waldron, eds. *The Poems of the Pearl Manuscript*. Exeter: University of Exeter, 1987.
Anttila, Raimo. "Sound Preference in Alliteration." *Statistical Methods in Linguistics* 5 (1969): 44-48.
Attridge, Derek. *The Rhythms of English Poetry*. London: Longman, 1982.
Attridge, Derek. *Poetic Rhythm: An Introduction*. Cambridge: Cambridge University Press, 1995.
Ballard, Kim. *The Frameworks of English: Introducing Language Structures*. Basingstoke: Palgrave, 2007.
Baltzer, Rebecca A., Thomas Cable, and James I. Wimsatt, eds. *The Union of Words and Music in Medieval Poetry*. Austin: University of Texas Press, 1991.
Barber, Charles. *The English Language: A Historical Introduction*. Cambridge: Cambridge University Press, 1993.
Baugh, Albert, and Thomas Cable. *A History of the English Language*. Fifth edn. Upper Saddle River, New Jersey: Prentice Hall, 2002.
Beaver, Joseph C. "The Rules of Stress in English Verse." *Language* 47 (1971): 586-614.
Bennett, J. W. A. "Survivals and Revivals of Alliterative Modes." *Leeds Studies of English* 14 (1983): 26-43.
Bernhart, A. W. "Complexity and Metricality." *Poetics* 12 (1974): 113-41.
Blake, Norman F. "Rhythmical Alliteration." *Modern Philology* 67 (1969): 118-24.
Blake, Norman F. *An Introduction to the Language of Literature*. Basingstoke: Macmillan, 1990.
Blake, Norman F. *The Cambridge History of the English Language. vol 2. 1066-1476*. Cambridge: Cambridge University Press, 1992.
Bliss, Alan. *An Introduction to Old English Metre*. Oxford: Basil Blackwell, 1962.
Boomsliter, Paul C., Warren Creel, and George S. Hastings. "Perception and English Poetic Meter." *PMLA* 88 (1973): 200-08.
Borroff, Marie. *Sir Gawain and the Green Knight: A Stylistic and Metrical Study*. New Haven and London: Yale University Press, 1962.
Borroff, Marie. "Reading the Poem Aloud." *Approaches to Teaching* Sir Gawain and the Green Knight. Eds. M. Miller and J. Chance. New York: Modern Language Association of America, 1986. 191-98.
Borroff, Marie. "Systematic Sound Symbolism in the Long Alliterative Line in *Beowulf* and *Sir Gawain*." *English Historical Metrics*. Eds. C. McCully, and J. Anderson.

Cambridge: Cambridge University Press, 1996. 120-33.

Bradford, Richard. *A Linguistic History of English Poetry*. London and New York: Routledge, 1993.

Bunt, Gerrit H. V. "Alliterative Patterning and the Editing of Middle English Poetry." *English Historical Metrics*. Eds. C. McCully, and J. Anderson. Cambridge: Cambridge University Press, 1996. 175-84.

Burrow, John A. "Reduncancy in Alliterative Verse: *St Erkenwald.*" *Individuality and Achievement in Middle English Poetry*. Ed. O. Pickering. Woodbridge, Sufffolk: D. S. Brewer, 1997. 119-28.

Burrow, J., and Thorlac Turville-Petre. *A Book of Middle English*. Oxford: Blackwell, 2005.

Cable, Thomas. "Timers, Stressers, and Linguists: Contention and Compromise." *Modern Language Quarterly* 33 (1972): 227-39.

Cable, Thomas. "Middle English Meter and its Theoretical Implications." *Yearbook of Langland Studies* 2 (1988): 47-69.

Cable, Thomas. "Standards from the Past: The Conservative Syllable Structure of the Alliterative Revival." *Standardizing English: Essays in the History of Language Change in Honor of John Hurt Fisher*. Ed. J. Trahern, Jr. Knoxville: University of Tennessee Press, 1989. 42-56.

Cable, Thomas. *The English Alliterative Tradition*. Philadelphia: University of Pennsylvania Press, 1991.

Cable, Thomas. "Grammar, Spelling, and the Rhythm of the Alliterative Long Line." *Prosody and Poetics in the Early Middle Ages: Essays in Honour of C. B. Hieatt*. Ed. M. Toswell. Toronto: University of Toronto Press, 1995. 13-22.

Cable, Thomas. "Clashing Stress in the Metres of Old, Middle, and Renaissance English." *English Historical Metrics*. Eds. C. McCully, and J. Anderson. Cambridge: Cambridge University Press, 1996. 7-29.

Camargo, Martin. "Oral Tradition Structure in *Sir Gawain and the Green Knight.*" *Comparative Research on Oral Traditions*. Ed. J. Foley. Columbus: Slavica, 1987. 121-37.

Campbell, Alastair. "The Old English Epic Style." *English and Medieval Studies Presented to J. R .R. Tolkien on the Occasion of his Seventieth Birthday*. Eds. N. Davis and C. Wrenn. London: Allen and Unwin, 1962. 13-26.

Campbell, J. J. "Oral Poetry in *The Seafarer.*" *Speculum* 35 (1960): 87-96.

Chamberlin, John S. "What Makes *Piers Plowman* So Hard to Read?" *Style* 23 (1989): 32-48.

Chatman, Seymour. *A Theory of Meter*. The Hague: Mouton, 1965.

Chomsky, Noam, and Morris Halle. *The Sound Pattern of English*. Cambridge, MA and

London: MIT Press, 1991.
Chomsky, Noam, Morris Halle, and F. Lukoff. "On Accent and Juncture in English." *For Roman Jakobson*. Eds. M. Halle, H. Lunt, H. McLean. and G. van Schooneveld. The Hague: Mouton, 1956. 65-80.
Clark, John W. "On Certain 'Alliterative' and 'Poetic' Words in the Poems Attributed to 'The Gawain-Poet.'" *Modern Language Quartery* 12 (1951): 387-98.
Couper-Kuhlen, Elizabeth. *An Introduction to English Prosody*. London: Edward Arnold, 1986.
Couper-Kuhlen, Elizabeth. *English Speech Rhythm: Form and Function in Everyday Verbal Interaction*. Amsterdam: John Benjamins, 1993.
Creed, Robert P. *Reconstructing the Rhythm of Beowulf*. Columbia: University of Missouri Press, 1990.
Crystal, David. *The Cambridge Encyclopedia of Language*. Cambridge and New York: Cambridge University Press, 1987.
Cureton, Richard D. *Rhythmic Phrasing in English Verse*. London: Longman, 1992.
Cureton, Richard D. "Rhythm and Verse Study." *Language and Literature* 3 (1994): 105-24.
Donner, Morton. "A Grammatical Perspective on Word Play in *Pearl*." *Chaucer Review* 22 (1988): 322-31.
Duggan, Hoyt N. "The Role of Formulas in the Dissemination of a Middle English Alliterative Romance." *Studies in Bibliography* 29 (1976): 265-88.
Duggan, Hoyt N. "Strophic Patterns in Middle English Alliterative Poetry." *Modern Philology* 74 (1976-77): 223-47.
Duggan, Hoyt N. "The Shape of the B-Verse in Middle English Alliterative Poetry." *Speculum* 61 (1986): 564-92.
Duggan, Hoyt N. "Final -*e* and the Rhythmic Structure of the B-Verse in Middle English Alliterative Poetry." *Modern Philology* 86 (1988): 119-45.
Duggan, Hoyt N. "Stress Assignment in Middle English Alliterative Poetry." *Journal of English and Germanic Philology* 89 (1990): 309-29.
Duggan, Hoyt N. "The Role and Distribution of –*ly* Adverbs in Middle English Alliterative Verse." *Loyal Letters: Studies on Medieval Alliterative Poetry and Prose*. Eds. L. Houwen and A. MacDonald. Groningen: Egbert Forsten, 1994. 131-54.
Eadie, J. "The Alliterative *Morte Arthure*: Structure and Meaning." *English Studies* 63 (1982): 1-12.
Ebbs, John Dale. "Stylistic Mannerisms of the Gawain-Poet." *Journal of English and Germanic Philology* 57 (1958): 522-25.
Everett, Dorothy. *Essays on Middle English Literature*. West Port: Greenwood Press, 1978.

Fabb, Nigel. *Linguistics and Literature: Language in the Verbal Arts of the World.* Oxford: Blackwell, 1997.

Finlayson, John. "Formulaic Technique in *Morte Arthure.*" *Anglia* 81 (1963): 372-93.

Finnegan, Ruth H. *Oral Traditions and the Verbal Arts.* London and New York: Routledge, 1992.

Fisiak, Jacek. *Studies in Middle English Linguistics.* Berlin and New York: Mouton de Gruyter, 1997.

Fisiak, Jacek. *Advances in English Historical Linguistics.* Hawthorne, NY: Mouton de Gruyter, 1998.

Foley, John M. "Tradition-Dependent and-Independent Features in Oral Literature: A Comparative View of the Formula." *Oral Traditional Literature: A Festschrift for A. B. Lord.* Ed. J. Foley. Columbus, OH: Slavica, 1981. 262-81.

Foley, John M. *Oral-Formulaic Theory and Research: An Introduction and Annotated Bibliography.* New York: Garland, 1985.

Frankis, John. "Word-Formation by Blending in the Vocabulary of Middle English Alliterative Verse." *Five Hundred Years of Words and Sounds: A Festschrift for Eric Dobson.* Eds. E. Stanley and D. Gray. Cambridge: Brewer, 1983. 29-38.

Freeborn, Dennis. *Style: Text Analysis and Linguistic Criticism.* Basingstoke and London: Macmillan, 1996.

Frye, Northrop, ed. *Sound and Poetry.* New York: Columbia University Press, 1957.

Fulk, Robert D. *A History of Old English Meter.* Philadelphia: University of Pennsylvania Press, 1992.

Furniss, Tom, and Michael Bath. *Reading Poetry: An Introduction.* Harlow: Pearson Longman, 2007.

Fussell, Paul, Jr., *Poetic Meter and Poetic Form.* Revised edn. New York: Random House, 1979.

Gardner, John. *The Complete Works of the Gawain-Poet.* Chicago and London: University of Chicago Press, 1967.

Giegerich, Heinz J. *Metrical Phonology and Phonological Structure: German and English.* Cambridge: Cambridge University Press, 1985.

Giegerich, Heinz J. *English Phonology: An Introduction.* Cambridge: Cambridge University Press, 1992.

Gilligan, Janet. "Numerical Composition in the Middle English *Patience.*" *Studia Neophilologica* 61 (1989): 7-11.

Gilmour-Bryson, Anne, ed. *Computer Applications to Medieval Studies.* Kalamazoo: Western Michigan University, 1984.

Goldsmith, Ulrich K. "Alliteration." *Princeton Encyclopedia of Poetry and Poetics.* Third edn. Ed. A. Preminger. Princeton: Princeton University Press, 1974.

15-16.
Göller, Karl H., ed. The Alliterative Morte Arthure: *A Reacessment of the Poem*. Cambridge: Brewer, 1981.
Görlach, Manfred. *Text Types and the History of English*. Berlin, New York: Mouton de Gruyter, 2004.
Graddol, David, Dick Leith, and Joan Swann. *English: History, Diversity and Change*. London: Routledge, 1996.
Gradon, Pamela. *Form and Style in Early English Literature*. London: Methuen, 1974.
Green, D. C. "Formulas and Syntax in Old English Poetry." *Computers and the Humanities* 6 (1971): 85-93.
Green, Richard H. "Medieval Poetics." *Approaches to Teaching* Sir Gawain and the Green Knight. Eds. M. Miller and J. Chance. New York: Modern Language Association of America, 1986. 102-08.
Gross, L. "The Meaning and Oral-Formulaic Use of Riot in the Alliterative *Morte Authure*." *Annuale Mediaevale* 9 (1968): 98-102.
Guest, Edwin. *A History of English Rhythms*. London: Pickering, 1838. Revised edn. Ed. W. Skeat. New York: Haskell House, 1968.
Hagen, Karl. T. "Adverbial Distribution in Middle English Alliterative Verse." *Modern Philology* 90 (1992): 159-71.
Halle, Morris, and Samuel J. Keyser. *English Stress: Its Form, its Growth and its Role in Verse*. New York: Harper and Row, 1971.
Hamel, Mary. Morte Arthure: *A Critical Edition*. New York: Garland, 1984.
Hanna, Ralph, III. "Defining Middle English Alliterative Poetry." *The Endless Knot: Essays on Old and Middle English in Honor of Marie Borroff*. Eds. M. Tavormina and R. Yeager. Cambridge: D. S. Brewer, 1995. 43-64.
Hanna, Ralph, III. "Alliterative Poetry." *The Cambridge History of Medieval English Literature*. Ed. D. Wallace. Cambridge: Cambridge University Press, 1999. 488-512.
Harding, D. W. *Words into Rhythm: English Speech Rhythm in Verse and Prose*. Cambridge: Cambridge University Press, 1976.
Hartle, Paul N. *Hunting the Letter: Middle English Alliterative Verse and the Formulaic Theory*. Frankfurt am Main: Peter Lang, 1999.
Haugen, Einar. "The Syllable in Linguistic Description." *For Roman Jakobson*. Eds. M. Halle, H. Lunt, H. McLean, and G. van Schooneveld. The Hague: Mouton, 1956. 213-21.
Hayes, Bruce. *A Metrical Theory of Stress Rules*. New York: Garland, 1985.
Hayes, Bruce. "The Prosodic Hierarchy in Meter." *Phonetics and Phonology I: Rhythm and Meter*. Eds. P. Kiparsky and G. Youmans. San Diego: Academic Press,

1989. 201-60.

Hayes, Bruce. *Metrical Stress Theory: Principles and Case Studies*. Chicago; University of Chicago Press, 1995.

Haynes, John. *Style*. London, New York: Routledge, 1995.

Hieatt, Constance B. "The Rhythm of the Alliterative Long Line." *Chaucer and Middle English Studies in Honour of Rossell Hope Robbins*. Ed. B. Rowland. London: Allen and Unwin, 1974. 119-30.

Hobsbaum, Philip. *Metre, Rhythm and Verse Form*. London and New York: Routledge, 1996.

Hogg, Richard, and C. B. McCully. *Metrical Phonology: A Coursebook*. Cambridge: Cambridge University Press, 1987.

Hoover, David L. *A New Theory of Old English Meter*. New York: Bern and Frankfurt am Main: Peter Lang, 1985.

Horobin, Simon, and Jeremy Smith. *An Introduction to Middle English*. New York: Oxford University Press, 2002.

Hulbert, J. R. "A Hypothesis Concerning the Alliterative Revival." *Modern Philology* 28 (1931): 405-22.

Huntsman-Mc, Jeffrey F. "The Celtic Heritage of *Sir Gawain and the Green Knight*." Approaches to Teaching Sir Gawain and the Green Knight. Eds. M. Miller and J. Chance. New York: Modern Language Association of America, 1986. 177-81.

Hutcheson, Bellenden R. *Old English Poetic Metre*. Cambridge: D. S. Brewer, 1995.

Jakobson, Roman. "Closing Statement: Linguistics and Poetics." *Style in Language*. Ed. T. Sebeok. Cambridge, MA: MIT Press, 1960. 350-77.

Jakobson, Roman. *On Language*. Eds. L. Wauch and M. Monville-Burston. Cambridge, MA: Harvard University Press, 1990.

Jespersen, Otto. "Notes on Meter." *The Structure of Verse: Modern Essays on Prosody*. Ed. H. Gross. Greenwich, CT: Fawcett, 1966. 111-30.

Johnson, James D. "Formulaic Thrift in the Alliterative *Morte Arthure*." *Medium Ævum* 47 (1978): 255-61.

Jordan, Richard. *Handbook of Middle English Grammar: Phonology*. Trans. and Rev. E. Crook. The Hague: Mouton, 1934/1974.

Kaluza, Max. *A Short History of English Versification from the Earliest Times to the Present Day*. Trans. A. Dunstan. Norwood, PA: Norwood Editions, 1978.

Kane, George. "Music Neither Unpleasant Nor Monotonous." *Chaucer and Langland: Historical and Textual Approaches*. Ed. G. Kane. London: Athlone, 1989. 77-89.

Kaye, Jonathan. "Do You Believe in Magic? The Story of $s + C$ Sequences." *A Festschrift for Edmund Gussmann from his Friends and Colleagues*. Eds. H. Karde-

la and B. Szymanek. Lublin: University Press of the Catholic University of Lublin, 1996. 155-77.
Keiser, George R. "Narrative Structure in the Alliterative *Morte Arthure*, 26-720." *Chaucer Review* 9 (1974): 130-44.
Kelly, M. H., and D. C. Rubin. "Natural Rhythmic Patterns in English Verse: Evidence from Child and Counting-Out Rhymes." *Journal of Memory and Language* 27 (1988): 718-40.
Kendall, Calvin B. *The Metrical Grammar of* Beowulf. Cambridge: Cambridge University Press, 1991.
Kiparsky, Paul. "The Rhythmic Structure of English Verse." *Linguistic Inquiry* 8 (1977): 189-247.
Kiparsky, Paul, and G. Youmans, eds. *Phonetics and Phonology I: Rhythm and Meter*. San Diego: Academic Press, 1989.
Krishna, Valerie S., ed. The Alliterative Morte Arthure: *A Critical Edition*. New York: Franklin, 1976.
Krishna, Valerie S. "Parataxis, Formulaic Density, and Thrift in the Alliterative *Morte Arthure*." *Speculum* 57 (1982): 63-83.
Lass, Roger. *Old English: A Historical Linguistic Companion*. Cambridge: Cambridge University Press, 1994.
Lass, Roger. *Historical Linguistics and Language Change*. Cambridge: Cambridge University Press, 1997.
Lawrence, R. F. "The Formulaic Theory and its Application to English Alliterative Poetry." *Essays on Style and Language: Linguistic and Critical Approaches to Literary Style*. Ed. R. Fowler. London: Routledge and K. Paul, 1966. 166-83.
Lawrence, R. F. "Formula and Rhythm in *the Wars of Alexander*." *English Studies* 51 (1970): 97-112.
Lawton, David A. "Larger Patterns of Syntax in Middle English Unrhymed Alliterative Verse." *Neophilologus* 64 (1980): 604-18.
Lawton, David A., ed. *Middle English Alliterative Poetry and its Literary Background: Seven Essays*. Cambridge: Brewer, 1982.
Lawton, David A. "The Unity of Middle English Alliterative Poetry." *Speculum* 58 (1983): 72-94.
Lawton, David A. "The Diversity of Middle English Alliterative Poetry." *Leeds Studies in English* 20 (1989): 143-72.
Leech, Geoffrey. *A Linguistic Guide to English Poetry*. Harlow: Longman, 1969.
Lehiste, Ilse. *Suprasegmentals*. Cambridge, MA: MIT Press, 1970.
Leonard, William. E. "The Scansion of Middle English Alliterative Verse." *University of Wisconsin Studies in Language and Literature* 11 (1920): 58-104.

Le Page, R. B. "Alliterative Patterns as a Test of Style in Old English Poetry." *Journal of English and Germanic Philology* 58 (1959): 434-41.
Lester, Godfrey A. *The Language of Old and Middle English Poetry*. London: Macmillan Press, 1996.
Levy, Bernard S., and Paul E. Szarmach, eds. *The Alliterative Tradition in the Fourteenth Century*. Kent: Kent State University Press, 1981.
Lewis, C. S. "The Alliterative Metre." *Selected Literary Essays*. Ed. W. Hooper. Cambridge: Cambridge University Press, 1969. 15-26.
Lord, Albert B. *Epic Singers and Oral Tradition*. Ithaca: Cornell University Press, 1991.
Lord, Albert B. *The Singer of Tales*. 2nd edn. Cambridge, MA: Harvard University Press, 2000.
McColly, William. "Style and Structure in the Middle English Poem *Cleanness*." *Computers and the Humanities* 21 (1987): 169-76.
McCully, C. B., and J. J. Anderson, eds. *English Historical Metrics*. Cambridge: Cambridge University Press, 1996.
Macrae-Gibson, O. D. "*Pearl*: The Link-Words and the Thematic Structure." *Neophilologus* 52 (1968): 54-64.
Macrae-Gibson, O. D., and J. R. Lishman. "Computer Assistance in the Analysis of Old English Metre: Methods and Results-A Provisional Report." *Prosody and Poetics in the Early Middle Ages: Essays in Honour of C. B. Hieatt*. Ed. M. Toswell. Toronto: University of Toronto Press, 1995. 102-16.
Magoun, Francis, P., Jr. "The Oral-Formulaic Character of Anglo-Saxon Narrative Poetry." *Speculum* 28 (1953): 446-67.
Malof, Joseph. "The Native Rhythm of English Meters." *Texas Studies in Literature and Language* 5 (1964): 580-94.
Matonis, Anne T. E. "Middle English Alliterative Poetry." *So Meny People, Longages and Tonges: Philological Essays in Scots and Medieval English Presented to Angus McIntosh*. Eds. M. Benskin and M. Samuels. Edinburgh: M. Benskin and M. Samuels, 1981. 341-54.
Matonis, Anne T. E. "A Reexamination of the Middle English Alliterative Long Line." *Modern Philology* 81 (1984): 339-60.
Meredith, Joel L. *Adventures in Alliteration*. www.Xlibris.com: Xlibris, 2000.
Miletich, J. S. "The Quest for the 'Formula': A Comparative Reappraisal." *Modern Philology* 74 (1976): 111-23.
Miller, Miriam Y., and Jane Chance, eds. *Approaches to Teaching* Sir Gawain and the Green Knight. New York: Modern Language Association of America, 1986.
Milroy, James. "*Pearl*: The Verbal Texture and the Linguistic Theme." *Neophilologus* 55

(1971): 195-208.

Minkova, Donka. *The History of Final Vowels in English: The Sound of Muting.* Berlin: Mouton de Gruyter, 1991.

Minkova, Donka. "Non-Primary Stress in Early Middle English Accnetual-Syllabic Verse." *English Historical Metrics.* Eds. C. McCully, and J. Anderson. Cambridge: Cambridge University Press, 1996. 95-120.

Minkova, Donka. "Constraint Ranking in Middle English Stress-Shifting." *Journal of English Language and Linguistics* 1 (1997): 135-75.

Minkova, Donka. *Alliteration and Sound Change in Early English.* Cambridge: Cambridge University Press, 2003.

Mitchell, Bruce, and Fred Robinson. *A Guide to Old English.* Seventh edn. Oxford: Blackwell, 2007.

Moorman, Charles. "The Origins of the Alliterative Revival." *Southern Quarterly* 7 (1969): 345-71.

Moriya, Yasuyo. "Alliteration and Metrical Subordination in the Alliterative *Morte Arthure*." *ICU Language Research Bulletin* 11 (1996): 149-61.

Moriya, Yasuyo. "The Meter of the Verse Line of the Middle English *Pearl*." *Studies in Medieval English Language and Literature* 11 (1996): 49-79.

Moriya, Yasuyo. "Alliteration Devices in the Poems of the *Pearl* Manuscript." *Studies in Medieval English Language and Literature* 14 (1999): 27-49.

Moriya, Yasuyo. "Identical Alliteration in *The Alliterative Morte Arthure.*" *English Language Notes* 38 (2000): 1-16.

Moriya, Yasuyo. "The Line Boundary of Middle English Alliterative Meter Compared to That of Old English Alliterative Meter." *Neuphilologische Mitteilungen* 101 (2000): 387-401.

Moriya, Yasuyo. "The Role of the Sound "r" in the Meter of *The Alliterative Morte Arthure.*" *Poetica* 53 (2000): 1-13.

Moriya, Yasuyo. "Metrical Constraints of King Arthur's Round Table in *The Alliterative Morte Arthure.*" *Publications of the Medieval Association of the Midwest* 8 (2001): 1-19.

Moriya, Yasuyo. "Habitual Collocations of Words in the Second Half-Line of Middle English Alliterative Verse." *ICU Language Research Bulletin* 18 (2003): 161-75.

Moriya, Yasuyo. "Alliteration Versus Natural Speech Rhythm in Determining the Meter of Middle English Alliterative Verse." *English Studies* 85 (2004): 498-507.

Moriya, Yasuyo. "Vertical Alliteration in Middle English Alliterative Poems: Sound Repetition Beyond the Verse Line." *NOWELE (North-Western European Language Evolution)* 48 (2006): 45-66.

守屋　靖代 「中英語頭韻詩にみる繰り返しとリズム」『ことばの楽しみ――東西の

文化を越えて』田島松二編　南雲堂　2006. 91-102.

Nagy, Gregory. "Formula and Meter." *Oral Literature and the Formula*. Eds. B. Stolz and R. Shannon, III. Ann Arbor: Center for the Coordination of Ancient and Modern Studies, University of Michigan, 1976. 239-60.

Nespor, Marina, and Irene Vogel. *Prosodic Phonology*. Dordrecht: Foris, 1986.

Niles, John D. "Formula and Formulaic System in *Beowulf*." *Oral Traditional Literature: A Festschrift for A. B. Lord*. Ed. J. Foley. Columbus, OH: Slavica, 1981. 391-415.

Noble, J. "Typological Patterns in the Middle English *Joseph of Arimathea*." *Chaucer Review* 1 (1992): 177-88.

Northup, Clark S. "A Study of the Metrical Structure of the Middle English Poem *The Pearl*." *PMLA* 12 (1897): 326-40.

Oakden, James P. "The Survival of a Stylistic Feature of Indo-European Poetry in Germanic, Especially in Middle English." *Review of English Studies* 9 (1933): 50-53.

Oakden, James P. *Alliterative Poetry in Middle English: The Dialectal and Metrical Survey*. Manchester: Manchester University Press, 1930, 1935. Reprint. Archon Books, 1968.

O' Loughlin, J. L. N. "The Middle English Alliterative *Morte Arthure*." *Medium Ævum* 4 (1935): 153-68.

Osberg, Richard H. "The Prosody of Middle English *Pearl* and the Alliterative Lyric Tradition." *English Historical Metrics*. Eds. C. McCully, and J. Anderson. Cambridge: Cambridge University Press, 1996. 150-174.

Parks, Ward. "The Oral-formulaic Theory in Middle English Studies." *Oral Tradition* 1 (1986): 636-94.

Payne, R. C. "Formulaic Poetry in Old English and its Backgrounds." *Studies in Medieval Culture* 11 (1977): 41-49.

Pearsall, Derek A. *Old English and Middle English Poetry*. London: Routledge and Kegan Paul, 1977.

Pearsall, Derek A. "The Origins of the Alliterative Revival." *The Alliterative Tradition in the Fourteenth Century*. Eds. B. Levy and P. Szarmach. Kent, OH: Kent State University Press, 1981. 1-24.

Pearsall, Derek A. "The Alliterative Revival: Origins and Social Backgrounds." *Middle English Alliterative Poetry and its Literary Background: Seven Essays*. Ed. D. Lawton. Cambridge: Brewer, 1982. 34-54.

Peters, Timothy, and Eugene Green. " 'P' Alliteration and Latin-English Contrasts in Langland's *Piers Plowman*." *Neuphilologische Mitteilungen* 93 (1992): 193-97.

Petronella, V. F. "*St Erkenwald*: Style as the Vehicle for Meaning." *Journal of English and Germanic Philology* 66 (1967): 532-40.

Pope, John C. *The Rhythm of* Beowulf: *An Interpretation of the Normal and Hypermetric Verse-Forms in Old English Poetry*. Revised edn. New Haven, CT: Yale University Press, 1966.

Preminger, Alex, ed. *The New Princeton Encyclopedia of Poetry and Poetics*. Princeton: Princeton University Press, 1993.

Putter, Ad. *An Introduction to the Gawain-Poet*. New York: Longman, 1996.

Quirk, Randolph. "Poetic Language and Old English Metre." *Early English and Norse Studies Presented to Hugh Smith in Honour of his Sixtieth Birthday*. Eds. A. Brown and P. Foote. London: Methuen, 1963. 149-71.

Richards, I. A. "Rhythm and Metre." *The Structure of Verse: Modern Essays on Prosody*. Ed. H. Gross. Greenwich, CT: Fawcett, 1966. 42-51.

Richardson, F. E. "*The Pearl*: A Poem and its Audience." *Neophilologus* 46 (1962): 308-16.

Riddy, Felicity. "The Alliterative Revival." *The History of Scottish Literature Volume 1: Origins to 1660*. Ed. R. Jack. Aberdeen: Aberdeen University Press, 1988. 39-54.

Ritzke-Rutherford, Jean. "Formulaic Macrostructure: The Theme of Battle." The Alliterative Morte Arthure: *A Reassessment of the Poem*. Ed. K. Göller. Cambridge: Brewer, 1981. 83-95.

Ritzke-Rutherford, Jean. "Formulaic Microstructure: The Cluster." The Alliterative Morte Arthure: *A Reassessment of the Poem*. Ed. K. Göller. Cambridge: Brewer, 1981. 70-82.

Roach, Peter. "On the Distinction between 'Stress-Timed' and 'Syllable-Timed' Languages." *Linguistic Controversies: Essays in Linguistic Theory and Practice in Honor of F. R. Palmer*. Ed. D. Crystal. London: Arnold, 1982. 73-79.

Roach, Peter. *English Phonetics and Phonology: A Practical Course*. Second edn. Cambridge: Cambridge University Press, 1991.

Robertson, Michael. "Stanzaic Symmetry in *Sir Gawain and the Green Knight*." *Speculum* 57 (1982): 779-85.

Røstvig, Maren-Sofie. "Numerical Composition in *Pearl*: A Theory." *English Studies* 48 (1967): 326-32.

Russom, Geoffrey. *Old English Meter and Linguistic Theory*. Cambridge: Cambridge University Press, 1987.

Russom, Geoffrey. Beowulf *and Old Germanic Metre*. Cambridge: Cambridge University Press, 1998.

Sadowski, Piotr. "The Sound-Symbolic Quality of Word-Initial GR-Cluster in Middle English Alliterative Verse." *Neuphilologische Mitteilungen* 102 (2001): 37-47.

Saintsbury, George. *A History of English Prosody from the Twelfth Century to the Present Day*. Second edn. New York: Macmillan, 1923.

Salmon, Paul. "Anomalous Alliteration in Germanic Verse." *Neophilologus* 42 (1958): 223-41.

Salter, Elizabeth. "The Alliterative Revival." *Modern Philology* 64 (1966): 146-50, 233-37.

Salter, Elizabeth. "Alliterative Modes and Affiliations in the Fourteenth Century." *Neuphilologische Mitteilungen* 79 (1978): 25-35.

Salter, Elizabeth. "A Complaint Against Blacksmiths." *Literature and History* 5 (1979): 195-215.

Sapora, Robert W., Jr. *A Theory of Middle English Alliterative Meter with Critical Applications*. Boston, MA: Mediaeval Academy of America, 1977.

Schaar, C. "On a New Theory of Old English Poetic Diction." *Neophilologus* 40 (1956): 301-05.

Schaefer, Ursula. "Twin Collocations in the Early Middle English Lives of the *Katherine* Group." *Orality and Literacy in Early Middle English*. Ed. H. Pitch. Tübingen: Gunter Narr Verlag, 1996. 179-98.

Schiller, Andrew. "The Gawain Rhythm." *Language and Style* 1 (1968): 268-94.

Schipper, Jakob. *A History of English Versification*. Folcroft, PA: Folcroft Library Editions, 1973.

Schmidt, A. V. C. *The Clerkly Maker: Langland's Poetic Art*. Woodbridge, Suffolk: D. S. Brewer, 1987.

Schotter, Anne Howland. "The Poetic Function of Alliterative Formulas of Clothing in the Portrait of the Pearl Maiden." *Studia Neophilologica* 51 (1979): 189-95.

Schreiber, Earl G. "The Structure of *Cleanness*." *The Alliterative Tradition in the Fourteenth Century*. Eds. B. Levy and P. Szarmach. Kent, OH: Kent State University Press, 1981. 131-52.

Shepherd, Geoffrey T. "The Nature of Alliterative Poetry in Late Medieval England." *Proceedings of the British Academy* 56 (1970): 57-76. Rpt. in *Middle English Literature: British Academy Gollancz Lectures*. Ed. J. Burrow. Oxrord University Press for British Academy, 1989. 141-60.

Sievers, Eduard. "Old Germanic Metrics and Old English Metrics." *Essential Articles for the Study of Old English Poetry*. Eds. J. Bessinger, Jr. and S. Kahrl. Hamden, CT: Archon Books, 1968. 1-38.

Sisam, Kenneth, ed. *Fourteenth Century Verse and Prose*. Oxford: Clarendon Press, 1975.

Smith, Jeremy. *An Historical Study of English: Function, Form and Change*. London and New York: Routledge, 1996.

Smith, Jeremy. *Essentials of Early English*. London, New York: Routledge, 1999.
Smith, Jeremy. "Semantics and Metrical Form in *Sir Gawain and the Green Knight*." *New Perspectives on Middle English Texts: A Festschrift for R. A. Waldron*. Eds. S. Powell and J. Smith. Woodbridge, Suffolk and Rochester, NY: D. S. Brewer, 2000. 87-103.
Spearing, A. C. *The Gawain-Poet: A Critical Study*. Cambridge: Cambridge University Press, 1970.
Starr, David. "Metrical Changes: From Old to Middle English." *Modern Philology* 68 (1970): 1-9.
Stevenson, Charles L. "The Rhythm of English Verse." *Journal of Aesthetics and Art Criticism* 28 (1970): 327-44.
Stevick, Robert D. *English and its History: The Evolution of a Language*. Boston: Allyn and Bacon, 1968.
Stewart, George R. "The Meter of *Piers Plowman*." *PMLA* 42 (1927): 113-28.
Stewart, George R. *The Technique of English Verse*. New York: Holt, 1930.
Stockwell, Robert P. "On Recent Theories of Metrics and Rhythm in *Beowulf*." *English Historical Metrics*. Eds. C. McCully, and J. Anderson. Cambridge: Cambridge University Press, 1996. 73-94.
Stockwell, Robert P., and Donka Minkova. "Old English Metrics and the Phonology of Resolution. *Germanic Studies in Honor of Anatoly Liberman, NOWELE (North-Western European Language Evolution)* 31/32 (1997): 389-406.
Stratyner, Leslie. "The Middle English Romance and the Alliterative Tradition." *Teaching Oral Traditions*. Ed. J. Foley. New York: Modern Language Association, 1998. 365-72.
Sweet, Henry. *A History of English Sounds: From the Earliest Period*. Oxford: Clarendon Press, 1988.
Tarlinskaja, Marina. *English Verse: Theory and History*. The Hague: Mouton, 1976.
Tavormina, M. Teresa, and R. F. Yeager, eds. *The Endless Knot: Essays on Old and Middle English in Honor of Marie Borroff*. Cambridge: D. S. Brewer, 1995.
Thun, Nils. *Reduplicative Words in English: A Study of Formations of the Types 'Tick-Tock,' 'Hurly-Burly,' and 'Shilly-Shally*.' Lund: Carl Bloms, 1963.
Tolkien, J. R. R., and E. V. Gordon, eds. *Sir Gawain and the Green Knight*. Ed. N. Davis. Revised edn. Oxford: Clarendon Press, 1967.
Toswell, M. ed. *Prosody and Poetics in the Early Middle Ages*. Toronto: University of Toronto Press, 1995.
Townsend, Peter. "Essential Groupings of Meaningful Force: Rhythm in Literary Discourse." *Language and Style* 16 (1983): 313-33.
Treharne, Elaine M., and Duncan Wu. *Old and Middle English Poetry*. Oxford: Black-

well, 2002.

Treiman, Rebecca, Jennifer Gross, and Annemarie Cwikiel-Glavin. "The Syllabification of /s/ Clusters in English." *Journal of Phonetics* 20 (1992): 383-402.

Turco, Lewis. *The New Book of Forms: A Handbook of Poetics.* Hanover, MA and London: University Press of New England, 1986.

Turville-Petre, Joan. "The Metre of *Sir Gawain and the Green Knight.*" *English Studies* 57(1976): 310-28.

Turville-Petre, Thorlac. *The Alliterative Revival.* Cambridge: D. S. Brewer and Totowa, NJ: Rowman Littlefield, 1977.

Turville-Petre, Thorlac. *Alliterative Poetry of the Later Middle Ages: An Anthology.* London: Routledge, 1989.

Vantuono, William, ed. *Old and Middle English Texts with Accompanying Textual and Linguistic Apparatus,* New York: Peter Lang, 1994

Vaughan, M. F. "Consecutive Alliteration, Strophic Patterns, and the Composition of the Alliterative *Morte Arthure.*" *Modern Philology* 77 (1979): 1-9.

Verdonk, Peter. *Stylistics.* Oxford and New York: Oxford University Press, 2002.

Waldron, Ronald A. "Oral-Formulaic Technique and Middle English Alliterative Poetry." *Speculum* 32 (1957): 792-804.

Waldron, Ronald A., ed. *Sir Gawain and the Green Knight.* London: Arnold, Evanston: North Western University Press, 1970.

Whallon, W. "The Diction of *Beowulf.*" *PMLA* 76 (1961): 309-19.

Whallon, W. *Formula, Character and Context: Studies in Homeric, Old English and Old Testament Poetry.* Cambridge, MA: Harvard University Press, 1969.

Whitman, F. H. "The Meaning of 'Formulaic' in Old English Verse Composition." *Neuphilologische Mitteilungen* 76 (1975): 529-37.

Whitman, F. H. *A Comparative Study of Old English Metre.* Toronto: University of Toronto Press, 1993.

Williams, D. J. "Alliterative Poetry in the Fourteenth and Fifteenth Centuries." *The New History of Literature Vol. 1: The Middle Ages.* Ed. W. Bolton. New York: Peter Bedrick, 1986. 119-67.

Wilson, Peter. "Word Play and the Interpretation of *Pearl.*" *Medium Ævum* 40 (1971): 116-34.

Wilson, Peter. "Reading a Line Metrically: The Practical Implications of Using the Halle-Keyser System." *Language and Style* 12 (1979): 146-57.

Wimsatt, William K., ed. *Versification: Major Language Types.* New York: Modern Language Association of America, 1972.

Wimsatt, William K., and Monroe C. Beardsley. "The Concept of Meter: An Exercise in Abstraction." *PMLA* 74 (1959): 585-98.

Windelberg, M. L. "How (Not) to Define the Epic Formula." *Olifant* 8 (1980): 29-50.
Wittig, S. "Formulaic Style and the Problem of Redundancy." *Centrum* 1 (1973): 123-36.
Wrenn, Charles L. "On the Continuity of English Poetry." *Anglia* 76 (1958): 41-59.
Wu, Duncan, ed. *Old and Middle English Poetry*. Oxford, Malden: Blackwell, 2002.
Youmans, Gilbert. "Introduction: Rhythm and Meter." *Phonetics and Phonology I: Rhythm and Meter*. Eds. P. Kiparsky and G. Youmans. San Diego: Academic Press, 1989. 1-14.
Youmans, Gilbert. "Reconsidering Chaucer's Prosody." *English Historical Metrics*. Eds. C. McCully, and J. Anderson. Cambridge: Cambridge University Press, 1996. 185-210.
Ziolkowski, Jan. "A Narrative Structure in the Alliterative *Morte Arthure* 1-1221 and 3150-4346." *Chaucer Review* 22 (1988): 234-45.
Zumthor, Paul. *Toward a Medieval Poetics*. Minneapolis, MN: University of Minnesota Press, 1992. Trans. Philip Bennett. First Published in 1972 by Sevil.

Notes to the Data

Information in Each Column:
§ The database that follows these notes consists of four columns, showing Stage One for all the poems. The first column shows the line number, the second one the whole line with slashes where the *a*-verse ends and where the word containing the first beat of the *b*-verse starts. Lines with only one slash have no unstressed syllables between the half lines. The third column indicates what kind of parts of speech falls between the half-lines whereas the slash mark (/) means that there is no such a syllable in that particular position. The final column shows the collocation of words in the *b*-verse. Note that Column 4, the collocation part, is shadowed for all the poems in order to clearly separate Column 3 and Column 4. As to *Wynnere and Wastoure*, all the four stages are shown. The shadowed column for Stages Two-Four is the key element that the data have been sorted out for each stage.

Column 1	Column 2	Column 3	Column 4
WW 1	Sythen that Bretayne was biggede / and / Bruyttus it aughte,	C	N H X
WW 2	Thurgh the takynge of Troye / with / tresone withinn,	P	N Z
WW 3	There hathe selcouthes bene sene / in / seere kynges tymes,	P	A N N
WW 4	Bot never so many as nowe / by the / nyne dele.	P D	A N

Orthographic Conventions
The punctuation marks are kept as shown in the text. The modern *th* is used for þ and ð. The letter *é* is simply indicated as *e*. The distinction between the upper- and lower-cases of 3/ʒ is made as much as possible.

List of Symbols for Parts of Speech:

A：Adjective	*G*：Present Participle	*P*：Preposition
C：Conjunction	*H*：Pronoun	*V*：Verb
D：Determiner	*I*：Interjection	*X*：Auxiliary Verb
E：Past Participle	*N*：Noun	*Z*：Adverb

Possible Determiners (D):

§ The determiners include, according to Ballard, articles (*the, a/an*), possessive determiners (*my, his*, etc.), wh-determiners (*what, which*, etc.), indefinite determiners (*many, no, every, much, other*, etc.), demonstrative determiners (*this, those*, etc.), and numerals (*two, third, quarter*, etc.). Typical determiners used in ME alliterative verse are as follows in modern spelling:

a, an, any, both, her, his, last, many, my, our, other, saint, some, the, that, their, these, those, thy, whose, your, numerals (*three, five*), etc.

§ In the line-middle position, namely, the unstressed position between the *a*-verse and the *b*-verse, the determiner is marked as *D*. It is marked as either *D* or *A* within the *b*-verse especially when the determiner is supposed to alliterate. Thus, the following difference in marking:

G 682   Who knew euer any kyng/ <u>such</u> /counsel to take
                              D   *N*   *to V*

G 707   Thay seȝe neuer no segge/ that watz of /<u>suche</u> hwez
                          that be *P*   *A*   *N*

G 396   I may be funde vpon folde, /and /foch the such wage
                                C   *V*   *H* *D*   *N*

§ In cases like *G* 396 in which determiners do not alliterate, the phrase containing a possible determiner in the second half-line may be shown in either of the following:

such many other	*A A H* or *D D H*
all other things	*A A N* or *D D N*
ten thousand helms	*A A N* or *D D N*

Possible Pronouns (H):

§ All personal pronouns (*I, him*, etc.), *both, each, else, one, other, third*, numerals (*two, ten, hundred*, etc.), etc. can be marked as *H*.

Possible Varieties in Marking:

§ The following words may have multiple grammatical functions:

all	*D, H, Z*
as	*C, P*

at	P, Q, that
be	be, V
both	A, D, H, Z
but	C, P, Z
each	A, D, H, Z
else	A, Z
full	A, Z
many	A, D, H, A (when alliterating or at the line end)
ne, na, not	A, D, H, Z, not
numerals (ten, first, etc.)	A, D, H, N
other	A, D, H, Z
so	A, C, Z
than	C, P, Z
that	D, H, that
there	Q, Z
this	D, H
to	C, P, Z (too), to [marked as to before V]
what	H, Q
when/where	C, Q
the + A (such as the rich):	D N (A) or D A

§ No definite distinction between A and G, between A and E, between N and G, between V and E, between V and X: e.g. *blessed, sacred*, etc. marked as either E or A.

§ Compound nouns and verbs are either marked as one single word or combination of two words:

G 2190	This oritore is vgly, with <u>erbez ouergrowen;</u>	N E (or N Z E)
G 1483	And connez not of compaynye the <u>costez vndertake,</u>	N V or (N Z V)
MA 1508	Raunson me resonabillye, as I may <u>ouerreche</u>	Z V (or V)
G 1641	"Now ar we euen," quoth the hathel, "in this <u>euentide</u>	N N (or N)

§ The following frequent phrases are marked as follows:

more than	A P
the same	D A
vs vchon	H H

§ There are many cases in which a word can be P or Z. When a noun precedes or follows, words such as *about, around, before, in, on, out*, etc. are likely to be marked as P, but it depends upon the context if it is actually marked as P or Z.

§ It has been a tradition to separate the two half-lines. The lexical items between the half-lines are usually considered to belong to the second half-line. Yet in certain cases, the unstressed syllables between the two half-lines do not coincide with the traditional line-boundary:

G 217   A lace lapped / aboute, that / louked at the hede,
             Z   that   V   P D   N

G 1272   For the costes that I haf knowen / vpon the, / knyȝt, here,
                                   P   H   N   Z

G 1796   Sykande ho sweȝe / doun and / semly hym kyssed,
              Z   C   Z   H   V

§ When the first word in the second half-line starts with an unstressed syllable or is a compound with an unstressed syllable at the beginning, the unstressed syllable is included in the second half-line:

G 879   Of a broun bleeaunt, / enbrauded ful ryche
                              /   E   Z   A

§ In the same manner when the last word in the first half-line ends with an unstressed syllable that is clearly linked to its preceding syllable, the unstressed syllable is not included in the middle part:

G 907   Comen to that Krystmasse, / as / case hym then lymped.
                              C

§ The unalliterating noun under the metrical subordination of the alliterating adjective is not considered between the two half-lines:

A 607   As any ȝare ȝeten gold, / ȝalow was the tothire.

§ The unalliterating adjective under the metrical subordination of the alliterating noun is not considered between the two half-lines:

A 530   Many peralus pull, / grete payne suffirs,

§ When an adverbial phrase falls in the line-middle position and the initial stressed position of the second half-line, both words are marked as Z:

G 256   "Nay, as help me," quoth the hathel, / "he that on / hyȝe syttes,
                                              H that Z   Z   V

Adverbial Phrases Marked as Single Z:

(Modern spellings if available; Middle English words italicized):

a little	at once	*na nother (nothir)*
a lofte	*at ryhgtys*	*ne other*
a neuen	at this ones	never the less
a quyle	*ayther other*	no better
a stounde	*bi stoundez*	*no ferre*
a throwe	by thane	no further (*ferrire,*
a twynne	by the last	*ferryre, forthire,*
a while	each other	*fryye)*
al about	for ever	*no lasse*
al ny3t	*for sothe*	no little
all day	*for the nones*	no longer (*lenger,*
all over	in a while	*langere)*
all together	in fast	no more
alle samen	in haste	*no nother (nothire)*
als fast	*in hy3e*	no while
any fe(y)rre	in land	non other
any forthire	*in lo3e*	none nerre
any more	in no wyse	*o ferrom*
appon (apon) lofte	in samen	of first
(loft)	*in sondire (sonder,*	*of sone*
at (*att*) ones (*ones*)	*sondere, sondre,*	*oft sythis*
at (the) last	*sondyre)*	upon high
at anys	in sunder	upon loft
at first	*lowe undir*	*vche tyme*
on a quile	one highte	*vchon other (othir)*
on fast	*oure one*	*vpon erthe*
on first	the less	*vpon hy3t (hy3te)*
on high	the more	*vpon lofte*
on hy3t	upon end	*with hast*
on land	upon first	*yn faste*
on loft	upon haste	
on low	*upon hepez*	
at little	*min/his/oure one*	

Database Sample
Saint Erkenwald

E 1	At London in Englond noȝt . . .	not Z	long sythen	Z Z
E 2	Sythen Crist suffrid on crosse . . .	C	Cristendome stablyd,	N V
E 3	Ther was a byschop in that . . .	/	blessyd and sacryd;	A C A
E 4	Saynt Erkenwolde as I hope . . .	D	holy mon hatte.	A N V
E 5	In his tyme in that toun the . . .	D	temple alder-grattyst	N A
E 6	Was drawen doun, that one dole, . . .	to	dedifie new,	V Z
E 7	For hit hethen had bene in . . .	be P	Hengyst dawes	N N
E 8	That the Saxones vnsaȝt . . .	have	sende hyder.	E Z

List of the Poems and the Number of Lines Included:

Wynnere and Wastoure (*W*) — 503 lines
    (Stage One, Stage Two, Stage Three, Stage Four)
Saint Erkenwald (*E*) — 352 lines
The Parlement of the Thre Ages (*AG*) — 661 lines
The Siege of Jerusalem (*J*) — 1134 lines
Patience (*Pat*) — 531 lines
Cleanness (*C*) — 1812 lines
Sir Gawain and the Green Knight (*G*) — 2020 lines
    (Excluding the Bob and the Wheel)
The Alliterative Morte Arthure (*MA*) — 1991 lines
The Wars of Alexander (*A*) — 2005 lines

Data

Wynner and Wastoure 115

    (Stage One, Stage Two, Stage Three, Stage Four)

Saint Erkenwald 144

The Parlement of the Thre Ages 150

The Siege of Jerusalem 160

Patience 178

Cleanness 186

Sir Gawain and the Green Knight 212

The Alliterative Morte Arthure 241

The Wars of Alexander 270

Middle English texts reproduced by the kind permission of Professor Thorlac Turville-Petre, Professor Hoyt Duggan, the Council of the Early English Text Society, the University of Exeter Press, and the Medieval Institute of Western Michigan University.

Wynner and Wastoure

Stage One

WW	1	Sythen that Bretayne was biggede / and / Bruyttus it aughte,	C	N H X
WW	2	Thurgh the takynge of Troye / with / tresone withinn,	P	N Z
WW	3	There hathe selcouthes bene sene / in / seere kynges tymes,	P	A N N
WW	4	Bot never so many as nowe / by the / nyne dele.	P D	A N
WW	5	For nowe alle es witt and wyles / that / we with delyn,	that	H Z V
WW	6	Wyse wordes and slee, / and icheon / wryeth othere.	C H	V H
WW	7	Dare never no westren wy / while this / werlde lasteth	C D	N V
WW	8	Send his sone southewarde / to / see ne to here,	to	V not to V
WW	9	That he ne schall holden byhynde / when he / hore eldes.	C H	A V
WW	10	Forthi sayde was a sawe / of / Salomon the wyse -	P	N D N(A)
WW	11	It hyeghte harde appone honde, / hope I no nother -	/	V H Z
WW	12	When wawes waxen schall wilde / and / walles bene doun,	C	N be Z
WW	13	And hares appon herthe-stones / schall / hurcle in hire fourme,	X	V P D N
WW	14	And eke boyes of blode / with / boste and with pryde,	P	N C P N
WW	15	Schall wedde ladyes in londe / and / lede hem at will,	C	V H P N
WW	16	Thene dredfull Domesdaye / it / draweth neghe aftir.	H	V Z Z
WW	17	Bot whoso sadly will see / and the / sothe telle,	C D	N V
WW	18	Say it newely will neghe / or es / neghe here.	C be	V Z
WW	19	Whylome were lordes in londe / that / loved in thaire hertis	that	V P D N
WW	20	To here makers of myrthes / that / matirs couthe fynde,	that	N X V
WW	21	And now es no frenchipe in fere / bot / fayntnesse of hert,	P	N P N
WW	22	Wyse wordes withinn / that / wroghte were never,	that	E be Z
WW	23	Ne redde in no romance / that ever / renke herde.	that Z	N V
WW	24	Bot now a childe appon chere, / withowtten / renke herde.	P	N N
WW	25	That never wroghte thurgh witt / thies / wordes togedire,	D	N Z
WW	26	Fro he can jangle als a jaye / and / japes telle,	C	N V
WW	27	He schall be levede and lovede / and / lett of a while	C	V Z Z
WW	28	Wele more than the man / that / made it hymselven.	that	V H H self
WW	29	Bot, never-the-lattere, at the laste / when / ledys bene knawen,	C	N be E
WW	30	Werke wittnesse will bere / who / wirche kane beste.	Q	V X Z
WW	31	Bot I schall tell yow a tale / that me / bytyde ones	that H	V Z
WW	32	Als I went in the weste, / wandrynge myn one,	/	G Z
WW	33	Bi a bonke of a bourne; / bryghte was the sone	/	A be D N
WW	34	Undir a worthiliche wodde / by a / wale medewe:	P D	A N
WW	35	Fele floures gan folde / ther my / fote steppede.	Q D	N V
WW	36	I layde myn hede one ane hill / ane / hawthorne besyde;	D	N P
WW	37	The throstills full throly / they / threpen togedire,	H	V Z
WW	38	Hipped up heghwalles / fro / heselis tyll othire,	P	N P H
WW	39	Bernacles with thayre billes / one / barkes thay roungen,	P	N H V
WW	40	The jay janglede one heghe, / jarmede the foles.	/	V D N
WW	41	The bourne full bremly rane / the / bankes bytwene;	D	N P
WW	42	So ruyde were the roughe stremys / and / raughten so heghe	C	V Z Z
WW	43	That it was neghande nyghte / or I / nappe myghte,	C H	V X
WW	44	For dyn of the depe watir / and / dadillyng of fewllys.	C	N(G) P N
WW	45	Bot as I laye at the laste / than / lowked myn eghne,	C	V D N
WW	46	And I was swythe in a sweven / sweped belyve.	/	E Z
WW	47	Me thoghte I was in the werlde, / I ne / wiste in whate ende,	H not	V P Q N
WW	48	One a loveliche lande / that was / ylike grene,	that be	Z A
WW	49	That laye loken by a lawe / the / lengthe of a myle.	D	N P D N
WW	50	In aythere holte was ane here / in / hawberkes full brighte,	P	N Z A
WW	51	Harde hattes appon hedes / and / helmys with crestys;	C	N P N
WW	52	Brayden owte thaire baners, / bown for to blawe,	/	A for to V
WW	53	Schowen owte of the schawes, / in / schiltrons thay felle,	P	N H V
WW	54	And bot the lengthe of a launde / thies / lordes bytwene.	D	N P
WW	55	And alle prayed for the pese / till the / prynce come,	C D	N V
WW	56	For he was worthiere in witt / than any / wy ells	P D	N A
WW	57	For to ridde and to rede / and to / rewlyn the wrothe	C to	V D N(A)
WW	58	That aythere here appon hate / had untill othere.	/	V P H
WW	59	At the creste of a clyffe / a / caban was rerede,	D	N be E
WW	60	Alle raylede with rede / the / rofe and the sydes,	D	N C D N
WW	61	With Ynglysse besantes full brighte, / betyn of golde,	/	E P N
WW	62	And ichone gayly umbygone / with / garters of inde,	P	N P N
WW	63	And iche a gartare of golde / gerede full riche.	/	E Z Z
WW	64	Then were ther wordes in the webbe / werped of he,	/	E P H

WW	65	Payntted of plunket, / and / poyntes bytwene,	C	N P
WW	66	That were fourried full fayre / appon / fresche lettres,	P	A N
WW	67	And alle was it one sawe / appon / Ynglysse tonge,	P	A N
WW	68	"Hethyng have the hathell / that any / harme thynkes."	that D	N V
WW	69	Now the kyng of this kythe / kepe hym oure Lorde!	/	V H D N
WW	70	Upon heghe one the holt / ane / hathell up stondes,	D	N Z V
WW	71	Wroghte als a wodwyse / alle in / wrethyn lokkes,	Z P	E N
WW	72	With ane helme one his hede, / ane / hatte appon lofte,	D	N Z
WW	73	And one heghe one the hatte / ane / hattfull beste,	D	A N
WW	74	A lighte lebarde and a longe, / lokande full kene,	/	G Z A
WW	75	Yarked alle of yalowe golde / in full / yape wyse.	P Z	A N
WW	76	Bot that that hillede the helme / byhynde in the nekke	/	Z P D N
WW	77	Was casten full clenly / in / quarters foure:	P	N A
WW	78	Two with flowres of Fraunce / before and behynde,	/	Z C Z
WW	79	And two out of Ynglonde / with sex / grym bestes,	P D	A N
WW	80	Thre leberdes one lofte / and / thre on lowe undir;	C	N Z Z
WW	81	At iche a cornere a knoppe / of full / clene perle,	P Z	A N
WW	82	Tasselde of tuly silke, / tuttynge out fayre.	/	G Z Z
WW	83	And by the cabane I knewe / the / knyghte that I see,	D	N that H V
WW	84	And thoghte to wiete or I went / wondres ynewe.	/	N A
WW	85	And als I waytted withinn / I was / warre sone	H be	A Z
WW	86	Of a comliche kynge / crowned with golde,	/	E P N
WW	87	Sett one a silken bynche, / with / septure in honde,	P	N P N
WW	88	One of the lovelyeste ledis, / whoso / loveth hym in hert,	Q	V H P N
WW	89	That ever segge under sonn / sawe with his eghne.	/	V P D N
WW	90	This kynge was comliche clade / in / kirtill and mantill -	P	N C N
WW	91	Bery-brown was his berde - / brouderde with fewlys,	/	E P N
WW	92	Fawkons of fyne golde, / flakerande with wynges,	/	G P N
WW	93	And ichone bare in ble / blewe als me thoghte	/	A C H V
WW	94	A grete gartare of ynde / gerede full riche.	/	E Z A
WW	95	Full gayly was that grete lorde / girde in the myddis:	/	E P D N
WW	96	A brighte belte of ble / broudirde with fewles,	/	E P N
WW	97	With drakes and with dukkes - / daderande tham semede	/	G H V
WW	98	For ferdnes of fawkons fete, / lesse / fawked thay were.	C	E H be
WW	99	And ever I sayd to myselfe, / "Full / selly me thynke	Z	A H V
WW	100	Bot if this renke to the revere / ryde umbestonde."	/	V Z
WW	101	The kyng biddith a beryn / by hym that stondeth,	/	P H that V
WW	102	One of the ferlyeste frekes / that / faylede hym never:	that	V H Z
WW	103	"Thynke I dubbede the knyghte / with / dynttis to dele!	P	N to V
WW	104	Wende wightly thy waye / my / willes to kythe.	D	N to V
WW	105	Go, bidd thou yondere bolde batell / that one the / bent hoves,	that P D	N V
WW	106	That they never neghe / nerre togedirs;	/	Z Z
WW	107	For if thay strike one stroke / stynte thay ne thynken."	/	V H not V
WW	108	"Yis, lorde," said the lede, / "while my / life dures."	C D	N V
WW	109	He dothe hym doun one the bonke, / and / dwellys awhile	C	V Z
WW	110	Whils he busked and bown / was one his / beste wyse.	be P D	A N
WW	111	He laped his legges in yren / to the / lawe bones,	P D	A N
WW	112	With pysayne and with pawnce / polischede full clene,	/	E Z Z
WW	113	With brases of broun stele / brauden full thikke,	/	E Z Z
WW	114	With plates buklede at the bakke / the / body to yeme,	D	N to V
WW	115	With a jupown full juste / joynede by the sydes,	/	E P D N
WW	116	A brod chechun at the bakke; / the / breste had another,	D	N V H
WW	117	Thre wynges inwith / wroghte in the kynde,	/	E P D N
WW	118	Umbygon with a gold wyre. / When I that / gome knewe,	C H D	N V
WW	119	What! he was yongeste of yeris / and / yapeste of witt	C	A P N
WW	120	That any wy in this werlde / wiste of his age.	/	V Z N V
WW	121	He brake a braunche in his hande, / and / caughte it swythe,	C	V H Z
WW	122	Trynes one a grete trotte / and / takes his waye	C	V D N
WW	123	There bothe thies ferdes folke / in the / felde hoves.	P D	N V
WW	124	Sayd, "Loo! the kyng of this kyth, / ther / kepe hym oure Lorde!	Q	V H D N
WW	125	Send his erande / by me, als hym / beste lyketh,	P H C H	Z V
WW	126	That no beryn be so bolde, / one / bothe his two eghne,	P	A D D N
WW	127	Ones to strike one stroke, / no / stirre none nerre	not	V Z
WW	128	To lede rowte in his rewme, / so / ryall to thynke	Z	Z to V
WW	129	Pertly with youre powers / his / pese to disturbe.	D	N to V
WW	130	For this es the usage here / and / ever schall worthe:	C	Z X N
WW	131	If any beryn be so bolde / with / banere for to ryde	P	N for to V
WW	132	Withinn the kyngdome riche / bot the / kynge one,	P D	N A
WW	133	That he schall losse the londe / and his / lyfe aftir.	C D	N Z
WW	134	Bot sen ye knowe noghte this kythe / ne the / kynge ryche,	not D	N A
WW	135	He will forgiffe yow this gilt / of his / grace one.	P D	N A

WW	136	Full wyde hafe I walked / amonges thies / wyes one,	P D	N A
WW	137	Bot sawe I never siche a syghte, / segge, with myn eghne;	/	N P D N
WW	138	For here es all the folke of Fraunce / ferdede besyde,		E Z
WW	139	Of Lorreyne, of Lumbardye, / and of / Lawe Spayne;	C P	N N
WW	140	Wyes of Westwale, / that in / were duellen;	that P	N V
WW	141	Of Ynglonde, of Yrlonde, / Estirlynges full many,	/	N Z A
WW	142	That are stuffede in stele, / strokes to dele.	/	N to V
WW	143	And yondere a banere of blake / that one the / bent hoves,	that P D	N V
WW	144	With thre bulles of ble white / brouden withinn,	/	E Z
WW	145	And iche one hase of henppe / hynged a corde,	/	E D N
WW	146	Seled with a sade lede; / I / say als me thynkes,	H	V C H V
WW	147	That hede es of holy kirke / I / hope he be there,	H	V H be Z
WW	148	Alle ferse to the fighte / with the / folke that he ledis.	P D	N that H V
WW	149	Another banere es upbrayde / with a / bende of grene,	P D	N P N
WW	150	With thre hedis white-herede / with / howes one lofte,	P	N Z
WW	151	Croked full craftyly / and / kembid in the nekke:	C	E P D N
WW	152	Thies are ledis of this londe / that schold oure / lawes yeme,	that X D	N V
WW	153	That thynken to dele this daye / with / dynttis full many.	P	N Z A
WW	154	I holde hym bot a fole that fightis / whils / flyttynge may helpe,	C	N(G) X V
WW	155	When he hase founden his frende / that / fayled hym never.	that	V H Z
WW	156	The thirde banere one bent / es of / blee whitte,	be P	N A
WW	157	With sexe galegs, I see, / of / sable withinn,	P	N Z
WW	158	And iche one has a brown brase / with / bokels twayne.	P	N A
WW	159	Thies are Sayn Franceys folke, that sayen / alle schall / fey worthe;	H X	A V
WW	160	They aren so ferse and so fresche, / thay / feghtyn bot seldom.	H	V C Z
WW	161	I wote wele for wynnynge / thay / wentten fro home;	H	V P N
WW	162	His purse weghethe full wele / that / wanne thaym all hedire.	that	V H Z Z
WW	163	The fourte banere one the bent / was / brayde appon lofte,	be	E Z
WW	164	With bothe the brerdes of blake, / a / balle in the myddes,	D	N P D N
WW	165	Reghte siche as the sone / es in / someris tyde,	be P	N N
WW	166	When it hase moste of the mayne / one / Missomer Even.	P	N N
WW	167	That was Domynyke this daye / with / dynttis to dele;	P	N to V
WW	168	With many a blesenande beryn / his / banere es stuffede.	D	N be E
WW	169	And sythen the pope es so priste / thies / prechours to helpe,	D	N to V
WW	170	And Fraunceys with his folke / es / forced besyde,	be	E Z
WW	171	And alle the ledis of the lande / ledith thurgh witt,	/	V P N
WW	172	There es no man appon molde / to / machen thaym agayne,	to	V H P
WW	173	Ne gete no grace appon grounde, / undir / God hymselven.	P	N H self
WW	174	And yitt es the fyfte appon the felde / the / faireste of tham alle,	D	A P H Z
WW	175	A brighte banere of blee whitte / with three / bore-hedis;	P D	N N
WW	176	Be any crafte that I kan / Carmes thaym semyde,	/	N H V
WW	177	For thay are the ordire that loven / oure / Lady to serve.	D	N to V
WW	178	If I scholde say the sothe, / it / semys no nothire	H	V Z
WW	179	Bot that the freris with othere folke / shall the / felde wynn.	X D	N V
WW	180	The sexte es of sendell, / and / so are thay alle,	C	Z be H Z
WW	181	Whitte als the whalles bone, / whoso the / sothe tellys,	Q D	N V
WW	182	With beltys of blake / bocled togedir,	/	E Z
WW	183	The poyntes pared off rowndé, / the / pendant awaye,	D	N Z
WW	184	And alle the lethire appon lofte / that one / lowe hengeth	that Z	Z V
WW	185	Schynethe alle for scharpynynge / of the / schavynge iren:	P D	G N
WW	186	The ordire of the Austyns, / for / oughte that I wene,	C	X that H V
WW	187	For by the blussche of the belte / the / banere I knewe.	D	N H V
WW	188	And othere synes I seghe / sett appon lofte,	/	E Z
WW	189	Some wittenesse of wolle, / and some of / wyne tounnes,	C H P	N N
WW	190	Some of merchandes merke, / so / many and so thikke	Z	A C Z A
WW	191	That I ne wote in my witt / for alle this / werlde riche	P D D	N A
WW	192	Whatt segge under the sonne / can the / sowme rekken.	X D	N V
WW	193	And sekere one that other syde / are / sadde men of armes,	be	A N P N
WW	194	Bolde sqwyeres of blode, / bowmen many,	/	N A
WW	195	That if thay strike one stroke / stynt thay ne thynken	/	V H not V
WW	196	Till owthir here appon hethe / be / hewen to dethe.	be	E P N
WW	197	Forthi I bid yow bothe / that thaym / hedir broghte	that H	Z V
WW	198	That ye wend with me, / are any / wrake falle,	be D	N V
WW	199	To oure comely kyng / that this / kythe owethe;	that D	N V
WW	200	And fro he wiete wittirly / where the / wronge ristyth,	Q D	N V
WW	201	Thare nowthir wye be wrothe / to / wirche als he demeth."	to	V C H V
WW	202	Off ayther rowte thar rode / owte a / renke als me thoghte,	Z D	N C H V
WW	203	Knyghtis full comly / one / coursers attyred,	P	N E
WW	204	And sayden, "Sir sandisman, / sele the betyde!	/	N H V
WW	205	Wele knowe we the kyng; / he / clothes us bothe,	H	V H A
WW	206	And hase us fosterde and fedde / this / fyve and twenty wyntere.	D	A C A N

WW	207	Now fare thou byfore / and we schall / folowe aftire."	C H X	V Z
WW	208	And now are thaire brydells upbraydc / and / bown one thaire wayes.	C	A P D N
WW	209	Thay lighten doun at the launde / and / leved thaire stedis,	C	V D N
WW	210	Kayren up at the clyffe / and one / knees fallyn.	C P	N V
WW	211	The kynge henttis by the handes / and / hetys tham to ryse,	C	V H to V
WW	212	And sayde, "Welcomes, heres, as hyne / of oure / house bothen."	P D	N A
WW	213	The kynge wayttede one wyde, / and the / wyne askes;	C D	N V
WW	214	Beryns broghte it anone / in / bolles of silvere.	P	N P N
WW	215	Me thoghte I sowpped so sadly / it / sowrede bothe myn eghne.	H	V D D N
WW	216	And he that wilnes of this werke / to / wete any forthire,	to	V Z
WW	217	Full freschely and faste, / for here a / fitt endes."	C Z D	N V
WW	218	Bot than kerpede the kynge, / sayd, / "Kythe what ye hatten,	V	V Q H V
WW	219	And whi the hates aren so hote / youre / hertis bytwene.	D	N P
WW	220	If I schall deme yow this day, / dothe me to here."	/	V H to V
WW	221	"Now certys, lorde," sayde / that one, "the / sothe for to telle,	D H D	N for to V
WW	222	I hatt Wynnere, a wy / that alle this / werlde helpis,	that D D	D
WW	223	For I lordes cane lere / thurgh / ledyng of witt.	P	N(G) P N
WW	224	Thoo that spedfully will spare / and / spende not to grete,	C	V not Z Z
WW	225	Lyve appon littill-whattes, / I / lufe hym the bettir.	H	V H D Z
WW	226	Witt wiendes me with, / and / wysses me faire;	C	V H A
WW	227	Aye when gadir my gudes / than / glades myn hert.	C	V D N
WW	228	Bot this felle false thefe / that / byfore yowe standes	that	P H V
WW	229	Thynkes to strike or he styntt / and / stroye me for ever.	C	V H Z
WW	230	Alle that I wynn thurgh witt / he / wastes thurgh pryde;	H	V P N
WW	231	I gedir, I glene, / and he lattys / goo sone;	C H V	V Z
WW	232	I pryke and I pryne, / and he he / purse opynes.	C H D	N V
WW	233	Why hase this cayteffe no care / how men / corne sellen?	Q N	N V
WW	234	His londes liggen alle ley, / his / lomes aren solde,	D	N be E
WW	235	Downn bene his dowfehowses, / drye bene his poles;	/	A be D N
WW	236	The devyll wounder one the wele / he / weldys at home,	H	V P N
WW	237	Bot hungere and heghe howses / and / howndes full kene.	C	N Z A
WW	238	Safe a sparthe and a spere / sparrede in ane hyrne,	/	E P D N
WW	239	A bronde at his bede-hede, / biddes he no nother	/	V H Z
WW	240	Bot a cuttede capill / to / cayre with to his frendes.	to	V Z P D N
WW	241	Then will he boste with his brande / and / braundesche hym ofte,	C	V H Z
WW	242	This wikkede weryed thefe / that / Wastoure men calles,	that	N N V
WW	243	That if he life may longe / this / lande will he stroye.	D	N X H V
WW	244	Forthi deme us this daye / for / Drightyns love in heven	P	N N P N
WW	245	To fighte furthe with oure folke / to owthire / fey worthe."	C H	A V
WW	246	"Yee, Wynnere," quod Wastoure, / "thi / wordes are hye:	D	N be A
WW	247	Bot I schall tell the a tale / that / tene schall the better.	that	V X H Z
WW	248	When thou haste waltered and went / and / wakede alle the nyghte,	C	E Z D N
WW	249	And iche a wy in this werlde / that / wonnes the abowte,	that	V H Z
WW	250	And hase werpede thy wyde howses / full of / wolle sakkes -	A P	N N
WW	251	The bemys benden at the rofe, / siche / bakone there hynges,	D	N Z V
WW	252	Stuffed are sterlynges / undere / stelen bowndes -	P	N N
WW	253	What scholde worthe of that wele / if no / waste come?	C D	N V
WW	254	Some rote, some ruste, / some / ratons fede.	D	N V
WW	255	Let be thi cramynge of thi kystes / for / Cristis lufe of heven!	P	N N P N
WW	256	Late the peple and the pore / hafe / parte of thi silvere;	V	N P D N
WW	257	For if thou wydwhare scholde walke / and / waytten the sothe,	C	V D N
WW	258	Thou scholdeste reme for rewthe, / in siche / ryfe bene the pore.	P D	N be H N(A)
WW	259	For and thou lengare thus lyfe, / leve thou no nother,	/	V H Z
WW	260	Thou scholde be hanged in helle / for that thou / here sparestе;	C that H	Z V
WW	261	For siche a synn haste thou solde / thi / soule into helle,	D	N P N
WW	262	And there es ever wellande woo, / worlde withowtten ende."	/	N P N
WW	263	"Late be thi worde, Wastoure," / quod / Wynnere the riche;	V	N D N(A)
WW	264	"Thou melleste of a mater, / thou / madiste it thiselven.	H	V H H self
WW	265	With thi sturte and thi stryffe / thou / stroyeste up my gudes	H	V Z D N
WW	266	In playinge and in wakynge / in / wynttres nyghttis,	P	N N
WW	267	In owttrage, in unthrifte, / in / augarte pryde.	P	A N
WW	268	There es no wele in this werlde / to / wasschen thyn handes	to	V D N
WW	269	That ne es gyffen and grounden / are thou it / getyn have.	be H H	E have
WW	270	Thou ledis renkes in thy rowte / wele / rychely attyrede;	be	Z E
WW	271	Some hafe girdills of golde / that more / gude coste	that A	N V
WW	272	Than alle the faire fre londe / that ye / byfore haden.	that H	Z V
WW	273	Ye folowe noghte youre fadirs / that / fosterde yow alle	that	V H Z
WW	274	A kynde herveste to cache / and / cornes to wynn	C	N to V
WW	275	For the colde wynttter and the kene / with / gleterand frostes,	P	G N
WW	276	Sythen dropeles drye / in the / dede monethe.	P D	A N
WW	277	And thou wolle to the taverne, / byfore the / tonne-hede,	P D	N N

WW Stage I

WW	278	Iche beryne redy with a bolle / to / blerren thyn eghne,	to	V D N
WW	279	Hete the whatte thou have schalte / and whatt thyn / hert lykes,	C Q D	N V
WW	280	Wyfe, wedowe, or wenche / that / wonnes there aboute.	that	V Z Z
WW	281	Then es there bott "fille in" and "feche / forthe," / florence to schewe,	Z	N to V
WW	282	"Wee hee," and "worthe / up," / wordes ynewe.	Z	N A
WW	283	Bot when this wele es awaye, / the / wyne moste be payede fore;	D	N X be E Z
WW	284	Than lympis yowe weddis to laye / or youre / londe selle.	C D	N V
WW	285	For siche wikked werkes / wery the oure Lorde!	/	V H D N
WW	286	And forthi God laughte that he lovede / and / levede that other,	C	V D H
WW	287	Iche freke one felde / ogh the / ferdere be to wirche.	X H	A be to V
WW	288	Teche thy men for to tille / and / tynen thyn feldes;	C	V D N
WW	289	Rayse up thi rent-howses, / ryme up thi yerdes,	/	V Z D N
WW	290	Owthere hafe as thou haste done / and / hope aftir werse -	C	V Z A
WW	291	That es firste the faylynge of fode, / and than the / fire aftir,	C Z D	N Z
WW	292	To brene the alle at a birre / for thi / bale dedis.	P D	A N
WW	293	The more colde es to come, / als me a / clerke tolde."	C H D	N V
WW	294	"Yee, Wynnere," quod Wastoure, / "thi / wordes are vayne.	D	N be A
WW	295	With oure festes and oure fare / we / feden the pore;	H	V D N(A)
WW	296	It es plesynge to the Prynce / that / Paradyse wroghte.	that	N V
WW	297	When Cristes peple hath parte / Hym / payes alle the better	H	V Z Z
WW	298	Then here ben hodirde and hidde / and / happede in cofers,	C	E P N
WW	299	That it no sonn may see / thurgh / seven wyntter ones,	P	A N Z
WW	300	Owthir freres it feche / when thou / fey worthes,	C H	A V
WW	301	To payntten with thaire pelers / or / pergett with thaire walles.	C	V P D N
WW	302	Thi sone and thi sektours, / ichone / slees othere;	H	V H
WW	303	Maken dale aftir thi daye, / for thou / durste neuer.	C H	V Z
WW	304	Mawngery ne myndale / ne never / myrthe lovediste.	not Z	N V
WW	305	A dale aftir thi daye / dose the no mare	/	V H Z
WW	306	Than a lighte lanterne / late appone nyghte	/	A P N
WW	307	When it es borne at thi bakke, / beryn, be my trouthe.	/	N be D N
WW	308	Now wolde God that it hathe / als I / wisse couthe,	C H	V X
WW	309	That thou, Wynnere, thou wriche, / and / Wanhope thi brothir,	C	N D N
WW	310	And eke ymbryne dayes, / and / evenes of sayntes,	C	N P N
WW	311	The Frydaye and his fere / one the / ferrere syde,	P D	A N
WW	312	Were drownede in the depe see / there never / droghte come,	Q Z	N V
WW	313	And dedly synn for thayre dede / were / endityde with twelve,	be	E P N
WW	314	And thies beryns one the bynches / with / howes one lofte,	P	N Z
WW	315	That bene knowen and kydde / for / clerkes of the beste,	P	N P D A
WW	316	Als gude als Arestotle / or / Austyn the wyse,	C	N D N(A)
WW	317	That alle schent were those schalkes / and / Scharshull iztwiste,	C	N Z
WW	318	That saide I prikkede with powere / his / pese to distourbe!	D	N to V
WW	319	Forthi, comely kynge, / that oure / case heris,	that D	N V
WW	320	Late us swythe with oure swerdes / swyngen togedirs;	/	V Z
WW	321	For nowe I se it es full sothe / that / sayde es full yore -	that	E be Z Z
WW	322	The richere of ranke wele, / the / rathere will drede:	D	Z X V
WW	323	The more havende that he hathe, / the more of / hert feble."	D A P	N A
WW	324	Bot than this wrechede Wynnere / full / wrothely he lukes,	Z	Z H V
WW	325	Sayse, "this es spedles speche / to / speken thies wordes.	to	V D N
WW	326	Loo! this wrechide Wastoure, / that / wydewhare es knawenn,	that	Z be E
WW	327	Ne es nothir kaysser, ne kynge, / ne / knyghte that the folowes,	D	N that H V
WW	328	Barone, ne bachelere, / ne / beryn that thou loveste,	D	N that H V
WW	329	Bot foure felawes or fyve, / that the / fayth owthe;	that D	N V
WW	330	And he schall dighte thaym to dyne / with / dayntethes so many	P	N Z A
WW	331	That iche a wy in this werlde / may / wepyn for sorowe.	X	V P N
WW	332	The bores-hede schall be broghte / with / plontes appon lofte,	P	N Z
WW	333	Buk-tayles full brode / in / brothes there besyde,	P	N Z Z
WW	334	Venyson with the frumentee, / and / fesanttes full riche,	C	N Z A
WW	335	Baken mete therby / one the / burde sett,	P D	N E
WW	336	Chewettes of choppede flesche, / charbiande fewlis,	/	A N
WW	337	And iche a segge that I see / has / sexe mens doke.	V	A N N
WW	338	If this were nedles note, / anothir comes aftir,	/	H V Z
WW	339	Roste with the riche sewes / and the / ryalle spyces,	C D	A N
WW	340	Kiddes cloven by the rigge, / quarterd swannes,	/	E N
WW	341	Tartes of ten ynche, / that / tenys myn hert	that	V D N
WW	342	To see the borde overbrade / with / blasande disches,	P	G N
WW	343	Als it were a rayled rode / with / rynges and stones.	P	N C N
WW	344	The thirde mese to me / were / mervelle to rekken -	be	N to V
WW	345	For alle es Martynmesse mete / that I with / most dele,	that H Z	X V
WW	346	Noghte bot worttes with the flesche, / withowt / wilde fowle	P	A N
WW	347	Save ane hene to hym / that the / howse owethe -	that D	N V
WW	348	And he will hafe birdes bownn / one a / broche riche,	P D	N A

WW	349	Barnakes and buturs / and many / billed snyppes,	C D	E N
WW	350	Larkes and lyngwhues / lapped in sogoure,	/	F P N
WW	351	Wodcokkes and wodwales / full / wellande hote,	Z	G A
WW	352	Teeles and titmoyses / to / take what him lykes;	to	V Q H V
WW	353	[Caudel]s of conynges / and / custadis swete,	C	N A
WW	354	[Dario]ls and dische-metis / that ful / dere coste,	that Z	Z V
WW	355	[Maw]mene that men stepen / your / mawes to fill,	D	N to V
WW	356	[Ich]e a mese at a merke / bytwen / twa men,	P	A N
WW	357	[That s]othe bot brynneth for bale / your / bowells within.	D	N P
WW	358	[Me t]enyth at your trompers, / thay / tounen so heghe	H	V Z Z
WW	359	[That ic]he a gome in the gate / goullyng may here:	/	G X V
WW	360	Then wil thay say to thamselfe, / as thay / samen ryden,	C H	Z V
WW	361	Ye hafe no myster of the helpe / of the / heven kyng.	P D	N N
WW	362	Thus are ye scorned by skyll, / and / schathed theraftir,	C	E Z
WW	363	That rechen for a repaste / a / rawnsom of silver.	D	N P N
WW	364	Bot ones I herd in a haule / of a / herdmans tong:	P D	N N
WW	365	"Better were meles many / than a / mery nyghte."	C D	A N
WW	366	And he that wilnes of this werke / for to / wete forthe,	for to	V Z
WW	367	Full freschely and faste, / for here a / fit endes.	C Z D	N V
WW	368	"Yee, Wynnere," quod Wastour, / "I / wote well myselven	H	V Z H self
WW	369	What sall lympe of the lede, / within/ fewe yeris.	P	A N
WW	370	Thurgh the poure plenté of corne / that the / peple sowes,	that D	N V
WW	371	That God will graunte of his grace / to / growe on the erthe,	to	V P D N
WW	372	Ay to appaire the pris, / and it / passe nott to hye,	C H	V not Z Z
WW	373	Schal make the to waxe wod / for / wanhope in erthe,	P	N P N
WW	374	To hope aftir an harde yere / to / honge thiselven.	to	V H self
WW	375	Woldeste thou hafe lordis to lyfe / as / laddes on fote?	P	N P N
WW	376	Prelates als prestes / that the / parischen yemes?	that D	N V
WW	377	Prowde marchandes of pris / as / pedders in towne?	P	N P N
WW	378	Late lordes lyfe als tham liste, / laddes as tham falles;	/	N C H V
WW	379	Thay the bacon and beefe, / thay / botours and swannes,	H	N C N
WW	380	Thay the roughe of the rye, / thay the / rede whete,	H D	A N
WW	381	Thay the grewell gray, / and thay the / gude sewes;	C H D	A N
WW	382	And then may the peple hafe parte / in / povert than standes,	P	N that V
WW	383	Sum gud morsell of mete / to / mend with thair chere.	to	V P D N
WW	384	If fewlis flye schold forthe / and / fongen be never,	C	E be Z
WW	385	And wild bestis in the wodde / wone al thaire lyve,	/	V Z D N
WW	386	And fisches flete in the flode, / and ichone / ete other,	C H	V H
WW	387	Ane henne at ane halpeny / by/ halfe yeris ende,	P	A N N
WW	388	Schold not a ladde be in londe / a / lorde for to serve.	D	N for to V
WW	389	This wate thou full wele / witterly thiselven,	/	Z H self
WW	390	Whoso wele schal wyn, / a / wastour moste he fynde,	D	N X H V
WW	391	For if it greves one gome, / it / gladdes another."	H	V H
WW	392	"Now," quod Wynner to Wastour, / "me / wondirs in hert	H	V P N
WW	393	Of thies poure penyles men / that / peloure will by,	that	N X V
WW	394	Sadills of sendale, / with / sercles full riche.	P	N Z A
WW	395	Lesse and ye wrethe your wifes, / thaire / willes to folowe,	D	N to V
WW	396	Ye sellyn wodd aftir wodde / in a / wale tyme,	P D	A N
WW	397	Bothe the oke and the assche / and / all that ther growes;	C	H that Z V
WW	398	The spyres and the yonge sprynge / ye / spare to your children,	H	V P D N
WW	399	And sayne God wil graunt it his grace / to / grow at the last,	to	V Z
WW	400	For to save to your sones: / bot the / schame es your ownn.	C D	N be D A
WW	401	Nedeles save ye the soyle, / for / sell it ye thynken.	C	V H H V
WW	402	Your forfadirs were fayne, / when any / frende come,	C D	N V
WW	403	For to schake to the schawe / and / schewe hym the estres,	C	V H D N
WW	404	In iche holt that thay had / ane / hare for to fynde,	D	N for to V
WW	405	Bryng to the brod lande / bukkes ynewe	/	N A
WW	406	To lache and to late goo, / to / lighten thaire hertis.	to	V D N
WW	407	Now es it sett and solde, / my / sorowe es the more,	D	N be D A
WW	408	Wastes alle wilfully, / your / wyfes to paye.	D	N to V
WW	409	That are had lordes in londe / and / ladyes riche,	C	N A
WW	410	Now are thay nysottes of the new gett, / so / nysely attyred,	Z	Z E
WW	411	With side slabbande sleves, / sleght to the grounde,	/	E P D N
WW	412	Ourlede all umbtourne / with / ermyn aboute,	P	N Z
WW	413	That es as harde, as I hope, / to / handil in the derne,	to	V P D N
WW	414	Als a cely symple wenche / that never / silke wroghte.	that Z	N V
WW	415	Bot whoso lukes on hir lyre, / oure / Lady of Heven,	D	N P N
WW	416	How scho fled for ferd / ferre out of hir kythe,	/	Z P P D N
WW	417	Appon ane amblande asse, / withowtten more pride,	/	P A N
WW	418	Safe a barne in hir barme, / and a / broken heltre	C D	E N
WW	419	That Joseph held in hys hande, / that / hend for to yeme,	D	N(A) for to V

WW	420	Allthofe scho walt al this werlde, / hir / wedes wer pore	D	N be A
WW	421	For to gyf ensample of siche, / for to / schewe other	for to	V C
WW	422	For to leve pompe and pride, / that / poverté ofte schewes."	that	N Z V
WW	423	Than the Wastour wrothly / castes up his eghne,	/	V Z D N
WW	424	And said, "Thou Wynnere, thou wriche, / me / wondirs in hert	H	V P N
WW	425	What hafe oure clothes coste / the, / caytef, to by,	H	N to V
WW	426	That thou schal birdes upbrayd / of thair / bright wedis,	P D	A N
WW	427	Sythen that we vouchesafe / that the / silver payen.	that D	N V
WW	428	It lyes wele for a lede / his/ leman to fynde,	D	N to V
WW	429	Aftir hir faire chere / to / forthir hir herte.	to	V D N
WW	430	Then will scho love hym lelely / as hir / lyfe one,	P D	N A
WW	431	Make hym bolde and bown / with / brandes to smytte,	P	N to V
WW	432	To schonn schenchipe and schame / ther / schalkes ere gadird;	Q	N be E
WW	433	And if my peple ben prode, / me / payes alle the better	H	V Z Z
WW	434	To see tham faire and free / tofore with myn eghne.	/	Z P D N
WW	435	And ye negardes appon nyghte / ye / nappen so harde,	H	V Z Z
WW	436	Routten at your raxillyng, / raysen your hurdes;	/	V D N
WW	437	Ye beden wayte one the wedir, / then / wery ye the while	Z	V H D N
WW	438	That ye nade hightilde up your houses / and your / hyne raysed.	C D	N E
WW	439	Forthi, Wynnere, with wronge / thou / wastes thi tyme;	H	V D N
WW	440	For gode day ne glade / getys thou never.	/	V H Z
WW	441	The devyll at thi dede-day / schal / delyn thi gudis;	X	V D N
WW	442	Tho thou woldest that it were, / wyn thay it never;	/	V H H Z
WW	443	Thi skathill sectours / schal / sever tham aboute,	X	V H Z
WW	444	And thou hafe helle full hotte / for that thou / here saved.	for that H	Z V
WW	445	Thou tast tent one a tale / that / tolde was full yore:	that	E be Z Z
WW	446	I hold hym madde that mournes / his / make for to wyn	D	N for to V
WW	447	Hent hir that hir haf / schal, and / hold hir his while,	X C	V H D N
WW	448	Take the coppe as it comes, / the / case as it falles,	Q H	N C H V
WW	449	For whoso lyfe may lengeste / lympes to feche	/	V to V
WW	450	Woodd that he waste / schall to / warmen hys helys,	X to	V D N
WW	451	Ferrere than his fadir dide / by / fyvetene myle.	P	A N
WW	452	Now kan I carpe no more; / bot, Sir / Kyng, by thi trouthe,	P D	N P D N
WW	453	Deme us where we duell / schall: me thynke the / day hyes.	X H V D	N A
WW	454	Yit harde sore es myn hert / and / harmes me more	C	V H Z
WW	455	Ever to see in my syghte / that I in / soule hate."	that H P	N V
WW	456	The kynge lovely lokes / on the/ ledis twayne,	P D	N A
WW	457	Says, "Blynnes, beryns, of youre brethe / and of youre / brode worde,	C P D	A N
WW	458	And I schal deme yow this day / where ye / duelle schall,	Q H	V X
WW	459	Aythere lede in a lond / ther he es / loved moste.	Q H be	V Z
WW	460	Wende, Wynnere, thi waye / over the / wale stremys,	P D	A N
WW	461	Passe forthe by Paris / to the / Pope of Rome;	P D	N P N
WW	462	The cardynalls ken the wele, / will / kepe the ful faire,	X	V H Z Z
WW	463	And make thi sydes in silken / schetys to lygge,	/	N to V
WW	464	And fede the and foster / the and / forthir thyn hert,	H C	V D N
WW	465	As leefe to worthen wode / as the to / wrethe ones.	C H to	V Z
WW	466	Bot loke, lede, be thi lyfe, / when I / lettres sende,	C H	N V
WW	467	That thou hy te to me home / on / horse or one fote;	P	N C P N
WW	468	And when I knowe thou will co[me], / he schall / cayre uttire,	H X	V Z
WW	469	And lenge with another lede, / til thou thi / lefe [take];	C H D	N V
WW	470	For thofe thou bide in this burgh / to thi / be[ryinge-daye],	P D	G N
WW	471	With hym happyns the never / a / fote for [to holde].	D	N for to V
WW	472	And thou, Wastoure, I will / that thou / wonn[e scholde]	that H	V X
WW	473	Ther moste waste es of wele, / and / wyng [ther until].	C	V Z Z
WW	474	Chese the forthe into the Chepe, / a / chambre thou rere,	D	N H V
WW	475	Loke thi wyndowe be wyde, / and / wayte the aboute,	C	V H P
WW	476	Where any potet beryn / thurgh the / burgh passe;	P D	N V
WW	477	Teche hym to the taverne / till he / tayte worthe;	C H	A V
WW	478	Doo hym drynk al nyghte / that he / dry be at morow,	that H	A be P N
WW	479	Sythen ken hym to the crete / to / comforth his vaynes,	to	V D N
WW	480	Brynge hym to Bred Strete, / bikken thi fynger,	/	V D N
WW	481	Schew hym of fatt chepe / scholdirs ynewe,	/	N A
WW	482	"Hotte for the hungry," / a / hen other twayne,	D	N C N
WW	483	Sett hym softe one a sege, / and sythen / send after,	C Z	V Z
WW	484	Bryng out of the burgh / the / best thou may fynde,	D	A H X V
WW	485	And luke thi knave hafe a knoke / bot he the / clothe sprede.	C H D	N V
WW	486	Bot late hym paye or he passe, / and / pik hym so clene	C	V H Z A
WW	487	That fynd a peny in his purse / and / put owte his eghe.	C	V Z D N
WW	488	When that es dronken and don, / duell then no lenger,	/	V Z Z
WW	489	Bot teche hym owt of the townn / to / trotte aftir more.	to	V Z Z
WW	490	Then passe to the Pultrie, / the / peple the knowes,	D	N H V

WW	491	And ken wele thi katour / to / knawen thi fode,		to	V D N
WW	492	The herons, the hastelet[ez], the / henne wele serve,		D	N Z V
WW	493	The pertrikes, the plovers, / the other / pulled byrddes,		D H	E N
WW	494	The albus, this other foules, / the / egretes dere;		D	N A
WW	495	The more thou wastis thi wele, / the / better the Wynner lykes.		D	Z D N V
WW	496	And wayte to me, thou Wynnere, / if thou wilt / wele chefe,		C H X	N V
WW	497	When I wende appon werre / my / wyes to lede;		D	N to V
WW	498	For at the proude pales / of / Parys the riche		P	N D N(A)
WW	499	I thynk to do it in ded, / and / dub the to knyghte,		C	V H P N
WW	500	And giff giftes full grete / of / golde and of silver,		P	N C P N
WW	501	To ledis of my legyance / that / lufen me in hert.		that	V H P N
WW	502	And sythen kayre as I come, / with / knyghtes that me foloen,		P	N that H V
WW	503	To the kirk of Colayne / ther the / kynges ligges. . . .		Q D	N V

Stage Two (by caesura)

WW	33b	/	bryghte was the sone	A be D N
WW	235b	/	drye bene his poles;	A be D N
WW	93b	/	blewe als me thoghte	A C H V
WW	52b	/	bown for to mete,	A for to V
WW	336b	/	charbiande fewlis,	A N
WW	306b	/	late appone nyghte	A P N
WW	145b	/	hynged a corde,	E D N
WW	340b	/	quarterd swannes,	E N
WW	95b	/	girde in the myddis:	E P D N
WW	115b	/	joynede by the sydes,	E P D N
WW	411b	/	sleght to the grounde,	E P D N
WW	238b	/	sparrede in ane hyrne,	E P D N
WW	117b	/	wroghte in the kynde,	E P D N
WW	64b	/	werped of he,	E P H
WW	61b	/	betyn of golde,	E P N
WW	91b	/	brouderde with fewlys,	E P N
WW	96b	/	broudirde with fewles,	E P N
WW	86b	/	crowned with golde,	E P N
WW	350b	/	lapped in sogoure,	E P N
WW	182b	/	bocled togedir,	E Z
WW	144b	/	brouden withinn,	E Z
WW	138b	/	ferdede besyde,	E Z
WW	188b	/	sett appon lofte,	E Z
WW	46b	/	sweped belyve.	E Z
WW	94b	/	gerede full riche.	E Z A
WW	113b	/	brauden full thikke,	E Z Z
WW	63b	/	gerede full riche.	E Z Z
WW	112b	/	polischede full clene,	E Z Z
WW	97b	/	daderande tham semede	G H V
WW	92b	/	flakerande with wynges,	G P N
WW	359b	/	goullyng may here:	G X V
WW	32b	/	wandrynge myn one,	G Z
WW	74b	/	lokande full kene,	G Z A
WW	82b	/	tuttynge out fayre.	G Z Z
WW	338b	/	anothir comes aftir,	H V Z
WW	194b	/	bowmen many,	N A
WW	405b	/	bukkes ynewe	N A
WW	481b	/	scholdirs ynewe,	N A
WW	84b	/	wondres ynewe.	N A
WW	307b	/	beryn, be my trouthe.	N be D N
WW	378b	/	laddes as tham falles;	N C H V
WW	176b	/	Carmes thaym semyde,	N H V
WW	204b	/	sele the betyde!	N H V
WW	137b	/	segge, with myn eghne;	N P D N
WW	262b	/	worlde withowtten ende."	N P N
WW	463b	/	schetys to lygge,	N to V
WW	142b	/	strokes to dele.	N to V
WW	141b	/	Estirlynges full many,	N Z A
WW	417b	/	withowtten more pride,	P A N
WW	101b	/	by hym that stondeth,	P H that V
WW	480b	/	bikken thi fynger,	V D N

WW	40b	/	jarmede the foles.	V D N
WW	436b	/	raysen your hurdes;	V D N
WW	69b	/	kepe hym oure Lorde!	V H D N
WW	285b	/	wery the oure Lorde!	V H D N
WW	442b	/	wyn thay it never;	V H H Z
WW	195b	/	stynt thay ne thynken	V H not V
WW	107b	/	stynte thay ne thynken."	V H not V
WW	220b	/	dothe me to here."	V H to V
WW	239b	/	biddes he no nother	V H Z
WW	305b	/	dose the no mare	V H Z
WW	440b	/	getys thou never.	V H Z
WW	11b	/	hope I no nother -	V H Z
WW	259b	/	leve thou no nother,	V H Z
WW	89b	/	sawe with his eghne.	V P D N
WW	58b	/	had untill othere.	V P H
WW	171b	/	ledith thurgh witt,	V P N
WW	449b	/	lympes to feche	V to V
WW	100b	/	ryde umbestonde."	V Z
WW	320b	/	swyngen togedirs;	V Z
WW	423b	/	castes up his eghne,	V Z D N
WW	289b	/	ryme up thi yerdes,	V Z D N
WW	120b	/	wiste of his age.	V Z D N
WW	385b	/	wone al thaire lyve,	V Z D N
WW	488b	/	duell ther no lenger,	V Z Z
WW	78b	/	before and behynde,	Z C Z
WW	389b	/	witterly thiselven,	Z H self
WW	76b	/	byhynde in the nekke	Z P D N
WW	434b	/	tofore with myn eghne.	Z P D N
WW	416b	/	ferre out of hir kythe,	Z P P D N
WW	106b	/	nerre togedirs;	Z Z
WW	250b	A P	wolle sakkes -	N N
WW	193b	be	sadde men of armes,	A N P N
WW	313b	be	enditye with twelve,	E P N
WW	196b	be	hewen to dethe.	E P N
WW	163b	be	brayde appon lofte,	E Z
WW	170b	be	forced besyde,	E Z
WW	344b	be	mervelle to rekken -	N to V
WW	270b	be	rychely attyrede;	Z E
WW	198b	be D	wrake falle,	N V
WW	269b	be H H	getyn have.	E have
WW	156b	be P	blee whitte,	N A
WW	165b	be P	someris tyde,	N N
WW	110b	be P D	beste wyse.	A N
WW	208b	C	bown one thaire wayes.	A P D N
WW	119b	C	yapeste of witt	A P N
WW	384b	C	fongen be never,	E be Z
WW	98b	C	fawked thay were.	E H be
WW	151b	C	kembid in the nekke:	E P D N
WW	298b	C	happede in cofers,	E P N
WW	362b	C	schathed theraftir,	E Z
WW	248b	C	wakede alle the nyghte,	E Z D N
WW	353b	C	custadis swete,	N A
WW	409b	C	ladyes riche,	N A
WW	29b	C	ledys bene knawen,	N be E
WW	12b	C	walles bene doun,	N be Z
WW	309b	C	Wanhope thi brothir,	N D N
WW	316b	C	Austyn the wyse,	N D N(A)
WW	1b	C	Bruyttus it aughte,	N H X
WW	65b	C	poyntes bytwene,	N P
WW	310b	C	evenes of sayntes,	N P N
WW	51b	C	helmys with crestys;	N P N
WW	274b	C	cornes to wynn	N to V
WW	26b	C	japes telle,	N V
WW	317b	C	Scharshull itwiste,	N Z
WW	334b	C	fesanttes full riche,	N Z A
WW	237b	C	howndes full kene.	N Z A
WW	80b	C	thre on lowe undir;	N Z Z
WW	44b	C	dadillyng of fewllys.	N(G) P N
WW	154b	C	flyttynge may helpe,	N(G) X V
WW	286b	C	levede that other,	V D H
WW	227b	C	glades myn hert.	V D N

WW 209b	C	leved thaire stedis,	V D N
WW 43b	C	lowked myn eghne,	V D N
WW 122b	C	takes his waye	V D N
WW 288b	C	tynen thyn feldes;	V D N
WW 257b	C	waytten the sothe,	V D N
WW 226b	C	wysses me faire;	V H A
WW 403b	C	schewe hym the estres,	V H D N
WW 401b	C	sell it ye thynken.	V H H V
WW 475b	C	wayte the aboute,	V H P
WW 499b	C	dub the to knyghte,	V H P N
WW 15b	C	lede hem at will,	V H P N
WW 211b	C	hetys tham to ryse,	V H to V
WW 241b	C	braundesche hym ofte,	V H Z
WW 121b	C	caughte it swythe,	V H Z
WW 454b	C	harmes me more	V H Z
WW 229b	C	stroye me for ever.	V H Z
WW 486b	C	pik hym so clene	V H Z A
WW 224b	C	spende not to grete,	V not Z Z
WW 301b	C	pergett with thaire walles.	V P D N
WW 109b	C	dwellys awhile	V Z
WW 290b	C	hope aftir werse -	V Z A
WW 487b	C	put owte his eghe.	V Z D N
WW 27b	C	lett of a while	V Z Z
WW 42b	C	raughten so heghe	V Z Z
WW 473b	C	wyng [ther untill].	V Z Z
WW 186b	C	oughte that I wene,	X that H V
WW 180b	C	so are thay alle,	Z be H Z
WW 130b	C	ever schall worthe:	Z X V
WW 397b	C	all that ther growes;	H that Z V
WW 18b	C be	neghe here.	V Z
WW 365b	C D	mery nyghte."	A N
WW 339b	C D	ryalle spyces,	A N
WW 349b	C D	billed snyppes,	E N
WW 418b	C D	broken heltre	E N
WW 400b	C D	schame es your ownn.	N be D A
WW 438b	C D	hyne raysed.	N E
WW 402b	C D	frende come,	N V
WW 108b	C D	life dures."	N V
WW 284b	C D	londe selle.	N V
WW 55b	C D	prynce come,	N V
WW 17b	C D	sothe telle,	N V
WW 253b	C D	waste come?	N V
WW 7b	C D	werlde lasteth	N V
WW 213b	C D	wyne askes;	N V
WW 133b	C D	lyfe aftir.	N Z
WW 245b	C H	fey worthe."	A V
WW 300b	C H	fey worthes,	A V
WW 9b	C H	hore eldes.	A V
WW 477b	C H	tayte worthe;	A V
WW 466b	C H	lettres sende,	N V
WW 386b	C H	ete other,	V H
WW 6b	C H	wryeth othere.	V H
WW 372b	C H	passe nott to hye,	V not Z Z
WW 43b	C H	nappe myghte,	V X
WW 308b	C H	wisse couthe,	V X
WW 303b	C H	durste never.	V Z
WW 360b	C H	samen ryden,	Z V
WW 381b	C H D	gude sewes;	A N
WW 293b	C H D	clerke tolde."	N V
WW 485b	C H D	clothe sprede.	N V
WW 118b	C H D	gome knewe,	N V
WW 469b	C H D	lefe [take].	N V
WW 232b	C H D	purse opynes.	N V
WW 189b	C H P	wyne tounnes,	N V
WW 465b	C H to	wrethe ones.	V Z
WW 231b	C H V	goo sone;	V Z
WW 496b	C H X	wele chefe,	N V
WW 207b	C H X	folowe aftire."	V Z
WW 139b	C P	Lawe Spayne;	N N
WW 210b	C P	knees fallyn.	N V
WW 457b	C P D	brode worde,	A N

WW Stage II

WW	279b	C Q D	hert lykes,	N V
WW	260b	C that H	here spareste;	Z V
WW	57b	C to	rewlyn the wrothe	V D N(A)
WW	483b	C Z	send after,	V Z
WW	367b	C Z D	fit endes.	N V
WW	217b	C Z D	fitt endes.	N V
WW	291b	C Z D	fire aftir,	N Z
WW	206b	D	fyve and twenty wyntere.	A C A N
WW	484b	D	best thou may fynde,	A H X V
WW	73b	D	hattfull beste,	A N
WW	174b	D	faireste of tham alle,	A P H Z
WW	494b	D	egretes dere;	N A
WW	420b	D	wedes wer pore	N be A
WW	294b	D	wordes are vayne.	N be A
WW	246b	D	wordes are hye:	N be A
WW	407b	D	sorowe es the more,	N be D A
WW	168b	D	banere es stuffede.	N be E
WW	59b	D	caban was rerede,	N be E
WW	234b	D	lomes aren solde,	N be E
WW	60b	D	rofe and the sydes,	N C D N
WW	448b	D	case as it falles,	N C H V
WW	482b	D	hen other twayne,	N C N
WW	471b	D	fote for [to holde].	N for to V
WW	404b	D	hare for to fynde,	N for to V
WW	388b	D	lorde for to serve.	N for to V
WW	446b	D	make for to wyn	N for to V
WW	187b	D	banere I knewe.	N H V
WW	474b	D	chambre thou rere,	N H V
WW	490b	D	peple the knowes,	N H V
WW	41b	D	bankes bytwene;	N P
WW	357b	D	bowells within.	N P
WW	36b	D	hawthorne besyde;	N P
WW	219b	D	hertis bytwene.	N P
WW	54b	D	lordes bytwene.	N P
WW	164b	D	balle in the myddes,	N P D N
WW	49b	D	lengthe of a myle.	N P D N
WW	415b	D	Lady of Heven,	N P N
WW	363b	D	rawnsom of silver.	N P N
WW	261b	D	soule into helle,	N P N
WW	328b	D	beryn that thou loveste,	N that H V
WW	83b	D	knyghte that I see,	N that H V
WW	327b	D	knyghte that the folowes,	N that H V
WW	114b	D	body to yeme,	N to V
WW	177b	D	Lady to serve.	N to V
WW	428b	D	leman to fynde,	N to V
WW	355b	D	mawes to fill,	N to V
WW	318b	D	pese to distourbe!	N to V
WW	129b	D	pese to disturbe.	N to V
WW	169b	D	prechours to helpe,	N to V
WW	395b	D	willes to folowe,	N to V
WW	104b	D	willes to kythe.	N to V
WW	497b	D	wyes to lede;	N to V
WW	408b	D	wyfes to paye.	N to V
WW	254b	D	ratons fede.	N V
WW	116b	D	breste had another,	N V H
WW	283b	D	wyne moste be payede fore;	N X be E Z
WW	243b	D	lande will he stroye.	N X H V
WW	390b	D	wastour moste he fynde,	N X H V
WW	72b	D	hatte appon lofte,	N Z
WW	25b	D	wordes togedire,	N Z
WW	183b	D	pendant awaye,	N Z
WW	251b	D	bakone there hynges,	N Z V
WW	70b	D	hathell up stondes,	N Z V
WW	492b	D	henne wele serve,	N Z V
WW	419b	D	hend for to yeme,	N(A) for to V
WW	495b	D	better the Wynner lykes.	Z D N V
WW	322b	D	rathere will drede:	Z X V
WW	323b	D A P	hert feble."	N A
WW	493b	D H	pulled byrddes,	E N
WW	221b	D H D	sothe for to telle,	N for to V
WW	444b	for that H	here saved.	Z V

WW	421b	for to	schewe other	V C
WW	388b	for to	wete forthe,	V ?
WW	379b	H	botours and swannes,	N C N
WW	425b	H	caytef, to by,	N to V
WW	146b	H	say als me thynkes,	V C H V
WW	160b	H	feghtyn bot seldom.	V C Z
WW	215b	H	sowrede bothe myn eghne.	V D D N
WW	439b	H	wastes thi tyme;	V D N
WW	295b	H	feden the pore;	V D N(A)
WW	391b	H	gladdes another."	V H
WW	302b	H	slees othere;	V H
WW	205b	H	clothes us bothe,	V H A
WW	147b	H	hope he be there,	V H be Z
WW	225b	H	lufe hym the bettir.	V H D Z
WW	264b	H	madiste it thiselven.	V H H self
WW	398b	H	spare to your children,	V P D N
WW	230b	H	wastes thurgh pryde;	V P N
WW	236b	H	weldys at home,	V P N
WW	161b	H	wentten fro home;	V P N
WW	392b	H	wondirs in hert	V P N
WW	424b	H	wondirs in hert	V P N
WW	178b	H	semys no nothire	V Z
WW	37b	H	threpen togedire,	V Z
WW	265b	H	stroyeste up my gudes	V Z D N
WW	368b	H	wote well myselven	V Z H self
WW	358b	H	tounen so heghe	V Z Z
WW	16b	H	draweth neghe aftir.	V Z Z
WW	435b	H	nappen so harde,	V Z Z
WW	297b	H	payes alle the better	V Z Z
WW	433b	H	payes alle the better	V Z Z
WW	85b	H be	warre sone	A Z
WW	464b	H C	forthir thyn hert,	V D N
WW	380b	H D	rede whete,	A N
WW	47b	H not	wiste in whate ende,	V P Q N
WW	159b	H X	fey worthe;	A V
WW	468b	H X	cayre uttire,	V Z
WW	127b	not	stirre none nerre	V Z
WW	134b	not D	kynge ryche,	N A
WW	304b	not Z	myrthe lovediste.	N V
WW	126b	P	bothe his two eghne,	A D D N
WW	356b	P	twa men,	A N
WW	267b	P	augarte pryde.	A N
WW	369b	P	fewe yeris.	A N
WW	66b	P	fresche lettres,	A N
WW	451b	P	fyvetene myle.	A N
WW	346b	P	wilde fowle	A N
WW	67b	P	Ynglysse tonge,	A N
WW	387b	P	halfe yeris ende,	A N N
WW	3b	P	seere kynges tymes,	A N N
WW	299b	P	seven wyntter ones,	A N Z
WW	342b	P	blasande disches,	G N
WW	275b	P	gleterand frostes,	G N
WW	158b	P	bokels twayne.	N A
WW	77b	P	quarters foure:	N A
WW	90b	P	kirtill and mantill -	N C N
WW	343b	P	rynges and stones.	N C N
WW	14b	P	boste and with pryde,	N C P N
WW	500b	P	golde and of silver,	N C P N
WW	467b	P	horse or one fote;	N C P N
WW	498b	P	Parys the riche	N D N(A)
WW	10b	P	Salomon the wyse -	N D N(A)
WW	203b	P	coursers attyred,	N E
WW	131b	P	banere for to ryde	N for to V
WW	173b	P	God hymselven.	N H self
WW	39b	P	barkes thay roungen,	N H V
WW	53b	P	schiltrons thay felle,	N H V
WW	166b	P	Missomer Even.	N N
WW	24b	P	renke herde.	N N
WW	252b	P	stelen bowndes -	N N
WW	266b	P	wynttres nyghttis,	N N
WW	255b	P	Cristis lufe of heven!	N N P N

WW Stage II

WW	244b	P	Drightyns love in heven	N N P N
WW	315b	P	clerkes of the beste,	N P D A
WW	38b	P	heselis tyll othire,	N P H
WW	373b	P	wanhope in erthe,	N P N
WW	214b	P	bolles of silvere.	N P N
WW	21b	P	fayntnesse of hert,	N P N
WW	62b	P	garters of inde,	N P N
WW	377b	P	pedders in towne?	N P N
WW	87b	P	septure in honde,	N P N
WW	375b	P	laddes on fote?	N P N
WW	502b	P	knyghtes that me foloen,	N that H V
WW	382b	P	povert that standes,	N that V
WW	431b	P	brandes to smytte,	N to V
WW	103b	P	dynttis to dele!	N to V
WW	167b	P	dynttis to dele;	N to V
WW	412b	P	ermyn aboute,	N Z
WW	150b	P	howes one lofte,	N Z
WW	314b	P	howes one lofte,	N Z
WW	332b	P	plontes appon lofte,	N Z
WW	157b	P	sable withinn,	N Z
WW	2b	P	tresone withinn,	N Z
WW	330b	P	dayntethes so many	N Z A
WW	153b	P	dynttis full many.	N Z A
WW	50b	P	hawberkes full brighte,	N Z A
WW	394b	P	sercles full riche.	N Z A
WW	333b	P	brothes there besyde,	N Z Z
WW	223b	P	ledyng of witt.	N(G) P N
WW	292b	P D	bale dedis,	A N
WW	426b	P D	bright wedis,	A N
WW	276b	P D	dede monethe.	A N
WW	311b	P D	ferrere syde,	A N
WW	79b	P D	grym bestes,	A N
WW	111b	P D	lawe bones,	A N
WW	4b	P D	nyne dele.	A N
WW	34b	P D	wale medewe:	A N
WW	460b	P D	wale stremys,	A N
WW	396b	P D	wale tyme,	A N
WW	470b	P D	be[ryinge-daye],	G N
WW	185b	P D	schavynge iren:	G N
WW	132b	P D	bot the / kynge one,	N A
WW	348b	P D	broche riche,	N A
WW	135b	P D	grace one.	N A
WW	212b	P D	house bothen."	N A
WW	456b	P D	ledis twayne,	N A
WW	430b	P D	lyfe one,	N A
WW	56b	P D	wy ells	N A
WW	136b	P D	wyes one,	N A
WW	258b	P D	ryfe bene the pore.	N be H N(A)
WW	335b	P D	burde sett,	N E
WW	175b	P D	bore-hedis;	N N
WW	364b	P D	herdmans tong:	N N
WW	361b	P D	heven kyng.	N N
WW	277b	P D	tonne-hede,	N N
WW	452b	P D	Kyng, by thi trouthe,	N P D N
WW	149b	P D	bende of grene,	N P N
WW	461b	P D	Pope of Rome;	N P N
WW	148b	P D	folke that he ledis.	N that H V
WW	476b	P D	burgh passe;	N V
WW	123b	P D	felde hoves.	N V
WW	191b	P D D	werlde riche	N A
WW	125b	P H C H	beste lyketh,	Z V
WW	81b	P Z	clene perle,	A N
WW	75b	P Z	yape wyse.	A N
WW	432b	Q	schalkes ere gadird;	N be E
WW	124b	Q	kepe hym oure Lorde!	V H D N
WW	88b	Q	loveth hym in hert,	V H P N
WW	30b	Q	wirche kane beste.	V X Z
WW	35b	Q D	fote steppede.	N V
WW	503b	Q D	kynges ligges. . . .	N V
WW	181b	Q D	sothe tellys,	N V
WW	200b	Q D	wronge ristyth,	N V

WW	458b	Q H	duelle schall,	V X
WW	439b	Q H bc	loved monte,	V Z
WW	233b	Q N	corne sellen?	N V
WW	312b	Q Z	droghte come,	N V
WW	22b	that	wroghte were never,	E be Z
WW	321b	that	sayde es full yore -	E be Z Z
WW	445b	that	tolde was full yore:	E be Z Z
WW	5b	that	we with delyn,	H Z V
WW	242b	that	Wastoure men calles,	N N V
WW	296b	that	Paradyse wroghte.	N V
WW	20b	that	matirs couthe fynde,	N X V
WW	393b	that	peloure will by,	N X V
WW	422b	that	poverté ofte schewes."	N Z V
WW	228b	that	byfore yowe standes	P H V
WW	341b	that	tenys myn hert	V D N
WW	28b	that	made it hymselven.	V H H self
WW	501b	that	lufen me in hert.	V H P N
WW	155b	that	fayled hym never.	V H Z
WW	102b	that	faylede hym never:	V H Z
WW	273b	that	fosterde yow alle	V H Z
WW	249b	that	wonnes the abowte,	V H Z
WW	162b	that	wanne thaym all hedire.	V H Z Z
WW	19b	that	loved in thaire hertis	V P D N
WW	247b	that	tene schall the better.	V X H Z
WW	280b	that	wonnes there aboute.	V Z Z
WW	326b	that	wydewhare es knawenn,	Z be E
WW	271b	that A	gude coste	N V
WW	48b	that be	ylike grene,	Z A
WW	319b	that D	case heris,	N V
WW	329b	that D	fayth owthe;	N V
WW	68b	that D	harme thynkes."	N V
WW	347b	that D	howse owethe -	N V
WW	199b	that D	kythe owethe;	N V
WW	376b	that D	parischen yemes?	N V
WW	370b	that D	peple sowes,	N V
WW	427b	that D	silver payen.	N V
WW	222b	that D D	werlde helpis,	N V
WW	478b	that H	dry be at morow,	A be P N
WW	472b	that H	wonn[e scholde]	V X
WW	31b	that H	bytyde ones	V Z
WW	272b	that H	byfore haden.	Z V
WW	197b	that H	hedir broghte	Z V
WW	455b	that H P	soule hate."	N V
WW	345b	that H Z	most dele,	X V
WW	140b	that P	were duellen;	N V
WW	143b	that P D	bent hoves,	N V
WW	105b	that P D	that one the / bent hoves,	N V
WW	152b	that X D	lawes yeme,	N V
WW	23b	that Z	renke herde.	N V
WW	414b	that Z	silke wroghte.	N V
WW	354b	that Z	dere coste,	Z V
WW	184b	that Z	lowe hengeth	Z V
WW	201b	to	wirche als he demeth."	V C H V
WW	278b	to	blerren thyn eghne,	V D N
WW	479b	to	comforth his vaynes,	V D N
WW	429b	to	forthir hir herte.	V D N
WW	491b	to	knawen thi fode,	V D N
WW	406b	to	lightten thaire hertis.	V D N
WW	325b	to	speken thies wordes.	V D N
WW	268b	to	wasschen thyn handes	V H P
WW	172b	to	machen thaym agayne,	V H P
WW	374b	to	honge thiselven.	V H self
WW	8b	to	see ne to here,	V not to V
WW	371b	to	growe on the erthe,	V P D N
WW	413b	to	handil in the derne,	V P D N
WW	383b	to	mend with thair chere.	V P D N
WW	352b	to	take what him lykes;	V Q H V
WW	399b	to	grow at the last,	V Z
WW	216b	to	wete any forthire,	V Z
WW	240b	to	cayre with to his frendes.	V Z P D N
WW	489b	to	trotte aftir more.	V Z Z

WW	337b	V	sexe mens doke.	A N N
WW	263b	V	Wynnere the riche;	N D N(A)
WW	256b	V	parte of thi silvere;	N P D N
WW	218b	V	Kythe what ye hatten,	V Q H V
WW	441b	X	delyn thi gudis;	V D N
WW	443b	X	sever tham aboute,	V H Z
WW	462b	X	kepe the ful faire,	V H Z Z
WW	13b	X	hurcle in hire fourme,	V P D N
WW	331b	X	wepyn for sorowe.	V P N
WW	447b	X C	hold hir his while,	V H D N
WW	179b	X D	felde wynn.	N V
WW	192b	X D	sowme rekken.	N V
WW	287b	X H	ferdere be to wirche.	A be to V
WW	453b	X H V D	day hyes.	N A
WW	450b	X to	warmen his helys,	V D N
WW	190b	Z	many and so thikke	A C Z A
WW	99b	Z	selly me thynke	A H V
WW	351b	Z	wellande hote,	G A
WW	282b	Z	wordes ynewe.	N A
WW	281b	Z	florence to schewe,	N to V
WW	437b	Z	wery ye the while	V H D N
WW	410b	Z	nysely attyred,	Z E
WW	324b	Z	wrothely he lukes,	Z H V
WW	128b	Z	ryall to thynke	Z to V
WW	202b	Z D	renke als me thoghte,	N C H V
WW	71b	Z P	wrethyn lokkes,	E N

Stage Three (by the first word of the *b*-verse)

WW	397b	C	all that ther growes;	H that Z V
WW	338b	/	anothir comes aftir,	H V Z
WW	267b	P	augarte pryde.	A N
WW	316b	C	Austyn the wyse,	N D N(A)
WW	251b	D	bakone there hynges,	N Z V
WW	292b	P D	bale dedis.	A N
WW	164b	D	balle in the myddes,	N P D N
WW	168b	D	banere es stuffede.	N be E
WW	131b	P	banere for to ryde	N for to V
WW	187b	D	banere I knewe.	N H V
WW	41b	D	bankes bytwene;	N P
WW	39b	P	barkes thay roungen,	N H V
WW	470b	P D	be[ryinge-daye],	G N
WW	78b	/	before and behynde,	Z C Z
WW	149b	P D	bende of grene,	N P N
WW	143b	that P D	bent hoves,	N V
WW	328b	D	beryn that thou loveste,	N that H V
WW	307b	/	beryn, be my trouthe.	N be D N
WW	484b	D	best thou may fynde	A H X V
WW	125b	P H C H	beste lyketh,	Z V
WW	110b	be P D	beste wyse.	A N
WW	495b	D	better the Wynner lykes.	Z D N V
WW	61b	/	betyn of golde,	E P N
WW	239b	/	biddes he no nother	V H Z
WW	480b	/	bikken thi fynger,	V D N
WW	349b	C D	billed snyppes,	E N
WW	342b	P	blasande disches,	G N
WW	156b	be P	blee whitte,	N A
WW	278b	to	blerren thyn eghne,	V D N
WW	93b	/	blewe als me thoghte	A C H V
WW	182b	/	bocled togedir,	E Z
WW	114b	D	body to yeme,	N to V
WW	158b	P	bokels twayne.	N A
WW	214b	P	bolles of silvere.	N P N
WW	175b	P D	bore-hedis;	N N
WW	14b	P	boste and with pryde,	N C P N
WW	132b	P D	bot the / kynge one,	N A
WW	126b	P	bothe his two eghne,	A D D N

WW	379b	H	botours and swannes,		N C N
WW	357b	D	bowellȝ within.		N P
WW	194b	/	bowmen many,		N A
WW	52b	/	bown for to mete,		A for to V
WW	208b	C	bown one thaire wayes.		A P D N
WW	431b	P	brandes to smytte,		N to V
WW	113b	/	brauden full thikke,		E Z Z
WW	241b	C	braundesche hym ofte,		V H Z
WW	163b	be	brayde appon lofte,		E Z
WW	116b	D	breste had another,		N V H
WW	426b	P D	bright wedis,		A N
WW	348b	P D	broche riche,		N A
WW	457b	C P D	brode worde,		A N
WW	418b	C D	broken heltre		E N
WW	333b	P	brothes there besyde,		N Z Z
WW	144b	/	brouden withinn,		E Z
WW	91b	/	brouderde with fewlys,		E P N
WW	96b	/	broudirde with fewles,		E P N
WW	1b	C	Bruyttus it aughte,		N H X
WW	33b	/	bryghte was the sone		A be D N
WW	405b	/	bukkes ynewe		N A
WW	335b	P D	burde sett,		N E
WW	476b	P D	burgh passe;		N V
WW	101b	/	by hym that stondeth,		P H that V
WW	272b	that H	byfore haden.		Z V
WW	228b	that	byfore yowe standes		P H V
WW	76b	/	byhynde in the nekke		Z P D N
WW	31b	that H	bytyde ones		V Z
WW	59b	D	caban was rerede,		N be E
WW	176b	/	Carmes thaym semyde,		N H V
WW	448b	D	case as it falles,		N C H V
WW	319b	that D	case heris,		N V
WW	423b	/	castes up his eghne,		V Z D N
WW	121b	C	caughte it swythe,		V H Z
WW	468b	H X	cayre uttire,		V Z
WW	240b	to	cayre with to his frendes.		V Z P D N
WW	425b	H	caytef, to by,		N to V
WW	474b	D	chambre thou rere,		N H V
WW	336b	/	charbiande fewlis,		A N
WW	81b	P Z	clene perle,		A N
WW	293b	C H D	clerke tolde."		N V
WW	315b	P	clerkes of the beste,		N P D A
WW	485b	C H D	clothe sprede.		N V
WW	205b	H	clothes us bothe,		V H A
WW	479b	to	comforth his vaynes,		V D N
WW	233b	Q N	corne sellen?		N V
WW	274b	C	cornes to wynn		N to V
WW	203b	P	coursers attyred,		N E
WW	255b	P	Cristis lufe of heven!		N N P N
WW	86b	/	crowned with golde,		E P N
WW	353b	C	custadis swete,		N A
WW	97b	/	daderande tham semede		G H V
WW	44b	C	dadillyng of fewllys.		N(G) P N
WW	453b	X H V D	day hyes.		N A
WW	330b	P	dayntethes so many		N Z A
WW	276b	P D	dede monethe.		A N
WW	441b	X	delyn thi gudis;		V D N
WW	354b	that Z	dere coste,		Z V
WW	305b	/	dose the no mare		V H Z
WW	220b	/	dothe me to here."		V H to V
WW	16b	H	draweth neghe aftir.		V Z Z
WW	244b	P	Drightyns love in heven		N N P N
WW	312b	Q Z	droghte come,		N V
WW	478b	that H	dry be at morow,		A be P N
WW	235b	/	drye bene his poles;		A be D N
WW	499b	C	dub the to knyghte,		V H P N
WW	488b	/	duell ther no lenger,		V Z Z
WW	458b	Q H	duelle schall,		V X
WW	303b	C H	durste never.		V Z
WW	109b	C	dwellys awhile		V Z
WW	153b	P	dynttis full many.		N Z A

WW	103b	P	dynttis to dele!	N to V
WW	167b	P	dynttis to dele;	N to V
WW	494b	D	egretes dere;	N A
WW	313b	be	enditye with twelve,	E P N
WW	412b	P	ermyn aboute,	N Z
WW	141b	/	Estirlynges full many,	N Z A
WW	386b	C H	ete other,	V H
WW	310b	C	evenes of sayntes,	N P N
WW	130b	C	ever schall worthe:	Z X V
WW	174b	D	faireste of tham alle,	A P H Z
WW	98b	C	fawked thay were.	E H be
WW	155b	that	fayled hym never.	V H Z
WW	102b	that	faylede hym never:	V H Z
WW	21b	P	fayntnesse of hert,	N P N
WW	329b	that D	fayth owthe;	N V
WW	295b	H	feden the pore;	V D N(A)
WW	160b	H	feghtyn bot seldom.	V C Z
WW	123b	P D	felde hoves.	N V
WW	179b	X D	felde wynn.	N V
WW	138b	/	ferdede besyde,	E Z
WW	287b	X H	ferdere be to wirche.	A be to V
WW	416b	/	ferre out of hir kythe,	Z P P D N
WW	311b	P D	ferrere syde,	A N
WW	334b	C	fesanttes full riche,	N Z A
WW	369b	P	fewe yeris.	A N
WW	245b	C H	fey worthe."	A V
WW	159b	H X	fey worthe;	A V
WW	300b	C H	fey worthes,	A V
WW	291b	C Z D	fire aftir,	N Z
WW	367b	C Z D	fit endes.	N V
WW	217b	C Z D	fitt endes.	N V
WW	92b	/	flakerande with wynges,	G P N
WW	281b	Z	florence to schewe,	N to V
WW	154b	C	flyttynge may helpe,	N(G) X V
WW	148b	P D	folke that he ledis.	N that H V
WW	207b	C H X	folowe aftire."	V Z
WW	384b	C	fongen be never,	E be Z
WW	170b	be	forced besyde,	E Z
WW	429b	to	forthir hir herte.	V D N
WW	464b	H C	forthir thyn hert,	V D N
WW	273b	that	fosterde yow alle	V H Z
WW	471b	D	fote for [to holde].	N for to V
WW	35b	Q D	fote steppede.	N V
WW	402b	C D	frende come,	N V
WW	66b	P	fresche lettres,	A N
WW	206b	D	fyve and twenty wyntere.	A C A N
WW	451b	P	fyvetene myle.	A N
WW	62b	P	garters of inde,	N P N
WW	94b	/	gerede full riche.	E Z A
WW	63b	/	gerede full riche.	E Z Z
WW	269b	be H H	getyn have.	E have
WW	440b	/	getys thou never.	V H Z
WW	95b	/	girde in the myddis:	E P D N
WW	391b	H	gladdes another."	V H
WW	227b	C	glades myn hert.	V D N
WW	275b	P	gleterand frostes,	G N
WW	173b	P	God hymselven.	N H self
WW	500b	P	golde and of silver,	N C P N
WW	118b	C H D	gome knewe,	N V
WW	231b	C H V	goo sone;	V Z
WW	359b	/	goullyng may here:	G X V
WW	135b	P D	grace one.	N A
WW	399b	to	grow at the last,	V Z
WW	371b	to	growe on the erthe,	V P D N
WW	79b	P D	grym bestes,	A N
WW	271b	that A	gude coste	N V
WW	381b	C H D	gude sewes;	A N
WW	58b	/	had untill othere.	V P H
WW	387b	P	halfe yeris ende,	A N N
WW	413b	to	handil in the derne,	V P D N
WW	298b	C	happede in cofers,	E P N

WW	404b	D	hare for to fynde,	N for to V
WW	68b	that D	harme thynkes."	N V
WW	454b	C	harmes me more	V H Z
WW	70b	D	hathell up stondes,	N Z V
WW	72b	D	hatte appon lofte,	N Z
WW	73b	D	hattfull beste,	A N
WW	50b	P	hawberkes full brighte,	N Z A
WW	36b	D	hawthorne besyde;	N P
WW	197b	that H	hedir broghte	Z V
WW	51b	C	helmys with crestys;	N P N
WW	482b	D	hen other twayne,	N C N
WW	419b	D	hend for to yeme,	N(A)for to V
WW	492b	D	henne wele serve,	N Z V
WW	364b	P D	herdmans tong:	N N
WW	444b	for that H	here saved.	Z V
WW	260b	C that H	here spareste;	Z V
WW	323b	D A P	hert feble."	N A
WW	279b	C Q D	hert lykes,	N V
WW	219b	D	hertis bytwene.	N P
WW	38b	P	heselis tyll othire,	N P H
WW	211b	C	hetys tham to ryse,	V H to V
WW	361b	P D	heven kyng.	N N
WW	196b	be	hewen to dethe.	E P N
WW	447b	X C	hold hir his while,	V H D N
WW	374b	to	honge thiselven.	V H self
WW	290b	C	hope aftir werse -	V Z A
WW	147b	H	hope he be there,	V H be Z
WW	11b	/	hope I no nother -	V H Z
WW	9b	C H	hore eldes.	A V
WW	467b	P	horse or one fote;	N C P N
WW	212b	P D	house bothen."	N A
WW	150b	P	howes one lofte,	N Z
WW	314b	P	howes one lofte,	N Z
WW	237b	C	howndes full kene.	N Z A
WW	347b	that D	howse owethe -	N V
WW	13b	X	hurcle in hire fourme,	V P D N
WW	438b	C D	hyne raysed.	N E
WW	145b	/	hynged a corde,	E D N
WW	26b	C	japes telle,	N V
WW	40b	/	jarmede the foles.	V D N
WW	115b	/	joynede by the sydes,	E P D N
WW	151b	C	kembid in the nekke:	E P D N
WW	69b	/	kepe hym oure Lorde!	V H D N
WW	124b	Q	kepe hym oure Lorde!	V H D N
WW	462b	X	kepe the ful faire,	V H Z Z
WW	90b	P	kirtill and mantill -	N C N
WW	491b	to	knawen thi fode,	V D N
WW	210b	C P	knees fallyn.	N V
WW	83b	D	knyghte that I see,	N that H V
WW	327b	D	knyghte that the folowes,	N that H V
WW	502b	P	knyghtes that me foloen,	N that H V
WW	452b	P D	Kyng, by thi trouthe,	N P D N
WW	134b	not D	kynge ryche,	N A
WW	503b	Q D	kynges ligges. . . .	N V
WW	199b	that D	kythe owethe;	N V
WW	218b	V	Kythe what ye hatten,	V Q H V
WW	378b	/	laddes as tham falles;	N C H V
WW	375b	P	laddes on fote?	N P N
WW	415b	D	Lady of Heven,	N P N
WW	177b	D	Lady to serve.	N to V
WW	409b	C	ladyes riche,	N A
WW	243b	D	lande will he stroye,	N X H V
WW	350b	/	lapped in sogoure,	E P N
WW	306b	/	late appone nyghte	A P N
WW	111b	P D	lawe bones,	A N
WW	139b	C P	Lawe Spayne;	N N
WW	152b	that X D	lawes yeme,	N V
WW	15b	C	lede hem at will,	V H P N
WW	456b	P D	ledis twayne,	N A
WW	171b	/	ledith thurgh witt,	V P N
WW	223b	P	ledyng of witt.	N(G) P N

WW	29b	C	ledys bene knawen,	N be E
WW	469b	C H D	lefe [take];	N V
WW	428b	D	leman to fynde,	N to V
WW	49b	D	lengthe of a myle.	N P D N
WW	27b	C	lett of a while	V Z Z
WW	466b	C H	lettres sende,	N V
WW	259b	/	leve thou no nother,	V H Z
WW	209b	C	leved thaire stedis,	V D N
WW	286b	C	levede that other,	V D H
WW	108b	C D	life dures."	N V
WW	406b	to	lightten thaire hertis.	V D N
WW	74b	/	lokande full kene,	G Z A
WW	234b	D	lomes aren solde,	N be E
WW	284b	C D	londe selle.	N V
WW	388b	D	lorde for to serve.	N for to V
WW	54b	D	lordes bytwene.	N P
WW	19b	that	loved in thaire hertis	V P D N
WW	459b	Q H be	loved moste.	V Z
WW	88b	Q	loveth hym in hert,	V H P N
WW	184b	that Z	lowe hengeth	Z V
WW	45b	C	lowked myn eghne,	V D N
WW	225b	H	lufe hym the bettir.	V H D Z
WW	501b	that	lufen me in hert.	V H P N
WW	133b	C D	lyfe aftir.	N Z
WW	430b	P D	lyfe one,	N A
WW	449b	/	lympes to feche	V to V
WW	172b	to	machen thaym agayne,	V H P
WW	28b	that	made it hymselven.	V H H self
WW	264b	H	madiste it thiselven.	V H H self
WW	446b	D	make for to wyn	N for to V
WW	190b	Z	many and so thikke	A C Z A
WW	20b	that	matirs couthe fynde,	N X V
WW	355b	D	mawes to fill,	N to V
WW	383b	to	mend with thair chere.	V P D N
WW	344b	be	mervelle to rekken -	N to V
WW	365b	C D	mery nyghte."	A N
WW	166b	P	Missomer Even.	N N
WW	345b	that H Z	most dele,	X V
WW	304b	not Z	myrthe lovediste.	N V
WW	43b	C H	nappe myghte,	V X
WW	435b	H	nappen so harde,	V Z Z
WW	18b	C be	neghe here.	V Z
WW	106b	/	nerre togedirs;	Z Z
WW	4b	P D	nyne dele.	A N
WW	410b	Z	nysely attyred,	Z E
WW	186b	C	oughte that I wene,	X that H V
WW	296b	that	Paradyse wroghte.	N V
WW	376b	that D	parischen yemes?	N V
WW	256b	V	parte of thi silvere;	N P D N
WW	498b	P	Parys the riche	N D N(A)
WW	372b	C H	passe nott to hye,	V not Z Z
WW	297b	H	payes alle the better	V Z Z
WW	433b	H	payes alle the better	V Z Z
WW	377b	P	pedders in towne?	N P N
WW	393b	that	peloure will by,	N X V
WW	183b	D	pendant awaye,	N Z
WW	370b	that D	peple sowes,	N V
WW	490b	D	peple the knowes,	N H V
WW	301b	C	pergett with thaire walles.	V P D N
WW	318b	D	pese to distourbe!	N to V
WW	129b	D	pese to disturbe.	N to V
WW	486b	C	pik hym so clene	V H Z A
WW	332b	P	plontes appon lofte,	N Z
WW	112b	/	polischede full clene,	E Z Z
WW	461b	P D	Pope of Rome;	N P N
WW	382b	P	povert that standes,	N that V
WW	422b	that	poverté ofte schewes."	N Z V
WW	65b	C	poyntes bytwene,	N P
WW	169b	D	prechours to helpe,	N to V
WW	55b	C D	prynce come,	N V
WW	493b	D H	pulled byrddes,	E N

WW	232b	C H D	purse opynes.	N V
WW	487b	C	put owte his eghe,	V Z D N
WW	340b	/	quarterd swannes,	E N
WW	77b	P	quarters foure:	N A
WW	322b	D	rathere will drede:	Z X V
WW	254b	D	ratons fede.	N V
WW	42b	C	raughten so heghe	V Z Z
WW	363b	D	rawnsom of silver.	N P N
WW	436b	/	raysen your hurdes;	V D N
WW	380b	H D	rede whete,	A N
WW	202b	Z D	renke als me thoghte,	N C H V
WW	24b	P	renke herde.	N N
WW	23b	that Z	renke herde.	N V
WW	57b	C to	rewlyn the wrothe	V D N(A)
WW	60b	D	rofe and the sydes,	N C D N
WW	128b	Z	ryall to thynke	Z to V
WW	339b	C D	ryalle spyces,	A N
WW	270b	be	rychely attyrede;	Z E
WW	100b	/	ryde umbestonde."	V Z
WW	258b	P D	ryfe bene the pore.	N be H N(A)
WW	289b	/	ryme up thi yerdes,	V Z D N
WW	343b	P	rynges and stones.	N C N
WW	157b	P	sable withinn,	N Z
WW	193b	be	sadde men of armes,	A N P N
WW	10b	P	Salomon the wyse -	N D N(A)
WW	360b	C H	samen ryden,	Z V
WW	89b	/	sawe with his eghne.	V P D N
WW	146b	H	say als me thynkes,	V C H V
WW	321b	that	sayde es full yore -	E be Z Z
WW	432b	Q	schalkes ere gadird;	N be E
WW	400b	C D	schame es your ownn.	N be D A
WW	317b	C	Scharshull itwiste,	N Z
WW	362b	C	schathed theraftir,	E Z
WW	185b	P D	schavynge iren:	G N
WW	463b	/	schetys to lygge,	N to V
WW	403b	C	schewe hym the estres,	V H D N
WW	421b	for to	schewe other	V C
WW	53b	P	schiltrons thay felle,	N H V
WW	481b	/	scholdirs ynewe,	N A
WW	8b	to	see ne to here,	V not to V
WW	3b	P	seere kynges tymes,	A N N
WW	137b	/	segge, with myn eghne;	N P D N
WW	204b	/	sele the betyde!	N H V
WW	401b	C	sell it ye thynken.	V H H V
WW	99b	Z	selly me thynke	A H V
WW	178b	H	semys no nothire	V Z
WW	483b	C Z	send after,	V Z
WW	87b	P	septure in honde,	N P N
WW	394b	P	sercles full riche.	N Z A
WW	188b	/	sett appon lofte,	E Z
WW	299b	P	seven wyntter ones,	A N Z
WW	443b	X	sever tham aboute,	V H Z
WW	337b	V	sexe mens doke.	A N N
WW	414b	that Z	silke wroghte.	N V
WW	427b	that D	silver payen.	N V
WW	302b	H	slees othere;	V H
WW	411b	/	sleght to the grounde,	E P D N
WW	180b	C	so are thay alle,	Z be H Z
WW	165b	be P	someris tyde,	N N
WW	407b	D	sorowe es the more,	N be D A
WW	221b	D H D	sothe for to telle,	N for to V
WW	17b	C D	sothe telle,	N V
WW	181b	Q D	sothe tellys,	N V
WW	455b	that H P	soule hate."	N V
WW	261b	D	soule into helle,	N P N
WW	192b	X D	sowme rekken.	N V
WW	215b	H	sowrede bothe myn eghne.	V D D N
WW	398b	H	spare to your children,	V P D N
WW	238b	/	sparrede in ane hyrne,	E P D N
WW	325b	to	speken thies wordes.	V D N
WW	224b	C	spende not to grete,	V not Z Z

WW	252b	P	stelen bowndes -	N N	
WW	127b	not	stirre none nerre	V Z	
WW	142b	/	strokes to dele.	N to V	
WW	229b	C	stroye me for ever.	V H Z	
WW	265b	H	stroyeste up my gudes	V Z D N	
WW	195b	/	stynt thay ne thynken	V H not V	
WW	107b	/	stynte thay ne thynken."	V H not V	
WW	46b	/	sweped belyve.	E Z	
WW	320b	/	swyngen togedirs;	V Z	
WW	352b	to	take what him lykes;	V Q H V	
WW	122b	C	takes his waye	V D N	
WW	477b	C H	tayte worthe;	A V	
WW	247b	that	tene schall the better.	V X H Z	
WW	341b	that	tenys myn hert	V D N	
WW	105b	that P D	that one the / bent hoves,	N V	
WW	80b	C	thre on lowe undir;	N Z Z	
WW	37b	H	threpen togedire,	V Z	
WW	434b	/	tofore with myn eghne.	Z P D N	
WW	445b	that	tolde was full yore:	E be Z Z	
WW	277b	P D	tonne-hede,	N N	
WW	358b	H	tounen so heghe	V Z Z	
WW	2b	P	tresone withinn,	N Z	
WW	489b	to	trotte aftir more.	V Z Z	
WW	82b	/	tuttynge out fayre.	G Z Z	
WW	356b	P	twa men,	A N	
WW	288b	C	tynen thyn feldes;	V D N	
WW	248b	C	wakede alle the nyghte,	E Z D N	
WW	34b	P D	wale medewe:	A N	
WW	460b	P D	wale stremys,	A N	
WW	396b	P D	wale tyme,	A N	
WW	12b	C	walles bene doun,	N be Z	
WW	32b	/	wandrynge myn one,	G Z	
WW	373b	P	wanhope in erthe,	N P N	
WW	309b	C	Wanhope thi brothir,	N D N	
WW	162b	that	wanne thaym all hedire.	V H Z Z	
WW	450b	X to	warmen his helys,	V D N	
WW	85b	H be	warre sone	A Z	
WW	268b	to	wasschen thyn handes	V D N	
WW	253b	C D	waste come?	N V	
WW	439b	H	wastes thi tyme;	V D N	
WW	230b	H	wastes thurgh pryde;	V P N	
WW	390b	D	wastour moste he fynde,	N X H V	
WW	242b	that	Wastoure men calles,	N N V	
WW	475b	C	wayte the aboute,	V H P	
WW	257b	C	waytten the sothe,	V D N	
WW	5b	that	we with delyn,	H Z V	
WW	420b	D	wedes wer pore	N be A	
WW	236b	H	weldys at home,	V P N	
WW	496b	C H X	wele chefe,	N V	
WW	351b	Z	wellande hote,	G A	
WW	161b	H	wentten fro home;	V P N	
WW	331b	X	wepyn for sorowe.	V P N	
WW	140b	that P	were duellen;	N V	
WW	222b	that D D	werlde helpis,	N V	
WW	7b	C D	werlde lasteth	N V	
WW	191b	P D D	werlde riche	N A	
WW	64b	/	werped of he,	E P H	
WW	285b	/	wery the oure Lorde!	V H D N	
WW	437b	Z	wery ye the while	V H D N	
WW	216b	to	wete any forthire,	V Z	
WW	366b	for to	wete forthe,	V Z	
WW	346b	P	wilde fowle	A N	
WW	395b	D	willes to folowe,	N to V	
WW	104b	D	willes to kythe,	N to V	
WW	201b	to	wirche als he demeth."	V C H V	
WW	30b	Q	wirche kane beste.	V X Z	
WW	308b	C H	wisse couthe,	V X	
WW	47b	H not	wiste in whate ende,	V P Q N	
WW	120b	/	wiste of his age.	V Z D N	
WW	417b	/	withowtten more pride,	P A N	
WW	389b	/	witterly thiselven,	Z H self	

WW	250b	A P	wolle sakkes -	N N
WW	392b	H	wondire in hert	V P N
WW	424b	H	wondirs in hert	V P N
WW	84b	/	wondres ynewe.	N A
WW	385b	/	wone al thaire lyve,	V Z D N
WW	472b	that H	wonn[e scholde]	V X
WW	249b	that	wonnes the abowte,	V H Z
WW	280b	that	wonnes there aboute.	V Z Z
WW	246b	D	wordes are hye:	N be A
WW	294b	D	wordes are vayne.	N be A
WW	25b	D	wordes togedire,	N Z
WW	282b	Z	wordes ynewe.	N A
WW	262b	/	worlde withowtten ende."	N P N
WW	368b	H	wote well myselven	V Z H self
WW	198b	be D	wrake falle,	N V
WW	465b	C H to	wrethe ones.	V Z
WW	71b	Z P	wrethyn lokkes,	E N
WW	117b	/	wroghte in the kynde,	E P D N
WW	22b	that	wroghte were never,	E be Z
WW	200b	Q D	wronge ristyth,	N V
WW	324b	Z	wrothely he lukes,	Z H V
WW	6b	C H	wryeth othere.	V H
WW	56b	P D	wy ells	N A
WW	326b	that	wydewhare es knawenn,	Z be E
WW	136b	P D	wyes one,	N A
WW	497b	D	wyes to lede;	N to V
WW	408b	D	wyfes to paye.	N to V
WW	442b	/	wyn thay it never;	V H H Z
WW	213b	C D	wyne askes;	N V
WW	283b	D	wyne moste be payede fore;	N X be E Z
WW	189b	C H P	wyne tounnes,	N N
WW	473b	C	wyng [ther until].	V Z Z
WW	263b	V	Wynnere the riche;	N D N(A)
WW	266b	P	wyntres nyghttis,	N N
WW	226b	C	wysses me faire;	V H A
WW	75b	P Z	yape wyse.	A N
WW	119b	C	yapeste of witt	A P N
WW	48b	that be	ylike grene,	Z A
WW	67b	P	Ynglysse tonge,	A N

Stage Four (by collocation of the *b*-verse)

WW	33b	/	bryghte was the sone	A be D N
WW	235b	/	drye bene his poles;	A be D N
WW	478b	that H	dry be at morow,	A be P N
WW	287b	X H	ferdere be to wirche.	A be to V
WW	206b	D	fyve and twenty wyntere.	A C A N
WW	93b	/	blewe als me thoghte	A C H V
WW	190b	Z	many and so thikke	A C Z A
WW	126b	P	bothe his two eghne,	A D D N
WW	52b	/	bown for to mete,	A for to V
WW	99b	Z	selly me thynke	A H V
WW	484b	D	best thou may fynde,	A H X V
WW	336b	/	charbiande fewlis,	A N
WW	110b	be P D	beste wyse.	A N
WW	365b	C D	mery nyghte."	A N
WW	339b	C D	ryalle spyces,	A N
WW	381b	C H D	gude sewes;	A N
WW	457b	C P D	brode worde,	A N
WW	73b	D	hattfull beste,	A N
WW	380b	H D	rede whete,	A N
WW	356b	P	twa men,	A N
WW	267b	P	augarte pryde.	A N
WW	369b	P	fewe yeris.	A N
WW	66b	P	fresche lettres,	A N
WW	451b	P	fyvetene myle.	A N
WW	346b	P	wilde fowle	A N

WW	67b	P	Ynglysse tonge,	A N
WW	292b	P D	bale dedis.	A N
WW	426b	P D	bright wedis,	A N
WW	276b	P D	dede monethe.	A N
WW	311b	P D	ferrere syde,	A N
WW	79b	P D	grym bestes,	A N
WW	111b	P D	lawe bones,	A N
WW	4b	P D	nyne dele.	A N
WW	34b	P D	wale medewe:	A N
WW	460b	P D	wale stremys,	A N
WW	396b	P D	wale tyme,	A N
WW	81b	P Z	clene perle,	A N
WW	75b	P Z	yape wyse.	A N
WW	387b	P	halfe yeris ende,	A N N
WW	3b	P	seere kynges tymes,	A N N
WW	337b	V	sexe mens doke.	A N N
WW	193b	be	sadde men of armes,	A N P N
WW	299b	P	seven wyntter ones,	A N Z
WW	208b	C	bown one thaire wayes.	A P D N
WW	174b	D	faireste of tham alle,	A P H Z
WW	306b	/	late appone nyghte	A P N
WW	119b	C	yapeste of witt	A P N
WW	245b	C H	fey worthe."	A V
WW	300b	C H	fey worthes,	A V
WW	9b	C H	hore eldes.	A V
WW	477b	C H	tayte worthe;	A V
WW	159b	H X	fey worthe;	A V
WW	85b	H be	warre sone	A Z
WW	384b	C	fongen be never,	E be Z
WW	22b	that	wroghte were never,	E be Z
WW	321b	that	sayde es full yore -	E be Z Z
WW	445b	that	tolde was full yore:	E be Z Z
WW	145b	/	hynged a corde,	E D N
WW	98b	C	fawked thay were.	E H be
WW	269b	be H H	getyn have.	E have
WW	340b	/	quarterd swannes,	E N
WW	349b	C D	billed snyppes,	E N
WW	418b	C D	broken heltre	E N
WW	493b	D H	pulled byrddes,	E N
WW	71b	Z P	wrethyn lokkes,	E N
WW	95b	/	girde in the myddis:	E P D N
WW	115b	/	joynede by the sydes,	E P D N
WW	411b	/	sleght to the grounde,	E P D N
WW	238b	/	sparrede in ane hyrne,	E P D N
WW	117b	/	wroghte in the kynde,	E P D N
WW	151b	C	kembid in the nekke:	E P D N
WW	64b	/	werped of he,	E P H
WW	61b	/	betyn of golde,	E P N
WW	91b	/	brouderde with fewlys,	E P N
WW	96b	/	broudirde with fewles,	E P N
WW	86b	/	crowned with golde,	E P N
WW	313b	be	endityde with twelve,	E P N
WW	196b	be	hewen to dethe.	E P N
WW	298b	C	happede in cofers,	E P N
WW	350b	/	lapped in sogoure,	E P N
WW	182b	/	bocled togedir,	E Z
WW	144b	/	brouden withinn,	E Z
WW	138b	/	ferdede besyde,	E Z
WW	188b	/	sett appon lofte,	E Z
WW	46b	/	sweped belyve.	E Z
WW	163b	be	brayde appon lofte,	E Z
WW	170b	be	forced besyde,	E Z
WW	362b	C	schathed theraftir,	E Z
WW	94b	/	gerede full riche.	E Z A
WW	248b	C	wakede alle the nyghte,	E Z D N
WW	113b	/	brauden full thikke,	E Z Z
WW	63b	/	gerede full riche.	E Z Z
WW	112b	/	polischede full clene,	E Z Z
WW	351b	Z	wellande hote,	G A
WW	97b	/	daderande tham semede	G H V
WW	342b	P	blasande disches,	G N

WW	275b	P	gleterand frostes,	G N
WW	470b	P D	be[ryinge daye],	G N
WW	185b	P D	schavynge iren:	G N
WW	92b	/	flakerande with wynges,	G P N
WW	359b	/	goullyng may here:	G X V
WW	32b	/	wandrynge myn one,	G Z
WW	74b	/	lokande full kene,	G Z A
WW	82b	/	tuttynge out fayre.	G Z Z
WW	397b	C	all that ther growes;	H that Z V
WW	338b	/	anothir comes aftir,	H V Z
WW	5b	that	we with delyn,	H Z V
WW	194b	/	bowmen many,	N A
WW	405b	/	bukkes ynewe	N A
WW	481b	/	scholdirs ynewe,	N A
WW	84b	/	wondres ynewe.	N A
WW	156b	be P	blee whitte,	N A
WW	353b	C	custadis swete,	N A
WW	409b	C	ladyes riche,	N A
WW	494b	D	egretes dere;	N A
WW	323b	D A P	hert feble."	N A
WW	134b	not D	kynge ryche,	N A
WW	158b	P	bokels twayne.	N A
WW	77b	P	quarters foure:	N A
WW	132b	P D	bot the / kynge one,	N A
WW	348b	P D	broche riche,	N A
WW	135b	P D	grace one.	N A
WW	212b	P D	house bothen."	N A
WW	456b	P D	ledis twayne,	N A
WW	430b	P D	lyfe one,	N A
WW	56b	P D	wy ells	N A
WW	136b	P D	wyes one,	N A
WW	191b	P D D	werlde riche	N A
WW	453b	X H V D	day hyes.	N A
WW	282b	Z	wordes ynewe.	N A
WW	420b	D	wedes wer pore	N be A
WW	294b	D	wordes are vayne.	N be A
WW	246b	D	wordes are hye:	N be A
WW	400b	C D	schame es your own.	N be D A
WW	407b	D	sorowe es the more,	N be D A
WW	307b	/	beryn, be my trouthe.	N be D N
WW	29b	C	ledys bene knawen,	N be E
WW	168b	D	banere es stuffede.	N be E
WW	59b	D	caban was rerede,	N be E
WW	234b	D	lomes aren solde,	N be E
WW	432b	Q D	schalkes ere gadird;	N be E
WW	258b	P D	ryfe bene the pore.	N be H N(A)
WW	12b	C	walles bene doun,	N be Z
WW	60b	D	rofe and the sydes,	N C D N
WW	378b	/	laddes as tham falles;	N C H V
WW	448b	D	case as it falles,	N C H V
WW	202b	Z D	renke als me thoghte,	N C H V
WW	482b	D	hen other twayne,	N C N
WW	379b	H	botours and swannes,	N C N
WW	90b	P	kirtill and mantill -	N C N
WW	343b	P	rynges and stones.	N C N
WW	14b	P	boste and with pryde,	N C P N
WW	500b	P	golde and of silver,	N C P N
WW	467b	P	horse or one fote;	N C P N
WW	309b	C	Wanhope thi brothir,	N D N
WW	316b	C	Austyn the wyse,	N D N(A)
WW	498b	P	Parys the riche	N D N(A)
WW	10b	P	Salomon the wyse -	N D N(A)
WW	263b	V	Wynnere the riche;	N D N(A)
WW	438b	C D	hyne raysed.	N E
WW	203b	P	coursers attyred,	N E
WW	335b	P D	burde sett,	N E
WW	471b	D	fote for [to holde].	N for to V
WW	404b	D	hare for to fynde,	N for to V
WW	388b	D	lorde for to serve.	N for to V
WW	446b	D	make for to wyn	N for to V
WW	221b	D H D	sothe for to telle,	N for to V

WW	131b	P	banere for to ryde	N for to V
WW	173b	P	God hymselven.	N H self
WW	176b	/	Carmes thaym semyde,	N H V
WW	204b	/	sele the betyde!	N H V
WW	187b	D	banere I knewe.	N H V
WW	474b	D	chambre thou rere,	N H V
WW	490b	D	peple the knowes,	N H V
WW	39b	P	barkes thay roungen,	N H V
WW	53b	P	schiltrons thay felle,	N H V
WW	1b	C	Bruyttus it aughte,	N H X
WW	250b	A P	wolle sakkes -	N N
WW	165b	be P	someris tyde,	N N
WW	189b	C H P	wyne tounnes,	N N
WW	139b	C P	Lawe Spayne;	N N
WW	166b	P	Missomer Even.	N N
WW	24b	P	renke herde.	N N
WW	252b	P	stelen bowndes -	N N
WW	266b	P	wynttres nyghttis,	N N
WW	175b	P D	bore-hedis;	N N
WW	364b	P D	herdmans tong:	N N
WW	361b	P D	heven kyng.	N N
WW	277b	P D	tonne-hede,	N N
WW	255b	P	Cristis lufe of heven!	N N P N
WW	244b	P	Drightyns love in heven	N N P N
WW	242b	that	Wastoure men calles,	N N V
WW	65b	C	poyntes bytwene,	N P
WW	41b	D	bankes bytwene;	N P
WW	357b	D	bowells within.	N P
WW	36b	D	hawthorne besyde,	N P
WW	219b	D	hertis bytwene.	N P
WW	54b	D	lordes bytwene.	N P
WW	315b	P	clerkes of the beste,	N P D A
WW	137b	/	segge, with myn eghne;	N P D N
WW	164b	D	balle in the myddes,	N P D N
WW	49b	D	lengthe of a myle.	N P D N
WW	452b	P D	Kyng, by thi trouthe,	N P D N
WW	256b	V	parte of thi silvere;	N P D N
WW	38b	P	heselis tyll othire,	N P H
WW	262b	/	worlde withowtten ende."	N P N
WW	310b	C	evenes of sayntes,	N P N
WW	51b	C	helmys with crestys;	N P N
WW	415b	D	Lady of Heven,	N P N
WW	363b	D	rawnsom of silver.	N P N
WW	261b	D	soule into helle,	N P N
WW	373b	P	wanhope in erthe,	N P N
WW	214b	P	bolles of silvere.	N P N
WW	21b	P	fayntnesse of hert,	N P N
WW	62b	P	garters of inde,	N P N
WW	377b	P	pedders in towne?	N P N
WW	87b	P	septure in honde,	N P N
WW	149b	P D	bende of grene,	N P N
WW	461b	P D	Pope of Rome;	N P N
WW	375b	P	laddes on fote?	N P N
WW	328b	D	beryn that thou loveste,	N that H V
WW	83b	D	knyghte that I see,	N that H V
WW	327b	D	knyghte that the folowes,	N that H V
WW	502b	P	knyghtes that me foloen,	N that H V
WW	148b	P D	folke that he ledis.	N that H V
WW	382b	P	povert that standes,	N that V
WW	463b	/	schetys to lygge,	N to V
WW	142b	/	strokes to dele.	N to V
WW	344b	be	mervelle to rekken -	N to V
WW	274b	C	cornes to wynn	N to V
WW	114b	D	body to yeme,	N to V
WW	177b	D	Lady to serve.	N to V
WW	428b	D	leman to fynde,	N to V
WW	355b	D	mawes to fill,	N to V
WW	318b	D	pese to distourbe!	N to V
WW	129b	D	pese to disturbe.	N to V
WW	169b	D	prechours to helpe,	N to V
WW	395b	D	willes to folowe,	N to V

WW 104b	D		willes to kythe.	N to V
WW 497b	D		wyeo to ledoi	N to V
WW 408b	D		wyfes to paye.	N to V
WW 425b	H		caytef, to by,	N to V
WW 431b	P		brandes to smytte,	N to V
WW 103b	P		dynttis to dele!	N to V
WW 167b	P		dynttis to dele;	N to V
WW 281b	Z		florence to schewe,	N to V
WW 198b	be D		wrake falle.	N V
WW 26b	C		japes telle,	N V
WW 402b	C D		frende come,	N V
WW 108b	C D		life dures."	N V
WW 284b	C D		londe selle.	N V
WW 55b	C D		prynce come,	N V
WW 17b	C D		sothe telle,	N V
WW 253b	C D		waste come?	N V
WW 7b	C D		werlde lasteth	N V
WW 213b	C D		wyne askes;	N V
WW 466b	C H		lettres sende,	N V
WW 293b	C H D		clerke tolde."	N V
WW 485b	C H D		clothe sprede.	N V
WW 118b	C H D		gome knewe,	N V
WW 469b	C H D		lefe [take];	N V
WW 210b	C P		knees fallyn.	N V
WW 279b	C Q D		hert lykes,	N V
WW 367b	C Z D		fit endes.	N V
WW 217b	C Z D		fitt endes.	N V
WW 254b	D		ratons fede.	N V
WW 476b	P D		burgh passe;	N V
WW 123b	P D		felde hoves.	N V
WW 35b	Q D		fote steppede.	N V
WW 503b	Q D		kynges ligges....	N V
WW 181b	Q D		sothe tellys,	N V
WW 200b	Q D		wronge ristyth,	N V
WW 233b	Q N		corne sellen?	N V
WW 312b	Q Z		droghte come,	N V
WW 296b	that		Paradyse wroghte.	N V
WW 271b	that A		gude coste	N V
WW 319b	that D		case heris,	N V
WW 329b	that D		fayth owthe;	N V
WW 68b	that D		harme thynkes."	N V
WW 347b	that D		howse owethe -	N V
WW 199b	that D		kythe owethe;	N V
WW 376b	that D		parischen yemes?	N V
WW 222b	that D D		werlde helpis,	N V
WW 455b	that H P		soule hate."	N V
WW 140b	that P		were duellen;	N V
WW 143b	that P D		bent hoves,	N V
WW 105b	that P D		that one the / bent hoves,	N V
WW 152b	that X D		lawes yeme,	N V
WW 23b	that Z		renke herde.	N V
WW 414b	that Z		silke wroghte.	N V
WW 179b	X D		felde wynn.	N V
WW 232b	C H D		purse opynes,	N V
WW 496b	C H X		wele chefe,	N V
WW 304b	not Z		myrthe lovediste.	N V
WW 370b	that D		peple sowes,	N V
WW 427b	that D		silver payen.	N V
WW 192b	X D		sowme rekken.	N V
WW 116b	D		breste had another,	N V H
WW 283b	D		wyne moste be payede fore;	N X be E Z
WW 243b	D		lande will he stroye.	N X H V
WW 390b	D		wastour moste he fynde,	N X H V
WW 20b	that		matirs couthe fynde,	N X V
WW 393b	that		peloure will by,	N X V
WW 317b	C		Scharshull itwiste,	N Z
WW 133b	C D		lyfe aftir.	N Z
WW 291b	C Z D		fire aftir,	N Z
WW 72b	D		hatte appon lofte,	N Z
WW 25b	D		wordes togedire,	N Z
WW 412b	P		ermyn aboute,	N Z

WW	150b	P	howes one lofte,	N Z
WW	314b	P	howes one lofte,	N Z
WW	332b	P	plontes appon lofte,	N Z
WW	157b	P	sable withinn,	N Z
WW	2b	P	tresone withinn,	N Z
WW	183b	D	pendant awaye,	N Z
WW	141b	/	Estirlynges full many,	N Z A
WW	334b	C	fesanttes full riche,	N Z A
WW	237b	C	howndes full kene.	N Z A
WW	330b	P	dayntethes so many	N Z A
WW	153b	P	dynttis full many.	N Z A
WW	50b	P	hawberkes full brighte,	N Z A
WW	394b	P	sercles full riche.	N Z A
WW	251b	D	bakone there hynges,	N Z V
WW	70b	D	hathell up stondes,	N Z V
WW	492b	D	henne wele serve,	N Z V
WW	422b	that	poverté ofte schewes."	N Z V
WW	80b	C	thre on lowe undir;	N Z Z
WW	333b	P	brothes there besyde,	N Z Z
WW	419b	D	hend for to yeme,	N(A) for to V
WW	44b	C	dadillyng of fewllys.	N(G) P N
WW	223b	P	ledyng of witt.	N(G) P N
WW	154b	C	flyttynge may helpe,	N(G) X V
WW	417b	/	withowtten more pride,	P A N
WW	101b	/	by hym that stondeth,	P H that V
WW	228b	that	byfore yowe standes	P H V
WW	421b	for to	schewe other	V C
WW	146b	H	say als me thynkes,	V C H V
WW	201b	to	wirche als he demeth."	V C H V
WW	160b	H	feghtyn bot seldom.	V C Z
WW	215b	H	sowrede bothe myn eghne,	V D H N
WW	286b	C	levede that other,	V D H
WW	480b	/	bikken thi fynger,	V D N
WW	40b	/	jarmede the foles.	V D N
WW	436b	/	raysen your hurdes;	V D N
WW	227b	C	glades myn hert.	V D N
WW	209b	C	leved thaire stedis,	V D N
WW	45b	C	lowked myn eghne,	V D N
WW	122b	C	takes his waye	V D N
WW	288b	C	tynen thyn feldes;	V D N
WW	257b	C	waytten the sothe,	V D N
WW	439b	H	wastes thi tyme;	V D N
WW	341b	that	tenys myn hert	V D N
WW	278b	to	blerren thyn eghne,	V D N
WW	479b	to	comforth his vaynes,	V D N
WW	429b	to	forthir hir herte.	V D N
WW	491b	to	knawen thi fode,	V D N
WW	406b	to	lightten thaire hertis.	V D N
WW	325b	to	speken thies wordes.	V D N
WW	268b	to	wasschen thyn handes	V D N
WW	441b	X	delyn thi gudis;	V D N
WW	450b	X to	warmen his helys,	V D N
WW	464b	H C	forthir thyn hert,	V D N
WW	57b	C to	rewlyn the wrothe	V D N(A)
WW	295b	H	feden the pore;	V D N(A)
WW	386b	C H	ete other,	V H
WW	6b	C H	wryeth othere.	V H
WW	391b	H	gladdes another."	V H
WW	302b	H	slees othere;	V H
WW	226b	C	wysses me faire;	V H A
WW	205b	H	clothes us bothe,	V H A
WW	147b	H	hope he be there,	V H be Z
WW	69b	/	kepe hym oure Lorde!	V H D N
WW	285b	/	wery the oure Lorde!	V H D N
WW	403b	C	schewe hym the estres,	V H D N
WW	124b	Q	kepe hym oure Lorde!	V H D N
WW	447b	X C	hold hir his while,	V H D N
WW	437b	Z	wery ye the while	V H D N
WW	225b	H	lufe hym the bettir.	V H D Z
WW	264b	H	madiste it thiselven.	V H H self
WW	28b	that	made it hymselven.	V H H self

WW 401b	C		sell it ye thynken.	V H H V
WW 442b	/		wyn thay it never;	V H H ?
WW 195b	/		stynt thay ne thynken	V H not V
WW 107b	/		stynte thay ne thynken."	V H not V
WW 475b	C		wayte the aboute,	V H P
WW 172b	to		machen thaym agayne,	V H P
WW 499b	C		dub the to knyghte,	V H P N
WW 15b	C		lede hem at will,	V H P N
WW 88b	Q		loveth hym in hert,	V H P N
WW 501b	that		lufen me in hert.	V H P N
WW 374b	to		honge thiselven.	V H self
WW 220b	/		dothe me to here."	V H to V
WW 211b	C		hetys tham to ryse,	V H to V
WW 239b	/		biddes he no nother	V H Z
WW 305b	/		dose the no mare	V H Z
WW 440b	/		getys thou never.	V H Z
WW 11b	/		hope I no nother -	V H Z
WW 259b	/		leve thou no nother,	V H Z
WW 241b	C		braundesche hym ofte,	V H Z
WW 121b	C		caughte it swythe,	V H Z
WW 454b	C		harmes me more	V H Z
WW 229b	C		stroye me for ever.	V H Z
WW 155b	that		fayled hym never.	V H Z
WW 102b	that		faylede hym never.	V H Z
WW 273b	that		fosterde yow alle	V H Z
WW 249b	that		wonnes the abowte,	V H Z
WW 443b	X		sever tham aboute,	V H Z
WW 486b	C		pik hym so clene	V H Z A
WW 162b	that		wanne thaym all hedire.	V H Z Z
WW 462b	X		kepe the ful faire,	V H Z Z
WW 8b	to		see ne to here,	V not to V
WW 224b	C		spende not to grete,	V not Z Z
WW 372b	C H		passe nott to hye,	V not Z Z
WW 89b	/		sawe with his eghne.	V P D N
WW 301b	C		pergett with thaire walles.	V P D N
WW 398b	H		spare to your children,	V P D N
WW 19b	that		loved in thaire hertis	V P D N
WW 371b	to		growe on the erthe,	V P D N
WW 413b	to		handil in the derne,	V P D N
WW 383b	to		mend with thair chere.	V P D N
WW 13b	X		hurcle in hire fourme,	V P D N
WW 58b	/		had untill othere.	V P H
WW 171b	/		ledith thurgh witt,	V P N
WW 230b	H		wastes thurgh pryde;	V P N
WW 236b	H		weldys at home,	V P N
WW 161b	H		wentten fro home;	V P N
WW 392b	H		wondirs in hert	V P N
WW 424b	H		wondirs in hert	V P N
WW 331b	X		wepyn for sorowe.	V P N
WW 47b	H not		wiste in whate ende,	V P Q N
WW 352b	to		take what him lykes;	V Q H V
WW 218b	V		Kythe what ye hatten,	V Q H V
WW 449b	/		lympes to feche	V to V
WW 43b	C H		nappe myghte,	V X
WW 308b	C H		wisse couthe,	V X
WW 458b	Q H		duelle schall,	V X
WW 472b	that H		wonn[e scholde]	V X
WW 247b	that		tene schall the better.	V X H Z
WW 30b	Q		wirche kane beste.	V X Z
WW 100b	/		ryde umbestonde."	V Z
WW 320b	/		swyngen togedirs;	V Z
WW 109b	C		dwellys awhile	V Z
WW 18b	C be		neghe here.	V Z
WW 303b	C H		durste never.	V Z
WW 465b	C H to		wrethe ones.	V Z
WW 231b	C H V		goo sone;	V Z
WW 207b	C H X		folowe aftire."	V Z
WW 483b	C Z		send after,	V Z
WW 366b	for to		wete forthe,	V Z
WW 178b	H		semys no nothire	V Z
WW 37b	H		threpen togedire,	V Z

WW	468b	H X	cayre uttire,	V Z
WW	127b	not	stirre none nerre	V Z
WW	459b	Q H be	loved moste.	V Z
WW	31b	that H	bytyde ones	V Z
WW	399b	to	grow at the last,	V Z
WW	216b	to	wete any forthire,	V Z
WW	290b	C	hope aftir werse -	V Z A
WW	423b	/	castes up his eghne,	V Z D N
WW	289b	/	ryme up thi yerdes,	V Z D N
WW	120b	/	wiste of his age.	V Z D N
WW	385b	/	wone al thaire lyve,	V Z D N
WW	265b	H	stroyeste up my gudes	V Z D N
WW	487b	C	put owte his eghe.	V Z D N
WW	368b	H	wote well myselven	V Z H self
WW	240b	to	cayre with to his frendes.	V Z P D N
WW	488b	/	duell ther no lenger,	V Z Z
WW	27b	C	lett of a while	V Z Z
WW	42b	C	raughten so heghe	V Z Z
WW	473b	C	wyng [ther until].	V Z Z
WW	358b	H	tounen so heghe	V Z Z
WW	16b	H	draweth neghe aftir.	V Z Z
WW	435b	H	nappen so harde,	V Z Z
WW	297b	H	payes alle the better	V Z Z
WW	433b	H	payes alle the better	V Z Z
WW	280b	that	wonnes there aboute.	V Z Z
WW	489b	to	trotte aftir more.	V Z Z
WW	186b	C	oughte that I wene,	X that H V
WW	345b	that H Z	most dele,	X V
WW	48b	that be	ylike grene,	Z A
WW	326b	that	wydewhare es knawenn,	Z be E
WW	180b	C	so are thay alle,	Z be H Z
WW	78b	/	before and behynde,	Z C Z
WW	495b	D	better the Wynner lykes.	Z D N V
WW	270b	be	rychely attyrede;	Z E
WW	410b	Z	nysely attyred,	Z E
WW	389b	/	witterly thiselven,	Z H self
WW	324b	Z	wrothely he lukes,	Z H V
WW	76b	/	byhynde in the nekke	Z P D N
WW	434b	/	tofore with myn eghne.	Z P D N
WW	416b	/	ferre out of hir kythe,	Z P P D N
WW	128b	Z	ryall to thynke	Z to V
WW	360b	C H	samen ryden,	Z V
WW	260b	C that H	here spareste;	Z V
WW	444b	for that H	here saved.	Z V
WW	125b	P H C H	beste lyketh,	Z V
WW	272b	that H	byfore haden.	Z V
WW	197b	that H	hedir broghte	Z V
WW	354b	that Z	dere coste,	Z V
WW	184b	that Z	lowe hengeth	Z V
WW	130b	C	ever schall worthe:	Z X V
WW	322b	D	rathere will drede:	Z X V
WW	106b	/	nerre togedirs;	Z Z

Saint Erkenwald

E	1	At London in Englond / no3t full / long sythen	not Z	Z Z
E	2	Sythen Crist suffrid on crosse / and / Cristendome stablyd,	C	N V
E	3	Ther was a byschop in that burgh, / blessyd and sacryd;	/	A C A
E	4	Saynt Erkenwolde as I hope / that / holy mon hatte.	D	A N V
E	5	In his tyme in that toun / the / temple alder-grattyst	D	N A
E	6	Was drawen doun, that one dole, / to / dedifie new,	to	V Z
E	7	For hit hethen had / bene in / Hengyst dawes	be P	N N
E	8	That the Saxones vnsa3t / haden / sende hyder.	have	E Z
E	9	Thai bete oute the Bretons / and / bro3t hom into Wales	C	V H P N
E	10	And peruertyd all the pepul / that in that / place dwellid;	that P D	N V
E	11	Then wos this reame renaide / mony / ronke 3eres,	D	A N
E	12	Til Saynt Austyn into Sandewich / was / send fro the pope.	be	E P D N
E	13	Then prechyd he here the pure faythe / and / plantyd the trouthe,	C	V D N
E	14	And conuertyd all the communnates / to / Cristendame newe,	P	N Z
E	15	He turnyd temples that tyme / that / temyd to the deuell,	that	V P D N
E	16	And clansyd hom in Cristes nome / and / kyrkes horn callid.	C	N H V
E	17	He hurlyd owt hor ydols / and / hade hym in sayntes,	C	V H P N
E	18	And chaungit cheuely hor nomes / and / chargit hom better;	C	V H Z ?
E	19	That ere was of Appolyn / is / now of Saynt Petre,	be	Z P N N
E	20	Mahoun to Saynt Margrete / othir to / Maudelayne,	C P	N
E	21	The Synagoge of the Sonne / was / sett to oure Lady,	be	E P D N
E	22	Jubiter and Jono / to / Jesu othir to James.	P	N C to N
E	23	So he hom dedifiet and dyght / all to / dere halowes	Z P	A N
E	24	That ere wos sett of Sathanas / in / Saxones tyme.	P	N N
E	25	Now that London is neuenyd hatte / the / New Troie,	D	A N
E	26	The metropol and the mayster-toun / hit / euermore has bene;	H	Z have E
E	27	The mecul mynster / therinne a / maghty deuel aght,	Z D	A N V
E	28	And the title of the temple / bitan was his name,	/	E be D N
E	29	For he was dryghtyn derrest / of / ydols praysid,	P	N E
E	30	And the solempnest of his sacrifices / in / Saxon londes.	P	A N
E	31	The thrid temple hit wos tolde / of / Triapolitanes:	P	N
E	32	By all Bretaynes bonkes / were / bot othire twayne.	be	C A N
E	33	Now of this Augustynes art / is / Erkenwolde bischop	be	N N
E	34	At loue London toun / and the / lagh teches,	C D	N V
E	35	Syttes semely in the sege / of / Saynt Paule mynster	P	N N N
E	36	That was the temple Triapolitan / as I / tolde are.	C H	V Z
E	37	Then was hit abatyd and beten / doun and / buggyd efte new,	Z C	V Z Z
E	38	A noble note for the nones / and / New Werke hit hatte;	C	A N H V
E	39	Mony a mery mason / was / made ther to wyrke,	be	E Z to V
E	40	Harde stones for to hewe / with / eggit toles,	P	E N
E	41	Mony grubber in grete / the / grounde for to seche	D	N for to V
E	42	That the fundement on fyrst / shuld the / fote halde;	X D	N V
E	43	And as thai makkyd and mynyd / a / meruayle thai founden	D	N H V
E	44	As 3et in crafty cronceles / is / kydde the memorie,	be	A(E) D N
E	45	For as thai dy3t and dalfe / so / depe into the erthe	Z	Z P D N
E	46	Thai founden fourmyt on a flore / a / ferly faire toumbe;	D	A A N
E	47	Hit was a throgh of thykke ston / thryuandly hewen,	/	Z E
E	48	With gargeles garnysht / aboute alle of / gray marbre.	Z Z P	A N
E	49	The sperl of the spelunke / that / spradde hit olofte	that	V H Z
E	50	Was metely made of the marbre / and / menskefully planed	C	Z E
E	51	And the bordure enbelicit / with / bry3t golde lettres;	P	A A N
E	52	Bot roynyshe were the resones / that ther on / row stoden.	that Q P	N V
E	53	Full verray were the vigures / ther / auisyd hom mony,	Q	V H A
E	54	Bot all muset hit to mouth / and quat hit / mene shuld,	C Q H	V X
E	55	Mony clerke in that clos / with / crownes ful brode	P	N Z A
E	56	Ther besiet hom aboute / no3t to / bryng hom in wordes.	not to	V H P N
E	57	Quen tithynges token to the toun / of the / toumbe-wonder	P D	N
E	58	Mony hundrid hende men / highid thider sone;	/	V Z Z
E	59	Burgeys boghit / therto, / bedels and othire,	Z	N C H
E	60	And mony a mesters mon / of / maners dyuerse;	C	N A
E	61	Laddes laften hor werke / and / lepen thiderwardes,	P	V Z
E	62	Ronnen radly in route / with / ryngand noyce;	P	G N
E	63	Ther comen thider of all kynnes / so / kenely mony	Z	Z A
E	64	That as all the worlde were thider walon / within a hondequile.	/	P D N
E	65	Quen the maire with his meynye / that / meruaile aspied,	that	N V
E	66	By assent of the sextene / the / sayntuaré thai kepten,	D	N H V

144

E	67	Bede vnlouke the lidde / and / lay hit byside;	C	V H Z	
E	68	Thai wold loke on that lome / quat / lengyd withinne.	Q	V Z	
E	69	Wyʒt werkemen / with that / wenten thertill,	P that	V Z	
E	70	Putten prises / therto, / pinchid one-vnder,	Z	V P	
E	71	Kaghten by the corners / with / crowes of yrne,	P	N P A	
E	72	And were the lydde neuer so large / thai / laide hit by sone.	H	V H Z Z	
E	73	Bot then wos wonder to wale / on / wehes that stoden	P	N that V	
E	74	That myʒt not come to to knowe / a / quontyse strange,	D	N A	
E	75	So was the glode within gay, / al with / golde payntyd,	Z P	N E	
E	76	And a blisfull body / opon the / bothum lyggid,	P D	N V	
E	77	Araide on a riche wise / in / riall wedes;	P	A N	
E	78	Al with glisnande golde / his / gowne wos hemmyd,	D	N be E	
E	79	With mony a precious perle / picchit theron,	/	A(E) Z	
E	80	And a gurdill of golde / bigripid his mydell;	/	V D N	
E	81	A meche mantel on lofte / with / menyuer furrit,	P	N E	
E	82	The clothe of camelyn ful clene / with / cumly bordures,	P	A N	
E	83	And on his coyfe wos kest / a / coron ful riche	D	N Z A	
E	84	And a semely septure / sett in his honde.	/	E P D	
E	85	Als wemles were his wedes / withouten any tecche	/	P D N	
E	86	Othir of moulyng othir of motes / othir / moght-freten,	C	N-E	
E	87	And als bryʒt of hor blee / in / blysnande hewes	P	G N	
E	88	As thai hade ʒepely in that ʒorde / bene / ʒisturday shapen;	be	Z E	
E	89	And als freshe hym the face / and the / flesh nakyd	C D	N A	
E	90	Bi his eres and bi his hondes / that / openly shewid	that	Z V	
E	91	With ronke rode as the rose / and two / rede lippes,	C D	A N	
E	92	As he in sounde sodanly / were / slipped opon slepe.	be	E P N	
E	93	Ther was spedeles space / to / spyr vschon othir	to	V Z	
E	94	Quat body hit myʒt be / that / buried wos ther;	that	E be Z	
E	95	How long had he ther layne, / his / lere so vnchaungit,	D	N A A(E)	
E	96	And al his wede vnwemmyd? / Thus ylka / weghe askyd.	C D	N V	
E	97	'Hit myʒt not be bot such a mon in mynde / stode long.	/	V Z	
E	98	He has ben kyng of this kith, / as / couthely hit semes;	C	Z H V	
E	99	He lyes doluen thus depe; / hit is a / derfe wonder	H be D	A N	
E	100	Bot summe segge couthe say / that he hym / sene hade.'	that H H	E have	
E	101	Bot that ilke note wos noght, / for / nourne none couthe,	C	V H X	
E	102	Nothir by title ne token / ne by / tale nobir,	not P	N Z	
E	103	That euer wos breuyt in burgh / ne in / boke notyd	not P	N E	
E	104	That euer mynnyd such a mon, / more ne lasse.	/	Z C Z	
E	105	The bodeword to the byschop / was / broght on a quile	be	E Z	
E	106	Of that buried body / al the / bolde wonder;	Z D	A N	
E	107	The primate with his prelacie / was / partyd fro home,	be	E P N	
E	108	In Esex was Sir Erkenwolde / an / abbay to visite.	D	N to V	
E	109	Tulkes tolden hym the tale / with / troubull in the pepul,	P	N P D N	
E	110	And suche a cry aboute a cors / crakit euermore,	/	V Z	
E	111	The bischop sende hit to blynne / by / bedels and lettres	P	N C N	
E	112	And buskyd thiderwarde bytyme / on his / blonke after.	P D	N Z	
E	113	By that he come to the kyrke / kydde of Saynt Paule,	/	A(E) P D N	
E	114	Mony hym metten on that meere / the / meruayle to tell,	D	N to V	
E	115	He passyd into his palais / and / pes he comaundit	C	N H V	
E	116	And deuoydit fro the dede / and / ditte the durre after.	C	V D N Z	
E	117	The derke nyʒt ouerdrofe / and / day-belle ronge,	C	N V	
E	118	And Sir Erkenwolde was vp / in the / vghten ere then,	P D	N P Z	
E	119	That welnegh al the nyʒt / hade / naityd his houres	have	E D N	
E	120	To biseche his souerayn / of / his swete grace	P D	A N	
E	121	To vouchesafe to reuele / hym hit by a / visoun or elles.	H H P D	N C H	
E	122	Thagh I be vnworthi', / al / wepand he sayde,	H Z	G H V	
E	123	Thurgh his deere debonerté / pite hym my Lorde;	/	V H D N	
E	124	In confirmyng thi cristen faith, / fulsen me to kenne	/	V H to V	
E	125	The mysterie of this meruaile / that / men opon wondres.'	that	N Z V	
E	126	And so long he grette after grace / that he / graunte hade	that H	E have	
E	127	An ansuare of the Holy Goste, / and / afterwarde hit dawid.	C	Z H V	
E	128	Mynster-dores were makyd opon / quen / matens were songen,	C	N be E	
E	129	The byschop hym shope solemply / to / synge the hegh masse.	to	V D A N	
E	130	The prelate in pontificals / was / prestly atyrid,	be	Z E	
E	131	Manerly with his ministres / the / masse he begynnes	D	N H V	
E	132	Of Spiritus Domini for his spede / on / sutile wise,	P	A N	
E	133	With queme questis of the quere / with ful / quaynt notes.	P Z	A N	
E	134	Mony a gay grete lorde / was / gedrid to herken hit,	be	E to V H	
E	135	As the rekenest of the reame / repairen thider ofte,	/	V Z Z	
E	136	Till cessyd was the seruice / and / sayde the later ende;	C	V D A N	
E	137	Then heldyt fro the autere / all the / hegh gynge.	Z D	A N	

E	138	The prelate passid on the playn / ther / plied to hym lordes,	Q	V P H N
E	139	As riche reuestid / as he was he / laykcd to the toumbe,	C H be H	V P D N
E	140	Men vnclosid hym the cloyster / with / clustred keies,	P	E N
E	141	Bot pyne wos with the grete prece / that / passyd hym after.	that	V H P
E	142	The byschop come to the burynes, / him / barones besyde,	H	N P
E	143	The maire with mony maʒti men / and / macers before hym;	C	N P H
E	144	The dene of the dere place / deuysit al on fyrst,	/	V Z Z
E	145	The fyndynge of that ferly / with / fynger he mynte.	P	N H V
E	146	`Lo, lordes,' quod that lede, / 'suche a / lyche here is,	D D	N Z be
E	147	Has layn loken here on logh, / how / long is vnknawen;	Q	Z be A(E)
E	148	And ʒet his colour and his clothe / has / caʒt no defaute,	have	E D N
E	149	Ne his lire ne the lome / that he is / layde inne.	that H be	E Z
E	150	Ther is no lede opon lyfe / of so / long age	P Z	A N
E	151	That may mene in his mynde / that suche a / mon regnyd,	that D D	N V
E	152	Ne nothir his nome ne his note / nourne of one speche,	/	V P D N
E	153	Quether mony porer in this place / is / putte into graue	be	E P N
E	154	That merkid is in oure martilage / his / mynde foreuer;	D	N Z
E	155	And we haue oure librarie laitid / thes / long seuen dayes,	D	A A N
E	156	Bot one cronicle of this kyng / con we neuer fynde.	/	X H Z V
E	157	He has non layne here so long, / to / loke hit by kynde,	to	V H P N
E	158	To malte so out of memorie / bot / meruayle hit were.'	C	N H be
E	159	Thou says sothe,' quod the segge / that / sacrid was byschop,	that	A be N
E	160	`Hit is meruaile to men / that / mountes to litell	that	V Z Z
E	161	Toward the prouidenes of the prince / that / paradis weldes,	that	N V
E	162	Quen hym luste to vnlouke / the / leste of his myʒtes.	D	A P D N
E	163	Bot quen matyd is monnes myʒt / and his / mynde passyd,	C D	N E
E	164	And al his resons are torent / and / redeles he stondes,	C	A H V
E	165	Then lettes hit hym ful litell / to / louse wyt a fynger	to	V P D N
E	166	That all the hondes vnder heuen / halde myʒt neuer.	/	V X Z
E	167	Thereas creatures crafte / of / counsell oute swarues,	P	N Z V
E	168	The comforth of the Creatore / byhoues the / cure take;	V D	N V
E	169	And so do we now oure dede, / deuyne we no fyrre;	/	V H no Z
E	170	To seche the soth at oureselfe / ʒee / se ther no bote;	H	V Z D N
E	171	Bot glow we all opon Godde / and his / grace aske,	C D	N V
E	172	That careles is of counsell / and / comforthe to sende;	C	N to V
E	173	And that in fastynge of ʒour faith / and of / fyne bileue,	C P	A N
E	174	I shal auay ʒow so verrayly / of / vertues his	P	N D
E	175	That ʒe may leue vpon long / that he is / lord myʒty,	that H be	N A
E	176	And fayne ʒour talent to fulfille / if ʒe hym / frende leues.'	C H H	N V
E	177	Then he turnes to the toumbe / and / talkes to the corce,	C	V P D N
E	178	Lyftand vp his egh-lyddes / he / loused such wordes:	H	V D N
E	179	`Now, lykhame that thus lies, / layne thou no lenger!	/	V H Z
E	180	Sythen Jesus has juggit today / his / joy to be schewyd,	D	N to be E
E	181	Be thou bone to his bode, / I / bydde in his behalue,	H	V P D N
E	182	As he was bende on a beme / quen he his / blode schadde,	C H D	N V
E	183	As thou hit wost wyterly / and we hit / wele leuen,	C H H	Z V
E	184	Ansuare here to my sawe, / concele no trouthe!	/	V D N
E	185	Sithen we wot not qwo / thou art, / witere vs thiselwen	H be	V H -self
E	186	In worlde quat weghe / thou was and / quy thow thus ligges,	H be C	Q H Z V
E	187	How long thou has layne / here and quat / lagh thou vsyt,	Z C Q	N H V
E	188	Quether art bou joyned to joy / othir / juggid to pyne.'	C	E P N
E	189	Quen the segge hade thus sayde / and / syked therafter,	C	V Z
E	190	The bryʒt body in the burynes / brayed a litell,	/	V Z
E	191	And with a dery dreme / he / dryues owte wordes	H	V Z N
E	192	Thurgh sum lant goste of lyfe / of hym that / lyfe redes.	P H that	N V
E	193	Bisshop,' quod this ilke body, / 'thi / boode is me dere;	D	N be H A
E	194	I may not bot bogh to thi bone / for / bothe myn eghen.	P	A D N
E	195	To the name that thou neuenyd / has and / nournet me after	have C	V H P
E	196	Al heuen and helle heldes / to and / erthe bitwene.	P C	N P
E	197	Fyrst to say the the sothe / quo / myselfe were,	Q	H self be
E	198	One the vnhapnest hathel / that euer on / erth ʒode,	that Z P	N V
E	199	Neuer kyng ne cayser / ne ʒet no / knyʒt nothyre,	not Z D	N Z
E	200	Bot a lede of the lagh / that then this / londe vsit.	that Z D	N V
E	201	I was committid and made, / a / mayster-mon here	D	N N Z
E	202	To sytte vpon sayd causes, / this / cité I ʒemyd	D	N H V
E	203	Vnder a prince of parage / of / paynymes lagh,	P	N N
E	204	And vche segge that him sewid / the / same fayth trowid.	D	A N V
E	205	The lengthe of my lying here / that is a / lewid date,	that be D	A N
E	206	Hit is to meche to any mon / to / make of a nombre;	to	V P D N
E	207	After that Brutus this burgh / had / buggid on fyrste,	have	E Z
E	208	Noʒt bot fife hundred ʒere / ther / aghtene wontyd	Q	A V

E	209	Before that kynned 3our Criste / by / cristen acounte:	P		N N
E	210	A thousand 3ere and thritty mo / and 3et / threnen aght.	C Z		A A
E	211	I was an heire of anoye / in the / New Troie	P D		A N
E	212	In the regne of the riche kyng / that / rewlit vs then,	that		V H Z
E	213	The bolde Breton Sir Belyn - / Sir / Berynge was his brothire;	D		N be D N
E	214	Mony one was the busmare / boden hom bitwene	/		E H P
E	215	For hor wrakeful werre quil / hor / wrath lastyd.	D		N V
E	216	Then was I juge here enjoynyd / in / gentil lawe.'	P		A N
E	217	Quil he in spelunke thus spake, / ther / sprange in the pepull	Q		V P D N
E	218	In al this worlde no worde / ne / wakenyd no noice,	not		V D N
E	219	Bot al as stille as the ston / stoden and listonde	/		V C V
E	220	With meche wonder forwrast, / and / wepid ful mony.	C		V Z H
E	221	The bisshop biddes that body: / 'Biknowe the cause,	/		V D N
E	222	Sithen thou was kidde for no kynge, / quy thou the / croun weres.	Q H D		N V
E	223	Quy haldes thou so hegh / in / honde the septre	P		N D N
E	224	And hades no londe of lege men ne life / ne / lym aghtes?'	not		N V
E	225	Dere sir,' quod the dede body, / 'deuyse the I thenke,	/		V H H V
E	226	Al was hit neuer my wille / that / wroght thus hit were.	that		E Z H be
E	227	I wos deputate and domesmon / vnder a / duke noble,	P D		N A
E	228	And in my power this place / was / putte altogeder.	be		E Z
E	229	I justifiet this joly toun / on / gentil wise	P		A N
E	230	And euer in fourme of gode faithe, / more then / fourty wynter;	A P		A N
E	231	The folke was felonse and fals / and / frowarde to reule -	C		A to V
E	232	I hent harmes ful ofte / to / holde hom to ri3t;	to		V H to N
E	233	Bot for wothe ne wele / ne / wrathe ne drede,	D		N D N
E	234	Ne for maystrie ne for mede / ne for no / monnes aghe,	not P D		N N
E	235	I remewit neuer fro the ri3t / by / reson myn awen	P		N D A
E	236	For to dresse a wrang dome, / no / day of my lyue.	D		N P D N
E	237	Declynet neuer my consciens / for / couetise on erthe	P		N P N
E	238	In no gynful jugement / no / japes to make;	D		N to V
E	239	Were a renke neuer so riche, / for / reuerens sake,	P		N N
E	240	Ne for no monnes manas, / ne / meschefe ne routhe,	D		N D N
E	241	Non gete me fro the hegh gate / to / glent out of ry3t	to		V P P N
E	242	Als ferforthe as my faith / confourmyd my hert.	/		V D N
E	243	Thagh had bene my fader bone, / I / bede hym no wranges,	H		V H D N
E	244	Ne fals fauour to my fader, / thagh / fell hym be hongyt;	C		V H be E
E	245	And for I was ry3twis and reken / and / redy of the laghe,	C		A P D N
E	246	Quen I deghed for dul / denyed all Troye;	/		V Z N
E	247	Alle menyd my dethe, / the / more and the lasse,	D		A C D A
E	248	And thus to bounty my body / thai / buriet in golde,	H		V P N
E	249	Cladden me for the curtest / that / courte couthe then holde,	that		N X Z V
E	250	In mantel for the mekest / and / monlokest on benche,	C		A P N
E	251	Gurden me for the gouernour / and / graythist of Troie,	C		A P N
E	252	Furrid me for the fynest / of / faith me withinne.	P		N H Z
E	253	For the honour of myn honesté / of / heghest enprise,	P		A N
E	254	Thai coronyd me the kidde kynge / of / kene justises	P		A N
E	255	Ther euer was tronyd in Troye / othir / trowid euer shulde,	C		E Z X
E	256	And for I rewardid euer ri3t / thai / raght me the septre.'	H		V H D N
E	257	The bisshop baythes / hym 3et with / bale at his hert,	H Z P		N P D N
E	258	Thagh men menskid / him so, how hit / my3t worthe	H Z Q H		X V
E	259	That his clothes were so clene. / `In / cloutes, me thynkes,	P		N H V
E	260	Hom burde haue rotid and bene rent / in / rattes long sythen.	P		N Z Z
E	261	Thi body may be enbawmyd, / hit / bashis me noght	H		V H not
E	262	That hit thar ryne no rote / ne no / ronke wormes:	not D		A N
E	263	Bot thi coloure ne thi clothe - / I / know in no wise	H		V P D N
E	264	How hit my3t lye by monnes lore / and / last so longe.'	C		V Z Z
E	265	`Nay, bisshop,' quod that body, / 'enbawmyd wos I neuer,	/		E be H Z
E	266	Ne no monnes counsell my cloth / has / kepyd vnwemmyd,	have		E E
E	267	Bot the riche kyng of reson, / that / ri3t euer alowes	that		N Z V
E	268	And loues al the lawes lely / that / longen to trouthe;	that		V P N
E	269	And moste he menskes men / for / mynnyng of ri3tes	P		G P N V
E	270	Then for al the meritorie medes / that / men on molde vsen,	that		N P N V
E	271	And if renkes for ri3t / thus me / arayed has,	C H		E have
E	272	He has lant me to last / that / loues ry3t best.'	that		V N Z
E	273	3ea, bot sayes thou of thi saule,' / sayd the bisshop;	C		V D N
E	274	Quere is ho stablid and stadde, / if thou so / stre3t wroghtes?	C H Z		Z V
E	275	He that rewardes vche a renke / as he has / ri3t seruyd	C H have		N E
E	276	My3t euel forgo the gyfe / of his / grace summe brawnche.	P D		N D N
E	277	For as he says in his sothe / psalmyde writtes:	/		A(E) N
E	278	"The skilfulle and the vnskathely / skelton ay to me."	/		V Z P H
E	279	Forthi say me of thi soule, / in / sele quere ho wonnes,	P		N Q H V

E	280	And of the riche restorment / that / raʒt hyr oure Lorde.'	that	V H D N
E	281	Then hummyd he that ther lay / and his / hedde waggyd,	C D	N V
E	282	And gefe a gronyng ful grete / and to / Godde sayde:	C P	N V
E	283	`Maʒty maker of men, / thi / myghtes are grete;	D	N be A
E	284	How myʒt thi mercy / to me / amounte any tyme?	P H	V D N
E	285	Nas I a paynym vnpreste / that neuer thi / plite knewe,	that Z D	N V
E	286	Ne the mesure of thi mercy / ne thi / mecul vertue,	not D	A N
E	287	Bot ay a freke faitheles / that / faylid thi laghes	that	V D N
E	288	That euer thou, Lord, wos louyd in? Allas / the / harde stoundes!	D	A N
E	289	I was non of the nombre / that thou with / noy boghtes	that H D	N V
E	290	With the blode of thi body / vpon the / blo rode;	P D	A N
E	291	Quen thou herghdes helle-hole, / and / hentes hom theroute,	C	V H Z
E	292	Thi loffynge oute of limbo, / thou / laftes me ther,	H	V H Z
E	293	And ther sittes my soule / that / se may no fyrre,	that	V X no Z
E	294	Dwynande in the derke deth / that / dyʒt vs oure fader,	that	V H D N
E	295	Adam oure alder, / that / ete of that appull	that	V P D N
E	296	That mony a plyʒtles pepul / has / poysned for euer.	have	E Z
E	297	ʒe were entouchid with his teche / and / take in the glotte,	C	V P D N
E	298	Bot mendyd with a medecyn / ʒe are / made for to lyuye -	H be	E for to V
E	299	That is fulloght in fonte / with / faithefule bileue,	P	A N
E	300	And that han we myste alle merciles, / myselfe and my soule.	/	H self C D N
E	301	Quat wan we with oure wele-dede / that / wroghtyn ay riʒt,	that	V Z N
E	302	Quen we are dampnyd dulfully / into the / depe lake,	P D	A N
E	303	And exilid fro that soper / so, that / solempne fest,	C D	A N
E	304	Ther richely hit arne refetyd / that after / right hungride?	that P	N V
E	305	My soule may sitte ther in sorow / and / sike ful colde,	C	N Z Z
E	306	Dymly in that derke dethe / ther / dawes neuer morowen,	Q	V Z N
E	307	Hungrie inwith helle-hole, / and / herken after meeles	C	V P N
E	308	Longe er ho bat soper se / othir / segge hyr to lathe.'	D	N H to V
E	309	Thus dulfully this dede body / deuisyt hit sorowe	/	V H N
E	310	That alle wepyd for woo / the / wordes that herden,	D	N that V
E	311	And the bysshop balefully / bere doun his eghen,	/	V Z D N
E	312	That hade no space to speke, / so / spakly he ʒoskyd,	Z	Z H V
E	313	Til he toke hym a tome / and to the / toumbe lokyd,	C P D	N V
E	314	To the liche ther hit lay, / with / lauande teres.	P	G N
E	315	Oure Lord lene', quod that lede, / `that thou / lyfe hades,	that H	N V
E	316	By Goddes leue, as longe / as I myʒt / lacche water,	C H X	V N
E	317	And cast vpon thi faire cors / and / carpe thes wordes:	C	V D N
E	318	"I folwe the in the Fader nome / and his / fre Childes	C D	N V
E	319	And of the gracious Holy Goste", / and not one / grue lenger.	C not D	N A
E	320	Then thof thou droppyd doun dede, / hit / daungerde me lasse.'	H	V H Z
E	321	With that worde that he warpyd, / the / wete of his eghen	D	N P D N
E	322	And teres trillyd / adoun and on the / toumbe lighten,	Z C P D	N V
E	323	And one felle on his face, / and the / freke syked;	C D	N V
E	324	Then sayd he with a sadde soun: / 'Oure / Sauyoure be louyd!	D	N be E
E	325	Now herid be thou, hegh God, / and thi / hende Moder,	C D	N N
E	326	And blissid be that blisful houre / that ho the / here in!	that H H	V P
E	327	And also be thou, bysshop, / the / bote of my sorowe	D	N P D N
E	328	And the relefe of the lodely lures / that my / soule has leuyd in!	that D	N have E Z
E	329	For the wordes that thou werpe / and the / water that thou sheddes,	C D	N that H V
E	330	The bryʒt bourne of thin eghen, / my / bapteme is worthyn.	D	N be E
E	331	The fyrst slent that on me slode / slekkyd al my tene;	/	V Z D N
E	332	Ryʒt now to soper my soule / is / sette at the table;	be	E P D N
E	333	For with the wordes and the water / that / wesche vs of payne,	that	V H P N
E	334	Liʒtly lasshit ther a leme / loghe in the abyme;	/	Z P D N
E	335	That spakly sprent my spyryt / with / vnsparid murthe	P	A(E) N
E	336	Into the cenacle solemply / ther / soupen all trew;	Q	V Z A
E	337	And ther a marciall hyr mette / with / menske alder-grattest,	P	N A
E	338	And with reuerence a rowme / he / raʒt hyr foreuer.	H	V H Z
E	339	I heere therof my hegh God / and / also the, bysshop,	C	Z H N
E	340	Fro bale has broʒt vs to blis, / blessid thou worth!'	/	A(E) H V
E	341	Wyt this cessyd his sowne, / sayd he no more,	/	V H Z
E	342	Bot sodenly his swete chere / swyndid and faylid	/	V C V
E	343	And all the blee of his body / wos / blakke as the moldes,	be	A P D N
E	344	As roten as the rottok / that / rises in powdere.	that	V P N
E	345	For as sone as the soule / was / sesyd in blisse,	be	E P N
E	346	Corrupt was that othir crafte / that / couert the bones,	that	V D N
E	347	For the ay-lastande life / that / lethe shall neuer	that	V X Z
E	348	Deuoydes vche a vayneglorie / that / vayles so litelle.	that	V Z Z
E	349	Then wos louyng oure Lord / with / loves vphalden,	P	N E
E	350	Meche mournyng and myrthe / was / mellyd togeder;	be	E Z

E	351	Thai passyd forthe in procession / and alle the / pepull folowid,	C D D	N V
E	352	And all the belles in the burgh / beryd at ones.	/	V Z

The Parlement of the Thre Ages

AG 1	In the monethe of Maye / when /mirthes bene fele,	C	N be A
AG 2	And the sesone of somere / when / softe bene the wedres,	C	A be D N
AG 3	Als I went to the wodde / my / werdes to dreghe,	D	N to V
AG 4	Into the schawes myselfe / a / schotte me to gete	D	N H to V
AG 5	At ane hert or ane hynde, / happen as it myghte;	/	V C H X
AG 6	And as Dryghtyn the day / drove frome the heven,	/	V P D N
AG 7	Als I habade one a banke / be a / bryme syde,	P D	N N
AG 8	There the gryse was grene, / growen with floures,	/	E P N
AG 9	The primrose, the pervynke, / and / piliole the riche,	C	N D N(A)
AG 10	The dewe appon dayses / donkede full faire,	/	V Z Z
AG 11	Burgons and blossoms / and / braunches full swete,	C	N Z A
AG 12	And the mery mystes / full / myldely gane falle;	Z	Z V V
AG 13	The cukkowe, the cowschote, / kene were thay bothen,	/	A be H Z
AG 14	And the throstills full throly / threpen in the bankes,	/	V P D N
AG 15	And iche foule in that frythe / faynere than other	/	A C H
AG 16	That the derke was done / and the / daye lightenede.	C D	N E
AG 17	Hertys and hyndes / one / hillys thay gouen,	P	N H V
AG 18	The foxe and the filmarte / thay / flede to the erthe;	H	V P D N
AG 19	The hare hurkles by hawes / and / harde thedir dryves,	C	Z Z V
AG 20	And ferkes faste to hir fourme / and / fatills hir to sitt.	C	V H to V
AG 21	Als I stode in that stede / one / stalkynge I thoghte:	P	N H V
AG 22	Bothe my body and my bowe / I / buskede with leves,	H	V P N
AG 23	And turnede towardes a tree / and / tariede there a while.	C	V Z Z
AG 24	And als I lokede to a launde / a / littill me besyde,	Z	Z H P
AG 25	I seghe ane hert with ane hede, / ane / heghe for the nones:	Z	Z Z
AG 26	Alle unburneschede was the beme, / full / borely the mydle,	Z	A D N
AG 27	With iche feetur as thi fote, / forfrayed in the greves,	/	E P D N
AG 28	With auntlers one aythere syde / eghelyche longe.		Z A
AG 29	The ryalls full richely / raughten frome the myddes,	/	V P D N
AG 30	With surryals full semely / appon / sydes twayne;	P	N A
AG 31	And he assommet and sett / of / six and of fyve,	P	N C P N
AG 32	And therto borely and brode / and of / body grete,	C P	N A
AG 33	And a coloppe for a kynge, / cache hym who myghte.	/	V H Q N
AG 34	Bot there sewet hym a sorwe / that / servet hym full yerne,	that	V H Z Z
AG 35	That woke and warned / hym when the / wynde faylede,	H C D	N V
AG 36	That none so sleghe in his slepe / with / sleghte scholde hym dere,	P	N X H V
AG 37	And went the wayes hym byfore / when any / wothe tyde.	C D	N V
AG 38	My lyame than full lightly / lete I doun falle,	/	V H Z V
AG 39	And to the bole of a birche / my / berselett I cowchide;	D	N H V
AG 40	I waitted wiesly the wynde / by / waggynge of leves,	P	N P N
AG 41	Stalkede full stilly / no / stikkes to breke,	D	N to V
AG 42	And crepite to a crabtre / and / coverede me therundere.	C	V H Z
AG 43	Then I bende up my bowe / and / bownede me to schote,	C	V H to V
AG 44	Tighte up my tylere / and / taysede at the hert.	C	V P D N
AG 45	Bot the sowre that hym sewet / sett up the nese,	/	V Z D N
AG 46	And waytttede wittyly / abowte and / wyndide full yerne.	Z C	V Z Z
AG 47	Then I moste stonde als I stode / and / stirre no fote ferrere,	C	V D N Z
AG 48	For had I myntid or movede / or / made any synys,	C	V D N
AG 49	Alle my layke hade bene loste / that I hade / longe wayttede.	that H have	Z E
AG 50	Bot gnattes gretely me grevede / and / gnewen myn eghne;	C	V D N
AG 51	And he stotayde and stelkett / and / starede full brode,	C	V Z Z
AG 52	Bot at the laste he loutted / doun and / laughte till his mete,	Z C	V P D N
AG 53	And I hallede to the hokes / and the / hert smote.	C D	N V
AG 54	And happenyd that I hitt / hym / byhynde the lefte scholdire,	H	P D A N
AG 55	That the blode braste / owte appon / bothe the sydes;	Z P	Z D N
AG 56	And he balkede and brayed / and / bruschede thurgh the greves,	C	V P D N
AG 57	As alle had hurlede one ane hepe / that in the / holte longede.	that P D	N V
AG 58	And sone the sowre that hym sewet / resorte to his feris,	/	V P D N
AG 59	And thay, forfrayede of his fare, / to the / fellys thay hyen,	P D	N H V
AG 60	And I hyede to my hounde / and / hent hym up sone,	C	V H Z Z
AG 61	And louset my lyame / and / lete hym umbycaste.	C	V H V
AG 62	The breris and the brakans / were / blody byronnen;	be	Z E
AG 63	And he assentis to that sewte / and / seches hym aftire	C	V H P
AG 64	There he was crepyde into a krage / and / crouschede to the erthe.	C	E P D N
AG 65	Dede als a dore-nayle / doun was he fallen;	C	Z be H E
AG 66	And I hym hent by the hede / and / heryett hym uttire,	/	V H Z

150

The Parlement of the Thre Ages 151

AG 67	Turned his troches / and / tachede thaym into the erthe,	C		V H P D N
AG 68	Kest up that keuduart / and / kutt of his tonge,	C		V Z D N
AG 69	Brayde owte his bewells / my / bereselet to fede.	D		N to V
AG 70	And I slitte hym at the assaye / to / see how me semyde,	to		V Q H V
AG 71	And he was floreschede full faire / of two / fyngere brede.	P D		N N
AG 72	I chese to the chawylls / chefe to begynn,	/		Z to V
AG 73	And ritte doun at a rase / reghte to the tayle,	/		Z P D N
AG 74	And than the herbere anone / aftir I makede;	/		C H V
AG 75	I raughte the righte legge / byfore /, ritt it theraftir.	Z		V H Z
AG 76	And so fro legge to legge / I / lepe thaym aboute;	H		V H Z
AG 77	And the felle fro the fete / fayre I departede,	/		Z H V
AG 78	And flewe it doun with my fiste / faste to the rigge.	/		Z P D N
AG 79	I tighte owte my trenchore / and / toke of the scholdirs,	C		V Z D N
AG 80	Cuttede corbyns bone / and / keste it awaye.	C		V H Z
AG 81	I slitte hym full sleghely / and / slyppede in my fyngere,	C		V P D N
AG 82	Lesse the poynte scholde perche / the / pawnche or the guttys;	D		N C D N
AG 83	I soughte owte my sewet / and / semblete it togedire,	C		V H Z
AG 84	And pullede oute the pawnche / and / putt it in an hole.	C		V H P D N
AG 85	I grippede owte the guttes / and / graythede thaym besyde,	C		V H P
AG 86	And than the nombles anone / name I thereaftire;	/		V H Z
AG 87	Rent up fro the rygge / reghte to the myddis,	/		Z P D N
AG 88	And then the fourches full fayre / I / fonge fro the sydes,	H		V P D N
AG 89	And chynede hym chefely / and / choppede of the nekke,	C		V Z D N
AG 90	And the hede and the haulse / homelyde in sondree.	/		V Z
AG 91	The fete of the fourche / I / feste thurgh the sydis,	H		V P D N
AG 92	And hevede all into ane hole / and / hidde it with ferne,	C		V H P N
AG 93	With hethe and with horemosse / hilde it about,	/		V H P
AG 94	That no fostere of the fee / scholde / fynde it theraftir;	X		V H Z
AG 95	Hid the hornes and the hede / in ane / hologhe oke,	P D		A N
AG 96	That no hunte scholde it hent / ne / have it in sighte.	not		V H P N
AG 97	I foundede faste therefro / for / ferde to be wryghede,	P		E to be E
AG 98	And sett me oute one a syde / to / see how it chevede	to		V Q H V
AG 99	To wayte it frome wylde swyne / that / wyse bene of nesse.	that		A be P N
AG 100	And als I satte in my sette / the / sone was so warme,	D		N be Z A
AG 101	And I for slepeles was slome / and / slomerde a while.	C		V Z
AG 102	And there me dremed in that dowte / a full / dreghe swevynn,	D Z		A N
AG 103	And whate I seghe in my saule / the / sothe I schall telle.	D		N H X V
AG 104	I seghe thre thro men / threpden full yerne,	/		V Z Z
AG 105	And moted of myche-whate / and / maden thaym full tale.	C		V H Z A
AG 106	And ye will, ledys, me listen / ane / hande-while,	D		Z(N)
AG 107	I schall reken thaire araye / redely for sothe,	/		Z P N
AG 108	And to yowe neven thaire names / naytly thereaftire.	/		Z Z
AG 109	The firste was a ferse freke, / fayrere than thies othire,	/		A C D H
AG 110	A bolde beryn one a blonke / bownne for to ryde,	/		A for to V
AG 111	A hathelle on ane heghe horse / with / hauke appon hande.	P		N P N
AG 112	He was balghe in the breste / and / brode in the scholdirs,	C		A P D N
AG 113	His axles and his armes / were / iliche longe,	be		Z A
AG 114	And in the medill als a mayden / menskfully schapen,	/		Z E
AG 115	Longe legges and large, / and / lele for to schewe.	C		A for to V
AG 116	He streghte hym in his sterapis / and / stode uprightes;	C		V Z
AG 117	He ne hade no hode ne no hatte / bot his / here one,	P D		N Z
AG 118	A chaplet one his chefelere / chosen for the nones,	/		E P D N
AG 119	Raylede alle with rede rose, / richeste of floures,	/		A P N
AG 120	With trayfoyles and trewloves / of full / triede perles,	P Z		E N
AG 121	With a chefe charebocle / chosen in the myddes.	/		E P D N
AG 122	He was gerede alle in grene, / alle with / golde bywevede,	Z P		N E
AG 123	Enbroddirde alle with besanttes / and / beralles full riche;	C		N Z A
AG 124	His colere with calsydoynnes / clustrede full thikke,	/		E Z Z
AG 125	With many dyamandes full dere / dighte one his sleves.	/		E P D N
AG 126	The semys with saphirs / sett were full many,	/		E be Z A
AG 127	With emeraudes and amatistes / appon / iche syde,	/		A N
AG 128	With full riche rubyes / raylede by the hemmes;	/		E P D N
AG 129	The price of that perry were worthe / powndes full many.	/		N Z A
AG 130	His sadill was of sykamoure / that he / satt inn,	that H		V Z
AG 131	His bridell alle of brente golde / with / silke brayden raynes,	P		N E N
AG 132	His cropoure was of tartaryne / that / traylede to the erthe;	that		V P D N
AG 133	And he throly was thryven / of / thritty yere of elde,	P		A N P N
AG 134	And therto yonge and yape, / and / Youthe was his name,	C		N be D N
AG 135	And the semelyeste segge / that I / seghe ever.	that H		V Z
AG 136	The seconde segge in his sete / satte at his ese,	/		V P D N
AG 137	A renke alle in rosette / that / rowmly was schapyn,	that		Z be E

AG 138 In a golyone of graye / girde in the myddes,	/	E P D N
AG 139 And Iehe bagge In his bosome / bctih than othere.		A C H
AG 140 One his golde and his gude / gretly he mousede,	/	Z H V
AG 141 His renttes and his reches / rekened he full ofte,	/	V H Z Z
AG 142 Of mukkyng, of marlelyng, / and / mendynge of howses,	C	G P N
AG 143 Of benes of his bondemen, / of / benefetis many,	P	N A
AG 144 Of presanttes of polayle, / of / pufilis als;	P	N Z
AG 145 Of purches of ploughe-londes, / of / parkes full faire,	P	N Z A
AG 146 Of profettis of his pasturs, / that his / purse mendis;	that D	N V
AG 147 Of stiewardes, of storrours, / stirkes to bye,	/	N to V
AG 148 Of clerkes, of countours, / his / courtes to holde;	D	N to V
AG 149 And alle his witt in this werlde / was one his / wele one.	be P D	N Z
AG 150 Hym semyde for to see / to of / sexty yere elde,	P P	A N N
AG 151 And therfore men in his marche / Medill Elde hym callede.	/	N N H E
AG 152 The thirde was a laythe lede / lenyde one his syde,	/	V P D N
AG 153 A beryne bownn alle in blake / with / bedis in his hande,	P	N P D N
AG 154 Croked and courbede, / encrampeschett for elde;	/	E P N
AG 155 Alle disfygured was his face / and / fadit his hewe,	C	E D N
AG 156 His berde and browes / were / blanchede full whitte,	be	E Z A
AG 157 And the hare one his hede / hewede of the same.	/	E P D A
AG 158 He was ballede and blynde / and alle / babirlippede,	C Z	E
AG 159 Totheles and tenefull, / I / tell yowe for sothe;	H	V H P N
AG 160 And ever he momelide and ment / and / mercy he askede,	C	N H V
AG 161 And cried kenely one Criste / and his / crede sayde,	C D	N V
AG 162 With sawtries full sere tymes / to / sayntes in heven;	P	N P N
AG 163 Envyous and angrye, / and / Elde was his name.	C	N be D N
AG 164 I helde hym be my hopynge / a / hundrethe yeris of age,	D	A N P N
AG 165 And bot his cruche and his couche / he / carede for no more.	H	V Z Z
AG 166 Now hafe I rekkende yow theire araye / redely the sothe,	/	Z D N
AG 167 And also namede yow thaire names / naytly thereaftire,	/	Z Z
AG 168 And now thaire carpynge I sall kythe - / knowe it if yowe liste.	/	V H C H V
AG 169 Now this gome alle in grene / so / gayly attyrede,	Z	Z E
AG 170 This hathelle one this heghe horse / with / hauke one his fiste,	P	N P D N
AG 171 He was yonge and yape / and / yernynge to armes,	C	G P N
AG 172 And pleynede hym one paramours / and / peteuosely syghede.	C	Z V
AG 173 He sett hym up in his sadill / and / seyde theis wordes:	C	C H V
AG 174 "My lady, my leman, / that I hafe / luffede ever,	that H have	E Z
AG 175 My wele and my wirchip / in / werlde where thou duellys,	P	N Q H V
AG 176 My playstere of paramours, my lady / with / pappis full swete,	P	N Z A
AG 177 Alle my hope and my hele, / myn / herte es thyn ownn!	D	N be D A
AG 178 I byhete the heste / and / heghely I avowe,	C	Z H V
AG 179 There schall no hode ne no hatt / one my / hede sitt	P D	N V
AG 180 Till that I joyntly with a gesserante / justede hafe with onere,	/	E have P N
AG 181 And done dedis for thi love, / doghety in armes."	/	A P N
AG 182 Bot then this gome alle in graye / greved with this wordes,	/	V P D N
AG 183 And sayde, "Felowe, be my faythe / thou / fonnes full yerne,	H	V Z Z
AG 184 For alle es fantome / and / foly that thou with faris.	C	N that H P V
AG 185 Where es the londe and the lythe / that thou arte / lorde over?	that H be	N Z
AG 186 For alle thy ryalle araye / renttis hase thou none,	/	N V H not
AG 187 Ne for thi pompe and thi pride / penyes bot fewe,	/	N P H
AG 188 For alle thi golde and thi gude / gloes one thi clothes,	/	V P D N
AG 189 And thou hafe caughte thi kaple / thou / cares for no fothire.	H	V Z Z
AG 190 Bye the stirkes with thi stede / and / stalles thaym make,	C	N H V
AG 191 Thi brydell of brent golde / wolde / bullokes the gete,	X	N H V
AG 192 The pryce of thi perrye / wolde / purches the londes,	X	V D N
AG 193 And wonne, wy, in thi witt, / for / wele neghe thou spilles."	C	Z H V
AG 194 Than the gome alle in grene / greved full sore,	/	V Z Z
AG 195 And sayd, "Sir, be my soule, / thi / counsell es feble.	D	N be A
AG 196 Bot thi golde and thi gude / thou hase no / god ells;	H have D	N Z
AG 197 For, be the Lorde and the laye / that I / leve inne,	that H	V Z
AG 198 And by the Gode that me gaffe / goste and soule,	/	N C N
AG 199 Me were levere one this launde / lengen a while,	/	V Z
AG 200 Stoken in my stele-wede / one my / stede bakke,	P D	N N
AG 201 Harde haspede in my helme / and in my / here-wedys,	C P D	N N
AG 202 With a grym grownden glayfe / graythely in myn honde,	/	Z P D N
AG 203 And see a kene knyghte come / and / cowpe with myselven,	C	V P H self
AG 204 That I myghte halde that I hafe highte / and / heghely avowede,	C	Z V
AG 205 And parfourme my profers / and / proven my strengthes,	C	V D N
AG 206 Than alle the golde and the gude / that thoue / gatt ever,	that H	V Z
AG 207 Than alle the londe and the lythe / that thoue arte / lorde over;	that H be	N Z
AG 208 And ryde to a revere / redily thereaftir,	/	Z Z

The Parlement of the Thre Ages

AG 209	With haukes full hawtayne / that / heghe willen flye,	that		A X V
AG 210	And when the fewlis bene founden / fawkoneres hyenn	/		N V
AG 211	To lache oute thaire lessches / and / lowsen thaym sone,	C		V H Z
AG 212	And keppyn of thaire caprons / and / casten fro honde;	C		V P N
AG 213	And than the hawteste in haste / hyghes to the towre,	/		V P D N
AG 214	With theire bellys so brighte / blethely thay ryngen,	/		Z H V
AG 215	And there they hoven appon heghte / as it were / heven angelles.	C H be		N N
AG 216	Then the fawkoners full fersely / to / floodes thay hyen,	P		N H V
AG 217	To the revere with thaire roddes / to / rere up the fewles,	to		V Z D N
AG 218	Sowssches thaym full serely / to / serven thaire hawkes.	to		V D N
AG 219	Than tercelettes full tayttely / telys doun striken;	/		N Z V
AG 220	Laners and lanerettis / lighten to thes endes,	/		V P D N
AG 221	Metyn with the maulerdes / and / many doun striken;	C		H Z V
AG 222	Fawkons thay founden / freely to lighte,	/		Z to V
AG 223	With hoo and howghe to the heron / thay / hitten hym full ofte,	H		V H Z Z
AG 224	Buffetyn hym, betyn / hym, and / bryngus hym to sege,	H C		V H P N
AG 225	And saylen hym full serely / and / sesyn hym thereaftire.	C		V H Z
AG 226	Then fawkoners full fersely / founden tham aftire,	/		V H P
AG 227	To helpen thaire hawkes / thay / hyen thaym full yerne,	H		V H Z Z
AG 228	For the bitt of his bill / bitterly he strikes.	/		Z H V
AG 229	They knelyn doun one theire knees / and / krepyn full lowe,	C		V Z Z
AG 230	Wynnen to his wynges / and / wrythen thaym togedire,	C		V H Z
AG 231	Brosten the bones / and / brekyn thaym in sondire,	C		V H Z
AG 232	Puttis owte with a penn / the / maryo one his glove,	D		N P D N
AG 233	And quopes thaym to the querrye / that / quelled hym to the dethe.	that		V H P D N
AG 234	He quyrres thaym and quotes / thaym, / quyppeys full lowde,	H		V Z Z
AG 235	Cheres thaym full chefely / ecchekkes to leve,	/		N to V
AG 236	Than henttis thaym one honde / and / hodes thaym theraftire,	C		V H Z
AG 237	Cowples up theire cowers / thaire / caprons to holde,	D		N to V
AG 238	Lowppes in thaire lesses / thorowe / vertwells of silvere.	P		N P N
AG 239	Than he laches to his luyre / and / lokes to his horse,	C		V P D N
AG 240	And lepis upe one the lefte syde / als the / laghe askes.	C D		N V
AG 241	Portours full pristly / putten upe the fowlis,	/		V Z D N
AG 242	And taryen for theire tercelettis / that / tenyn thaym full ofte,	that		V H Z Z
AG 243	For some chosen to the echecheke / thoghe some / chefe bettire.	C H		V Z
AG 244	Spanyells full spedily / thay / spryngen abowte,	H		V Z
AG 245	Bedagged for dowkynge / when / digges bene enewede;	C		N be E
AG 246	And than kayre to the courte / that I / come fro,	that H		V Z
AG 247	With ladys full lovely / to / lappyn in myn armes,	to		V P D N
AG 248	And clyp thaym and kysse / thaym and / comforthe myn hert,	H C		V D N
AG 249	And than with damesels dere / to / daunsen in thaire chambirs,	to		V P D N
AG 250	Riche romance to rede / and / rekken the sothe	C		V D N
AG 251	Of kempes and of conquerours, / of / kynges full noblee,	P		N Z A
AG 252	How thay wirchipe and welthe / wanne in thaire lyves;	/		V P D N
AG 253	With renkes in ryotte / to / revelle in haulle,	to		V P N
AG 254	With coundythes and carolles / and / compaynyes sere,	C		N A
AG 255	And chese me to the chesse / that / chefe es of gamnes:	that		A be P N
AG 256	And this es life for to lede / while I schalle / lyfe here.	C H X		V Z
AG 257	And thou with wandrynge and woo / schalte / wake for thi gudes,	X		V P D N
AG 258	And be thou dolven and dede / thi / dole schall be schorte,	D		N X be A
AG 259	And he that thou leste luffes / schall / layke hym therewith,	X		V H Z
AG 260	And spend that thou haste longe sparede, / the / devyll spede hym els!"	D		N V H Z
AG 261	Than this renke alle in rosett / rothelede thies wordes:	/		V D N
AG 262	He sayde, "Thryfte and thou have threpid / this / thirtene wynter;	D		A N
AG 263	I seghe wele samples bene sothe / that / sayde bene yore:	that		E be Z
AG 264	Fole es that with foles delys; / flyte we no lengare."	/		V H Z
AG 265	Than this beryn alle in blake / bownnes hym to speke,	/		V H to V
AG 266	And sayde, "Sirres, by my soule, / sottes bene ye bothe!	/		N be H Z
AG 267	Bot will ye hendely me herken / ane / hande-while,	D		Z (N)
AG 268	And I schalle stynte your stryffe / and / stillen your threpe.	C		V D N
AG 269	I sett ensample bi myselfe / and / sekis it no forthire:	C		V H Z
AG 270	While I was yonge in my youthe / and / yape of my dedys,	C		A P D N
AG 271	I was als everrous in armes / as / outher of youreselven,	C		H P H self
AG 272	And as styffe in a stourre / one my / stede bake,	P D		N N
AG 273	And as gaye in my gere / als any / gome ells,	C D		N Z
AG 274	And as lelly byluffede / with / ladyse and maydens.	P		N C N
AG 275	My likame was lovely, / es / lothe nowe to schewe,	be		A Z to V
AG 276	And as myche wirchip I wane, / iwis, as ye bothen.	/		Z C H Z
AG 277	And aftir irkede me with this / and / ese was me levere,	C		N be H A
AG 278	Als man in his medill elde / his / makande wolde have.	D		N X V
AG 279	Than I mukkede and marlede / and / made up my howses,	C		V Z D N

AG 280	And purcheste me ploughe-londes / and / pastures full noble,	C	N Z A
AG 281	Gatte gude and golde / full / gaynly to honde,	Z	Z P N
AG 282	Reches and renttes / were / ryfe to myselven.	be	A P H self
AG 283	Bot Elde undireyode / me are / I laste wiste,	H C	H Z V
AG 284	And alle disfegurede my face / and / fadide my hewe;	C	V D N
AG 285	Bothe my browes and my berde / blawnchede full whitte,	/	V Z A
AG 286	And when he sotted my syghte / than / sowed myn hert,	C	V D N
AG 287	Croked me, cowrbed / me, / encrapeschet myn hondes,	H	V D N
AG 288	That I ne may hefe tham to my hede / ne noghte / helpe myselven,	not not	V H -self
AG 289	Ne stale stonden one my fete / bot I my / staffe have.	C H D	N V
AG 290	Makes youre mirrours / bi me, / men, bi youre trouthe:	P H	N P D N
AG 291	This schadowe in my schewere / schunte ye no while.	/	V H Z
AG 292	And now es dethe at my dore / that I / drede moste;	that H	V Z
AG 293	I ne wot wiche day ne when / ne / whate tyme he comes,	not	Q N H V
AG 294	Ne whedirwardes, ne whare, / ne / whatte to do aftire.	not	Q to V Z
AG 295	Bot many modyere / than I, / men one this molde,	C H	N P D N
AG 296	Hafe passed the pase / that I schall / passe sone,	that H X	V Z
AG 297	And I schall neven yow the names / of / nyne of the beste	P	A P D A
AG 298	That ever wy in this werlde / wiste appon erthe,	/	V P N
AG 299	That were conquerours full kene / and / kiddeste of other.	C	A P H
AG 300	The firste was Sir Ector / and / aldeste of tyme,	C	A P N
AG 301	When Troygens of Troye / were / tried to fighte	be	E to V
AG 302	With Menylawse the mody kynge / and / men out of Grece,	C	N P P N
AG 303	That thaire cité assegede / and / sayled it full yerne,	C	V H Z Z
AG 304	For Elayne his ownn quene / that / thereinn was halden,	that	Z be E
AG 305	That Pareschte the proude knyghte / paramours lovede.	/	Z V
AG 306	Sir Ectore was everous / als the / storye telles,	C D	N V
AG 307	And als clerkes in the cronycle cownten the sothe:	/	V D N
AG 308	Nowmbron thaym to nynetene / and / nyne mo by tale	C	N A P N
AG 309	Of kynges with crounes / he / killede with his handes,	H	V P D N
AG 310	And full fele other folke, / als / ferly were ellis.	C	A be Z
AG 311	Then Achilles his adversarye / undide with his werkes,	/	V P D N
AG 312	With wyles and no wirchipe / woundede hym to dethe	/	V H P N
AG 313	Als he tentid to a tulke / that he / tuke of were.	that H	V Z N
AG 314	And he was slayne for that slaughte / sleghely theraftir	/	Z Z
AG 315	With the wyles of a woman / as he had / wroghte byfore.	C H have	E Z
AG 316	Than Menylawse the mody kynge / hade / myrthe at his hert,	have	N P D N
AG 317	That Ectore hys enymy / siche / auntoure hade fallen,	D	N have E
AG 318	And with the Gregeis of Grece / he / girde over the walles,	H	V P D N
AG 319	The prowde paleys / dide he / pulle doun to the erthe,	V H	V Z P D N
AG 320	That was rialeste of araye / and / rycheste undir the heven.	C	A P D N
AG 321	And then the Trogens of Troye / teneden full sore,	/	V Z Z
AG 322	And semblen thaym full serely / and / sadly thay foughten.	C	Z H V
AG 323	Bot the lure at the laste / lighte appon Troye,	/	V P N
AG 324	For there Sir Priamus the prynce / put was to dethe,	/	E be P N
AG 325	And Pantasilia the quene / paste hym byfore.	/	V H Z
AG 326	Sir Troylus, a trewe knyghte / that / tristyly hade foghten,	that	Z have E
AG 327	Neptolemus, a noble knyghte / at / nede that wolde noghte fayle,	P	N that X not V
AG 328	Palamedes, a prise knyghte / and / preved in armes,	C	E P N
AG 329	Ulixes and Ercules, / that full / everrous were bothe,	that Z	A be Z
AG 330	And other fele of that ferde / fared of the same,	/	V P D A
AG 331	As Dittes and Dares / demeden togedir.	/	V Z
AG 332	Aftir this Sir Alysaunder / alle the / worlde wanne,	D D	N V
AG 333	Bothe the see and the sonde / and the / sadde erthe,	C D	A N
AG 334	The iles of the Oryent / to / Ercules boundes -	P	N N
AG 335	Ther Ely and Ennoke / ever hafe bene sythen,	/	Z have E Z
AG 336	And to the come of Antecriste / unclosede be thay never -	/	E be H Z
AG 337	And conquered Calcas / knyghtly theraftire,	/	Z Z
AG 338	Ther jentille Jazon the Grewe / wane the / flese of golde.	V D	N P N
AG 339	Then grathede he hym to Gadres / the / gates full righte,	D	N Z Z
AG 340	And there Sir Gadyfere the gude / the / Gaderayns assemblet,	D	N V
AG 341	And rode oute full ryally / to / rescowe the praye;	to	V D N
AG 342	And than Emenyduse hym mete / and / made hym full tame,	C	V H Z A
AG 343	And girdes Gadyfere to the grounde, / gronande full sore,	/	E Z Z
AG 344	And there that doughty was dede / and mekill / dole makede.	C D	N V
AG 345	Then Alixander the Emperour, / that / athell kynge hymselven,	that	A N H self
AG 346	Arayed hym for to ryde / with the / renkes that he hade:	P D	N that H V
AG 347	Ther was the mody Meneduse, / a / mane of Artage -	D	N P N
AG 348	He was Duke of that douth / and a / dussypere -	C D	N
AG 349	Sir Filot and Sir Florydase, / full / ferse men of armes,	Z	A N P N
AG 350	Sir Clyton and Sir Caulus, / knyghtis full noble,	/	N Z A

AG 351	And Sir Garsyene the gaye, / a / gude man of armes,	D	A N P N
AG 352	And Sir Lyncamoure thaym ledys / with a / lighte will.	P D	A N
AG 353	And than Sir Cassamus thaym kepide, / and the / kyng prayede	C D	N V
AG 354	To fare into Fesome / his / frendis to helpe;	D	N to V
AG 355	For one Carrus the kynge / was / comen owte of Inde,	be	E P P N
AG 356	And hade Fozome affrayede / and / Fozayne asegede	C	N E
AG 357	For Dame Fozonase the faire / that he of / lufe bysoughte.	that H P	N V
AG 358	The kynge agreed hym to goo / and / graythed hym sone,	C	V H Z
AG 359	In mendys of Amenyduse / that he / hade mysdone.	that H	have E
AG 360	Then ferde he towarde Facron / and by the / flode abydes,	C P D	N V
AG 361	And there he tighte up his tentis / and / taried there a while.	C	V Z Z
AG 362	There knyghtis full kenely/ caughten theire leve	/	V D N
AG 363	To fare into Fozayne / Dame / Fozonase to see,	D	N to V
AG 364	And Idores and Edease / all bydene;	/	Z Z
AG 365	And there Sir Porus and his prynces / to the / poo avowede.	P D	N V
AG 366	Was never speche byfore spoken / sped bettir aftir,	/	V Z Z
AG 367	For als thay demden to doo / thay / deden full even.	H	V Z Z
AG 368	For there Sir Porus the prynce / into the / prese thrynges,	P D	N V
AG 369	And bare the batelle one bake / and / abaschede thaym swythe.	C	V H Z
AG 370	And than the bolde Bawderayne / bowes to the kyng,	/	V P D N
AG 371	And brayde owte the brighte brande / owt of the / kynges hande,	P P D	N N
AG 372	And Florydase full freschely / foundes hym aftir,	/	V H P
AG 373	And hent the helme of his hede / and the / halse crakede.	C D	N V
AG 374	Than Sir Gadefere the gude / gripis his axe,	/	V D N
AG 375	And into the Indyans ofte / auntirs hym sone,	/	V H Z
AG 376	And thaire stiffe standerte / to / stikkes he hewes.	P	N H V
AG 377	And than Sir Cassamus the kene / Carrus releves:	/	N V
AG 378	When he was fallen appon fote / he / fet hym his stede.	H	V H D N
AG 379	And aftyr that Sir Cassamus / Sir / Carus he drepitt,	D	N H V
AG 380	And for that poynte Sir Porus / perset hym to dethe.	/	V H P N
AG 381	And than the Indyans ofte / uttire tham droghen,	/	Z H V
AG 382	And fledden faste of the felde / and / Alexandere suede.	C	N V
AG 383	When thay were skaterede and skayled / and / skyftede in sondere,	C	E Z
AG 384	Alyxandere oure athell kyng / ames hym to lenge,	/	V H to V
AG 385	And fares into Fozayne / festes to make,	/	N to V
AG 386	And weddis wy unto wy / that / wildede togedire.	that	V Z
AG 387	Sir Porus the pryce knyghte / moste / praysed of othere	Z	E P H
AG 388	Fonge Fozonase to fere, / and / fayne were thay bothe;	C	A be H Z
AG 389	The bolde Bawderayne of Baderose, / Sir / Cassayle hymselven,	D	N H self
AG 390	Bele Edyas the faire birde / bade he no nother;	/	V H Z
AG 391	And Sir Betys the beryne / the / beste of his tyme,	D	A P D N
AG 392	Idores his awnn lufe / aughte he hymselven;	/	V H H self
AG 393	Then iche lede hade the love / that he hade / longe yernede.	that H have	Z E
AG 394	Sir Alixander oure Emperour / ames hym to ryde,	/	V H to V
AG 395	And bewes towardes Babyloyne / with the / beryns that were levede,	P D	N that be E
AG 396	Bycause of Dame Candace / that / comfortheed hym moste;	that	V H Z
AG 397	And that cité he bysegede / and / assaylede it aftire,	C	V H Z
AG 398	While hym the gatis were yete / and / yolden the keyes.	C	E D N
AG 399	And there that pereles prynce / was / puysonede to dede,	be	E P A
AG 400	Thare he was dede of a drynke, / as / dole es to here,	C	N be to V
AG 401	That the curssede Cassander / in a / cowpe hym broghte.	P D	N H V
AG 402	He conquered with conqueste / kyngdomes twelve,	/	N A
AG 403	And dalte thaym to his dussypers / when he the / dethe tholede;	C H D	N V
AG 404	And thus the worthieste of this werlde / went to his ende.	/	V P D N
AG 405	Thane Sir Sezere hymselven, / that / Julyus was hatten,	that	N be E
AG 406	Alle Inglande he aughte / at his / awnn will,	P D	A N
AG 407	When the Bruyte in his booke / Bretayne it callede.	/	N H V
AG 408	The trewe toure of Londone / in his / tyme he makede,	P D	N H V
AG 409	And craftely the condithe / he / compaste thereaftire,	H	V Z
AG 410	And then he droghe hym to Dovire / and / duellyde there a while,	C	V Z Z
AG 411	And closede ther a castelle / with / cornells full heghe,	P	N Z A
AG 412	Warnestorede it full wiesely, / als / witnesses the sothe,	C	V D N
AG 413	For there es hony in that holde, / holden sythen his tyme.	/	V P D N
AG 414	Than rode he into Romayne / and / rawnsede it sone,	C	V H Z
AG 415	And Cassabalount the kynge / conquerede thereaftire.	/	V Z
AG 416	Then graythed he hym into Grece / and / gete hym belyve;	C	V H Z
AG 417	The semely cité Alexaunder / seside he theraftire;	/	V H Z
AG 418	Affrike and Arraby / and / Egipt the noble,	C	N D N(A)
AG 419	Surry and Sessoyne / sessede he togedir,	/	V H Z
AG 420	With alle the iles of the see / appon / iche a syde.	P	A D N
AG 421	Thies thre were paynymes full priste / and / passed alle othire.	C	V D H

AG 422	Of thre Jewes full gentill / jugge we aftir,	/	V H Z
AG 423	In the Olde Testament / as the / storye tellis,	C D	N V
AG 424	In a booke of the Bible / that / breves of kynges,	that	V Z N
AG 425	And renkes that rede / kane / Regum it callen.	X	N H V
AG 426	The firste was gentill Josue / that was a / Jewe noble,	that be D	N A
AG 427	Was heryet for his holynes / into / hevenriche.	P	N
AG 428	When Pharaoo had flayede / the / folkes of Israelle,	D	N P N
AG 429	Thay ranne into the Rede See / for / radde of hymselven,	P	A P H self
AG 430	And than Josue the Jewe / Jhesu he prayed	/	N H V
AG 431	That the peple myghte passe / unpereschede that tyme.	/	E Z
AG 432	And than the see sett / up appon / sydes twayne,	Z P	N A
AG 433	In manere of a mode walle / that / made were with hondes,	that	E be P N
AG 434	And thay soughten over the see / sownnde alle togedir.	/	A Z Z
AG 435	And Pharaoo full fersely / folowede thaym aftire,	/	V H P
AG 436	And efte Josue the Jewe / Jhesus he prayede,	/	N H V
AG 437	And the see sattillede / agayne and / sanke thaym thereinn -	Z C	V H Z
AG 438	A soppe for the Sathanas; / unsele have theire bones!	/	N V D N
AG 439	And aftire Josue the Jewe / full / gentilly hym bere,	Z	Z H V
AG 440	And conquerede kynges / and / kyngdomes twelve,	C	N A
AG 441	And was a conqueroure full kene / and moste / kyd in his tyme.	C Z	E P D N
AG 442	Than David the doughty / thurghe / Drightynes sonde	P	N N
AG 443	Was caughte from kepyng of schepe / and a / kyng made.	C D	N V
AG 444	The grete grym Golyas / he to / grounde broghte	H P	N V
AG 445	And sloughe hym with his slynge / and with no / sleghte ells.	C P D	N Z
AG 446	The stone thurghe his stele helme / stong into his brayne,	/	V P D N
AG 447	And he was dede of that dynt - / the / Devyll hafe that reche!	D	N V D V
AG 448	And than was David full dere / to / Drightyn hymselven,	P	N H self
AG 449	And was a prophete of pryse / and / praysed full ofte.	C	E Z Z
AG 450	Bot yit greved he his God / gretely theraftire,	/	Z Z
AG 451	For Urye his awnn knyghte / in / aventure he wysede	P	N H V
AG 452	There he haten at that dede, / as / dole es to here;	C	N be to V
AG 453	For Bersabee his awnn birde / was alle that / bale rerede.	be Z D	N E
AG 454	The gentill Judas Machabee / was a / Jewe kene,	be D	N A
AG 455	And thereto worthy in were / and / wyse of his dedis.	C	A P D N
AG 456	Antiochus and Appolyne / aythere he drepide,	/	Z H V
AG 457	And Nychanore, another kynge, / full / naytly thereaftire,	Z	Z Z
AG 458	And was a conqueour kydde / and / knawen with the beste.	C	E P D A
AG 459	Thies thre were Jewes full joly / and / justers full noble,	C	N Z A
AG 460	That full loughe have bene layde / sythen / gane full longe tyme:	C	V Z A N
AG 461	Of siche doughety doers looke / what es worthen.	/	Q be E
AG 462	Of the thre Cristen to carpe / couthely thereaftir,	/	Z Z
AG 463	That were conquerours full kene / and / kyngdomes wonnen,	C	N V
AG 464	Areste was Sir Arthure / and / eldeste of tyme,	C	A P N
AG 465	For alle Inglande he aughte / at his / awnn will,	P D	A N
AG 466	And was kynge of this kythe / and the / crowne hade.	C D	N V
AG 467	His courte was at Carlele / comonly holden,	/	Z E
AG 468	With renkes full ryalle / of his / Rownnde Table,	P D	A N
AG 469	That Merlyn with his maystries / made in his tyme,	/	V P D N
AG 470	And sett the Sege Perilous / so / semely one highte,	Z	Z Z
AG 471	There no segge scholde sitt / bot hym scholde / schame tyde,	C H X	N V
AG 472	Owthir dethe withinn the thirde daye / demed to hymselven,	/	E P H self
AG 473	Bot Sir Galade the gude / that the / gree wanne.	that D	N V
AG 474	There was Sir Launcelot de Lake / full / lusty in armes,	Z	A P N
AG 475	And Sir Gawayne the gude / that never / gome harmede,	that Z	N V
AG 476	Sir Askanore, Sir Ewayne, / Sir / Errake Fytz Lake,	D	N N N
AG 477	And Sir Kay the kene / and / kyd of his dedis,	C	E P D N
AG 478	Sir Percevalle de Galeys / that / preved had bene ofte,	that	E have been Z
AG 479	Mordrede and Bedwere, men / of / mekyll myghte,	P	A N
AG 480	And othere fele of that ferde, / folke of the beste.	/	N P D A
AG 481	Then Roystone the riche kyng, / full / rakill of his werkes,	Z	A P D N
AG 482	He made a blyot to his bride / of the / berdes of kynges,	P D	N P N
AG 483	And aughtilde Sir Arthures / berde one scholde be;	/	E H X be
AG 484	Bot Arthure oure athell kynge / another he thynkes,	/	H H V
AG 485	And faughte with hym in the felde / till he was / fey worthen.	C H be	A E
AG 486	And than Sir Arthure oure kyng / ames hym to ryde;	/	V H to V
AG 487	Uppon Sayn Michaells Mounte / mervaylles he wroghte,	/	N H V
AG 488	There a dragone he dreped / that / drede was full sore.	that	E be Z Z
AG 489	And than he sayled over the see / into / sere londes,	P	A N
AG 490	Whils alle the beryns of Bretayne / bewede hym to fote.	/	V H PRE N
AG 491	Gascoyne and Gyane / gatt he thereaftir,	/	V H Z
AG 492	And conquered kyngdomes / and / contrees full fele.	C	N Z A

The Parlement of the Thre Ages 157

AG	493	Than ames he into Inglonde / into his / awnn kythe;	P D	A N
AG	494	The gates towardes Glasshenbery / full / graythely he rydes.	Z	Z H V
AG	495	And ther Sir Mordrede hym mett / by a / more syde,	P D	N N
AG	496	And faughte with hym in the felde / to alle were / fey worthen,	P H be	A E
AG	497	Bot Arthur oure athell kyng / and / Wawayne his knyghte.	C	N D N
AG	498	And when the felde was flowen / and / fey bot thaymselven,	C	A P H self
AG	499	Than Arthure Sir Wawayne / athes by his trouthe	/	V P D N
AG	500	That he swiftely his swerde / scholde / swynge in the mere,	X	V P D N
AG	501	And whatt selcouthes he see / the / sothe scholde he telle.	D	N X H V
AG	502	And Sir Wawayne swith to the swerde / and / swange it in the mere,	C	V H P D N
AG	503	And ane hande by the hiltys / hastely it grippes,	/	Z H V
AG	504	And brawndeschet that brighte swerde / and / bere it awaye.	C	V H Z
AG	505	And Wawayne wondres of this werke, / and / wendes bylyve	C	V Z
AG	506	To his lorde there he hym lefte, / and / lokes abowte,	C	V Z
AG	507	And he ne wiste in alle this werlde / where he was bycomen.	/	Q H be E
AG	508	And then he hyghes hym in haste / and / hedis to the mere,	C	V P D N
AG	509	And seghe a bote from the banke / and / beryns thereinn.	C	N Z
AG	510	Thereinn was Sir Arthure / and / othire of his ferys,	C	H P D N
AG	511	And also Morgn la Faye that myche / couthe of sleghte.	/	V P N
AG	512	And ther ayther segge seghe othir laste, / for / sawe he hym no more.	C	V H H Z
AG	513	Sir Godfraye de Bolenn / siche / grace of God hade	D	N P N V
AG	514	That alle Romanye he rode / and / rawnnsunte it sone;	C	V H Z
AG	515	The Amorelle of Antyoche / aftire he drepit,	C	C H V
AG	516	That was called Corboraunt, / kiluarde of dedis;	/	A P N
AG	517	And aftir he was callede kynge / and the / crownn hade	C D	N V
AG	518	Of Jerasalem and of the Jewes / gentill togedir,	/	A Z
AG	519	And with the wirchipe of this werlde / he / went to his ende.	H	V P D N
AG	520	Than was Sir Cherlemayne chosen / chefe kynge of Fraunce,	/	A N P N
AG	521	With his doghty doussypers, / to / do als hym lykede;	to	V C H V
AG	522	Sir Rowlande the riche / and Duke / Raynere of Jene,	C D	N P N
AG	523	Olyver and Aubrye / and / Ogere Deauneys,	C	N N
AG	524	And Sir Naymes at the nede / that / never wolde fayle,	that	Z X V
AG	525	Turpyn and Terry, / two full / tryed lordes,	D Z	E N
AG	526	And Sir Sampsone hymselfe / of the / Mounte Ryalle,	P D	N N
AG	527	Sir Berarde de Moundres, / a / bolde beryn in armes,	D	A N P N
AG	528	And gud Sir Gy de Burgoyne, / full / gracyous of dedis;	Z	A P N
AG	529	The katur fitz Emowntez / were / kydde knyghtes alle,	be	E N Z
AG	530	And other moo than I may myne / or any / man elles.	C D	N Z
AG	531	And then Sir Cherlles the chefe / ches for to ryde,	/	V for to V
AG	532	And paste towardes Polborne / to / proven his strenghte;	to	V D N
AG	533	Salamadyne the Sowdane / he / sloghe with his handis,	H	V P D N
AG	534	And that cité he bysegede / and / saylede it full ofte.	C	V H Z Z
AG	535	While hym his yernynge was yett / and the / gates opynede;	C D	N V
AG	536	And Witthyne thaire waryed kynge / wolde nott abyde,	/	X not V
AG	537	Bot soghte into Sessoyne / socoure hym to gete;	/	N H to V
AG	538	And Cherlemayne oure chefe kynge / cheses into the burgh,	/	V P D N
AG	539	And Dame Nioles anone / he / name to hymselven,	H	V P H self
AG	540	And maried hir to Maundevyle / that scho hade / myche lovede;	that H have	Z V
AG	541	And spedd hym into hethyn Spayne / spedely thereaftire,	/	Z Z
AG	542	And fittilled hym by Flagott / faire for to loge.	/	Z for to V
AG	543	There Olyver the everous / aunterde hymselven,	/	V H self
AG	544	And faughte with Sir Ferambrace / and / fonge hym one were;	C	V H P N
AG	545	And than they fologhed hym in a fonte / and / Florence hym callede.	C	N H V
AG	546	And than moved he hym to Mawltryple / Sir / Balame to seche,	D	N to V
AG	547	And that Emperour at Egremorte / aftir he takes,	/	C H V
AG	548	And wolde hafe made Sir Balame / a / man of oure faythe,	D	N P D N
AG	549	And garte feche forthe / a / founte by-fore-with his eghne,	D	N P D N
AG	550	And he dispysede it and spitte / and / spournede it to the erthe,	C	V H P D N
AG	551	And one swyftely with a swerde / swapped of his hede.	/	V P D N
AG	552	And Dame Floripe the faire / was / cristened thereaftire,	be	E Z
AG	553	And kende thaym to the corownne / that / Criste had one hede,	that	N V P N
AG	554	And the nayles anone / nayttly thereaftire,	/	Z Z
AG	555	When he with passyoun and pyne / was / naylede one the rode.	be	E P D N
AG	556	And than those relikes so riche / redely he takes,	/	Z H V
AG	557	And at Sayne Denys he thaym dide, / and / duellyd there forever.	C	V Z Z
AG	558	And than bodworde unto Merchill / full / boldly he sendys,	Z	Z H V
AG	559	And bade hym Cristyne bycome / and one / Criste leve,	C P	N V
AG	560	Or he scholde bette doun his borowes / and / brenn hym thereinn;	C	V H Z
AG	561	And garte Genyone goo that erande / that / grevede thaym alle.	that	V H Z
AG	562	Thane rode he to Rowncyvale, / that / rewed hym aftire,	that	V H P
AG	563	There Sir Rowlande the ryche Duke / refte was his lyfe,	/	E be D N

AG	564	And Olyver his awnn fere / that / ay had bene trewe,	that	Z have been A
AG	565	And Sir Turpyn the newe, / that full / triste was at nede,	that Z	A be P N
AG	566	And full fele othir folke, / als / ferly were elles.	C	A be Z
AG	567	Then suede he the Sarazenes / seven yere and more,	/	A N C A
AG	568	And the Sowdane at Saragose / full / sothely he fyndis,	Z	Z H V
AG	569	And there he bett downn the burghe / and Sir / Merchill he tuke,	C D	N H V
AG	570	And that daye he dide hym to the dethe / als he had / wele servede.	C H have	Z V
AG	571	Bot by than his wyes were wery / and / woundede full many,	C	V Z A
AG	572	And he fared into France / to / fongen thaire riste,	to	V D N
AG	573	And neghede towarde Nerbone, / that / noyede thaym full sore.	that	V H Z Z
AG	574	And that cité he asseggede / appone / sere halfves,	P	A N
AG	575	While hym the gates were yette / and / yolden the keyes,	C	E D N
AG	576	And Emorye made Emperour / even at that tyme,	/	Z P D N
AG	577	To have and to holde / it to / hym and to his ayers.	H P	H C P D N
AG	578	And then thay ferden into Fraunce / to / fongen thaire ese,	to	V D N
AG	579	And at Sayn Denys he dyede / at his / dayes tyme.	P D	N N
AG	580	Now hafe I nevened yow the names / of / nyne of the beste	P	N P D A
AG	581	That ever were in this werlde / wiste appon erthe,	/	V P N
AG	582	And the doghtyeste of dedis / in thaire / dayes tyme,	P D	N N
AG	583	Bot doghetynes when dede comes / ne / dare noghte habyde.	not	V not V
AG	584	Of wyghes that were wysette / will ye now here,	/	X H Z V
AG	585	And I schall shortly yow schewe / and / schutt me ful sone.	C	V H Z Z
AG	586	Arestotle he was arste / in / Alexander tyme,	P	N N
AG	587	And was a fyne philozophire / and a / fynour noble,	C D	N A
AG	588	The grete Alexander to graythe / and / gete golde when hym liste,	C	V N C H V
AG	589	And multiplye metalles / with / mercurye watirs,	P	N N
AG	590	And with his ewe ardaunt / and / arseneke pouders,	C	N N
AG	591	With salpetir and sal-jeme / and / siche many othire,	C	A A H
AG	592	And menge his metalles / and / make fyne silvere,	C	V A N
AG	593	And was a blaunchere of the beste / thurgh / blaste of his fyre.	P	N P D N
AG	594	Then Virgill thurgh his vertus / verrayle he maket	/	Z H V
AG	595	Bodyes of brighte brasse / full / boldely to speke,	Z	Z to V
AG	596	To telle whate betydde / had and whate / betyde scholde,	have C Q	E X
AG	597	When Dioclesyane was dighte / to be / dere Emperour;	to be	A N
AG	598	Of Rome and of Romanye / the / rygalté he hade.	D	N H V
AG	599	Than Sir Salomon hymselfe / sett hym by hym one;	/	V H P H Z
AG	600	His bookes in the Bible / bothe bene togedirs.	/	both V Z
AG	601	That one of wisdome and of witt / wondirfully teches;	/	Z V
AG	602	His sampills and his sawes / bene / sett in the tother:	be	E P D H
AG	603	And he was the wyseste in witt / that ever / wonnede in erthe,	that Z	V P N
AG	604	And his techynges will bene trowede / whills the / werlde standes,	C D	N V
AG	605	Bothe with kynges and knyghtis / and / kaysers therinn.	C	N Z
AG	606	Merlyn was a mervayllous man / and / made many thynges,	C	V D N
AG	607	And naymely nygromancye / nayttede he ofte,	/	V H Z
AG	608	And graythed Galyan a boure / to / kepe hyr therin,	to	V H Z
AG	609	That no wy scholde hir wielde / ne / wynne from hymselven.	not	V P H self
AG	610	Theis were the wyseste in the worlde / of / witt that ever yitt were,	P	N that Z H be
AG	611	Bot dethe wondes for no witt / to / wende were hym lykes.	to	V Q H V
AG	612	Now of the prowdeste in presse / that / paramoures loveden	that	Z V
AG	613	I schalle titly yow telle / and / tary yow no lengere.	C	V H Z
AG	614	Amadase and Edoyne / in / erthe are thay bothe,	P	E be H Z
AG	615	That in golde and in grene / were / gaye in thaire tyme;	be	A P D N
AG	616	And Sir Sampsone hymselfe / full / savage of his dedys,	Z	A P D N
AG	617	And Dalyda his derelynge, / now / dethe has tham bothe.	Z	N V H Z
AG	618	Sir Ypomadonn de Poele / full / priste in his armes,	P	A P D N
AG	619	The faire Fere de Calabre, / now / faren are they bothe.	Z	E be H Z
AG	620	Generides the gentill / full / joly in his tyme,	Z	A P D N
AG	621	And Clarionas that was so clere, / are / bothe nowe bot erthe.	be	H Z P N
AG	622	Sir Eglamour of Artas / full / everous in armes,	Z	A P N
AG	623	And Cristabelle the clere maye / es / crept in hir grave,	be	E P D N
AG	624	And Sir Tristrem the trewe, / full / triste of hymselven,	Z	A P H self
AG	625	And Ysoute his awnn lufe, / in / erthe are thay bothe.	P	N V H Z
AG	626	Whare es now Dame Dido / was / qwene of Cartage?	be	N P N
AG	627	Dame Candace the comly / was / called quene of Babyloyne?	be	E N P N
AG	628	Penelopie that was price / and / passed alle othere,	C	V D H
AG	629	And Dame Gaynore the gaye, / nowe / graven are thay bothen,	Z	E be H Z
AG	630	And othere moo than I may mene / or any / man elles.	C D	N Z
AG	631	Sythen doughtynes when dede / comes ne / dare noghte habyde.	V not	V not V
AG	632	Ne dethe wondes for no witt / to / wende where hym lykes,	to	V Q H V
AG	633	And therto paramours and pride / puttes he full lowe,	/	V H Z Z
AG	634	Ne there es reches ne rent / may / rawnsone your lyves,	X	V D N

The Parlement of the Thre Ages 159

AG 635	Ne noghte es sekire to youreselfe / in / certayne bot dethe,	P	A P N
AG 636	And he es so uncertayne / that / sodaynly he comes,	that	Z H V
AG 637	Me thynke the wele of this werlde / worthes to noghte.	/	V P N
AG 638	Ecclesiastes the clerke / declares in his booke	/	V P D N
AG 639	Vanitas vanitatum et omnia vanitas,	L	(L)
AG 640	That alle es vayne and vanytes / and / vanyte es alle.	C	N be Z
AG 641	Forthi amendes youre mysse / whills ye are / men here,	C H be	N Z
AG 642	Quia in inferno nulla est redempcio -	L	(L)
AG 643	For in Helle es no helpe, / I / hete yow for sothe.	H	V H P N
AG 644	Als God in his gospelle / graythely yow teches,	/	Z H V
AG 645	Ite ostendite vos sacerdotibus,	L	(L)
AG 646	To schryve yow full schirle / and / schewe yow to prestis.	C	V H P N
AG 647	Et ecce omnia munda sunt vobis,	L	(L)
AG 648	And ye that wronge wroghte / schall / worthen full clene.	X	V Z A
AG 649	Thou man in thi medill elde / hafe / mynde whate I saye!	have	N Q H V
AG 650	I am thi sire and thou my sone, / the / sothe for to telle,	D	N for to V
AG 651	And he the sone of thiselfe, / that / sittis one the stede,	that	V P D N
AG 652	For Elde es sire of Midill Elde, / and / Midill Elde of Youthe.	C	A N P N
AG 653	And haves gud daye, for now I go - / to / grave moste me wende.	P	N X H V
AG 654	Dethe dynges one my dore, / I / dare no lengare byde."	H	V Z V
AG 655	When I had lenged and layne / a full / longe while,	D Z	A N
AG 656	I herde a bogle one a bonke / be / blowen full lowde.	be	E Z Z
AG 657	And I wakkened therwith / and / waytted me umbe.	C	V H Z
AG 658	Than the sone was sett / and / syled full loughe,	C	E Z Z
AG 659	And I founded appon fote / and / ferkede towarde townn.	C	V P N
AG 660	And in the monethe of Maye / thies / mirthes me tydde,	D	N H V
AG 661	Als I schurtted me in a schelfe / in the / schawes faire,	P D	N A
AG 662	And belde me in the birches / with / bewes full smale,	P	N Z A
AG 663	And lugede me in the leves / that / lighte were and grene.	that	A be C A
AG 664	There dere Drightyne this daye / dele us of thi blysse,	/	V H P D N
AG 665	And Marie that es mylde qwene / amende us of synn. Amen Amen.	/	V H P N

The Siege of Jerusalem

J	1	In Tiberyus tyme / the / trewe emperour	D	A N
J	2	Sir Sesar hym sulf / seysed in Rome	/	V P N
J	3	Whyle Pylat was prouost / vnder that / prince riche	P D	N A
J	4	And Iewen iustice / also in / Judeus londis	Z P	N N
J	5	Herodes vnder his emperie / as / heritage wolde	C	N X
J	6	Kyng of Galile ycalled / whan that / Crist deyed	C D	N V
J	7	They Sesar sakles / wer that oft / synne hatide	be that Z	N V
J	8	Throw Pylat pyned / he was and / put on the rode	H be C	E P D N
J	9	A pyler pyȝt / was doun vpon the / playn erthe	be Z P D	A N
J	10	His body bonden / ther to / beten with scourgis	Z to	V P N
J	11	Whyppes of quyrboyle / by-wente his white sides	/	V D A N
J	12	Til he al on rede blode ran / as / rayn [i]n the strete	C	N P D N
J	13	Suth stoked hym on a stole / with / styf Mannes hondis	P	A N N
J	14	Blyndfelled hym as a be / and / boffetis hym raȝte	C	N H V
J	15	Ȝif thou be prophete of pris / prophecie they sayde	/	N H V
J	16	Whiche [beryn] her aboute / bolled the laste	/	V D N
J	17	A thrange thornen croune / was / thraste on his hed	be	E P D N
J	18	Vmbe-casten hym with a cry / and on a / croys slowen	C P D	N E
J	19	For al the harme that he hadde / hasted he noȝt	/	V H not
J	20	On hem the vyleny to venge / that his / veynys brosten	that D	N V
J	21	Bot ay taried ouer the tyme / ȝif they / tourne wolde	C H	V X
J	22	Ȝaf hem space that hym spilide / they hit / spedde lyte	H H	V Z
J	23	Forty wynter as y fynde / and no / fewer ȝyrys	C D	A N
J	24	Or princes presed / in hem that hym to / pyne wroȝt	P H that H P	N V
J	25	Til hit tydde on a tyme / that / Tytus of Rome	that	N P N
J	26	That alle Gascoyne gate / and / Gyan the noble	C	N D A
J	27	Whyle noye noyet / hym in / Neroes tyme	H P	N N
J	28	He hadde a malady vn-meke / a-myd[dis] the face	/	P D N
J	29	The lyppe lyth on a lumpe / lyuered on the cheke	/	V P D N
J	30	So a canker vnclene / hit / clocheth to gedres	H	V Z
J	31	Also hit fader of flesche / is / ferly bytide	be	N E
J	32	A biker of waspen bees / bredde on his nose	/	V P D N
J	33	Hyued vpon his hed / he / hadde hem of ȝouthe	H	V H P N
J	34	And Waspasian was caled / the / waspene bees after	D	N N P
J	35	Was neuer syknes sorer / than this / sir tholed	C D	N V
J	36	For in a liter he lay / laser at Rome	/	A P N
J	37	Out of Galace was gon / to / glade hym a stounde	to	V H Z
J	38	For in that cuthe he was kyng / they he / car tholede	H H	N V
J	39	Nas ther no leche vpon lyue / this / lordes couth helpe	D	N X V
J	40	Ne no grace growyng to gayne / her / grym sores	H	A N
J	41	Now was ther on N[a]than / Neymes sone of Grec[e]	/	N N P N
J	42	That souȝt oft ouer the se / fram / cyte to other	P	N P H
J	43	Knewe contreys fele / kyngdomes manye	/	N A
J	44	And was a marener myche / and / marchaunt bothe	C	N Z
J	45	Sensceus out of Surye / sent hym to Rome	/	V H P N
J	46	To the athel Emperour / an / eraunde fram the Jewes	D	N P D N
J	47	Caled Nero by name / that hym to / noye wroȝt	that H P	N V
J	48	Of his tribute to telle / that they / withtake wolde	that H	V X
J	49	Nathan toward Nero / nome on his way	/	V P D N
J	50	Ouer the Grekys grounde / myd the / grym ythes	P D	A N
J	51	An heye setteth the sayl / ouer the / [salte] water	P D	A N
J	52	And with a dromound on the deep / drof on faste	/	V Z Z
J	53	The wolco[n] wanned / anon and the / water skeweth	Z C D	N V
J	54	Cloudes clateren gon / as they / cleue wolde	C H	V X
J	55	The racke myd a rede wynde / roos on the myddel	/	V P D N
J	56	And sone sette on the se / out of the / south side	P P D	N N
J	57	Blewe on the brode se / bolned vp harde	/	V Z Z
J	58	Nathannys naue / a-non on [the] / north dryueth	Z P D	N V
J	59	So the wedour and the wynd / on the / water metyn	P D	N V
J	60	That alle hurtled on an hepe / that the / helm ȝemyd	that D	N V
J	61	Nathan flatte for ferde / and / ful vnder hacchys	C	Z P N
J	62	Lete the wedour and the wynde / worthe as hit lyked	/	V C H V
J	63	The schip scher vpon schore / schot froward Rome	/	V P N
J	64	Toward vncouth costes / keuereth the ythes	/	V D N
J	65	Rapis vnradly / vmbe / ragged tourres	P	E N
J	66	The brode sail at o brayd / to-bresteth a twynne	/	V Z

The Siege of Jerusalem

J	67	That on ende of the sschip / was / ay toward heuen	be	Z P N
J	68	That other doun in the deep / as alle / drenche wolde	C H	V X
J	69	Ouer wilde wawes he wende / as alle / walte scholde	C H	V X
J	70	St[a]rke stremes throw / yn / stormes and wyndes	P	N C N
J	71	With mychel langour atte laste / as our / lord wolde	C D	N X
J	72	Alle was born at a by[rre] / to / Burdewes hauene	P	N N
J	73	By that wer bernes atte banke / barouns and kny3tes	/	N C N
J	74	And [citezeins] of the sy3t / selcouth [hem] tho3t	/	A H V
J	75	That euer barge other bot / or / berne vpon lyue	C	N P N
J	76	Vnpersched passed / hadde the / peryles wer so many	had D	N be Z A
J	77	They token hym to Titus / for he the / tonge couthe	C H D	N V
J	78	And he [hem] fraynes how fer / the / flode hadde yferked	D	N had E
J	79	Sir out of Surre / he / seide y am come	H	V H be E
J	80	To Nero sondis-man sent / the / [seygnour] of Rome	D	N P N
J	81	Ffram Sensceus his seriant / with / certayn leteres	P	A N
J	82	That is iustise and iuge / of / Jewen lawe	P	A N
J	83	Me wer leuer at that londe / le[ngede] that y wer	/	E that H be
J	84	Than alle the gold other good / that euer / god made	that Z	N V
J	85	The kyng in to conseyl / calleth hym sone	/	V H Z
J	86	And saide Canste thou any cur / or / craft vpon erthe	C	N P N
J	87	To softe the grete sore / that / sitteth on my cheke	that	V P D N
J	88	And y schal the redly rewarde / and to / Rome sende	C P	N V
J	89	Nathan nyckes hym with nay / sayde he / non couthe	V H	not V
J	90	Bot wer thou kyng in that kuththe / ther that / Crist deyed	Q that	N V
J	91	Ther is a worlich wif / a / womman ful clene	D	N Z A
J	92	That hath softyng and salue / for eche / sore out	P D	N Z
J	93	Telle me tyt quoth Titus / and the schal / tyde better	C H X	V Z
J	94	What medecyn is most / that that / may vseth	that that	N V
J	95	Whether gommes other graces / or any / goode drenches	C D	A N
J	96	Other chauntementes or charmes / y / charge the to say	H	V H to V
J	97	Nay non of tho quoth Nathan / bot / now wole y [telle]	C	Z X H V
J	98	Ther was a lede in our londe / while he / lif hadde	C H	N V
J	99	Preued for a prophete / throw / preysed dedes	P	E N
J	100	And born in Bethleem one by / of a / burde schene	P D	N A
J	101	And 3o a mayde vnmarred / that neuer / man touched	that Z	N V
J	102	As clene as clef / ther / cristalle sprynges	D	N N
J	103	Without hosebondes helpe / saue the / holy goste	P D	A N
J	104	A kyng and a knaue child / 3o / conceyued at ere	H	V P N
J	105	A touche of the trinyte / touched hir hadde	/	V D N
J	106	Thre persones in o place / preued to gedres	/	E Z
J	107	Eche grayn is o god / and o / god bot alle	C D	N P H
J	108	And alle thre ben bot one / as / eldres vs tellen	C	N H V
J	109	The first is the fader / that / fourmed was neuer	that	E be Z
J	110	The secunde is the sone / of his / sede growyn	P D	N E
J	111	The thridde in heuen myd hem / is the / holy goste	be D	A N
J	112	Nether merked ne made / bot / mene fram hem passyth	but	N P H V
J	113	Alle ben they endeles / and / euer of o my3t	C	Z P D N
J	114	And weren endeles euer / [er] the / world was bygonne	C D	N be E
J	115	As sone was the sone / as the / self fader	P D	self N
J	116	The holy goste with hem / hadde they euer	/	V H Z
J	117	The secunde persone the sone / sent was to erthe	/	E be P N
J	118	To take careynes kynde / of a / clene mayde	P D	A N
J	119	And so vnknowen he came / caytifes to helpe	/	N to V
J	120	And wro3t wondres ynowe ay / tille he / wo driede	C H	N V
J	121	Wyne he wro3t of water / at o / word ene	P D	N Z
J	122	Ten lasares at a logge / he / leched at enys	H	V Z
J	123	Pyned myd p[ar]il[sye] / he / putte to hele	H	V P N
J	124	And ded men fro the deth / eche / day rered	D	N V
J	125	Croked and cancred / he / keuered hem alle	H	V H Z
J	126	Both the dombe and the deue / myd his / der wordes	P D	A N
J	127	Dide myracles mo / than y in / mynde haue	than H P	N V
J	128	Nis no clerk with countours / couthe aluendel rekene	/	X N V
J	129	Fyf thousand of folke / is / ferr to here	be	A to V
J	130	With two fisches he fedde / and / fif ber loues	C	N Z V
J	131	That eche freke hadde his fulle / and 3it / ferre leued	C H	Z V
J	132	Of brede and of broken mete / basckettes twelue	/	N A
J	133	Ther suwed hym out of an cite / [seuenty] and twey	/	N C N
J	134	To do what he dempte / disciples wer hoten	D	N be E
J	135	Hem to citees he sende / his / sawes to preche	D	N to V
J	136	Ay by two and by two / til hy wer a-twynne	/	C H be Z
J	137	Hym suwed of an-other cite / semeliche twelue	/	Z N

J	138	Pore men and noȝt prute / apostelles wer hoten	/	N be E
J	139	That of cay[ti]fes he ches / holy churche to encreasche	/	A N to V
J	140	The out-wale of this worlde / this / wer her names	D	be D N
J	141	Peter James and Jon / and / Jacob the ferthe	C	N D N
J	142	And the fifthe of his felawys / Phelip was hoten	/	N be E
J	143	The sixte Symond was caled / and the / seueth eke	C D	N Z
J	144	Bertholomewe that his bone / neuer / breke nolde	Z	V X
J	145	The eyȝt man was Mathu / that is / myche yloued	that be	Z E
J	146	Tadde and Tomas / her ben / ten euen	Z be	N A
J	147	And Andreu the elleueth / that / auntred hym myche	that	V H Z
J	148	Byfor princes to preche / was / Petrus brother	be	N N
J	149	The laste man was vnlele / and / luther of his dedis	C	A P D N
J	150	Judas that Jesu Crist / to the / Jewes solde	P D	N V
J	151	Suth hymsulf he slowe / for / sorow of that dede	P	N P D N
J	152	His body on a balwe tree / to-breste on the myddel	/	V P D N
J	153	Whan Crist hadde heried helle / and was [to] / heuen passed	C be to	N V
J	154	For that mansed man / Mathie they chossyn	/	N H V
J	155	Ȝit vnbaptized wer bothe / Barnabe and Poule	/	N C N
J	156	And noȝt knewen of Crist / bot / comen sone after	C	V Z Z
J	157	The princes and the prelates / aȝen the / paske tyme	Z D	N N
J	158	Alle thei hadde hym in hate / for his / holy werkes	P D	A N
J	159	Hit was a doylful dede / whan they his / deth caste	C H D	N V
J	160	Throw Pilat pyned / he was the / prouost of Rome	H be D	A P N
J	161	And that worliche wif / that arst / was ynempned	that Z	be E
J	162	Hath his visage in hir veil / Veronyk ȝo hatte	/	N H V
J	163	Peynted priuely and playn / that no / poynt wanteth	that D	N V
J	164	For loue he left / hit hir til hir / lyues ende	H H C D	N V
J	165	Ther is no gome [o]n this [grounde] / that is / grym wounded	that be	Z E
J	166	Meselry ne meschef / ne / man vpon erthe	D	N P N
J	167	That kneleth doun to that cloth / and on / Crist leueth	C P	N V
J	168	Bot alle hapneth to hele / in [ane] / hand whyle	P D	N N
J	169	At Rome reyned the emperour / quoth the / kyng riche than	V D	N A Z
J	170	Cesar synful wrecche / that / sent hym fram Rome	that	V H P N
J	171	Why nadde thy lycam be leyd / low vnder erthe	/	E Z P N
J	172	Whan Pilat prouost / was made suche a / prince to jugge	be E D D	N to V
J	173	And or his wordes wer [well] / wonne to the ende	/	V P D N
J	174	The canker that the kyng / hadde / clenly was heled	had	Z be E
J	175	With out faute the face / of / flesche and of hyde	P	N C P N
J	176	As newe as the nebbe / that / neuer was wemmyd	that	Z be E
J	177	A corteys Crist / seide / kyng riche than	V D	N A Z
J	178	Was neuer worke that y wroȝt / worthy the to telle	/	A H to V
J	179	Ne dede that y haue don / bot thy / deth mened	C D	N E
J	180	Ne neuer sey the in siȝt / goddis sone der	/	N N A
J	181	Bot now [be] bayne [to] my bone / blessed lord	/	E N
J	182	To stire Nero with noye / and / newen hir sorowe	C	V D N
J	183	And y schal buske me boun / hem / bale to wyrche	H	A to V
J	184	To do the deueles of dawe / and thy / deth venge	C D	N V
J	185	Telle me tit quoth Titus / what / tokne he lafte	Q	N H V
J	186	To hem that knew hym for Crist / and his / crafte leued	C D	N V
J	187	Nempne the trinyte by name / quoth / Nathan at thries	V	N P Z
J	188	And ther myd baptemed be / in / blessed water	P	E N
J	189	Forth they fetten a font / and / foulled hym ther	C	V H Z
J	190	Made hym cristen kyng / that for / Crist werred	that P	N be
J	191	Corrours in to eche coste / than the / cours nomen	Z D	N V
J	192	And alle his baronage broȝt / to / Burdewes hauen	P	N N
J	193	Suth with the sondes-man / he / [s]ouȝt to Rome	H	V P N
J	194	The ferly and the fair cure / his / fader to schewe	D	N to V
J	195	And he gronnand glad / grete god thanked	/	A N V
J	196	And loude criande on Crist / carped and saide	/	V C V
J	197	Worthy wemlese God / in / whom y byleue	P	H H V
J	198	[Als] thou in Bethleem was born / of a / bryȝt mayde	P D	A N
J	199	Sende me hele of my hurt / and / heyly y a-fowe	C	Z H V
J	200	To be ded for thy deth / bot hit be / der ȝolden	C H be	Z E
J	201	That tyme peter was pope / and / preched in rome	C	V P N
J	202	The lawe and the lore / that our / byleue asketh	that D	N V
J	203	Folowed faste on the folke / and to the / fayth tourned	C P D	N V
J	204	And crist wroȝt for that wye / wondres ynow	/	N A
J	205	Ther of waspasian was war / that the / waspys hadde	that D	N V
J	206	Sone sendeth / hym to and the / sothe tolde	H P C D	N V
J	207	Of crist and the kerchef / that / keuered the sike	that	V D N(A)
J	208	As nathan neymes sone seide / that [was to / nero] come	that be P	N V

The Siege of Jerusalem

J	209	Than to consayl was called / the / knyȝtes of rome	D		N P N
J	210	And assenteden sone / to / sende messages	P		V N
J	211	Twenti knyȝtes wer cud / the / ker[ch]yf to fecche	D		N to V
J	212	And asked trewes of the emperour / that / erand to done	that		N to V
J	213	Ac without tribute or trewes / tenfulle wyes	/		A N
J	214	The knyȝtes with the kerchef / comen ful blyue	/		V Z Z
J	215	The pope ȝaf pardoun / to hem that / passed ther aȝens	P H	that	V D N
J	216	With processioun and pres / princes and dukes	/		N C N
J	217	And whan the womman was war / that the / wede owede	that D		N V
J	218	[Of] seint peter the pope / ȝo / platte to the grounde	H		V P D N
J	219	Vmbefelde his fete / and to the / freke saide	C P D		N V
J	220	Of this kerchef and my cors / the / kepyng y the take	D		G H H V
J	221	Than bygan the burne / biterly to wepe	/		Z to V
J	222	For the doylful deth of / of his / der mayster	P D		A N
J	223	And longe stode in the stede / or he / stynte myȝt	C H		V X
J	224	Whan he vnclosed the clothe / that / cristes body touched	that		N N V
J	225	The wede fram the womman / [he] / warpe atte laste	H		V Z
J	226	Receyued hit myd reuerence / and / rennande teris	C		G N
J	227	Out of the place myd pres / they / passed on swythe	H		V Z Z
J	228	And ay held hit on hey / that alle / byhold myȝt	that H		V X
J	229	Than twelf barouns bolde / the / emperour bade wende	D		N V V
J	230	And the pope departe / fram the / pople faste	P D		N Z
J	231	Veronyk and the vail / waspasian they broȝt	/		N H V
J	232	And seint peter the pope / presented bothe	/		V Z
J	233	Bot a ferly byfelle / forth myd hem alle	/		Z P H Z
J	234	In her temple bytidde / tenful thynges	/		A V
J	235	The mahound and the mametes / tomortled to peces	/		V P N
J	236	And al tocrased as the cloth / throȝ the / kirke passed	P D		N V
J	237	Into the palice with the printe / than the / pope ȝede	C D		N V
J	238	Knyȝtes kepten the clothe / and on / knees fallen	C P		N V
J	239	A flauour flambeth / ther fro they / felleden hit alle	Q P H		V H A
J	240	Was neuer odour ne eyr / vpon / erthe swetter	P		N A
J	241	The kerchef clansed hit self / and so / cler wexed	C Z		A V
J	242	Myȝt no lede on hit loke / for / liȝt that hit schewed	P		N that H V
J	243	As hit aproched to the prince / he / put vp his hed	H		V Z D N
J	244	For comfort of the cloth / he / cried wel loude	H		V Z Z
J	245	Lo lordlynges / her the / lyknesse of crist	D D		N P N
J	246	Of whom my botnyng y bidde / for his / bitter woundis	P D		A N
J	247	Than was wepyng and wo / and / wryngyng of hondis	C		N(V) P N
J	248	With loude dyn and dit / for / doil of hym one	P		N P H Z
J	249	The pope availed the vaile / and his / visage touched	C D		N V
J	250	The body suth al aboute / blessed hit thrye	/		V H Z
J	251	The waspys wenten away / and alle the / wo after	C D D		N P
J	252	That er lasar was longe / lyȝtter was neuere	/		A be Z
J	253	Than was pypyng and play / his / pyne was awey	D		N be Z
J	254	They ȝelden grace to god / this two / grete lordes	D D		A N
J	255	The kerchef arieth fram alle / and in the / eyr hangyth	C P D		N V
J	256	That the symple myȝt hit se / in to / soper tyme	P P		N N
J	257	The veronycle after veronyk / waspasian hit called	/		N H V
J	258	Garde hit gayly agysen / in / gold and in seluere	P		N C P N
J	259	ȝit is the visage in the vail / as / veronyk hym broȝt	C		N H V
J	260	The romaynes at rome / a / relyk hit holden	D		N H V
J	261	This whyle nero hadde noye / and non / nyȝtes reste	C D		N N
J	262	For his tribute was [tynt] / as / nathan hit broȝte	C		N E had
J	263	He commaundith knyȝtes to come / consail to holde	/		N to V
J	264	Erles and alle men / the / emperour aboute	D		N P
J	265	Assembled the senatours / sone vpon haste	/		Z Z
J	266	To iugge who jewes / myȝt best vpon the / jewys take	X Z P D		N V
J	267	And alle demeden by dome / tho / dukes to wende	D		N to V
J	268	That wer cured throw crist / that they on / croys slowen	that H P		N V
J	269	That on waspasian was / of the / wyes twey	P D		N A
J	270	That the trauail vndertoke / and / titus an other	C		N D H
J	271	A bold burne on a blonke / and of his / body comyn	C P D		N V
J	272	No ferther sib to hymself / bot his / sone der	P D		N A
J	273	Crouned kynges bothe / and mychel / crist loued	C Z		N V
J	274	That hadde hem [g]euen of his grace / and her / grem stroyed	C D		N E
J	275	Moste thei hadde hit in hert / her / hestes to kepe	D		N to V
J	276	And her forwardis to fulfille / that thei / byfor made	that H		Z V
J	277	Than was rotlyng in rome / robbyng of brynnyes	/		N(V) P N
J	278	Schewyng of scharpe [stele] / scheldes ydressed	/		N E
J	279	Lauȝte leue at that lord / leften his sygne	/		V D N

J	280	A grete dragoun of gold / and alle the / [g]lyng folwed	C D D	N V
J	281	By that schippis wer schred / yschot on the depe	/	E P D A
J	282	Takled and atired / on / talterande ythes	P	G N
J	283	Ffresch water and wyn / wounden yn faste	/	E Z
J	284	And stof of alle maner store / that hem / strengthe scholde	that H	V X
J	285	Ther wer floynes a flot / farcostes many	/	N A
J	286	Cogges and crayers / ycasteled alle	/	E Z
J	287	Galees of grete streyngthe / with / golden fanes	P	A N
J	288	[the brede] on the brod se / aboute four myle	/	P A N
J	289	They ty3ten vp tal-sail / whan the / tide asked	C D	N V
J	290	Hadde byr at the bake / and the / bonke lefte	C D	N V
J	291	Sou3te ouer the se / with / soudeours manye	P	N A
J	292	And [ioyned in to] port jaf / in / judeis londys	P	N N
J	293	Suree cesaris londe / thou may / seken euer	H X	V Z
J	294	Ful mychel wo m[o]n be wro3te / in thy / [w]lonk tounes	P D	A N
J	295	Cytees vnder s[yon] / now is 3our / sorow uppe	Z be D	N Z
J	296	The deth of the dereworth crist / der schal be 3olden	/	Z X be E
J	297	Now is bethleem thy bost / ybro3t to an ende	/	E P D N
J	298	Jerusalem and ierico / for / juggyd wrecchys	P	E N
J	299	Schal neuer kyng of 3our kynde / with / croune be ynoyntid	P	N be E
J	300	Ne jewe for jesu sake / [i]ouke in 3ou more	/	V P H Z
J	301	They setten vpon eche side / surrie withyn	/	N P
J	302	Brente ay at the bak / and [all] / bar laften	C H	A V
J	303	Was no3t bot roryng and r[u]th / in alle the / riche tounne	P D D	A N
J	304	And red laschyng lye / alle the / londe ouer	D D	N P
J	305	Token tour and tour / teldes ful fele	/	N Z A
J	306	Brosten 3ates of brass / and many / borwe wonnen	C D	N V
J	307	Holy the hethen here / hewyn to grounde	/	V P N
J	308	Both in bent and in borwe / that / abide wolde	that	V X
J	309	The jewes to ierusalem / th[ere] / josephus dwelde	Q	N V
J	310	Flowen as the foule doth / that / faucoun wolde strike	that	N X V
J	311	A cite vnder syon / sett was ful noble	/	E be Z Z
J	312	With many toret and tour / that / toun to defende	D	N to V
J	313	Princes and prelates / and / poreil of the londe	C	N P D N
J	314	Clerkes and comens / of / contrees aboute	P	N Z
J	315	Wer schacked to that cite / sacrifice to make	/	N to V
J	316	At paske tyme as preched / hem / prestes of the lawe	H	N P D N
J	317	Many swykel at the sweng / to the / swerd 3ede	P D	N V
J	318	For penyes passed / non tho3 he / pay wolde	H C H	V X
J	319	Bot diden alle to the dethe / and / drowen hem after	C	V H P
J	320	With engynes to jerusalem / ther / jewes wer thykke	Q	N be A
J	321	They sette sadly a sege / the / cite alle aboute	D	N Z Z
J	322	Pi3ten pauelouns / doun of / pallen webbes	Z P	E N
J	323	With ropis of riche silk / raysen vp swythe	/	V Z Z
J	324	Grete tentis as a toun / of / torke[is] clothys	P	A N
J	325	Choppyn ouer the cheuentayns / with / charboklis four	P	N A
J	326	A gay egle of gold / on a / gilde appul	P D	A N
J	327	With grete dragouns grym / alle in / gold wro3te	Z P	N E
J	328	Lyk to lyouns / also / lyande thervnder	Z	G Z
J	329	Paled and paynted / the / paueloun was vmbe	D	N be Z
J	330	Stoked ful of storijs / strayned myd armys	/	E P N
J	331	Of quaynte colour to know / kerneld alofte	/	N Z
J	332	An hundred stondyng on stage / in that / stede one	P D	N A
J	333	Toured with torettes / was the / tente thanne	be D	N Z
J	334	Suth britaged aboute / bri3t to byholde	/	A to V
J	335	Er alle the sege was sette / 3it of the / cite comyn	Z P D	N E
J	336	Messengeres wer made / fram / maistres of the lawe	P	N P D N
J	337	To the chef cheuentayn / they / chosen her wey	H	V D N
J	338	Deden mekly by mouthe / her / message attonys	D	N Z
J	339	Sayen the cite hath [vs] sent / to / serche 3our wille	to	V D N
J	340	To here the cause of 3our comyng / [and what] 3e / coueyte wolde	C Q H	V X
J	341	Waspasian no word / to the / wyes schewed	P D	N V
J	342	Bot sendeth sondismen / a3en twelf / siker kny3tes	Z D	A N
J	343	[gert hem greithely] to go / and the / gomes telle	C D	N V
J	344	That alle the cause of her com[e] / was / crist forto venge	be	N for to V
J	345	Sayth y bidde hem be boun / bishopes and other	/	N C H
J	346	Tomorow or [mydday] / [alle / modur-nakyd]	D	A E
J	347	Vp her 3ates to 3elde / with / 3erdes an hande	P	N P N
J	348	Eche whi3t in a white scherte / and no / wede ellys	C D	N Z
J	349	Jewyse for iesu crist / by / juggemente to take	P	N to V
J	350	And make hem come that iesu crist / thro3 / conseil bytrayede	P	N V

J	351	Or y to the walles schal wende / and / walten alle ouere	C	V Z Z
J	352	Schal no ston vpon ston / stonde by y passe	/	V C H V
J	353	This sondismen sadly / to the / cite ȝede	P D	N V
J	354	Ther the lordes of the londe / lent weren alle	/	E be Z
J	355	Tit tolden her tale / and / wonder towe made	C	Z A V
J	356	Of crist and of cayphas / and how they / come scholde	C Q H	V X
J	357	And when the knyȝtes of crist / carpyn bygonn	/	V V
J	358	The jewes token alle twelf / without / tale mor	P	N A
J	359	Her hondis bounden at her bak / with / borden stauys	P	A N
J	360	And of flocken her fa[x] / and her / fair berdis	C D	A N
J	361	Made hem naked as a nedel / to the / nether houe	P D	A N
J	362	Her visages blecken with bleche / and al the / body after	C D D	N P
J	363	Suth knyt with a corde / to eche / knyȝtes swer	P D	N N
J	364	A chese and charged / hem her / chyuentayn to ber	H D	N to V
J	365	Sayth vnbuxum we beth / his / biddyng to ȝete	D	G to V
J	366	Ne noȝt dreden his dom / his / deth haue we atled	D	N have H E
J	367	He schal vs fynde in the felde / ne no / ferr seke	not not	Z V
J	368	Tomorowe pryme or hit passe / and so ȝour / prince tellith	C Z D	N V
J	369	The burnes busken out of burwe / bounden alle twelf	/	V A N
J	370	Aȝen message to make / fram the / maister jewes	P D	N N
J	371	Was neuer waspasian so wrothe / as whan the / wyes come	C C D	N V
J	372	That wer scorned and schende / vpon / schame wyse	P	N N
J	373	This knyȝtes byfor the kyng / vpon / knees fallen	P	N V
J	374	And tolden the tale / as hit / tid hadde	C H	E have
J	375	Of thy manace ne thy myȝt / they / make bot lyte	H	V C A
J	376	Thus ben we tourned of our tyre / in / tokne of the sothe	P	N P D N
J	377	And bounden for our bolde speche / the / batail they willeth	D	N H V
J	378	Tomorowe prime or hit passe / they / put hit no ferre	H	V H Z
J	379	Hit schal be satled on thy-self / the / same that thou atlest	D	N that H V
J	380	Thus han they certifiet the [to saye] / and / sende the this cheses	C	V H D N
J	381	Wode wedande wroth / waspasian was thanne	/	N be Z
J	382	Layde wecche to the walle / and / warned in haste	C	V Z
J	383	That alle maner of men / in the / morowe scholde	P D	N X
J	384	Be sone after the sonne / assembled in the felde	/	V P D N
J	385	He streyȝt up a standard / in a / stour wyse	P D	A N
J	386	Bild as a belfray / bretful of wepne	/	A P N
J	387	Whan oȝt fauted in the folke / that to the / feld longed	that P D	N V
J	388	Atte the belfray to be / botnyng to fynde	/	N to V
J	389	A dragoun was dressed / drawyn a lofte	/	E Z
J	390	Wyde gapande of gold / gomes to swelwe	/	N to V
J	391	With arwes armed in the mouthe / and / also he hadde	C	Z H V
J	392	A fauch[ou]n vnder his feet / with / four kene bladdys	P	A A N
J	393	Therof the poyntes wer piȝt / in / partyis four	P	N A
J	394	Of this wlonfulle wor[l]de / ther thei / werr fondyn	Q H	N V
J	395	In forbesyn to the folke / this / fauchoun hengeth	D	N V
J	396	That they hadde wonnen with [werre] / al the / world riche	D D	N A
J	397	A bal of brennande gold / the / beste was on sette	D	A be Z E
J	398	His taille trayled / ther aboute that / tourne scholde he neuere	Q Z that	V X H Z
J	399	Whan he was lifte vp[his liche] / ther the / lord werred	Q D	N V
J	400	Bot ay lokande on the londe / tille that al / lauȝte wer	C that H	E be
J	401	Ther by the cite myȝt se / no / setlyng wolde rise	D	G X V
J	402	Ne no trete of no trewes / bot the / toun ȝelde	C D	N V
J	403	Or ride on the romayns / for they han her / rede take	C H have D	N V
J	404	Ther britned to be / or the / [burghe] wynne	C D	N V
J	405	His wynges [brighte wer and brade] / boun forto flee	/	A for to V
J	406	With belles bordored aboute / al of / briȝt seluere	Z P	A N
J	407	Redy whan ouȝte runnen / to / rynge ful loude	to	V Z Z
J	408	With eche [wap] of a [wynde] / that to the / wynges sprongyn	that P D	N V
J	409	Ibrytaged aboute / the / belfray was thanne	D	N be Z
J	410	With a tenful tour / that ouer the / toun gawged	that Z D	N V
J	411	The b[est] by the briȝtnesse / burnes myȝt knowe	/	N X V
J	412	Four myle ther fro / so the / feldes schonen	C D	N V
J	413	And on eche pomel wer pyȝt / penseles hyȝe	/	N A
J	414	Of selke and sendel / with / seluere ybetyn	P	N E
J	415	Hit glitered as gled fur / ful of / gold riche	A C	N A
J	416	Ouer al the cite to se / as the / sonne bemys	P D	N N
J	417	Byfor the four ȝates / he / formes to lenge	H	V to V
J	418	Sixtene thousand by somme / while the / sege lasteth	C D	N V
J	419	Sette ward [to] the walles / that noȝt / awey scaped	that not	Z V
J	420	Sixe thousand in sercle / the / cite alle aboute	D	N Z P
J	421	Was noȝt while the nyȝt laste / bot / nehyng of stedis	C	G P N

J	422	Strogelyng in stele wede / and / stuffyng of helmes	C	G P N
J	423	With armyng of olyfauntes / and / other arwe bestes	C	A A N
J	424	Aȝen the cristen to come / with / castels on bake	P	N P N
J	425	Waspasya[n] in stele wede / and his / wyes alle	C D	N Z
J	426	Weren diȝt forth by day / and / drowen to the vale	C	V P D N
J	427	Of josophat ther jesu crist / schal / juggen alle thinges	X	V D N
J	428	Bigly batayled / hym ther to / bide[n] this other	H Z to	V D H
J	429	The fauward titus toke / to / telle vpon ferste	to	V P Z
J	430	With six thousand soudiours / assyned for the nones	/	E Z
J	431	And mony in the mydward wer / merked to lenge	/	E to V
J	432	Ther waspasian was / with / princes and dukes	P	N C N
J	433	And sixtene thousand in the thridde / with a / thryuande knyȝt	P D	G N
J	434	Sir sabyn of surrie / a / siker man of armes	D	A N P N
J	435	That prince was of prouynce / and michel / peple ladde	C D	N V
J	436	Fourty hundred in helmes / and / harnays to schewe	C	N to V
J	437	And ten thousand atte tail / at the / tentis lafte	P D	N V
J	438	Hors and harnays / fram / harmyng to kepe	P	N to V
J	439	By that bemys on the burwe / blowen ful loude	/	V Z Z
J	440	And baners beden / hem forth now / blesse vs our lorde	H Z Z	V H D N
J	441	The jewes assembled wer sone / and of the / cite come	C P D	N V
J	442	An hundred thousand on hors / with / hamberkes atired	P	N E
J	443	Without folke vpon fot / at the / four ȝates	P D	A N
J	444	That preset to the place / with / pauyes on hande	P	N P N
J	445	Fyf and twenti olyfauntes / defensable bestes	/	A N
J	446	With brode castels on bak / out of / burwe come	P P	N V
J	447	And on eche olyfaunte / armed men manye	/	E N A
J	448	Ay an hundred an hey / an / hundred withyn	D	N P
J	449	Tho drowen dromedarius / doun / deuelich thicke	Z	Z A
J	450	[an] hundred thousand and yheled / with / harnays of mayle	P	N P N
J	451	Eche beste with a big tour / ther / bold men wer ynne	Q	A N be Z
J	452	Twenty told by tale / in eche / tour euene	P D	N Z
J	453	Cameles closed in stele / comen out thanne	/	V Z Z
J	454	Faste toward the feld / a / ferlich nonbr	D	A N
J	455	Busked to batail / and on / bak hadde	C P	N V
J	456	Echon a toret of tre / with / ten men of armes	P	A N P N
J	457	Chares ful of chosen / charged with wepne	/	V P N
J	458	A wonder nonbr ther was / who so / wite lyste	Q Z	V V
J	459	Many douȝti that day / that was / adradde neuer	that be	A Z
J	460	Wer fond fey in the feld / er that / fiȝt endid	C D	N V
J	461	An olyfaunt yarmed / came out at the laste	/	V Z Z
J	462	Keuered myd a castel / was / craftily ywroȝt	be	Z E
J	463	A tabernacle in the tour / atyred was riche	/	E be Z
J	464	Piȝt as a paueloun / on / pileres of seluere	P	N P N
J	465	A which of white seluere / wal[w]ynde ther-ynne	/	G Z
J	466	On four goions of gold / that hit fram / grounde bar	that H P	N V
J	467	A c[h]osen chayr / therby on / charbokeles twelfe	Z P	N A
J	468	Betyn al with barn[d] gold / with / brennande sergis	P	G N
J	469	The chekes of the chayr / wer / cha[r]-bokles fyue	be	N A
J	470	Couered myd a riche clothe / ther / cayphas was sette	Q	N be E
J	471	A plate of pulsched gold / was / piȝt on his breste	be	E P D N
J	472	With many preciose perle / and / pured stones	C	A N
J	473	Lered men of the lawe / that / loude couthe synge	that	Z X V
J	474	With sawters seten / hym by and the / psalmys tolde	H P C D	N V
J	475	Of douȝty david the kyng / and other / der storijs	C D	A N
J	476	Of joseph the noble jewe / and / judas the knyȝt	C	N D N
J	477	Cayphas of the kyst / kyppid a rolle	/	V D N
J	478	And radde how the folke ran / throȝ the / re[d]e wa[ters]	P D	A N
J	479	Whan pharao and his ferde / wer in the / floode drouned	be P D	N E
J	480	And myche of moyses lawe / he / mynned that tyme	H	V D N
J	481	Whan this faithles folke / to the / feld comen	P D	N V
J	482	And batayled after the bent / with many / burne kene	P D	N A
J	483	For baneres that blased / and / bestes yarmed	C	N E
J	484	Myȝt no man se throw the sonne / ne the / cite knowe	not D	N V
J	485	Waspasian dyuyseth / the / vale alle aboute	D	N Z Z
J	486	That was with baneres ouer[brade] / to the / borwe wallis	P D	N N
J	487	To barouns and bold men / that hym / aboute wer	that H	P be
J	488	Seith lordlynges aloude / lestenyth my speche	/	V D N
J	489	Her nys king nother knyȝt / comen to this place	/	V P D N
J	490	Baroun ne burges / ne / burne that me folweth	not	N that H V
J	491	That the cause of his come / nys / crist forto venge	be	N for to V
J	492	Vpon the faithles folke / that hym / fayntly slowen	that H	Z V

J	493	Byholdeth the hethyng / and the / harde woundes	C D	A N
J	494	The betyng and the byndyng / that the / body hadde	that D	N V
J	495	Lat neuer this lawles ledis / laȝ at his harmys	/	V P D N
J	496	That bouȝt vs fram bale / with / blod of his herte	P	N P D N
J	497	[i] quyckeclayme the querels / of alle / quyk burnes	P D	A N
J	498	And clayme of euereche kyng / saue of / crist one	P P	N A
J	499	That this peple to pyne / no / pite ne hadde	D	N not V
J	500	That preueth his passioun / who so the / paas redeth	Q Z D	N V
J	501	Hit nedith noȝt at this note / of / nero to mynde	P	N to V
J	502	Ne to trete of no trewe / for / tribute that he asketh	P	N that H V
J	503	That querel y quikcleyme / [qwether] he ne wilneth	/	C H not V
J	504	Of this rebel to rome / bot / resoun to haue	C	N to V
J	505	Bot mor thing in our mynde / myneth [vs] today	/	V H Z
J	506	That by resoun to rome / the / regnance fallyth	D	N V
J	507	Bothe the myȝt and the mayn / [and] / mais[trie] on e[rthe]	C	N P N
J	508	And lord[chipe] of eche londe / that / lithe vnder heuen	that	V P N
J	509	Lat neuer this faithles folke / with / fiȝt vs wynne	P	N H V
J	510	Hors ne harnays / bot they hit / hard byen	C H H	Z V
J	511	Plate ne pesan / ne / pendauntes ende	D	N N
J	512	While any lyme may laste / or we the / lif haue	C H D	N V
J	513	For thei ben feyn[t] at the fiȝt / fals of byleue	/	A P N
J	514	And wel wenen at a wap / alle the / wo[r]ld quelle	D D	N V
J	515	Nother grounded on god / ne on no / grace tristen	not P D	N V
J	516	Bot alle in st[erynne]s of stour / and in / strength one	C P	N A
J	517	And we ben diȝt today / driȝten to serue	/	N to V
J	518	Hey heuen kyng / [take] / hede to his owne	V	N P D A
J	519	The ledes louten / hym alle and / aloude sayde	H Z C	Z V
J	520	Today that flethe any fote / the / fende haue his soule	D	N V D N
J	521	Bemes blowen / anon / blonkes to neȝeȝ	Z	N to V
J	522	Stedis stampen in the felde / stif steil vnder	/	A N P
J	523	Stithe men in stiropys / striden alofte	/	V Z
J	524	Knyȝtes croysen / hemself / cacchen her helmys	H self	V D N
J	525	With loude clarioun cry / and alle / kyn pypys	C D	N N
J	526	Tymbris and tabourris / tonelande loude	/	G Z
J	527	ȝeuen a schillande schout / schrynken the jewes	/	V D N
J	528	As womman [welter solde in swounn] / whan hir the / water neȝeth	C H D	N V
J	529	Lacchen launces / anon / lepyn to-gedris	Z	V Z
J	530	As fur out of flynt ston / ferde hem bytwene	/	V H P
J	531	Doust drof vpon lofte / dymedyn alle aboute	/	V Z Z
J	532	As thonder and thicke rayn / throwolande in skyes	/	G P N
J	533	[thei] beren burnes throw / brosten launces	/	V N
J	534	Knyȝtes crosschen / doun to the / cold erthe	Z P D	A N
J	535	Ffouȝt faste in the felde / and ay the / fals vnder	C Z D	N P
J	536	Doun swowande [one] swelt / with out / swar more	P P	N A
J	537	Tytus tourneth / hym to / tolles of the beste	H P	V P D A
J	538	Forjustes the jolieste / with / joyn[yng] of werr	P	G P N
J	539	Suth with a briȝt bronde / he / betith on harde	H	V Z Z
J	540	Tille the brayn and the blod / on the / bent ornen	P D	N V
J	541	Souȝt throȝ an other side / with a / sore wepne	P D	A N
J	542	Bet on the broun stele / while the / bladde laste	C D	N V
J	543	An hey breydeth the brond / and as a / bore loketh	C C D	N V
J	544	How hetterly doun hente / who so wolde	/	Q Z X
J	545	Alle briȝtned the bent / as / bemys of sonne	P	N P N
J	546	Of the gilden ger / and the / goode stones	C D	A N
J	547	Ffor schyueryng of sche[l]des / and / schynyng of helmes	C	G P N
J	548	Hit ferde as alle the firmament / vpon a / fur wer	P D	N V
J	549	Waspasian in the vale / the / fanward by-holdeth	D	N V
J	550	How the hethyn / her / heldith to grounde	H	V P N
J	551	Cam with a fair ferde / the / fals men to mete	D	A N to V
J	552	As greued griffouns / girden in samen	/	V Z
J	553	Spakly her speres / on / sprotes thay ȝeden	P	N H V
J	554	Scheldes as schidwod / on / scholdres tocleuen	P	N V
J	555	Schoken out of schepes / that / scharpe w[ere] ygrounde	that	Z be E
J	556	And mallen metel / throȝ / vnmylt hertes	P	A N
J	557	Hewen on the hethen / hurtlen togedr	/	V Z
J	558	Forschorne gilt schroud / sch[o]dered burne[s]	/	V N
J	559	Baches woxen ablode / aboute in the vale	/	Z P D N
J	560	And goutes fram gold wede / as / goteres they runne	C	N H V
J	561	Sir sabyn setteth / hym vp whan hit / so ȝede	H Z C H	Z V
J	562	Rideth myd the rereward / and alle the / route folweth	C D D	N V
J	563	Kenely the castels / came to assayle	/	V to V

J	564	That the bestes on her bake / out of / burwe ladden	P P	N V
J	565	Atles on the olyfauntes / that / orıble wer	that	A be
J	566	Girdith out the guttes / with / grounden speres	P	G N
J	567	R[o]ppis rispen / forth that / redles an hundred	Z that	Z D N
J	568	Scholde be busy to burie / that on a / bent lafte	that P D	N V
J	569	Castels clateren / doun / cameles brosten	Z	N V
J	570	Dromedaries to the deth / drowen ful swythe	/	V Z Z
J	571	The blode fomed hem fro / in the / flasches aboute	P D	N Z
J	572	Th[at] knedepe in the dale / dascheden stedes	/	V N
J	573	The burnes in the bretages / that / aboue wer	that	Z be
J	574	For the doust and the dyn / as alle / doun ȝede	C H	Z V
J	575	Al forstoppette in stele / storteblynde wexen	/	A V
J	576	Whan hurdiȝs and hard erthe / hurtled togedre	/	V Z
J	577	And vnder dromedaries doun / diȝten hem sone	/	V H Z
J	578	Was non left vpon lyue / that a / lofte standeth	that Z	Z V
J	579	Saue [ane] olepy olyfaunt / at the / grete ȝate	P D	A N
J	580	Theras cayphas the clerke / in / castel rideth	P	N V
J	581	He say the wrake on hem wende / and / away tourneth	C	Z V
J	582	With twelf maystres made / of / moyses lawe	P	N N
J	583	An hundred helmed men / hien hem after	/	V H P
J	584	Er they of castel myȝt come / cauȝten hem alle	/	V H Z
J	585	Bounden the bischup / on / bycchyd wyse	P	E N
J	586	That the blode out barst / eche / band vnder	D	N P
J	587	And broȝten [to] the [berfraye] / alle [tho] / bew clerkes	D D	A N
J	588	Ther the standard stode / and / stadded hem ther	C	V H Z
J	589	The beste and the britage / and alle the / briȝt ger	C D D	A N
J	590	Chair and chaundelers / and / charbokel stones	C	N N
J	591	The rolles that they redden / [on] and alle the / riche bokes	Z C D D	A N
J	592	They broȝte myd the bischup / thou hym / bale thouȝte	C H	A V
J	593	Anon the feythles folke / fayleden herte	/	V N
J	594	Tourned toward the toun / and / tytus hem after	C	N H P
J	595	Ffe[l]de of the fals ferde / in the / felde lefte	P D	N V
J	596	An hundred in her helmes / myd his / honde one	P D	N A
J	597	The fals jewes in the felde / fallen so thicke	/	V Z Z
J	598	As hail froward heuen / hepe ouer other	/	Z P H
J	599	So was the bent ouerbrad / blody byrunne	/	A E
J	600	With ded bodies aboute / alle the / brod vale	D D	A N
J	601	Myȝt no stede doun stap / bot on / stele wede	C P	N N
J	602	Or on burne other on beste / or on / briȝt scheldes	C P	A N
J	603	So myche was the multitude / that on the / molde lafte	that P D	N V
J	604	Ther so many wer mar[red] / mereuail wer ellis	/	N be Z
J	605	ȝit wer the romayns as rest / as they fram / rome come	C H P	N V
J	606	[vnrevyn] eche a renk / and noȝt a / ryng brosten	C not D	N V
J	607	Was no poynt perschid / of alle her / pris armur	P D D	A N
J	608	So crist his knyȝtes gan kepe / tille / complyn tyme	P	N N
J	609	An hundred thousand helmes / of the / hethen syde	P D	A N
J	610	Wer fey fallen in the felde / [that no / freke skapide]	that D	N V
J	611	Saue seuen thousand of the somme / that to the / cite flowen	that P D	N V
J	612	And wy[nn]en with mychel wo / the / walles with-ynne	D	N P
J	613	Ledes lepen / to a-non / louken the ȝates	to Z	V D N
J	614	Barren hem bigly / with / boltes of yren	P	N P N
J	615	Brayden vp brigges / with / brouden chaynes	P	E N
J	616	And portecolis with pile / picchen to grounde	/	V P N
J	617	Thei wynnen vp whyȝtly / the / walles to kepe	D	N to V
J	618	Fr[e]sche vnfonded folke / and / grete defence made	C	A N V
J	619	Tyeth in-to tourres / tonnes ful manye	/	N Z A
J	620	With grete stones of gret / and of / gray marble	C P	A N
J	621	Kepten kenly with caste / the / kernels alofte	D	N Z
J	622	Quar[r]en qu[a]rels / out with / quart[ote]s attonys	P P	N Z
J	623	That other folke at the fote / freshly assayled	/	Z V
J	624	Tille eche dale with dewe / was / donked aboute	be	E Z
J	625	With-drowen hem fro the diche / dukes and other	/	N C H
J	626	[for] the caste was so kene / that / come fram the walles	that	V P D N
J	627	Comen forthe with the kyng / clene as they ȝede	/	Z C H V
J	628	W[ant]ed noȝt o wye / ne non that / wem hadde	not not that	N V
J	629	Princes to her pauelouns / passen on swythe	/	V Z Z
J	630	Vnarmen hem as tyt / and alle the / nyȝt resten	C D D	N V
J	631	With wacche vmbe the walles / to many / wyes sorowe	P D	N N
J	632	They wolle noȝt the hethen / her so / harmeles be lafte	H Z	A be E
J	633	Sone as the rede day / ros [o]n the schye	/	V P D N
J	634	Bemes blowen / anon / burnes to aryse	Z	N to V

The Siege of Jerusalem

J	635	The kyng comaundeth a cry / that / comsed was sone	that	E be Z
J	636	The ded bodies on the bonke / barforto make	/	N V
J	637	To spoyle the spilt folke / spar scholde none	/	V X H
J	638	Geten girdeles and ger gold / and / goode stones	C	A N
J	639	Byes broches bryȝt / besauntes riche	/	N A
J	640	Helmes hewen of gold / hamberkes manye	/	N A
J	641	Kesten ded vpon ded / was / deil to byholde	be	N to V
J	642	Made wide weyes / and to the / walles comen	C P D	N V
J	643	Assembleden at the cite / saut to bygynne	/	N to V
J	644	Ffolke ferlich thycke / at the / four ȝate	P D	A N
J	645	They broȝten toures of tre / that they / taken hadde	that H	E had
J	646	A-ȝen euereche ȝate / ȝarken hem hey	/	V H Z
J	647	By-gonnnen at the grettist / a / garrite to rer	D	N to V
J	648	Groded vp fro the grounde / on twelfe / grete postes	P D	A N
J	649	[it] was wonderlich wide / wroȝt vpon hyȝte	/	E Z
J	650	Ffyue hundred in frounte / to / fiȝten at the walles	P	N P D N
J	651	Hardy men vp-on haste / hyen at the grecys	/	V P D N
J	652	And bygonnnen with bir / the / borow to assayle	D	N to V
J	653	Quarels flambande of fur / flowen out harde	/	V Z Z
J	654	And arwes [vn]arwely / with / attyr enuenymyd	P	N E
J	655	Taysen at the toures / tachen on the jewes	/	V P D N
J	656	Throȝ kernels cacchen her deth / many / kene burnes	D	A N
J	657	Brenten and beten / doun that / bilde was wel thycke	Z that	E be Z Z
J	658	Brosten the britages / and the / brode toures	C D	A N
J	659	By that was many bold burne / the / burwe to assayle	D	N to V
J	660	The hole batail boun / a-boute the / brode walles	P D	A N
J	661	That wer byg and brode / and / bycchet to wynne	C	E to V
J	662	Wonder heye to byholde / with / holwe diches vnder	Z	E N P
J	663	Heye bonked a-bou[t]e / vpon / bothe sydes	P	A N
J	664	Riȝt wicked to wynne / bot ȝif / wyles helpe	C C	N V
J	665	Bow-men atte bonke / benden her ger	/	V D N
J	666	Schoten vp scharply / to the / schene walles	P D	A N
J	667	With arwes and arblastes / and alle that / harme myȝt	C D that	V X
J	668	To affray the folke / that / defence made	that	N V
J	669	The jewes werien the walles / with / wyles ynowe	P	N A
J	670	Hote [p]ll[ay]ande picche / a-monge the / peple ȝeten	P D	N V
J	671	Brenn[a]n[d] leed and brynston / barels fulle	/	N A
J	672	Schoten schynande / doun riȝt as / schyr water	Z Z C	A N
J	673	Waspasian wendeth fram the walles / wariande hem alle	/	G H Z
J	674	Other busked wer boun / benden engynes	/	V N
J	675	Kesten at the kernels / and / clustred tounes	C	E N
J	676	And monye der daies worke / dongen to grounde	/	V P N
J	677	By that wriȝtes han wroȝt / a / wonder stronge pale	D	Z A N
J	678	Alle aboute the burwe / with / bastiles manye	P	N A
J	679	That [no freke in myȝt fonde / with-owttyn / fethyrhames]	P	N
J	680	[ne] no segge vnder sonne / myȝt fram the / cite passe	X P D	N V
J	681	Suth dommyn the diches / with the / ded corses	P D	A N
J	682	Crammen hit myd karayn / the / kirnels vnder	D	N P
J	683	That the stynk of the steem / myȝt / strike ouer the walles	X	V P D N
J	684	To cothe the corsed folke / that hem / kepe scholde	that H	V X
J	685	The cors of the condit / that / comen to [the] toun	that	V P D N
J	686	Stoppen euereche a streem / ther any / str[ande] ȝede	Q D	N V
J	687	With stockes and stones / and / stynkande bestes	C	G N
J	688	That they no water myȝt wynne / that / weren enclosed	that	be E
J	689	Waspasian tourneth to his tente / with / titus and other	P	N C H
J	690	Commaundeth consail / anon on / cayphas to sitte	Z P	N to V
J	691	W[hat] deth by dome / that he / dey scholde	that H	V X
J	692	With the lettered ledes / that they / lauȝte hadde	that H	E have
J	693	Domes-men vpon de[y]s / demeden swythe	/	V Z
J	694	That ech freke wer quyk fleyn / the / felles of clene	D	N P Z
J	695	Then to be on a bent / with / blonkes to-drawe	P	N E
J	696	And suth honget on an hep / vpon / heye galwes	D	A N
J	697	The feet to the firmament / alle / folke to byholden	D	N to V
J	698	With hony vpon ech [halfe] / the / hydeles anoynted	D	N E
J	699	Corres and cattes / with / claures ful scharpe	P	N Z A
J	700	Ffour kagge[d] and knyt / to / cayphases theyes	P	N N
J	701	Twey apys at his armes / to / angren hym mor	to	V H Z
J	702	That renten the rawe flesche / vpon / rede peces	P	A N
J	703	So was he pyned fram prime / with / perschèd sides	P	E N
J	704	Tille the sonne doun souȝt / in / sommere-tyme	P	N N
J	705	The lered men of the lawe / a / litel bynythe	Z	Z Z

J	706	Weren tourmented on a tre / topsail walten	/	Z V	
J	707	Knyt to euerech clerke kene / corres twey	/	N A	
J	708	That alle the cite myȝt se / the / sorow that they dryuen	D	N that H V	
J	709	The jewes walten ouer the walles / for / wo at that tyme	P	N P D N	
J	710	Seuen hundred slow hem-self / for / sorow of her clerkes	P	N P D N	
J	711	Somme hent her heer / and fram the / hed pulled	C P D	N V	
J	712	And somme [down] for deil / dasch[e]de to grounde	/	V P N	
J	713	The kyng lete drawen hem a-doun / whan they / dede wer	C H	A be	
J	714	Bade a bole-fur betyn / to / brennen the corses	to	V D N	
J	715	Kesten cayphas / ther-yn and his / clerkes twelf	Z C D	N A	
J	716	And brenten euereche bon / in-to the / browne askes	P D	A N	
J	717	Suth went to the walle / on the / wynde syde	P D	N N	
J	718	And alle a-brod on the burwe / blewen the powder	/	V D N	
J	719	Ther is doust [to] ȝour drynke / a / du[ke] to hem crieth	D	N P H V	
J	720	And bade hem bible of that broth / for the / bischopes soule	P D	N N	
J	721	Thus ended coursed cayphas / and his / clerkes alle	C D	N A	
J	722	Al to-brused myd bestes / brent at the laste	/	E Z	
J	723	In tokne of tresoun / and / trey that he wroȝt	C	N that H V	
J	724	Whan crist throw his conseil / was / cacched to deth	be	E P N	
J	725	By that was the day don / dym[m]ed the skyes	/	V D N	
J	726	Merked [the] montayns / and / mores a-boute	C	N P	
J	727	Foules fallen to fote / and her / fethres r[y]s[t]en	C D	N V	
J	728	The nyȝt-wacche to the walle / and / waytes to blowe	C	N to V	
J	729	Bryȝt fures a-boute betyn / a-brode in the oste	/	Z P D N	
J	730	The kyng and his consail / carpen to-gedr	/	V Z	
J	731	Chosen chyuentayns / out and / chiden no mor	Z C	V Z	
J	732	Bot charged the chek-wecche / and to / chambr wenten	C P	N V	
J	733	Kynges and knyȝtes / to / cacchen hem reste	to	V H N	
J	734	Waspasian lyth in his logge / litel he slepith	/	Z H V	
J	735	Bot walwyth and wyndith / and / waltreth a-boute	C	V Z	
J	736	Ofte tourneth for tene / and on the / toun thynketh	C P D	N V	
J	737	Whan schadewes and schir day / scheden attwynne	/	V Z	
J	738	Leuerockes vpon lofte / lyften her steuenes	/	V D N	
J	739	Burnes busken hem out of bedde / with / bemes loude	P	N A	
J	740	Bothe blowyng on bent / and on the / burwe walles	C P D	N N	
J	741	Waspasian bounys of bedde / busked hym fayr	/	V H A	
J	742	Fram the fote to the fourche / in / fyne gold clothes	P	A A N	
J	743	Suth putteth the prince / ouer his / pal[l]e[n] wedes	P D	E N	
J	744	A brynye browded thicke / with a / brest-plate	P D	N N	
J	745	[the] gra[te was] of gray steel / and of / gold riche	C P	N A	
J	746	Ther-ouer he casteth a cote / colour[ede] of his armys	/	E P D N	
J	747	A grete girdel of gold / with-out / ger other	P	N A	
J	748	Layth vmbe his lendis / with / lacchetes ynow	P	N A	
J	749	A bryȝt burnesched sword / he / belteth alofte	H	V Z	
J	750	Of pur purged gold / the / pomel and the hulte	D	N C D N	
J	751	A brod schynande scheld / on / scholdir he hongith	P	N H V	
J	752	Bocklyd myd briȝt gold / abou[t]e at the necke	/	Z P D N	
J	753	The glowes of gray steel / that wer with / gold hemmyd	that be P	N E	
J	754	Hauleth [ouer] harnays / and his / hors asketh	C D	N V	
J	755	The gold hewen helme / haspeth he blyue	/	V H Z	
J	756	With viser and with a-vental / deuysed for the nones	/	V Z	
J	757	A croune of clene gold / was / closed vpon lofte	be	E Z	
J	758	Rybaunde vmbe the rounde helm / ful of / riche stones	A P	A N	
J	759	Pyȝt prudely with perles / in-to the / pur corners	P D	A N	
J	760	And so with saphyres sett / the / sydes a-boute	D	N P	
J	761	He strideth on a stif stede / and / striketh ouer the bente	C	V P D N	
J	762	Liȝt as a lyoun / wer / loused out of cheyne	be	E P P N	
J	763	His segges se[y]en / hym alle and echon / sayth to other	H Z C H	V P H	
J	764	This is a comlich kyng / knyȝtes to lede	/	N to V	
J	765	He boweth to the barres / or he / bide wolde	C H	V X	
J	766	Betynge on with the brond / on the / bras rynges	P D	N N	
J	767	Cometh caytifes / forth ȝe that / crist slowen	Z H that	N V	
J	768	Knoweth hym for ȝour kyng / or ȝe / cacche mor	C H	V Z	
J	769	Wayteth doun fro the walle / what / wo is on hande	Q	N be P N	
J	770	May ȝe fecche ȝou no fode / thoȝ ȝe / fey worthe	C H	A V	
J	771	And thoȝ ȝe waterles wede / wynne ȝe noȝt o droppe	/	V H not D N	
J	772	Thoȝ ȝe deth scholde dey / daies in ȝour lyue	/	N P D N	
J	773	The pale that i piȝt / haue / passe hit who myȝt	have	V H Q X	
J	774	That is so byg on the bonke / and hat the / burowe closed	C have D	N E	
J	775	Ffourty to fyȝten / aȝens / fyue hundred	P	A N	
J	776	Thoȝ ȝe wer etnes echon / in / scholde [ȝ]e [tourne]	P	X H V	

J	777	And more manschyp / wer hit ʒit / mercy by-seche	be H Z	N V
J	778	Than metles marr / ther no / myʒt helpys	Q D	N V
J	779	Was non that warpith a word / bot / waytes her poyntes	C	V D N
J	780	ʒif [any] stertis on st[r]ay / with / stones hem to kylle	P	N H to V
J	781	Than wroth as a wode bore / he / wendeth his bridul	H	V D N
J	782	ʒif ʒe as dogges wol dey / than / deuel haue that recche	D	N V D N
J	783	And or i wende fro this walle / ʒe schul / wordes schewe	H X	N V
J	784	And efte spakloker speke / or y ʒour / speche owene	C P D	N A
J	785	By that a jewe josophus / the / gentyl clerke	D	A N
J	786	Hadde wroʒt a wonder wyle / whan hem / water fayled	C H	N V
J	787	Made wedes of wolle / in / wete for to plunge	P	N for to V
J	788	Water-waschen as they wer / and on the / walle hengen	C P D	N V
J	789	The wedes dropeden doun / d[r]yed ʒerne	/	V Z
J	790	Rich rises / hem fro the / romayns byholden	H P D	N V
J	791	Wenden wel her wedes / hadde / wasschyng so ryue	had	N A A
J	792	That no wye in the wone / water schold fayle	/	N X V
J	793	Waspasian the wile / wel ynow knewe	/	Z Z V
J	794	Loude lawʒ[eth] / ther-at and / lordlynges byddis	Z C	N V
J	795	No burne abasched / be thoʒ they this / bost make	be C H D	N V
J	796	Hit beth bot wyles of werr / for / water hem fayleth	C	N H V
J	797	Than was no-thyng bot a newe / note to bygynne	/	N to V
J	798	Assaylen on eche a side / the / cite by halues	D	N P N
J	799	Merken myd manglouns / ful / vn-mete dyntes	A	A N
J	800	And myche of masouns note / they / marden that tyme	H	V D N
J	801	Ther-of was josophus war / that myche of / werr couthe	D H P	N V
J	802	And sette on the walle side / sakkes myd chaf		N P N
J	803	Aʒens the streyngthe of the stroke / ther the / stones hytte	Q D	N V
J	804	That alle dered noʒt a dyʒs / bot / grete dy[n] made	C	A N V
J	805	The romayns runne / to a-non and on / roddes knytte	P Z C P	N V
J	806	Sithes for the sackes / that / selly wer kene	that	Z be A
J	807	Raʒten to the ropis / rent hem in sonder	/	V H Z
J	808	That alle dasschande doun / in-to the / diche flatten	P D	N V
J	809	Bot josophus the gynful / her / engynes alle	D	N A
J	810	Brente with brennande oyle / and myche / bale wroʒt	C Z	A V
J	811	Waspasian wounded / was ther / wonderlich sore	be Z	Z Z
J	812	Throw the hard of the hele / with an / hande-darte	P D	N N
J	813	That boot throw the bote / and the / bone nayled	C D	N V
J	814	Of the frytted fote / in the / folis syde	P D	N N
J	815	Sone assembled / hym to many / sadde hundred	H P D	A N
J	816	That wolden wrecken the wounde / other / wo habben	D	N V
J	817	They bowyn to the barres / bekered ʒerne	/	V Z
J	818	Fouʒt riʒt felly / foyned with speres		V P N
J	819	Jo[k]ken jewes / throʒ / engynes by thanne	P	N Z
J	820	Wer manye bent at the bonke / and to the / burwe threwen	C P D	N V
J	821	Ther wer selcouthes sen / as / segges mowe here	C	N X V
J	822	A burne with a balwe-ston / was the / brayn cloue	be D	N E
J	823	The gretter pese of the panne / the / pyble forth striketh	D	N Z V
J	824	That hit flow in-to the feld / a / forlong or more	D	N C A
J	825	A womman bounden with a barn / was on the / body hytte	be P D	N E
J	826	With the ston o[f] a staf[-slyng] / as the / storyj telleth	C D	N V
J	827	That the barn out brayde / fram the / body clene	P D	N A
J	828	And was born vp as a bal / ouer the / burwe walles	P D	N N
J	829	Burnes wer brayned / and / brosed to deth	C	E P N
J	830	Wymmen wide open / walte vnder stones	/	E P N
J	831	Frosletes fro the ferst / to the / flor thrylled	P D	N V
J	832	And many toret doun tilte / the / temple a-boute	D	N P
J	833	The cite had ben seised / myd / saut at that tyme	P	N P D N
J	834	Nad the folke be so fers / that the / fende serued	that D	N V
J	835	That kilden on the cristen / and / kepten the walles	C	V D N
J	836	With arwes and arblastes / and / archers manye	C	N A
J	837	With speres and spryngoldes / sponnen out hard	/	V Z Z
J	838	Dryuen dartes a-doun / ʒeuen / depe woundes	V	A N
J	839	That manye renke out of rome / [by] / rest[ing] of th[e] s[o]nne	P	G P D N
J	840	Was mychel leuer a leche / than / layke myd his ton	C	N P D N
J	841	Waspasian stynteth of the stour / steweth his burnes	/	V D N
J	842	That wer for-beten and bled / vnder / bryʒt yren	P	A N
J	843	Tyen to her tentis / myd / tene that they hadde	P	N that H V
J	844	Al wery of that werk / and / wounded ful sore	C	E Z A
J	845	Helmes and hamberkes / hadden of sone	/	V Z
J	846	Leches by torche-liʒt / loken her hurtes	/	V D N
J	847	Waschen woundes with wyn / and with / wolle stoppen	C P	N V

J	848	With oyle and orisoun / ordeyned in charme	/	V P N
J	849	Suth euereche a segge / to the / soper ȝede	P D	N V
J	850	Thoȝ they wounded wer / was no / wo nempned	be D	N E
J	851	Bot daunsyng and no deil / with / dynnyng of pipis	P	N P N
J	852	And the nakerer noyse / alle the / nyȝt-tyme	D D	N N
J	853	Whan the derk was doun / and the / day spr[o]ngen	C D	N V
J	854	Sone after the sonne / sembled the grete	/	V D N(A)
J	855	Comen forth-with the kyng / conseil to her	/	N P V
J	856	Alle the knyȝthod clene / that for / crist werred	that P	N V
J	857	Waspasian waiteth a-wide / his / wyes byholdeth	D	N V
J	858	That wer frescher to fiȝt / than at the / furst tyme	C P D	A N
J	859	Prayeth princes on ernest / and alle the / peple after	C D D	N P
J	860	That eche wye of that werr / schold his / wille specke	X D	N V
J	861	For or this toun be tak / and this / toures heye	C D	N A
J	862	Michel tor[fere] and tene / vs / tides on hande	H	V P N
J	863	Thay tourned alle to titus / and hym the / tale scheweth	C H D	N V
J	864	Of the cite and the sege / to / seyn for hem alle	P	E P H Z
J	865	Than titus tourneth / hem to and / talkyng bygynneth	H P C	N(V) V
J	866	Thus to layke with this les[e folke] / vs / lympis the worse	H	V D A
J	867	For they ben fel[l]e of defence / ferce men and noble	/	A N C A
J	868	And this toured toun / is / tenful to wynne	be	A to V
J	869	The worst wrecche in the wone / may on / walle lygge	X P	N V
J	870	Strike doun with a ston / and / stuny many knyȝtes	C	V A N
J	871	Whan we schul houe and byholde / and litel / harme wirche	C D	N V
J	872	And ay the lothe of the layk / liȝt on vs-selue	/	V P H self
J	873	Now mowe they ferke no ferr / her / fode forto wynne	D	N for to V
J	874	Wolde we stynt of our strif / whyle they her / stor ma[r]-den	C H D	N V
J	875	We scholde with [hunger] hem honte / to / hoke out of toun	P	V P P N
J	876	[with-owttyn weme or wounde / or any / wo ells]	C D	N Z
J	877	For ther as fayleth the fode / ther is / feynt strengthe	Q be	A N
J	878	And ther as hunger is hote / hertes ben feble	/	N be A
J	879	Alle assenteden to the sawe / that to the / [sege] longed	that P D	N V
J	880	Apaied as the prince / and the / peple wolde	C D	N V
J	881	To the kyng wer called / constables thanne	/	N Z
J	882	Marchals maser[s] / men that he to tristith	/	N that H to V
J	883	He chargeth hem che[f]ly / for / chaunce that may falle	P	N that X V
J	884	With wacche of waled men / the / walles to kepe	D	N to V
J	885	For we wol hunten at the hart / this / hethes aboute	D	N P
J	886	And hur racches renne / a-monge this / rowe bonkes	P D	A N
J	887	Ride to the reuer / and / rer vp the foules	C	V Z D N
J	888	Se faucouns fle / fole of the beste	/	N P D A
J	889	Ech segge to the solas / that / hym-self lyked	that	H self V
J	890	Princes out of pauelouns / presen on stedes	/	V P N
J	891	Torn[ei]en trifflyn / and on the / toun wayten	C P D	N V
J	892	This lyf they ledde longe / and / [lord] ȝyue vs grace	C	N V H N
J	893	In rome nero hath now / mychel / noye wroȝt	D	N V
J	894	To deth pyned the pope / and mychel / peple quelled	C D	N V
J	895	Petr apostlen prince / and seint / poule [also]	C D	N Z
J	896	Senek and the senatours / and alle the / cite fured	C D D	N E
J	897	His modir and his my[l]de wif / murdred to dethe	/	E P N
J	898	Combred cristen fele / that on / crist leued	that P	N V
J	899	The romayns resen / a-non whan they th[i]s / rewthe seyen	Z C H D	N V
J	900	To quelle the emperour quyk / that hem / vnquemed hadde	that H	E had
J	901	They pressed to his paleys / porayle and other	/	N C H
J	902	To br[it]ten the bold kyng / in his / burwe riche	P D	N A
J	903	The cite and the senatours / assented hem bothe	/	V H Z
J	904	Non other dede was to doun / they han his / dome ȝolden	H have D	N E
J	905	Than flowe that freke / frendles alone	/	N Z
J	906	Out at a pore posterne / and alle the / peple folwed	C D D	N V
J	907	With a tronchoun of tre / toke he no more	/	V H Z
J	908	Of alle the glowande gold / that he on / grounde hadde	that H P	N V
J	909	On that tronchoun with his teth / he / toggeth and byteth	H	V C V
J	910	Tille hit was piked at the poynt / as a / pokes ende	C D	N N
J	911	Than abideth that burne / and / biterlych speketh	C	Z V
J	912	To alle the wyes that ther wer / wordes aloude	/	N Z
J	913	Tourneth traytours aȝen / schal neuer the / tale rise	X Z D	N V
J	914	Of no karl by the coppe / how he his / kyng quelde	Q H D	N V
J	915	Hym-self he stryketh myd that staf / streȝt to the hert	/	Z P D N
J	916	That the colke to-clef / and the / kyng deyed	C D	N V
J	917	Six monthe after and no mor / this / myschef bytydde	D	N V
J	918	That waspasian was went / to / werry on the jewes	to	V P D N

The Siege of Jerusalem

J	919	Four mettyn myle out of rome / to / mynde for euere	to	V Z
J	920	That erst was emperour / of alle thus / ended in sorow	P H Z	V P N
J	921	The grete to-gedres / than / [gete] hem an-other	C	V H H
J	922	On gabba a gome / that mychel / grem hadde	that D	N V
J	923	Throȝ othis I[ucy]us a lord / that hym / longe hated	that H	Z V
J	924	And at the last that lord / out of / lyf hym broȝt	P P	N H V
J	925	Amydde the market of rome / the[y] / mette to-gedres	H	V Z
J	926	Othis fallith hym fey / ȝaf hym / fale woundes	V H	A N
J	927	That four monthes and [no] mor / hadde / mayntened the croune	had	E D N
J	928	And tho deyed the duke / and the / diademe lefte	C D	N V
J	929	And whan that gabba was gon / and to / grounde broȝt	C P	N E
J	930	Othis entrith on ernest / and / emperour was made	C	N be E
J	931	The man in his maieste / was / monthes bot thre	be	N P N
J	932	Than he ȝeldeth sathanas the soule / and / hym-self quelled	C	H self V
J	933	The romayns risen vp a renk / rome for to kepe	/	N for to V
J	934	A knyȝt that vitel was calde / and hym the / croune rauȝte	C H D	N V
J	935	Bot for sir sabyns sake / a / segge that was noble	D	N that be A
J	936	Waspasian brother of blode / [that] he / brytned hadde	that H	E had
J	937	Waspasian vpon vitel / to / vengen his brother	to	V D N
J	938	S[en]t out of surrie / segges to rome	/	N P N
J	939	That [a]s naked as an nedul / the / newe emperour	D	A N
J	940	For sir sabyns sake / alle the / cite drowe hym	D D	N V H
J	941	Suth gored the gome / that his / guttes alle	D D	N A
J	942	As a bowe[l]ed beste / in-to his / breche felle	P D	N V
J	943	Doun ȝer[m]ande he ȝede / and / ȝeldeth the soule	C	V D N
J	944	And [they] kayȝt the cors / and / kast in-to tybre	C	V P N
J	945	Seuen monthes this [segge] / hadde / septre on hande	had	N P N
J	946	And thus loste he the lyf / for his / luther dedes	P D	A N
J	947	An other segge was to seke / that / septre schold haue	that	N X V
J	948	For alle this grete ben gon / and neuer / agayn tournen	C Z	Z E
J	949	Now of the cite and of the sege / wolle y / sey mor	X H	V Z
J	950	How this comelich kyng / that for / crist werreth	that P	N V
J	951	Hath holden yn the hethen men / this other / half wynter	D D	A N
J	952	That neuer burne was so bold / the / burwe for to passe	D	N for to V
J	953	As he to dyner on a day / with / dukes was sette	P	N be E
J	954	Comen renkes fram rome / rapande swythe	/	G Z
J	955	In bruneys and in bryȝt wede / with / bodeworde newe	P	N A
J	956	Louten alle to the lord / letres hym rauȝten	/	N H V
J	957	Sayn comelich kyng / the / knyȝthod of rome	D	N P N
J	958	Throȝ the senatours assent / and alle the / cite ellis	C D D	N Z
J	959	Han chosen the her chyuentayn / her / chef lord to worthe	D	A N to V
J	960	And riche emperour of rome / thus / redeth this letres	C	V D N
J	961	The lord vnlappeth the lef / this / letres byholdeth	D	N V
J	962	Ouer-loketh ech a lyne / to the / last ende	P D	A N
J	963	Bordes born wer doun / and the / burne riseth	C D	N V
J	964	Calleth consail / a-non and / kytheth this speche	Z C	V D N
J	965	ȝe ben burnes of my blod / that y / best wolde	that H	Z V
J	966	My sone is next to my-self / and other / sib manye	C D	A H
J	967	Sir sabyn of surrie / a / segge that y triste	D	N that H V
J	968	And other frendes fele / that me / fayth owen	that H	N A
J	969	Now is me bodeword of blys / broȝt froward rome	/	V P N
J	970	To be lord ouer that lond / as this/ letres speketh	C D	N V
J	971	Sir sabyn of surrie / sey the by-houyth	/	V H V
J	972	How y myȝt sauy my-self / and i / so wroȝt	C H	Z V
J	973	Ffor y haue heylych / heyȝt her forto lenge	/	E H for to V
J	974	[tille] me the ȝates ben ȝet / and / ȝolden the keyes	C	E D N
J	975	[and] i this toured [t]oun / ha[ue] / taken at wille	have	E P N
J	976	And suth houshed on hem / that this / hold kepyn	that D	N V
J	977	Brosten and betyn / doun this / britages heye	Z D	N A
J	978	That neuer ston in that stede / stond vpon other	/	V P H
J	979	Kythe th[i] consail sir knyȝt / this / kyng to hym sayde	D	N P H V
J	980	For y wol worche by thy witt / ȝif / worschip may folowe	C	N X V
J	981	Than seith sir sabyn / a-non / semelich lord	Z	A N
J	982	We ben wyes the with / thy / worschup to further	D	N to V
J	983	Of longe tyme bylafte / and / ledes thyn owen	C	N D A
J	984	That we doun is thy dede / may no man / demen elles	X D N	V Z
J	985	The dom demed / was ther who so / doth by another	be Z Q Z	V P H
J	986	Schal be soferayn hym-self / sein in the werke	/	V P D N
J	987	For as fers is the freke / atte / ferr ende	P	A N
J	988	That of fleis the fel / as he that / foot holdeth	C H that	N V
J	989	Bytake tytus thy sone / this / toun for to kepe	D	N for to V

J	990	And to the douȝti duke / domyssian his brother	/	N D N
J	991	Her ı holde vp myn honde / myd / hem for to lenge	P	N for to V
J	992	With alle the here that i haue / while my / herte lasteth	C D	N V
J	993	And thou schalt ride to rome / and / receyue the croune	C	V D N
J	994	In honour emperour to be / as thyn / eure schapith	C D	N V
J	995	So may thy couenaunt be kept / that thou to / crist made	that H P	N V
J	996	Thy-self dest that thy soudiours / by thyn / assent worchen	P D	N V
J	997	Than with a liouns lote / he / lifte vp the eyen	H	V Z D N
J	1098	To voiden alle by vile deth / that / vitelys destruyed	that	N V
J	1099	Wymmen and weyke folke / that / weren of olde age	that	be P A N
J	1100	Myȝt noȝt stonde in stede / bot her / stor mardyn	C D	N V
J	1101	After [thay] touche of trewe / to / trete with the lord	to	V P D N
J	1102	Bot Titus grauntteth noȝt for gile / that the / gomes thence	that D	N Z
J	1103	For he is wise that is war / or hym / wo hape	C H	N V
J	1104	And with falsede a-fer / is / fairest to dele	be	A to V
J	1105	To worchyn vnder the wal / w[a]yes they casten	/	N H V
J	1106	Whan Tytus nold no trewe / to the / toun graunte	P D	N V
J	1107	With mynours and masouns / myne they bygonne	/	V H V
J	1108	Grobben faste [i]n the grounde / and / god ȝyue vs joye	C	N V H N
J	1109	As Tytus after [on] a tyme / vmbe the / toun r[i]deth	P D	N V
J	1110	Wyth sixty speres of the sege / segges a fewe	/	N D A
J	1111	Alle outwith the ost / out of a kaue	/	P P D N
J	1112	Vp a buschment brake / alle of / briȝt hedis	H D	A N
J	1113	Fyf hundred fiȝtyng men / fellen hem aboute	/	V H P
J	1114	In jepouns and jambers / Jewes they wer	/	N H be
J	1115	Hadde wroȝt hem a wey / and the / wal myned	C D	N E
J	1116	And Titus tourneth / hem to without / tale mor	H P P	N A
J	1117	Schaftes schedred wer sone / and / scheldes ythrelled	C	N E
J	1118	[And many schalke thurghe schotte / with the / scharpe ende]	P D	A N
J	1119	Brunyes and briȝt wede / blody by-runne	/	Z E
J	1120	And many segge at that saute / souȝte to the grounde	/	V P D N
J	1121	Hacchen vpon hard steel / with an / herty wylle	P D	A N
J	1122	That fur out flowe / as of / flynt stonys	C P	N N
J	1123	Of the helm and the hed / hewen at-tonys	/	V Z
J	1124	The stompe vnder stede feet / in the / steel leueth	P D	N V
J	1125	The ȝong duk Domycian / of the / dyn herde	P D	N V
J	1126	And issed out of the ost / with / eȝte hundred speres	P	A A N
J	1127	Ffel on the fals folke / vmbe-feldes hem sone	/	V H Z
J	1128	As bestes bretnes / hem alle and hath his / brother holpen	H Z C have D	N E
J	1129	Than Titus toward his tentis / tourneth hym sone	/	V H Z
J	1130	Maketh mynour[s] and men / the / myne to stoppe	D	N to V
J	1131	After profreth pes / for / pyte that he hadde	P	N that H V
J	1132	Whan he wist of her wo / that / wer withyn stoken	that	be Z E
J	1133	Bot Jon the jenfulle / that the / Jewes ladde	that D	N V
J	1134	An other Symond of his assent / forsoke the profre	/	V D N
J	1135	Sayn leuer in this lif / lengen hem wer	/	V H be
J	1136	Than any renke out of Rome / [re]joycid her sorowe	/	V D N
J	1137	Sale in the cite / was / cesed with thanne	be	E Z Z
J	1138	Was noȝt for besauntes to bye / that / men bite myȝt	that	N V X
J	1139	For a ferthyng-worth of fode / floryns an hundred	/	N A N
J	1140	Princes profren in the toun / to / pay in the fuste	to	V P D N
J	1141	Bot alle was boteles bale / f[or] who so / bred hadde	P Q Z	E have
J	1142	Nold a goet haue [g]ouen / for / goode vpon [erth]e	P	A P N
J	1143	Wymmen falwed faste / and her / face chaungen	C D	N V
J	1144	Ffeynte and fallen / doun that so / fair wer	Z that Z	A be
J	1145	S[ome] swallen as swyn / som / swart wexen	H	A V
J	1146	Som lene on to loke / as / la[n]terne-hornes	P	N N
J	1147	The morayne was so myche / that no / man couthe telle	that D	N X V
J	1148	Wher to burie in the burwe / the / bodies that wer ded	D	N that be A
J	1149	Bot wenten with hem to the walle / and / walten [hem o]uere	C	V H P
J	1150	In-to the depe of the diche / the / ded doun fallen	D	N(A) Z V
J	1151	Whan Titus told was the tale / to / trewe god he vouched	P	A N H V
J	1152	That [he] hadde profred hem pes / and / grete pite hadde	C	A N V
J	1153	Tho praied he Josophus to preche / the / peple [to en-for]me	D	N to V
J	1154	[For] to saue hemself / and the / cite ȝelde	C D	N V
J	1155	Bot Jon forsoke the sawe / so for to wyrche	/	Z for to V
J	1156	With Symond that other segge / that the / cyte ladde	that D	N V
J	1157	Myche peple for the prechyng / at the / posterne ȝatis	P D	A N
J	1158	Tyen out of the toun / and / Tytus bysecheth	C	N V
J	1159	To for[g]yue hem the gult / that they to / god wroȝt	that H P	N V
J	1160	And he grauntteth hem grace / and / gaylers bytauȝt	C	N V

J	1161	Bot whan they metten with mete / vnmyȝty they wer	/	A H be
J	1162	Any fode to defye / so / faynt was her strengthe	Z	A be D N
J	1163	Fful the gottes of gold / eche / gome hadde	D	N V
J	1164	Lest fomen fongen / hem schold her / floreyns they eten	H X H	N H V
J	1165	Whan hit was broȝt vp abrode / and the / bourd aspyed	C D	N E
J	1166	[Withou]ten leue of that lord / ledes hem slowen	/	N H V
J	1167	[G]oren euereche a gome / and the / gold taken	C D	N V
J	1168	Ffayn[ere] of the floreyns / [than of] the / frekes alle	P P D	N A
J	1169	Ay wer the ȝates vn[ȝ]et / tille two / ȝeres ende	C D	N V
J	1170	So longe they [s]ouȝt hit by sege / or they the / [cite] hadde	C H D	N V
J	1171	Eleuen hundred thousand Jewes / in the / mene whyle	P D	A N
J	1172	Swalten while the sweng last / by / swerd and by hunger	P	N C P N
J	1173	Now Titus conseil hath take / the / toun to assayle	D	N to V
J	1174	To wynne hit on eche [wise] / of / warwolues handes	P	N N
J	1175	Neuer pyte ne pees / profre hem more	/	V H Z
J	1176	Ne gome that he gete / may to no / grace taken	X P D	N V
J	1177	[thei] armen hem as tyt / alle for the werr	/	H P D N
J	1178	Tyen euen to the toun / with / trompis and pypys	P	N C N
J	1179	With nakerers and grete noyce / neȝen the walles	/	V D N
J	1180	Ther many styf man and stour / stondith alofte	/	V Z
J	1181	Sir Sabyn of Surrye / on a / syde ȝede	P D	N N
J	1182	The ȝong duke Domycian / drow to an other	/	V P D H
J	1183	XV thousand [fiȝtynge] men / eche / freke hadde	D	N V
J	1184	With many maner of engyne / and / mynours ynowe	C	N A
J	1185	Tytus at the toun ȝate / with / ten thousand helmes	P	A A N
J	1186	Merketh mynour[s] at the wal / wher they / myne scholde	Q H	V X
J	1187	On ech side for the assaute / setteth engynes	/	V N
J	1188	And bold-brayned men / in / belfrayes heye	P	N A
J	1189	Was noȝt bot dyn and dyt / as alle / deye scholde	C H	V X
J	1190	So eche lyuande lyf / layeth on other	/	V P H
J	1191	At eche kernel was cry / and / quasschyng of wepne	C	N P N
J	1192	And many burne atte brayd / brayned to deth	/	E P N
J	1193	Sir Sabyn of Surrye / whyle the / saute laste	C D	N V
J	1194	Leyth a ladder to the wal / and / alofte clymyth	C	Z V
J	1195	Wendeth wyȝtly / theron thoȝ hym / wo happned	Z C H	N V
J	1196	And vp stondith for ston[es] / or for / steel gere	C P	N N
J	1197	Syx he slow on the wal / sir / Sabyn alone	D	N Z
J	1198	The seueth hitteth on hym / an / vnhende dynte	D	A N
J	1199	That the brayn out brast / at / both nose-thrylles	P	A N N
J	1200	And Sabyn ded of the dynt / in-to the / diche falleth	P D	N V
J	1201	Than Tytus wepyth for wo / and / warieth the tyme	C	V D N
J	1202	Syth he the lede hath lost / that he / loue scholde	that H	V X
J	1203	Ffor now is a duke ded / the / douȝtiest y trowe	D	A H V
J	1204	That euer stede bystrode / or any / steel wered	C D	N V
J	1205	Tytus on the same side / setteth an engyne	/	V D N
J	1206	A sowe wroȝt for the werr / and to the / wal dryueth	C P D	N V
J	1207	That alle ouerwalte ther he went / and / wyes an hundred	C	N A A
J	1208	Wer ded of that dynt / and in the / diche lyȝten	C P D	N V
J	1209	Than Tytus heueth vp the honde / and / heuen kyng thonketh	C	N N V
J	1210	That they the dukes deth / han so / der bouȝte	have Z	Z V
J	1211	The Jewes praien the pees / this was the / paske-euene	H be D	N N
J	1212	And the comelich kyng / the / keyes out rauȝten	D	N Z V
J	1213	Nay traytours quoth Tytus / now / take hem ȝourselfen	Z	V H H self
J	1214	Ffor schal no ward on ȝour wal / vs the / way lette	H D	N V
J	1215	We han geten vs a gate / a[g]en ȝour wille	/	P D N
J	1216	That schal be satled sour / on ȝour / sory kynde	P D	A N
J	1217	Or the ȝates wer ȝolden / thre / ȝer byfore	D	N P
J	1218	Ouer the cyte wer seyn / selcouthe thynges	/	A N
J	1219	A bryȝt bren[n]yng swerd / ouer the / burwe henged	P D	N V
J	1220	Without hond other helpe / saue [of] / heuen one	P P	N Z
J	1221	Armed men in the ayer / vpon / ost-wyse	P	N N
J	1222	Ouer the cyte wer seyn / sundrede tymes	/	A N
J	1223	A calf aȝen kynde / calued in the temple	/	V P D N
J	1224	And eued an ewe-lombe / at [the] / offryng-tyme	P D	N N
J	1225	A wye on the wal cried / wonder heye	/	Z Z
J	1226	Voys fram est and fram west / and fram the / four wyndis	C P D	A N
J	1227	And sayd Wo wo wo / worth on ȝou bothe	/	V P H Z
J	1228	Jerusalem the Jewen toun / and the / joly temple	C D	A N
J	1229	ȝif sayth the wye on the walle / o / word mor	D	N A
J	1230	Wo to this worldly wone / and / wo to my-selue	C	N P H self
J	1231	And deyd whan he don / hadde throw / dynt of [a] slynge	have P	N P D N

J	1232	And haplich was had away / how / wyst I neuere	Q	V H Z
J	1233	And than they deuysed hem / and / vengaunce hit helde	C	N H V
J	1234	And wyten her wo / the / wronge that they wro3te	D	N(A) that H V
J	1235	Whan they brutned in the burwe / the / byschup seint Jame	D	N D N
J	1236	No3t wolde acounte hit for Crist / the / car that they hadde	D	N that H V
J	1237	Bot vp 3eden her 3ates / [they] / 3elden hem alle	H	V H Z
J	1238	Without brunee and bri3t wede / in her / bar chertes	P D	A N
J	1239	Fram none tille the merke ny3t / neuer ne cesed	/	Z not V
J	1240	Bot man after man / mercy bysou3t	/	N V
J	1241	Tytus into the toun / taketh his way	/	V D N
J	1242	My3t no man st[e]ken [i]n the stret / for / stynke of ded corses	P	N P A N
J	1243	The peple in the pauyment / was / pite to byholde	be	N to V
J	1244	That we enfamy[n]ed for defaute / whan hem / fode wanted	C H	N V
J	1245	Was no3t on ladies lafte / bot the / lene bones	P D	A N
J	1246	That wer fleschy byfor / and / fayr on to loke	C	A Z to V
J	1247	Burges with bafies / as / barels or that tyme	C	N C D N
J	1248	No gretter than a grehounde / to / grype on the medil	to	V P D N
J	1249	Tytus tarieth / no3t for that bot to the / temple wendith	not P H C P D	N V
J	1250	That was rayled the roof / with / rebies grete	P	N A
J	1251	With perles and peritotes / alle the / place ferde	D D	N V
J	1252	As glowande gledfur / that on / gold st[r]iketh	that P	N V
J	1253	The dores ful of dyemauntes / dryuen wer thicke	/	E be A
J	1254	And made merueylous lye / with / margeri perles	P	A N
J	1255	Derst no candel be [ky]nde / whan / clerkes scholde rise	C	N X V
J	1256	So wer they lemaunde ly3t / and as a / lampe schonen	C C D	N V
J	1257	The Romayns wayten on the werke / warien the toune	/	V D N
J	1258	That euer so precious a place / scholde / persche for her synne	X	V P D N
J	1259	Out the tresour to take / Tytus commaundyth	/	N V
J	1260	Doun bete the bilde / brenne hit in-to grounde	/	V H P N
J	1261	Ther was plente in the place / of / precious stonys	P	A N
J	1262	Grete gaddes of gold / who-so / grype lyste	Q	V V
J	1263	Platis pecis of peys / pulsched vessel	/	E N
J	1264	Bassynes of brend gold / and other / bry3t ger	C D	A N
J	1265	Pelours masly made / of / metals fele	P	N A
J	1266	In cop[r]e craftly cast / and in / clene seluere	C P	A N
J	1267	Peynted [with] pur gold / alle the / place was ouer	D D	N be Z
J	1268	The Romayns renten / hem doun and to / Rome ledyn	H Z C P	N V
J	1269	Whan they the cyte han sou3t / vpon the / same wyse	P D	A N
J	1270	Telle couthe no tonge / the / tresours that thei ther foundn	D	N that H Z V
J	1271	Jewels for joly men / je[mewes] riche	/	N A
J	1272	Ffloreyns of [fyne] gold / no / freke wanted	D	N V
J	1273	Riche pelour and pane / princes to wer	/	N to V
J	1274	Besantes bies of gold / broches and rynges	/	N C N
J	1275	Clene clothes of selke / many / carte-fulle	D	N N(A)
J	1276	Wele wanteth no wye / bot / wale[th] what hym lyketh	C	V Q H V
J	1277	Now masouns and mynours / han the / molde sou3te	have D	N E
J	1278	With pykeyse and ponsone / persched the walles	/	V D N
J	1279	Hewen throw hard ston / hadde hem to grounde	/	V H P N
J	1280	That alle derkned the diche / for / doust of the pouder	P	N P D N
J	1281	So they wrou3ten at the wal / alle the / woke-tyme	D D	N N
J	1282	Tille the cyte was serched / and / sou3t al aboute	C	E Z Z
J	1283	Maden wast at [a] wappe / ther the / walle stode	Q D	N V
J	1284	Bothe in temple and in tour / alle the / toun ouer	D D	N P
J	1285	Nas no ston in the stede / stondande alofte	/	G Z
J	1286	Morter ne m[o]de walle / bot alle to / mulle fallen	C Z P	N V
J	1287	Nother tymbr ne tre / temple ne other	/	N not H
J	1288	Bot doun betyn and brent / into / blake erthe	P	A N
J	1289	And whan the temple was ouertourned / Tytus commaundys	/	N V
J	1290	In plowes to putte / and alle the / place erye	C D D	N V
J	1291	Suth sow hit with salt / and / seide this wordes	C	V D N
J	1292	Now is this stalwourthe stede / distroied for euere	/	E Z
J	1293	Tytus suth sett / hym on a / sete riche	H P D	N A
J	1294	As juge Jewes to jugge / justise hym-self	/	N H self
J	1295	Criour[s] callen hem forth / as hy that / Crist slowen	C H that	N V
J	1296	And beden Pilat apere / that / prouost was thanne	that	N be Z
J	1297	Pilat proffrith / hym forth / apered at the bar	H Z	V P D N
J	1298	And he frayneth the freke / alle with / fair wordis	Z P	A N
J	1299	Whan Crist of dawe was don / and to the / deth 3ede	C P D	N V
J	1300	Of the he[th]yng that he hadde / and the / hard woundis	C D	A N
J	1301	Than melys the man / and the / matere tolde	C D	N V
J	1302	How alle the ded was don / whan he / deth tholed	C H	N V

J	1303	For thritty penyes in a poke / his / postel hym solde	D	N H V
J	1304	So was he bargayned and bouȝt / and as a / beste quelled	C C D	N V
J	1305	Now corsed be he quoth the kyng / that the / cate made	that D	N V
J	1306	He wexe marchaunte amys / that the / money fenged	that D	N V
J	1307	To sille so precyous a prince / for / penyes so fewe	P	N A A
J	1308	[Thoghe ilke a ferthynge had bene ful / florence an hundrethe]	/	N A N
J	1309	Bot I schal marchaundise make / in / mynde of that other	P	N P H A
J	1310	That schal be hethyng to hem / or I / hennes passe	C H	Z V
J	1311	Alle that here bodyes wol by / or / bargaynes make	C	N V
J	1312	By lower pris for to passe / than they the / prophete solde	C H D	N V
J	1313	He made in myddel of [the] ost / a / market to crye	D	N to V
J	1314	Alle that cheffare wolde chepe / chepis to haue	/	N to V
J	1315	Ay for a peny of pris / who-so / pay wolde	Q	V X
J	1316	Thrytty Jewes in a throm / throngen in ropis	/	E P N
J	1317	So wer they bargayned and bouȝt / and / broȝt out of londe	C	E P P N
J	1318	Neuer suth [on] that syde / cam / segge of hem after	V	N P H Z
J	1319	Ne non that leued in her lawe / scholde in that / londe dwelle	X P D	N V
J	1320	That tormented trewe God / thus / Titus commaundyth	C	N V
J	1321	Josophus the gentile clerke / a-jorneyd was to Rome	/	E be P N
J	1322	Ther of this mater and mo / he / made fayr bokes	H	V A N
J	1323	And Pilat to prisoun / was do to / pyne for euere	be E to	N Z
J	1324	At Viterbe ther he veniaunce / and / vile deth tholed	C	N N V
J	1325	The wye that hym warded / wente on a tyme	/	V P D N
J	1326	Hym-self fedyng with frut / and / feffyt hym with a per	C	V H P D N
J	1327	And forto paren his pere / he / praieth hym ȝerne	H	V H Z
J	1328	Of a knyf and the kempe / kest hym a trenchour	/	V H D N
J	1329	And with the same he schef / hymself to the herte	/	H self P D N
J	1330	And so the kaytif as his kynde / corsedlich deied	/	Z V
J	1331	Whan alle was demed and d[on]e / thei / drow vp tentis	H	V Z N
J	1332	Trossen her tresour / and / trompen vp the sege	C	V Z D N
J	1333	Wenten syngyng away / and han her / wille forthred	C have D	N E
J	1334	And hom riden to Rome / Now / rede ous our lord	Z	V H D N

Patience

Pat 1	Pacience is a poynt, / thaʒ hit / displese ofte.	C H	V Z
Pat 2	When heuy herttes ben hurt / wyth / hethyng other elles,	P	N H Z
Pat 3	Suffraunce may aswagen / hem and the /swelme lethe,	H C D	N V
Pat 4	For ho quelles vche a qued / and / quenches malyce;	C	V N
Pat 5	For quoso suffer cowthe syt, / sele wolde folʒe,	/	N X V
Pat 6	And quo for thro may noʒt thole, / the / thikker he sufferes.	D	Z H V
Pat 7	Then is better to abyde / the / bur vmbestoundes	D	N Z
Pat 8	Then ay throw forth my thro, / thaʒ me / thynk ylle.	C H	V A
Pat 9	I herde on a halyday, / at a / hyʒe masse,	P D	A N
Pat 10	How Mathew melede that his Mayster / His / meyny con teche.	D	N X V
Pat 11	Aʒt happes He hem hyʒt / and / vcheon a mede,	C	H D N
Pat 12	Sunderlupes, for hit dissert, / vpon a / ser wyse:	P D	A N
Pat 13	Thay arn happen that han / in / hert pouerté,	P	N N
Pat 14	For hores is the heuen-ryche / to / holde for euer;	to	V Z
Pat 15	Thay ar happen also / that / haunte mekenesse,	that	V N
Pat 16	For thay schal welde this worlde / and alle her / wylle haue;	C D D	N V
Pat 17	Thay ar happen also / that for her / harme wepes,	that P D	N V
Pat 18	For thay schal comfort encroche / in / kythes ful mony;	P	N Z A
Pat 19	Thay ar happen also / that / hungeres after ryʒt,	that	V P N
Pat 20	For thay schal frely be refete/ ful of alle gode;	/	Z P D A(N)
Pat 21	Thay ar happen also that han / in / hert rauthe,	P	N N
Pat 22	For mercy in alle maneres / her / mede schal worthe;	D	N X V
Pat 23	Thay ar happen also / that arn of / hert clene,	that be P	N A
Pat 24	For thay her Sauyour in sete / schal / se with her yʒen;	X	V P D N
Pat 25	Thay ar happen also / that / halden her pese,	that	V D N
Pat 26	For thay the gracious Godes sunes / schal / godly be called;	X	Z be E
Pat 27	Thay ar happen also / that con her / hert stere,	that X D	N V
Pat 28	For hores is the heuen-ryche, / as I / er sayde.	C H	Z V
Pat 29	These arn the happes alle aʒt / that vus / bihyʒt weren,	that H	E be
Pat 30	If we thyse ladyes wolde lof / in / lyknyng of thewes:	P	N P N
Pat 31	Dame Pouert, Dame Pitée, / Dame / Penaunce the thrydde,	D	N D N
Pat 32	Dame Mekenesse, Dame Mercy, / and / miry Clannesse,	C	A N
Pat 33	And thenne Dame Pes, and Pacyence / put in therafter.	/	V Z Z
Pat 34	He were happen that hade one; / alle were the better.	/	H be D A
Pat 35	Bot syn I am put to a poynt / that / pouerté hatte,	that	N V
Pat 36	I schal me poruay pacyence / and / play me with bothe,	C	V H P H
Pat 37	For in the tyxte there thyse two / arn in / teme layde,	be P	N E
Pat 38	Hit arn fettled in on forme, / the / forme and the laste,	D	N C D N
Pat 39	And by quest of her quoyntyse / enquylen on mede.	/	V P N
Pat 40	And als, in myn vpnynyoun, / hit arn of on kynde:	/	H be P N
Pat 41	For theras pouert hir proferes / ho nyl be / put vtter,	H X be	E Z
Pat 42	Bot lenge wheresoeuer hir lyst, / lyke other greme:	/	V C V
Pat 43	And thereas pouert enpresses, / thaʒ mon / pyne thynk,	C N	N V
Pat 44	Much, maugré his mun, / he / mot nede suffer;	H	X V V
Pat 45	Thus pouerté and pacyence / arn / nedes playferes.	be	N N
Pat 46	Sythen I am sette with hem samen, / suffer me byhoues;	/	V H V
Pat 47	Thenne is me lyʒtloker hit lyke / and her / lotes prayse,	C D	N V
Pat 48	Thenne wyther wyth and be wroth / and the / wers haue.	C D	N(A) V
Pat 49	ʒif me be dyʒt a destyné / due to haue,	/	N to V
Pat 50	What dowes me the dedayn, / other / dispit make?	D	N V
Pat 51	Other ʒif my lege lorde lyst / on / lyue me to bidde	P	N H to V
Pat 52	Other to ryde other to renne / to / Rome in his ernde,	P	N P D N
Pat 53	What graythed me the grychchyng / bot / grame more seche?	C	N D V
Pat 54	Much ʒif he me nade, / maugref my chekes,	/	P D N
Pat 55	And thenne thrat moste I thole / and / vnthonk to mede,	C	V P N
Pat 56	The had bowed to his bode / bongré my hyure.	/	P D N
Pat 57	Did not Jonas in Judé / suche / jape sumwhyle?	D	N Z
Pat 58	To sette hym to sewrté, / vnsounde he hym feches.	C	N H H V
Pat 59	Wyl ʒe tary a lyttel tyne / and / tent me a whyle,	C	V H Z
Pat 60	I schal wysse yow therwyth / as / holy wryt telles.	C	A N V
Pat 61	Hit bitydde sumtyme / in the / termes of Judé,	P D	N P N
Pat 62	Jonas joyned / watz therinne / Jentyle prophete;	be Z	A N
Pat 63	Goddes glam to hym glod / that hym / vnglad made,	that H	A V
Pat 64	With a roghlych rurd / rowned in his ere:	/	V P D N
Pat 65	'Rys radly,' / He says, 'and / rayke forth euen;	H V C	V Z Z
Pat 66	Nym the way to Nynyue / wythouten / other speche,	P	A N

178

Patience

Pat 67	And in that ceté My saȝes / soȝhe alle aboute,	/	V Z Z
Pat 68	That in that place, at the poynt, / I / put in thi hert.	H	V P D N
Pat 69	For iwysse hit arn so wykke / that in that / won dowellez	that P D	N V
Pat 70	And her malys is so much, / I / may not abide,	H	X not V
Pat 71	Bot venge Me on her vilanye / and / venym bilyue;	C	V Z
Pat 72	Now sweȝe Me thider swyftly / and / say Me this arende.'	C	V H D N
Pat 73	When that steuen watz stynt / that / stowned his mynde,	that	V D N
Pat 74	Al he wrathed in his wyt, / and / wytherly he thoȝt:	C	Z H V
Pat 75	'If I bowe to His bode / and / bryng hem this tale,	C	V H D N
Pat 76	And I be nummen in Nuniue, / my / nyes begynes:	D	N V
Pat 77	He telles me those traytoures / arn / typped schrewes;	be	E N
Pat 78	I com wyth those tythynges, / thay / ta me bylyue,	H	V H Z
Pat 79	Pynez me in a prysoun, / put me in stokkes,	/	V H P N
Pat 80	Wrythe me in a warlok, / wrast out myn yȝen.	/	V P D N
Pat 81	This is a meruayl message / a / man for to preche	D	N for to V
Pat 82	Amonge enmyes so mony / and / mansed fendes,	C	E N
Pat 83	Bot if my gaynlych God / such / gref to me wolde,	D	N P H V
Pat 84	For desert of sum sake / that I / slayn were.	that H	E be
Pat 85	At alle peryles,' quoth the prophete, / 'I / aproche hit no nerre.	H	V H Z
Pat 86	I wyl me sum other waye / that He ne / wayte after;	that H not	V Z
Pat 87	I schal tee into Tarce / and / tary there a whyle,	C	V Z Z
Pat 88	And lyȝtly when I am lest / He / letes me alone.'	H	V H Z
Pat 89	Thenne he ryses radly / and / raykes bilyue,	C	V Z
Pat 90	Jonas toward port Japh, / ay / janglande for tene	Z	G P N
Pat 91	That he nolde thole for nothyng / non of those pynes,	/	H P D N
Pat 92	Thaȝ the Fader that hym formed / were / fale of his hele.	be	A P D N
Pat 93	'Oure Syre syttes,' / he says, 'on / sege so hyȝe	H V P	N Z Z
Pat 94	In His glowande glorye, / and / gloumbes ful lyttel	C	N Z A
Pat 95	Thaȝ I be nummen in Nunniue / and / naked dispoyled,	C	E E
Pat 96	On rode rwly torent / with / rybaudes mony.'	P	N A
Pat 97	Thus he passes to that port / his / passage to seche,	D	N to V
Pat 98	Fyndes he a fayr schyp / to the / fare redy,	P D	A N
Pat 99	Maches hym with the maryneres, / makes her paye	/	V D N
Pat 100	For to towe hym into Tarce / as / tyd as thay myȝt.	C	Z C H X
Pat 101	Then he tron on tho tres, / and thay her / tramme ruchen,	C H D	N V
Pat 102	Cachen vp the crossayl, / cables thay fasten,	/	N H V
Pat 103	Wiȝt at the wyndas / weȝen her ankres,	/	V D N
Pat 104	Spende spak to the sprete / the / spare bawelyne,	D	A N
Pat 105	Gederen to the gyde-ropes, / the / grete cloth falles,	D	A N V
Pat 106	Thay layden in on ladde borde, / and the / lofe wynnes.	C D	N V
Pat 107	The blythe brethe at her bak / the / bosum he fyndes;	H	N H V
Pat 108	He swenges me thys swete schip / swefte fro the hauen.	/	Z P D N
Pat 109	Watz neuer so joyful a Jue / as / Jonas watz thenne,	C	N be Z
Pat 110	That the daunger of Dryȝtyn / so / derfly ascaped;	Z	Z V
Pat 111	He wende wel that that Wyȝ / that al the / world planted	that D D	N E
Pat 112	Hade no maȝt in that mere / no / man for to greue.	D	N for to V
Pat 113	Lo, the wytles wrechche! / For he / wolde noȝt suffer,	C H	X not V
Pat 114	Now hatz he put hym in plyt / of / peril wel more.	P	N Z Z
Pat 115	Hit watz a wenyng vnwar / that / welt in his mynde,	that	V P D N
Pat 116	Thaȝ he were soȝt fro Samarye, / that / God seȝ no fyrre.	that	N V Z
Pat 117	ȝise, He blusched ful brode: / that / burde hym by sure;	that	V H Z Z
Pat 118	That ofte kyd hym the carpe / that / kyng sayde,	that	N V
Pat 119	Dyngne Dauid on des / that / demed this speche	that	V D N
Pat 120	In a psalme that he set / the / sauter withinne:	D	N P
Pat 121	'O folez in folk, / felez otherwhyle	/	V Z
Pat 122	And vnderstondes vmbestounde, / thaȝ ȝe be / stapen in folé:	C H be	E P N
Pat 123	Hope ȝe that He heres / not that / eres alle made?	not that	N Z V
Pat 124	Hit may not be that He is blynde / that / bigged vche yȝe.'	that	V D N
Pat 125	Bot he dredes no dynt / that / dotes for elde.	that	V P N
Pat 126	For he watz fer in the flod / foundande to Tarce,	/	G P N
Pat 127	Bot I trow ful tyd / ouertan that he were,	/	E that H be
Pat 128	So that schomely to schort / he / schote of his ame.	H	V P D N
Pat 129	For the Welder of wyt / that / wot alle thynges,	that	V D N
Pat 130	That ay wakes and waytes, / at / wylle hatz He slyȝtes.	P	N V H N
Pat 131	He calde on that ilk crafte / He / carf with His hondes;	H	V P D N
Pat 132	Thay wakened wel the wrotheloker / for / wrothely He cleped:	C	Z H V
Pat 133	'Ewrus and Aquiloun / that / on / est sittes	that P	N V
Pat 134	Blowes bothe at My bode / vpon / blo watteres.'	P	A N
Pat 135	Thenne watz no tom ther bytwene / His/ tale and her dede,	D	N C D N
Pat 136	So bayn wer thay bothe / two His / bone for to wyrk.	D D	N for to V
Pat 137	Anon out of the north-est / the / noys bigynes,	D	N V

Pat 138	When bothe brethes con blowe / vpon / blo watteres.	P	A N
Pat 139	Roȝ rakkes ther ros / with / rudnyng anvnder;	P	G Z
Pat 140	The see souȝed ful sore, / gret selly to here;	/	A N to V
Pat 141	The wyndes on the wonne water / so / wrastel togeder	Z	V Z
Pat 142	That the wawes ful wode / waltered so hiȝe	/	V Z Z
Pat 143	And efte busched to the abyme, / that / breed fysches	that	E N
Pat 144	Durst nowhere for roȝ / arest at the bothem.	/	V P D N
Pat 145	When the breth and the brok / and the / bote metten,	C D	N V
Pat 146	Hit watz a joyles gyn / that / Jonas watz inne,	that	N be P
Pat 147	For hit reled on roun / vpon the / roȝe ythes.	P D	A N
Pat 148	The bur ber to hit baft, / that / braste alle her gere,	that	V D D N
Pat 149	Then hurled on a hepe / the / helme and the sterne;	D	N C D N
Pat 150	Furst tomurte mony rop / and the / mast after;	C D	N P
Pat 151	The sayl sweyed on the see, / thenne / suppe bihoued	Z	V V
Pat 152	The coge of the colde water, / and thenne the / cry ryses.	C Z D	N V
Pat 153	Ȝet coruen thay the cordes / and / kest al theroute;	C	V Z Z
Pat 154	Mony ladde ther forth lep / to / laue and to kest —	to	V C to V
Pat 155	Scopen out the scathel water / that / fayn scape wolde —	that	Z V X
Pat 156	For þe monnes lode neuer so luther, / the/ lyf is ay swete.	D	N be Z A
Pat 157	Ther watz busy ouer borde / bale to kest,	/	N to V
Pat 158	Her bagges and her fether-beddes / and her / bryȝt wedes,	C D	A N
Pat 159	Her kysttes and her coferes, / her / caraldes alle,	D	N Z
Pat 160	And al to lyȝten that lome, / ȝif / lethe wolde schape.	C	N X V
Pat 161	Bot euer watz ilyche loud / the / lot of the wyndes,	D	N P D N
Pat 162	And euer wrother the water / and / wodder the stremes.	C	A D N
Pat 163	Then tho wery forwroȝt / wyst no bote,	/	V D N
Pat 164	Bot vchon glewed on his god / that / gayned hym beste:	that	V H Z
Pat 165	Summe to Vernagu ther vouched / avowes solemne,	/	V Z
Pat 166	Summe to Diana deuout / and / derf Neptune,	C	A N
Pat 167	To Mahoun and to Mergot, / the / mone and the sunne,	D	N C D N
Pat 168	And vche lede as he loued / and / layde had his hert.	C	E have D N
Pat 169	Thenne bispeke the spakest, / dispayred wel nere:	/	E Z be
Pat 170	'I leue here be sum losynger, / sum / lawles wrech,	D	A N
Pat 171	That hatz greued his god / and / gotz here amonge vus.	C	V Z P H
Pat 172	Lo, al synkes in his synne / and for his / sake marres.	C P D	N V
Pat 173	I lovue that we lay lotes / on / ledes vchone,	P	N A
Pat 174	And whoso lympes the losse, / lay hym theroute;	/	V H Z
Pat 175	And quen the gulty is gon, / what may / gome trawe	Q X	N V
Pat 176	Bot He that rules the rak / may / rwe on those other?'	X	V P D H
Pat 177	This watz sette in asent, / and / sembled thay were,	C	E H be
Pat 178	Herȝed out of vche hyrne / to / hent that falles.	to	V that V
Pat 179	A lodesmon lyȝtly / lep vnder hachches,	/	V P N
Pat 180	For to layte mo ledes / and hem to / lote bryng.	C H to	N V
Pat 181	Bot hym fayled no freke / that he / fynde myȝt,	that H	V X
Pat 182	Saf Jonas the Jwe, / that / jowked in derne.	that	V P N
Pat 183	He watz flowen for ferde / of the / flode lotes	P D	N N
Pat 184	Into the bothem of the bot, / and on a / brede lyggede,	C P D	N G
Pat 185	Onhelde by the hurrok, / for the / heuen wrache,	P D	N N
Pat 186	Slypped vpon a sloumbe-selepe, / and / sloberande he routes.	C	G H V
Pat 187	The freke hym frunt with his fot / and / bede hym ferk vp:	C	V H V Z
Pat 188	Ther Ragnel in his rakentes / hym / rere of his dremes!	H	V P D N
Pat 189	Bi the haspede hater / he / hentes hym thenne,	H	V H Z
Pat 190	And broȝt hym vp by the brest / and vpon / borde sette,	C P	N V
Pat 191	Arayned hym ful runyschly / what / raysoun he hade	Q	N H V
Pat 193	In such slaȝtes of sorȝe / to / slepe so faste.	to	V Z Z
Pat 193	Sone haf thay her sortes sette / and / serelych deled,	C	Z E
Pat 194	And ay the lote vpon laste / lymped on Jonas.	/	V P N
Pat 195	Thenne ascryed thay hym sckete / and / asked ful loude:	C	V Z Z
Pat 196	'What the deuel hatz thou don, / doted wrech?	/	E N
Pat 197	What seches thou on see, / synful schrewe,	/	A N
Pat 198	With thy lastes so luther / to / lose vus vchone?	to	V H H
Pat 199	Hatz thou, gome, no gouernour / ne / god on to calle,	not	N P to V
Pat 200	That thou thus slydes on slepe / when thou / slayn worthes?	C H	E V
Pat 201	Of what londe art thou lent, / what / laytes thou here,	Q	V H Z
Pat 202	Whyder in worlde that thou wylt, / and / what is thyn arnde?	C	Q be D N
Pat 203	Lo, thy dom is the dyȝt, / for thy / dedes ille.	P D	N A
Pat 204	Do gyf glory to thy god, / er thou / glyde hens.'	C H	V Z
Pat 205	'I am an Ebru,' / quoth he, 'of / Israyl borne;	V H P	N E
Pat 206	That Wyȝe I worchyp, iwysse, / that / wroȝt alle thynges,	that	V D N
Pat 207	Alle the worlde with the welkyn, / the / wynde and the sternes,	D	N C D N
Pat 208	And alle þat wonez ther withinne, / at a / worde one.	P D	N A

Pat 209	Alle this meschef for me / is / made at thys tyme,	be		E P D N
Pat 210	For I haf greued my God / and / gulty am founden;	C		A be E
Pat 211	Forthy berez me to the borde / and / bathes me theroute,	C		V H Z
Pat 212	Er gete ʒe no happe, / I / hope forsothe.'	H		V Z
Pat 213	He ossed hym by vnnynges / that thay / vndernomen	that H		V
Pat 214	That he watz flawen fro the face / of / frelych Dryʒtyn;	P		A N
Pat 215	Thenne such a ferde on hem fel / and / flayed hem withinne	C		V H P
Pat 216	That thay ruyt hym to rowwe, / and letten the / rynk one.	C V D		N Z
Pat 217	Hatheles hyʒed in haste / with / ores ful longe,	P		N Z A
Pat 218	Syn her sayl watz hem aslypped, / on / sydez to rowe,	P		N to V
Pat 219	Hef and hale vpon hyʒt / to / helpen hymseluen,	to		V H self
Pat 220	Bot al watz nedles note: / that / nolde not bityde.	that		X not V
Pat 221	In bluber of the blo flod / bursten her ores.	/		V D N
Pat 222	Thenne hade thay noʒt in her honde / that hem / help myʒt;	that H		V X
Pat 223	Thenne nas no coumfort to keuer, / ne / counsel non other,	not		N Z
Pat 224	Bot Jonas into his juis / jugge bylyue.	/		V Z
Pat 225	Fyrst thay prayen to the Prynce / that / prophetes seruen	that		N V
Pat 226	That He gef hem the grace / to / greuen Hym neuer,	to		V H Z
Pat 227	That thay in balelez blod / ther / blenden her handez,	Z		V D N
Pat 228	Thaʒ that hathel wer His / that thay / here quelled.	that H		Z V
Pat 229	Tyd by top and bi to / that / token hym synne;	H		V H Z
Pat 230	Into that lodlych loʒe / thay/ luche hym sone.	H		V H Z
Pat 231	He watz no tytter outtulde / that / tempest ne sessed:	that		N not V
Pat 232	The se saʒtled / therwith as / sone as ho moʒt.	Z C		Z C H X
Pat 233	Thenne thaʒ her takel were torne / that / totered on ythes,	that		V P N
Pat 234	Styffe stremes and streʒt / hem / strayned a whyle,	H		V Z
Pat 235	That drof hem dryʒlych / adoun the / depe to serue,	Z D		N(A) to V
Pat 236	Tyl a swetter ful swythe / hem / sweʒed to bonk.	H		V P N
Pat 237	Ther watz louyng on lofte, / when thay the / londe wonnen,	C H D		N V
Pat 238	To oure mercyable God, / on / Moyses wyse,	P		N N
Pat 239	With sacrafyse vpset, / and / solempne vowes,	C		Z V
Pat 240	And graunted Hym on to be God / and / graythly non other.	C		Z Z
Pat 241	Thaʒ thay be jolef for joye, / Jonas ʒet dredes;	/		N Z V
Pat 242	Thaʒ he nolde suffer no sore, / his / seele is on anter;	D		N be P N
Pat 243	For whatso worthed of that wyʒe / fro he in / water dipped,	Z H P		N V
Pat 244	Hit were a wonder to wene, / ʒif / holy wryt nere.	C		A N be
Pat 245	Now is Jonas the Jwe / jugged to drowne;	/		E to V
Pat 246	Of that schended schyp / men / schowued hym sone.	N		V H Z
Pat 247	A wylde walterande whal, / as / Wyrde then schaped,	C		N Z V
Pat 248	That watz beten fro the abyme, / bi that / bot flotte,	P D		N G
Pat 249	And watz war of that wyʒe / that the / water soʒte,	that D		N V
Pat 250	And swyftely swenged hym to swepe, / and his / swolʒ opened;	C D		N V
Pat 251	The folk ʒet haldande his fete, / the / fysch hym tyd hentes;	D		N H Z V
Pat 252	Withouten towche of any tothe / he / tult in his throte.	H		V P D N
Pat 253	Thenne he swengez and swayues / to the / se bothem,	P D		N N
Pat 254	Bi mony rokkez ful roʒe / and / rydelande strondes,	C		G N
Pat 255	Wyth the mon in his mawe / malskred in drede,	/		E P N
Pat 256	As lyttel wonder hit watz, / ʒif he / wo dreʒed,	C H		N V
Pat 257	For nade the hyʒe Heuen-Kyng, / thurʒ His / honde myʒt,	P D		N N
Pat 258	Warded this wrech man / in / warlowes guttez,	P		N N
Pat 259	What lede moʒt leue / bi / lawe of any kynde,	P		N P D N
Pat 260	That any lyf myʒt be lent / so / longe hym withinne?	Z		Z H P
Pat 261	Bot he watz sokored by that Syre / that / syttes so hiʒe,	that		V Z Z
Pat 262	Thaʒ were wanlez of wele / in / wombe of that fissche,	P		N P D N
Pat 263	And also dryuen thurʒ the depe / and in / derk walterez.	C P		A N
Pat 264	Lorde, colde watz his cumfort, / and his / care huge,	C D		N A
Pat 265	For he knew vche a cace / and / kark that hym lymped,	C		N that H V
Pat 266	How fro the bot into the blober / watz with a / best lachched,	be P D		N E
Pat 267	And thrwe in at hit throte / withouten / thret more,	P		N A
Pat 268	As mote in at a munster dor, / so / mukel wern his chawlez.	Z		A be D N
Pat 269	He glydes in by the giles / thurʒ / glaym ande glette,	P		N C N
Pat 270	Relande in by a rop, / a / rode that hym thoʒt,	D		N that H V
Pat 271	Ay hele ouer hed / hourlande aboute,	/		G Z
Pat 272	Til he blunt in a blok / as / brod as a halle;	C		A C D N
Pat 273	And ther he festnes the fete / and / fathmez aboute,	C		N Z
Pat 274	And stod vp in his stomak / that / stank as the deuel.	that		V P D N
Pat 275	Ther in saym and in sorʒe / that / sauoured as helle,	that		V P N
Pat 276	Ther watz bylded his bour / that wyl no / bale suffer.	that X D		N V
Pat 277	And thenne he lurkkes and laytes / where watz / le best,	Q be		N A
Pat 278	In vche a nok of his nauel, / bot / nowhere he fyndez	C		Z H V
Pat 279	No rest ne recouerer, / bot / ramel ande myre,	P		N C N

Pat 280	In wych gut so euer he gotz, / bot euer is / God swete;	C Z be	N A
Pat 281	And ther he lenged at the last, / and to the / Lede called:	C P D	N V
Pat 282	'Now, Prynce, of Thy prophete / pité Thou haue.	/	N H V
Pat 283	Thaȝ I be fol and fykel / and / falce of my hert,	C	A P D N
Pat 284	Dewoyde now Thy vengaunce, / thurȝ / vertu of rauthe;	P	N P N
Pat 285	Thaȝ I be gulty of gyle, / as / gaule of prophetes,	P	N P N
Pat 286	Thou art God, and alle gowdez / ar / graythely Thyn owen.	be	Z D A
Pat 287	Haf now mercy of Thy man / and his / mysdedes,	C D	N
Pat 288	And preue The lyȝtly a Lorde / in / londe and in water.'	P	N C P N
Pat 289	With that he hitte to a hyrne / and / helde hym therinne,	C	V H Z
Pat 290	Ther no defoule of no fylthe / watz / fest hym abute;	be	Z H P
Pat 291	Ther he sete also sounde, / saf for merk one,	/	P P N Z
Pat 292	As in the bulk of the bote / ther he / byfore sleped.	Q H	Z V
Pat 293	So in a bouel of that best / he / bidez on lyue,	H	V P N
Pat 294	Thre dayes and thre nyȝt, / ay / thenkande on Dryȝtyn,	Z	G P N
Pat 295	His myȝt and His merci, / His / mesure thenne.	D	N Z
Pat 296	Now he knawez Hym in care / that / couthe not in sele.	that	V not P N
Pat 297	Ande euer walteres this whal / bi / wyldren depe,	P	N A
Pat 298	Thurȝ mony a regioun ful roȝe, / thurȝ / ronk of his wylle;	P	N P D N
Pat 299	For that mote in his mawe / mad hym, I trowe,	/	V H H V
Pat 300	Thaȝ hit lyttel were hym wyth, / to / wamel at his hert;	to	V P D N
Pat 301	Ande as sayled the segge, / ay / sykerly he herde	Z	Z H V
Pat 302	The bygge borne on his bak / and / bete on his sydes.	C	V P D N
Pat 303	Then a prayer ful prest / the / prophete ther maked;	D	N Z V
Pat 304	On this wyse, as I wene, / his / wordez were mony:	D	N be A
Pat 305	'Lorde, to The haf I cleped / in / carez ful stronge;	P	N Z A
Pat 306	Out of the hole Thou me herde / of / hellen wombe;	P	N N
Pat 307	I calde, and Thou knew / myn / vncler steuen.	D	A N
Pat 308	Thou diptez me of the depe se / into the / dymme hert,	P D	A N
Pat 309	The grete flem of Thy flod / folded me vmbe;	/	V H P
Pat 310	Alle the gotez of Thy guferes / and / groundelez powlez,	C	A N
Pat 311	And Thy stryuande stremez / of / stryndez so mony,	P	N Z A
Pat 312	In on daschande dam / dryuez me ouer.	/	V H P
Pat 313	And ȝet I sayde as I seet / in the / se bothem:	P D	N N
Pat 314	"Careful am I, kest / out fro Thy / cler ȝen	P P D	A N
Pat 315	And deseuered fro Thy syȝt; / ȝet / surely I hope	Z	Z H V
Pat 316	Efte to trede on Thy temple / and / teme to Thyseluen."	C	V P H self
Pat 317	I am wrapped in water / to my / wo stoundez;	P D	N V
Pat 318	The abyme byndes the body / that I / byde inne;	that H	V Z
Pat 319	The pure poplande hourle / playes on my heued;	/	V P D N
Pat 320	To laste mere of vche a mount, / Man, am I fallen;	/	N be H E
Pat 321	The barrez of vche a bonk / ful / bigly me haldes,	Z	Z H V
Pat 322	That I may lachche no lont, / and Thou my / lyf weldes.	C H D	N V
Pat 323	Thou schal releue me, Renk, / whil Thy / ryȝt slepez,	C D	N V
Pat 324	Thurȝ myȝt of Thy mercy, / that / mukel is to tryste.	that	Z be to V
Pat 325	For when th' acces of anguych / watz / hid in my sawle,	be	E P D N
Pat 326	Thenne I remembered me ryȝt / of my / rych Lorde,	P D	A N
Pat 327	Prayande Him for peté / His / prophete to here,	D	N to V
Pat 328	That into His holy hous / myn / orisoun moȝt entre.	D	N X V
Pat 329	I haf meled with Thy maystres / mony longe day,	/	A A N
Pat 330	Bot now I wot wyterly / that those / vnwyse ledes	that D	A N
Pat 331	That affyen hym in vanyté / and in / vayne thynges	C P	A N
Pat 332	For think that mountes to noȝt / her / mercy forsaken;	D	N E
Pat 333	Bot I dewoutly awowe, / that / verray betz halden,	that	Z be E
Pat 334	Soberly to do The sacrafyse / when I schal / saue worthe,	C H X	A V
Pat 335	And offer The for my hele / a ful / hol gyfte,	D Z	A N
Pat 336	And halde goud that Thou me hetes: / haf here my trauthe.'	/	V Z D N
Pat 337	Thenne oure Fader to the fysch / ferslych biddez	/	Z V
Pat 338	That he hym sput spakly / vpon / spare drye.	P	A N
Pat 339	The whal wendez at His wylle / and a / warthe fyndez,	C D	N V
Pat 340	And ther he brakez vp the buyrne / as / bede hym oure Lorde.	C	V H D N
Pat 341	Thenne he swepe to the sonde / in / sluchched clothes:	P	E N
Pat 342	Hit may wel be that mester / were his / mantyle to wasche.	be D	N to V
Pat 343	The bonk that he blosched / to and / bode hym bisyde	P C	V H P
Pat 344	Wern of the regiounes ryȝt / that he / renayed hade.	that H	E have
Pat 345	Thenne a wynde of Goddez worde / efte the / wyȝe bruxlez:	Z D	N V
Pat 346	'Nylt thou neuer to Nuniue / bi no / kynnez wayez?'	P D	N N
Pat 347	'Ȝisse, Lorde,' quoth the lede, / 'lene me Thy grace	/	V H D N
Pat 348	For to go at Thi gre: / me / gaynez non other.	H	V Z
Pat 349	'Ris, aproche then to prech, / lo, the / place here.	I D	N Z
Pat 350	Lo, My lore is in the loke, / lauce hit therinne.'	/	V H Z

Patience

Pat 351	Thenne the renk radly / ros as he myȝt,	/	V C H X
Pat 352	And to Niniue that naȝt / he / neȝed ful euen;	H	V Z Z
Pat 353	Hit watz a ceté ful syde / and / selly of brede;	C	A P N
Pat 354	On to threnge therthurȝe / watz / thre dayes dede.	be	A N N
Pat 355	That on journay ful joynt / Jonas hym ȝede,	/	N H V
Pat 356	Er euer he warpped any worde / to / wyȝe that he mette,	P	N that H V
Pat 357	And thenne he cryed so cler / that / kenne myȝt alle	that	V X H
Pat 358	The trwe tenor of his teme; / he / tolde on this wyse:	H	V P D N
Pat 359	'ȝet schal forty dayez fully / fare to an ende,	/	V P D N
Pat 360	And thenne schal Niniue be nomen / and to / noȝt worthe;	C to	not V
Pat 361	Truly this ilk toun / schal / tylte to grounde;	X	V P N
Pat 362	Vp-so-doun schal ȝe dumpe / depe to the abyme,	/	Z P D N
Pat 363	To be swolȝed swyftly / wyth the / swart erthe,	P D	A N
Pat 364	And alle that lyuyes / hereinne / lose the swete.'	Z	V D N
Pat 365	This speche sprang in that space / and / spradde alle aboute,	C	V Z Z
Pat 366	To borges and to bacheleres / that in that / burȝ lenged;	that P D	N V
Pat 367	Such a hidor hem hent / and a / hatel drede,	C D	A N
Pat 368	That al chaunged her chere / and / chylled at the hert.	C	V P D N
Pat 369	The segge sesed / not ȝet, bot / sayde euer ilyche:	not Z C	V Z Z
Pat 370	'The verray vengaunce of God / schal / voyde this place!'	X	V D N
Pat 371	Thenne the peple pitosly / pleyned ful stylle,	/	V Z Z
Pat 372	And for the drede of Dryȝtyn / doured in hert;	/	V P N
Pat 373	Heter hayrez thay hent / that / asperly bited,	that	Z V
Pat 374	And those thay bounden to her bak / and to her / bare sydez,	C P D	A N
Pat 375	Dropped dust on her hede, / and / dymly bisoȝten	C	Z V
Pat 376	That that penaunce plesed / Him that / playnez on her wronge.	H that	V P D N(A)
Pat 377	And ay he cryes in that kyth / tyl / the / kyng herde,	C D	N V
Pat 378	And he radly vpros / and / ran fro his chayer,	C	V P D N
Pat 379	His ryche robe he torof / of his / rigge naked,	P D	N A
Pat 380	And of a hep of askes / he / hitte in the myddez.	H	V P D N
Pat 381	He askez heterly a hayre / and / hasped hym vmbe,	C	V H P
Pat 382	Sewed a sekke / therabof, and / syked ful colde;	Z C	V Z Z
Pat 383	Ther he dared in that duste, / with / droppande teres,	P	G N
Pat 384	Wepande ful wonderly / alle his / wrange dedes.	D D	A N
Pat 385	Thenne sayde he to his serjauntes: / 'Samnes yow bilyue;	/	V H Z
Pat 386	Do dryue out a decre, / demed of myseluen,	/	V P H self
Pat 387	That alle the bodyes that ben / withinne this / borȝ quyk,	P D	N A
Pat 388	Bothe burnes and bestes, / burdez and childer,	/	N C N
Pat 389	Vch prynce, vche prest, / and / prelates alle,	C	N A
Pat 390	Alle faste frely / for her / falce werkes;	P D	A N
Pat 391	Sesez childer of her sok, / soghe hem so neuer,	/	V H Z Z
Pat 392	Ne best bite on no brom, / ne no / bent nauther,	not D	N Z
Pat 393	Passe to no pasture, / ne / pike non erbes,	not	V D N
Pat 394	Ne non oxe to no hay, / ne no / horse to water.	not D	N P N
Pat 395	Al schal crye, forclemmed, / with alle oure / clere strenthe;	P D D	A N
Pat 396	The rurd schal ryse / to Hym that / rawthe schal haue;	P H that	N X V
Pat 397	What wote other wyte / may ȝif the / Wyȝe lykes,	X C D	N V
Pat 398	That is hende in the hyȝt / of / His gentryse?'	P	D N
Pat 399	I wot His myȝt is much, / thaȝ He be / myssepayed,	C H be	E
Pat 400	That in His mylde amesyng / He / mercy may fynde.	H	N X V
Pat 401	And if we leuen the layk / of oure / layth synnes,	P D	A N
Pat 402	And stylle steppen in the styȝe / He / styȝtlez Hymseluen,	H	V H self
Pat 403	He wyl wende of His wodschip / and His / wrath leue,	C D	N V
Pat 404	And forgif vus this gult, / ȝif we Hym / God leuen.'	C H H	N V
Pat 405	Thenne al leued on His lawe / and / laften her synnes,	C	V D N
Pat 406	Parformed alle the penaunce / that the / prynce radde;	that D	N V
Pat 407	And God thurȝ His godnesse / forgef as He sayde;	/	V C H V
Pat 408	Thaȝ He other bihyȝt, / withhelde His vengaunce.	/	V D N
Pat 409	Muche sorȝe thenne satteled / vpon / segge Jonas;	P	N N
Pat 410	He wex as wroth as the wynde / towarde oure Lorde.	/	P D N
Pat 411	So hatz anger onhit / his / hert, he callez	D	N H V
Pat 412	A prayer to the hyȝe Prynce, / for / pyne, on thys wyse:	P	N P D N
Pat 413	'I bische The, Syre, / now Thou / self jugge;	Z H	self V
Pat 414	Watz not this ilk worde / that / worthen is nouthe,	that	E be Z
Pat 415	That I kest in my cuntré, / when Thou Thy / carp sendez	C H D	N V
Pat 416	That I schulde tee to thys toun / Thi / talent to preche?	D	N to V
Pat 417	Wel knew I Thi cortaysye, / Thy / quoynt soffraunce,	D	A N
Pat 418	Thy bounté of debonerté / and Thy / bene grace,	C D	A N
Pat 419	Thy longe abydyng wyth lur, / Thy / late vengaunce;	D	A N
Pat 420	And ay Thy mercy is mete, / be / mysse neuer so huge.	P	N Z Z
Pat 421	I wyst wel, when I hade worded / quatsoeuer I cowthe	/	Q H V

Pat 422	To manace alle thise mody men / that in this / mote dowellez,	that P D	N V
Pat 423	Wyth a prayer and a pyne / thay myʒt her / peşe gete,	H X D	N V
Pat 424	And therfore I wolde haf flowen / fer into Tarce.	/	Z P N
Pat 425	Now, Lorde, lach out my lyf, / hit / lastes to longe.	H	V Z Z
Pat 426	Bed me bilyue my bale-stour / and / bryng me on ende,	C	V H P N
Pat 427	For me were swetter to swelt / as / swythe, as me thynk,	C	Z C H V
Pat 428	Then lede lenger Thi lore / that thus me / les makez.'	that C H	A V
Pat 429	The soun of oure Souerayn / then / swey in his ere,	Z	V P D N
Pat 430	That vpbraydes this burne / vpon a / breme wyse:	P D	A N
Pat 431	'Herk, renk, is this ryʒt / so / ronkly to wrath	Z	Z to V
Pat 432	For any dede that I haf don / other / demed the ʒet?'	H	V H Z
Pat 433	Jonas al joyles / and / janglande vpryses,	C	N (G) V
Pat 434	And haldez out on est half / of the / hyʒe place,	P D	A N
Pat 435	And farandely on a felde / he / fettelez hym to bide,	H	V H to V
Pat 436	For to wayte on that won / what schulde / worthe after.	Q X	V Z
Pat 437	Ther he busked hym a bour, / the / best that he myʒt,	D	N(A) that H X
Pat 438	Of hay and of euer-ferne / and / erbez a fewe,	C	N A
Pat 439	For hit watz playn in that place / for / plyande greuez,	P	G N
Pat 440	For to schylde fro the schene / other any / schade keste.	D D	N V
Pat 441	He bowed vnder his lyttel bothe, / his / bak to the sunne,	D	N P D N
Pat 442	And ther he swowed and slept / sadly al nyʒt,	/	Z Z
Pat 443	The whyle God of His grace / ded / growe of that soyle	V	V P D N
Pat 444	The fayrest bynde hym abof / that euer / burne wyste.	that Z	N V
Pat 445	When the dawande day / Dryʒtyn con sende,	/	N X V
Pat 446	Thenne wakened the wyʒ / vnder / wodbynde,	P	N
Pat 447	Loked alofte on the lef / that / lylled grene;	that	V A
Pat 448	Such a lefsel of lof / neuer / lede hade,	Z	N V
Pat 449	For hit watz brod at the bothem, / boʒted on lofte,	/	V Z
Pat 450	Happed vpon ayther half, / a / hous as hit were,	D	N C H be
Pat 451	A nos on the north syde / and / nowhere non ellez,	C	Q not Z
Pat 452	Bot al schet in a schaʒe / that / schaded ful cole.	that	V Z Z
Pat 453	The gome glyʒt on the grene / graciouse leues,	/	A N
Pat 454	That euer wayued a wynde / so / wythe and so cole;	Z	A C Z A
Pat 455	The schyre sunne hit vmbeschon, / thaʒ no / schafte myʒt	C D	N X
Pat 456	The mountaunce of a lyttel mote / vpon that / man schyne.	P D	N V
Pat 457	Thenne watz the gome so glad / of his / gay logge,	P D	A N
Pat 458	Lys loltrande / therinne / lokande to toune;	Z	G P N
Pat 459	So blythe of his wodbynde / he / balteres thervnder,	H	V Z
Pat 460	That of no diete that day / the / deuel haf he roʒt.	D	N V H V
Pat 461	And euer he laʒed as he loked / the / loge alle aboute,	D	N Z Z
Pat 462	And wysched hit were in his kyth / ther he / wony schulde,	Q H	V X
Pat 463	On heʒe vpon Effraym / other / Ermonnes hillez:	D	N N
Pat 464	'Iwysse, a worthloker won / to / welde I neuer keped.'	to	V H Z V
Pat 465	And quen nit neʒed to naʒt / nappe hym bihoued;	/	V H V
Pat 466	He slydez on a sloumbe-slep / sloghe vnder leues,	/	Z P N
Pat 467	Whil God wayned a worme / that / wrot vpe the rote,	that	V Z D N
Pat 468	And wyddered watz the wodbynde / bi that the / wyʒe wakned;	P that D	N V
Pat 469	And sythen He warnez the west / to / waken ful softe,	to	V Z Z
Pat 470	And sayez vnte Zeferus / that he / syfle warme,	that H	V Z
Pat 471	That ther quikken no cloude / bifore the / cler sunne,	P D	A N
Pat 472	And ho schal busch vp ful brode / and / brenne as a candel.	C	V P D N
Pat 473	Then wakened the wyʒe / of his / wyl dremes,	P D	A N
Pat 474	And bluschet to his wodbynde / that / brothely watz marred,	that	Z be E
Pat 475	Al welwed and wasted / tho / worthelych leues;	D	A N
Pat 476	The schyre sunne hade hem schent / er euer the / schalk wyst.	C Z D	N V
Pat 477	And then hef vp the hete / and / heterly brenned;	C	Z V
Pat 478	The warm wynde of the weste, / wertes he swythez.	/	N H V
Pat 479	The man marred on the molde / that / moʒt hym not hyde;	that	X H not V
Pat 480	His wodbynde watz away, / he / weped for sorʒe;	H	V P N
Pat 481	With hatel anger and hot, / heterly he callez:	/	Z H V
Pat 482	'A, Thou Maker of man, / what / maystery The thynkez	Q	N H V
Pat 483	Thus Thy freke to forfare / forbi alle other?	/	P D H
Pat 484	With alle meschef that Thou may, / neuer Thou / me sparez;	Z H	H V
Pat 485	I keuered me a cumfort / that now is / caʒt fro me,	that Z be	E P H
Pat 486	My wodbynde so wlonk / that / wered my heued.	that	V D N
Pat 487	Bot now I se Thou art sette / my / solace to reue;	D	N to V
Pat 488	Why ne dyʒttez Thou me to diʒe? / I / dure to longe.'	H	V Z Z
Pat 489	ʒet oure Lorde to the lede / laused a speche:	/	V D N
Pat 490	'Is this ryʒtwys, thou renk, / alle thy / ronk noyse,	D D	A N
Pat 491	So wroth for a wodbynde / to / wax so sone?	to	V Z Z
Pat 492	Why art thou so waymot, / wyʒe, for so lyttel?'	/	N P Z Z

Pat 493	'Hit is not lyttel,' quoth the lede, / 'bot / lykker to ryȝt;	C	N(A) P N
Pat 494	I wolde I were of this worlde / wrapped in moldez.'	/	E P N
Pat 495	'Thenne bythenk the, mon, / if the / forthynk sore,	C H	V Z
Pat 496	If I wolde help My hondewerk, / haf thou no wonder;	/	V H D N
Pat 497	Thou art waxen so wroth / for thy / wodbynde,	P D	N
Pat 498	And trauayledez neuer to tent / hit the / tyme of an howre,	H D	N P D N
Pat 499	Bot at a wap hit here wax / and / away at another,	C	Z P H
Pat 500	And ȝet lykez the so luther, / thi / lyf woldez thou tyne.	D	N X H V
Pat 501	Thenne wyte not Me for the werk, / that I hit / wolde help,	that H H	X V
Pat 502	And rwe on tho redles / that / remen for synne;	that	V P N
Pat 503	Fyrst I made hem Myself / of / materes Myn one,	P	N D Z
Pat 504	And sythen I loked hem ful longe / and hem on / lode hade.	C H P	N V
Pat 505	And if I My trauayl schulde tyne / of / termes so longe,	P	N Z Z
Pat 506	And type doun ȝonder toun / when hit / turned were,	C H	E be
Pat 507	The sor of such a swete place / burde / synk to My hert,	V	V P D N
Pat 508	So mony malicious mon / as / mournez therinne.	C	V Z
Pat 509	And of that soumme ȝet arn summe, / such / sottez formadde,	D	N A
Pat 510	Bitwene the stele and the stayre / disserne noȝt cunen,	/	V not X
Pat 511	What rule renes in roun / bitwene the / ryȝt hande	P D	A N
Pat 512	And hys lyfte, thaȝ his lyf / schulde / lost be therfor;	X	E be Z
Pat 513	As lyttel barnez on barme / that neuer / bale wroȝt,	that Z	N V
Pat 514	And wymmen vnwytté / that / wale ne couthe	that	V not X
Pat 515	That on hande fro that other, / for alle this / hyȝe worlde.	P D D	A N
Pat 516	And als ther ben doumbe bestez / in the / burȝ mony,	P D	N A
Pat 517	That may not synne in no syt / hemseluen to greue.	/	H self to V
Pat 518	Why schulde I wrath / wyth hem, sythen / wyȝez wyl torne,	P H C	N X V
Pat 519	And cum and cnawe Me for Kyng / and My / carpe leue?	C D	N V
Pat 520	Wer I as hastif as thou heere, / were / harme lumpen;	be	N E
Pat 521	Couthe I not thole bot as thou, / ther / thryued ful fewe.	Q	V Z A
Pat 522	I may not be so malicious / and / mylde be halden,	C	A be E
Pat 523	For malyse is noȝt to mayntyne / boute / mercy withinne.'	P	N Z
Pat 524	Be noȝt so gryndel, godman, / bot / go forth thy wayes,	C	V Z D N
Pat 525	Be preue and be pacient / in / payne and in joye;	P	N C P N
Pat 526	For he that is to rakel / in to / renden his clothez	to	V D N
Pat 527	Mot efte sitte with more vnsounde / to / sewe hem togeder.	to	V H Z
Pat 528	Forthy when pouerté me enprecez / and / paynez innoȝe	C	V Z
Pat 529	Ful softly with suffraunce / saȝttel me bihouez;	/	V H V
Pat 530	Forthy penaunce and payne / topreue hit in syȝt	/	V H P N
Pat 531	That pacience is a nobel poynt, / thaȝ hit / displese ofte.	C H	V Z

Cleanness

CL 1	Clannesse whoso kyndly / cowthe comende,	/	X V
CL 2	And rekken vp alle the resounz / that ho by / riʒt askez,	that H P	N V
CL 3	Fayre formez myʒt he fynde / in / fortheriung his speche,	P	G D N
CL 4	And in the contraré kark / and / combraunce huge.	C	N A
CL 5	For wonder wroth is the Wyʒ / that / wroʒt alle thinges	that	V D N
CL 6	Wyth the freke that in fylthe / folʒes Hym after –	/	V H P
CL 7	As renkez of relygioun / that / reden and syngen,	that	V C V
CL 8	And aprochen to Hys presens, / and / prestez arn called;	C	N be E
CL 9	Thay teen vnto His temmple / and / temen to Hymseluen,	C	V P H self
CL 10	Reken with reuerence / thay / rychen His auter,	H	V D N
CL 11	Thay hondel ther His aune body / and / vsen hit bothe.	C	V H Z
CL 12	If thay in clannes be clos / thay / cleche gret mede;	H	V A N
CL 13	Bot if thay conterfete crafte / and / cortaysye wont,	C	N V
CL 14	As be honest vtwyth / and / inwith alle fylthez,	C	Z D N
CL 15	Then ar thay synful hemself, / and / sulpen altogeder	C	V Z
CL 16	Bothe God and His gere, / and Hym to / greme cachen.	C H P	N V
CL 17	He is so clene in His courte, / the / Kyng that al weldez,	D	N that H V
CL 18	And honeste in His housholde, / and / hagherlych serued	C	Z V
CL 19	With angelez enourled / in / alle that is clene,	P	H that be A
CL 20	Bothe withinne and withouten / in / wedez ful bryʒt;	P	N Z A
CL 21	Nif He nere scoymus and skyg, / and non / scathe louied,	C D	N V
CL 22	Hit were a meruayl to much, / hit / moʒt not falle.	H	X not V
CL 23	Kryst kydde / hit Hymseif in a / carp onez,	H H self PD	N Z
CL 24	Theras He heuened aʒt happez / and / hyʒt hem her medez.	C	V H H N
CL 25	Me mynez on one amonge other, / as / Mathew recordez,	C	N V
CL 26	That thus of clannesse vnclosez / a ful / cler speche:	D Z	A N
CL 27	'The hathel clene of his hert / hapenez ful fayre,	/	V Z Z
CL 28	For he schal loke on oure Lorde / with a / leue chere' ;	P D	A N
CL 29	As so saytz, to that syʒt / seche schal he neuer	/	V X H Z
CL 30	That any vnclannesse hatz on, / auwhere abowte;	/	Q P
CL 31	For He flemus vch fylthe / fer fro His hert	/	Z P D N
CL 32	May not byde that burre / that hit His / body neʒe.	that H D	N V
CL 33	Forthy hyʒ not to heuen / in / haterez totorne,	P	N E
CL 34	Ne in the harlatez hod, / and / handez vnwaschen.	C	N E
CL 35	For what vrthly hathel / that / hyʒ honour haldez	that	A N V
CL 36	Wolde lyke if a ladde com / lytherly attyred,	/	Z E
CL 37	When he were sette solempnely / in a / sete ryche,	P D	N A
CL 38	Abof dukez on dece, / with / dayntys serued?	P	N E
CL 39	Then the harlot with haste / helded to the table,	/	V P D N
CL 40	With rent cokrez at the kne / and his / clutte traschez,	C D	E N
CL 41	And his tabarde totorne, / and his / totez oute,	C D	N Z
CL 42	Other ani on of alle thyse, / he schulde be / halden vtter,	H X be	E Z
CL 43	With mony blame ful bygge, / a / boffet perauntter,	D	N Z
CL 44	Hurled to the halle doré / and / harde theroute schowued,	C	Z Z V
CL 45	And be forboden that borʒe / to / bowe thider neuer,	to	V Z Z
CL 46	On payne of enprysonment / and / puttyng in stokkez;	C	G P N
CL 47	And thus schal he be schent / for his / schrowde feble,	P D	N A
CL 48	Thaʒ neuer in talle ne in tuch / he / trespas more.	H	V Z
CL 49	And if vnwelcum he were / to a / wordlych prynce,	P D	A N
CL 50	ʒet hym is the hyʒe Kyng / harder in heuen;	/	Z P N
CL 51	As Mathew melez in his masse / of that / man ryche,	P D	N A
CL 52	That made the mukel mangerye / to / marie his here dere,	to	V D N A
CL 53	And sende his sonde then to say / that thay / samne schulde,	that H	V X
CL 54	And in comly quoyntis / to / com to his feste:	to	V P D N
CL 55	'For my boles and my borez / arn / bayted and slayne,	be	E C E
CL 56	And my fedde foulez / fatted with sclaʒt,	/	E P N
CL 57	My polyle that is penne-fed / and / partrykez bothe,	C	N Z
CL 58	Wyth scheldez of wylde swyn, / swanez and cronez,	C	N C N
CL 59	Al is rotheled and rosted / ryʒt to the sete;	/	Z P D N
CL 60	Comez cof to my corte, / er hit / colde worthe.'	C H	A V
CL 61	When thay knewen his cal / that thider / com schulde,	that Z	V X
CL 62	Alle excused hem by the skyly / he / scape by moʒt.	H	V Z X
CL 63	On hade boʒt hym a borʒ, / he sayde, / by hys trawthe:	H V	P D N
CL 64	'Now turne I theder als tyd / the / toun to byholde.'	D	N to V
CL 65	Another nayed / also and / nurned this cawse:	Z C	V D N
CL 66	'I haf ʒerned and ʒat / ʒokkez of oxen,	/	N P N

CL 67	And for my hyȝez hem boȝt; / to / bowe haf I mester,	to	V V H N
CL 68	To see hem pulle in the plow / aproche me byhouez.	/	V H V
CL 69	'And I haf wedded a wyf,' / so / wer hym the thryd;		be H D H
CL 70	'Excuse me at the court, / I may not / com there.'	H X not	V Z
CL 71	Thus thay droȝ hem adreȝ / with / daunger vchone,	P	N H
CL 72	That non passed to the place / thaȝ he / prayed were.	C H	E be
CL 73	Thenne the ludych lorde / lyked ful ille,	/	V Z Z
CL 74	And hade dedayn of that dede; / ful / dryȝly he carpez.	Z	Z H V
CL 75	He saytz: 'Now for her owne sorȝe / thay / forsaken habbez;	H	E have
CL 76	More to wyte is her wrange / then any / wylle gentyl.	C D	N A
CL 77	Thenne gotz forth, my gomez, / to the / grete streetez,	P D	A N
CL 78	And forsettez on vche a syde / the / ceté aboute;	D	N P
CL 79	The wayferande frekez, / on / fote and on hors,	P	N C P N
CL 80	Bothe burnez and burdez, / the / better and the wers,	D	A C D A
CL 81	Lathez hem alle luflyly / to / lenge at my fest,	to	V P D N
CL 82	And bryngez hem blythly to borȝe / as / barounez thay were,	C	N H be H A
CL 83	So that my palays plat / ful be / pyȝt al aboute;	Z be	E Z
CL 84	Thise other wrechez iwysse / worthy noȝt wern.'	/	A not be
CL 85	Then thay cayred and com / that the / cost waked,	that D	N V
CL 86	Broȝten bachelerez / hem wyth that thay by / bonkez metten,	H P that H P	N V
CL 87	Swyerez that swyftly / swyed on blonkez,	/	V P N
CL 88	And also fele vpon fote, / of / fre and of bonde.	P	N(A) C P N
CL 89	When thay com to the courte / keppte wern thay fayre,	/	E be H A
CL 90	Styȝtled with the stewarde, / stad in the halle,	/	E P D N
CL 91	Ful manerly with marchal / mad for to sitte,	/	E for to V
CL 92	As he watz dere of degré / dressed his seete.	/	E D N
CL 93	Thenne seggez to the souerayn / sayden therafter:	/	V Z
CL 94	'Lo! lorde, with your leue, / at your / lege heste	P D	A N
CL 95	And at thi banne we haf broȝt, / as thou / beden habbez,	C H	E have
CL 96	Mony renischche renkez, / and ȝet is / roum more.'	C Z be	N A
CL 97	Sayde the lorde to tho ledez, / 'Laytez ȝet ferre,	/	V Z Z
CL 98	Ferkez out in the felde, / and / fechez mo gestez;	C	V A N
CL 99	Waytez gorstez and greuez, / if ani / gomez lyggez;	C D	N V
CL 100	Whatkyn folk so ther fare, / fechez hem hider;	/	V H Z
CL 101	Be thay fers, be thay feble, / forlotez none,	/	V H
CL 102	Be thay hol, be thay halt, / be thay / onyȝed,	be H	E
CL 103	And thaȝ thay ben bothe blynde / and / balterande cruppelez,	C	G N
CL 104	That my hous may holly / by / halkez by fylled.	P	N be E
CL 105	For, certez, thyse ilk renkez / that me / renayed habbe,	that H	E have
CL 106	And denounced me noȝt / now at this tyme,	/	Z P D N
CL 107	Schul neuer sitte in my sale / my / soper to fele,	D	N to V
CL 108	Ne suppe on sope of my seve, / thaȝ thay / swelt schulde.'	C H	V X
CL 109	Thenne the sergauntez, at that sawe, / swengen theroute,	/	V Z
CL 110	And diden the dede that watz demed, / as he / deuised hade,	C H	E have
CL 111	And with peple of alle plytez / the / palays thay fyllen;	D	N H V
CL 112	Hit weren not alle on wyuez sunez, / wonen with on fader.	/	E P D N
CL 113	Whether thay wern worthy other wers, / wel wern thay stowed,	/	Z be H E
CL 114	Ay the best byfore / and / bryȝtest atyred,	C	Z E
CL 115	The derrest of the hyȝe dese, / that / dubbed wer fayrest,	that	E be Z
CL 116	And sythen on lenthe biiooghe / ledez inogh.	/	N A
CL 117	And ay as seggez serly / semed by her wedez,	/	V P D N
CL 118	So with marschal at her mete / mensked thay were.	/	E H be
CL 119	Clene men in companye / forknowen wern lyte,	/	E be Z
CL 120	And ȝet the symplest in that sale / watz / serued to the fulle,	be	E P D N
CL 121	Bothe with menske and with mete / and / mynstrasy noble,	C	N A
CL 122	And alle the laykez that a lorde / aȝt in / londe schewe.	X P	N V
CL 123	And thay bigonne to be glad / that / god drink haden,	that	A N V
CL 124	And vch mon with his mach / made hym at ese.	/	V H P N
CL 125	Now inmyddez the mete / the / mayster hym bithoȝt	D	N H V
CL 126	That he wolde se the semblé / that / samned was there,	that	E be Z
CL 127	And rehayte rekenly / the / riche and the poueren,	D	N(A) C D N(A)
CL 128	And cherisch hem alle with his cher, / and / chaufen her joye.	C	V D N
CL 129	Then he bowez fro his bour / into the / brode halle	P D	A N
CL 130	And to the best on the bench, / and / bede hym be myry,	C	V H be A
CL 131	Solased hem with semblaunt / and / syled fyrre,	C	V Z
CL 132	Tron fro table to table / and / talkede ay myrthe.	C	G Z N
CL 133	Bot as he ferked ouer the flor, / he / fande with his yȝe –	H	V P D N
CL 134	Hit watz not for a halyday / honestly arayed –	/	Z E
CL 135	A thral thryȝt in the throng / vnthryuandely clothed,	/	Z E
CL 136	Ne no festiuial frok, / bot / fyled with werkkez,	C	E P N
CL 137	The gome watz vngarnyst / with / god men to dele.	P	A N to V

CL 138	And gremed therwith the grete lorde, / and / greue hym he thozt.	C	V H H V	
CL 139	'Say me, frende,' quoth the freke / with a / felle chere,	P D	A N	
CL 140	'Hov wan thou into this won / in / wedez so fowle?'	P	N Z A	
CL 141	The abyt that thou hatz vpon, / no / halyday hit menskez:	D	N H V	
CL 142	Thou, burne, for no brydale / art / busked in wedez.	be	E P N	
CL 143	How watz thou hardy this hous / for thyn / vnhap to neze	P D	N to V	
CL 144	In on so ratted a robe / and / rent at the sydez?	C	E P D N	
CL 145	Thow art a gome vngoderly / in that / goun febele;	P D	N A	
CL 146	Thou praysed me and my place / ful / pouer and ful gnede,	Z	Z C Z Z	
CL 147	That watz so prest to aproche / my / presens hereinne.	D	N Z	
CL 148	Hopez thou I be a harlot / thi / erigaut to prayse?'	D	N to V	
CL 149	That other burne watz abayst / of his / brothe wordez,	P D	A N	
CL 150	And hurkelez doun with his hede, / for / vrthe he biholdez;	D	N H V	
CL 151	He watz so scoumfit of his scylle, / lest he / skathe hent,	C H	V V	
CL 152	That he ne wyst on worde / what he / warp schulde.	Q H	V X	
CL 153	Then the lorde wonder loude / laled and cryed,	/	V C V	
CL 154	And talkez to his tormenttourez: / 'Takez hym,' he biddez,	/	V H H V	
CL 155	'Byndez byhynde, at his bak, / bothe two his handez,	/	A D D N	
CL 156	And felle fetterez to his fete / festenez bylyue;	/	V Z	
CL 157	Stik hym stifly in stokez, / and / stekez hym therafter	C	V H Z	
CL 158	Depe in my doungoun / ther / doel euer dwellez,	Q	N Z V	
CL 159	Greuing and gretyng / and / gryspyng harde	C	G Z	
CL 160	Of tethe tenfully togeder, / to / teche hym be quoynt.'	to	V H be E	
CL 161	Thus comparisunez Kryst / the / kyndom of heuen	D	N P N	
CL 162	To this frelych feste / that / fele arn to called;	that	H be P E	
CL 163	For alle arn lathed luftyly, / the / luther and the better,	D	N(A) C D N(A)	
CL 164	That euer wern fulzed in font, / that / fest to haue.	that	N to V	
CL 165	Bot war the wel, if thou wylt, / thy / wedez ben clene	D	N be A	
CL 166	And honest for the halyday, / lest thou / harme lache,	C D	N V	
CL 167	For aproch thou to that Prynce / of / parage noble,	P	N A	
CL 168	He hates felle / no more then / hem that ar sowlé.	Z C	H that be A	
CL 169	Wich arn thenne thy wedez / thou / wrappez the inne,	H	V H P	
CL 170	That schal schewe hem so schene / schrowde of the best?	/	N P D N(A)	
CL 171	Hit arn thy werkez, wyterly, / that thou / wrozt hauez,	that H	E have	
CL 172	And lyued with the lykyng / that / lyze in thyn hert;	that	V P D N	
CL 173	That tho be frely and fresch / fonde in thy lyue,	/	V P D N	
CL 174	And fetyse of a fayr forme / to / fote and to honde,	P	N C P N	
CL 175	And sythen alle thyn other lymez / lapped ful clene;	/	V Z Z	
CL 176	Thenne may thou se thy Sauior / and His / sete ryche.	C D	N A	
CL 177	For feler fautez may a freke / forfete his blysse,	/	V D N	
CL 178	That he the Souerayn ne se, / then for / slauthe one;	C P	N Z	
CL 179	As for bobaunce and bost / and / bolnande priyde	C	G N	
CL 180	Throly into the deuelez throte / man / thryngez bylyue.	H	V Z	
CL 181	For couetyse and colwarde / and / croked dedez,	C	E N	
CL 182	For monsworne and menscla3t / and to / much drynk,	C Z	A N	
CL 183	For thefte and for threpyng, / vnthonk may mon haue;	/	N X N V	
CL 184	For roborrye and riboudrye / and / resounez vntrwe,	C	N A	
CL 185	And dysheriete and depryue / dowrie of wydoez,	/	N P N	
CL 186	For marryng of maryagez / and / mayntnaunce of schrewez,	C	N P N	
CL 187	For traysoun and trichcherye / and / tyrauntyré bothe,	C	N Z	
CL 188	And for fals famacions / and / fayned lawez;	C	V N	
CL 189	Man may mysse the myrthe / that / much is to prayse	that	A be to V	
CL 190	For such vnthewez as thise, / and / thole much payne,	C	V D N	
CL 191	And in the Creatores cort / com neuermore,	/	V Z	
CL 192	Ne neuer see Hym with syzt / for such / sour tournez.	P D	A N	
CL 193	Bot I haue herkned and herde / of mony / hyze clerkez,	P D	A N	
CL 194	And als in resounez of ryzt / red hit myseluen,	/	V H H self	
CL 195	That that ilk proper Prynce / that / paradys weldez	D	N V	
CL 196	Is displesed at vch a poynt / that / plyes to scathe;	that	V to V	
CL 197	Bot neuer zet in no boke / breued I herde	/	E H V	
CL 198	That euer He wrek so wytherly / on / werk that He made,	P	N that H V	
CL 199	Ne venged for no vilté / of / vice ne synne,	P	N not N	
CL 200	Ne so hastyfly watz hot / for / hatel of His wylle,	P	N(A) P D N	
CL 201	Ne neuer so sodenly sozt / vnsoundely to weng,	/	Z to V	
CL 202	As for fylthe of the flesch / that / foles han vsed;	that	N have E	
CL 203	For, as I fynde, ther He forzet / alle His / fre thewez,	D D	A N	
CL 204	And wex wod to the wrache / for / wrath at His hert.	P	N P D N	
CL 205	For the fyrste felonye / the / falce fende wrozt	D	A N V	
CL 206	Whyl he watz hyze in the heuen / houen vpon lofte,	/	E Z	
CL 207	Of alle thyse athel aungelez / attled the fayrest:	/	E D A	
CL 208	And he vnkyndely, as a karle, / kydde a reward.	/	V D N	

CL 209	He seȝ noȝt bot hymself / how / semly he were,	Q	A H be
CL 210	Bot his Souerayn he forsoke / and / sade thyse wordez:	C	V D N
CL 211	'I schal telde vp my trone / in the / tramountayne,	P D	N
CL 212	And by lyke to that Lorde / that the / lyft made.'	that D	N V
CL 213	With this worde that he warp, / the / wrake on hym lyȝt:	D	N P H V
CL 214	Dryȝtyn with His dere dom / hym / drof to the abyme,	H	V P D N
CL 215	In the measure of His mode, / His / metz neuer the lasse.	D	N Z
CL 216	Bot ther He tynt the tythe dool / of His / tour ryche:	P D	N A
CL 217	Thaȝ the feloun were so fers / for his / fayre wedez	P D	A N
CL 218	And his glorious glem / that / glent so bryȝt,	that	V Z Z
CL 219	As sone as Dryȝtynez dome / drof to hymseluen,	/	V P H self
CL 220	Thikke thowsandez thro / thrwen theroute,	/	V Z
CL 221	Fellen fro the fyrmament / fendez ful blake,	/	N Z A
CL 222	Sweued at the fyrst swap / as the / snaw thikke,	P D	N A
CL 223	Hurled into helle-hole / as the / hyue swarmez.	C D	N V
CL 224	Fylter fenden folk / forty dayez lencthe,	/	A N N
CL 225	Er that styngande storme / stynt ne myȝt;	/	V not X
CL 226	Bot as smylt mele vnder smal siue / smokez forthikke,	/	V Z
CL 227	So fro heuen to helle / that / hatel schor laste,	D	A N V
CL 228	On vche syde of the worlde / aywhere ilyche.	/	Q Z
CL 229	Ȝis, hit watz a brem brest / and a / byge wrache,	C D	A N
CL 230	And ȝet wrathed not the Wyȝ; / ne the / wrech saȝtled,	not D	N V
CL 231	Ne neuer wolde, for wylfulnes, / his / worthy God knawe,	D	A N V
CL 232	Ne pray Hym for no pité, / so / proud watz his wylle.	Z	A be D N
CL 233	Forthy thaȝ the rape were rank, / the / rawthe watz lyttel;	D	N be A
CL 234	Thaȝ he be kest into kare, / he / kepes no better.	H	V Z
CL 235	Bot that other wrake that wex, / on / wyȝez hit lyȝt	P	N H V
CL 236	Thurȝ the faut of a freke / that / fayled in trawthe,	that	V P N
CL 237	Adam inobedyent, / ordaynt to blysse.	/	E P N
CL 238	Ther pryuély in paradys / his / place watz devised,	D	N be E
CL 239	To lyue ther in lykyng / the / lenthe of a terme,	D	N P D N
CL 240	And thenne enherite that home / that / aungelez forgart;	that	N V
CL 241	Bot thurȝ the eggyng of Eue / he / ete of an apple	H	V P D N
CL 242	That enpoysened alle peplez / that / parted fro hem bothe,	that	V P H Z
CL 243	For a defence that watz dyȝt / of / Dryȝtyn Seluen,	P	N self
CL 244	And a payne theron put / and / pertly halden.	C	Z E
CL 245	The defence watz the fryt / that the / freke towched,	that D	N V
CL 246	And the dom is the dethe / that / drepez vus alle;	that	V H Z
CL 247	Al in mesure and methe / watz / mad the vengiaunce,	be	E D N
CL 248	And efte amended with a mayden / that / make had neuer.	D	N V Z
CL 249	Bot in the thryd watz forthrast / al that / thryue schuld:	H that	V X
CL 250	Ther watz malys mercyles / and / mawgré much scheued,	C	N Z E
CL 251	That watz for fylthe vpon folde / that the / folk vsed,	that D	N V
CL 252	That then wonyed in the worlde / withouten any maysterz.	/	P D N
CL 253	Hit wern the fayrest of forme / and of / face als,	C P	N Z
CL 254	The most and the myriest / that / maked wern euer,	that	E be Z
CL 255	The styfest, the stalworthest / that / stod euer on fete,	that	V Z P N
CL 256	And lengest lyf in hem lent / of / ledez alle other.	P	N A A
CL 257	For hit was the forme foster / that the / folde bred,	that D	N V
CL 258	The athel aunceterez sunez / that / Adam watz called,	that	N be E
CL 259	To whaum God hade geuen / alle that / gayn were,	H that	E be
CL 260	Alle the blysse boute blame / that / bodi myȝt haue,	that	N X V
CL 261	And those lykkest to the lede, / that / lyued next after;	that	V Z Z
CL 262	Forthy so semly to see / sythen wern none.	/	C be H
CL 263	Ther watz no law to hem layd / bot / loke to kynde,	C	V P N
CL 264	And kepe to hit, and alle hit cors / clanly fulfylle.	/	Z V
CL 265	And thenne founden thay fylthe / in / fleschlych dedez,	P	A N
CL 266	And controeued agayn kynde / contraré werkez,	/	A N
CL 267	And vsed hem vnthryftyly / vchon on other,	/	H P H
CL 268	And als with other, wylsfully, / upon a / wrange wyse:	P D	A N
CL 269	So ferly fowled her flesch / that the / fende loked	that D	N V
CL 270	How the deȝter of the douthe / wern / derelych fayre,	be	Z A
CL 271	And fallen in felaȝschyp / with hem on / folken wyse,	P H P	N N
CL 272	And engendered on hem jeauntez / with her / japez ille.	P D	N A
CL 273	Those wern men methelez / and / maȝty on vrthe,	C	A P N
CL 274	That for her lodlych laykez / alosed thay were;	/	E H be
CL 275	He watz famed for fre / that / feȝt loued best,	that	N V Z
CL 276	And ay the bigest in bale / the / best watz halden.	D	N(A) be E
CL 277	And thenne euelez on erthe / ernestly grewen	/	Z E
CL 278	And multyplyed monyfolde / inmongez mankynde,	/	P N
CL 279	For that the maȝty on molde / so / marre thise other	Z	A D H

CL 280	That the Wyȝe that al wroȝt / ful / wrothly bygynnez.		Z	Z V
CL 281	When He knew vche contre / coruppte in hitseluen,		/	V P H self
CL 282	And vch freke forloyned / fro the / ryȝt wayez,		P D	A N
CL 283	Felle temptande tene / towched His hert.		/	V D N
CL 284	As wyȝe wo hym withinne, / werp to Hymseluen:		/	V P H self
CL 285	'Me forthynkez ful much / that euer I / mon made,		that Z H	N V
CL 286	Bot I schal delyuer and do / away that / doten on this molde,		Z that	V P D N
CL 287	And fleme out of the folde / al that / flesch werez,		D D	N be
CL 288	Fro the burne to the best, / fro / bryddez to fyschez;		P	N P N
CL 289	Al schal doun and be ded / and / dryuen out of erthe		C	E P P N
CL 290	That euer I sette saule / inne; and / sore hit Me rwez		Z C	N H H V
CL 291	That euer I made hem Myself; / bot if I / may herafter,		C C H	X Z
CL 292	I schal wayte to be war / her / wrenchez to kepe.'		/	N to V
CL 293	Thenne in worlde watz a wyȝe / wonyande on lyue,		/	G P N
CL 294	Ful redy and ful ryȝtwys, / and / rewled hym fayre,		C	V H Z
CL 295	In the drede of Dryȝtyn / his / dayez he vsez,		D	N H V
CL 296	And ay glydande wyth his God, / his / grace watz the more.		D	N be D A
CL 297	Hym watz the nome Noe, / as is / innoghe knawen.		C be	Z E
CL 298	He had thre thryuen sunez, / and thay / thre wyuez:		C H	A N
CL 299	Sem sothly that on, / that / other hyȝt Cam,		that	H V N
CL 300	And the jolef Japheth / watz / gendered the thryd.		be	E D H
CL 301	Now God in nwy / to / Noe con speke		P	N X V
CL 302	Wylde wrakful wordez, / in His / wylle greued:		P D	N V
CL 303	'The ende of alle kynez flesch / that on / vrthe meuez		that P	N V
CL 304	Is fallen forthwyth My face, / and / forther hit I thenk.		C	V H H V
CL 305	With her vnworthelych werk / Me / wlatez withinne;		H	V Z
CL 306	The gore therof Me hatz greued / and the / glette nwyed.		C D	N V
CL 307	I schal strenkle My distresse, / and / strye al togeder,		C	V Z
CL 308	Bothe ledez and londe / and alle that / lyf habbez.		C D D	N V
CL 309	Bot make to the a mancioun, / and that is / My wylle,		C H be	D N
CL 310	A cofer closed of tres, / clanlych planed.		/	Z E
CL 311	Wyrk wonez therinne / for / wylde and for tame,		P	N(A) C P N(A)
CL 312	And thenne cleme hit with clay / comly withinne,		/	Z Z
CL 313	And alle the endentur dryuen / daube withouten.		/	V Z
CL 314	And thus of lenthe and of large / that / lome thou make:		D	N H V
CL 315	Thre hundred of cupydez / thou / holde to the lenthe,		H	V P D N
CL 316	Of fyfty fayre ouerthwert / forme the brede;		/	V D N
CL 317	And loke euen that thyn ark haue / of / heȝthe thretté,		P	N N
CL 318	And a wyndow wyd vponande / wroȝt vpon lofte,		/	E Z
CL 319	In the compas of a cubit / kyndely sware;		/	Z A
CL 320	A wel dutande dor, / don on the syde;		/	E P D N
CL 321	Haf hallez therinne / and / halkez ful mony,		C	N Z A
CL 322	Bothe boskenz and bourez / and wel / bounden penez.		C Z	E N
CL 323	For I schal waken vp a water / to / wasch alle the worlde,		to	V D D N
CL 324	And quelle alle that is quik / with / quauende flodez,		P	G N
CL 325	Alle that glydez and gotz / and / gost of lyf habbez;		C	N P N V
CL 326	I schal wast with My wrath / that / wons vpon vrthe.		that	V P N
CL 327	Bot My forwarde with the / I / festen on this wyse,		H	V P D N
CL 328	For thou in reysoun hatz rengned / and / ryȝtwys ben euer:		C	A be Z
CL 329	Thou schal enter this ark / with thyn / athel barnez		P D	A N
CL 330	And thy wedded wyf; / with the thou take		/	P H H V
CL 331	The makez of thy myry sunez; / this / meyny of aȝte		D	N P N
CL 332	I schal saue of monnez saulez, / and / swelt those other.		C	V D H
CL 333	Of vche best that berez lyf / buck the a cupple,		/	V H D N
CL 334	Of vche clene comly kynde / enclose seuen makez,		/	V A N
CL 335	Of vche horwed in ark / halde bot a payre,		/	V P D N
CL 336	For to saue Me the sede / of alle / ser kyndez.		P D	A N
CL 337	And ay thou meng with the malez / the / mete ho-bestez,		D	A N
CL 338	Vche payre by payre / to / plese ayther other;		to	V Z
CL 339	With alle the fode that may be founde / frette thy cofer,		/	V D N
CL 340	For sustnaunce to yowself / and / also those other.'		C	Z D H
CL 341	Ful graythely gotz this god man / and dos / Godez hestes;		C V	N N
CL 342	In dryȝ dred and daunger / that / durst no don other.		that	V V D H
CL 343	Wen hit watz fettled and forged / and to the / fulle graythed,		C P D	Z E
CL 344	Thenn con Dryȝttyn hym dele / dryȝly thyse wordez.		/	Z D N
CL 345	'Now Noe, quoth oure Lorde, / art thou / al redy?		be H	Z A
CL 346	Hatz thou closed thy kyst / with / clay alle aboute?'		P	N Z Z
CL 347	'Ȝe, Lorde, with Thy leue,' / sayde the / lede thenne,		V D	N Z
CL 348	'Al is wroȝt at Thi worde, / as Thou me / wyt lantez.'		C H H	N V
CL 349	'Enter in, thenn,' quoth He, / 'and / haf thi wyf with the,		C	V D N P H
CL 350	Thy thre sunez, withouten threp, / and her / thre wyuez;		C D	A N

CL 351	Bestez, as I bedene / haue, / bosk therinne als,	have	V Z Z
CL 352	And when ȝe arn staued, styfly / stekez yow therinne.	/	V H Z
CL 353	Fro seuen dayez ben seyed / I / sende out bylyue	H	V Z Z
CL 354	Such a rowtande ryge / that / rayne schal swythe	that	N X Z
CL 355	That schal wasch alle the worlde / of / werkez of fylthe;	P	N P N
CL 356	Schal no flesch vpon folde / by / fonden onlyue,	C	E A
CL 357	Outtaken yow aȝt / in this / ark staued	P D	N E
CL 358	And sed that I wyl saue / of thyse / ser bestez.'	P D	A N
CL 359	Now Noe neuer styntez-/ that / niyȝt he bygynnez-	that	N H V
CL 360	Er al wer stawed and stoken / as the / steuen wolde.	C D	N V
CL 361	Thenne sone com the seuenthe day, / when / samned wern alle,	C	E be H
CL 362	And alle woned in the whichche, / the / wylde and the tame.	D	N(A) C D N(A)
CL 363	Then bolned the abyme, / and / bonkez con ryse,	C	N X V
CL 364	Waltes out vch walle-heued / in ful / wode stremez;	P Z	A N
CL 365	Watz no brymme that abod / vnbrosten bylyue;	/	E Z
CL 366	The mukel lauande loghe / to the / lyfte rered.	P D	N V
CL 367	Mony clustered clowde / clef alle in clowtez;	/	V Z P N
CL 368	Torent vch a rayn-ryfte / and / rusched to the vrthe,	C	V P D N
CL 369	Fon neuer in forty dayez. / And then the / flod ryses,	C Z D	N V
CL 370	Ouerwaltez vche a wod / and the / wyde feldez.	C D	A N
CL 371	For when the water of the welkyn / with the / worlde mette,	P D	N V
CL 372	Alle that deth moȝt dryȝe / drowned therinne.	/	V Z
CL 373	Ther watz moon for to make / when / meschef was cnowen,	C	N be E
CL 374	That noȝt dowed bot the deth / in the / depe stremez;	P D	A N
CL 375	Water wylger ay wax, / wonez that stryede,	/	N that V
CL 376	Hurled into vch hous, / hent that ther dowelled.	/	V H Q V
CL 377	Fyrst feng to the flyȝt / alle that / fle myȝt;	H that	V X
CL 378	Vuche burde with her barne / the / byggyng thay leuez	D	N H V
CL 379	And bowed to the hyȝ bonk / ther / brentest hit wern,	Q	A H be
CL 380	And heterly to the hyȝe hyllez / thay / haled on faste.	H	V Z
CL 381	Bot al watz nedlez her note, / for / neuer cowthe stynt	P	Z A N
CL 382	The roȝe raynande ryg, / the / raykande wawez,	D	G N
CL 383	Er vch bothom watz brurdful / to the / bonkez eggez,	P D	N N
CL 384	And vche a dale so depe / that / demmed at the brynkez.	that	V P D N
CL 385	The moste mountaynez on mor / thenne watz no / more dryȝe,	Z be Z	Z A
CL 386	And theron flokked the folke, / for / ferde of the wrake.	P	N P D N
CL 387	Sythen the wylde of the wode / on the / water flette;	P D	N V
CL 388	Summe swymmed theron that saue / hemself trawed,	/	H self V
CL 389	Summe styȝe to a stud / and / stared to the heuen,	C	V P D N
CL 390	Rwly wyth a loud rurd / rored for drede.	/	V P N
CL 391	Harez, herttez also, / to the / hyȝe runnen;	P D	N(A) V
CL 392	Bukkez, bausenez, and bulez / to the / bonkkez hyȝed;	P D	N V
CL 393	And alle cryed for care / to the / Kyng of heuen,	P D	N P N
CL 394	Recouerer of the Creator / thay / cryed vchone,	H	V H
CL 395	That amounted the mase / His / mercy watz passed,	D	N be E
CL 396	And alle His pyté departed / fro / peple that He hated.	P	N that H V
CL 397	Bi that the flod to her fete / floȝed and waxed,	/	V C V
CL 398	Then vche a segge seȝ / wel that / synk hym byhoued.	Z that	V H V
CL 399	Frendez fellen in fere / and / fathmed togeder,	C	V Z
CL 400	To dryȝ her delful destyné / and / dyȝen alle samen;	C	V Z
CL 401	Luf lokez to luf / and his / leue takez,	C D	N V
CL 402	For to ende alle at onez / and for / euer twynne.	C Z	Z V
CL 403	By forty dayez wern faren, on folde / no / flesch styryed	D	N V
CL 404	That the flod nade al freten / with / feȝtande waȝez;	P	G N
CL 405	For hit clam vche a clyffe, / cubites fyftene	/	N A
CL 406	Ouer the hyȝest hylle / that / hurkled on erthe.	that	V P N
CL 407	Thenne mourkne in the mudde / most ful nede	/	A A N
CL 408	Alle that spyrakle inspranc-/ no / sprawlyng awayled-	D	G V
CL 409	Saue the hathel vnder hach / and his / here straunge,	C D	N A
CL 410	Noe that ofte neuened / the / name of oure Lorde,	D	N P D N
CL 411	Hym aȝtsum in that ark, / as / athel God lyked,	C	A N V
CL 412	Ther alle ledez in lome / lenged druye.	/	V A
CL 413	The arc houen watz on hyȝe / with / hurlande gotez,	P	G N
CL 414	Kest to kythez vncouthe / the / clowdez ful nere.	D	N Z P
CL 415	Hit waltered on the wylde flod, / went as hit lyste,	/	V C H V
CL 416	Drof vpon the depe dam, / in / daunger hit semed,	P	N H V
CL 417	Withouten mast, other myke, / other / myry bawelyne,	D	A N
CL 418	Kable, other capstan / to / clyppe to her ankrez,	to	V P D N
CL 419	Hurrok, other hande-helme / hasped on rother,	/	E P N
CL 420	Other any swaende sayl / to / seche after hauen,	to	V P N
CL 421	Bot flote forthe with the flyt / of the / felle wyndez.	P D	A N

CL 422	Whederwarde so the water / wafte, hit rebounde;	/	V H V
CL 423	Ofte hit roled on rounde / and / rered on ende,	C	V P N
CL 424	Nyf oure Lorde hade ben her lodezmon / hem had / lumpen harde.	H have	V Z
CL 425	Of the lenthe of Noe lyf / to / lay a lel date,	to	V D A N
CL 426	The sex hundreth of his age / and none / odde ʒerez,	C D	A N
CL 427	Of secounde monyth / the / seuententhe day ryʒtez,	D	A N Z
CL 428	Towalten alle thyse welle-hedez / and the / water flowed;	C D	N V
CL 429	And thryez fyfty the flod / of / folwande dayez;	P	G N
CL 430	Vche hille watz ther hidde / with / ythez ful graye.	P	N Z A
CL 431	Al watz wasted that wonyed / the / worlde withinne,	D	N P
CL 432	That euer flote, other flwe, / other on / fote ʒede,	C P	N V
CL 433	That roʒly watz the remnaunt / that the / rac dryuez	that D	N V
CL 434	That alle gendrez so joyst / wern / joyned wythinne.	be	E Z
CL 435	Bot quen the Lorde of the lyfte / lyked Hymseluen	/	V H self
CL 436	For to mynne on His mon / His / meth that abydez,	D	N that V
CL 437	Then He wakened a wynde / on / watterez to blowe;	P	N to V
CL 438	Thenne lasned the llak / that / large watz are.	that	A be Z
CL 439	Then He stac vp the stangez, / stoped the wellez,	/	V D N
CL 440	Bed blynne of the rayn: / hit / batede as fast;	H	V Z Z
CL 441	Thenne lasned the loʒ / lowkande togeder.	/	G Z
CL 442	After harde dayez wern / out an / hundreth and fyfté,	Z D	N C N
CL 443	As that lyftande lome / luged aboute,	/	V Z
CL 444	Where the wynde and the weder / warpen hit wolde,	/	V H X
CL 445	Hit saʒtled on a softe day, / synkande to grounde;	/	G P N
CL 446	On a rasse of a rok / hit / rest at the laste,	H	V Z
CL 447	On the mounte of Ararach / of / Armene hilles,	P	A N
CL 448	That otherwayez on Ebrv / hit / hat the Thanes.	H	V D N
CL 449	Bot thaʒ the kyste in the cragez / were / closed to byde,	be	E to V
CL 450	ʒet fyned not the flod / ne / fel to the bothemez,	not	V P D N
CL 451	Bot the hyʒest of the eggez / vnhuled wern a lyttel,	/	E be Z
CL 452	That the burne bynne borde / byhelde the bare erthe.	/	V D A N
CL 453	Thenne wafte he vpon his wyndowe, / and / wysed theroute	C	V Z
CL 454	A message fro that meyny / hem / moldez to seche:	H	N to V
CL 455	That watz the rauen so ronk, / that / rebel watz euer;	that	A be Z
CL 456	He watz colored as the cole, / corbyal vntrwe.	/	N A
CL 457	And he fongez to the flyʒt / and / fannez on the wyndez,	C	V P D N
CL 458	Halez hyʒe vpon hyʒt / to / herken tythyngez.	to	V N
CL 459	He croukez for comfort / when / carayne he fyndez	C	N H V
CL 460	Kast vp on a clyffe / ther / costese lay drye;	Q	N V A
CL 461	He hade the smelle of the smach / and / smoltes theder sone,	C	V Z Z
CL 462	Fallez on the foule flesch / and / fyllez his wombe,	C	V D N
CL 463	And sone ʒederly forʒete / ʒisterday steuen,	/	N N
CL 464	How the cheuetayn hym charged / that the / chyst ʒemed.	that D	N V
CL 465	The rauen raykez / hym forth, that / reches ful lyttel	H Z that	V Z Z
CL 466	How alle fodez ther fare, / ellez he / fynde mete;	C H	V N
CL 467	Bot the burne bynne borde / byhelde / that / bod to hys come	that	V P D N
CL 468	Banned hym ful bytterly / with / bestes alle samen.	P	N Z
CL 469	He sechez another sondezmon, / and / settez on the douue,	C	V P D N
CL 470	Bryngez that bryʒt vpon borde, / blessed, and sayde:	/	V C V
CL 471	'Wende, worthelych wyʒt, / vus / wonez to seche;	H	N to V
CL 472	Dryf ouer this dymme water; / if thou / druye fyndez	C H	N(A) V
CL 473	Bryng bodworde to bot / blysse to vus alle.'	/	N P H Z
CL 474	Thaʒ that fowle be false, / fre be thou euer.	/	A be H Z
CL 475	Ho wyrled out on the weder / on / wyngez ful scharpe,	P	N Z A
CL 476	Dreʒly alle alonge day / that / dorst neuer lyʒt;	that	V Z V
CL 477	And when ho fyndez no folde / her / fote on to pyche,	D	N P to V
CL 478	Ho vmbekestez the coste / and the / kyst sechez.	C D	N V
CL 479	Ho hittez on the euentyde / and on / the / ark sittez;	C P D	N V
CL 480	Noe nymmes hir anon / and / naytly hir stauez.	C	Z D N
CL 481	Noe on another day / nymmez efte the dowue,	/	V Z D N
CL 482	And byddez hir bowe ouer the borne / efte / bonkez to seche;	Z	N to V
CL 483	And ho skyrmez vnder skwe / and / skowtez aboute,	C	V Z
CL 484	Tyl hit watz nyʒe at the naʒt, / and / Noe then sechez.	C	N Z V
CL 485	On ark on an euentyde / houez the dowue;	/	V D N
CL 486	On stamyn ho stod / and / stylle hym abydez.	C	Z H V
CL 487	What! ho broʒt in hir beke / a / bronch of olyue,	D	N P N
CL 488	Gracyously vmbegrouen / al with / grene leuez;	Z P	A N
CL 489	That watz the syngne of sauyté / that / sende hem oure Lorde,	that	V H D N
CL 490	And the saʒtlyng of Hymself / with tho / sely bestez.	P D	A N
CL 491	Then watz ther joy in that gyn / where / jumpred er dryʒed,	Q	V C V
CL 492	And much comfort in that cofer / that watz / clay-daubed.	that be	N E

CL 493	Myryly on a fayr morn, / monyth the fyrst,	/		N D H
CL 494	That fallez formast in the 3er, / and the / fyrst day,	C D		A N
CL 495	Ledez lo3en in that lome / and / loked theroute,	C		V Z
CL 496	How that watterez wern woned / and the / worlde dryed.	C D		N V
CL 497	Vchon loued oure Lorde, / bot / lenged ay stylle	C		V Z Z
CL 498	Tyl thay had tythyng fro the Tolke / that / tyned hem therinne.	that		V H Z
CL 499	Then Godez glam to hem glod / that / gladed hem alle,	that		V H Z
CL 500	Bede hem drawe to the dor: / delyuer hem He wolde.	/		V H H X
CL 501	Then went thay to the wykket, / hit / walt vpon sone;	H		V Z Z
CL 502	Bothe the burne and his barnez / bowed theroute,	/		V Z
CL 503	Her wyuez walkez hem wyth / and the / wylde after,	C D		N(A) P
CL 504	Throly thrublande in thronge, / throwen ful thykke.	/		E Z Z
CL 505	Bot Noe of vche honest kynde / nem out an odde,	/		V Z D N
CL 506	And heuened vp an auter / and / hal3ed hit fayre,	C		V H Z
CL 507	And sette a sakerfyse / theron of vch a / ser kynde	Z P H D		A N
CL 508	That watz comly and clene: / God / kepez non other.	N		V Z
CL 509	When bremly brened those bestez, / and the / brethe rysed,	C D		N V
CL 510	The sauour of his sacrafyse / so3t to Hym euen	/		V P H Z
CL 511	That al spedez and spyllez; / He / spekes with that ilke	H		V P D H
CL 512	In comly comfort ful clos / and / cortays wordez:	C		A N
CL 513	'Now, Noe, no more / nel I / neuer wary	X H		Z V
CL 514	Alle the mukel mayny on molde / for no / mannez synnez,	P D		N N
CL 515	For I se wel that hit is sothe / that alle / seggez wyttez	that D		N N
CL 516	To vnthryfte arn alle thrawen / with / tho3t of her herttez,	P		N P D N
CL 517	And ay hatz ben, and wyl be / 3et; fro her / barnage	Z P D		N
CL 518	Al is the mynde of the man / to / malyce enclyned.	P		N E
CL 519	Forthy schal I neuer schende / so / schortly at ones	Z		Z Z
CL 520	As dysstrye al for manez dedez, / dayez of this erthe.	/		N P D N
CL 521	Bot waxez now and wendez / forth and / worthez to monye,	Z C		V Z A
CL 522	Multyplyez on this molde, / and / menske yow bytyde.	C		N H V
CL 523	Sesounez schal yow neuer sese / of / sede ne of heruest,	P		N not P N
CL 524	Ne hete, ne no harde forst, / vmbre ne dro3the,	/		N not N
CL 525	Ne the swetnesse of somer, / ne the / sadde wynter,	D D		A N
CL 526	Ne the ny3t, ne the day, / ne the / newe 3erez,	D D		A N
CL 527	Bot euer renne restlez: / rengnez 3e therinne.'	/		V H Z
CL 528	Therwyth He blessez vch a best, / and / byta3t hem this erthe.	C		V H D N
CL 529	Then watz a skylly skyualde, / quen / scaped alle the wylde,	C		V D D N
CL 530	Vche fowle to the fly3t / that / fytherez my3t serue,	that		N X V
CL 531	Vche fysch to the flod / that / fynne couthe nayte,	that		N X V
CL 532	Vche beste to the bent / that / bytes on erbez;	that		N P N
CL 533	Wylde wormez to her won / wrythez in the erthe,	/		V P D N
CL 534	The fox and the folmarde / to the / fryth wyndez,	P D		N V
CL 535	Herttes to hy3e hethe, / harez to gorstez,	/		N P N
CL 536	And lyounez and lebardez / to the / lake-ryftes;	P D		N N
CL 537	Hernez and hauekez / to the / hy3e rochez,	P D		A N
CL 538	The hole-foted fowle / to the / flod hy3ez,	P D		N V
CL 539	And vche best at a brayde / ther hym / best lykez;	Q H		Z V
CL 540	The fowre frekez of the folde / fongez the empyre.	/		V D N
CL 541	Lo! suche a wrakful wo / for / wlatsum dedez	P		A N
CL 542	Parformed the hy3e Fader / on / folke that He made;	P		N that H V
CL 543	That He chysly hade cherisched / He / chastysed ful hardee,	H		V Z Z
CL 544	In devoydynge the vylanye / that / venkquyst His thewez.	that		V D N
CL 545	Forthy war the now, wy3e / that / worschyp desyres	that		N V
CL 546	In His comlych courte / that / Kyng is of blysse,	that		N be P N
CL 547	In the fylthe of the flesch / that / thou be / founden neuer,	that H be		E Z
CL 548	Tyl any water in the worlde / to / wasche the fayly.	to		V H V
CL 549	For is no segge vnder sunne / so / seme of his craftez,	Z		A P D N
CL 550	If he be sulped in synne, / that / syttez vnclene;	that		V A
CL 551	On spec of a spote / may / spede to mysse	X		V to V
CL 552	Of the sy3te of the Souerayn / that / syttez so hy3e;	that		V Z Z
CL 553	For that schewe me schale / in tho / schyre howsez,	P D		A N
CL 554	As the beryl bornyst / byhouez be clene,	/		V V A
CL 555	That is sounde on vche a syde / and no / sem habes-	C D		N V
CL 556	Withouten maskle other mote, /as / margerye-perle.	P		N N
CL 557	Sythen the Souerayn in sete / so / sore fortho3t	Z		Z V
CL 558	That euer He man vpon molde / merked to lyuy,	/		V to V
CL 559	For he in fylthe watz fallen, / felly He uenged,	/		Z H V
CL 560	Quen fourferde alle the flesch / that He / formed hade.	that H		E have
CL 561	Hym rwed that He hem vprerde / and / ra3t hem lyflode;	C		V H N
CL 562	And efte that He hem vndyd, / hard hit Hym tho3t.	/		A H H V
CL 563	For quen the swemande sor3e / so3t to His hert,	/		V P D N

CL 564	He knyt a couenaunde cortaysly / with / monkynde there,	P	N Z
CL 565	In the mesure of His mode / and / mebe of Hio wylle,	C	N P D N
CL 566	That He schulde neuer for no syt / smyte al at onez,	/	V Z Z
CL 567	As to quelle alle quykez / for / qued that myʒt falle,	P	N that X V
CL 568	Whyl of the lenthe of the londe / lastez the terme.	/	V D N
CL 569	That ilke skyl for no scathe / ascaped Hym neuer.	/	V H Z
CL 570	Wheder wonderly He wrak / on / wykked men after,	P	E N Z
CL 571	Ful felly for that ilk faute / forferde a kyth ryche,	/	V D N A
CL 572	In the anger of His ire, / that / arʒed mony;	that	V H
CL 573	And al watz for this ilk euel, / that / vnhappen glette,	that	V N
CL 574	The venym and the vylanye / and the / vycios fylthe	C D	A N
CL 575	That bysulpez mannez saule / in / vnsounde hert,	P	A N
CL 576	That he Saueour ne see / with / syʒt of his yʒen.	P	N P D N
CL 577	Alle illez He hates / as / helle that stynkkez;	P	N that V
CL 578	Bot non nuyez Hym on naʒt / ne / neuer vpon dayez	not	Z P N
CL 579	As harlottrye vnhonest, / hethyng of seluen:	/	N P self
CL 580	That schamez for no schrewedschyp, / schent mot he worthe.	/	E X H V
CL 581	Bot sauyour, mon, in thyself, / thaʒ thou a / sotte lyuie,	C H D	N V
CL 582	Thaʒ thou bere thyself babel, / bythenk the sumtyme	/	V H Z
CL 583	Whether He that stykked vche a stare / in vche / steppe yʒe-	P D	A N
CL 584	ʒif Hymself be bore blynde / hit is a / brod wonder;	H be D	A N
CL 585	And He that fetly in face / fettled alle eres,	/	V D N
CL 586	If He hatz losed the lysten / hit / lyftez meruayle:	H	V N
CL 587	Trave thou neuer that tale-/ vntrwe thou hit fyndez.	/	A H H V
CL 588	Ther is no dede so derne / that / dittez His yʒen;	that	V D N
CL 589	Ther is no wyʒe in his werk / so / war ne so stylle	Z	A not Z A
CL 590	That hit ne thrawez to Hym thro / er he hit / thoʒt haue.	C H H	E have
CL 591	For He is the gropande God, / the / grounde of alle dedez,	D	N P D N
CL 592	Rypande of vche a ring / the / reynyez and hert.	D	N C N
CL 593	And there He fyndez al fayre / a / freke wythinne,	D	N P
CL 594	With hert honest and hol, / that / hathel He honourez,	D	N H V
CL 595	Sendez hym a sad syʒt: / to / se His auen face,	to	V D A N
CL 596	And harde honysez thise other, / and of His / erde flemez.	C P D	N V
CL 597	Bot of the dome of the douthe / for / dedez of schame-	P	N P N
CL 598	He is so skoymos of that skathe, / He / scarrez bylyue;	H	V Z
CL 599	He may not dryʒe to draw / allyt, bot / drepez in hast:	Z C	V P N
CL 600	And that watz schewed schortly / by a / schathe onez.	P D	N Z
CL 601	Olde Abraham in erde / onez he syttez,	/	Z H V
CL 602	Euen byfore his hous-dore, / vnder an / oke grene;	P D	N A
CL 603	Bryʒt blykked the bem / of the / brode heuen;	P D	A N
CL 604	In the hyʒe hete / therof / Abraham bidez:	Z	N V
CL 605	He watz schunt to the schadow / vnder / schyre leuez.	P	A N
CL 606	Thenne watz he war on the waye / of / wlonk Wyʒez thrynne;	P	A N A
CL 607	If Thay wer farande and fre / and / fayre to beholde	C	A to V
CL 608	Hit is ethe to leue / by the / last ende.	P D	A N
CL 609	For the lede that ther laye / the / leuez anvnder,	D	N P
CL 610	When he hade to Hem syʒt / he / hyʒez bylyue,	H	V Z
CL 611	And as to God the goodmon / gos Hem agaynez	/	V H P
CL 612	And haylsed Hem in onhede, / and sayde: / 'Hende Lorde,	C V	A N
CL 613	ʒif euer Thy mon vpon molde / merit disserued,	/	N V
CL 614	Lenge a lyttel here / therof / I / loʒly biseche:	H	Z V
CL 615	Passe neuer fro Thi pouere, / ʒif I hit / pray durst,	C H H	V V
CL 616	Er Thou haf biden with Thi burne / and vnder / boʒe resttes,	C P	N E
CL 617	And I schal wynne Yow woʒt / of / water a lyttel,	P	N Z
CL 618	And fast aboute schal I fare / Your / fette wer waschene.	D	N be E
CL 619	Resttez here on this rote / and I schal / rachche after	C H X	V Z
CL 620	And brynge a morsel of bred / to / baume Your hertte.'	to	V D N
CL 621	'Fare forthe,' quoth the Frekez, / 'and / fech as thou seggez;	C	V C H V
CL 622	By bole of this brode tre / We / byde the here.'	H	V H Z
CL 623	Thenne orppedly into his hous / he / hyʒed to Saré,	H	V P N
CL 624	Comaunded hir to be cof / and / quyk at this onez:	C	A Z
CL 625	'Thre mettez of mele menge / and / ma kakez;	C	V N
CL 626	Vnder askez ful hote / happe hem bylyue;	/	V H Z
CL 627	Quyl I fete sumquat fat, / thou the / fyr bete,	H D	N V
CL 628	Prestly at this ilke poynte / sum / polment to make.'	C D	N V
CL 629	He cached to his covhous / and a / calf bryngez,	V	V P D N
CL 630	That watz tender and not toʒe, / bed / vnfor of the hyde,	that H H	V Z
CL 631	And sayde to his seruaunt / that he hit / sethe faste;	/	V H Z
CL 632	And he deruely at his dome / dyʒt hit bylyue.	/	V H Z
CL 633	The burne to be bare-heued / buskez hym thenne,	/	V H Z
CL 634	Clechez to a clene clothe / and / kestez on the grene,	C	V P D N(A)

CL 635	Thrwe thryftyly / theron tho thre / therue kakez,	Z D D	A N
CL 636	And bryngez butter / wythal and by the / bred settez;	Z C P D	N V
CL 637	Mete messez of mylke / he / merkkez bytwene,	H	V Z
CL 638	Sythen potage and polment / in / plater honest.	P	N A
CL 639	As sewer in a god assyse / he / serued Hem fayre,	H	V H Z
CL 640	Wyth sadde semblaunt and swete / of / such as he hade;	P	H C H V
CL 641	And God as a glad gest / mad / god chere	V	A N
CL 642	That watz fayn of his frende, / and his / fest praysed.	C D	N V
CL 643	Abraham, al hodlez, / with / armez vp-folden,	P	N E
CL 644	Mynystred mete byfore tho Men / that / myʒtes al weldez.	that	X H V
CL 645	Thenne Thay sayden as Thay sete / samen alle thrynne,	/	Z D H
CL 646	When the mete watz remued / and Thay of / mensk speken,	C H P	N V
CL 647	'I schal efte hereaway, / Abram,' Thay sayden,	/	N H V
CL 648	'ʒet er thy lyuez lyʒt / lethe vpon erthe,	/	V P N
CL 649	And thenne schal Saré consayue / and a / sun bere,	C D	N V
CL 650	That schal be Abrahamez ayre / and / after hym wynne	C	P H V
CL 651	With wele and wyth worschyp / the / worthely peple	D	A N
CL 652	That schal halde in heritage / that I / haf men ʒarked.'	that H	have N E
CL 653	Thenne the burde byhynde the dor / for / busmar laʒed;	P	N V
CL 654	And sayde sothly to hirself / Saré madde:	/	N H A
CL 655	'May thou traw for tykle / that thou / teme moʒtez,	that H	V X
CL 656	And I so hyʒe out of age, / and / also my lorde?'	C	Z D N
CL 657	For sothely, as says the wryt, / he wern of / sadde elde,	H be P	A N
CL 658	Bothe the wyʒe and his wyf, / such / werk watz hem fayled	D	N be H E
CL 659	Fro mony a brod day byfore; / ho / barayn ay bydene,	H	A Z Z
CL 660	That selue Saré, withouten sede / into that / same tyme.	P D	A N
CL 661	Thenne sayde oure Syre ther He sete: 'Se! / so / Saré laʒes,	C	N V
CL 662	Not trawande the tale / that / I the to schewed.	that	H H P V
CL 663	Hopez ho oʒt may be harde / My / hondez to work?	D	N to V
CL 664	And ʒet I avow verayly / the / avaunt that I made;	D	N that H V
CL 665	I schal ʒeply aʒayn / and / ʒelde that I hyʒt,	C	V that H V
CL 666	And sothely sende to Saré / a / soun and an hayre.'	D	N C D N
CL 667	Thenne swenged forth Saré / and / swer by hir trawthe	C	V P D N
CL 668	That for lot that Thay laused / ho / laʒed neuer.	H	V Z
CL 669	'Now innoghe: hit is not / so,' thenne / nurned the Dryʒtyn,	Z Z	V D N
CL 670	'For thou laʒed aloʒ, / bot / let we hit one.'	C	V H H Z
CL 671	With that Thay ros vp radly, / as Thay / rayke schulde,	C H	V X
CL 672	And setten toward Sodamas / Her / syʒt alle at onez;	H	V Z Z
CL 673	For that cité therbysyde / watz / sette in a vale,	be	E P D N
CL 674	No mylez fro Mambre / mo then tweyne,	/	A P N
CL 675	Whereso wonyed this ilke wyʒ, / that / wendez with oure Lorde	that	V P D N
CL 676	For to tent Hym with tale / and / teche Hym the gate.	C	V H D N
CL 677	Then glydez forth God; / the / godmon Hym folʒez;	D	N H V
CL 678	Abraham heldez Hem / wyth, / Hem to conueye	P	H to V
CL 679	Towarde the cety of Sodamas / that / synned had thenne	that	E have Z
CL 680	In the faute of this fylthe. / The / Fader hem thretes,	D	N H V
CL 681	And sayde thus to the segg / that / sued Hym after:	that	V H P
CL 682	'How myʒt I hyde Myn hert / fro / Habraham the trwe,	P	N D N(A)
CL 683	That I ne dyscouered to his corse / My / counsayl so dere,	D	N Z A
CL 684	Sythen he is chosen to be chef / chyldryn fader,	/	N N
CL 685	That so folk schal falle / fro to / flete alle the worlde,	P to	V D D N
CL 686	And vche blod in that burne / blessed schal worthe?	/	E X V
CL 687	Me bos telle to that tolk / the / tene of My wylle,	D	N P D N
CL 688	And alle Myn atlyng to Abraham / vnhaspe bilyue.	/	V Z
CL 689	The grete soun of Sodamas / synkkez in Myn erez,	/	V P D N
CL 690	And the gult of Gomorre / garez Me to wrath.	/	V H to V
CL 691	I schal lyʒt into that led / and / loke Myseluen	C	V H self
CL 692	If thay haf don as the dyne / dryuez on lofte.	/	V Z
CL 693	Thay han lerned a lyst / that / lykez me ille,	that	V H Z
CL 694	That thay han founden in her flesch / of / fautez the werst:	P	N D A
CL 695	Vch male matz his mach / a / man as hymseluen,	D	N P H self
CL 696	And fylter folyly in fere / on / femmalez wyse.	P	N N
CL 697	I compast hem a kynde crafte / and / kende hit hem derne,	C	V H H Z
CL 698	And amed hit in Myn ordenaunce / oddely dere,	/	Z A
CL 699	And dyʒt drwry / therinne, / doole alther-swettest,	Z	N A A
CL 700	And the play of paramorez / I / portrayed Myseluen,	H	V H self
CL 701	And made therto a maner / myriest of other:	/	A P H
CL 702	When two true togeder / had / tyʒed hemseluen,	have	E H self
CL 703	Bytwene a male and his make / such / merthe schulde come,	D	N X V
CL 704	Welnyʒe pure paradys / moʒt / preue no better;	X	V Z
CL 705	Ellez thay moʒt honestly / ayther other welde,	/	Z V

CL 706	At a stylle stollen steuen, / vnstered wyth sy3t,	/		E P N
CL 707	Luf-lowe / hem bytwene / lasched so hote		II P	V Z A
CL 708	That alle the meschefez on mold / mo3t hit not sleke.	/		X H not V
CL 709	Now haf thay skyfted My skyl / and / scorned natwre,	C		V N
CL 710	And henttez hem in hethyng / an / vsage vnclene.	D		N A
CL 711	Hem to smyte for that smod / smartly I thenk,	/		Z H V
CL 712	That wy3ez schal be by hem war, / worlde withouten ende.'	/		N P N
CL 713	Thenne ar3ed Abraham / and alle his / mod chaunged,	C D D		N V
CL 714	For hope of the harde hate / that / hy3t hatz oure Lorde.	that		E have D N
CL 715	Al sykande he sayde: / 'Sir, with Yor leue,	/		N P D N
CL 716	Schal synful and saklez / suffer al on payne?	/		V Z P N
CL 717	Wether euer hit lyke my Lorde / to / lyfte such domez	to		V D N
CL 718	That the wykked and the worthy / schal on / wrake suffer,	X P		N V
CL 719	And weye vpon the worre half / that / wrathed The neuer?	that		V H Z
CL 720	That watz neuer Thy won / that / wro3tez vus alle.	that		V H Z
CL 721	Now fyfty fyn frendez / wer / founde in 3onde toune,	be		E P D N
CL 722	In the cety of Sodamas / and / also Gomorre,	C		Z N
CL 723	That neuer lakked Thy laue, / bot / loued ay trauthe,	C		V Z N
CL 724	And re3tful wern and resounable / and / redy The to serue,	C		A H to V
CL 725	Schal thay falle in the faute / that other / frekez wro3t,	that D		N V
CL 726	And joyne to her juggement, / her / juise to haue?	D		N to V
CL 727	That nas neuer Thyn note, / vnneuened hit worthe,	/		E H V
CL 728	That art so gaynly a God / and of / goste mylde.'	C P		N A
CL 729	'Nay, for fyfty,' quoth the Fader, / 'and thy / fayre speche,	C D		A N
CL 730	And thay be founden in that folk / of her / fylthe clene,	P D		N A
CL 731	I schal forgyue alle the gylt / thur3 My / grace one,	P D		N Z
CL 732	And let hem smolt al unsmyten / smothely at onez.'	/		Z Z
CL 733	'Aa! blessed be Thow,' quoth the burne, / 'so / boner and thewed,	Z		A C A
CL 734	And al haldez in Thy honde, / the / heuen and the erthe;	D		N C D N
CL 735	Bot, for I towched haf this talke, / tatz to non ille	/		V P D N
CL 736	3if I mele a lyttel more / that / mul am and askez.	that		N be C V
CL 737	What if fyue faylen / of / fyfty the noumbre,	P		N D N
CL 738	And the remnaunt be reken, / how / restes Thy wylle?'	Q		V D N
CL 739	'And fyue wont of fyfty,' quoth God, / 'I schal / for3ete alle	V N H X		V H
CL 740	And wythhalde My honde / for / hortyng on lede.'	P		G P N
CL 741	'And quat if faurty be fre / and / fauty thyse other:	C		A D H
CL 742	Schalt Thow schortly al schende / and / schape non other?'	Z		V Z
CL 743	'Nay, tha3 faurty forfete, / 3et / fryst I a whyle,	Z		V H Z
CL 744	And voyde away My vengaunce, / tha3 Me / vyl thynk.'	C H		A V
CL 745	Then Abraham obeched Hym / and / lo3ly Him thonkkez:	C		Z H V
CL 746	'Now sayned be Thou, Sauiour, / so / symple in Thy wrath!	Z		A P D N
CL 747	I am bot erthe ful euel / and / vsle so blake,	C		N Z A
CL 748	For to mele wyth such a Mayster / as / my3tez hatz alle.	C		N V H
CL 749	Bot I haue bygonnen wyth my God, / and He hit / gayn thynkez;	C H H		A V
CL 750	3if I forloyne as a fol / Thy / fraunchyse may serue.	D		N X V
CL 751	What if thretty thryuande / be / thrad in 3on tounez,	be		E P D N
CL 752	What schal I leue of my Lorde-/ if He hem / lethe wolde?'	C H H		V X
CL 753	Thenne the godlych God / gef hym onsware:	/		V H N
CL 754	'3et thretty in throng / I schal My / thro steke,	H X D		N V
CL 755	And spare spakly of spyt / in / space of My thewez,	P		N P D N
CL 756	And My rankor refrayne / four thy / reken wordez.'	D D		A N
CL 757	'What for twenty,' quoth the tolke, / 'vntwynez Thou hem thenne?'	/		V H H Z
CL 758	'Nay, 3if thou 3ernez hit 3et, / 3ark I hem grace,'	/		V H H N
CL 759	If that twenty be trwe, / I / tene hem no more,	H		V H Z
CL 760	Bot relece alle that regioun / of her / ronk werkkez.'	P D		A N
CL 761	'Now, athel Lorde,' quoth Abraham, / 'onez a speche,	/		Z D N
CL 762	And I schal schape no more / tho / schalkkez to helpe.	D		N to V
CL 763	If ten trysty in toune / be / tan in Thi werkkez,	be		E P D N
CL 764	Wylt Thou mese Thy mode / and / menddyng abyde?'	C		N V
CL 765	'I graunt,' quoth the grete God, / 'Graunt mercy,' that other;	/		A N D H
CL 766	And thenne arest the renk / and / ra3t no fyrre.	C		V Z
CL 767	And Godde glydez His gate / by those / grene wayez,	P D		A N
CL 768	And he conueyen Hym con / with / cast of his y3e;	P		N P D N
CL 769	And als he loked along / thereas oure / Lorde passed,	Z D		N V
CL 770	3et he cryed Hym after / with / careful steuen:	P		A N
CL 771	'Meke Mayster, on Thy mon / to / mynne if The lyked,	to		V C H V
CL 772	Loth lengez in 3on leede / that is my / lef brother;	that be D		A N
CL 773	He syttez ther in Sodomis, / Thy / seruaunt so pouere,	D		N Z A
CL 774	Among tho mansed men / that han The / much greued.	that have H		Z E
CL 775	3if Thou tynez that toun, / tempre Thyn yre,	/		V D N
CL 776	As Thy mersy may malte, / Thy/ meke to spare.'	D		N to V

CL 777	Then he wendez his way, / wepande for care,	/	G P N
CL 778	Towarde the mere of Mambre, / mornande for sorewe;	/	G P N
CL 779	And there in longyng al nyȝt / he / lengez in wones,	H	V P N
CL 780	Whyl the Souerayn to Sodamas / sende to spye.	/	V to V
CL 781	His sonde into Sodamas / watz / sende in that tyme,	be	E P D N
CL 782	In that ilk euentyde, / by / aungels tweyne,	P	N A
CL 783	Meuand mekely / togeder as / myry men ȝonge,	Z P	A N A
CL 784	As Loot in a loge dor / lened hym alone,	/	V H Z
CL 785	In a porche of that place / pyȝt to the ȝates,	/	E P D N
CL 786	That watz ryal and ryche / so watz the / renkes seluen.	C be D	N self
CL 787	As he stared into the strete / ther / stout men played,	Q	A N V
CL 788	He syȝe ther swey in asent / swete men tweyne;	/	A N A
CL 789	Bolde burnez wer thay bothe / with / berdles chynnez,	P	A N
CL 790	Ryol rollande fax / to / raw sylk lyke,	P	A N A
CL 791	Of ble as the brere-flour / whereso the / bare scheweed.	Q D	N V
CL 792	Ful clene watz the countenaunce / of her / cler yȝen;	P D	A N
CL 793	Wlonk whit watz her wede / and / wel hit hem semed.	C	A H H V
CL 794	Of alle feturez ful fyn / and / fautlez bothe;	C	A Z
CL 795	Watz non aucly in outher, / for / aungels hit wern,	P	N H be
CL 796	And that the ȝep underȝede / that in the / ȝate syttez;	that P D	N V
CL 797	He ros vp ful radly / and / ran hem to mete,	C	V H to V
CL 798	And loȝe he loutez / hem to, / Loth, to the grounde,	H P	N P D N
CL 799	And sythen soberly: / 'Syrez, I yow byseche	/	N H H V
CL 800	That ȝe wolde lyȝt at my loge / and / lenge therinne.	C	V Z
CL 801	Comez to your knaues kote, / I / craue at this onez;	H	V P D H
CL 802	I schal fette yow a fatte / your / fette for to wasche;	D	N for to V
CL 803	I norne yow bot for on nyȝt / neȝe me to lenge,	/	V H to V
CL 804	And in the myry mornyng / ȝe / may youre waye take.'	H	X D N V
CL 805	And thay nay that thay nolde / neȝ no howsez,	/	V D N
CL 806	Bot stylly ther in the strete / as thay / stadde wern	C H	E be
CL 807	Thay wolde lenge the long / naȝt and / logge theroute:	not C	V Z
CL 808	Hit watz hous innoȝe to hem / the / heuen vpon lofte.	D	N Z
CL 809	Loth lathed so longe / wyth / luflych wordez	D	A N
CL 810	That thay hym grauntted to go / and / gruȝt no lenger.	C	V Z
CL 811	The bolde to his byggyng / bryngez hem bylyue,	/	V H Z
CL 812	That watz ryally arayed, / for he watz / ryche euer.	C H be	A Z
CL 813	The wyȝez wern welcom / as the / wyf couthe;	C D	N X
CL 814	His two dere doȝterez / deuoutly hem haylsed,	/	Z H V
CL 815	That wer maydenez ful meke, / maryed not ȝet,	/	E not Z
CL 816	And thay wer semly and swete, / and / swythe wel arayed.	C	Z Z E
CL 817	Loth thenne ful lyȝtly / lokez hym aboute,	/	V H P
CL 818	And his men amonestes / mete for to dyȝt:	/	N for to V
CL 819	'Bot thenkkez on hit be threfte / what / thynk so ȝe make,	Q	V Z H V
CL 820	For wyth no sour ne no salt / seruez hym neuer.'	/	V H Z
CL 821	Bot ȝet I wene that the wyf / hit / wroth to dyspyt,	H	V P N
CL 822	And sayde softely to hirself: / 'This / vnsauere hyne	D	E N
CL 823	Louez no salt in her sauce; / ȝet hit no / skyl were	C H D	N be
CL 824	That other burne be boute, / thaȝ / bothe be nyse.'	C	H be A
CL 825	Thenne ho sauerez with salt / her / seuez vchone,	D	N H
CL 826	Agayne the bone of the burne / that hit / forboden hade,	that H	E had
CL 827	And als ho scelt hem in scorne / that wel her / skyl knewen.	that Z D	N E
CL 828	Why watz ho, wrech, so wod? / Ho / wrathed oure Lorde.	H	V D N
CL 829	Thenne seten thay at the soper, / wern / serued bylyue,	be	E Z
CL 830	The gestes gay and ful glad, / of / glam debonere,	P	N A
CL 831	Welawynnely wlonk, / tyl thay / waschen hade,	C H	E have
CL 832	The trestes tylt to the woȝe / and the / table bothe.	C D	N Z
CL 833	Fro the seggez haden souped / and / seten bot a whyle,	C	E Z Z
CL 834	Er euer thay bosked to bedde, / the / borȝ watz al vp,	D	N be Z Z
CL 835	Alle that weppen myȝt welde, / the / wakker and the stronger,	D	N(A) C D N(A)
CL 836	To vmbelyȝe Lothez hous / the / ledez to take.	D	N to V
CL 837	In grete flokkez of folk / thay / fallen to his ȝatez;	H	V P D N
CL 838	As a scowte-wach scarred / so the / asscry rysed;	C D	N V
CL 839	With kene clobbez of that clos / thay / clatrez on the wowez,	H	V P D N
CL 840	And wyth a schrylle scharp schout / thay / schewe thyse wordez:	H	V D N
CL 841	'If thou louyez thy lyf, / Loth, in thyse wones,	/	N P D N
CL 842	ȝete vus out those ȝong men / that / ȝore-whyle here entred,	that	Z Z V
CL 843	That we may here hym of lof, / as oure / lyst biddez,	C D	N V
CL 844	As is the asyse of Sodomas / to / seggez that passen.'	P	N that V
CL 845	Whatt! thay sputen and speken / of so / spitous fylthe,	P Z	A N
CL 846	What! thay ȝeȝed and ȝolped / of / ȝestande sorȝe,	P	G N
CL 847	That ȝet the wynd and the weder / and the / worlde stynkes	C D	N V

CL 848	Of the bryeh that vpbraydez / those / brothelych wordez.	D	A N
CL 849	The godman glytte with that glam / and / gloped for noyse,	C	V P N
CL 850	So scharpe schame to hym schot, / he / schrank at the hert.	H	V P D N
CL 851	For he knew the costoum / that / kythed those wrechez,	that	V D N
CL 852	He doted neuer for no doel / so / depe in his mynde.	Z	Z P D N
CL 853	'Allas!' sayd hym thenne Loth, / and / lyʒtly he rysez,	C	Z H V
CL 854	And bowez forth fro the bench / into the / brode ʒates.	P D	A N
CL 855	What! he wonded no wothe / of / wekked knauez,	P	E N
CL 856	That he ne passed the port / the / peril to abide.	D	N to V
CL 857	He went forthe at the wyket / and / waft hit hym after,	C	V H H P
CL 858	That a clyket hit cleʒt / clos hym byhynde.	/	Z H P
CL 859	Thenne he meled to tho men / mesurable wordez,	/	A N
CL 860	For harlotez with his hendelayk / he / hoped to chast:	H	V to V
CL 861	'Oo, my frendez so fre, / your / fare is to strange;	D	N be Z A
CL 862	Dotz away your derf dyn / and / derez neuer my gestes.	C	V Z D N
CL 863	Avoy! hit is your vylaynye, / ʒe / vylen yourseluen;	H	V H self
CL 864	And ʒe are jolyf gentylmen, / your / japez ar ille.	D	N be A
CL 865	Bot I schal kenne yow by kynde / a / crafte that is better:	D	N that be A
CL 866	I haf a tresor in my telde / of / tow my fayre deʒter,	P	N D A N
CL 867	That ar maydenez vnmard / for alle / men ʒette;	P D	N Z
CL 868	In Sodamas, thaʒ I hit say, / non / semloker burdes;	D	A N
CL 869	Hit arn ronk, hit arn rype, / and / redy to manne;	C	A P N
CL 870	To samen wyth tho semly / the / solace is better.	D	N be A
CL 871	I schal biteche yow tho two / that / tayt arn and quoynt,	that	A be C A
CL 872	And laykez wyth hem as yow lyst, / and / letez my gestes one.'	C	V D N Z
CL 873	Thenne the rebaudez so ronk / rerd such a noyse	/	V D D N
CL 874	That aʒly hurled in his erez / her / harlotez speche:	D	N N
CL 875	'Wost thou not wel that thou wonez / here a / wyʒe strange,	Z D	N A
CL 876	An outcomlyng, a carle? / We / kylle of thyn heued!	H	V P D N
CL 877	Who joyned the be jostyse / oure / japez to blame,	D	N to V
CL 878	That com a boy to this borʒ, / thaʒ thou be / burne ryche?'	C H be	N A
CL 879	Thus thay throbled and throng / and / thrwe vmbe his erez,	C	V Z D N
CL 880	And distresed hym wonder strayt / with / strenkthe in the prece,	P	N P D N
CL 881	Bot that the ʒonge men, so ʒepe, / ʒornen theroute,	/	V Z
CL 882	Wapped vpon the wyket / and / wonnen hem tylle,	C	V H P
CL 883	And by the hondez hym hent / and / horyed hym withinne,	C	V H P
CL 884	And steken the ʒates ston-harde / wyth / stalworth barrez.	P	A N
CL 885	Thay blwe a boffet / inblande that / banned peple,	P D	E N
CL 886	That thay blustered, as blynde / as / Bayard watz euer;	C	N be Z
CL 887	Thay lest of Lotez logging / any / lysoun to fynde,	D	N to V
CL 888	Bot nyteled ther alle the nyʒt / for / noʒt at the last.	P	N Z
CL 889	Thenne vch tolke tyʒt hem, / that hade of / tayt fayled,	H that have P	N E
CL 890	And vchon rotheled to the rest / that he / reche moʒt;	that H	V X
CL 891	Bot thay wern wakned al wrank / that ther in / won lenged,	that Z P	N V
CL 892	Of on the vglokest vnhap / euer on erd suffred.	/	Z P N V
CL 893	Ruddon of the day-rawe / ros vpon vʒten,	/	V P N
CL 894	When merk of the mydnyʒt / moʒt no more last.	/	X Z V
CL 895	Ful erly those aungelez / this / hathel thay ruthen,	D	N H V
CL 896	And glopnedly on Godez halue / gart hym vpryse;	/	V H V
CL 897	Fast the freke ferkez / vp ful / ferd at his hert;	Z Z	E P D N
CL 898	Thay comaunded hym cof / to / cach that he hade,	to	V Q H V
CL 899	'Wyth thy wyf and thy wyʒez / and thy / wlonc deʒtters,	C D	A N
CL 900	For we lathe the, sir Loth, / that thou thy / lyf haue.	that H D	N V
CL 901	Cayre tid of this kythe / er / combred thou worthe,	C	E H V
CL 902	With alle thi here vpon haste, / tyl thou a / hil fynde;	C H D	N V
CL 903	Foundez faste on your fete; / bifore your / face lokes,	C D	N V
CL 904	Bot bes neuer so bolde / to / blusch yow bihynde,	to	V H P
CL 905	And loke ʒe stemme no stepe, / bot / strecheʒ on faste;	C	V Z
CL 906	Til ʒe reche to a reset, / rest ʒe neuer.	/	V H Z
CL 907	For we schal tyne this toun / and / traythely disstrye,	C	Z V
CL 908	Wyth alle thise wyʒez so wykke / wyʒtly devoyde,	/	Z V
CL 909	And alle the londe with thise ledez / we / losen at onez;	H	V Z
CL 910	Sodomas schal ful sodenly / synk into groude,	/	V P N
CL 911	And the grounde of Gomorre / gorde into helle,	/	V P N
CL 912	And vche a koste of this kythe / clater vpon hepes.'	/	V P N
CL 913	Then laled Loth: / 'Lorde, what is best?	/	N Q be A
CL 914	If I me fele vpon fote / that I / fle moʒt,	that H	V X
CL 915	Hov schulde I huyde me fro Hym / that hatz His / hate kynned	that have D	N E
CL 916	In the brath of His breth / that / brennez alle thinkez?	that	V D N
CL 917	To crepe fro my Creatour / I / know not wheder,	H	V not Q
CL 918	Ne whether His fooschip me folʒez / bifore other bihynde.'	/	Z H P

CL 919	The freke sayde: 'No foschip / oure / Fader hatz the schewed,	D	N have H E
CL 920	Bot hiȝly heuened thi hele / fro / hem that arn combred.	P	H that be E
CL 921	Nov wale the a wonnyng / that the / warisch myȝt,	that H	V X
CL 922	And He schal saue hit for thy sake / that hatz vus / sende hider,	that have H	E Z
CL 923	For thou art oddely thyn one / out of this fylthe,	/	P P D N
CL 924	And als Abraham thyn eme / tho / maydenez schulde wedde;	H P	H self V
CL 925	'Lorde, loued He worthe,' / quoth / Loth, 'vpon erthe!	V	N P N
CL 926	Ther is a cité herbisyde / that / Segor hit hatte-	that	N H V
CL 927	Here vtter on a rounde hil / hit / houez hit one.	H	V H P
CL 928	I wolde, if His wylle wore, / to that / won scape.'	P D	N V
CL 929	'Thenn fare forth,' quoth that fre, / 'and / fyne thou neuer,	C	V H Z
CL 930	With those ilk that thow wylt / that / threnge the after,	that	V H P
CL 931	And ay goande on your gate, / wythouten / agayn-tote,	P	Z N
CL 932	For alle this londe schal be lorne longe / er the / sonne rise.'	C D	N V
CL 933	The wyȝe wakened his wyf / and his / wlonk deȝteres,	C D	A N
CL 934	And other two myri men / tho / maydenez schulde wedde;	D	N X V
CL 935	And thay token hit as tayt / and / tented hit lyttel;	C	V H Z
CL 936	Thaȝ fast lathed hem Loth, / thay / leȝen ful stylle.	H	V Z Z
CL 937	The aungelez hasted thise other / and / aȝly hem thratten,	C	Z H V
CL 938	And enforsed alle fawre / forth at the ȝatez:	/	Z P D N
CL 939	Tho wern Loth and his lef, / his / luflyche deȝter;	D	A N
CL 940	Ther soȝt no mo to sauement / of / cities athel fyue.	P	N A H
CL 941	Thise aungelez hade hem by hande / out at the ȝatez,	/	Z P D N
CL 942	Prechande hem the perile, / and / beden hem passe fast:	C	V H V Z
CL 943	'Lest ȝe be taken in the teche / of / tyrauntez here,	P	N Z
CL 944	Loke ȝe bowe now bi bot; / bowez fast hence!'	/	V Z Z
CL 945	And thay kayre ne con, / and / kenely flowen.	C	Z V
CL 946	Erly, er any heuen-glem, / thay to a / hil comen.	H P D	N V
CL 947	The grete God in His greme / bygynnez on lofte	/	V Z
CL 948	To waken wederez so wylde; / the / wyndez He callez,	D	N H V
CL 949	And thay wrothely vpwafte / and / wrastled togeder,	C	V Z
CL 950	Fro fawre half of the folde / flytande loude.	/	G Z
CL 951	Clowdez clustered / bytwene / kesten vp torres,	Z	V Z N
CL 952	That the thik thunder-thrast / thirled hem ofte.	/	V H Z
CL 953	The rayn rueled / adoun, / ridlande thikke	Z	G Z
CL 954	Of felle flaunkes of fyr / and / flakes of soufre,	C	N P N
CL 955	Al in smolderande smoke / smachande ful ille,	/	G Z Z
CL 956	Swe aboute Sodamas / and hit / sydez alle,	C H	N Z
CL 957	Gorde to Gomorra, / that the / grounde laused,	that D	N V
CL 958	Abdama and Syboym, / thise / ceteis alle faure	D	N D H
CL 959	Al birolled wyth the rayn, / rostted and brenned,	/	E C E
CL 960	And ferly flayed that folk / that in those / fees lenged.	that P D	N V
CL 961	For when that the Helle herde / the / houndez of heuen,	D	N P N
CL 962	He watz ferlyly fayn, / vnfolded bylyue;	/	E Z
CL 963	The grete barrez of the abyme / he / barst vp at onez,	H	V Z Z
CL 964	That alle the regioun torof / in / riftes ful grete,	/	N Z A
CL 965	And clouen alle in lyttel cloutes / the / clyffez aywhere,	D	N Z
CL 966	As lauce leuez of the boke / that / lepes in twynne.	that	V P N
CL 967	The brethe of the brynston / bi that hit / blende were,	P H H	E be
CL 968	Al tho citees and her sydes / sunkken to helle.	/	V P N
CL 969	Rydelles wern tho grete rowtes / of / renkkes withinne,	P	N Z
CL 970	When thay wern war of the wrake / that no / wyȝe achaped;	that D	N V
CL 971	Such a ȝomerly ȝarm / of / ȝellyng ther rysed,	P	G Z V
CL 972	Therof clatered the cloudes, / that / Kryst myȝt haf rawthe.	that	N X V N
CL 973	The segge herde that soun / to / Segor that ȝede,	P	N that V
CL 974	And the wenches hym wyth / that by the / way folȝed;	that P D	N V
CL 975	Ferly ferde watz her flesch / that / flowen ay ilyche,	that	V Z Z
CL 976	Trynande ay a hyȝe trot, / that / torne neuer dorsten.	that	V Z V
CL 977	Loth and tho luly-whit, / his / lefly two deȝter,	D	A A N
CL 978	Ay folȝed here face, / bifore her bothe yȝen;	/	P D D N
CL 979	Bot the balleful burde, / that neuer / bode keped,	that Z	N V
CL 980	Blusched byhynden her bak / that / bale for to herkken.	D	N for to V
CL 981	Hit watz lusty Lothes wyf / that ouer her / lyfte schulder	that P D	A N
CL 982	Ones ho bluschet to the burȝe, / bot / bod ho no lenger	C	V H Z
CL 983	That ho nas stadde a stiffe ston, / a / stalworth image,	D	A N
CL 984	Al so salt as ani se-/ and / so ho ȝet standez.	C	Z H Z V
CL 985	Thay slypped bi and syȝe / hir not that wern hir / samen-feres,	H not that be D	N N
CL 986	Tyl thay in Segor wern sette, / and / sayned our Lorde;	C	V D N
CL 987	Wyth lyȝt louez vplyfte / thay / loued Hym swythe,	H	V H Z
CL 988	That so His seruauntes wolde see / and / saue of such wothe.	/	V P D N
CL 989	Al watz dampped and don / and / drowned by thenne;	C	E P Z

CL	990	The ledez of that lyttel toun / wern / lopen out for drede	be	E Z P N
CL	991	Into that malscrande mere, / marred bylyue,	/	V Z
CL	992	That noȝt saued watz bot Segor, / that / sat on a lawe.	that	V P D N
CL	993	The thre ledez therin lent, / Loth and his deȝter;	/	N C D N
CL	994	For his make watz myst, / that on the / mount lenged	that P D	N V
CL	995	In a stonen statue / that / salt sauor habbes,	that	N N V
CL	996	For two fautes that the fol / watz / founde in mistrauthe:	be	E P N
CL	997	On, ho serued at the soper / salt bifore Dryȝtyn,	/	N P N
CL	998	And sythen, ho blusched hir bihynde, / thaȝ hir / forboden were;	C H	E be
CL	999	For on ho standes a ston, / and / salt for that other,	C	N P D H
CL	1000	And alle lyst on hir lik / that arn on / launde bestes.	that be P	N N
CL	1001	Abraham ful erly / watz / vp on the morne,	be	Z P D N
CL	1002	That alle naȝt much niye / hade / nomen in hert,	have	E P D N
CL	1003	Al in longing for Loth / leyen in a wache;	/	E P D N
CL	1004	Ther he lafte hade oure Lorde / he is on / lofte wonnen;	H be Z	Z V
CL	1005	He sende toward Sodomas / the / syȝt of his yȝen,	D	N P D N
CL	1006	That euer hade ben an erde / of / erthe the swettest,	P	N D A
CL	1007	As aparaunt to paradis, / that / plantted the Dryȝtyn;	that	V D N
CL	1008	Nov is hit plunged in a pit / like of / pich fylled.	C P	N E
CL	1009	Suche a rothun of a reche / ros fro the blake,	/	V P D N
CL	1010	Askez vpe in the ayre / and / vsellez ther flowen,	C	N Z V
CL	1011	As a fornes ful of flot / that vpon / fyr boyles	that P	N V
CL	1012	When bryȝt brennande brondez / ar / bet theranvnder.	be	E Z
CL	1013	This watz a uengaunce violent / that / voyded thise places,	that	V D N
CL	1014	That foundered hatz so fayr a folk / and the / folde sonkken.	C D	N E
CL	1015	Ther the fyue citées wern set / nov is a / see called,	Z be D	N E
CL	1016	That ay is drouy and dym, / and / ded in hit kynde,	C	A P D N
CL	1017	Blo, blubrande, and blak, / vnblythe to neȝe;	/	A to V
CL	1018	As a stynkande stanc / that / stryed synne,	that	V N
CL	1019	That euer of smelle and of smach / smart is to fele.	/	A be to V
CL	1020	Forthy the derk Dede See / hit is / demed euermore,	H be	E Z
CL	1021	For hit dedez of dethe / duren there ȝet;	/	V Z Z
CL	1022	For hit is brod and bothemlez, / and / bitter as the galle,	C	A P D N
CL	1023	And noȝt may lenge in that lake / that any / lyf berez,	that D	N V
CL	1024	And alle the costez of kynde / hit / combrez vchone.	H	V Z
CL	1025	For lay theron a lump of led, / and hit on / loft fletez,	C H Z	Z V
CL	1026	And folde theron a lyȝt fyther, / and hit to / founs synkkez;	C H P	N V
CL	1027	And ther water may walter / to / wete any erthe	to	V D N
CL	1028	Schal neuer grene theron growe, / gresse ne wod nawther.	/	N not N not
CL	1029	If any schalke to be schent / wer / schowued therinne,	be	E Z
CL	1030	Thaȝ he bode in that bothem / brothely a monyth,	/	Z D N
CL	1031	He most ay lyue in that loȝe / in / losyng euermore,	P	N Z
CL	1032	And neuer dryȝe no dethe / to / dayes of ende.	P	N P N
CL	1033	And as hit is corsed of kynde / and hit / coostez als,	C D	N Z
CL	1034	The clay that clenges / therby arn / corsyes strong,	Z be	N A
CL	1035	As alum and alkaran, / that / angré arn bothe,	that	A be Z
CL	1036	Soufre sour and saundyuer, / and other / such mony;	C D	A H
CL	1037	And ther waltez of that water / in / waxlokes grete	P	N A
CL	1038	The spumande aspaltoun / that / spyserez sellen;	that	V N
CL	1039	And suche is alle the soyle / by that / se halues,	P D	N N
CL	1040	That fel fretes the flesch / and / festres bones.	C	V N
CL	1041	And ther ar tres by that terne / of / traytoures,	P	N
CL	1042	And thay borgounez and beres / blomez ful fayre,	/	N Z A
CL	1043	The fayrest fryt / that may on / folde growe,	that X P	N V
CL	1044	As orenge and other fryt / and / apple-garnade,	C	N N
CL	1045	Also red and so ripe / and / rychely hwed	C	Z E
CL	1046	As any dom myȝt deuice / of / dayntyez oute;	P	N Z
CL	1047	Bot quen hit is brused other broken, / other / byten in twynne,	H	E P N
CL	1048	No worldez goud hit wythinne, / bot / wyndowande askes.	C	G N
CL	1049	Alle thyse ar teches and tokenes / to / trow vpon ȝet;	to	V Z Z
CL	1050	And wittnesse of that wykked werk, / and the / wrake after	C D	N P
CL	1051	That oure Fader forthrede / for / fylthe of those ledes.	P	N P D N
CL	1052	Thenne vch wyȝe may wel wyt / that He he / wlonk louies;	that H D	N(A) V
CL	1053	And if He louyes clene layk / that is oure / Lorde ryche,	that be D	N A
CL	1054	And to be couthe in His courte / thou / coueytes thenne,	H	V Z
CL	1055	To se that Semly in sete / and His / swete face,	C D	A N
CL	1056	Clerrer counseyl / con I non, bot that thou / clene worthe.	X H not C that H	A V
CL	1057	For Clopyngnel in the compas / of his / clene Rose,	P D	A N
CL	1058	Ther he expouned a speche / to hym that / spede wolde	P H that	V X
CL	1059	Of a lady to be loued: / 'Loke to hir sone	/	V P D N
CL	1060	Of wich beryng that ho be, / and wych ho / best louyes,	C Q H	Z V

CL	1061	And be ryȝt such in vch a borȝe / of / body and of dedes,	P	N C P N
CL	1062	And folȝ the fet of that fere / that thou / fre haldes;	that H	A V
CL	1063	And if thou wyrkkes on this wyse, / thaȝ ho / wyk were,	C H	A be
CL	1064	Hir schal lyke that layk / that / lyknes hir tylle.'	that	V H P
CL	1065	If thou wyl dele drwrye / wyth / Dryȝtyn thenne,	P	N Z
CL	1066	And lelly louy thy Lorde / and His / leef worthe,	C D	N(A) V
CL	1067	Thenne confourme the to Kryst, / and the / clene make,	C H	A V
CL	1068	That euer is polyced als playn / as the / perle seluen.	P D	N self
CL	1069	For, loke, fro fyrst that He lyȝt / withinne the / lel mayden,	P D	A N
CL	1070	By how comly a kest / He watz / clos there,	H be	A Z
CL	1071	When venkkyst watz no vergynyté, / ne / vyolence maked,	D	N V
CL	1072	Bot much clener watz hir corse, / God / kynned therinne.	N	E Z
CL	1073	And efte when He borne / watz in / Bethelen the ryche,	be P	N D N(A)
CL	1074	In wych puryté thay departed; / thaȝ thay / pouer were,	C H	A be
CL	1075	Watz neuer so blysful a bour / as watz a / bos thenne,	C be D	N Z
CL	1076	Ne no schroude hous no schene / as a / schepon thare,	P D	N Z
CL	1077	Ne non so glad vnder God / as ho that / grone schulde.	C H that	V X
CL	1078	For ther watz seknesse al sounde / that / sarrest is halden,	that	N be E
CL	1079	And ther watz rose reflayr / where / rote hatz ben euer,	Q	N have E Z
CL	1080	And ther watz solace and songe / wher / sorȝ hatz ay cryed;	Q	N have Z E
CL	1081	For aungelles with instrumentes / of / organes and pypes,	P	N C N
CL	1082	And rial ryngande rotes / and the / reken fythel,	C D	A N
CL	1083	And alle hende that honestly / moȝt an / hert glade,	X D	N V
CL	1084	Aboutte my lady watz lent / quen ho / delyuer were.	C H	A be
CL	1085	Thenne watz her blythe Barne / burnyst so clene	/	E Z A
CL	1086	That bothe the ox and the asse / Hym / hered at ones;	H	V Z
CL	1087	Thay knewe Hym by His clannes / for / Kyng of nature,	P	N P N
CL	1088	For non so clene of such a clos / com neuer er thenne.	/	V Z Z Z
CL	1089	And ȝif clanly He thenne com, / ful / cortays therafter,	Z	A Z
CL	1090	That alle that longed to luther / ful / lodly He hated,	Z	Z H V
CL	1091	By nobleye of His norture / He / nolde neuer towche	H	X Z V
CL	1092	Oȝt that watz vngoderly / other / ordure watz inne.	D	N be Z
CL	1093	ȝet comen lodly to that Lede, / as / lazares monye,	P	N A
CL	1094	Summe lepre, summe lome, / and / lomerande blynde,	C	G A
CL	1095	Poysened, and parlatyk, / and / pyned in fyres,	C	E P N
CL	1096	Drye folk and ydropike, / and / dede at the laste,	C	A Z
CL	1097	Alle called on that Cortayse / and / claymed His grace.	C	V D N
CL	1098	He heled hem wyth hynde speche, / of that thay / ask after,	P that H	V Z
CL	1099	For whatso hit towched also tyd / tourned to hele,	/	V P N
CL	1100	Wel clanner then any crafte / cowthe devyse.	/	X V
CL	1101	So hende watz His hondelyng / vche / ordure hit schoniend	D	N H V
CL	1102	And the gropyng so goud / of / God and Man bothe,	P	N C N Z
CL	1103	That for fetys of His fyngeres / fonded He neuer	/	V H Z
CL	1104	Nauther to cout ne to kerue / wyth / knyf ne wyth egge;	P	N not P N
CL	1105	Forthy brek He the bred / blades wythouten,	/	N P
CL	1106	For hit ferde freloker in fete / in His / fayre honde,	P D	A N
CL	1107	Displayed more pryuyly / when He hit / part schulde,	C H H	V X
CL	1108	Thenne alle the toles of Tolowse / moȝt / tyȝt hit to kerue.	X	V H to V
CL	1109	Thus is He kyryous and clene / that thou His / cort askes:	that H D	N V
CL	1110	Hov schulde thou com to His kyth / bot if thou / clene were?	C C H	A be
CL	1111	Nov ar we sore and synful / and / sovly vchone;	C	A H
CL	1112	How schulde we se, then may we say, / that / Syre vpon throne?	D	N P N
CL	1113	ȝis, that Mayster is mercyable, / thaȝ thou be / man fenny,	C H be	N A
CL	1114	And al tomarred in myre / whyle thou on / molde lyuyes;	C H P	N V
CL	1115	Thou may schyne thurȝ schryfte, / thaȝ thou haf / schome serued,	C H have	N E
CL	1116	And pure the with penaunce / tyl thou a / perle worthe.	C H D	N V
CL	1117	Perle praysed is prys / ther / perré is schewed,	Q	N be E
CL	1118	Thaȝ hyt not derrest be demed / to / dele for penies.	to	V P N
CL	1119	Quat may the cause be called / bot for hir / clene hwes,	P P D	A N
CL	1120	That wynnes worschyp / abof alle / whyte stones?	P D	A N
CL	1121	For ho schynes so schyr / that is of / schap rounde,	that be P	N A
CL	1122	Wythouten faut other fylthe / ȝif ho / fyn were,	C H	A be
CL	1123	And wax euer in the worlde / in / weryng so olde,	P	G Z A
CL	1124	ȝet the perle payres / not whyle ho in / pryse lasttes;	not C H P	N V
CL	1125	And if hit cheue the chaunce / vncheryst ho worthe,	/	A H V
CL	1126	That ho blyndes of ble / in / bour ther ho lygges,	P	N Q H V
CL	1127	Nobot wasch hir wyth wourchyp / in / wyn as ho askes,	P	N C H V
CL	1128	Ho by kynde schal becom / clerer then are.	/	A Z Z
CL	1129	So if folk be defowled / by / vnfre chaunce,	P	A N
CL	1130	That he be sulped in sawle, / seche to schryfte,	/	V P N
CL	1131	And he may polyce hym at the prest, / by / penaunce taken,	P	N E

CL 1132	Wel bryȝter then the beryl / other / browden perles.	D	E N
CL 1133	Dot wai the wel, if thou be waschen / wyth / water of schryfte,	P	N P N
CL 1134	And polysed als playn / as / parchmen schauen,	P	N E
CL 1135	Sulp no more thenne in synne / thy / saule therafter,	D	N Z
CL 1136	For thenne thou Dryȝtyn dyspleses / with / dedes ful sore,	P	N Z A
CL 1137	And entyses Hym to tene / more / traythly then euer,	D	Z Z Z
CL 1138	And wel hatter to hate / then / hade thou not waschen.	C	have H not E
CL 1139	For when a sawele is saȝtled / and / sakred to Dryȝtyn,	C	E P N
CL 1140	He holly haldes hit His / and / haue hit He wolde;	C	V H H X
CL 1141	Thenne efte lastes hit likkes, / He / loses hit ille,	H	V H Z
CL 1142	As hit were rafte wyth vnryȝt / and / robbed wyth thewes.	C	E P N
CL 1143	War the thenne for the wrake: / His / wrath is achaufed	D	N be E
CL 1144	For that that ones watz His / schulde / efte be vnclene,	X	Z be A
CL 1145	Thaȝ hit be bot a bassyn, / a / bolle other a scole,	D	N C D N
CL 1146	A dysche other a dobler, / that / Dryȝtyn onez serued.	that	N Z V
CL 1147	To defowle hit euer vpon folde / fast He forbedes,	/	Z H V
CL 1148	So is He scoymus of scathe / that / scylful is euer.	that	A be Z
CL 1149	And that watz bared in Babyloyn / in / Baltazar tyme,	P	N N
CL 1150	Hov harde vnhap ther hym hent / and / hastyly sone,	C	Z Z
CL 1151	For he the vesselles avyled / that / vayled in the temple	that	V P D N
CL 1152	In seruyse of the Souerayn / sumtyme byfore.	/	Z Z
CL 1153	Ȝif ȝe wolde tyȝt me a tom / telle hit I wolde,	/	V H H X
CL 1154	Hov charged more watz his chaunce / that hem / cherych nolde	that H	V X
CL 1155	Then his fader forloyne / that / feched hem wyth strenthe,	that	V H P N
CL 1156	And robbed the relygioun / of / relykes alle.	P	N Z
CL 1157	Danyel in his dialokez / devysed sumtyme,	/	V Z
CL 1158	As ȝet is proued expresse / in his / profecies,	P D	N
CL 1159	Hov the gentryse of Juise / and / Jherusalem the ryche	C	N D N(A)
CL 1160	Watz disstryed wyth distres, / and / drawen to the erthe.	C	E P D N
CL 1161	For that folke in her fayth / watz / founden vntrwe,	be	E A
CL 1162	That haden hyȝt the hyȝe God / to / halde of Hym euer;	to	V P H Z
CL 1163	And He hem halȝed for His / and / help at her nede	C	V P D N
CL 1164	In mukel meschefes mony, / that / meruayl is to here.	that	A be to V
CL 1165	And thay forloyne her fayth / and / folȝed other goddes,	C	V D N
CL 1166	And that wakned His wrath / and / wrast hit so hyȝe	C	V H Z Z
CL 1167	That He fylsened the faythful / in the / falce lawe	P D	A N
CL 1168	To forfare the falce / in the / faythe trwe.	P D	N A
CL 1169	Hit watz sen in that sythe / that / Zedechyas rengned	that	N V
CL 1170	In Juda, that justised / the / Juyne kynges.	D	N N
CL 1171	He sete on Salamones solie / on / solemne wyse,	P	A N
CL 1172	Bot of leauté he watz lat / to his / Lorde hende:	P D	N A
CL 1173	He vsed abominaciones / of / idolatrye,	P	N
CL 1174	And lette lyȝt bi the lawe / that he watz / lege tylle.	that H be	E P
CL 1175	Forthi oure Fader vpon folde / a / foman hym wakned:	D	N H V
CL 1176	Nabigodenozar / nuyed hym swythe.	/	V H Z
CL 1177	He pursued into Palastyn / with / proude men mony,	P	A N A
CL 1178	And ther he wast wyth werre / the / wones of thorpes;	D	N P N
CL 1179	He herȝed vp alle Israel / and / hent of the beste,	C	V P D N(A)
CL 1180	And the gentylest of Judée / in / Jerusalem biseged,	P	N V
CL 1181	Vmbewalt alle the walles / wyth / wyȝes ful stronge,	P	N Z A
CL 1182	At vche a dor a doȝty duk, / and / dutte hem wythinne;	C	V H P
CL 1183	For the borȝ watz so bygge / batayled alofte,	/	E Z
CL 1184	And stoffed wythinne with stout men / to / stalle hem theroute.	to	V H Z
CL 1185	Thenne watz the sege sette / the / ceté aboute,	D	N P
CL 1186	Skete skarmoch skelt, / much / skathe lached;	D	N V
CL 1187	At vch brugge a berfray / on / basteles wyse	P	N N
CL 1188	That seuen sythe vch a day / asayled the ȝates;	/	V D N
CL 1189	Trwe tulkkes in toures / teueled wythinne,	/	V Z
CL 1190	In bigge brutage of borde / bulde on the walles;	/	E P D N
CL 1191	Thay feȝt and thay fende / of, and / fylter togeder	Z C	V Z
CL 1192	Til two ȝer ouertorned, / ȝet / tok thay hit neuer.	C	V H H Z
CL 1193	At the laste, vpon longe, / tho / ledes wythinne,	D	N P
CL 1194	Faste fayled hem the fode, / enfamined monie;	/	V H
CL 1195	The hote hunger / wythinne / hert hem wel sarre	P	V H Z Z
CL 1196	Then any dunt of that douthe / that / dowelled theroute.	that	V Z
CL 1197	Thenne wern the rowtes redles / in tho / ryche wones;	P D	A N
CL 1198	Fro that mete watz myst, / megre thay wexen,	/	A H V
CL 1199	And thay stoken so strayt / that thay ne / stray myȝt	that H not	V X
CL 1200	A fote fro that forselet / to / forray no goudes.	to	V D N
CL 1201	Thenne the kyng of the kyth / a / counsayl hym takes	D	N H V
CL 1202	Wyth the best of his burnes, / a / blench for to make;	D	N for to V

CL	1203	Thay stel out on a stylle ny3t / er any / steuen rysed,	C D	N V
CL	1204	And harde hurles thur3 the oste / er / enmies hit wyste.	C	N H V
CL	1205	Bot er thay atwappe ne mo3t / the / wach wythoute	D	N P
CL	1206	Hi3e skelt watz the askry / the / skewes anvnder.	D	N P
CL	1207	Loude alarom vpon launde / lulted watz thenne;	/	E be Z
CL	1208	Ryche, ruthed of her rest, / ran to here wedes,	/	V P D N
CL	1209	Hard hattes thay hent / and on / hors lepes;	C P	N V
CL	1210	Cler claryoun crak / cryed on lofte.	/	V Z
CL	1211	By that watz alle on a hepe / hurlande swythee,	/	G Z
CL	1212	Fol3ande that other flote, / and / fonde hem bilyue,	C	V H Z
CL	1213	Ouertok hem as tyd, / tult hem of sadeles,	/	V H P N
CL	1214	Tyl vche prynce hade his per / put to the grounde.	/	E P D N
CL	1215	And ther watz the kyng ka3t / wyth / Caldé pryncez,	P	N N
CL	1216	And alle hise gentyle forjusted / on / Jerico playnes,	P	N N
CL	1217	And presented wern as presoneres / to the / prynce rychest,	P D	N A
CL	1218	Nabigodenozar, / noble in his chayer;	/	A P D N
CL	1219	And he the faynest freke / that he his / fo hade,	that H D	N V
CL	1220	And speke spitously / hem to, and / spylt therafter.	H P C	V Z
CL	1221	The kynges sunnes in his sy3t / he / slow euervch one,	H	V D H
CL	1222	And holkked out his auen y3en / heterly bothe,	/	Z Z
CL	1223	And bede the burne to be bro3t / to / Babyloyn the ryche,	P	N D N(A)
CL	1224	And there in dongoun be don / to / dre3e ther his wyrdes.	to	V Z D N
CL	1225	Now se, so the Souerayn / set hatz His wrake:	/	E have D N
CL	1226	Nas hit not for Nabugo / ne his / noblé nauther	D D	N(A) Z
CL	1227	That other depryued watz of pryde / with / paynes stronge,	P	N A
CL	1228	Bot for his beryng so badde / agayn his / blythe Lorde;	Z D	A N
CL	1229	For hade the Fader ben his frende, / that hym / bifore keped,	that H	P V
CL	1230	Ne neuer trespast / to Him in / teche of mysseleue,	P H P	N P N
CL	1231	To colde wer alle Caldé / and / kythes of Ynde,	C	N P N
CL	1232	3et take Torkye / hem wyth-her / tene hade ben little.	H P D	N have E A
CL	1233	3et nolde neuer Nabugo / this ilke / note leue	D D	N V
CL	1234	Er he hade tyrued this town / and / torne hit to grounde.	C	E H P N
CL	1235	He joyned vnto Jerusalem / a / gentyle duc thenne-	D	A N Z
CL	1236	His name watz Nabuzardan-/ to / noye the Jues;	to	V D N
CL	1237	He watz mayster of his men / and / my3ty himseluen,	C	A H self
CL	1238	The chef of his cheualrye / his / chekkes to make;	D	N to V
CL	1239	He brek the bareres as bylyue, / and the / bur3 after,	C D	N P
CL	1240	And enteres in ful ernestly, / in / yre of his hert.	P	N P D N
CL	1241	What! the maysterry watz mene: / men wern away,	D	N be Z
CL	1242	The best bo3ed wyth the burne / that the / bor3 3emed,	that D	N V
CL	1243	And tho that byden wer so biten / with the / bale hunger	P D	N N
CL	1244	That on wyf hade ben worthe / the / welgest fourre.	D	A N
CL	1245	Nabizardan no3t / forthy / nolde not spare,	C	X not V
CL	1246	Bot bede al to the bronde / vnder / bare egge;	P	A N
CL	1247	Thay slowen of swettest / semlych burdes,	/	A N
CL	1248	Bathed barnes in blod / and her / brayn spylled;	C D	N V
CL	1249	Prestes and prelates / thay / presed to dethe,	H	V P N
CL	1250	Wyues and wenches / her / wombes tocoruen,	D	N V
CL	1251	That her boweles outborst / aboute the diches,	/	P D N
CL	1252	And al watz carfully kylde / that thay / cach my3t.	that H	V X
CL	1253	And alle that swypped, vnswol3ed / of the / sworde kene,	P D	N A
CL	1254	Thay wer cagged and ka3t / on / capeles al bare,	P	N Z A
CL	1255	Festned fettres to her fete / vnder / fole wombes,	P	N N
CL	1256	And brothely bro3t to Babyloyn / ther / bale to suffer,	Q	N to V
CL	1257	To sytte in seruage and syte, / that / sumtyme wer gentyle.	that	Z be A
CL	1258	Now ar chaunged to chorles / and / charged wyth werkkes,	C	E P N
CL	1259	Bothe to cayre at the kart / and the / kuy mylke,	C D	N N
CL	1260	That sumtyme sete in her sale / syres and burdes.	/	N C N
CL	1261	And 3et Nabuzardan nyl / newer stynt	/	Z V
CL	1262	Er he to the temppe tee / wyth his / tulkkes alle;	P D	N Z
CL	1263	Betes on the barers, / brestes vp the 3ates,	/	V Z D N
CL	1264	Slouen alle at a slyp / that / serued therinne,	that	V Z
CL	1265	Pulden prestes bi the polle / and / plat of her hedes,	C	V Z D N
CL	1266	Di3ten dekenes to dethe, / dungen doun clerkkes,	/	V Z N
CL	1267	And alle the maydenes of the munster / ma3tyly hokyllen	/	Z V
CL	1268	Wyth the swayf of the sworde / that / swol3ed hem alle.	that	V H Z
CL	1269	Thenne ran thay to the relykes / as / robbors wylde,	C	N X
CL	1270	And pyled alle the apparement / that / pented to the kyrke-	that	V P D N
CL	1271	The pure pyleres of bras / pourtrayd in golde,	/	E P N
CL	1272	And the chef chaundeler / charged with the ly3t,	/	E P D
CL	1273	That ber the lamp vpon lofte / that / lemed euermore	that	V Z

CL 1274	Bifore the sancta sanctorum / ther / selcouth watz ofte.	Q	N be Z
CL 1275	Thay caȝt away that condelstik, / and the / crowne als	C D	N Z
CL 1276	That the auter hade vpon, / of / athel golde ryche,	P	A N A
CL 1277	The gredirne and the goblotes / garnyst of syluer,	/	E P N
CL 1278	The bases of the bryȝt postes / and / bassynes so schyre,	C	N Z A
CL 1279	Dere disches of golde / and / dubleres fayre,	C	N A
CL 1280	The vyoles and the vesselment / of / vertuous stones.	P	A N
CL 1281	Now hatz Nabuzardan nomen / alle thyse / noble thynges,	D D	A N
CL 1282	And pyled that precious place / and / pakked those godes;	C	V D N
CL 1283	The golde of the gazafylace / to swythe / gret noumbre,	P D	A N
CL 1284	Wyth alle the vrnmentes of that hous, / he / hamppred togeder;	H	V Z
CL 1285	Alle he spoyled spitously / in a / sped whyle	P D	N N
CL 1286	That Salomon so mony a sadde ȝer / soȝt to make.	/	V to V
CL 1287	Wyth alle the coyntyse that he cowthe / clene to wyrke,	/	Z to V
CL 1288	Deuised he the vesselment, / the / vestures clene;	D	N A
CL 1289	Wyth slyȝt of his ciences, / his / Souerayn to loue,	D	N to V
CL 1290	The hous and the anournementes / he / hyȝtled togedere.	H	V Z
CL 1291	Now hatz Nabuzardan / nummen hit al samen,	/	V H Z Z
CL 1292	And sythen bet doun the burȝ / and / brend hit in askes.	C	V H P N
CL 1293	Thenne wyth legiounes of ledes / ouer / londes he rydes,	P	N H V
CL 1294	Herȝez of Israel / the / hyrnez aboute;	D	N P
CL 1295	Wyth charged chariotes / the / cheftayn he fyndez,	D	N H V
CL 1296	Bikennes the catel to the kyng, / that he / caȝt hade;	that H	E have
CL 1297	Presented him the prisoneres / in / pray that thay token-	P	N that H V
CL 1298	Moni a worthly wyȝe / whil her / worlde laste,	C D	N V
CL 1299	Moni semly syre soun, / and / swythe rych maydenes,	C	A A N
CL 1300	The pruddest of the prouince, / and / prophetes childer,	C	N N
CL 1301	As Ananie, and Azarie, / and / als Mizael,	C	Z N
CL 1302	And dere Daniel / also, that watz / deuine noble,	Z that be	N A
CL 1303	With moni a modey moder-chylde / mo then innoghe.	/	A P Z
CL 1304	And Nabugodenozar / makes much joye,	/	V A N
CL 1305	Nov he the kyng hatz conquest / and the / kyth wunnen,	C D	N E
CL 1306	And dreped alle the doȝtyest / and / derrest in armes,	C	N(A) P N
CL 1307	And the lederes of her lawe / layd to the grounde,	/	V P D N
CL 1308	And the pryce of the profecie / prisoners maked.	/	N V
CL 1309	Bot the joy of the juelrye / so / gentyle and ryche,	Z	A C A
CL 1310	When hit watz schewed hym so schene, / scharp watz his wonder;	/	A be D N
CL 1311	Of such vessel auayed, / that / vayled so huge,	that	V Z Z
CL 1312	Neuer ȝet nas / Nabugodenozar er thenne.	/	N Z Z
CL 1313	He sesed hem with solemneté, / the / Souerayn he praysed	D	N H V
CL 1314	That watz athel ouer alle, / Israel Dryȝtyn;	/	N N
CL 1315	Such god, such gounes, / such / gay vesselles,	D	A N
CL 1316	Comen neuer out of kyth / to / Caldée reames.	P	N N
CL 1317	He trussed hem in his tresorye / in a / tryed place,	P D	E N
CL 1318	Rekenly, wyth reuerens, / as he / ryȝt hade;	C H	N V
CL 1319	And ther he wroȝt as the wyse, / as ȝe may / wyt hereafter,	C H X	V Z
CL 1320	For hade he let of hem lyȝt, / hym moȝt haf / lumpen worse.	H X have	E A
CL 1321	That ryche in gret rialté / rengned his lyue,	/	V D N
CL 1322	As conquerour of vche a cost / he / cayser watz hatte,	H	N be E
CL 1323	Emperour of alle the erthe / and / also the saudan,	C	Z D N
CL 1324	And als the god of the grounde / watz / grauen his name.	be	E D N
CL 1325	And al thurȝ dome of Daniel, / fro he / deuised hade	P H	E have
CL 1326	That alle goudes com of God, / and / gef hit hym bi samples,	C	V H H P N
CL 1327	That he ful clanly bicnv / his / carp bi the laste,	D	N Z
CL 1328	And ofte hit mekned his mynde, / his / maysterful werkkes.	D	A N
CL 1329	Bot al drawes to dyȝe / with / doel vpon ende.	P	N Z
CL 1330	Bi a hathel neuer so hyȝe, / he / heldes to grounde.	H	V P N
CL 1331	And so Nabugodenozar, / as he / nedes moste,	C H	V Z
CL 1332	For alle his empire so hiȝe / in / erthe is he grauen.	P	N be H E
CL 1333	Bot thenn the bolde Baltazar, / that watz his / barn aldest,	that be D	N A
CL 1334	He watz stalled in his stud, / and / stabled the rengne	C	V D N
CL 1335	In the burȝ of Babiloyne, / the / biggest he trawed,	D	N(A) H V
CL 1336	That nauther in heuen ne on erthe / hade no pere;	/	V D N
CL 1337	For he bigan in alle the glori / that hym the / gome lafte,	that H D	N V
CL 1338	Nabugodenozar, / that watz his / noble fader.	that be D	A N
CL 1339	So kene a kyng in Caldée / com neuer er thenne;	/	V Z Z Z
CL 1340	Bot honoured he not Hym / that in / heuen wonies.	that P	N V
CL 1341	Bot fals fantummes of fendes, / formed with handes,	/	E P N
CL 1342	Wyth tool out of harde tre, / and / telded on lofte,	C	E Z
CL 1343	And of stokkes and stones, / he / stoute goddes callz,	H	A N V
CL 1344	When thay ar gilde al with golde / and / gered wyth syluer;	C	E P N

CL	1345	And there he kneles and callez / and / clepes after help.	C	V P N
CL	1346	And thay reden him ry3t / rewarde he hem hetes,	/	N H H V
CL	1347	And if thay gruchen him his grace, / to / gremen his hert,	to	V D N
CL	1348	He cleches to a gret klubbe / and / knokkes hem to peces.	C	V H P N
CL	1349	Thus in pryde and olipraunce / his / empyre he haldes,	D	N H V
CL	1350	In lust and in lecherye / and / lothelych werkkes,	C	A N
CL	1351	And hade a wyf for to welde, / a / worthelych quene,	D	A N
CL	1352	And mony a lemman, neuer the later, / that / ladis wer called.	that	N be E
CL	1353	In the clernes of his concubines / and / curious wedez,	C	A N
CL	1354	In notyng of nwe metes / and of / nice gettes,	C P	A N
CL	1355	Al watz the mynde of that man / on / misschapen thinges,	P	A N
CL	1356	Til the Lorde of the lyfte / liste hit abate.	/	V H V
CL	1357	Thenne this bolde Baltazar / bithenkkes hym ones	/	V H Z
CL	1358	To vouche on avayment / of his / vayneglorie;	P D	N
CL	1359	Hit is not innoghe to the nice / al / no3ty think vse	D	A N V
CL	1360	Bot if alle the worlde wyt / his / wykked dedes.	D	A N
CL	1361	Baltazar thur3 Babiloyn / his / banne gart crye,	D	N V N
CL	1362	And thur3 the cuntré of Caldée / his / callyng con spryng,	D	N X V
CL	1363	That alle the grete vpon grounde / schulde / geder hem samen	X	V H Z
CL	1364	And assemble at a set day / at the / saudans fest.	P D	N N
CL	1365	Such a mangerie to make / the / man watz auised,	D	N be E
CL	1366	That vche a kythyn kyng / schuld / com thider,	X	V Z
CL	1367	Vche duk wyth his duthe, / and other / dere lordes,	C D	A N
CL	1368	Schulde com to his court / to / kythe hym for lege,	to	V H P N(A)
CL	1369	And to reche hym reuerens, / and his / reuel herkken,	C D	N V
CL	1370	To loke on his lemanes / and / ladis hem calle.	C	N H V
CL	1371	To rose hym in his rialty / rych men so3tten,	/	A N V
CL	1372	And mony a baroun ful bolde, / to / Babyloyn the noble.	P	N D N(A)
CL	1373	Ther bowed toward Babiloyn / burnes so mony,	/	N Z A
CL	1374	Kynges, cayseres ful kene, / to the / court wonnen,	P D	N V
CL	1375	Mony ludisch lordes / that / ladies bro3ten,	that	N V
CL	1376	That to neuen the noumbre / to much / nye were.	P D	A be
CL	1377	For the bour3 watz so brod / and so / bigge alce,	C Z	A Z
CL	1378	Stalled in the fayrest stud / the / sterrez anvnder,	D	N P
CL	1379	Prudly on a plat playn, / plek alther-fayrest,	/	N A
CL	1380	Vmbesweyed on vch a syde / with / seuen grete wateres,	P	A A N
CL	1381	With a wonder wro3t walle / wruxeled ful hi3e,	/	E Z Z
CL	1382	With koynt carneles / aboue, / coruen ful clene,	Z	E Z Z
CL	1383	Troched toures / bitwene, / twenty spere lenthe,	/	A N N
CL	1384	And thiker throwen vmbethour / with / ouerthwert palle.	P	E N
CL	1385	The place that plyed / the / pursaunt wythinne	D	N P
CL	1386	Watz longe and ful large / and euer / ilych sware,	C Z	Z A
CL	1387	And vch a syde vpon soyle / helde / seuen myle,	V	A N
CL	1388	And the saudans sete / sette in the myddes.	/	E P D N
CL	1389	That watz a palayce of pryde / passande alle other,	/	G D H
CL	1390	Bothe of werk and of wunder, / and / walled al aboute;	C	E Z Z
CL	1391	He3e houses / withinne, the / halle to hit med,	P D	N P H A
CL	1392	So brod bilde in a bay / that / blonkkes my3t renne.	that	N X V
CL	1393	When the terme of the feste / watz / towched of the feste,	be	E P D N
CL	1394	Dere dro3en therto / and vpon / des metten,	C P	N V
CL	1395	And Baltazar vpon bench / was / busked to sete,	be	E P N
CL	1396	Stepe stayred stones / of his / stoute throne.	P D	A N
CL	1397	Thenne watz alle the halle flor / hiled with kny3tes,	/	E P N
CL	1398	And barounes at the sidebordes / bounet aywhere,	/	E Z
CL	1399	For non watz dressed vpon dece / bot the / dere seluen,	P D	A self
CL	1400	And his clere concubynes / in / clothes ful bry3t.	P	N Z A
CL	1401	When alle segges were ther set / then / seruyse bygynnes,	Z	N V
CL	1402	Sturne trumpen strake / steuen in halle,	/	N P N
CL	1403	Aywhere by the wowes / wrasten krakkes,	/	V N
CL	1404	And brode baneres / therbi / blusnande of gold,	Z	G P N
CL	1405	Burnes berande the bredes / vpon / brode skeles	P	A N
CL	1406	That were of sylueren sy3t, / and / served therwyth,	C	E Z
CL	1407	Lyfte logges / therouer and on / lofte coruen,	Z C Z	Z E
CL	1408	Pared out of paper / and / poynted of golde,	C	E P N
CL	1409	Brothe baboynes / abof, / besttes anvnder,	Z	N P
CL	1410	Foles in foler / flakerande bitwene,	/	G Z
CL	1411	And al in asure and ynde / enaumayld ryche;	/	E Z
CL	1412	And al on blonkken bak / bere hit on honde.	/	V H P N
CL	1413	And ay the nakeryn noyse, / notes of pipes,	/	N P N
CL	1414	Tymbres and tabornes, / tulket among,	/	V Z
CL	1415	Symbales and sonetez / sware the noyse,	/	V D N

CL	1416	And bougounz busch / batered so thikke.	/	V Z Z
CL	1417	3o watz serued fele sythe / the / sale alle aboute,	D	N Z P
CL	1418	With solace at the sere course, / bifore the / self lorde,	P D	self N
CL	1419	Ther the lede and alle his loue / lenged at the table;	/	V P D N
CL	1420	So faste thay we3ed to him wyne / hit / warmed his hert	H	V D N
CL	1421	And breythed vppe into his brayn / and / blemyst his mynde,	C	V D N
CL	1422	And al waykned his wyt, / and / welne3e he foles;	C	Z H V
CL	1423	For he waytez on wyde, / his / wenches he byholdes,	D	N H V
CL	1424	And his bolde baronage / aboute bi the wo3es.	/	Z P D N
CL	1425	Thenne a dotage ful depe / drof to his hert,	/	V P D N
CL	1426	And a caytif counsayl / he / ca3t bi hymseluen;	H	V P H self
CL	1427	Maynly his marschal / the / mayster vpon calles,	D	N P V
CL	1428	And comaundes hym cofly / coferes to lauce,	/	N to V
CL	1429	And fech forth the vessel / that his / fader bro3t,	that D	N V
CL	1430	Nabugodenozar, / noble in his strenthe,	/	A P D N
CL	1431	Conquered with his kny3tes / and of / kyrk rafte	C P	N V
CL	1432	In Judé, in Jerusalem, / in / gentyle wyse:	P	A N
CL	1433	'Bryng hem now to my borde, / of / beuerage hem fylles,	P	N H V
CL	1434	Let thise ladyes of hem lape-/ I / luf hem in hert;	H	V H P N
CL	1435	That schal I cortaysly kythe, / and thay schin / knawe sone,	C H X	V Z
CL	1436	Ther is no bounté in burne / lyk / Baltazar thewes.'	P	N N
CL	1437	Thenne towched to the tresour / this / tale watz sone,	D	N be Z
CL	1438	And he with keyes vncloses / kystes ful mony;	/	N Z A
CL	1439	Mony burthen ful bry3t / watz / bro3t into halle,	be	E P N
CL	1440	And couered mony a cupborde / with / clothes ful quite.	P	N Z A
CL	1441	The jueles out of Jerusalem / with / gemmes ful bry3t	P	N Z A
CL	1442	Bi the syde of the sale / were / semely arayed;	be	Z E
CL	1443	The athel auter of brasse / watz / hade into place,	be	E P N
CL	1444	The gay coroun of golde / gered on lofte.	/	E Z
CL	1445	That hade ben blessed bifore / wyth / bischopes hondes	P	N N
CL	1446	And wyth besten blod / busily anoynted,	/	Z E
CL	1447	In the solempne sacrefyce / that / goud sauor hade	that	A N V
CL	1448	Bifore the Lorde of the lyfte / in / louyng Hymseluen,	P	G H self
CL	1449	Now is sette, for to serue / Satanas the blake,	/	N D N(A)
CL	1450	Bifore the bolde Baltazar / wyth / bost and wyth pryde;	P	N C P N
CL	1451	Houen vpon this auter / watz / athel vessel	be	A N
CL	1452	That wyth so curious a crafte / coruen watz wyly.	/	E be Z
CL	1453	Salamon sete him seuen 3ere / and a / sythe more,	C D	N A
CL	1454	With alle the syence that hym sende / the / souerayn Lorde,	D	A N
CL	1455	For to compas and kest / to haf hem / clene wro3t.	to have H	Z E
CL	1456	For ther wer bassynes ful bry3t / of / brende golde clere,	P	E N A
CL	1457	Enaumaylde with azer, / and / eweres of sute,	C	N P N
CL	1458	Couered cowpes foul clene, / as / casteles arayed,	P	N E
CL	1459	Enbaned vnder batelment / with / bantelles quoynt,	P	N E
CL	1460	And fyled out of fygures / of / ferlylé schappes.	P	A N
CL	1461	The coperounes of the couacles / that on the / cuppe reres	that P D	N V
CL	1462	Wer fetysely formed / out in / fylyoles longe;	Z P	N A
CL	1463	Pinacles py3t ther apert / that / profert bitwene,	that	V Z
CL	1464	And al bolled abof / with / braunches and leues,	P	N C N
CL	1465	Pyes and papejayes / purtrayed withinne,	/	E Z
CL	1466	As thay prudly hade piked / of / pomgarnades;	P	N
CL	1467	For alle the blomes of the bo3es / wer / blyknande perles,	be	G N
CL	1468	And alle the fruyt in tho formes / of / flaumbeande gemmes,	P	G N
CL	1469	Ande safyres, and sardiners, / and / semely topace,	C	A N
CL	1470	Alabaundarynes, and amaraunz, / and / amaffised stones,	C	N N
CL	1471	Casydoynes, and crysolytes, / and / clere rubies,	C	A N
CL	1472	Penitotes, and pynkardines, / ay / perles bitwene;	Z	N P
CL	1473	So trayled and tryfled / atrauerce wer alle,	/	Z be H
CL	1474	Bi vche bekyr ande bolle, / the / brurdes al vmbe;	D	N Z P
CL	1475	The gobelotes of golde / grauen aboute,	/	E Z
CL	1476	And fyoles fretted with flores / and / fleez of golde;	C	N P N
CL	1477	Vpon that avter watz al / aliche dresset.	/	Z E
CL	1478	The candelstik bi a cost / watz / cayred thider sone,	be	E Z Z
CL	1479	Vpon the pyleres apyked, / that / praysed hit mony,	that	V H H
CL	1480	Vpon hit basez of brasse / that / ber vp the werkes,	that	V Z D N
CL	1481	The bo3es bry3t therabof, / brayden of golde,	Z	E P N
CL	1482	Braunches bredande / theron, and / bryddes ther seten	Z C	N Z V
CL	1483	Of mony koynt kyndes, / of fele / kyn hues,	P D	N N
CL	1484	As thay with wynge vpon wynde / hade / waged her fytheres.	have	E D N
CL	1485	Inmong the leues of the lyndes / lampes wer graythed,	/	N be E
CL	1486	And other louflych ly3t / that / lemed ful fayre,	that	V Z Z

CL	1487	As mony morteres of wax / merkked withoute	/	V Z
CL	1488	With mony a borlych best / al of / brende golde.	H P	E N
CL	1489	Hit watz not wonte in that wone / to / wast no serges,	to	V D N
CL	1490	Bot in temple of the trauthe / trwly to stonde	/	Z to V
CL	1491	Bifore the sancta sanctorum, / ther / sothefast Dryȝtyn	Q	A N
CL	1492	Expouned His speche spiritually / to / special prophetes.	P	A N
CL	1493	Leue thou wel that the Lorde / that the / lyfte ȝemes	that D	N V
CL	1494	Displesed much at that play / in that / plyt stronge,	P D	N A
CL	1495	That His jueles so gent / wyth / jaueles wer fouled,	P	N be E
CL	1496	That presyous in His presens / wer / proued sumwhyle.	be	A Z
CL	1497	Soberly in His sacrafyce / summe wer anoynted,	/	H be E
CL	1498	Thurȝ the somones of Himselfe / that / syttes so hyȝe;	that	V Z Z
CL	1499	Now a boster on benche / bibbes therof	/	V Z
CL	1500	Tyl he be dronkken as the deuel, / and / dotes ther he syttes.	C	V Q H V
CL	1501	So the Worcher of this worlde / wlates therwyth	/	V Z
CL	1502	That in the poynt of her play / He / poruayes a mynde;	H	V D N
CL	1503	Bot er harme hem He / wolde in / haste of His yre,	X P	N P D N
CL	1504	He wayned hem a warnyng / that / wonder hem thoȝt.	that	A H V
CL	1505	Nov is alle this guere geten / glotounes to serue,	/	N to V
CL	1506	Stad in a ryche stal, / and / stared ful bryȝte;	C	V Z Z
CL	1507	Baltazar in a brayd: '/ Bede vus therof!'	/	V H Z
CL	1508	Weȝe wyn in this won! / Wassayl!' he cryes.	/	I H V
CL	1509	Swyfte swaynes ful swythe / swepen thertylle,	/	V Z
CL	1510	Kyppe kowpes in honde / kyngez to serue;	/	N to V
CL	1511	In bryȝt bollez ful bayn / birlen thise other,	/	V D H
CL	1512	And vche mon for his mayster / machches alone.	/	V Z
CL	1513	Ther watz rynging, on ryȝt, / of / ryche metalles,	P	A N
CL	1514	Quen renkkes in that ryche rok / rennen hit to cache;	/	V H to V
CL	1515	Clatering of couaclez / that / kesten tho burdes	that	V D N
CL	1516	As sonet out of sauteray / songe als myry.	/	V Z Z
CL	1517	Then the dotel on dece / drank that he myȝt;	/	V that H X
CL	1518	And thenne derfly arn dressed / dukez and pryncez,	/	N C N
CL	1519	Concubines and knyȝtes, / bi / cause of that merthe;	P	N P D N
CL	1520	As vchon hade hym inhelde / he / haled of the cuppe.	H	V P D N
CL	1521	So long likked thise lordes / thise / lykores swete,	D	N A
CL	1522	And gloryed on her falce goddes, / and her / grace calles,	/	N V
CL	1523	That were of stokkes and stones, / stille euermore-	/	A Z
CL	1524	Neuer steuen hem astel, / so / stoken is hor tonge.	Z	E be D N
CL	1525	Alle the goude golden goddes / the / gaulez ȝet neuenen,	D	N Z V
CL	1526	Belfagor and Belyal, / and / Belssabub als,	C	N Z
CL	1527	Heyred hem as hyȝly / as / heuen wer thayres,	C	N be H
CL	1528	Bot Hym that alle goudes giues, / that / God thay forȝeten.	that	N H V
CL	1529	Forthy a ferly bifel / that / fele folk seȝen;	that	A N V
CL	1530	Fyrst knew hit the kyng / and alle the / cort after:	C D D	N P
CL	1531	In the palays pryncipale, / vpon the / playn wowe,	P D	A N
CL	1532	In contrary of the candelstik, / ther / clerest hit schyned,	Q	Z H V
CL	1533	Ther apered a paume, / with / poyntel in fyngres,	P	N P N
CL	1534	That watz grysly and gret, / and / grymly he wrytes;	C	Z H V
CL	1535	Non other forme bot a fust / faylande the wryste	/	G D N
CL	1536	Pared on the parget, / purtrayed lettres.	/	V N
CL	1537	When that bolde Baltazar / blusched to that neue,	/	V P D N
CL	1538	Such a dasande drede / dusched to his hert	/	V P D N
CL	1539	That al falewed his face / and / fayled the chere;	C	V D N
CL	1540	The stronge strok of the stonde / strayned his joyntes,	/	V D N
CL	1541	His cnes cachches toclose, / and / cluchches his hommes,	C	V D N
CL	1542	And he with plattyng his paumes / dispyses his leres,	/	V D N
CL	1543	And romyes as a rad ryth / that / rorez for drede,	that	V P N
CL	1544	Ay biholdand the honde / til hit / hade al grauen	C H	have Z E
CL	1545	And rasped on the roȝ woȝe / runisch sauez.	/	A N
CL	1546	When hit the scrypture hade scraped / wyth a / scrof penne,	P D	A N
CL	1547	As a coltour in clay / cerues the forȝes,	/	V D N
CL	1548	Thenne hit vanist verayly / and / voyded of syȝt,	C	V P N
CL	1549	Bot the lettres bileued / ful / large vpon plaster.	Z	A P N
CL	1550	Sone so the kynge for his care / carping myȝt wynne,	/	N X V
CL	1551	He bede his burnes boȝ / to that were / bok-lered,	P that be	N E
CL	1552	To wayte the wryt that hit wolde, / and / wyter hym to say-	C	Z H to V
CL	1553	'For al hit frayes my flesche, / the / fyngres so grymme.'	D	N Z A
CL	1554	Scoleres skelten / theratte the / skyl for to fynde,	Z D	N for to V
CL	1555	Bot ther watz neuer on so wyse / couthe on / worde rede,	X P	N V
CL	1556	Ne what ledisch lore / ne / langage nauther,	D	N Z
CL	1557	What tythyng ne tale / tokened tho draȝtes.	/	V D N

CL 1558	Thenne the bolde Baltazar / bred ner wode,	/	V Z A
CL 1559	And bede the ceté to seche / segges thurȝout	/	N Z
CL 1560	That wer wyse of wychecrafte, / and / warlaȝes other	C	N A
CL 1561	That con dele wyth demerlayk / and / deuine lettres.	C	A N
CL 1562	'Calle hem alle to my cort, / tho / Caldé clerkkes,	D	N N
CL 1563	Vnfolde hem alle this ferly / that is / bifallen here,	that be	E Z
CL 1564	And calle wyth a hiȝe cry: / "He that the / kyng wysses,	H that D	N V
CL 1565	In expounyng of speche / that / spredes in thise lettres,	that	V P D N
CL 1566	And makes the mater to malt / my / mynde wythinne,	D	N P
CL 1567	That I may wyterly wyt / what that / wryt menes,	Q that	N V
CL 1568	He schal be gered ful gaye / in / gounes of porpre,	P	N P N
CL 1569	And a coler of cler golde / clos vmbe his throte;	/	A P D N
CL 1570	He schal be prymate and prynce / of / pure clergye,	P	A N
CL 1571	And of my threuenest lordez / the / thrydde he schal,	D	N H X
CL 1572	And of my reme the rychest / to / ryde wyth myseluen,	to	V P H self
CL 1573	Outtaken bare two, / and / thenne he the thrydde.'	C	Z H D H
CL 1574	This cry watz vpcaste, / and ther / comen mony	C Z	V H
CL 1575	Clerkes out of Caldye / that / kennest wer knauen,	that	A be E
CL 1576	As the sage sathrapas / that / sorsory couthe,	that	N V
CL 1577	Wychez and walkyries / wonnen to that sale,	/	V P D N
CL 1578	Deuinores of demorlaykes / that / dremes cowthe rede,	that	N X V
CL 1579	Sorsers of exorsismus / and fele / such clerkes;	C D	A N
CL 1580	And alle that loked on that letter / as / lewed thay were	C	A H be
CL 1581	As thay had loked in the lether / of my / lyft bote.	P D	A N
CL 1582	Thenne cryes the kyng / and / kerues his wedes.	C	V D N
CL 1583	What! he corsed his clerkes / and / calde hem chorles;	C	V H N
CL 1584	To henge the harlotes / he / heȝed ful ofte:	H	V Z
CL 1585	So watz the wyȝe wytles / he / wed wel ner.	H	V Z Z
CL 1586	Ho herde hym chyde to the chambre / that watz the / chef quene.	that be D	A N
CL 1587	When ho watz wytered bi wyȝes / what watz the cause-	/	Q be D N
CL 1588	Suche a chaungande chaunce / in the / chef halle-	P D	A N
CL 1589	The lady, to lauce that los / that the / lorde hade,	that D	N V
CL 1590	Glydes doun by the grece / and / gos to the kyng.	C	V P D N
CL 1591	Ho kneles on the colde erthe / and / carpes to hymseluen	C	V P H self
CL 1592	Wordes of worchyp / wyth a / wys speche.	P D	A N
CL 1593	'Kene kyng,' quoth the quene, / 'kayser of vrthe,	/	N P N
CL 1594	Euer laste thy lyf / in / lenthe of dayes!	P	N P N
CL 1595	Why hatz thou rended thy robe / for / redles hereinne,	P	N(A) Z
CL 1596	Thaȝ those ledes ben lewed / lettres to rede,	/	N to V
CL 1597	And hatz a hathel in thy holde, / as I haf / herde ofte,	C H have	E Z
CL 1598	That hatz the gost of God / that / gyes alle sothes?	that	V D N
CL 1599	His sawle is ful of syence, / saȝes to schawe,	/	N to V
CL 1600	To open vch a hide thyng / of / aunteres vncowthe.	P	N A
CL 1601	That is he that ful ofte / hatz / heuened thy fader	have	E D N
CL 1602	Of mony anger ful hote / with his / holy speche.	P D	A N
CL 1603	When Nabugodenozar / watz / nyed in stoundes,	be	E P N
CL 1604	He devysed his dremes / to the / dere trawthe;	P D	A N
CL 1605	He keuered hym with his counsayl / of / caytyf wyrdes;	P	A N
CL 1606	Alle that he spured hym, in space / he / expowned clene,	H	V Z
CL 1607	Thurȝ the sped of the spyryt, / that / sprad hym withinne,	that	V H P
CL 1608	Of the godeliest goddez / that / gaynes aywhere.	that	V Z
CL 1609	For his depe diuinité / and his / dere sawes,	C D	A N
CL 1610	Thy bolde fader Baltazar / bede by his name,	/	V P D N
CL 1611	That now is demed Danyel, / of / derne coninges,	P	A N
CL 1612	That caȝt watz in the captyuidé / in / cuntré of Jues;	P	N P N
CL 1613	Nabuzardan hym nome, / and / now is he here,	C	Z be H Z
CL 1614	A prophete of that prouince / and / pryce of the worlde.	C	N P D N
CL 1615	Sende into the ceté / to / seche hym bylyue,	to	V H Z
CL 1616	And wynne hym with the worchyp / to / wayne the bote;	to	V D N
CL 1617	And thaȝ the mater be merk / that / merked is ȝender,	that	E be Z
CL 1618	He schal declar hit also cler / as hit on / clay stande.'	C H P	N V
CL 1619	That gode counseyl at the quene / watz / cached as swythe;	be	E C Z
CL 1620	The burne byfore Baltazar / watz / broȝt in a whyle.	be	E Z
CL 1621	When he com bifore the kyng / and / clanly had halsed,	C	Z have E
CL 1622	Baltazar vmbebrayde / hym, and / 'Beue sir,' he sayde,	H C	A N H V
CL 1623	'Hit is tolde me bi tulkes / that thou / trwe were	that H	A be
CL 1624	Profete of that prouynce / that / prayed my fader,	that	V D N
CL 1625	Ande that thou hatz in thy hert / holy connyng,	/	A N
CL 1626	Of sapyence thi sawle / ful, / sothes to schawe;	Z	N to V
CL 1627	Goddes gost is the geuen / that / gyes alle thynges,	that	V D N
CL 1628	And thou vnhyles vch hidde / that / Heuen-Kyng myntes.	that	N N V

CL	1629	And here is a ferly byfallen, / and I / fayn wolde	C H	Z X
CL	1630	Wyt the wytte of the wryt / that on the / wowe clyues,	that P D	N V
CL	1631	For alle Caldé clerkes / han / cowwardely fayled.	have	Z E
CL	1632	If thou with quayntyse con quere / hit, I / quyte the thy mede:	H H	V H D N
CL	1633	For if thou redes hit by ryȝt / and hit to / resoun brynges,	C H P	N V
CL	1634	Fyrst telle me the tyxte / of the / tede lettres,	P D	E N
CL	1635	And sythen the mater of the mode / mene me therafter,	/	V H Z
CL	1636	And I schal halde the the hest / that I the / hyȝt haue,	that H H	E have
CL	1637	Apyke the in porpre clothe, / palle alther-fynest,	/	N A
CL	1638	And the byȝe of bryȝt golde / abowte thyn nekke,	/	P D N
CL	1639	And the thryd thryuenest / that / thrynges me after,	that	V H P
CL	1640	Thou schal be baroun vpon benche, / bede I the no lasse.'	/	V H H Z
CL	1641	Derfly thenne Danyel / deles thyse wordes:	/	V D N
CL	1642	'Ryche kyng of this regne, / rede the oure Lorde!	/	V H D N
CL	1643	Hit is surely soth / the / Souerayn of heuen	D	N P N
CL	1644	Fylsened euer thy fader / and vpon / folde cherychéd,	C P	N V
CL	1645	Gart hym grattest / to be of / gouernores alle,	to be P	N Z
CL	1646	And alle the worlde in his wylle / welde as hym lyked.	/	V C H V
CL	1647	Whoso wolde wel / do, / wel hym bityde,	V	Z H V
CL	1648	And quos deth so he dezyre, / he / dreped als fast;	H	V Z Z
CL	1649	Whoso hym lyked to lyft, / on / lofte watz he sone,	Z	Z be H Z
CL	1650	And quoso hym lyked to lay / watz / loȝed byluue.	be	E Z
CL	1651	So watz noted the note / of / Nabugodenozar,	P	N
CL	1652	Styfly stabled the regne / bi the / stronge Dryȝtyn;	P D	A N
CL	1653	For of the Hyȝest he hade / a / hope in his hert,	D	N P D N
CL	1654	That vche pouer past / out of that / Prynce euen.	P P D	N Z
CL	1655	And whyle that counsayl watz cleȝt / clos in his hert	/	Z P D N
CL	1656	There watz no mon vpon molde / of / myȝt as hymseluen;	P	N P H self
CL	1657	Til hit bitide on a tyme / towched hym pryde	/	V H N
CL	1658	For his lordeschyp so large / and his / lyf ryche;	C D	N A
CL	1659	He hade so huge an insyȝt / to his / aune dedes	P D	A N
CL	1660	That the power of the hyȝe Prynce / he / purely forȝetes.	H	Z V
CL	1661	Thenne blynnes he not of blasfemy / on to / blame the Dryȝtyn;	P to	V D N
CL	1662	His myȝt mete to Goddes / he / made with his wordes:	H	V P D N
CL	1663	"I am god of the grounde, / to / gye as me lykes.	to	V C H V
CL	1664	As He that hyȝe is in heuen, / His / aungeles that weldes.	D	N that V
CL	1665	If He hatz formed the folde / and / folk thervpone,	C	N Z
CL	1666	I haf bigged Babiloyne, / burȝ alther-rychest,	/	N A
CL	1667	Stabled therinne vche a ston / in / strenkthe of myn armes;	P	N P D N
CL	1668	Moȝt neuer myȝt bot myn / make such another."	/	V D H
CL	1669	Watz not this ilke worde / wonnen of his mowthe	/	V P D N
CL	1670	Er thenne the Souerayn saȝe / souned in his eres:	/	V P D N
CL	1671	"Now Nabugodenozar / innoȝe hatz spoken,	/	Z have E
CL	1672	Now is alle thy pryncipalté / past at ones,	/	E Z
CL	1673	And thou, remued fro monnes sunes, / on / mor most abide	P	N X V
CL	1674	And in wasturne walk / and wyth the / wylde dowelle,	C P D	N(A) V
CL	1675	As best, byte on the bent / of / braken and erbes,	P	N C N
CL	1676	With wrothe wolfes to won / and wyth / wylde asses."	C P	A N
CL	1677	Inmydde the poynt of his pryde / departed he there	/	V H Z
CL	1678	Fro the soly of his solempneté; / his / solace he leues,	D	N H V
CL	1679	And carfully was outkast / to / contré vnknawen,	P	N E
CL	1680	Fer into a fyr fryth / there / frekes neuer comen.	Q	N Z V
CL	1681	His hert heldet vnhole; / he / hoped non other	H	V Z
CL	1682	Bot a best that he be, / a / bol other an oxe.	D	N C D N
CL	1683	He fares forth on alle faure, / fogge watz his mete,	/	N be D N
CL	1684	And ete ay as a horce / when / erbes were fallen;	C	N be E
CL	1685	Thus he countes hym a kow / that watz a / kyng ryche,	that be D	N A
CL	1686	Quyle seuen sytheȝ were ouerseyed, / someres I trawe.	/	N H V
CL	1687	By that mony thik fythereȝ / thryȝt vmbe his lyre,	/	V P D N
CL	1688	That alle watz dubbed and dyȝt / in the / dew of heuen;	P D	N P N
CL	1689	Faxe, fyltered and felt, / floȝed hym vmbe,	/	V H P
CL	1690	That schad fro his schulderes / to his / schere-wykes,	P D	A N
CL	1691	And twenty-folde twynande / hit to his / tos raȝt,	H P D	N V
CL	1692	Ther mony clyuy as clyde / hit / clyȝt togeder.	H	V Z
CL	1693	His berde ibrad alle his brest / to the / bare vrthe,	P D	A N
CL	1694	His browes bresed as breres / aboute his / brode chekes;	P D	A N
CL	1695	Holȝe were his yȝen / and vnder / campe hores,	C P	A N
CL	1696	And al watz gray as the glede, / with ful / grymme clawres	P Z	A N
CL	1697	That were croked and kene / as the / kyte paune;	P D	N N
CL	1698	Erne-hwed he watz / and / al ouerbrawden,	C	Z E
CL	1699	Til he wyst ful wel / who / wroȝt alle myȝtes,	Q	V D N

CL	1700	And cowthe vche kyndam tokerue / and / keuer when Hym lyked.	C	V C H V
CL	1701	Thenne He wayned hym his wyt, / that hade / we offered,	that have	N E
CL	1702	That he com to knawlach / and / kenned hymseluen;	C	V H self
CL	1703	Thenne he loued that Lorde / and / leued in trawthe	C	V P N
CL	1704	Hit watz non other then He / that hade / al in honde.	that have	H P N
CL	1705	Thenne sone watz he sende / agayn, his / sete restored;	Z D	N E
CL	1706	His barounes boȝed / hym to, / blythe of his come,	H P	A P D N
CL	1707	Haȝerly in his aune hwef / his / heued watz couered,	D	N be E
CL	1708	And so ȝeply watz ȝarked / and / ȝolden his state.	C	V D N
CL	1709	Bot thou, Baltazar, his barne / and his / bolde ayre,	C D	A N
CL	1710	Seȝ these syngnes with syȝt / and / set hem at lyttel,	C	V H Z
CL	1711	Bot ay hatz hofen thy hert / agaynes the / hyȝe Dryȝtyn,	Z D	A N
CL	1712	With bobaunce and with blasfamye / bost at Hym kest,	/	N P N V
CL	1713	And now His vessayles avyled / in / vanyté vnclene,	P	N A
CL	1714	That in His hows Hym to honour / were / heuened of fyrst;	be	E Z
CL	1715	Bifore the barounz hatz hom broȝt, / and / byrled therinne	C	E Z
CL	1716	Wale wyne to thy wenches / in / waryed stoundes;	P	E N
CL	1717	Bifore thy borde hatz thou broȝt / beuerage in th'edé,	/	N P D N
CL	1718	That blythely were fyrst blest / with / bischopes hondes,	P	N N
CL	1719	Louande theron lese goddez / that / lyf haden neuer,	that	N V Z
CL	1720	Made of stokkes and stonez / that neuer / styry moȝt.	that Z	V X
CL	1721	And for that frothande fylthe, / the / Fader of heuen	D	N P N
CL	1722	Hatz sende into this sale / thise / syȝtes vncowthe,	D	N A
CL	1723	The fyste with the fyngeres / that / flayed thi hert,	that	V D N
CL	1724	That rasped renyschly the woȝe / with the / roȝ penne.	P D	A N
CL	1725	Thise ar the wordes here wryten, / withoute / werk more,	P	N A
CL	1726	By vch fygure, as I fynde, / as oure / Fader lykes:	C D	N V
CL	1727	Mane, Techal, Phares: / merked in thrynne,	/	E P N
CL	1728	That thretes the of thyn vnthryfte / vpon / thre wyse.	P	A N
CL	1729	Now expowne the this speche / spedly I thenk:	/	Z H V
CL	1730	Mane menes als much / as / "Maynful Gode	P	A N
CL	1731	Hatz counted thy kyndam / bi a / clene noumbre,	P D	A N
CL	1732	And fulfylled hit in fayth / to the / fyrre ende" .	P D	A N
CL	1733	To teche the of Techal, / that / terme thus menes:	that	N Z V
CL	1734	"Thy wale rengne is walt / in / weȝtes to heng,	P	N to V
CL	1735	And is funde ful fewe / of hit / fayth-dedes."	P D	N N
CL	1736	And Phares folȝes for those fawtes, / to / frayst the trawthe;	to	V D N
CL	1737	In Phares fynde I forsothe / thise / felle saȝes:	D	A N
CL	1738	"Departed is thy pryncipalté, / depryued thou worthes,	/	E D N
CL	1739	Thy rengne rafte / is the fro, and / raȝt is the Perses;	be H P C	E be D N
CL	1740	The Medes schal be maysteres / here, and thou of / menske schowued."'	Z C H P	N E
CL	1741	The kyng comaunded / anon to / clethe that wyse	Z to	V D N
CL	1742	In frokkes of fyn cloth, / as / forward hit asked;	C	N H V
CL	1743	Thenne sone watz Danyel dubbed / in ful / dere porpor,	P Z	A N
CL	1744	And a coler of cler golde / kest vmbe his swyre.	/	E P D N
CL	1745	Then watz demed a decre / bi the / duk seluen:	P D	N self
CL	1746	Bolde Baltazar bed / that hym / bowe schulde	that H	V X
CL	1747	The comynes al of Caldé / that to the / kyng longed,	that P D	N V
CL	1748	As to the prynce pryuyest / preued the thrydde,	/	V D H
CL	1749	Heȝest of alle other / saf / onelych tweyne,	P	A N
CL	1750	To boȝ after Baltazar / in / borȝe and in felde.	P	N C P N
CL	1751	Thys watz cryed and knawen / in / cort als fast,	P	N Z
CL	1752	And alle the folk therof fayn / that / folȝed hym tylle.	that	V H P
CL	1753	Bot howso Danyel watz dyȝt, / that / day ouerȝede,	that	N V
CL	1754	Nyȝt neȝed ryȝt now / with / nyes fol mony,	P	N Z A
CL	1755	For daȝed neuer another day, / that ilk / derk ayre,	D D	N P
CL	1756	Er dalt were that ilk dome / that / Danyel deuysed.	that	N V
CL	1757	The solace of the solempneté / in that / sale dured	P D	N V
CL	1758	Of that farand fest, / tyl / fayled the sunne;	C	V D N
CL	1759	Thenne blykned the ble / of the / bryȝt skwes,	P D	A N
CL	1760	Mourkenes the mery weder, / and the / myst dryues	C D	N V
CL	1761	Thorȝ the lyst of the lyfte, / bi the / loȝ medoes.	P D	A N
CL	1762	Vche hathel to his home / hyȝes ful fast,	/	V Z Z
CL	1763	Seten at her soper / and / songen therafter;	C	V Z
CL	1764	Then foundez vch a felaȝschyp / fyrre at forth naȝtes.	/	Z P D N
CL	1765	Baltazar to his bedd / with / blysse watz caryed;	P	N be E
CL	1766	Reche the rest / as hym lyst: he / ros neuer therafter.	C H V H	V Z Z
CL	1767	For his foes in the felde / in / flokkes ful grete,	P	N Z A
CL	1768	That longe hade layted that lede / his / londes to strye,	D	N to V
CL	1769	Now ar thay sodenly assembled / at the / self tyme.	P D	A N
CL	1770	Of hem wyst no wyȝe / that in that / won dowelled.	that P D	N V

CL	1771	Hit watz the dere Daryus, / the / duk of thise Medes,	D	N P D N
CL	1772	The prowde prynce of Perce, / and / Porros of Ynde,	C	N P N
CL	1773	With mony a legioun ful large, / with / ledes of armes,	P	N P N
CL	1774	That now hatz spyed a space / to / spoyle Caldéez.	to	V N
CL	1775	Thay throngen theder in the thester / on / thrawen hepes,	P	A N
CL	1776	Asscaped ouer the skyre watteres / and / scayled the walles,	C	V D N
CL	1777	Lyfte laddres ful longe / and vpon / lofte wonen,	C Z	Z V
CL	1778	Stelen stylly the toun / er any / steuen rysed.	C D	N V
CL	1779	Withinne an oure of the ni3t / an / entré thay hade,	D	N H V
CL	1780	3et afrayed thay no freke. / Fyrre thay passen,	/	Z H V
CL	1781	And to the palays pryncipal / thay / aproched ful stylle,	H	V Z Z
CL	1782	Thenne ran thay in on a res / on / rowtes ful grete;	P	N Z A
CL	1783	Blastes out of bry3t brasse / brestes so hy3e,	/	V Z Z
CL	1784	Ascry scarred on the scue, / that / scomfyted mony.	that	V H
CL	1785	Segges slepande were slayne / er thay / slyppe my3t;	C H	V X
CL	1786	Vche hous heyred / watz withinne a / hondewhyle.	be P D	N
CL	1787	Baltazar in his bed / watz / beten to dethe,	be	E P N
CL	1788	That bothe his blod and his brayn / blende on the clothes;	/	V P D N
CL	1789	The kyng in his cortyn / watz / ka3t bi the heles,	be	E P D N
CL	1790	Feryed out bi the fete / and / fowle dispysed.	C	N(A) V
CL	1791	That watz so do3ty that day / and / drank of the vessayl	C	V P D N
CL	1792	Now is a dogge also dere / that in a / dych lygges.	that P D	N V
CL	1793	For the mayster of thyse Medes / on the / morne ryses,	P D	N V
CL	1794	Dere Daryous that day / dy3t vpon trone,	/	V P N
CL	1795	That ceté seses ful sounde, / and / sa3tlyng makes	C	N V
CL	1796	Wyth alle the barounz theraboute, / that / bowed hym after.	that	V H P
CL	1797	And thus watz that londe lost / for the / lordes synne,	P D	N N
CL	1798	And the fylthe of the freke / that / defowled hade	that	E have
CL	1799	The ornementes of Goddez hous / that / holy were maked.	that	A be E
CL	1800	He watz corsed for his vnclannes, / and / cached therinne,	C	E Z
CL	1801	Done doun of his dyngneté / for / dedez vnfayre,	P	N A
CL	1802	And of thyse worldes worchyp / wrast out for euer,	/	V Z Z
CL	1803	And 3et of lykynges on lofte / letted, I trowe:	/	V H V
CL	1804	To loke on oure lofly Lorde / late bitydes.	/	Z V
CL	1805	Thus vpon thrynne wyses / I haf yow / thro schewed	H have H	Z E
CL	1806	That vnclannes tocleues / in / corage dere	P	N A
CL	1807	Of that wynnelych Lorde / that / wonyes in heuen,	that	V P N
CL	1808	Entyses Hym to be tene, / teldes vp His wrake;	/	V Z D N
CL	1809	Ande clannes is His comfort, / and / coyntyse He louyes,	C	N H V
CL	1810	And those that seme arn and swete / schyn / se His face.	X	V D N
CL	1811	That we gon gay in oure gere / that / grace He vus sende,	that	N H H V
CL	1812	That we may serue in His sy3t, / ther / solace neuer blynnez.	Q	N Z V

Sir Gawain and the Green Knight

G	1	Sithen the sege and the assaut / watz / sesed at Troye,	be	E P N
G	2	The borȝ brittened and brent / to / brondeȝ and askez,	P	N C N
G	3	The tulk that the trammes / of / tresoun ther wroȝt	P	N Z V
G	4	Watz tried for his tricherie, / the / trewest on erthe:	D	A P N
G	5	Hit watz Ennias the athel, / and his / highe kynde,	C D	A N
G	6	That sithen depreced prouinces, / and / patrounes bicome	C	N V
G	7	Welneȝe of al the wele / in the / west iles.	P D	N N
G	8	Fro riche Romulus to Rome / ricchis hym swythe,	/	V H Z
G	9	With gret bobbaunce that burȝe / he / biges vpon fyrst,	H	V P Z
G	10	And neuenes hit his aune nome, / as hit / now hat;	C H	Z V
G	11	Tirius to Tuskan / and / teldes bigynnes,	C	N V
G	12	Langaberde in Lumbardie / lyftes vp homes,	/	V P N
G	13	And fer ouer the French flod / Felix Brutus	/	N N
G	14	On mony bonkkes ful brode / Bretayn he settez	/	N H V
G	20	Ande quen this Bretayn watz bigged / bi this / burn rych,	P D	N A
G	21	Bolde bredden / therinne, / baret that lofden,	Z	N that V
G	22	In mony turned tyme / tene that wroȝten.	/	N that V
G	23	Mo ferlyes on this folde / han / fallen here oft	have	E Z Z
G	24	Then in any other that I wot, / syn that / ilk tyme.	P D	A N
G	25	Bot of alle that here bult, / of / Bretaygne kynges,	P	N N
G	26	Ay watz Arthur the hendest, / as I haf / herde telle.	C H have	E V
G	27	Forthi an aunter in erde / I / attle to schawe,	H	V to V
G	28	That a selly in siȝt / summe men hit holden,	/	A N H V
G	29	And an outtrage awenture / of / Arthurez wonderez.	P	N N
G	30	If ȝe wyl lysten this laye / bot on / littel quile,	P P	A N
G	31	I schal telle hit as-tit, / as I in / toun herde,	C H P	N V
G	37	This kyng lay at Camylot / vpon / Krystmasse	P	N
G	38	With mony luflych lorde, / ledez of the best,	/	N P D A
G	39	Rekenly of the Rounde Table / alle tho / rich brether,	D D	A N
G	40	With rych reuel oryȝt / and / rechles merthes.	C	A N
G	41	Ther tournayed tulkes / by / tymez ful mony,	P	N Z A
G	42	Justed ful jolilé / thise / gentyle kniȝtes,	D	A N
G	43	Sythen kayred to the court / caroles to make.	/	N to V
G	44	For ther the fest watz ilyche / ful / fiften dayes,	Z	A N
G	45	With alle the mete and the mirthe / that / men couthe avyse;	that	N X V
G	46	Such glaum ande gle / glorious to here,	/	A to V
G	47	Dere dyn vpon day, / daunsyng on nyȝtes,	/	G P N
G	48	Al watz hap vpon heȝe / in / hallez and chambrez	P	N C N
G	49	With lordez and ladies, / as / leuest him thoȝt.	C	A H V
G	50	With all the wele of the worlde / thay / woned ther samen,	H	V Z Z
G	51	The most kyd knyȝtez / vnder / Krystes seluen,	P	N self
G	52	And the louelokkest ladies / that euer / lif haden,	that Z	N V
G	53	And he the comlokest kyng / that the / court haldes;	that D	N V
G	54	For al watz this fayre folk / in her / first age,	P D	A N
G	60	Wyle Nw ȝer watz so ȝep / that hit watz / nwe cummen,	that H be	Z E
G	61	That day doubble on the dece / watz the / douth serued.	be D	N E
G	62	Fro the kyng watz cummen / with / knyȝtes into the halle,	P	N P D N
G	63	The chauntré of the chapel / cheued to an ende,	/	V P D N
G	64	Loude crye watz ther kest / of / clerkez and other,	P	N C H
G	65	Nowel nayted onewe, / neuened ful ofte;	/	V Z Z
G	66	And sythen riche forth runnen / to / reche hondeselle,	to	V N
G	67	Ȝeȝed ȝeres-ȝiftes on hiȝ, / ȝelde hem bi honde,	/	V H P N
G	68	Debated busyly / aboute tho giftes;	/	P D N
G	69	Ladies laȝed ful loude, / thoȝ thay / lost haden,	C H	E have
G	70	And he that wan watz not wrothe, / that may ȝe / wel trawe.	that X H	Z V
G	71	Alle this mirthe thay maden / to the / mete tyme;	P D	A N
G	72	When thay had waschen worthyly / thay / wenten to sete,	H	V to V
G	73	The best burne ay abof, / as hit / best semed,	C H	A V
G	74	Whene Guenore, ful gay, / graythed in the myddes,	/	V P D N
G	75	Dressed on the dere des, / dubbed al aboute,	/	E Z Z
G	76	Smal sendal bisides, / a / selure hir ouer	D	N H P
G	77	Of tryed tolouse, / and / tars tapites innoghe,	C	N N A
G	78	That were enbrawded and beten / wyth the / best gemmes	P D	A N
G	79	That myȝt be preued of prys / wyth / penyes to bye,	P	N to V
G	85	Bot Arthure wolde not ete / til / al were serued,	C	H be E
G	86	He watz so joly of his joyfnes, / and / sumquat childgered:	C	Z A(E)

G	87	His lif liked hym ly3t, / he / louied the lasse	H	V D N
G	88	Auther to longe lye / or to / longe sitte,	C Z	Z V
G	89	So bisied him his 3onge blod / and his / brayn wylde.	C D	N A
G	90	And also an other maner / meued him eke	/	V H Z
G	91	That he thur3 nobelay had nomen, / he wolde / neuer ete	H X	Z V
G	92	Vpon such a dere day / er hym / deuised were	C H	E be
G	93	Of sum auenturus thyng / an / vncouthe tale,	D	A N
G	94	Of sum mayn meruayle, / that he / my3t trawe,	that H	X V
G	95	Of alderes, of armes, / of / other auenturus,	P	A N
G	96	Other sum segg hym biso3t / of sum / siker kny3t	P D	A N
G	97	To joyne wyth hym in iustyng, / in / jopardé to lay,	P	N to V
G	98	Lede, lif for lyf, / leue vchon other,	/	V Z
G	99	As fortune wolde fulsun hom, / the / fayrer to haue.	D	N(A) to V
G	100	This watz the kynges countenaunce / where he in / court were,	Q H P	N be
G	101	At vch farand fest / among his / fre meny	P D	A N
G	107	Thus ther stondes in stale / the / stif kyng hisseluen,	D	A N H self
G	108	Talkkande bifore the hy3e table / of / trifles ful hende.	P	N Z A
G	109	There gode Gawan watz graythed / Gwenore bisyde,	/	N Z
G	110	And Agrauayn a la dure mayn / on that / other syde sittes,	P D	A N V
G	111	Bothe the kynges sistersunes / and ful / siker kni3tes;	C Z	A N
G	112	Bischop Bawdewyn / abof / biginez the table,	Z	V D N
G	113	And Ywan, Vryn son, / ette with hymseluen.	/	V P H self
G	114	Thise were di3t on the des / and / derworthly serued,	C	Z E
G	115	And sithen mony siker segge / at the / sidbordez.	P D	N
G	116	Then the first cors come / with / crakkyng of trumpes,	P	G P N
G	117	Wyth mony baner ful bry3t / that / therbi henged;	that	Z V
G	118	Nwe nakryn noyse / with the / noble pipes,	P D	A N
G	119	Wylde werbles and wy3t / wakned lote,	/	V N
G	120	That mony hert ful hi3e / hef at her towches.	/	V P D N
G	121	Dayntés dryuen / therwyth of ful / dere metes,	Z P Z	A N
G	122	Foysoun of the fresche, / and on so / fele disches	C P Z	A N
G	123	That pine to fynde the place / the / peple biforne	D	N P
G	124	For to sette the sylueren / that / sere sewes halden	that	A N V
G	130	Now wyl I of hor seruise / say yow no more,	/	V H Z
G	131	For vch wy3e may wel wit / no / wont that ther were.	D	N that Z be
G	132	An other noyse ful newe / ne3ed biliue,	/	V Z
G	133	That the lude my3t haf leue / liflode to cach;	/	N to V
G	134	For vnethe watz the noyce / not a whyle sesed,	/	not Z E
G	135	And the fyrst cource in the court / kyndely serued,	/	Z E
G	136	Ther hales in at the halle dor / an / aghlich mayster,	D	A N
G	137	On the most on the molde / on / mesure hyghe;	P	N A
G	138	Fro the swyre to the swange / so / sware and so thik,	Z	A C Z A
G	139	And his lyndes and his lymes / so / longe and so grete,	Z	A C Z A
G	140	Half etayn in erde / I / hope that he were,	H	V that H be
G	141	Bot mon most I algate / mynn hym to bene,	/	V H to be
G	142	And that the myriest in his muckel / that / my3t ride;	that	X V
G	143	For of bak and of brest / al were his / bodi sturne,	H be D	N A
G	144	Both his wombe and his wast / were / worthyly smale,	be	Z A
G	145	And alle his fetures fol3ande, / in / forme that he hade,	P	N that H V
G	151	Ande al graythed in grene / this / gome and his wedes:	D	N C D N
G	152	A strayte cote ful stre3t, / that / stek on his sides,	that	V P D N
G	153	A meré mantile / abof, / menskked withinne	P	E Z
G	154	With pelure pured apert, / the / pane ful clene	D	N Z A
G	155	With blythe blaunner ful bry3t, / and his / hod bothe,	C D	N Z
G	156	That watz la3t fro his lokkez / and / layde on his schulderes;	C	V P D N
G	157	Heme wel-haled / hose of that same,	/	N P D A
G	158	That spenet on his sparlyr, / and / clene spures vnder	C	A N P
G	159	Of bry3t golde, vpon silk bordes / barred ful ryche,	/	E Z A
G	160	And scholes vnder schankes / there the / schalk rides;	Q D	N V
G	161	And alle his vesture uerayly / watz / clene verdure,	be	A N
G	162	Bothe the barres of his belt / and other / blythe stones,	C D	A N
G	163	That were richely rayled / in his / aray clene	P D	N A
G	164	Aboutte hymself and his sadel, / vpon / silk werkez.	P	N N
G	165	That were to tor for to telle / of / tryfles the halue	P	N D N(A)
G	166	That were enbrauded abof, / wyth / bryddes and fly3es,	P	N C N
G	167	With gay gaudi of grene, / the / golde ay inmyddes.	D	N Z Z
G	168	The pendauntes of his payttrure, / the / proude cropure,	D	A N
G	169	His molaynes, and alle the metail / anamayld was thenne,	/	E be Z
G	170	The steropes that he stod / on / stayned of the same,	P	V P D A
G	171	And his arsounz al after / and his / athel skyrtes,	C D	A N
G	172	That euer glemered and glent / al of / grene stones;	Z P	A N

G	173	The fole that he ferkkes / on / fyn of that ilke,	P	Z P D H
G	179	Wel gay watz this gome / gered in grene,	/	E P N
G	180	And the here of his hed / of his / hors swete.	P D	N N
G	181	Fayre fannand fax / vmbefoldes his schulderes;	/	V D N
G	182	A much berd as a busk / ouer his / brest henges,	P D	N V
G	183	That wyth his hi3lich here / that of his / hed reches	that P D	N V
G	184	Watz euesed al vmbetorne / abof his elbowes,	/	P D N
G	185	That half his armes ther-vnder / were / halched in the wyse	be	E P D N
G	186	Of a kyngez capados / that / closes his swyre;	that	V D N
G	187	The mane of that mayn hors / much to hit lyke,	/	Z to H A
G	188	Wel cresped and cemmed, / wyth / knottes ful mony	P	N Z A
G	189	Folden in wyth fildore / aboute the / fayre grene,	P D	A N
G	190	Ay a herle of the here, / an / other of golde;	D	H P N
G	191	The tayl and his toppyng / twynnen of a sute,	/	E P D N
G	192	And bounden bothe wyth a bande / of a / bry3t grene,	P D	A N
G	193	Dubbed wyth ful dere stonez, / as the / dok lasted,	C D	N V
G	194	Sythen thrawen wyth a thwong / a / thwarle knot alofte,	D	A N Z
G	195	Ther mony bellez ful bry3t / of / brende golde rungen.	P	E N V
G	196	Such a fole vpon folde, / ne / freke that hym rydes,	D	N that H V
G	197	Watz neuer sene in that sale / wyth / sy3t er that tyme,	P	N P D N
G	203	Whether hade he no helme / ne / hawbergh nauther,	D	N Z
G	204	Ne no pysan ne no plate / that / pented to armes,	that	V P N
G	205	Ne no schafte ne no schelde / to / schwue ne to smyte,	to	V not to V
G	206	Bot in his on honde he hade / a / holyn bobbe,	D	N N
G	207	That is grattest in grene / when / greuez ar bare,	C	N be A
G	208	And an ax in his other, / a / hoge and vnmete,	H	A C A
G	209	A spetos sparthe to expoun / in / spelle, quoso my3t.	P	N Q X
G	210	The lenkthe of an eln3erde / the / large hede hade,	D	A N V
G	211	The grayn al of grene stele / and of / golde hewen,	C P	N E
G	212	The bit burnyst bry3t, / with a / brod egge	P D	A N
G	213	As wel schapen to schere / as / scharp rasores,	P	A N
G	214	The stele of a stif staf / the / sturne hit bi grypte,	D	N(A) H P V
G	215	That watz wounden wyth yrn / to the / wandez ende,	P D	N N
G	216	And al bigrauen with grene / in / gracios werkes;	P	A N
G	217	A lace lapped / aboute, that / louked at the hede,	Z that	V P D N
G	218	And so after the halme / halched ful ofte,	/	V Z Z
G	219	Wyth tryed tasselez / therto / tacched innoghe	Z	V Z
G	220	On botounz of the bry3t grene / brayden ful ryche.	/	E Z A
G	221	This hathel heldez / hym in and the / halle entres,	H P C D	N V
G	222	Driuande to the he3e dece, / dut he no wothe,	/	V H D N
G	223	Haylsed he neuer one, / bot / he3e he ouer loked.	C	Z H Z V
G	224	The fyrst word that he warp, / "Wher is", he sayd,	/	Q be H V
G	225	"The gouernour of this gyng? / Gladly I wolde	/	Z H X
G	226	Se that segg in sy3t, / and with / hymself speke	C P	H self V
G	232	Ther watz lokyng on lenthe / the / lude to beholde,	D	N to V
G	233	For vch mon had meruayle, / quat hit / mene my3t	Q H	V X
G	234	That a hathel and a horse / my3t such a / hwe lach,	X D D	N V
G	235	As growe grene as the gres / and / grener hit semed,	C	A H V
G	236	Then grene aumayl on golde / glowande bry3ter.	/	G A
G	237	Al studied that ther stod, / and / stalked hym nerre	C	V H P
G	238	Wyth al the wonder of the worlde / what he / worch schulde.	Q H	V X
G	239	For fele sellyez had thay sen, / bot / such neuer are;	C	H Z be
G	240	Forthi for fantoum and fayry3e / the / folk there hit demed.	D	N Z H V
G	241	Therfore to answare watz ar3e / mony / athel freke,	D	A N
G	242	And al stouned at his steuen / and / stonstil seten	C	A V
G	243	In a swoghe sylence / thur3 the / sale riche;	P D	N A
G	244	As al were slypped vpon slepe / so / slaked hor lotez	Z	V D N
G	250	Thenn Arthour bifore the hi3 dece/ that / auenture byholdez,	that	N V
G	251	And rekenly hym reuerenced, / for / rad was he neuer,	C	A be H Z
G	252	And sayde, "Wy3e, welcum / iwys to this place,	/	Z P D N
G	253	The hede of this ostel / Arthour I hat;	/	N H V
G	254	Li3t luflych / adoun and / lenge, I the praye,	Z C	V H H V
G	255	And quat-so thy wylle / is we schal / wyt after."	be H X	V Z
G	256	"Nay, as help me," quoth the hathel, / "he that on / hy3e syttes,	H that Z	Z V
G	257	To wone any quyle in this won, / hit / watz not myn ernde;	H	be not D N
G	258	Bot for the los of the, lede, / is / lyft vp so hy3e,	be	E Z Z Z
G	259	And thy bur3 and thy burnes / best ar holden,	/	A be E
G	260	Stifest vnder stel-gere / on / stedes to ryde,	P	N to V
G	261	The wy3test and the worthyest / of the / worldes kynde,	P D	N N
G	262	Preue for to play / wyth in other / pure laykez,	P P D	A N
G	263	And here is kydde cortaysye, / as I haf / herd carp,	C H have	V V

G	264	And that hatz wayned me hider, / iwyis, at this tyme.	/	Z P D N
G	265	3e may be seker bi this braunch / that I / bere here	that H	V Z
G	266	That I passe as in pes, / and no / ply3t seche;	C D	N V
G	267	For had I founded in fere / in / fe3tyng wyse,	P	A N
G	268	I haue a hauberghe at home / and a / helme bothe,	C D	N Z
G	269	A schelde and a scharp spere, / schinande bry3t,	/	G Z
G	270	Ande other weppenes to welde, / I / wene wel, als;	H	V Z Z
G	271	Bot for I wolde no were, / my / wedez ar softer.	D	N be A
G	272	Bot if thou be so bold / as alle / burnez tellen,	C D	N V
G	273	Thou wyl grant me godly / the / gomen that I ask	D	N that H V
G	279	"Nay, frayst I no fy3t, / in / fayth I the telle,	P	N H H V
G	280	Hit arn aboute on this bench / bot / berdlez chylder.	P	A N
G	281	If I were hasped in armes / on a / he3e stede,	P D	A N
G	282	Here is no mon me to mach, / for / my3tez so wayke.	P	N A A
G	283	Forthy I craue in this court / a / Crystemas gomen,	D	N N
G	284	For hit is 3ol and Nwe 3er, / and here ar / 3ep mony:	C Z be	A H
G	285	If any so hardy in this hous / holdez hymseluen,	/	V H self
G	286	Be so bolde in his blod, / brayn in hys hede,	/	A P D N
G	287	That dar stifly strike / a / strok for an other,	D	N P D H
G	288	I schal gif hym of my gyft / thys / giserne ryche,	D	N A
G	289	This ax, that is heué innogh, / to / hondele as hym lykes,	to	V C H V
G	290	And I schal bide the fyrst bur / as / bare as I sitte.	C	A C H V
G	291	If any freke be so felle / to / fonde that I telle,	to	V that H V
G	292	Lepe ly3tly / me to, and / lach this weppen,	H P C	V D N
G	293	I quit-clayme hit for euer, / kepe hit as his auen,	/	V H P D H
G	294	And I schal stonde hym a strok, / stif on this flet,	/	A P D N
G	295	Ellez thou wyl di3t me the dom / to / dele hym an other	to	V H D H
G	301	If he hem stowned vpon fyrst, / stiller were thanne	/	A be Z
G	302	Alle the heredmen in halle, / the / hy3 and the lo3e.	D	A C D A
G	303	The renk on his rouncé / hym / ruched in his sadel,	H	V P D N
G	304	And runischly his rede y3en / he / reled aboute,	H	V Z
G	305	Bende his bresed bro3ez, / blycande grene,	/	G A
G	306	Wayued his berde for to wayte / quo-so / wolde ryse.	Q	X V
G	307	When non wolde kepe hym with carp / he / co3ed ful hy3e,	H	V Z Z
G	308	Ande rimed hym ful richly, / and / ry3t hym to speke:	C	V H to V
G	309	"What, is this Arthures hous," / quoth the / hathel thenne,	V D	N Z
G	310	"That al the rous rennes / of thur3 / ryalmes so mony?	P P	N Z A
G	311	Where is now / your / sourquydrye and your conquestes,	D	N C D N
G	312	Your gryndellayk and your greme, / and your / grete wordes?	C D	A N
G	313	Now is the reuel and the renoun / of the / Rounde Table	P D	A N
G	314	Ouerwalt wyth a worde / of on / wy3es speche,	P P	N N
G	315	For al dares for drede / withoute / dynt schewed!"	P	N V
G	316	Wyth this he la3es so loude / that the / lorde greued;	that D	N V
G	317	The blod schot for scham / into his / schyre face	P D	A N
G	323	Ande sayde, "Hathel, by heuen, / thyn / askyng is nys,	D	G be A
G	324	And as thou foly hatz frayst, / fynde the behoues.	/	V H X
G	325	I know no gome that is gast / of thy / grete wordes;	P D	A N
G	326	Gif me now thy geserne, / vpon / Godez halue,	P	N N
G	327	And I schal baythen the bone / that thou / boden habbes."	that H	E have
G	328	Ly3tly lepez / he hym to, and / la3t at his honde.	H H P C	V P D N
G	329	Then feersly that other freke / vpon / fote ly3tis.	P	N V
G	330	Now hatz Arthure his axe, / and the / halme grypez,	C D	N V
G	331	And sturnely sturez / hit aboute, that / stryke wyth hit tho3t.	H P that	V P H V
G	332	The stif mon hym bifore / stod vpon hy3t,	/	V Z
G	333	Herre then ani in the hous / by the / hede and more.	P D	N C Z
G	334	Wyth sturne schere ther he stod / he / stroked his berde,	H	V D N
G	335	And wyth a countenaunce dry3e / he / dro3 doun his cote,	H	V Z D N
G	336	No more mate ne dismayd / for hys / mayn dintez	P D	A N
G	337	Then any burne vpon bench / hade / bro3t hym to drynk	have	E H to V
G	343	"Wolde 3e, worthilych lorde," / quoth / Wawan to the kyng,	V	N to D N
G	344	"Bid me bo3e fro this benche, / and / stonde by yow there,	C	V P H Z
G	345	That I wythoute vylanye / my3t / voyde this table,	X	V D N
G	346	And that my legge lady / lyked not ille,	/	V not A
G	347	I wolde com to your counseyl / bifore your / cort ryche.	P D	N A
G	348	For me think hit not semly, / as hit is / soth knawen,	C H be	N(A) E
G	349	Ther such an askyng is heuened / so / hy3e in your sale,	Z	A P D N
G	350	Tha3 3e 3ourself be talenttyf, / to / take hit to yourseluen,	to	V H P H self
G	351	Whil mony so bolde / yow aboute vpon / bench sytten,	H P P	N V
G	352	That vnder heuen I hope / non / ha3erer of wylle,	not	A P N
G	353	Ne better bodyes on bent / ther / baret is rered.	Q	N be E
G	354	I am the wakkest, I wot, / and of / wyt feblest,	C P	N A

G	355	And lest lur of my lyf, / quo / laytes the sothe-	Q	V D N
G	356	Bot for as much as ȝe ar myn em̃, / I am̃ / only to playse,	H be	A to V
G	357	No bounté bot your blod / I in my / bodé knowe;	H P D	N V
G	358	And sythen this note is so nys / that / noȝt hit yow falles,	that	not H H V
G	359	And I haue frayned hit at yow fyrst, / foldeȝ hit to me;	/	V H P H
G	360	And if I carp not comlyly, / let alle this / cort rych	let D D	N A
G	366	Then comaunded the kyng / the / knyȝt for to ryse;	D	N for to V
G	367	And he ful radly vpros, / and / ruchched hym fayre,	C	V H Z
G	368	Kneled doun bifore the kyng, / and / cacheȝ that weppen;	C	V D N
G	369	And he luflyly hit hym laft, / and / lyfte vp his honde,	C	V Z D N
G	370	And gef hym Goddeȝ blessyng, / and / gladly hym biddes	C	Z H V
G	371	That his hert and his honde / schulde / hardi be bothe.	X	A be Z
G	372	"Kepe the cosyn,"quoth the kyng, / "that thou on / kyrf sette,	that H P	N V
G	373	And if thou redeȝ hym ryȝt, / redly I trowe	/	Z H V
G	374	That thou schal byden the bur / that he schal / bede after."	that H X	V Z
G	375	Gawan gotȝ to the gome / with / giserne in honde,	P	N P N
G	376	And he baldly hym bydeȝ, / he / bayst neuer the helder.	H	V Z D A
G	377	Then carppeȝ to Sir Gawan / the / knyȝt in the grene,	D	N P D N
G	378	"Refourme we oure forwardes, / er we / fyrre passe.	C H	Z E
G	379	Fyrst I ethe the, hathel, / how that thou hattes	/	Q that H V
G	380	That thou me telle truly, / as I / tryst may."	C H	V X
G	381	"In god fayth," quoth the goode knyȝt, / "Gawan I hatte,	/	N H V
G	382	That bede the this buffet, / quat-so / bifalleȝ after,	Q	V Z
G	383	And at this tyme twelmonyth / take at the an other	/	V P H D H
G	384	Wyth what weppen so thou wylt, / and wyth no / wyȝ elleȝ	C P D	N Z
G	390	"Bigog," quoth the grene knyȝt, / "Sir / Gawan, me lykes	D	N H V
G	391	That I schal fange at thy fust / that I haf / frayst here.	that H have	V Z
G	392	And thou hatȝ redily rehersed, / bi / resoun ful trwe,	P	N Z A
G	393	Clanly al the couenaunt / that I the / kynge asked,	that H D	N V
G	394	Saf that thou schal siker / me, / segge, bi thi trawthe,	H	N P D N
G	395	That thou schal seche me thiself, / where-so thou hopes	/	Q H V
G	396	I may be funde vpon folde, / and / foch the such wages	C	V H D N
G	397	As thou deles me to-day / bifore this / douthe ryche."	P D	N A
G	398	"Where schulde I wale the," quoth Gauan, / "where is thy place?	/	Q be D N
G	399	I wot neuer where thou wonyes, / bi / hym that me wroȝt,	P	H that H V
G	400	Ne I know not the, knyȝt, / by / cort ne thi name.	P	N not D N
G	401	Bot teche me truly /therof, / telle me how thou hattes,	Z C	V H Q H V
G	402	And I schal ware alle my wyt / to / wynne me theder,	to	V H Z
G	403	And that I swere the for sothe, / and by my / seker traweth."	C P D	A N
G	404	"That is innogh in Nwe ȝer, / hit / nedes no more",	H	V Z
G	405	Quoth the gome in the grene / to / Gawan the hende;	P	N D A
G	406	"Ȝif I telle trwly, / quen I the / tape haue	Q H H	N V
G	407	And thou me smothely hatȝ smyten, / smartly I the teche	/	Z H H V
G	408	Of my hous and my home / and myn / owen nome,	C D	A N
G	409	Then may thou frayst my fare / and / forwardeȝ holde;	C	N V
G	410	And if I spende no speche, / thenne / spedeȝ thou the better,	Z	V H D Z
G	411	For thou may leng in thy londe / and / layt no fyrre-	C	V D N
G	417	The grene knyȝt vpon grounde / graythely hym dresses,	/	Z H V
G	418	A littel lut with the hede, / the / lere he discouereȝ,	H	N H V
G	419	His longe louelych lokkeȝ / he / layd ouer his croun,	H	V P D N
G	420	Let the naked nec / to the / note schewe.	P D	N V
G	421	Gauan gripped to his ax, / and / gedereȝ hit on hyȝt,	C	V H Z
G	422	The kay fot on the folde / he / before sette,	H	Z V
G	423	Let him doun lyȝtly / lyȝt on the naked,	/	V P D N(A)
G	424	That the scharp of the schalk / schyndered the bones,	/	V D N
G	425	And schrank thurȝ the schyire grece, / and / schade hit in twynne,	C	V H P A
G	426	That the bit of the broun stel / bot on the grounde.	/	V P D N
G	427	The fayre hede fro the halce / hit to the erthe,	/	V P D N
G	428	That fele hit foyned wyth her fete, / there hit / forth roled;	Q H	Z V
G	429	The blod brayd fro the body, / that / blykked on the grene;	that	V P D N
G	430	And nawther faltered ne fel / the / freke neuer the helder,	D	N Z D Z
G	431	Bot stythly he start / forth vpon / styf schonkes,	Z P	A N
G	432	And runyschly he raȝt / out, there as / renkkeȝ stoden,	Z Q C	N V
G	433	Laȝt to his lufly hed, / and / lyft hit vp sone;	C	V H P Z
G	434	And sythen boȝeȝ to his blonk, / the / brydel he cachcheȝ,	C	N H V
G	435	Steppeȝ into stelbawe / and / strydeȝ alofte,	/	V Z
G	436	And his hede by the here / in his / honde haldeȝ;	P D	N V
G	437	And as sadly the segge / hym in his / sadel sette	H P D	N V
G	438	As non vnhap had hym ayled, / thaȝ / hedleȝ he were	C	A H be
G	444	For the hede in his honde / he / haldeȝ vp euen,	H	V Z Z
G	445	Toward the derrest on the dece / he / dresseȝ the face,	H	V D N

G	446	And hit lyfte vp the yȝe-lyddez / and / loked ful brode,	C	V Z Z
G	447	And meled thus much with his muthe, / as ȝe / may now here:	C H	X Z V
G	448	"Loke, Gawan, thou be graythe / to / go as thou hettez,	to	V C H V
G	449	And layte as lelly / til thou me, / lude, fynde,	C H H	N V
G	450	As thou hatz hette in this halle, / herande thise knyȝtes;	/	G D N
G	451	To the grene chapel thou chose, / I / charge the, to fotte	H	V H to V
G	452	Such a dunt as thou hatz dalt-/ disserued thou habbez	/	E H V
G	453	To be ȝederly ȝolden / on / Nw ȝeres morn.	P	A N N
G	454	The knyȝt of the grene chapel / men / knowen me mony;	X	V H H
G	455	Forthi me for to fynde if thou fraystez, / faylez thou neuer.	/	V H Z
G	456	Therfore com, other recreaunt / be / calde the behoues."	be	E H X
G	457	With a runisch rout / the / raynez he tornez,	D	N H V
G	458	Halled out at the hal dor, / his / hed in his hande,	D	N P D N
G	459	That the fyr of the flynt flaȝe / fro / fole houes.	P	N N
G	460	To quat kyth he becom / knwe non there,	/	V not Z
G	461	Neuer more then thay wyste / from / quethen he watz wonnen.	P	Q H be E
G	467	Thaȝ Arther the hende kyng / at / hert hade wonder,	P	N V N
G	468	He let no semblaunt be sene, / bot / sayde ful hyȝe	C	V Z Z
G	469	To the comlych quene / wyth / cortays speche,	P	A N
G	470	"Dere dame, to-day / demay yow neuer;	/	V H Z
G	471	Wel bycommes such craft / vpon / Cristmasse,	P	N
G	472	Laykyng of enterludez, / to / laȝe and to syng,	to	V C to V
G	473	Among thise kynde caroles / of / knyȝtez and ladyez.	P	N C N
G	474	Neuer the lece to my mete / I / may me wel dres,	H	X H Z V
G	475	For I haf sen a selly, / I / may not forsake."	H	X not V
G	476	He glent vpon Sir Gawen, / and / gaynly he sayde,	C	Z H V
G	477	"Now, sir, heng vp thyn ax, / that hatz / innogh hewen";	that have	Z E
G	478	And hit watz don abof the dece / on / doser to henge,	P	N to V
G	479	Ther alle men for meruayl / myȝt on hit loke,	/	X P H V
G	480	And bi trwe tytel / therof to / telle the wonder.	Z to	V D N
G	481	Thenne thay boȝed to a borde / thise / burnes togeder,	D	N Z
G	482	The kyng and the gode knyȝt, / and / kene men hem serued	C	A N H V
G	483	Of alle dayntyez double, / as / derrest myȝt falle;	C	A X V
G	484	Wyth alle maner of mete / and / mynstralcie bothe,	C	N Z
G	485	Wyth wele walt thday, / til / worthed an ende	C	V D N
G	491	THIS hanselle hatz Arthur / of / auenturus on fyrst	P	N Z
G	492	In ȝonge ȝer, for he ȝerned / ȝelpyng to here.	/	N to V
G	493	Thaȝ hym wordez were wane / when thay to / sete wenten,	C H to	V V
G	494	Now ar thay stoken of sturne werk, / stafful her hond.	/	A D N
G	495	Gawan watz glad to begynne / those / gomnez in halle,	D	N P N
G	496	Bot thaȝ the ende be heuy / haf ȝe no wonder;	/	V H D N
G	497	For thaȝ men ben mery in mynde / quen thay han / mayn drynk,	C H have	A N
G	498	A ȝere ȝernes ful ȝerne, / and / ȝeldez neuer lyke,	C	V Z N(A)
G	499	The forme to the fynisment / foldez ful selden.	/	V Z Z
G	500	Forthi this ȝol ouerȝede, / and the / ȝere after,	C D	N P
G	501	And vche sesoun serlepes / sued after other:	/	V P H
G	502	After Crystenmasse com / the / crabbed lentoun,	D	A N
G	503	That fraystez flesch wyth the fysche / and / fode more symple;	C	N Z A
G	504	Bot thenne the weder of the worlde / wyth / wynter hit threpez,	P	N H V
G	505	Colde clengez / adoun, / cloudez vplyften,	Z	N V
G	506	Schyre schedez the rayn / in / schowrez ful warme,	P	N Z A
G	507	Fallez vpon fayre flat, / flowrez there schewen,	/	N Z V
G	508	Bothe groundez and the greuez / grene ar her wedez,	/	A be D N
G	509	Bryddez busken to bylde, / and / bremlych syngen	C	Z V
G	510	For solace of the softe somer / that / sues therafter	that	V Z
G	516	After the sesoun of somer / wyth the / soft wyndez	P D	A N
G	517	Quen Zeferus syflez hymself / on / sedez and erbez,	P	N C N
G	518	Wela wynne is the wort / that / waxes theroute,	that	V Z
G	519	When the donkande dewe / dropez of the leuez,	/	N P D N
G	520	To bide a blysful blusch / of the / bryȝt sunne.	P D	A N
G	521	Bot then hyȝes heruest, / and / hardenes hym sone,	C	V H Z
G	522	Warnez hym for the wynter / to / wax ful rype;	to	V Z A
G	523	He dryues wyth droȝt / the / dust for to ryse,	D	N for to V
G	524	Fro the face of the folde / to / flyȝe ful hyȝe;	to	V Z Z
G	525	Wrothe wynde of the welkyn / wrastelez with the sunne,	/	V P D N
G	526	The leuez lancen fro the lynde / and / lyȝten on the grounde,	C	V P D N
G	527	And al grayes the gres / that / grene watz ere;	that	A be Z
G	528	Thenne al rypez and rotez / that / ros vpon fyrst,	that	V Z
G	529	And thus ȝirnez the ȝere / in / ȝisterdayez mony,	P	N A
G	530	And wynter wyndez / aȝayn, as the / worlde askez,	Z C D	N A
G	536	Ȝet quyl Al-hal-day / with / Arther he lenges;	P	N H V

G	537	And he made a fare on that fest / for the / frekez sake,	P D	N N
G	538	With much reuel and ryche / of the / Rounde Table.	P D	A N
G	539	Kny3tez ful cortays / and / comlych ladies	C	A N
G	540	Al for luf of that lede / in / longynge thay were,	P	G H be
G	541	Bot neuer the lece ne the later / thay / neuened bot merthe:	H	V Z N
G	542	Mony ioylez for that ientyle / iapez ther maden.	/	N Z V
G	543	For aftter mete with mournyng / he / melez to his eme,	H	V P D N
G	544	And spekez of his passage, / and / pertly he sayde,	C	Z H V
G	545	Now, lege lorde of my lyf, / leue I yow ask;	/	N H H V
G	546	3e knowe the cost of this cace, / kepe I no more	/	V H Z
G	547	To telle yow tenez / therof / neuer bot trifel;	Z	Z Z N
G	548	Bot I am boun to the bur / barely to-morne	/	Z Z
G	549	To sech the gome of the grene, / as / God wyl me wysse."	C	N X H V
G	550	Thenne the best of the bur3 / bo3ed togeder,	/	V Z
G	551	Aywan, and Errik, / and / other ful mony,	C	H A A
G	552	Sir Doddinaual de Sauage, / the / duk of Clarence,	D	N P N
G	553	Launcelot, and Lyonel, / and / Lucan the gode,	C	N D A
G	554	Sir Boos, and Sir Byduer, / big men bothe,	/	A N Z
G	555	And mony other menskful, / with / Mador de la Port.	P	N P D N
G	556	Alle this compayny of court com / the / kyng nerre	D	N Z
G	557	For to counseyl the kny3t, / with / care at her hert.	P	N P D N
G	558	There watz much derue doel / driuen in the sale	/	E P D N
G	559	That so worthé as Wawan / schulde / wende on that ernde,	X	V P D N
G	560	To dry3e a delful dynt, / and / dele no more	C	V Z
G	566	He dowellez ther al that day, / and / dressez on the morn,	C	V P D N
G	567	Askez erly hys armez, / and / alle were thay bro3t.	C	H be H E
G	568	Fyrst a tulé tapit / ty3t ouer the flet,	/	E P D N
G	569	And miche watz the gyld gere / that / glent theralofte;	that	V Z
G	570	The stif mon steppez / theron, and the / stel hondelez,	Z C D	N V
G	571	Dubbed in a dublet / of a / dere tars,	P D	A N
G	572	And sythen a crafty capados, / closed aloft,	/	V Z
G	573	That wyth a bry3t blaunner / was / bounden withinne.	be	E Z
G	574	Thenne set thay the sabatounz / vpon the / segge fotez,	P D	N N
G	575	His legez lapped in stel / with / luflych greuez,	P	A N
G	576	With polaynez piched / therto, / policed ful clene,	Z	E Z A
G	577	Aboute his knez knaged / wyth / knotez of golde;	P	N P N
G	578	Queme quyssewes / then, that / coyntlych closed	Z that	Z V
G	579	His thik thrawen thy3ez, / with / thwonges to tachched;	P	N to V
G	580	And sythen the brawden bryné / of / bry3t stel ryngez	P	A N N
G	581	Vmbeweued that wy3 / vpon / wlonk stuffe,	P	A N
G	582	And wel bornyst brace / vpon his / bothe armes,	P D	A N
G	583	With gode cowters and gay, / and / glouez of plate,	C	N P N
G	584	And alle the godlych gere / that hym / gayn schulde	that H	V X
G	590	When he watz hasped in armes, / his / harnays watz ryche:	D	N be A
G	591	The lest lachet ouer loupe / lemed of golde.	/	V P N
G	592	So harnayst as he / watz he / herknez his masse,	be H	V D N
G	593	Offred and honoured / at the / he3e auter.	P D	A N
G	594	Sythen he comez to the kyng / and to his / cort-ferez,	C P D	N N
G	595	Lachez lufly his leue / at / lordez and ladyez;	P	N C N
G	596	And thay hym kyst and conueyed, / bikende hym to Kryst.	/	V H P N
G	597	Bi that watz Gryngolet grayth, / and / gurde with a sadel	C	E P D N
G	598	That glemed ful gayly / with mony / golde frenges,	P D	A N
G	599	Ayquere naylet ful nwe, / for that / note ryched;	P D	N V
G	600	The brydel barred / aboute, with / bry3t golde bounden;	Z P	A N E
G	601	The apparayl of the payttrure / and of the / proude skyrtez,	C P D	A N
G	602	The cropore and the couertor, / acorded wyth the arsounez;	/	V P D N
G	603	And al watz rayled on red / ryche golde naylez,	/	A A N
G	604	That al glytered and glent / as / glem of the sunne.	P	N P D N
G	605	Thenne hentes he the helme, / and / hastily hit kysses,	C	Z H V
G	606	That watz stapled stifly, / and / stoffed wythinne.	C	E Z
G	607	Hit watz hy3e on his hede, / hasped bihynde,	/	E Z
G	608	Wyth a ly3tly vrysoun / ouer the / auentayle,	P D	N
G	609	Enbrawden and bounden / wyth the / best gemmez	P D	A N
G	610	On brode sylkyn borde, / and / bryddez on semez,	C	N P N
G	611	As papiayez paynted / peruyng bitwene,	/	N P
G	612	Tortors and trulofez / entayled so thyk	/	E A A
G	613	As mony burde theraboute / had / ben seuen wynter	have be	A N
G	619	THEN thay schewed hym the schelde, / that was of / schyr goulez	that be P	A N
G	620	Wyth the pentangel depaynt / of / pure golde hwez.	P	A A N
G	621	He braydez hit by the bauderyk, / aboute the / hals kestes,	P D	N V
G	622	That bisemed the segge / semlyly fayre.	/	Z A

G	623	And quy the pentangel apendez / to that / prynce noble	P D	N A
G	624	I am in tent yow to telle, / thof / tary hyt me schulde:	C	V H H X
G	625	Hit is a syngne that Salamon / set sumquyle	/	V Z
G	626	In bytoknyng of trawthe, / bi / tytle that hit habbez,	P	N that H V
G	627	For hit is a figure that haldez / fyue poyntez,	/	A N
G	628	And vche lyne vmbelappez / and / loukez in other,	C	V P H
G	629	And ayquere hit is endelez; / and / Englych hit callen	C	N(A) H V
G	630	Oueral, as I here, / the / endeles knot.	D	A N
G	631	Forthy hit acordez to this kny3t / and to his / cler armez,	C P D	A N
G	632	For ay faythful in fyue / and sere / fyue sythez	C D	A N
G	633	Gawan watz for gode knawen, / and as / golde pured,	C P	N E
G	634	Voyded of vche vylany, / wyth / vertuez ennourned	P	N E
G	640	Fyrst he watz funden fautlez / in his / fyue wyttez,	P D	A N
G	641	And efte fayled neuer the freke / in his / fyue fyngres,	P D	A N
G	642	And alle his afyaunce vpon folde / watz in the / fyue woundez	be P D	A N
G	643	That Cryst ka3t on the croys, / as the / crede tellez;	C D	N V
G	644	And quere-so-euer thys mon / in / melly watz stad,	P	N be E
G	645	His thro tho3t watz in that, / thur3 / alle other thyngez,	P	A A N
G	646	That alle his forsnes he feng / at the / fyue joyez	P D	A N
G	647	That the hende heuen-quene / had of hir chylde;	/	V P D N
G	648	At this cause the kny3t / comlyche hade	/	Z V
G	649	In the inore half of his schelde / hir / ymage depaynted,	D	N E
G	650	That quen he blusched / therto his / belde neuer payred.	Z D	N Z V
G	651	The fyft fyue that I finde / that the / frek vsed	that D	N V
G	652	Watz fraunchyse and fela3schyp / forbe al thyng,	/	P A N
G	653	His clannes and his cortaysye / croked were neuer,	/	A be Z
G	654	And pité, that passez alle poyntez, / thyse / pure fyue	D	A N
G	655	Were harder happed / on that / hathel then on any other.	P D	N Z P D H
G	656	Now alle these fyue sythez, for sothe, / were / fetled on this kny3t,	be	E P D N
G	657	And vchone halched in other, / that non / ende hade,	that D	N V
G	658	And fyched vpon fyue poyntez, / that / fayld neuer,	that	V Z
G	659	Ne samned neuer in no syde, / ne / sundred nouther,	not	V Z
G	660	Withouten ende at any noke / I / oquere fynde,	H	Z V
G	661	Whereeuer the gomen bygan, / or / glod to an ende.	C	V P D N
G	662	Therfore on his schene schelde / schapen watz the knot	/	E be D N
G	663	Ryally wyth red golde / vpon / rede gowlez,	P	A N
G	664	That is the pure pentaungel / wyth the / peple called	P D	N V
G	670	He sperred the sted with the spurez / and / sprong on his way,	C	V P D N
G	671	So stif that the ston-fyr / stroke out therafter.	/	V Z Z
G	672	Al that se3 that semly / syked in hert,	/	V P N
G	673	And sayde sothly al same / segges til other,	/	N P H
G	674	Carande for that comly: / "Bi / Kryst, hit is scathe	P	N H be N
G	675	That thou, leude, schal be lost, / that art of / lyf noble!	that be P	N A
G	676	To fynde hys fere vpon folde, / in / fayth, is not ethe.	P	N be not A
G	677	Warloker to haf wro3t / had more / wyt bene,	have D	N E
G	678	And haf dy3t 3onder dere / a / duk to haue worthed;	D	N to V E
G	679	A lowande leder of ledez / in / londe hym wel semez,	P	N H Z V
G	680	And so had better haf ben / then / britned to no3t,	Z	E P N
G	681	Hadet wyth an aluisch mon, / for / angardez pryde.	P	A N
G	682	Who knew euer any kyng / such / counsel to take	D	N to V
G	683	As kny3tez in cauelaciounz / on / Crystmasse gomnez!"	P	N N
G	684	Wel much watz the warme water / that / waltered of y3en,	that	V P N
G	685	When that semly syre / so3t fro tho wonez	/	V P D N
G	691	Now ridez this renk / thur3 the / ryalme of Logres,	P D	N P N
G	692	Sir Gauan, on Godez halue, / tha3 hym no / gomen tho3t,	C H D	N V
G	693	Oft leudlez alone / he / lengez on ny3tez	H	V P N
G	694	Ther he fonde no3t hym byfore / the / fare that he lyked.	D	N that H V
G	695	Hade he no fere bot his fole / bi / frythez and dounez,	P	N C N
G	696	Ne no gome bot God / bi / gate wyth to karp,	P	N P to V
G	697	Til that he ne3ed ful neghe / into the / Northe Walez.	P D	A N
G	698	Alle the iles of Anglesay / on lyft / half he haldez,	P D	N H V
G	699	And farez ouer the fordez / by the / forlondez,	P D	N
G	700	Ouer at the Holy Hede, / til he / hade eft bonk	C H	V Z N
G	701	In the wyldrenesse of Wyrale; / wonde ther bot lyte	/	V Z Z A
G	702	That auther God other gome / wyth / goud hert louied.	P	A N V
G	703	And ay he frayned, as he ferde, / at / frekez that he met,	P	N that H V
G	704	If thay hade herde any karp / of a / kny3t grene,	P D	N A
G	705	In any grounde theraboute, / of the / grene chapel;	P D	A N
G	706	And al nykked hym wyth nay, / that / neuer in her lyue	that	Z P D N
G	707	Thay se3e neuer no segge / that watz of / suche hwez	that be P	A N
G	713	Mony klyf he ouerclambe / in / contrayez straunge,	P	N A

G	714	Fer floten fro his frendez / fremedly he rydez.	/	Z H V
G	715	At vche warþe oþer water / þer þe / wyʒe passed	Q D	N V
G	716	He fonde a foo hym byfore, / bot / ferly hit were,	C	A H be
G	717	And that so foule and so felle / that / feʒt hym byhode.	that	V H V
G	718	So mony meruayl bi mount / ther the / mon fyndez,	Q D	N V
G	719	Hit were to tore for to telle / of the / tenthe dole.	P D	A N
G	720	Sumwhyle wyth wormez he werrez, / and with / wolues als,	C P	N Z
G	721	Sumwhyle wyth wodwos, / that / woned in the knarrez,	that	V P D N
G	722	Bothe wyth bullez and berez, / and / borez otherquyle,	C	N Z
G	723	And etaynez, that hym anelede / of the / heʒe felle;	P D	A N
G	724	Nade he ben duʒty and dryʒe, / and / Dryʒtyn had serued,	C	N have E
G	725	Douteles he hade ben ded / and / dreped ful ofte.	C	E Z Z
G	726	For werre wrathed hym not so much / that / wynter nas wors,	that	N be A
G	727	When the colde cler water / fro the / cloudez schadde,	P D	N V
G	728	And fres er hit falle / myʒt to the / fale erthe;	X P D	A N
G	729	Ner slayn wyth the slete / he / sleped in his yrnes	H	V P D N
G	730	Mo nyʒtez then innoghe / in / naked rokkez,	P	A N
G	731	Ther as claterande fro the crest / the / colde borne rennez,	D	A N V
G	732	And henged heʒe ouer his hede / in / hard iisse-ikkles.	P	A N-N
G	733	Thus in peryl and payne / and / plytes ful harde	C	N Z A
G	734	Bi contray cayrez this knyʒt, / tyl / Krystmasse euen,	P	N N
G	740	Bi a mounte on the morne / meryly he rydes	/	Z H V
G	741	Into a forest ful dep, / that / ferly watz wylde,	that	Z be A
G	742	Hiʒe hillez on vche a halue, / and / holtwodez vnder	C	N P
G	743	Of hore okez ful hoge / a / hundreth togeder;	D	N Z
G	744	The hasel and the haʒthorne / were / harled al samen,	be	E Z Z
G	745	With roʒe raged mosse / rayled aywhere,	/	E Z
G	746	With mony bryddez vnblythe / vpon / bare twyges,	P	A N
G	747	That pitosly ther piped / for / pyne of the colde.	P	N P D N[A]
G	748	The gome vpon Gryngolet / glydez hem vnder,	/	V H P
G	749	Thurʒ mony misy and myre, / mon al hym one,	/	N Z H Z
G	750	Carande for his costes, / lest he ne / keuer schulde	C H not	V X
G	751	To se the seruyse of that syre, / that on that / self nyʒt	that P D	A N
G	752	Of a burde watz borne / oure / baret to quelle;	D	N to V
G	753	And therfore sykyng he sayde, / "I / beseche the, lorde,	H	V H N
G	754	And Mary, that is myldest / moder so dere,	/	N Z A
G	755	Of sum herber ther heʒly / I myʒt / here masse,	H X	V N
G	756	Ande thy matynez to-morne, / mekely I ask,	/	Z H V
G	757	And therto prestly I pray / my / pater and aue	D	N C N
G	763	NADE he sayned hymself, / segge, bot thrye,	/	N C N
G	764	Er he watz war in the wod / of a / won in a mote,	P D	N P D N
G	765	Abof a launde, on a lawe, / loken vnder boʒez	/	E P N
G	766	Of mony borelych bole / aboute bi the diches:	/	Z P D N
G	767	A castel the comlokest / that euer / knyʒt aʒte,	that Z	N V
G	768	Pyched on a prayere, / a / park al aboute,	D	N Z Z
G	769	With a pyked palays / pyned ful thik,	/	E Z Z
G	770	That vmbeteʒe mony tre / mo then two myle.	/	A C A N
G	771	That holde on that on syde / the / hathel auysed,	D	N V
G	772	As hit schemered and schon / thurʒ the / schyre okez;	P D	A N
G	773	Thenne hatz he hendly of his helme, / and / heʒly he thonkez	C	Z H N
G	774	Jesus and sayn Gilyan, / that / gentyle ar bothe,	that	A be Z
G	775	That cortaysly had hym kydde, / and his / cry herkened.	C D	N V
G	776	"Now bone hostel," cothe the burne, / "I / beseche yow ʒette!"	H	V H V
G	777	Thenne gerdez he to Gryngolet / with the / gilt helez,	P D	E N
G	778	And he ful chauncely hatz chosen / to the / chef gate,	P D	A N
G	779	That broʒt bremly the burne / to the / bryge ende	P D	N N
G	785	The burne bode on blonk, / that on / bonk houed	that P	N V
G	786	Of the depe double dich / that / drof to the place;	that	V P D N
G	787	The walle wod in the water / wonderly depe,	/	Z Z
G	788	Ande eft a ful huge heʒt / hit / haled vpon lofte	H	V Z
G	789	Of harde hewen ston / vp to the tablez,	/	Z P D N
G	790	Enbaned vnder the abataylment / in the / best lawe;	P D	A N
G	791	And sythen garytez ful gaye / gered bitwene,	/	E Z
G	792	Wyth mony luffych loupe / that / louked ful clene:	that	V Z Z
G	793	A better barbican that burne / blusched vpon neuer.	/	V Z Z
G	794	And innermore he behelde / that / halle ful hyʒe,	D	N Z A
G	795	Towres telded / bytwene, / trochet ful thik,	Z	E Z A
G	796	Fayre fylyolez that fyʒed, / and / ferlyly long,	C	Z A
G	797	With coroun coprounes / craftyly sleʒe.	/	Z A
G	798	Chalkwhyt chymnees / ther / ches he innoʒe	Q	V H A
G	799	Vpon bastel rouez, / that / blenked ful quyte;	that	V Z A

G	800	So mony pynakle payntet / watz / poudred ayquere,	be	E Z
G	801	Among the castel carnelez / clambred so thik,	/	E Z Z
G	802	That pared out of papure / purely hit semed.	/	Z H V
G	803	The fre freke on the fole / hit / fayr innoghe thoȝt,	H	A Z V
G	804	If he myȝt keuer to com / the / cloyster wythinne,	D	N P
G	805	To herber in that hostel / whyl / halyday lested,	C	N V
G	811	"Gode sir," quoth Gawan, / "woldez thou / go myn ernde	X H	V D N
G	812	To the heȝ lorde of this hous, / herber to craue?"	/	N to V
G	813	"Ȝe, Peter," quoth the porter, / "and / purely I trowee	C	Z H V
G	814	That ȝe be, wyȝe, welcum / to / won quyle yow lykez."	to	V C H V
G	815	Then ȝede the wyȝe ȝerne / and com / aȝayn swythe,	C V	Z Z
G	816	And folke frely / hym wyth, to / fonge the knyȝt.	H P to	V D N
G	817	Thay let doun the grete draȝt / and / derely out ȝeden,	C	Z Z V
G	818	And kneled doun on her knes / vpon the / colde erthe	P D	A N
G	819	To welcum this ilk wyȝ / as / worthy hom thoȝt;	C	A H V
G	820	Thay ȝolden hym the brode ȝate, / ȝarked vp wyde,	/	V Z Z
G	821	And he hem raysed rekenly, / and / rod ouer the brygge.	C	V P D N
G	822	Sere seggez hym sesed / by / sadel, quel he lyȝt,	P	N C H V
G	823	And sythen stabeled his stede / stif men innoȝe.	/	A N A
G	824	Knyȝtez and swyerez / comen doun thenne	/	V Z Z
G	825	For to bryng this buurne / wyth / blys into halle;	P	N P N
G	826	Quen he hef vp his helme, / ther / hiȝed innoghe	Q	V A
G	827	For to hent hit at his honde, / the / hende to seruen;	D	N(A) to V
G	828	His bronde and his blasoun / bothe thay token.	/	A H V
G	829	Then haylsed he ful hendly / tho / hathelez vchone,	D	N H
G	830	And mony proud mon ther pressed / that / prynce to honour.	D	N to V
G	831	Alle hasped in his heȝ wede / to / halle thay hym wonnen,	P	N H H V
G	832	Ther fayre fyre vpon flet / fersly brenned.	/	Z V
G	833	Thenne the lorde of the lede / loutez fro his chambre	/	V P D N
G	834	For to mete wyth menske / the / mon on the flor;	D	N P D N
G	835	He sayde, "ȝe ar welcum / to / welde as yow lykez	to	V C H V
G	836	That here is; al is yowre awen, / to / haue at yowre wylle	to	V P D N
G	842	Gawayn glyȝt on the gome / that / godly hym gret,	that	Z H V
G	843	And thuȝt hit a bolde burne / that the / burȝ aȝte,	that D	N V
G	844	A hoge hathel for the nonez, / and of / hyghe eldee;	C P	A N
G	845	Brode, bryȝt, watz his berde, / and al / beuer-hwed,	C D	N A
G	846	Sturne, stif on the strythþe / on / stalworth schonkez,	P	A N
G	847	Felle face as the fyre, / and / fre of hys speche;	C	A P D N
G	848	And wel hym semed, for sothe, / as the / segge thuȝt,	C D	N V
G	849	To lede a lortschyp in lee / of / leudez ful gode.	P	N Z A
G	850	The lorde hym charred to a chambre, / and / chefly cumaundez	C	Z V
G	851	To delyuer hym a leude, / hym / loȝly to serue;	H	Z to V
G	852	And there were boun at his bode / burnez innoȝe,	/	N A
G	853	That broȝt hym to a bryȝt boure, / ther / beddyng watz noble,	Q	N be A
G	854	Of cortynes of clene sylk / wyth / cler golde hemmez,	P	A A N
G	855	And couertorez ful curious / with / comlych panez	P	N(A) N
G	856	Of bryȝt blaunner / aboue, / enbrawded bisydez,	Z	E Z
G	857	Rudelez rennande on ropez, / red golde ryngez,	/	A A N
G	858	Tapitez tyȝt to the woȝe / of / tuly and tars,	P	N(A) C N
G	859	And vnder fete, on the flet, / of / folȝande sute.	P	A(G) N
G	860	Ther he watz dispoyled, / wyth / spechez of myerthe,	P	N P N
G	861	The burn of his bruny / and of his / bryȝt wedez.	C P D	A N
G	862	Ryche robes ful rad / renkkez hym broȝten,	/	N H V
G	863	For to charge, and to chaunge, / and / chose of the best.	C	V P D A
G	864	Sone as he on hent, / and / happed therinne,	C	V Z
G	865	That sete on hym semly / wyth / saylande skyrtez,	P	G N
G	866	The ver by his uisage / verayly hit semed	/	Z H V
G	867	Welneȝ to vche hathel, / alle on hwes	/	N(A) P N
G	868	Lowande and lufly / alle his / lymmez vnder,	Z D	N P
G	869	That a comloker knyȝt / neuer / Kryst made	Z	N V
G	875	A cheyer byfore the chemné, / ther / charcole brenned,	Q	N V
G	876	Watz graythed for Sir Gawan / graythely with clothez,	/	Z P N
G	877	Whyssynes vpon queldepoyntes / that / koynt wer bothe;	that	A be A(N)
G	878	And thenne a meré mantyle / watz on that / mon cast	be P D	N E
G	879	Of a broun bleeaunt, / enbrauded ful ryche	/	E Z A
G	880	And fayre furred / wythinne with / fellez of the best,	Z P	N P D A
G	881	Alle of ermyn in erde, / his / hode of the same;	D	N P D A
G	882	And he sete in that settel / semlych ryche,	/	Z A
G	883	And achaufed hym chefly, / and thenne his / cher mended.	C Z D	N V
G	884	Sone watz telded vp a tabil / on / trestez ful fayre,	P	N Z A
G	885	Clad wyth a clene clothe / that / cler quyt schewed,	that	A A V

G	886	Sanap, and salure, / and / syluerin sponez.	C	A N
G	887	The wyȝe wesche at his wylle, / and / went to his mete.	C	V P D N
G	888	Seggez hym serued / semly innoȝe	/	Z A
G	889	Wyth sere sewes and sete, / sesounde of the best.	/	E P D A
G	890	Double-felde, as hit fallez, / and / fele kyn fischez,	C	A N N
G	891	Summe baken in bred, / summe / brad on the gledez,	D	E P D N
G	892	Summe sothen, summe in sewe / sauered with spyces,	/	E P N
G	893	And ay sawes so sleȝe / that the / segge lyked.	that D	N V
G	894	The freke calde hit a fest / ful / frely and ofte	Z	Z C Z
G	895	Ful hendely, quen alle the hatheles / rehayted hym at onez,	/	V H Z
G	901	Thenne watz spyed and spured / vpon / spare wyse	P	Z Z
G	902	Bi preué poyntez of that prynce, / put to hymseluen,	/	V P H self
G	903	That he beknew cortaysly / of the / court that he were	P D	N that H be
G	904	That athel Arthure the hende / haldez hym one,	/	V H Z
G	905	That is the ryche ryal kyng / of the / Rounde Table,	P D	A N
G	906	And hit watz Wawen hymself / that in that / won syttez,	that P D	N V
G	907	Comen to that Krystmasse, / as / case hym then lymped.	C	N H Z V
G	908	When the lorde hade lerned / that he the / leude hade,	that H D	N V
G	909	Loude laȝed / he therat, so / lef hit hym thoȝt,	H Z Z	A H H V
G	910	And alle the men in that mote / maden much joye	/	V A N
G	911	To apere in his presense / prestly that tyme,	/	Z D N
G	912	That alle prys and prowes / and / pured thewes	C	E N
G	913	Apendes to hys persoun, / and / praysed is euer;	C	E be Z
G	914	Byfore alle men vpon molde / his / mensk is the most.	D	N be D A
G	915	Vch segge ful softly / sayde to his fere:	/	V P D N
G	916	"Now schal we semlych se / sleȝtez of thewez	/	N P N
G	917	And the teccheles termes / of / talkyng noble,	P	G A
G	918	Wich spede is in speche / vnspurd may we lerne,	/	A X H V
G	919	Syn we haf fonged that fyne / fader of nurture.	/	N P N
G	920	God hatz geuen vus his grace, / godly for sothe,	/	Z Z
G	921	That such a gest as Gawan / grauntez vus to haue,	/	V H to V
G	922	When burnez blythe / of his / burthe schal sitte	P D	N X V
G	928	Bi that the diner watz done / and the / dere vp	C D	N(A) Z
G	929	Hit watz neȝ at the niȝt / neȝed the tyme.	/	V D N
G	930	Chaplaynez to the chapeles / chosen the gate,	/	V D N
G	931	Rungen ful rychely, / ryȝt as thay schulden,	/	Z C H X
G	932	To the hersum euensong / of the / hyȝe tyde.	P D	A N
G	933	The lorde loutes / therto, and the / lady als,	Z C D	N Z
G	934	Into a cumly closet / coyntly ho entrez,	/	Z H V
G	935	Gawan glydez ful gay / and / gos theder sone;	C	V Z Z
G	936	The lorde laches hym by the lappe / and / ledez hym to sytte,	C	V H to V
G	937	And couthly hym knowez / and / callez hym his nome,	C	V H D N
G	938	And sayde he watz the welcomest / wyȝe of the worlde;	/	N P D N
G	939	And he hym thonkked throly, / and / halched other,	C H	V H
G	940	And seten soberly samen / the / seruise quyle.	D	N N
G	941	Thenne lyst the lady / to / loke on the knyȝt,	to	V P D N
G	942	Thenne com ho of hir closet / with mony / cler burdez.	P D	A N
G	943	Ho watz the fayrest in felle, / of / flesche and of lyre,	P	N C P N
G	944	And of compas and colour / and / costes, of alle other,	C	N P A H
G	945	And wener then Wenore, / as the / wyȝe thoȝt.	C D	N V
G	946	Ho ches thurȝe the chaunsel / to / rycheche that hende.	to	V D N(A)
G	947	An other lady hir lad / bi the / lyft honde,	P D	A N
G	948	That watz alder then ho, / an / auncian hit semed,	D	N(A) H V
G	949	And heȝly honowred / with / hatheleȝ aboute.	P	N Z
G	950	Bot vnlyke on to loke / tho / ladyes were,	D	N be
G	951	For if the ȝonge watz ȝep, / ȝolȝe watz that other;	/	A be D H
G	952	Riche red / on that on / rayled ayquere,	P that P	E Z
G	953	Rugh ronkled chekez / that / other on rolled;	that	H P V
G	954	Kerchofes of that on, / wyth mony / cler perlez,	P D	A N
G	955	Hir brest and hir bryȝt throte / bare displayed,	/	A V
G	956	Schon schyrer then snawe / that / schedez on hillez;	that	V P N
G	957	That other wyth a gorger / watz / gered ouer the swyre,	be	E P D N
G	958	Chymbled ouer hir blake chyn / with / chalkquyte vayles,	P	A N
G	959	Hir frount folden in sylk, / enfoubled ayquere,	/	E Z
G	960	Toreted and treleted / with / tryflez aboute,	P	N Z
G	961	That noȝt watz bare of that burde / bot the / blake broȝes,	P D	A N
G	962	The tweyne yȝen and the nase, / the / naked lyppez,	D	A N
G	963	And those were soure to se / and / sellyly blered;	C	Z E
G	964	A mensk lady on molde / mon may hir calle,	/	N X H V
G	970	When Gawayn glyȝt on that gay, / that / graciously loked,	that	Z V
G	971	Wyth leue laȝt of the lorde / he / lent hem aȝaynes;	H	V H P

G	972	The alder he haylses, / heldande ful lowe,	/	V Z Z
G	973	The loueloker he lappez / a / lyttel in armez,	Z	Z P N
G	974	He kysses hir comlyly, / and / kny3tly he melez.	C	Z he V
G	975	Thay kallen hym of aquoyntaunce, / and he hit / quyk askez	C H H	Z V
G	976	To be her seruaunt sothly, / if / hemself lyked.	C	H self V
G	977	Thay tan hym bytwene / hem, wyth / talkyng hym leden	H P	N(V) H V
G	978	To chambre, to chemné, / and / chefly thay asken	C	Z H V
G	979	Spycez, that vnsparely men / speded hom to bryng,	/	V H to V
G	980	And the wynnelych wyne / therwith vche tyme.	/	Z Z
G	981	The lorde luflych aloft / lepez ful ofte,	/	V Z Z
G	982	Mynned merthe to be made / vpon / mony sythez,	P	A N
G	983	Hent he3ly of his hode, / and on a / spere henged,	C P D	N V
G	984	And wayned hom to wynne / the / worchip therof,	D	N Z
G	985	That most myrthe my3t meue / that / Crystenmas whyle-	D	N N
G	986	"And I schal fonde, bi my fayth, / to / fylter wyth the best	to	V P D A
G	987	Er me wont the wede, / with / help of my frendez."	P	N P D N
G	988	Thus wyth la3ande lotez / the / lorde hit tayt makez,	D	N H A V
G	989	For to glade Sir Gawayn / with / gomnez in halle	P	N P N
G	995	On the morne, as vch mon / mynez that tyme	/	V D N
G	996	That Dry3tyn for oure destyné / to / de3e watz borne,	to	V be E
G	997	Wele waxez in vche a won / in / worlde for his sake;	P	N P D N
G	998	So did hit there on that day / thur3 / dayntés mony:	P	N A
G	999	Bothe at mes and at mele / messes ful quaynt	/	N Z A
G	1000	Derf men vpon dece / drest of the best.	/	V P D A
G	1001	The olde auncian wyf / he3est ho syttez,	/	Z H V
G	1002	The lorde lufly / her by / lent, as I trowe;	H P	V C H V
G	1003	Gawan and the gay burde / togeder thay seten,	/	Z H V
G	1004	Euen inmyddez, as the messe / metely come,	/	Z V
G	1005	And sythen thur3 al the sale / as hem / best semed.	C H	Z V
G	1006	Bi vche grome at his degré / graythely watz serued	/	Z be E
G	1007	Ther watz mete, ther watz myrthe, / ther watz / much ioye,	Z be	A N
G	1008	That for to telle therof / hit me / tene were,	H H	N be
G	1009	And to poynte hit 3et I pyned / me / parauenture.	H	Z
G	1010	Bot 3et I wot that Wawen / and the / wale burde	C D	A N
G	1011	Such comfort of her compaynye / ca3ten togeder	/	V Z
G	1012	Thur3 her dere dalyaunce / of her / derne wordez,	P D	A N
G	1013	Wyth clene cortays carp / closed fro fylthe,	/	E P N
G	1014	That hor play watz passande / vche / prynce gomen,	D	N N
G	1020	Much dut watz ther dryuen / that / day and that other,	D	N C D H
G	1021	And the thryd as thro / thronge in therafter;	/	V Z Z
G	1022	The ioye of sayn Jonez day / watz / gentyle to here,	be	A to V
G	1023	And watz the last of the layk, / leudez ther tho3ten.	/	N Z V
G	1024	Ther wer gestes to go / vpon the / gray morne,	P D	A N
G	1025	Forthy wonderly thay woke, / and the / wyn dronken,	C D	N V
G	1026	Daunsed ful dre3ly / wyth / dere carolez.	P	A N
G	1027	At the last, when hit watz late, / thay / lachen her leue,	H	V H N
G	1028	Vchon to wende on his way / that watz / wy3e stronge.	that be	N A
G	1029	Gawan gef hym god day, / the / godmon hym lachchez,	D	N H V
G	1030	Ledes hym to his awen chambre, / the / chymné by3e,	D	N P
G	1031	And there he dra3ez hym on dry3e, / and / derely hym thonkkez	C	Z H V
G	1032	Of the wynne worschip / that he hym / wayued hade,	that H H	E have
G	1033	As to honour his hous / on that / hy3e tyde,	P D	A N
G	1034	And enbelyse his bur3 / with his / bele chere:	P D	A N
G	1035	"Iwysse sir, quyl I leue, / me / worthez the better	H	V D A
G	1036	That Gawayn hatz ben my gest / at / Goddez awen fest."	P	N A N
G	1037	"Grant merci, sir," quoth Gawayn, / "in / god fayth hit is yowrez,	P	A N H be H
G	1038	Al the honour is your awen- / the / he3e kyng yow 3elde!	D	A N H V
G	1039	And I am wy3e at your wylle / to / worch youre hest,	to	V H N
G	1040	As I am halden / therto, in / hy3e and in lo3e,	Z Z	Z C Z
G	1046	Then frayned the freke / ful / fayre at himseluen	Z	Z P H self
G	1047	Quat derue dede had hym dryuen / at that / dere tyme	P D	A N
G	1048	So kenly fro the kyngez kourt / to / kayre al his one,	to	V Z Z
G	1049	Er the halidayez holly / were / halet out of toun.	be	V P P N
G	1050	"For sothe, sir," quoth the segge, / "3e / sayn bot the trawthe,	H	V P D N
G	1051	A he3e ernde and a hasty / me / hade fro tho wonez,	H	V P D N
G	1052	For I am sumned myselfe / to / sech to a place,	to	V P D N
G	1053	I ne wot in worlde whederwarde / to / wende hit to fynde.	to	V H to V
G	1054	I nolde bot if I hit negh / my3t on / Nw 3eres morne	X P	A N N
G	1055	For alle the londe inwyth Logres, / so me oure / lorde help!	C H D	N V
G	1056	Forthy, sir, this enquest / I / require yow here,	H	V H Z
G	1057	That 3e me telle with trawthe / if euer 3e / tale herde	C Z H	N V

G	1058	Of the grene chapel, / quere hit on / grounde stondez,	Q H P	N V
G	1059	And of the knyȝt that hit kepes, / of / colour of grene.	P	N P N
G	1060	Ther watz stabled bi statut / a / steuen vus bytwene	D	N H P
G	1061	To mete that mon at that mere, / ȝif I / myȝt last;	C H	X V
G	1062	And of that ilk Nw ȝere bot neked / now wontez,	/	Z V
G	1063	And I wolde loke on that lede, / if God me / let wolde,	C N H	V X
G	1064	Gladloker, bi Goddez sun, / then any / god welde!	Z D	N V
G	1065	Forthi, iwysse, bi ȝowre wylle, / wende me bihoues,	/	V H V
G	1066	Naf I now to busy / bot / bare thre dayez,	P	Z A N
G	1067	And me als fayn to falle feye / as / fayly of myyn ernde."	C	V P D N
G	1068	Thenne laȝande quoth the lorde, / "Now / leng the byhoues,	Z	V H V
G	1069	For I schal teche yow to that terme / bi the / tymez ende,	P D	N N
G	1070	The grene chapayle vpon grounde / greue yow no more;	/	V H Z
G	1071	Bot ȝe schal be in yowre bed, / burne, at thyn ese,	/	N P D N
G	1072	Quyle forth dayez, and ferk / on the / fyrst of the ȝere,	P D	N P D N
G	1073	And cum to that merk at mydmorn, / to / make quat yow likez	to	V Q H V
G	1079	Thenne watz Gawan ful glad, / and / gomenly he laȝed:	C	Z H V
G	1080	"Now I thonk yow thryuandely / thurȝ alle other thynge,	/	P A A N
G	1081	Now acheued is my chaunce, / I / schal at your wylle	H	X P D N
G	1082	Dowelle, and ellez / do quat ȝe demen."	/	V Q H V
G	1083	Thenne sesed hym the syre / and / set hym bysyde,	C	V H P
G	1084	Let the ladiez be fette / to / lyke hem the better.	to	V H D A
G	1085	Ther watz seme solace / by / hemself stille;	P	H self A
G	1086	The lorde let for luf / lotez so myry,	/	N Z A
G	1087	As wyȝ that wolde of his wyte, / ne / wyst quat he myȝt.	not	V Q H X
G	1088	Thenne he carped to the knyȝt, / criande loude,	/	G Z
G	1089	"ȝe han demed to do / the / dede that I bidde;	D	N that H V
G	1090	Wyl ȝe halde this hes / here at thys onez?"	/	Z Z
G	1091	"ȝe, sir, for sothe," sayd / the / segge trwe,	D	N A
G	1092	"Whyl I byde in yowre borȝe, / be / bayn to ȝowre hest."	be	A P D N
G	1093	"For ȝe haf trauayled," quoth the tulk, / "towen fro ferre,	/	E P Z
G	1094	And sythen waked me wyth, / ȝe arn not / wel waryst	H be not	Z E
G	1095	Nauther of sostnaunce ne of slepe, / sothly I knowe;	/	Z H V
G	1096	ȝe schal lenge in your lofte, / and / lyȝe in your ese	C	V P D N
G	1097	To-morn quyle the messequyle, / and to / mete wende	C P	N V
G	1098	When ȝe wyl, wyth my wyf, / that / wyth yow schal sitte	that	P H X V
G	1099	And comfort yow with compayny, / til I to / cort torne;	C H P	N V
G	1105	"ȝet firre," quoth the freke, / "a / forwarde we make:	D	N H V
G	1106	Quat-so-euer I wynne in the wod / hit / worthez to yourez,	H	V P H
G	1107	And quat chek so ȝe acheue / chaunge me therforne.	/	V H Z
G	1108	Swete, swap / we so, / sware with trawthe,	H Z	V P N
G	1109	Quether, leude, so lymp, / lere other better."	/	A A A
G	1110	"Bi God," quoth Gawayn the gode, / "I / grant thertylle,	H	V Z
G	1111	And that yow lyst for to layke, / lef hit me thynkes."	/	A H H V
G	1112	"Who bryngez vus this beuerage, / this / bargayn is maked":	D	N be E
G	1113	So sayde the lorde of that lede; / thay / laȝed vchone,	H	V H
G	1114	Thay dronken and daylyeden / and / dalten vntyȝtel,	C	V N
G	1115	Thise lordez and ladyez, / quyle that hem lyked;	/	C H H V
G	1116	And sythen with Frenkysch fare / and / fele fayre lotez	C	A A N
G	1117	Thay stoden and stemed / and / stylly speken,	C	Z V
G	1118	Kysten ful comlyly / and / kaȝten her leue.	C	V D N
G	1119	With mony leude ful lyȝt / and / lemande torches	C	V N
G	1120	Vche burne to his bed / watz / broȝt at the laste,	be	E Z
G	1126	Ful ely bifore the day / the / folk vprysen,	D	N V
G	1127	Gestes that go / wolde hor / gromez thay calden,	X D	N H V
G	1128	And thay busken vp bilyue / blonkkez to sadel,	/	N to V
G	1129	Tyffen her takles, / trussen her males,	/	V D N
G	1130	Richen hem the rychest, / to / ryde alle arayde,	to	V Z E
G	1131	Lepen vp lyȝtly, / lachen her brydeles,	/	V D N
G	1132	Vche wyȝe on his way / ther hym / wel lyked.	Q H	Z V
G	1133	The leue lorde of the londe / watz / not the last	be	not D A
G	1134	Arayed for the rydyng, / with / renkkez ful mony;	P	N Z A
G	1135	Ete a sop hastyly, / when he hade / herde masse,	C H have	E N
G	1136	With bugle to bent-felde / he / buskez bylyue.	H	V Z
G	1137	By that any daylyȝt / lemed vpon erthe	/	V P N
G	1138	He with his hatheles on hyȝe / horssses weren.	/	N be
G	1139	Thenne thise cacheres that couthe / cowpled hor houndez,	/	V D N
G	1140	Vnclosed the kenel dore / and / calde hem theroute,	C	V H Z
G	1141	Blwe bygly in buglez / thre / bare mote;	D	A N
G	1142	Braches bayed / therfore and / breme noyse maked;	C C	A N V
G	1143	And thay chastysed and charred / on / chasyng that went,	P	N(G) H V

G	1144	A hundreth of hunteres, / as I haf / herde telle,	C H have	E N
G	1150	At the fyrst quethe of the quest / quaked the wylde;	/	V D N(A)
G	1151	Der drof in the dale, / doted for drede,	/	E P N
G	1152	Hiȝed to the hyȝe, / bot / heterly thay were	C	Z H be
G	1153	Restayed with the stablye, / that / stoutly ascryed.	that	Z V
G	1154	Thay let the herttez haf the gate, / with the / hyȝe hedes,	P D	A N
G	1155	The breme bukkez / also with hor / brode paumez;	Z P D	A N
G	1156	For the fre lorde hade defende / in / fermysoun tyme	P	N N
G	1157	That ther schulde no mon meue / to the / male dere.	P D	A N
G	1158	The hindez were halden / in with / hay! and war!	P P	I C I
G	1159	The does dryuen with gret dyn / to the / depe sladez;	P D	A N
G	1160	Ther myȝt mon se, as thay slypte, / slentyng of arwes-	/	N(G) P N
G	1161	At vche wende vnder wande / wapped a flone-	/	V D N
G	1162	That bigly bote on the broun / with ful / brode hedez.	P Z	A N
G	1163	What! thay brayen, and bleden, / bi / bonkkez thay deȝen,	P	N H V
G	1164	And ay rachches in a res / radly hem folȝes,	/	Z H V
G	1165	Hunterez wyth hyȝe horne / hasted hem after	/	V H P
G	1166	Wyth such a crakkande kry / as / klyffes haden brusten.	C	N have E
G	1167	What wylde so atwaped / wyȝes that schotten	/	N that V
G	1168	Watz al toraced and rent / at the / resayt,	P D	N
G	1169	Bi thay were tened at the hyȝe / and / taysed to the wattrez;	C	E P D N
G	1170	The ledez were so lerned / at the / loȝe trysteres,	P D	A N
G	1171	And the grehoundez so grete, / that / geten hem bylyue	that	V H Z
G	1172	And hem tofylched, as fast / as / frekez myȝt loke,	C	N X V
G	1178	Thus laykez this lorde / by / lynde-wodez euez,	P	N-N N
G	1179	And Gawayn the god mon / in / gay bed lygez,	P	A N V
G	1180	Lurkkez quyl the daylyȝt / lemed on the wowes,	/	V P D N
G	1181	Vnder couertour ful clere, / cortyned aboute;	/	E Z
G	1182	And as in slomeryng he slode, / sleȝly he herde	/	Z H V
G	1183	A littel dyn at his dor, / and / dernly vpon;	/	Z Z
G	1184	And he heuez vp his hed / out of the clothes,	/	P P D N
G	1185	A corner of the cortyn / he / caȝt vp a lyttel,	H	V Z Z
G	1186	And waytez warly / thiderwarde quat hit be myȝt.	/	Z Q H be X
G	1187	Hit watz the ladi, / loflyest to beholde,	/	A to V
G	1188	That droȝ the dor / after hir ful / dernly and stylle,	P H Z	Z C Z
G	1189	And boȝed towarde the bed; / and the / burne schamed,	C D	N V
G	1190	And layde hym doun lystyly, / and / let as he slepte;	C	V C H V
G	1191	And ho stepped stilly / and / stel to his bedde,	C	V P D N
G	1192	Kest vp the cortyn / and / creped withinne,	C	V Z
G	1193	And set hir ful softly / on the / bed-syde,	P D	N N
G	1194	And lenged there selly longe / to / loke quen he wakened.	to	V C H V
G	1195	The lede lay lurked / a ful / longe quyle,	D Z	A N
G	1196	Compast in his concience / to quat that / cace myȝt	P Q that	N X
G	1197	Meue other amount- / to / meruayle hym thoȝt,	P	N H V
G	1198	Bot ȝet he sayde in hymself, / "More / semly hit were	Z	A H be
G	1199	To aspye wyth my spelle / in / space quat ho wolde."	Z	Z H H X
G	1200	Then he wakenede, and wroth, / and to hir / warde torned,	C P H	Z V
G	1201	And vnlouked his yȝe-lyddez, / and / let as hym wondered,	C	V C H V
G	1202	And sayned hym, as bi his saȝe / the / sauer to worthe,	D	A to V
G	1208	"God moroun, Sir Gawayn," / sayde that / gay lady,	V D	A N
G	1209	"Ȝe ar a sleper vnslyȝe, / that mon may / slyde hider;	that H X	V Z
G	1210	Now ar ȝe tan as-tyt! / Bot / true vus may schape,	C	N H X V
G	1211	I schal bynde yow in your bedde, / that / be ȝe trayst":	that	be H A
G	1212	Al laȝande the lady / lanced tho bourdez.	/	V D N
G	1213	"Goud moroun, gay," / quoth / Gawayn the blythe,	V	N D A
G	1214	"Me schal worthe at your wille, / and that me / wel lykez,	C that H	Z V
G	1215	For I ȝelde me ȝederly, / and / ȝeȝe after grace,	C	V P N
G	1216	And that is the best, be my dome, / for me / byhouez nede":	P H	V Z
G	1217	And thus he bourded aȝayn / with mony a / blythe laȝter.	P D D	A N
G	1218	"Bot wolde ȝe, lady louely, / then / leue me grante,	C	N H V
G	1219	And deprece your prysoun, / and / pray hym to ryse,	C	V H to V
G	1220	I wolde boȝe of this bed, / and / busk me better;	C	V H Z
G	1221	I schulde keuer the more comfort / to / karp yow wyth."	to	V H P
G	1222	"Nay for sothe, beau sir," / sayd that swete,	/	V D N(A)
G	1223	"Ȝe schal not rise of your bedde, / I / rych yow better,	H	V H Z
G	1224	I schal happe yow here / that / other half als,	that	A N Z
G	1225	And sythen karp wyth my knyȝt / that I / kaȝt haue;	that H	E have
G	1226	For I wene wel, iwysse, / Sir / Wowen ȝe are,	D	N H be
G	1227	That alle the worlde worchipez / quere-so ȝe ride;	/	Z H V
G	1228	Your honour, your hendelayk / is / hendely praysed	be	Z E
G	1229	With lordez, wyth ladyes, / with alle that / lyf bere.	P D D	N V

G	1230	And now ȝe ar here, iwysse, / and / we bot oure one;	C	H P D A
G	1231	My lorde and his ledez / ar on / lenthe faren,	be P	N F
G	1232	Other burnez in her bedde, / and my / burdez als,	C D	N Z
G	1233	The dor drawen and dit / with a / derf haspe;	P D	A N
G	1234	And sythen I haue in this hous / hym that / al lykez,	H that	Z V
G	1235	I schal ware my whyle wel, / quyl hit lastez,	/	C H V
G	1241	"In god fayth," quoth Gawayn, / "ȝayn hit me thynkkez,	/	N(A) H H V
G	1242	Thaȝ I be not now / he that / ȝe of speken;	H that	H P V
G	1243	To reche to such reuerence / as ȝe / reherce here	C H	V Z
G	1244	I am wyȝe vnworthy, / I / wot wel myseluen.	H	V Z H self
G	1245	Bi God, I were glad, / and yow / god thoȝt,	C H	A V
G	1246	At saȝe other at seruyce / that I / sette myȝt	that H	V X
G	1247	To the plesaunce of your prys- / hit were a / pure ioye."	H be D	A N
G	1248	"In god fayth, Sir Gawayn," / quoth the / gay lady,	V D	A N
G	1249	"The prys and the prowes / that / plesez al other,	that	V A H
G	1250	If I hit lakked other set at lyȝt, / hit were / littel daynté;	H be	A N
G	1251	Bot hit ar ladyes innoȝe / that / leuer wer nowthe	that	A be Z
G	1252	Haf the, hende, in hor holde, / as I the / habbe here,	C H H	V Z
G	1253	To daly with derely / your / daynté wordez,	D	A N
G	1254	Keuer hem comfort / and / colen her carez,	C	V D N
G	1255	Then much of the garysoun / other / golde that thay hauen.	D	N that H V
G	1256	Bot I louue that ilk lorde / that the / lyfte haldez,	that D	N V
G	1257	I haf hit holly in my honde / that I / al desyres,	that	H V
G	1263	"Madame," quoth the myry mon, / "Mary yow ȝelde,	/	N H V
G	1264	For I haf founden, in god fayth, / yowre / fraunchis nobele,	D	N A
G	1265	And other ful much of other folk / fongen bi hor dedez,	/	V P D N
G	1266	Bot the daynté that thay delen, / for my / disert nys euen,	P D	N be A
G	1267	Hit is the worchyp of yourself, / that noȝt bot / wel connez."	that not C	Z V
G	1268	"Bi Mary," quoth the menskful, / "me thynk hit an other;	/	H V H D H
G	1269	For were I worth al the wone / of / wymmen alyue,	P	N A
G	1270	And al the wele of the worlde / were in my honde,	/	be P D N
G	1271	And I schulde chepen and chose / to / cheue me a lorde,	to	V H D N
G	1272	For the costes that I haf knowen / vpon the, / knyȝt, here,	P H	N Z
G	1273	Of bewté and debonerté / and / blythe semblaunt,	C	A N
G	1274	And that I haf er herkkened / and / halde hit here trwee,	C	V H Z A
G	1275	Ther schulde no freke vpon folde / bifore yow be chosen."	/	C H be E
G	1276	"Iwysse, worthy," quoth the wyȝe, / "ȝe haf / waled wel better,	H have	E Z Z
G	1277	Bot I am proude of the prys / that ȝe / put on me,	that H	V P H
G	1278	And, soberly your seruaunt, / my / souerayn I holde yow,	D	N H V H
G	1279	And yowre knyȝt I becom, / and / Kryst yow forȝelde."	C	N H V
G	1280	Thus thay meled of muchquat / til / mydmorn paste,	C	N V
G	1281	And ay the lady let lyk / as hym / loued mych;	C H	V Z
G	1282	The freke ferde with defence, / and / feted ful fayre-	C	V Z Z
G	1283	"Thaȝ I were burde bryȝtest", / the / burde in mynde hade.	C	N P N V
G	1284	The lasse luf in his lode / for / lur that he soȝt	P	N that H V
G	1290	Thenne ho gef hym god day, / and wyth a / glent laȝed,	C P D	N V
G	1291	And as ho stod, ho stonyed / hym wyth ful / stor wordez:	H P Z	A N
G	1292	"Now he that spedez vche spech / this / disport ȝelde yow!	D	N V H
G	1293	Bot that ȝe be Gawan, / hit / gotz in mynde."	H	V P N
G	1294	"Querforeth" quoth the freke, / and / freschly he askez,	C	Z H V
G	1295	Ferde lest he hade fayled / in / fourme of his castes;	P	N P D N
G	1296	Bot the burde hym blessed, / and / "Bi this skyl" sayde:	C	P D N V
G	1297	"So god as Gawayn / gaynly is halden,	/	Z be E
G	1298	And cortaysye is closed / so / clene in hymseluen,	Z	P H self
G	1299	Couth not lyȝtly haf lenged / so / long wyth a lady,	Z	Z P D N
G	1300	Bot he had craued a cosse, / bi his / courtaysye,	P D	N
G	1301	Bi sum towch of summe tryfle / at sum / talez ende."	P D	N N
G	1302	Then quoth Wowen: "Iwysse, / worthe as yow lykez;	/	V C H V
G	1303	I schal kysse at your comaundement, / as a / knyȝt fallez,	C D	N V
G	1304	And fire, lest he displese / yow, so / plede hit no more."	H C	V H Z
G	1305	Ho comes nerre / with that, and / cachez hym in armez,	P H C	V H P N
G	1306	Loutez luflych / adoun and the / leude kyssez.	Z C D	N V
G	1307	Thay comly bykennen / to / Kryst ayther other;	P	N Z
G	1308	Ho dos hir forth at the dore / withouten / dyn more;	P	N A
G	1309	And he ryches hym to ryse / and / rapes hym sone,	C	V H Z
G	1310	Clepes to his chamberlayn, / choses his wede,	/	V D N
G	1311	Boȝez forth, quen he watz boun, / blythely to masse;	/	Z P N
G	1312	And thenne he meued to his mete / that / menskly hym keped,	that	Z H V
G	1313	And made myrry al day, / til the / mone rysed,	C D	N V
G	1319	And ay the lorde of the londe / is / lent on his gamnez,	be	E P D N
G	1320	To hunt in holtez and hethe / at / hyndez barayne;	P	N A

G	1321	Such a sowme he ther slowe / bi that the / sunne heldet,	P that D	N V
G	1322	Of dos and of other dere, / to / deme were wonder.	to	V be N
G	1323	Thenne fersly thay flokked / in / folk at the laste,	P	N Z
G	1324	And quykly of the quelled dere / a / querré thay maked.	D	N H V
G	1325	The best boȝed / therto with / burneȝ innoghe,	Z P	N A
G	1326	Gedered the grattest / of / greȝ that ther were,	P	N that Z be
G	1327	And didden hem derely vndo / as the / dede askeȝ;	C D	N V
G	1328	Serched hem at the asay / summe that ther were,	/	H that Z be
G	1329	Two fyngeres thay fonde / of the / fowlest of alle.	P D	A P H
G	1330	Sythen thay slyt the slot, / sesed the erber,	/	V D N
G	1331	Schaued wyth a scharp knyf, / and the / schyre knitten;	C D	N(A) V
G	1332	Sythen rytte thay the foure lymmes, / and / rent of the hyde,	C	V P D N
G	1333	Then brek thay the balé, / the / bowelez out token	D	N Z V
G	1334	Lystily for laucyng / the / lere of the knot;	D	N P D N
G	1335	Thay gryped to the gargulun, / and / graythely departed	C	Z V
G	1336	The wesaunt fro the wynt-hole, / and / walt out the guttez;	C	V Z D N
G	1337	Then scher thay out the schulderez / with her / scharp knyuez,	P D	A N
G	1338	Haled hem by a lyttel hole / to / haue hole sydes.	to	V N N
G	1339	Sithen britned thay the brest / and / brayden hit in twynne,	C	V H P N(A)
G	1340	And eft at the gargulun / bigyneȝ on thenne,	/	V Z Z
G	1341	Ryueȝ hit vp radly / ryȝt to the byȝt,	/	Z P D N
G	1342	Voydeȝ out the avanters, / and / verayly therafter	C	Z Z
G	1343	Alle the rymeȝ by the rybbeȝ / radly thay lance;	/	Z H V
G	1344	So ryde thay of by resoun / bi the / rygge boneȝ,	P D	N N
G	1345	Euenden to the haunche, / that / henged alle samen,	that	V Z
G	1346	And heuen hit vp al hole, / and / hwen hit of thenne,	C	V H P Z
G	1347	And that thay neme for the noumbles / bi / nome, as I trowe,	P	N C H V
G	1353	Bothe the hede and the hals / thay / hwen of thenne,	H	V P Z
G	1354	And sythen sunder thay the sydeȝ / swyft fro the chyne,	/	Z P D N
G	1355	And the corbeles fee / thay / kest in a greue;	H	V P D N
G	1356	Thay thurled thay ayther thik side / thurȝ bi the rybbe,	/	P P D N
G	1357	And henged thenne ayther / bi / hoȝez of the fourchez,	P	N P D N
G	1358	Vche freke for his fee, / as / fallez for to haue.	C	A(V) for to V
G	1359	Vpon a felle of the fayre best / fede thay thayr houndes	/	V H D N
G	1360	Wyth the lyuer and the lyȝtez, / the / lether of the paunchez,	D	N P D N
G	1361	And bred bathed in blod / blende theramongez.	/	E Z
G	1362	Baldely thay blw prys, / bayed thayr rachchez,	/	V D N
G	1363	Sythen fonge thay her flesche, / folden to home,	/	V P N
G	1364	Strakande ful stoutly / mony / stif motez.	D	A N
G	1365	Bi that the daylyȝt watz done / the / douthe watz al wonen	D	N be Z E
G	1366	Into the comly castel, / ther the / knyȝt bideȝ	Q D	N V
G	1372	Thenne comaunded the lorde in that sale / to / samen alle the meny,	to	V A D N
G	1373	Bothe the ladyes on loghe / to / lyȝt with her burdes	to	V P D N
G	1374	Bifore alle the folk on the flette, / frekez he beddez	/	N H V
G	1375	Verayly his venysoun / to / fech hym byforne,	to	V H P
G	1376	And al godly in gomen / Gawayn he called,	/	N H V
G	1377	Techeȝ hym to the tayles / of ful / tayt bestes,	P Z	A N
G	1378	Schewez hym the schyree grece / schorne vpon rybbes.	/	E P N
G	1379	"How payeȝ yow this play? / Haf I / prys wonnen?	have H	N E
G	1380	Haue I thryuandely thonk / thurȝ my / craft serued?"	P D	N V
G	1381	"Ȝe iwysse," quoth that other wyȝe, / "here is / wayth fayrest	Z be	N A
G	1382	That I seȝ this seuen ȝere / in / sesoun of wynter."	P	N P N
G	1383	"And al I gif yow, Gawayn," / quoth the / gome thenne,	V D	N Z
G	1384	"For by acordez of couenaunt / ȝe / craue hit as your awen."	H	V H C D A
G	1385	"This is soth," quoth the segge, / "I / say yow that ilke,	H	V H D H(A)
G	1386	That I haf worthyly wonnen / this / wonez wythinne,	D	N P
G	1387	Iwysse with as god wylle / hit / worthez to ȝourez."	H	V P H
G	1388	He hasppez his fayre hals / his / armez wythinne,	D	N P
G	1389	And kysses hym as comlyly / as he / couthe awyse:	C H	X V
G	1390	"Tas yow there my cheuicaunce, / I / cheued no more;	H	V Z
G	1391	I wowche hit saf fynly, / thaȝ / feler hit were."	C	A H be
G	1392	"Hit is god," quoth the godmon, / "grant mercy therfore.	/	V N Z
G	1393	Hit may be such hit is the better, / and / ȝe me / breue wolde	C H H	V X
G	1394	Where ȝe wan this ilk wele / bi / wytte of yorseluen."	P	N P H self
G	1395	"That watz not forward," / quoth he, / "frayst me no more.	V H	V H Z
G	1396	For ȝe haf tan that yow tydeȝ, / trawe non other	/	V Z
G	1402	And sythen by the chymné / in / chamber thay seten,	P	N H V
G	1403	Wyȝeȝ the walle wyn / weȝed to hem oft,	/	V P H Z
G	1404	And efte in her bourdyng / thay / baythen in the morn	H	V P D N
G	1405	To fylle the same forwardez / that thay / byfore maden:	that H	Z V
G	1406	Wat chaunce so bytydeȝ / hor / cheuysaunce to chaunge,	H	N to V

G	1407	What nwez so thay nome, / at / naȝt quen thay metten.	P	N C H V
G	1408	Thay acorded of the couenauntez / byfore the / court alle;	P D	N A
G	1409	The beuerage watz broȝt / forth in / bourde at that tyme,	Z P	N P D N
G	1410	Thenne thay louelych leȝten / leue at the last,	/	N Z
G	1411	Vche burne to his bedde / busked bylyue.	/	V Z
G	1412	Bi that the coke hade crowen / and / cakled bot thryse,	C	E C Z
G	1413	The lorde watz lopen of his bedde, / the / leudez vchone;	D	N H
G	1414	So that the mete and the masse / watz / metely delyuered,	be	Z E
G	1415	The douthe dressed to the wod, / er any / day sprenged,	C D	N V
G	1421	SONE thay calle of a quest / in a / ker syde,	P D	N N
G	1422	The hunt rehayted the houndez / that / hit fyrst mynged,	that	H Z V
G	1423	Wylde wordez hym warp / wyth a / wrast noyce;	P D	A N
G	1424	The howndez that hit herde / hastid thider swythe,	/	V Z Z
G	1425	And fellen as fast to the fuyt, / fourty at ones;	/	A Z
G	1426	Thenne such a glauer ande glam / of / gedered rachchez	P	E N
G	1427	Ros, that the rocherez / rungen aboute;	/	G Z
G	1428	Hunterez hem hardened / with / horne and wyth muthe.	P	N C P N
G	1429	Then al in a semblé / sweyed togeder,	/	V Z
G	1430	Bitwene a flosche in that fryth / and a / foo cragge;	C D	A N
G	1431	In a knot bi a clyffe, / at the / kerre syde,	P D	N N
G	1432	Ther as the rogh rocher / vnrydely watz fallen,	/	Z be E
G	1433	Thay ferden to the fyndyng, / and / frekez hem after;	C	N H P
G	1434	Thay vmbekesten the knarre / and the / knot bothe,	C D	N A
G	1435	Wyȝez, whyl thay wysten / wel / wythinne hem hit were,	Z	P H H be
G	1436	The best that ther breued / watz wyth the / blodhoundez.	be P D	N
G	1437	Thenne thay beten on the buskez, / and / bede hym vpryse,	C	V H V
G	1438	And he vnsoundyly out soȝt / seggez ouerthwert,	/	N P
G	1439	On the sellokest swyn / swenged out there,	/	V Z Z
G	1440	Long sythen fro the sounder / that / siȝed for olde,	that	V P A
G	1441	For he watz breme, bor / alther-grattest,	/	Z A
G	1442	Ful grymme quen he gronyed; / thenne / greued mony,	Z	V H
G	1443	For thre at the fyrst thrast / he / thryȝt to the erthe,	H	V P D N
G	1444	And sparred forth good sped / boute / spyt more.	P	N A
G	1445	Thise other halowed hyghe! ful hyȝe, / and / hay! hay! cryed,	C	I I V
G	1446	Haden hornez to mouthe, / heterly rechated;	/	Z V
G	1447	Mony watz the myry mouthe / of / men and of houndez	P	N C P N
G	1448	That buskkez after this bor / with / bost and wyth noyse	P	N C P N
G	1454	Schalkez to schote / at hym / schowen to thenne,	P H	V to Z
G	1455	Haled to hym fayr arewez, / hitten hym oft;	/	V H Z
G	1456	Bot the poyntez payred at the pyth / that / pyȝt in his scheldez,	that	V P D N
G	1457	And the barbez of his browe / bite non wolde-	/	V non X
G	1458	Thaȝ the schauen schaft / schyndered in pecez,	/	V P N
G	1459	The hede hypped / aȝayn / were-so-euer hit hitte.	Z	Z H V
G	1460	Bot quen the dyntez hym dered / of her / dryȝe strokez,	P D	A N
G	1461	Then, braynwod for bate, / on / burnez he rasez,	P	N H V
G	1462	Hurtez hem ful heterly / ther / he forth hyȝez,	Q	H Z V
G	1463	And mony arȝed therat, / and on / lyte droȝen.	C P	N V
G	1464	Bot the lorde on a lyȝt horce / launces hym after,	/	V H P
G	1465	As burne bolde vpon bent / his / bugle he blowez,	D	N H V
G	1466	He rechated, and rode / thurȝ / ronez ful thyk,	P	N Z A
G	1467	Suande this wylde swyn / til the / sunne schafted.	C D	N V
G	1468	This day wyth this ilk dede / thay / dryuen on this wyse,	H	V P D N
G	1469	Whyle oure luflych lede / lys in his bedde,	/	V P D N
G	1470	Gawayn graythely at home, / in / gerez ful ryche	P	N Z A
G	1476	Ho commes to the cortyn, / and at the / knyȝt totes.	C P D	N V
G	1477	Sir Wawen her welcumed / worthy on fyrst,	/	Z Z
G	1478	And ho wyth ȝeldez aȝayn / ful / ȝerne of hir wordez,	Z	Z P D N
G	1479	Settez hir softly by his syde, / and / swythely ho laȝez,	C	Z H V
G	1480	And wyth a luflych loke / ho / layde hym thyse wordez:	H	V H D N
G	1481	"Sir, ȝif ȝe be Wawen, / wonder me thynkkez,	/	N H V
G	1482	Wyȝe that is so wel / wrast alway to god,	/	E Z P N
G	1483	And connez not of companye / the / costez vndertake,	D	N V
G	1484	And if mon kennes yow hom to knowe, / ȝe / kest hom of your mynde;	H	V H P D N
G	1485	Thou hatz forȝeten ȝederly / that / ȝisterday I taȝtte	that	Z H V
G	1486	Bi alder-truest token / of / talk that I cowthe."	P	N that H V
G	1487	"What is that?" quoth the wyghe, / "Iwysse I wot neuer;	/	Z H V Z
G	1488	If hit be sothe that ȝe breue, / the / blame is myn awen."	D	N be D A
G	1489	"ȝet I kende yow of kyssyng," / quoth the / clere thenne,	V D	N(A) Z
G	1490	"Quere-so countenaunce is couthe / quikly to clayme;	/	Z to V
G	1491	That bicumes vche a knyȝt / that / cortaysy vses."	that	N V
G	1492	"Do way," quoth that derf mon, / "my / dere, that speche,	D	N(A) D N

G	1493	For that durst I not do, / lest I / deuayed were;	C H	E be
G	1494	If I were werned, I were wrang, / iwysse, ʒif I profered."	/	Z C H V
G	1495	"Ma fay," quoth the meré wyf, / "ʒe / may not be werned,	H	X not be E
G	1496	ʒe ar stif innoghe to constrayne / wyth / strenkthe, ʒif yow lykez,	P	N C H V
G	1497	ʒif any were so vilanous / that yow / devaye wolde."	that H	V X
G	1498	"ʒe, be God," quoth Gawayn, / "good is your speche,	/	A be D N
G	1499	Bot threte is vnthryuande / in / thede ther I lende,	P	N Q H V
G	1500	And vche gift that is geuen / not with / goud wylle.	not P	A N
G	1501	I am at your comaundement, / to / kysse quen yow lykez,	to	V C H V
G	1502	ʒe may lach quen yow lyst, / and / leue quen yow thynkkez,	C	V C H V
G	1508	"I woled wyt at onez, wyʒe," / that / worthy ther sayde,	D	N(A) Z V
G	1509	"And yow wrathed not therwyth, / what were the skylle	/	Q be D N
G	1510	That so ʒong and so ʒepe / as / ʒe at this tyme,	P	H P D N
G	1511	So cortayse, so knyʒtly, / as ʒe ar / knowen oute-	C H be	E Z
G	1512	And of alle cheualry to chose, / the / chef thyng alosed	D	A N E
G	1513	Is the lel layk of luf, / the / lettrure of armes;	D	N P N
G	1514	For to telle of this teuelyng / of this / trwe knyʒtez,	P D	A N
G	1515	Hit is the tytelet token / and / tyxt of her werkkez,	C	N P D N
G	1516	How ledes for her lele luf / hor / lyuez han auntered,	D	N have E
G	1517	Endured for her drury / dulful stoundez,	/	A N
G	1518	And after wenged with her walour / and / voyded her care,	C	V D N
G	1519	And broʒt blysse into boure / with / bountees hor awen-	P	N D A
G	1520	And ʒe ar knyʒt comlokest / kyd of your elde,	/	A(E) P D N
G	1521	Your worde and your worchip / walkez ayquere,	/	V Z
G	1522	And I haf seten by yourself / here / sere twyes,	Z	Z Z
G	1523	ʒet herde I neuer of your herd / helde no wordez	/	V D N
G	1524	That euer longed to luf, / lasse ne more;	/	A Z
G	1525	And ʒe, that ar so cortays / and / coynt of your hetes,	C	A P D N
G	1526	Oghe to a ʒonke / thynk / ʒern to schewe	V	Z to V
G	1527	And teche sum tokenez / of / trweluf craftes.	P	N N
G	1528	Why! ar ʒe lewed, / that alle the / los weldez?	that D D	N V
G	1529	Other elles ʒe demen me to dille / your / dalyaunce to herken?	D	N to V
G	1535	"In goud faythe," quoth Gawayn, / "God yow forʒelde!	/	N H V
G	1536	Gret is the gode gle, / and / gomen to me huge,	C	N P H A
G	1537	That so worthy as ʒe wolde / wynne hidere,	/	V Z
G	1538	And pyne yow with so pouer a mon, / as / play wyth your knyʒt	C	V P D N
G	1539	With anyskynnez countenaunce, / hit / keuerez me ese;	H	V H N
G	1540	Bot to take the toruayle to myself / to / trwluf expoun,	to	N V
G	1541	And towche the temez of tyxt / and / talez of armez	C	N P N
G	1542	To yow that, I wot wel, / weldez more slyʒt	/	V A N
G	1543	Of that art, bi the half, / or a / hundreth of seche	C D	N P H
G	1544	As I am, other euer / schal, in / erde ther I leue,	X P	N Q H V
G	1545	Hit were a folé felefolde, / my / fre, by my trawthe.	D	N(A) P D N
G	1546	I wolde yowre wylnyng / worche at my myʒt,	/	V P D N
G	1547	As I am hyʒly bihalden, / and / euermore wylle	C	Z X
G	1548	Be seruaunt to yourseluen, / so / saue me Dryʒtyn!"	C	V H N
G	1549	Thus hym frayned that fre, / and / fondet hym ofte,	C	V H Z
G	1550	For to haf wonnen hym to woʒe, / what-so scho thoʒt ellez;	/	H H V Z
G	1551	Bot he defended hym so fayr / that no / faut semed,	that D	N V
G	1552	Ne non euel on nawther halue, / nawther thay wysten	/	C H V
G	1558	Then ruthes hym the renk, / and / ryses to the masse,	C	V P D N
G	1559	And sithen hor diner watz dyʒt / and / derely serued.	/	Z E
G	1560	The lede with the ladyez / layked alle day,	/	V Z
G	1561	Bot the lorde ouer the londez / launced ful ofte,	/	V Z Z
G	1562	Swez his vncely swyn, / that / swyngez bi the bonkkez	that	V P D N
G	1563	And bote the best of his brachez / the / bakkez in sunder	D	N Z
G	1564	Ther he bode in his bay, / til / bawemen hit breken,	C	N H V
G	1565	And madee hym mawgref his hed / for to / mwe vtter,	for to	V Z
G	1566	So felle flonez ther flete / when the / folk gedered.	C D	N V
G	1567	Bot ʒet the styffest to start / bi / stoundez he made,	Z	Z H V
G	1568	Til at the last he watz so mat / he / myʒt no more renne,	H	X Z V
G	1569	Bot in the hast that he myʒt he / to a / hole wynnez	P D	N V
G	1570	Of a rasse bi a rokk / ther / rennez the boerne.	Q	V D N
G	1571	He gete the bonk at his bak, / bigynez to scrape,	/	V to V
G	1572	The frothe femed at his mouth / vnfayre bi the wykez,	/	A P D N
G	1573	Whettez his whyte tuschez; / with hym then irked	/	P H Z V
G	1574	Alle the burnez so bolde / that hym / by stoden	that H	P V
G	1575	To nye hym on-ferum, / bot / neʒe hym non durst	C	V H not V
G	1581	Til the knyʒt com / hymself, / kachande his blonk,	H self	V D N
G	1582	Syʒ hym byde at the bay, / his / burnez bysyde;	D	N P
G	1583	He lyʒtes luflych / adoun, / leuez his corsour,	Z	V D N

G	1584	Braydez out a bryȝt bront / and / bigly forth strydez,	C	Z Z V
G	1585	Foundez fast thurȝ the forth / ther the / felle bydon.	Q D	N(A) V
G	1586	The wylde watz war of the wyȝe / with / weppen in honde,	P	N P N
G	1587	Hef hyȝly the here, / so / hetterly he fnast	Z	Z H V
G	1588	That fele ferde for the freke, / lest / felle hym the worre.	C	V H D N(A)
G	1589	The swyn settez / hym out on the / segge euen,	H P P D	N Z
G	1590	That the burne and the bor / were / bothe vpon hepez	be	Z Z
G	1591	In the wyȝtest of the water; / the / worre hade that other,	D	N(A) have D H
G	1592	For the mon merkkez / hym wel, as thay / mette fyrst,	H Z C H	V Z
G	1593	Set sadly the scharp / in the / slot euen,	P D	N Z
G	1594	Hit hym vp to the hult, / that the / hert schyndered,	that D	N V
G	1595	And he ȝarrande hym ȝelde, / and / ȝedoun the water	C	V D N
G	1601	There watz blawyng of prys / in mony / breme horne,	P D	A N
G	1602	Heȝe halowing on hiȝe / with / hatheleȝ that myȝt,	P	N that X
G	1603	Brachetes bayed that best, / as / bidden the maysterez	C	V D N
G	1604	Of that chargeaunt chace / that were / chef huntes.	that be	A N
G	1605	Thenne a wyȝe that watz wys / vpon / wodcraftez	P	N
G	1606	To vnlace this bor / lufly bigynnez.	/	Z V
G	1607	Fyrst he hewes of his hed / and on / hiȝe settez,	C Z	Z V
G	1608	And sythen rendez him al roghe / bi the / rygge after,	P D	N Z
G	1609	Braydez out the boweles, / brennez hom on glede,	/	V H P N
G	1610	With bred blent / therwith his / braches rewardez.	Z D	N V
G	1611	Sythen he britnez out the brawen / in / bryȝt brode cheldez,	P	A A N
G	1612	And hatz out the hastlettez, / as / hiȝtly bisemez;	C	Z V
G	1613	And ȝet hem halchez al hole / the / halueȝ togeder,	D	N Z
G	1614	And sythen on a stif stange / stoutly hem henges.	/	Z H V
G	1615	Now with this ilk swyn / thay / swengen to home;	H	V P N
G	1616	The bores hed watz borne / bifore the / burnes seluen	P D	N self
G	1617	That him forferde in the forthe / thurȝ / forse of his honde	P	N P D N
G	1623	The lorde ful lowde with lote / and / laȝter myry,	C	N A
G	1624	When he seȝe Sir Gawayn, / with / solace he spekez;	P	N H V
G	1625	The goude ladyez were geten, / and / gedered the meyny,	C	V D N
G	1626	He schewez hem the scheldez, / and / schapes hem the tale	C	V H D N
G	1627	Of the largesse and the lenthe, / the / lithernez alse	D	N Z
G	1628	Of the were of the wylde swyn / in / wod ther he fled.	P	N Q H V
G	1629	That other knyȝt ful comly / comended his dedez,	/	V D N
G	1630	And praysed hit as gret prys / that he / proued hade,	that H	E have
G	1631	For suche a brawne of a best, / the / bolde burne sayde,	D	A N V
G	1632	Ne such sydes of a swyn / segh he neuer are.		V H Z Z
G	1633	Thenne hondeled thay the hoge hed, / the / hende mon hit praysed,	D	A N H V
G	1634	And let lodly / therat the / lorde for to here.	Z D	N for to V
G	1635	"Now, Gawayn," quoth the godmon, / "this / gomen is your awen	D	N be D A
G	1636	Bi fyn forwarde and faste, / faythely ȝe knowe."	/	Z H V
G	1637	"Hit is sothe," quoth the segge, / "and as / siker trwe	C C	Z A
G	1638	Alle my get I schal yow gif / agayn, bi my trawthe."	/	Z P D N
G	1639	He hent the hathel aboute the halse, / and / hendely hym kysses,	C	Z H V
G	1640	And eftersones of the same / he / serued hym there.	H	V H Z
G	1641	"Now ar we euen," / quoth the / hathel, "in this euentide	V D	N P D N
G	1642	Of alle the couenauntes that we knyt, / sythen I / com hider,	C H	V Z
G	1648	Thenne thay teldet tablez / trestes alofte,	/	N P
G	1649	Kesten clothen / vpon; / clere lyȝt thenne	P	A N Z
G	1650	Wakned bi woȝez, / waxen torches;	/	A N
G	1651	Seggez sette and serued / in / sale al aboute;	P	N Z Z
G	1652	Much glam and gle / glent vp therinne	/	V Z Z
G	1653	Aboute the fyre vpon flet, / and on / fele wyse	C P	A N
G	1654	At the soper and after, / mony / athel songez,	D	A N
G	1655	As coundutes of Krystmasse / and / carolez newe	C	N A
G	1656	With al the manerly merthe / that / mon may of telle,	that	N X P V
G	1657	And euer oure luflych knyȝt / the / lady bisyde.	D	N P
G	1658	Such semblaunt to that segge / semly ho made	/	Z H V
G	1659	Wyth stille stollen countenaunce, / that / stalworth to plese,	that	N(A) to V
G	1660	That al forwondered watz the wyȝe, / and / wroth with hymseluen,	C	A P H self
G	1661	Bot he nolde not for his nurture / nurne hir aȝaynez,	/	V H P
G	1662	Bot dalt with hir al in daynté, / how-se-euer the / dede turned	C D	N V
G	1668	Ande ther thay dronken, and dalten, / and / demed eft nwe	C	V Z Z
G	1669	To norne on the same note / on / Nwe ȝerez euen;	P	A N N
G	1670	Bot the knyȝt craued leue / to / kayre on the morn,	to	V P D N
G	1671	For hit watz neȝ at the terme / that / he to schulde.	that	H Z V
G	1672	The lorde hym letted / of that, to / lenge hym resteyed,	P H to	V H V
G	1673	And sayde, "As I am trwe segge, / I / siker my trawthe	H	V D N
G	1674	Thou schal cheue to the grene chapel / thy / charres to make,	D	N to V

G	1675	Leude, on Nw ȝerez lyȝt, / longe bifore pryme.	/	Z P N
G	1676	Forthy thow lye in thy loft / and / lach thyn ese,	C	V D N
G	1677	And I schal hunt in this holt, / and / halde the towchez,	C	V D N
G	1678	Chaunge wyth the cheuisaunce, / bi that I / charre hider;	P that H	V Z
G	1679	For I haf fraysted the twys, / and / faythful I fynde the.	C	A H V H
G	1680	Now "thrid tyme throwe / best" / thenk on the morne,	Z	V P D N
G	1681	Make we mery quyl we may / and / mynne vpon joye,	C	V P N
G	1682	For the lur may mon lach / when-so / mon lykez."	C	N V
G	1683	This watz graythely graunted, / and / Gawayn is lenged,	C	N be E
G	1684	Blithe broȝt watz hym drynk, / and thay to / bedde ȝeden	C H P	N V
G	1690	After messe a morsel / he and his / men token;	H C D	N V
G	1691	Miry watz the mornyng, / his / mounture he askes.	D	N H V
G	1692	Alle the hatheles that on horse / schulde / helden hym after	X	V H P
G	1693	Were boun busked on hor blonkkez / bifore the halle ȝatez.	/	P D N N
G	1694	Ferly fayre watz the folde, / for the / forst clenged;	C D	N V
G	1695	In rede rudede vpon rak / rises the sunne,	/	V D N
G	1696	And ful clere costez / the / clowdes of the welkyn.	D	N P D N
G	1697	Hunteres vnhardeled / bi a / holt syde,	P D	N N
G	1698	Rocheres roungen bi rys / for / rurde of her hornes;	P	N P D N
G	1699	Summe fel in the fute / ther the / fox bade,	Q D	N V
G	1700	Traylez ofte a traueres / bi / traunt of her wyles;	P	N P D N
G	1701	A kenet kyres / therof, the / hunt on hym calles;	Z D	N P H V
G	1702	His felaȝes fallen / hym to, that / fnasted ful thike,	H P that	V Z Z
G	1703	Runnen forth in a rabel / in his / ryȝt fare,	P D	A N
G	1704	And he fyskez hem byfore; / thay / founden hym sone,	H	V H Z
G	1705	And quen thay seghe hym with syȝt / thay / sued hym fast,	H	V H Z
G	1706	Wreȝande hym ful weterly / with a / wroth noyse;	P D	A N
G	1707	And he trantes and tornayeez / thurȝ mony / tene greue,	P D	A(N) N
G	1708	Hauilounez, and herkenez / bi / heggez ful ofte.	P	N Z Z
G	1709	At the last bi a littel dich / he / lepez ouer a spenne,	H	V P D N
G	1710	Stelez out ful stilly / bi a / strothe rande,	P D	N N
G	1711	Went haf wylt of the wode / with / wylez fro the houndes;	P	N P D N
G	1712	Thenne watz he went, er he wyst, / to a / wale tryster,	P D	A N
G	1713	Ther thre thro at a thrich / thrat hym at ones,	/	V H Z
G	1719	Thenne watz hit list vpon lif / to / lythen the houndez,	to	V D N
G	1720	When alle the mute hade hym met, / menged togeder:	/	E Z
G	1721	Suche a sorȝe at that syȝt / thay / sette on his hede	H	V P D N
G	1722	As alle the clamberande clyffes / hade / clatered on hepes;	have	E P N
G	1723	Here he watz halawed, / when / hathelez hym metten,	C	N H V
G	1724	Loude he watz ȝayned / with / ȝarande speche;	P	G N
G	1725	Ther he watz threted and ofte / thef called,	/	N E
G	1726	And ay the titlerez at his tayl, / that / tary he ne myȝt;	that	V H not X
G	1727	Ofte he watz runnen / at, when he / out rayked,	Z C H	Z V
G	1728	And ofte reled in aȝayn, / so / Reniarde watz wylé.	C	N be A
G	1729	And ȝe he lad hem bi lagmon, / the / lorde and his meyny,	D	N C D N
G	1730	On this maner bi the mountes / quyle / myd-ouer-vnder,	P	N
G	1731	Whyle the hende knyȝt at home / holsumly slepes	/	Z V
G	1732	Withinne the comly cortynes, / on the / colde morne.	P D	A N
G	1733	Bot the lady for luf / let not to slepe,	/	V not to V
G	1734	Ne the purpose to payre / that / pyȝt in hir hert,	that	E P D N
G	1735	Bot ros hir vp radly, / rayked hir theder	/	V H Z
G	1736	In a mery mantyle, / mete to the erthe,	/	A to D N
G	1737	That watz furred ful fyne / with / fellez wel pured,	P	N Z E
G	1738	No hwef goud on hir hede / bot the / haȝer stones	P D	A N
G	1739	Trased aboute hir tressour / be / twenty in clusteres;	P	N P N
G	1740	Hir thryuen face and hir throte / throwen al naked,	/	E Z A
G	1741	Hir brest bare bifore, / and / bihinde eke.	C	Z Z
G	1742	Ho comez withinne the chambre dore, / and / closes hit hir after,	C	V H H P
G	1743	Wayuez vp a wyndow, / and on the / wyȝe callez,	C P D	N V
G	1744	And radly thus rehayted / hym with hir / riche wordes,	H P D	A N
G	1750	In dreȝ droupyng of dreme / draueled that noble,	/	V D N(A)
G	1751	As mon that watz in mornyng / of / mony thro thoȝtes,	P	H P N
G	1752	How that destiné schulde that day / dele hym his wyrde	/	V H D N
G	1753	At the grene chapel, / when he the / gome metes,	C H D	N V
G	1754	And bihoues his buffet abide / withoute / debate more;	P	N A
G	1755	Bot quen that comly com / he / keuered his wyttes,	H	V D N
G	1756	Swenges out of the sweuenes, / and / swarez with hast.	C	V Z
G	1757	The lady luflych / com / laȝande swete,	V	G Z
G	1758	Felle ouer his fayre face, / and / fetly hym kyssed;	C	Z H V
G	1759	He welcumez hir worthily / with a / wale chere.	P D	A N
G	1760	He seȝ hir so glorious / and / gayly atyred,	C	Z E

G	1761	So fautles of hir fetures / and of so / fyne hewes,	C P Z	A N
G	1762	Wyȝt wallande joye / warmed his hert.	/	V D N
G	1763	With smothe smylyng and smolt / thay / smeten into merthe,	H	V P N
G	1764	That al watz blis and bonchef / that / breke hem bitwene,	that	V H P
G	1770	For that prynces of pris / depresed hym so thikke,	/	V H Z Z
G	1771	Nurned hym so neȝe the thred, / that / nede hym bihoued	that	Z H V
G	1772	Other lach ther hir luf, / other / lodly refuse.	H	Z V
G	1773	He cared for his cortaysye, / lest / crathayn were,	C	N H be
G	1774	And more for his meschef / ȝif he schulde / make synne,	C H X	V N
G	1775	And be traytor to that tolke / that that / telde aȝt.	that D	N V
G	1776	"God schylde," quoth the schalk, / "that / schal not befalle!"	that	X not V
G	1777	With luf-laȝyng a lyt / he / layd hym bysyde	H	V H P
G	1778	Alle the spechez of specialté / that / sprange of her mouthe.	that	V P D N
G	1779	Quoth that burde to the burne, / "Blame ȝe disserue,	/	N H V
G	1780	ȝif ȝe luf not that lyf / that ȝe / lye nexte,	that H	V Z
G	1781	Bifore alle the wyȝez in the worlde / wounded in hert,		E P N
G	1782	Bot if ȝe haf a lemman, a leuer, / that yow / lykez better,	that H	V Z
G	1783	And folden fayth to that fre, / festned so harde		E Z Z
G	1784	That yow lausen ne lyst- / and that I / leue nouthe;	C that H	V Z
G	1785	And that ȝe telle me that now / trwly I pray yow,	/	Z H V
G	1786	For alle the lufez vpon lyue / layne not the sothe	/	V not D N
G	1792	"That is a worde," quoth that wyȝt, / "that / worst is of alle,	that	A be P H
G	1793	Bot I am swared for sothe, / that / sore me thinkkez.	that	A H V
G	1794	Kysse me now comly, / and I schal / cach hethen,	C H X	V Z
G	1795	I may bot mourne vpon molde, / as / may that much louyes."	C	N that Z V
G	1796	Sykande ho sweȝe / doun and / semly hym kyssed,	Z C	Z H V
G	1797	And sithen ho seueres / hym fro / and says as ho stondes,	H P C	V C H V
G	1798	"Now, dere, at this departyng / do me this ese,	/	V H D N
G	1799	Gif me sumquat of thy gifte, / thi / gloue if hit were,	D	N C H be
G	1800	That I may mynne on the mon, / my / mournyng to lassen."	D	N to V
G	1801	"Now iwysse," quoth that wyȝe, / "I / wolde I hade here	H	V H V Z
G	1802	The leuest thing for thy luf / that I in / londe welde,	that H Z	Z V
G	1803	For ȝe haf deserued, for sothe, / sellyly ofte	/	Z Z
G	1804	More rewarde bi resoun / then I / reche myȝt;	C H	V X
G	1805	Bot to dele yow for drurye / that / dawed bot neked,	that	V C N
G	1806	Hit is not your honour / to / haf at this tyme	to	V P D N
G	1807	A gloue for a garysoun / of / Gawaynez giftez,	P	N N
G	1808	And I am here an erande / in / erdez vncouthe,	P	Z A
G	1809	And haue no men wyth no malez / with / menskful thingez;	P	A N
G	1810	That mislykez me, ladé, / for / luf at this tyme,	P	N P D N
G	1811	Iche tolke mon do as he is tan, / tas to non ille	P	V P H Z
G	1817	Ho raȝt hym a riche rynk / of / red golde werkez,	P	A A N
G	1818	Wyth a starande ston / stondande alofte	/	G Z
G	1819	That bere blusschande bemez / as the / bryȝt sunne;	P D	A N
G	1820	Wyt ȝe wel, hit watz worth / wele ful hoge.	/	N Z A
G	1821	Bot the renk hit renayed, / and / redyly he sayde,	C	Z H V
G	1822	"I wil no giftez, for Gode, / my / gay, at this tyme;	D	N(A) P D N
G	1823	I haf none yow to norne, / ne / noȝt wyl I take."	D	N X H V
G	1824	Ho bede hit hym ful bysily, / and he hir / bode wernes,	C H D	N V
G	1825	And swere swyfte by his sothe / that he hit / sese nolde,	that H H	V X
G	1826	And ho soré that he forsoke, / and / sayde therafter,	C	V Z
G	1827	"If ȝe renay my rynk, / to / ryche for hit semez,	to	A C H V
G	1828	ȝe wolde not so hyȝly / halden be to me,	/	E be P H
G	1829	I schal gif yow my girdel, / that / gaynes yow lasse."	that	V H Z
G	1830	Ho laȝt a lace lyȝtly / that / leke vmbe hir sydez,	that	V P D N
G	1831	Knit vpon hir kyrtel / vnder the / clere mantyle,	P D	A N
G	1832	Gered hit watz with grene sylke / and with / golde schaped,	C P	N A(E)
G	1833	Noȝt bot arounde brayden, / beten with fyngrez;	/	E P N
G	1834	And that ho bede to the burne, / and / blythely bisoȝt,	C	Z V
G	1835	Thaȝ hit vnworthi were, / that he hit / take wolde.	that H H	V X
G	1836	He nay that he nolde / neghe in no wyse	/	V Z
G	1837	Nauther golde ne garysoun, / er / God hym grace sende	C	N H N V
G	1838	To acheue to the chaunce / that he hade / chosen there.	that H have	E Z
G	1839	"And therfore, I pray yow, / displese yow noȝt,	H	V H not
G	1840	And lettez be your bisinesse, / for I / baythe hit yow neuer	C H	V H H Z
G	1846	"Now forsake ȝe this silke," / sayde the burde thenne,	/	V D N Z
G	1847	"For hit is symple in hitself? / And / so hit wel semez.	C	Z H Z V
G	1848	Lo! so hit is littel, / and / lasse hit is worthy;	C	Z H be A
G	1849	Bot who-so knew the costes / that / knit ar therinne,	that	E be Z
G	1850	He wolde hit prayse at more prys, / parauenture;	/	Z
G	1851	For quat gome so is gorde / with this / grene lace,	P D	A N

G	1852	While he hit hade hemely / halched aboute,	/	E Z
G	1853	Ther is no hathel vnder heuen / tohewe hym that myȝt,	/	V H that X
G	1854	For he myȝt not be slayn / for / slyȝt vpon erthe."	P	Z Z
G	1855	Then kest the knyȝt, / and hit / come to his hert	C H	V P D N
G	1856	Hit were a juel for the jopardé / that hym / iugged were:	that H	E be
G	1857	When he acheued to the chapel / his / chek for to fech,	D	N for to V
G	1858	Myȝt he haf slypped to be vnslayn, / the / sleȝt were noble.	D	N be A
G	1859	Thenne he thulged with hir threpe / and / tholed hir to speke,	C	V H to V
G	1860	And ho bere on hym the belt / and / bede hit hym swythe-	C	V H H Z
G	1861	And he granted and hym gafe / with a / goud wylle-	P D	A N
G	1862	And bisoȝt hym, for hir sake, / disceuer hit neuer,	/	V H Z
G	1863	Bot to lelly layne fro hir lorde; / the / leude hym acordez	D	N H V
G	1864	That neuer wyȝe schulde hit wyt, / iwysse, bot thay twayne	/	Z C H A
G	1870	Thenne lachchez ho hir leue, / and / leuez hym there,	C	V H Z
G	1871	For more myrthe of that mon / moȝt ho not gete.	/	X H not V
G	1872	When ho watz gon, Sir Gawayn / gerez hym sone,	/	V H Z
G	1873	Rises and riches / hym in / araye noble,	H P	N A
G	1874	Lays vp the luf-lace / the / lady hym raȝt,	D	N H V
G	1875	Hid hit ful holdely, / ther he hit / eft fonde.	Q H H	Z V
G	1876	Sythen cheuely to the chapel / choses he the waye,	/	V H D N
G	1877	Preuély aproched to a prest, / and / prayed hym there	C	V H Z
G	1878	That he wolde lyste his lyf / and / lern hym better	C	V H Z
G	1879	How his sawle schulde be saued / when he schuld / seye hethen.	C H X	V Z
G	1880	There he schrof hym schyrly / and / schewed his mysdedez,	C	V D N
G	1881	Of the more and the mynne, / and / merci besechez,	C	N V
G	1882	And of absolucioun / he on the / segge calles;	H P D	N V
G	1883	And he asoyled hym surely / and / sette hym so clene	C	V H Z A
G	1884	As domezday / schulde haf ben / diȝt on the morn.	X have been	E P D N
G	1885	And sythen he mace hym as mery / among the / fre ladyes,	P D	A N
G	1886	With comlych caroles / and alle / kynnes ioye,	C D	N N
G	1887	As neuer he did bot that daye, / to the / derk nyȝt,	P D	A N
G	1893	Now hym lenge in that lee, / ther / luf hym bityde!	Q	V H V
G	1894	ȝet is the lorde on the launde / ledande his gomnes.	/	G D N
G	1895	He hatz forfaren this fox / that he / folȝed longe;	that H	V Z
G	1896	As he sprent ouer a spenne / to / spye the schrewe,	to	V D N
G	1897	Ther as he herde the howndes / that / hasted hym swythe,	that	V H Z
G	1898	Renaud com richchande / thurȝ a / roȝe greue,	P D	A N
G	1899	And alle the rabel in a res / ryȝt at his helez.	/	Z P D N
G	1900	The wyȝe watz war of the wylde, / and / warly abides,	C	Z V
G	1901	And braydez out the bryȝt bronde, / and at the / best castez.	C P D	N V
G	1902	And he schunt for the scharp, / and / schulde haf arered;	C	X have E
G	1903	A rach rapes / hym to, / ryȝt er he myȝt,	H P	Z Z H X
G	1904	And ryȝt bifore the hors fete / thay / fel on hym alle,	H	V P H Z
G	1905	And woried me this wyly / wyth a / wroth noyse.	P D	A N
G	1906	The lorde lyȝtez bilyue, / and / lachez hym sone,	C	V H Z
G	1907	Rased hym ful radly / out of the / rach mouthes,	P P D	N N
G	1908	Haldez heȝe ouer his hede, / halowez faste,	/	V Z
G	1909	And ther bayen hym mony / brath houndez.	/	A N
G	1910	Huntes hyȝed / hem theder with / hornez ful mony,	H Z P	N Z A
G	1911	Ay rechatande aryȝt / til thay the / renk seȝen.	C H D	N V
G	1912	Bi that watz comen / his / compeyny noble,	D	N A
G	1913	Alle that euer ber bugle / blowed at ones,	/	V Z
G	1914	And alle thise other halowed / that / hade no hornes;	that	V D N
G	1915	Hit watz the myriest mute / that euer / men herde,	that Z	N V
G	1916	The rich rurd that ther watz raysed / for / Renaude saule	P	N N
G	1922	And thenne thay helden to home, / for hit watz / nieȝ nyȝt,	C H be	P N
G	1923	Strakande ful stoutly / in hor / store hornez.	P D	A N
G	1924	The lorde is lyȝt at the laste / at hys / lef home,	P D	A N
G	1925	Fyndez fire vpon flet, / the / freke ther-byside,	D	N Z
G	1926	Sir Gawayn the gode, / that / glad watz withalle,	that	A be Z
G	1927	Among the ladies for luf / he / ladde much ioye;	H	V A N
G	1928	He were a bleaunt of blwe / that / bradde to the erthe,	that	V P D N
G	1929	His surkot semed / hym wel that / softe watz forred,	H Z that	Z be E
G	1930	And his hode of that ilke / henged on his schulder,	/	V P D N
G	1931	Blande al of blaunner / were / bothe al aboute.	be	Z Z Z
G	1932	He metez me this godmon / inmyddez the flore,	/	P D N
G	1933	And al with gomen he hym gret, / and / goudly he sayde,	C	Z H V
G	1934	"I schal fylle vpon fyrst / oure / forwardez nouthe,	D	N Z
G	1935	That we spedly han spoken, / ther / spared watz no drynk."	Q	E be D N
G	1936	Then acoles he the knyȝt / and / kysses hym thryes,	C	V H Z
G	1937	As sauerly and sadly / as he hem / sette couthe.	C H H	V X

G	1938	"Bi Kryst," quoth that other knyȝt, / 'ȝe / cach much sele	H	V A N
G	1939	In cheuisaunce of this chaffer, / ȝif ȝe hade / goud chepez "	C H have	A N
G	1940	"ȝe, of the chepe no charg," / quoth / chefly that other,	V	Z D H
G	1941	"As is pertly payed / the / chepez that I aȝte."	D	N that H V
G	1942	"Mary," quoth that other mon, / "myn is bihynde,	/	H be Z
G	1943	For I haf hunted al this day, / and noȝt / haf I geten	C not	have H E
G	1944	Bot this foule fox felle- / the / fende haf the godez!-	D	N V D N
G	1945	And that is ful pore for to pay / for suche / prys thinges	P D	A N
G	1946	As ȝe haf thryȝt me here thro, / suche / thre cosses	D	A N
G	1952	With merthe and mynstralsye, / with / metez at hor wylle,	P	N P D N
G	1953	Thay maden as mery / as any / men moȝten-	C D	N X
G	1954	With laȝyne of ladies, / with / lotez of bordes	P	N P N
G	1955	Gawayn and the godemon / so / glad were thay bothe-	Z	A be H Z
G	1956	Bot if the douthe had doted, / other / dronken ben other.	D	A(E) E Z
G	1957	Bothe the mon and the meyny maden / mony iapez,	/	A N
G	1958	Til the sesoun watz seȝen / that thay / seuer moste;	that H	Z Z
G	1959	Burnez to hor bedde / behoued at the laste.	/	V Z
G	1960	Thenne loȝly his leue / at the / lorde fyrst	P D	N Z
G	1961	Fochchez this fre mon, / and / fayre he hym thonkkez:	C	A H H V
G	1962	"Of such a selly soiorne / as I haf / hade here,	C H have	E Z
G	1963	Your honour at this hyȝe fest, / the / hyȝe kyng yow ȝelde!	D	A N H V
G	1964	I ȝef yow me for on of yourez, / if / yowreself lykez,	C	H self V
G	1965	For I mot nedes, as ȝe wot, / meue to-morne,	/	V Z
G	1966	And ȝe me take sum tolke / to / teche, as ȝe hyȝt,	to	V C H V
G	1967	The gate to the grene chapel, / as / God wyl me suffer	C	N V H V
G	1968	To dele on Nw ȝerez day / the / dome of my wyrdes."	D	N P D N
G	1969	"In god faythe," quoth the godmon, / "wyth a / goud wylle	P D	A N
G	1970	Al that euer I yow hyȝt / halde schal I redé."	/	V X H A
G	1971	Ther asyngnes he a seruaunt / to / sett hym in the waye,	to	V H P D N
G	1972	And coundue hym by the downez, / that he no / drechch had,	that H D	N V
G	1973	For to ferk thurȝ the fryth / and / fare at the gaynest	C	V P D A
G	1979	With care and wyth kyssyng / he / carppez hem tille,	H	V H P
G	1980	And fele thryuande thonkkez / he / thrat hom to haue,	H	V H to V
G	1981	And thay ȝelden hym aȝayn / ȝeply that ilk;	/	Z D H
G	1982	Thay bikende hym to Kryst / with ful / colde sykyngez.	P Z	A N
G	1983	Sythen fro the meyny / he / menskly departes;	H	Z V
G	1984	Vche mon that he mette, / he / made hem a thonke	H	V H D N
G	1985	For his seruyse and his solace / and his / sere pyne,	C D	A N
G	1986	That thay wyth busynes had ben / aboute hym to serue;	/	Z H to V
G	1987	And vche segge as soré / to / seuer with hym there	to	V P H Z
G	1988	As thay hade wonde worthyly / with that / wlonk euer.	P D	N(A) Z
G	1989	Then with ledes and lyȝt / he watz / ladde to his chambre	H be	E P D N
G	1990	And blythely broȝt to his bedde / to / be at his rest.	to	V P D N
G	1991	ȝif he ne slepe soundyly / say ne dar I,	/	V not X H
G	1992	For he hade muche on the morn / to / mynne, ȝif he wolde,	to	V C H X
G	1998	Now neȝez the Nw ȝere, / and the / nyȝt passez,	C D	N V
G	1999	The day dryuez to the derk, / as / Dryȝtyn biddez;	C	N V
G	2000	Bot wylde wederez of the worlde / wakned theroute,	/	V Z
G	2001	Clowdes kesten kenly / the / colde to the erthe,	D	N(A) P D N
G	2002	Wyth nyȝe innoghe of the northe, / the / naked to tene;	D	N(A) to V
G	2003	The snawe snitered ful snart, / that / snayped the wylde;	that	V D N
G	2004	The werbelande wynde / wapped fro the hyȝe,	/	V P D A
G	2005	And drof vche dale / ful of / dryftes ful grete.	A P	N Z A
G	2006	The leude lystened / ful wel that / leȝ in his bedde,	Z Z that	V P D N
G	2007	Thaȝ he lowkez his liddez, / ful / lyttel he slepes;	Z	Z H V
G	2008	Bi vch kok that crue / he / knwe wel the steuen.	H	V Z D N
G	2009	Deliuerly he dressed / vp, er the / day sprenged,	Z C D	N V
G	2010	For there watz lyȝt of a laumpe / that / lemed in his chambre;	that	V P D N
G	2011	He called to his chamberlayn, / that / cofly hym swared,	that	Z H V
G	2012	And bede hym bryng hym his bruny / and his / blonk sadel;	C D	N V
G	2013	That other ferkez hym vp / and/ fechez hym his wedez,	C	V H D N
G	2014	And graythez me Sir Gawayn / vpon a / grett wyse.	P D	A N
G	2015	Fyrst he clad hym in his clothez / the / colde for to were,	D	N(A) for to V
G	2016	And sythen his other harnays, / that / holdely watz keped,	that	Z be E
G	2017	Bothe his paunce and his platez, / piked ful clene,	/	E Z Z
G	2018	The ryngez rokked of the roust / of his / riche bruny;	P D	A N
G	2019	And al watz fresch as vpon fyrst, / and he watz / fayn thenne	C H be	A Z
G	2025	Whyle the wlonkest wedes / he / warp on hymseluen-	H	V P H self
G	2026	His cote wyth the conysaunce / of the / clere werkez	P D	A N
G	2027	Ennurned vpon veluet, / vertuus stonez	/	A N
G	2028	Aboute beten and bounden, / enbrauded semez,	/	E V

G	2029	And fayre furred / withinne wyth / fayre pelures-	Z P	A N
G	2030	Ʒet laft he not the lace, / the / ladiez gifte,	D	N N
G	2031	That forgat not Gawayn / for / gode of hymseluen.	P	N P H self
G	2032	Bi he hade belted the bronde / vpon his / balƷe haunchez,	P D	A N
G	2033	Thenn dressed he his drurye / double hym aboute,	/	Z H P
G	2034	Swythe swethled vmbe his swange / swetely that knyƷt	/	Z D N
G	2035	The gordel of the grene silke, / that / gay wel bisemed,	that	N(A) Z V
G	2036	Vpon that ryol red clothe / that / ryche watz to schewe.	that	A be to V
G	2037	Bot wered not this ilk wyƷe / for / wele this gordel,	P	N D N
G	2038	For pryde of the pendauntez, / thaƷ / polyst thay were,	C	E H be
G	2039	And thaƷ the glyterande golde / glent vpon endez,	/	V P N
G	2040	Bot for to sauen hymself, / when / suffer hym byhoued,	C	V H X
G	2041	To byde bale withoute dabate / of / bronde hym to were	P	N H to V
G	2047	Thenne watz Gryngolet graythe, / that / gret watz and huge,	that	A be C A
G	2048	And hade ben soiourned sauerly / and in a / siker wyse,	C P D	A N
G	2049	Hym lyst prik for poynt, / that / proude hors thenne.	D	A N Z
G	2050	The wyƷe wynnez / hym to and / wytez on his lyre,	H P C	V P D N
G	2051	And sayde soberly hymself / and by his / soth swerez:	C P D	N(A) V
G	2052	"Here is a meyny in this mote / that on / menske thenkkez,	that P	N V
G	2053	The mon hem mayntenies, / ioy mot thay haue;	/	N X H V
G	2054	The leue lady on lyue / luf hir bityde;	/	N H V
G	2055	Ʒif thay for charyté / cherysen a gest,	/	V D N
G	2056	And halden honour in her honde, / the / hathel hem Ʒelde	D	N H V
G	2057	That haldez the heuen vpon hyƷe, / and / also yow alle!	C	Z H Z
G	2058	And Ʒif I myƷt lyf vpon londe / lede any quyle,	/	V D N
G	2059	I schuld rech yow sum rewarde / redyly, if I myƷt."	/	Z C H X
G	2060	Thenn steppez he into stirop / and / strydez alofte;	C	V Z
G	2061	His schalk schewed hym his schelde, / on / schulder he hit laƷt,	P	N H H V
G	2062	Gordez to Gryngolet / with his / gilt helez,	P D	E N
G	2063	And he startez on the ston, / stod he no lenger	/	V H Z
G	2069	The brygge watz brayde / doun, and the / brode Ʒatez	Z C D	A N
G	2070	Vnbarred and born open / vpon / bothe halue.	P	A N
G	2071	The burne blessed hym bilyue, / and the / bredez passed-	C D	N V
G	2072	Prayses the porter / bifore the / prynce kneled,	C D	N V
G	2073	Gef hym God and goud day, / that / Gawayn he saue-	that	N H V
G	2074	And went on his way / with his / wyƷe one,	P D	N Z
G	2075	That schulde teche hym to tourne / to that / tene place	P D	A(N) N
G	2076	Ther the ruful race / he schulde / resayue.	H X	V
G	2077	Thay boƷen bi bonkkez / ther / boƷez ar bare,	Q	N be A
G	2078	Thay clomben bi clyffez / ther / clengez the colde.	Q	V D N(A)
G	2079	The heuen watz vphalt, / bot / vgly ther-vnder;	C	A Z
G	2080	Mist muged on the mor, / malt on the mountez,	/	V P D N
G	2081	Vch hille hade a hatte, / a / myst-hakel huge.	D	N A
G	2082	Brokez byled and breke / bi / bonkkez aboute,	P	N Z
G	2083	Schyre schaterande on schorez, / ther thay / doun schowued.	Q H	Z V
G	2084	Wela wylle watz the way / ther thay bi / wod schulden,	Q H P	N X
G	2085	Til hit watz sone sesoun / that the / sunne ryses	that D	N V
G	2091	"For I haf wonnen yow hider, / wyƷe, at this tyme,	/	N P D N
G	2092	And now nar Ʒe not fer / fro that / note place	P D	E N
G	2093	That Ʒe han spied and spuryed / so / specially after;	Z	Z Z
G	2094	Bot I schal say yow for sothe, / sythen I yow knowe,	/	C H H V
G	2095	And Ʒe ar a lede vpon lyue / that I / wel louy,	that H	Z V
G	2096	Wolde Ʒe worch bi my wytte, / Ʒe / worthed the better.	H	V D A
G	2097	The place that Ʒe prece / to ful / perelous is halden;	Z Z	A be E
G	2098	Ther wonez a wyƷe in that waste, / the / worst vpon erthe,	D	N(A) P N
G	2099	For he is stiffe and sturne, / and to / strike louies,	C to	V V
G	2100	And more he is then any mon / vpon / myddelerde,	P	N
G	2101	And his body bigger / then the / best fowre	C D	A N
G	2102	That ar in ArthureƷ hous, / Hestor, other other.	/	N Z Z
G	2103	He cheuez that chaunce / at the / chapel grene,	P D	N A
G	2104	Ther passes non is that place / so / proude in his armes	Z	A P D N
G	2105	That he ne dyngez hym to dethe / with / dynt of his honde;	P	N P D N
G	2106	For he is a mon methles, / and / mercy non vses,	C	N not V
G	2107	For be hit chorle other chaplayn / that bi the / chapel rydes,	that P D	N V
G	2108	Monk other masseprest, / other any / mon elles,	D D	N Z
G	2109	Hym thynk as queme hym to quelle / as / quyk go hymseluen.	C	Z V H self
G	2110	Forthy I say the, as sothe / as Ʒe in / sadel sitte,	C H P	N V
G	2111	Com Ʒe there, Ʒe be kylled, / may the / knyƷt rede,	X D	N V
G	2112	Trawe Ʒe me that trwely, / thaƷ Ʒe had / twenty lyues	C H have	A N
G	2118	"Forthy, goude Sir Gawayn, / let the / gome one,	V D	N A
G	2119	And gotz away sum other gate, / vpon / Goddez halue!	P	N N

G	2120	Cayrez bi sum other kyth, / ther / Kryst mot yow spede,	Q	N X H V
G	2121	And I schal hyʒ me hom / aʒayn, and / hete yow fyrre	ZC	V H Z
G	2122	That I schal swere bi God / and alle his / gode halʒez,	C D D	A N
G	2123	As help me God and the halydam, / and / othez innoghe,	C	N A
G	2124	That I schal lelly yow layne, / and / lance neuer tale	C	V Z N
G	2125	That euer ʒe fondet to fle / for / freke that I wyst."	P	N that H V
G	2126	"Grant merci", quoth Gawayn, and / gruchyng he sayde:	C	G H V
G	2127	"Wel worth the, wyʒe, / that / woldez my gode,	that	V D N
G	2128	And that lelly me layne / I / leue wel thou woldez.	H	V Z H V
G	2129	Bot helde thou hit neuer so holde, / and I / here passed,	C H	Z V
G	2130	Founded for ferde for to fle, / in / fourme that thou tellez,	P	N that H V
G	2131	I were a knyʒt kowarde, / I / myʒt not be excused.	H	X not be E
G	2132	Bot I wyl to the chapel, / for / chaunce that may falle,	P	N that X V
G	2133	And talk wyth that ilk tulk / the / tale that me lyste,	D	N that H V
G	2134	Worthe hit wele other wo, / as the / wyrde lykez	C D	N V
G	2140	"Mary!" quoth that other mon, / "now thou so / much spellez,	Z H Z	N(A) V
G	2141	That thou wylt thyn awen nye / nyme to thyseluen,	/	V P H self
G	2142	And the lyst lese thy lyf, / the / lette I ne kepe.	H	V H not V
G	2143	Haf here thi helme on thy hede, / thi / spere in thi honde,	D	N P D N
G	2144	And ryde me doun this ilk rake / bi ʒon / rokke syde,	P D	N N
G	2145	Til thou be broʒt to the bothem / of the / brem valay;	P D	A N
G	2146	Thenne loke a littel on the launde, / on thi / lyfte honde,	P D	A N
G	2147	And thou schal se in that slade / the / self chapel,	D	A N
G	2148	And the borelych burne / on / bent that hit kepez.	P	N that H V
G	2149	Now farez wel, on Godez half, / Gawayn the noble!	/	N D A
G	2150	For alle the golde vpon grounde / I nolde / go wyth the,	H X	V P H
G	2151	Ne bere the felaʒschip thurʒ this fryth / on / fote fyrre."	P	N Z
G	2152	Bi that the wyʒe in the wod / wendez his brydel,	/	V D N
G	2153	Hit the hors with the helez / as / harde as he myʒt,	C	Z C H X
G	2154	Lepez hym ouer the launde, / and / leuez the knyʒt there	C	V D N Z
G	2160	Thenne gyrdez he to Gryngolet, / and / gederez the rake,	C	V D N
G	2161	Schowuez in bi a schore / at a / schaʒe syde,	P D	N N
G	2162	Ridez thurʒ the roʒe bonk / ryʒt to the dale;	/	Z P D N
G	2163	And thenne he wayted hym aboute, / and / wylde hit hym thoʒt,	C	A H H V
G	2164	And seʒe no syngne of resette / bisydez nowhere,	/	Z Z
G	2165	Bot hyʒe bonkkez and brent / vpon / bothe halue,	P	A N
G	2166	And ruʒe knokled knarrez / with / knorned stonez;	P	A(E) N
G	2167	The skwez of the scowtes / skayned hym thoʒt.	/	E H V
G	2168	Thenne he houed, and wythhylde / his / hors at that tyde,	D	N P D N
G	2169	And ofte chaunged his cher / the / chapel to seche:	D	N to V
G	2170	He seʒ non suche in no syde, / and / selly hym thoʒt,	C	A H V
G	2171	Saue, a lyttel on a launde, / a / lawe as hit were;	D	N C H be
G	2172	A balʒ berʒ bi a bonke / the / brymme bysyde,	D	N P
G	2173	Bi a forʒ of a flode / that / ferked thare;	that	V Z
G	2174	The borne blubred / therinne as hit / boyled hade.	Z C H	E have
G	2175	The knyʒt kachez his caple, / and / com to the lawe,	C	V P D N
G	2176	Liʒtez doun luflyly, / and at a / lynde tachez	C P D	N V
G	2177	The rayne and his riche / with a / roʒe braunche.	P D	A N
G	2178	Thenne he boʒez to the berʒe, / aboute hit he walkez,	/	P H H V
G	2179	Debatande with hymself / quat hit be myʒt.	/	H H be X
G	2180	Hit hade a hole on the ende / and on / ayther syde,	C P	A N
G	2181	And ouergrowen with gresse / in / glodes aywhere,	P	N Z
G	2182	And al watz holʒ inwith, / nobot an / olde caue,	Z D	A N
G	2183	Or a creuisse of an olde cragge, / he / couthe hit noʒt deme	H	X H not V
G	2189	"Now iwysse," quoth Wowayn, / "wysty is here;	/	A be Z
G	2190	This oritore is vgly, / with / erbez ouergrowen;	P	N E
G	2191	Wel bisemez the wyʒe / wruxled in grene	/	E P N
G	2192	Dele here his deuocioun / on the / deueler wyse.	P D	N N
G	2193	Now I fele hit is the fende, / in my / fyue wyttez,	P D	A N
G	2194	That hatz stoken me this steuen / to / strye me here.	to	V H Z
G	2195	This is a chapel of meschaunce, / that / chekke hit bytyde!	D	N H V
G	2196	Hit is the corsedest kyrk / that euer I / com inne!"	that Z H	V Z
G	2197	With heʒe helme on his hede, / his / launce in his honde,	D	N P D N
G	2198	He romez vp to the roffe / of the / roʒ wonez.	P D	A N
G	2199	Thene herde he of that hyʒe hil, / in a / harde roche	P D	A N
G	2200	Biʒonde the broke, in a bonk, / a / wonder breme noyse,	D	Z A N
G	2201	Quat! hit claterred in the clyff, / as hit / cleue schulde,	C H	V X
G	2202	As one vpon a gryndelston, / hade / grounden a sythe.	have	E D N
G	2203	What! hit wharred and whette, / as / water at a mulne;	P	N P D N
G	2204	What! hit rusched and ronge, / rawthe to here.	/	N to V
G	2205	Thenne "Bi Godde," quoth Gawayn, "that / gere, as I trowe,	D	N C H V

G	2206	Is ryched at the reuerence / me, / renk, to mete	H	N to V
G	2212	Thenne the kny3t con / calle ful hy3e:	/	V Z Z
G	2213	"Who sti3tlez in this sted / me / steuen to holde?	H	N to V
G	2214	For now is gode Gawayn / goande ry3t here.	/	G Z Z
G	2215	If any wy3e o3t wyl, / wynne hider fast,	/	V Z Z
G	2216	Other now other neuer, / his / nedez to spede."	D	N to V
G	2217	"Abyde", quoth on on the bonke / abouen ouer his hede,	/	Z P D N
G	2218	"And thou schal haf al in hast / that I the / hy3t ones."	that H H	V Z
G	2219	3et he rusched on that rurde / rapely a throwe.	/	Z Z
G	2220	And wyth quettyng awharf, / er he / wolde ly3t;	C H	X V
G	2221	And sythen he keuerez bi a cragge, / and / comez of a hole,	C	V P D N
G	2222	Whyrlande out of a wro / wyth a / felle weppen,	P D	A N
G	2223	A denez ax nwe dy3t, / the / dynt with to 3elde,	D	N P to V
G	2224	With a borelych bytte / bende by the halme,	/	E P D N
G	2225	Fyled in a fylor, / fowre fote large-	/	A N A
G	2226	Hit watz no lasse bi that lace / that / lemed ful bry3t-	that	V Z Z
G	2227	And the gome in the grene / gered as fyrst,	/	V C Z
G	2228	Bothe the lyre and the leggez, / lokkez and berde,	/	N C N
G	2229	Saue that fayre on his fote / he / foundez on the erthe,	H	V P D N
G	2230	Sette the stele to the stone, / and / stalked bysyde.	C	V Z
G	2231	When he wan to the watter, / ther he / wade nolde,	Q H	V X
G	2232	He hypped ouer on hys ax, / and / orpedly strydez,	C	Z V
G	2233	Bremly brothe on a bent / that / brode watz aboute,	that	A be Z
G	2239	"Gawayn," quoth that grene gome, / "God the mot loke!	/	N H X V
G	2240	Iwysse thou art welcom, / wy3e, to my place,	/	N P D N
G	2241	And thou hatz tymed thi trauayl / as / truee mon schulde,	C	A N X
G	2242	And thou knowez the couenauntez / kest vus bytwene:	/	V H P
G	2243	At this tyme twelmonyth / thou / toke that the falled,	H	V H H V
G	2244	And I schulde at this Nwe 3ere / 3eply the quyte.	/	Z H V
G	2245	And we ar in this valay / verayly oure one;	/	Z Z
G	2246	Here ar no renkes vs to rydde, / rele as vus likez.	/	V C H V
G	2247	Haf thy helme of thy hede, / and / haf here thy pay.	C	V Z D N
G	2248	Busk no more debate / then I the / bede thenne	C H H	V Z
G	2249	When thou wypped of my hede / at a / wap one."	P D	N A
G	2250	"Nay, bi God," quoth Gawayn, / "that me / gost lante,	that H	N V
G	2251	I schal gruch the no grwe / for / grem that fallez.	P	N that V
G	2252	Bot sty3tel the vpon on strok, / and I schal / stonde stylle	C H X	V Z
G	2253	And warp the no wernyng / to / worch as the lykez,	to	V C H V
G	2259	THEN the gome in the grene / graythed hym swythe,	/	V H Z
G	2260	Gederez vp hys grymme tole / Gawayn to smyte;	/	N to V
G	2261	With alle the bur in his body / he / ber hit on lofte,	H	V H Z
G	2262	Munt as ma3tyly / as / marre hym he wolde;	C	V H H X
G	2263	Hade hit dryuen adoun / as / dre3 as he atled,	C	Z C H V
G	2264	Ther hade ben ded of his dynt / that / do3ty watz euer.	that	A be Z
G	2265	Bot Gawayn on that giserne / glyfte hym bysyde,	/	V H P
G	2266	As hit com glydande / adoun on / glode hym to schende,	Z P	N H to V to D
G	2267	And schranke a lytel with the schulderes / for the / scharp yrne.	P D	A N
G	2268	That other schalk wyth a schunt / the / schene wythhaldez,	D	N(A) V
G	2269	And thenne repreued he the prynce / with mony / prowde wordez:	P D	A N
G	2270	"Thou art not Gawayn," quoth the gome, / "that is so / goud halden,	that be Z	A E
G	2271	That neuer ar3ed for no here / by / hylle ne be vale,	P	N not P N
G	2272	And now thou fles for ferde / er thou / fele harmez!	C H	V N
G	2273	Such cowardise of that kny3t / cowthe I neuer here.	/	X H Z V
G	2274	Nawther fyked I ne fla3e, / freke, quen thou myntest,	/	N C H V
G	2275	Ne kest no kauelacion / in / kyngez hous Arthor.	P	N N N
G	2276	My hede fla3 to my fote, / and 3et / fla3 I neuer;	C Z	V H Z
G	2277	And thou, er any harme hent, / ar3ez in hert;	/	V P N
G	2278	Wherfore the better burne / me / burde be called	H	X be E
G	2284	"Bot busk, burne, bi thi fayth, / and / bryng me to the poynt.	C	V H P D N
G	2285	Dele to me my destiné, / and / do hit out of honde,	C	V H P P N
G	2286	For I schal stonde the a strok, / and / start no more	C	V Z
G	2287	Til thyn ax haue me hitte: / haf here my trawthe."	/	V Z D N
G	2288	"Haf at the thenne!" quoth that other, / and / heuez hit alofte,	C	V H Z
G	2289	And waytez as wrothely / as he / wode were.	C H	A be
G	2290	He myntez at hym ma3tyly, / bot not the / mon rynez,	C not D	N V
G	2291	Withhelde heterly his honde, / er hit / hurt my3t.	C H	V X
G	2292	Gawayn graythely hit bydez, / and / glent with no membre,	C	V P D N
G	2293	Bot stode stylle as the ston, / other a / stubbe auther	C D	N C
G	2294	That ratheled is in roché grounde / with / rotez a hundreth.	P	N D N
G	2295	Then muryly efte con he mele, / the / mon in the grene:	D	N P D N
G	2296	"So, now thou hatz thi hert holle, / hitte me bihous.	/	V H V

G	2297	Halde the now the hyȝe hode / that / Arthur the raȝt,	that	N H V
G	2298	And kepe thy kauel at this kest, / ȝif hit / keuer may."	C H	V Y
G	2299	Gawayn ful gryndelly / with / greme thenne sayde:	P	N Z V
G	2300	"Wy! thresch on, thou thro mon, / thou / thretez to longe;	C	V Z Z
G	2301	I hope that thi hert arȝe / wyth thyn / awen seluen."	P D	A self
G	2302	"For sothe," quoth that other freke, / "so / felly thou spekez,	Z	Z H V
G	2303	I wyl no lenger on lyte / lette thin ernde	/	V D N
G	2309	He lyftes lyȝtly his lome, / and / let hit doun fayre	C	V H Z Z
G	2310	With the barbe of the bitte / bi the / bare nek;	P D	A N
G	2311	Thaȝ he homered heterly, / hurt hym no more	/	V H Z
G	2312	Bot snyrt hym on that on syde, / that / seuered the hyde.	that	V D N
G	2313	The scharp schrank to the flesche / thurȝ the / schyre grece,	P D	A N
G	2314	That the schene blod ouer his schulderes / schot to the erthe;	/	V P D N
G	2315	And quen the burne seȝ the blode / blenk on the snawe,	/	V P D N
G	2316	He sprit forth spenne-fote / more then a / spere lenthe,	A P D	N N
G	2317	Hent heterly his helme, / and on his / hed cast,	C P D	N V
G	2318	Schot with his schulderez / his / fayre schelde vnder,	D	A N P
G	2319	Braydez out a bryȝt sworde, / and / bremely he spekez-	C	Z H V
G	2320	Neuer syn that he watz burne / borne of his moder	/	E P D N
G	2321	Watz he neuer in this worlde / wyȝe half so blythe-	/	N Z A A
G	2322	"Blynne, burne, of thy bur, / bede me no mo!	/	V H Z
G	2323	I haf a stroke in this sted / withoute / stryf hent,	P	N V
G	2324	And if thow rechez me any mo, / I / redyly schal quyte,	H	Z X V
G	2325	And ȝelde ȝederly aȝayn- / and therto / ȝe tryst-	C Z	H V
G	2331	The hathel heldet / hym fro, and on his / ax rested,	H P C P D	N V
G	2332	Sette the schaft vpon schore, / and to the / scharp lened,	C P D	N(A) V
G	2333	And loked to the leude / that on the / launde ȝede,	that P D	N V
G	2334	How that doȝty, dredles, / deruely ther stondez	/	Z Z V
G	2335	Armed, ful aȝlez: / in / hert hit hym lykez.	P	N H H V
G	2336	Thenn he melez muryly / wyth a / much steuen,	P D	A N
G	2337	And wyth a rynkande rurde / he to the / renk sayde:	H P D	N V
G	2338	"Bolde burne, on this bent / be not so gryndel.	/	V not Z A
G	2339	No mon here vnmanerly / the / mysboden habbez,	D	E have
G	2340	Ne kyd bot as couenaunde / at / kyngez kort schaped.	P	N N V
G	2341	I hyȝt a strok and thou hit hatz, / halde the wel payed;	/	V H Z E
G	2342	I relece the of the remnaunt / of / ryȝtes alle other.	P	N A H
G	2343	Iif I deliuer had bene, / a / boffet paraunter	D	N Z
G	2344	I couthe wrotheloker haf waret, / to the haf / wroȝt anger.	P H have	E N
G	2345	Fyrst I mansed the muryly / with a / mynt one,	P D	N A
G	2346	And roue the wyth no rof-sore, / with / ryȝt I the profered	P	N H H V
G	2347	For the forwarde that we fest / in the / fyrst nyȝt,	P D	A N
G	2348	And thou trystyly the trawthe / and / trwly me haldez,	C	Z H V
G	2349	Al the gayne thow me gef, / as / god mon schulde.	C	A N X
G	2350	That other munt for the morne, / mon, I the profered,	/	N H H V
G	2351	Thou kyssedes my clere wyf- / the / cossez me raȝtez.	D	N H V
G	2352	For bothe two here I the bede / bot two / bare myntes	P D	A N
G	2358	"For hit is my wede that thou werez, / that ilke / wouen girdel,	that D	E N
G	2359	Myn owen wyf hit the weued, / I / wot wel for sothe.	H	V Z Z
G	2360	Now know I wel thy cosses, / and thy / costes als,	C D	N Z
G	2361	And the wowyng of my wyf: / I / wroȝt hit myseluen.	H	V H H self
G	2362	I sende hir to asay thi, the, / and / sothly me thynkkez	H C	A V
G	2363	On the fautlest freke / that euer on / fote ȝede,	that Z P	N V
G	2364	As perle bi the quite pese / is of / prys more,	be P	N A
G	2365	So is Gawayn, in god fayth, / bi other / gay knyȝtez.	P D	A N
G	2366	Bot here yow lakked a lyttel, / sir, and / lewté yow wonted;	N C	N H V
G	2367	Bot that watz for no wylyde werke, / ne / wowyng nauther,	not	N Z
G	2368	Bot for ȝe lufed your lyf; / the / lasse I yow blame."	D	Z H H V
G	2369	That other stif mon in study / stod a gret whyle,	/	V D A N
G	2370	So agreued for greme / he / gryed withinne;	H	V Z
G	2371	Alle the blode of his brest / blende in his face,	/	V P D N
G	2372	That al he schrank for schome / that the / schalk talked.	that D	N V
G	2373	The forme worde vpon folde / that the / freke meled:	that D	N V
G	2374	"Corsed worth cowarddyse / and / couetyse bothe!	C	N A
G	2375	In yow is vylany and vyse / that / vertue disstryez."	that	N V
G	2376	Thenne he kaȝt to the knot, / and he / kest lawsez,	C D	N V
G	2377	Brayde brothely the belt / to the / burne seluen:	P D	N self
G	2378	"Lo! ther the falssyng, / foule mot hit falle!	/	Z X H V
G	2379	For care of thy knokke / cowardyse me taȝt	/	N H V
G	2380	To acorde me with couetyse, / my / kynde to forsake,	D	N to V
G	2381	That is larges and lewté / that / longez to knyȝtez.	that	V P N
G	2382	Now am I fawty and falce, / and / ferde haf ben euer	C	E have E Z

Sir Gawain and the Green Knight

G	2383	Of trecherye and vntrawthe: / bothe / bityde sorȝe	H	V N
G	2389	Thenn loȝe that other leude / and / luflyly sayde:	C	Z V
G	2390	"I halde hit hardily hole, / the / harme that I hade.	D	N that H V
G	2391	Thou art confessed so clene, / beknowen of thy mysses,	/	E P D N
G	2392	And hatz the penaunce apert / of the / poynt of myn egge,	P D	N P D N
G	2393	I halde the polysed of that plyȝt, / and / pured as clene	C	E C A
G	2394	As thou hadez neuer forfeted / sythen thou watz / fyrst borne;	C H be	Z E
G	2395	And I gif the, sir, the gurdel / that is / golde-hemmed,	that be	N E
G	2396	For hit is grene as my goune. / Sir / Gawayn, ȝe maye	D	N H X
G	2397	Thenk vpon this ilke threpe, / ther thou / forth thryngez	Q H	Z V
G	2398	Among pryncez of prys, / and this a / pure token	C H D	A N
G	2399	Of the chaunce of the grene chapel / at / cheualrous knyȝtez.	P	A N
G	2400	And ȝe schal in this Nwe ȝer / aȝayn to my wonez,	/	Z P D N
G	2401	And we schyn reuel the remnaunt / of this / ryche fest	P D	A N
G	2407	"Nay, for sothe," quoth the segge, / and / sesed hys helme,	C	V D N
G	2408	And hatz hit hendely, / and the / hathel thonkkez,	C D	N V
G	2409	"I haf soiorned sadly; / sele yow bytyde,	/	N H V
G	2410	And he ȝelde hit yow ȝare / that / ȝarkkez al menskes!	that	V A N
G	2411	And comaundez me to that cortays, / your / comlych fere,	D	A N
G	2412	Bothe that on and that other, / myn / honoured ladyez,	D	E N
G	2413	That thus hor knyȝt wyth hor kest / han / koyntly bigyled.	have	Z E
G	2414	Bot hit is no ferly / thaȝ a / fole madde,	C D	N V
G	2415	And thurȝ wyles of wymmen / be / wonen to sorȝe,	be	E P N
G	2416	For so watz Adam in erde / with / one bygyled,	P	H V
G	2417	And Salamon with fele sere, / and / Samson eftsonez-	C	N Z
G	2418	Dalyda dalt hym hys wyrde- / and / Dauyth therafter	C	N Z
G	2419	Watz blended with Barsabe, / that much / bale tholed.	that D	N V
G	2420	Now these were wrathed wyth her wyles, / hit were a / wynne huge	H be D	N A
G	2421	To luf hom wel, and leue / hem not, a / leude that couthe	H not D	N H V
G	2422	For thes wer forne the freest, / that / folȝed alle the sele	that	V D D N
G	2423	Exellently of alle thyse other, / vnder / heuenryche	P	Z
G	2429	"Bot your gordel", quoth Gawayn, / "God yow forȝelde!	/	N H V
G	2430	That wyl I welde wyth goud wylle, / not for the / wynne golde,	not P D	A N
G	2431	Ne the saynt, ne the sylk, / ne the / syde pendaundes,	D D	A N
G	2432	For wele ne for worchyp, / ne for the / wlonk werkkez,	not P D	A N
G	2433	Bot in syngne of my surfet / I schal / se hit ofte,	H X	V H Z
G	2434	When I ride in renoun, / remorde to myseluen	/	V P H self
G	2435	The faut and the fayntyse / of the / flesche crabbed,	P D	N A
G	2436	How tender hit is to entyse / teches of fylthe;	/	N P N
G	2437	And thus, quen pryde schal me pryk / for / prowes of armes,	P	N P N
G	2438	The loke to this luf-lace / schal / lethe my hert.	X	V D N
G	2439	Bot on I wolde yow pray, / displeses yow neuer:	/	V H Z
G	2440	Syn ȝe be lorde of the ȝonder londe / ther I haf / lent inne	Q H have	E Z
G	2441	Wyth yow wyth worschyp- / the / wyȝe hit yow ȝelde	D	N H H V
G	2442	That vphaldez the heuen / and on / hyȝ sittez-	C Z	Z V
G	2443	How norne ȝe yowre ryȝt nome, / and thenne / no more?"	C Z	Z
G	2444	"That schal I telle the trwly," / quoth that / other thenne,	V D	H Z
G	2445	"Bertilak de Hautdesert / I / hat in this londe.	H	V P D N
G	2446	Thurȝ myȝt of Morgne la Faye, / that in my / hous lenges,	that P D	N V
G	2447	And koyntyse of clergye, / bi / craftes wel lerned,	P	N Z E
G	2448	The maystrés of Merlyn / mony hatz taken-	/	H have E
G	2449	For ho hatz dalt drwry / ful / dere sumtyme	Z	A Z
G	2450	With that conable klerk, / that / knowes alle your knyȝtez	that	V A D N
G	2456	"Ho wayned me vpon this wyse / to your / wynne halle	P D	A N
G	2457	For to assay the surquidré, / ȝif hit / soth were	C H	A be
G	2458	That rennes of the grete renoun / of the / Rounde Table;	P D	A N
G	2459	Ho wayned me this wonder / your / wyttez to reue,	D	N to V
G	2460	For to haf greued Gaynour / and / gart hir to dyȝe	C	E H to V
G	2461	With glopnyng of that ilke gome / that / gostlych speked	that	Z V
G	2462	With his hede in his honde / bifore the / hyȝe table.	P D	A N
G	2463	That is ho that is at home, / the / auncian lady;	D	A N
G	2464	Ho is euen thyn aunt, / Arthurez half-suster,	/	N A N
G	2465	The duches doȝter of Tyntagelle, / that / dere Vter after	D	A N P
G	2466	Hade Arthur vpon, / that / athel is nowthe.	that	A be Z
G	2467	Therfore I ethe the, hathel, / to / com to thyn aunt,	to	V P D N
G	2468	Make myry in my hous; / my / meny the louies,	D	N H V
G	2469	And I wol the as wel, / wyȝe, bi my faythe,	/	N P D N
G	2470	As any gome vnder God / for thy / grete trauthe."	P D	A N
G	2471	And he nikked hym naye, / he / nolde bi no wayes.	H	V P D N
G	2472	Thay acolen and kyssen / and / kennen ayther other	C	V H H
G	2473	To the prynce of paradise, / and / parten ryȝt there	C	V Z Z

G	2479	Wylde wayez in the worlde / Wowen now rydez	/	N Z V
G	2480	On Gryngolet, that the grace / hade / geten of his lyue;	have	E P D N
G	2481	Ofte he herbered in house / and / ofte al theroute,	C	Z Z Z
G	2482	And mony aventure in vale, / and / venquyst ofte,	C	V Z
G	2483	That I ne tyʒt at this tyme / in / tale to remene.	P	N to V
G	2484	The hurt watz hole / that he hade / hent in his nek,	that H have	E P D N
G	2485	And the blykkande belt / he / bere theraboute	H	V Z
G	2486	Abelef as a bauderyk / bounden bi his syde,	/	E P D N
G	2487	Loken vnder his lyfte arme, / the / lace, with a knot,	D	N P D N
G	2488	In tokenyng he watz tane / in / tech of a faute.	P	N P D N
G	2489	And thus he commes to the court, / knyʒt al in sounde.	/	N Z P N(A)
G	2490	Ther wakned wele in that wone / when / wyst the grete	C	V D N(A)
G	2491	That gode Gawayn watz commen; / gayn hit hym thoʒt.	/	N(A) H H V
G	2492	The kyng kyssez the knyʒt, / and the / whene alce,	C D	N Z
G	2493	And sythen mony syker knyʒt / that / soʒt hym to haylce,	that	V H to V
G	2494	Of his fare that hym frayned; / and / ferlyly he telles,	C	Z H V
G	2495	Biknowez alle the costes / of / care that he hade,	P	N that H V
G	2496	The chaunce of the chapel, / the / chere of the knyʒt,	D	N P D N
G	2497	The luf of the ladi, / the / lace at the last.	D	N Z
G	2498	The nirt in the nek / he / naked hem schewed	H	A H V
G	2499	That he laʒt for his vnleuté / at the / leudes hondes	P D	N N
G	2505	"Lo! lorde," quoth the leude, / and the / lace hondeled,	C D	N V
G	2506	"This is the bende of this blame / I / bere in my nek,	H	V P D N
G	2507	This is the lathe and the losse/ that I / laʒt haue	that H	E have
G	2508	Of couardise and couetyse / that I haf / caʒt thare;	that H have	E Z
G	2509	This is the token of vntrawthe / that I am / tan inne,	that H be	E Z
G	2510	And I mot nedez hit were / wyle I may last;	/	C H X V
G	2511	For mon may hyden his harme, / bot / vnhap ne may hit,	C	V not X H
G	2512	For ther hit onez is tachched / twynne wil hit neuer."	/	V X H Z
G	2513	The kyng comfortez the knyʒt, / and alle the / court als	C D D	N Z
G	2514	Laʒen loude / therat, and / luflyly acorden	Z C	Z V
G	2515	That lordes and ladis / that / longed to the Table,	that	V P D N
G	2516	Vche burne of the brotherhede, / a / bauderyk schulde haue,	D	N X V
G	2517	A bende abelef hym aboute / of a / bryʒt grene,	P D	A N
G	2518	And that, for sake of that segge, / in / swete to were.	P	N to V
G	2519	For that watz acorded the renoun / of the / Rounde Table,	P D	A N
G	2520	And he honoured that hit hade / euermore after,	/	Z Z
G	2521	As hit is breued in the best boke / of / romaunce.	P	N
G	2522	Thus in Arthurus day / this / aunter bitidde,	D	N V
G	2523	The Brutus bokez / therof / beres wyttenesse;	Z	V N
G	2524	Syphen Brutus, the bolde burne, / boʒed hider fyrst,	/	V Z Z
G	2525	After the segge and the asaute / watz / sesed at Troye,	be	E P N

The Alliterative Morte Arthure

MA 1	How grett glorious Godd, / thurgh / grace of Hym seluen,	P	N P H self
MA 2	And the precyous prayere / of Hys / prys Modyr,	P D	A N
MA 3	Schelde vs fro schamesdede / and / synfull werkes,	C	A N
MA 4	And gyffe vs grace to gye / and / gouerne vs here,	C	V H Z
MA 5	In this wrechyd werld, / thorowe / vertous lywynge,	P	A N
MA 6	That we may kayre til Hys courte, / the / kyngdom of Hevyne,	D	N P N
MA 7	When oure saules schall parte / and / sundyre fra the body,	C	V P D N
MA 8	Ewyre to belde and to byde / in / blysse wyth Hym seluen;	P	N P H self
MA 9	And wysse me to werpe / owte som / worde at this tym	Z D	N P D N
MA 10	That nothyre voyde be ne vayne, / bot / wyrchip till Hym selvyn,	C	N C H self
MA 11	Plesande and profitabill / to the / popule that them heres.	P D	N that H V
MA 12	3e that liste has to lyth / or / luffes for to here	C	V for to V
MA 13	Off elders of alde tym / and of theire / awke dedys,	C P D	A N
MA 14	How they were lele in theire lawe / and / louede God Almyghty,	C	V N A
MA 15	Herkynes me heyndly / and / holdys 3ow styll,	C	V H A
MA 16	And I sall tell 3ow a tale / that / trewe es and nobyll,	that	A be C A
MA 17	Off the ryeall renkys / of the / Rownnde Table,	P D	A N
MA 18	That chefe ware of cheualrye / and / cheftans nobyll,	C	N A
MA 19	Bathe ware in thire werkes / and / wyse men of armes,	C	A N P N
MA 20	Doughty in theire doyngs / and / dredde ay schame,	C	V Z N
MA 21	Kynde men and courtays / and / couthe of courte thewes;	C	A P N N
MA 22	How they whanne wyth / were / wyrchippis many,	be	N A
MA 23	Sloughe Lucyus the lythyre, / that / Lorde was of Rome,	that	N be P N
MA 24	And conqueryd that kyngryke / thorowe / craftys of armes;	P	N P N
MA 25	Herkenes now hedyrwarde / and / herys this storye.	C	V D N
MA 26	Qwen that the kyng Arthur / by / conqueste hade wonnyn	P	N have E
MA 27	Castells and kyngdoms / and / contreez many,	C	N A
MA 28	And he had couerede the coroun / of the / kyth ryche,	P D	N A
MA 29	Of all that Vter in erthe / aughte in his tym	/	V P D N
MA 30	Orgayle and Orkenay / and all this / owte iles,	C D D	A N
MA 31	Irelande vttirly, / as / occyane rynnys;	C	N V
MA 32	Scathyll Scottlande by skyll / he / skyftys as hym lykys,	P	V C H V
MA 33	And Wales of were / he / wane at hys will;	H	V P D N
MA 34	Bathe Flaundrez and Fraunce / fre til him seluyn,	/	Z P H self
MA 35	Holaund and Henawde / they / helde of hym bothen,	H	V P N Z
MA 36	Burgoyne and Brabane / and / Bretayn the Lasse,	C	N D N(A)
MA 37	Gyan and Gothelande / and / Grace the ryche;	C	N D A
MA 38	Bayon and Burdeux / he / beldytt full faire,	H	V Z Z
MA 39	Turoyn and Tholus, / with / toures full hye;	P	N Z A
MA 40	Off Peyters and of Prouynce / he was / prynce holdyn,	H be	N E
MA 41	Of Valence and Vyenne, / off / value so noble,	P	N Z A
MA 42	Of Ouergne and Anyou, / thos / erledoms ryche,	D	N A
MA 43	By conqueste full cruell / they / knewe hym fore lorde;	H	V H P N
MA 44	Of Nauerne and Norwaye / and / Normaundye eke,	C	N Z
MA 45	Of Almayne, of Estriche, / and / other ynowe;	C	H A
MA 46	Danmarke he dryssede / all by / drede of hym seluyn,	Z P	N P H self
MA 47	Fra Swynn vnto Swetherwyke, / with his / swerde kene.	P D	N A
MA 48	Qwenn he thes dedes had don, / he / doubbyd hys knyghtez,	H	V D N
MA 49	Dyuysyde dowcherys and delte / in / dyuerse remmes,	P	A N
MA 50	Mad of his cosyns / kyngys ennoyntede,	/	N E
MA 51	In kyth there they couaitte / crounes to bere.	/	N to V
MA 52	Whene he thys rewmes hade redyn / and / rewlyde the popule,	C	V D N
MA 53	Then rystede that ryall / and helde the / Rounde Tabyll;	C V D	A N
MA 54	Suggeourns that seson / to / solace hym seluen	to	V H self
MA 55	In Bretayn the Braddere, / as hym / beste lykes.	C H	A V
MA 56	Sythyn wente into Wales / with / wyes all,	P D	N A
MA 57	Sweys into Swaldye / with his / snell houndes,	P D	A N
MA 58	For to hunt at the hartes / in thas / hye laundes,	P D	A N
MA 59	In Glamorgan with glee, / thare / gladchipe was euere.	Q	N be Z
MA 60	And thare a citee he sette, / be / assentte of his lordys,	P	N P D N
MA 61	That Caerlyon was callid, / with / curius walles,	P	A N
MA 62	On the riche reuare / that / rynnys so faire,	that	V Z Z
MA 63	There he myghte semble his sorte / to / see whenn hym lykede.	to	V Q H V
MA 64	Thane aftyre at Carlele / a / Cristynmese he haldes,	D	N H V
MA 65	This ilke kyde conquerour, / and / helde hym for lorde,	C	V H P N
MA 66	Wyth dukez and duspers / of / dyuers rewmes,	P	A N

MA 67	Erles and ercheuesqes / and / other ynowe,	C	H A
MA 68	Byschopes and bachelers / and / banerettes nobill,	C	N A
MA 69	That bowes to his banere, / buske when hym lykys.	/	V C H V
MA 70	Bot on the Cristynmes Daye, / when they were / all semblyde,	C H be	Z E
MA 71	That comlyche conquerour / commaundez hym seluyn	/	V H self
MA 72	That ylke a lorde sulde lenge / and no / lefe take	C D	N V
MA 73	To the tende day fully / ware / takyn to the ende.	be	E P D N
MA 74	Thus on ryall araye he helde / his / Rounde Table,	D	A N
MA 75	With semblant and solace / and / selcouthe metes;	C	A N
MA 76	Whas neuer syche noblay / in no / manys tym	P D	N N
MA 77	Mad in mydwynter / in tha / weste marchys.	P D	N N
MA 78	Bot on the Newʒere Daye, / at the / none euyne,	P D	N Z
MA 79	As the bolde at the borde / was of / brede seruyde,	be P	N E
MA 80	So come in sodanly / a / senatour of Rome,	D	N P N
MA 81	Wyth sexten knyghtes in a soyte, / sewande hym one.	/	G N P
MA 82	He saluʒed the souerayne, / and the / sale aftyr,	C D	N P
MA 83	Ilke a kyng aftyre kyng, / and / mad his enclines;	C	V D N
MA 84	Gaynour in hir degre / he / grette as hym lykyde,	H	V C H V
MA 85	And syne agayne to the gome / he / gaffe vp his nedys:	H	V Z D N
MA 86	"Sir Lucius Iberius, / the / Emperour of Rome,	D	N P N
MA 87	Saluz the as sugett, / vndyre his / sele ryche;	P D	N A
MA 88	It es credens, Sir Kyng, / with / cruell wordez;	P	A N
MA 89	Trow it for no trufles: / his / targe es to schewe.	D	N be to V
MA 90	Now in this Newʒers Daye, / with / notaries synge,	P	N N
MA 91	I make the somouns in sale / to / sue for thi landys,	to	V P D N
MA 92	That on Lammesse Daye / thare be no / lette founden,	Q be D	N V
MA 93	That thow bee redy at Rome / with all thi / Rounde Table,	P D D	A N
MA 94	Appere in thy presens / with thy / price knyghtez,	P D	A N
MA 95	At pryme of the daye, / in / payne of ʒour lyvys,	P	N P D N
MA 96	In the kydd capytoile, / before the / kyng selvyn,	P D	N self
MA 97	When he and his senatours / bez / sette as them lykes,	be	E C H V
MA 98	To ansuere anely / why thow / ocupyes the laundez	Q H	V D N
MA 99	That awe homage of alde / till / hym and his eldyrs;	P	H C D N(A)
MA 100	Why thow has redyn and raymede / and / raunsound the pople,	C	V D N
MA 101	And kyllyde doun his cosyns, / kyngys ennoynttyde;	/	N E
MA 102	Thare schall thow gyffe rekkynyng / for all thy / Rounde Table	P D D	A N
MA 103	Why thow arte rebell to Rome / and / rentez them wytholdez.	C	N H V
MA 104	ʒiff thow theis somouns wythsytte, / he / sendes thie thies wordes:	H	V H D N
MA 105	He sall the seke ouer the see / wyth / sexten kynges,	P	A N
MA 106	Bryne Bretayn the Brade / and / bryttyn thy knyghtys,	C	V D N
MA 107	And bryng the bouxsomly as a beste / with / brethe whare hym lykes,	P	N Q H V
MA 108	That thow ne schall rowte ne ryste / vndyre the / heuene ryche,	P D	N A
MA 109	Thofe thow for reddour of Rome / ryne to the erthe;	/	V P D N
MA 110	For if thow flee into Fraunce / or / Freselaund owther,	C	N Z
MA 111	Thou sall be feched with force / and / ouersette fore euer!	C	E Z
MA 112	Thy fadyr mad fewtee, / we / fynde in oure rollez,	H	V P D N
MA 113	In the regestre of Rome, / who-so / ryghte lukez.	Q	A V
MA 114	Withowttyn more trouflyng / the / trebute we aske	D	N H V
MA 115	That Iulius Cesar wan / with his / ientill knyghttes."	P D	A N
MA 116	The Kyng blyschit on the beryn / with his / brode eghn,	P D	A N
MA 117	That full brymly for breth / brynte as the gledys,	/	V P D N
MA 118	Keste colours as Kyng, / with / crouell lates,	P	A N
MA 119	Luked as a lyon, / and on his / lyppe bytes.	C P D	N V
MA 120	The Romaynes for radnesse / ruschte to the erthe,	/	V P D N
MA 121	Fore ferdnesse of hys face, / as they / fey were;	C H	A be
MA 122	Cowchide as kenetez / before the / Kyng seluyn;	P D	N self
MA 123	Because of his contenaunce / confusede them semede.	/	E H V
MA 124	Then couerd vp a knyghte / and / criede ful lowde,	C	V Z Z
MA 125	"Kyng corounede of kynd, / curtays and noble,	/	A C A
MA 126	Misdoo no messangere / for / menske of thi seluyn,	P	N P H self
MA 127	Sen we are in thy manrede / and / mercy the besekes.	C	N H V
MA 128	We lenge with Sir Lucius, / that / Lorde es of Rome,	that	N be P N
MA 129	That es the meruelyousteste man / that on / molde lengez;	that P	N V
MA 130	It is lefull till vs / his / likyng till wyrche;	D	G Z V
MA 131	We come at his commaundment; / haue vs excusede."	/	V H E
MA 132	Then carpys the Conquerour / crewell wordez;		A N
MA 133	"Haa, crauaunde knyghte, / a / cowarde the semez!	D	N H V
MA 134	Thare [is] some segge in this sale, / and he ware / sare greuede,	C H be	Z E
MA 135	Thow durste noghte for all Lumberdye / luke on hym ones."	/	V P H Z
MA 136	"Sir," sais the Senatour, / "so / Crist mott me helpe,	C	N X H V
MA 137	The voute of thi vesage / has / woundyde vs all!	have	E H Z

MA 138	Thow arte the lordlyeste lede / that / euer I one lukyde;	that	Z H Z V
MA 139	By lukyng, withowttyn lesse, / a / lyon the semys!"	D	N H V
MA 140	"Thow has me somond," quod the Kyng, / "and / said what the lykes;	C	V Q H V
MA 141	Fore sake of thy soueraynge / I / suffre the the more;	H	V H Z
MA 142	Sen I [was] coround in kyth, / wyth / crysum enoyntede,	P	N E
MA 143	Was neuer creature / to me that / carpede so large.	P H that	V Z Z
MA 144	Bot I sall tak concell / at / kynges enoyntede,	P	N E
MA 145	Off dukes and duspers / and / doctours noble,	C	N A
MA 146	Offe peres of the parlement, / prelates and other,	/	N C H
MA 147	Off the richeste renkys / of the / Rounde Table;	P D	A N
MA 148	Thus schall I take avisemente / of / valiant beryns,	P	A N
MA 149	Wyrke aftyre the wytte / of my / wyes knyghttes;	P D	N N
MA 150	To warpe wordez in waste / no / wyrchip it were,	D	N H be
MA 151	Ne wilfully in this wrethe / to / wreken my seluen.	to	V H self
MA 152	Forthi sall thow lenge here / and / lugge wyth thise lordes,	C	V P D N
MA 153	This seuenyghte in solace, / to / suggourne 3our horses,	to	V D N
MA 154	To see whatte lyfe that wee leede / in thees / lawe laundes,	P D	A N
MA 155	Forby the realtee of Rome, / that / recheste was euere."	that	A be Z
MA 156	He command Sir Cayous, / "Take / kepe to thoos lordez,	V	N P D N
MA 157	To styghtyll tha steryn men / as theire / statte askys,	C D	N V
MA 158	That they bee herberde in haste / in thoos / heghe chambres,	P D	A N
MA 159	Sythin sittandly in sale / seruyde theraftyr.	/	V Z
MA 160	That they fynd na fawte / of / fude to thiere horsez,	P	N P D N
MA 161	Nowthire weyn, ne waxe, / ne / welthe in this erthe,	D	N P D N
MA 162	Spare for no spycerye, / bot / spende what the lykys,	C	V Q H V
MA 163	That there be largesce on lofte / and no / lake founden.	C D	N E
MA 164	If thou my wyrchip wayte, / wy, be my trouthe,	/	N P D N
MA 165	Thou sall haue gersoms full grett, / that / gayne sall the euere."	that	V X H Z
MA 166	Now er they herberde in hey / and in / oste holden,	C D	N V
MA 167	Hastyly wyth hende men / within thees / heghe wallez;	P D	A N
MA 168	In chambyrs with chympnes / they / chaungen theire wedez,	H	V D N
MA 169	And sythyn the chauncelere them fecchede / with / cheualrye noble.	P	N A
MA 170	Sone the Senatour was sett, / as hym / wele semyde;	C H	A V
MA 171	At the Kyngez ownn borde / twa / knyghtes hym seruede,	D	N H V
MA 172	Singulere sothely, / as / Arthure hym seluyn,	P	N H self
MA 173	Richely on the ryghte hannde / at the / Round Table,	P D	A N
MA 174	Be resoun that the Romaynes / whare so / ryche holden,	Q Z	A V
MA 175	As of the realeste blode / that / reynede in erthe.	that	V P N
MA 176	There come in at the fyrste coursse, / befor the / Kyng seluen,	P D	N self
MA 177	Bareheuedys that ware bryghte, / burnyste with syluer,	/	E P N
MA 178	All with taghte men and town / in / togers full ryche,	P	N Z A
MA 179	Of saunke reall in suyte, / sexty at ones;	/	N Z
MA 180	Flesch fluriste of fermyson / with / frumentee noble,	P	N A
MA 181	Therto wylde to wale / and / wynlyche bryddes,	C	A N
MA 182	Pacokes and plouers / in / platers of golde,	P	N P N
MA 183	Pygges of porke despyne / that / pasturede neuer,	that	V Z
MA 184	Sythen herons in hedoyne, / hyled full faire,	/	E Z A
MA 185	Grett swannes full swythe / in / silueryn chargeours,	P	A N
MA 186	Tartes of turky, / taste wham them lykys,	/	V Q H V
MA 187	Gumbaldes grathely, / full / gracious to taste,	Z	A to V
MA 188	Seyne bowes of wylde bores / with the / braune lechyde,	P D	N E
MA 189	Bernakes and botures / in / baterde dysches,	P	E N
MA 190	Thareby braunchers in brede, / bettyr was neuer,	/	A be Z
MA 191	With brestez of barowes / that / bryghte ware to schewe;	that	A be to V
MA 192	Seyn come ther sewes sere, / with / solace theraftyr,	P	N Z
MA 193	Ownd of azure all ouer / and / ardant them semyde,	C	A H V
MA 194	Of ilke a leche the lowe / launschide full hye,	/	V Z Z
MA 195	That all ledes myghte lyke / that / lukyde them apon;	that	V H P
MA 196	Than cranes and curlues / craftyly rosted,	/	Z E
MA 197	Connygez in cretoyne, / colourede full faire,	/	E Z A
MA 198	Fesauntez enflureschit / on / flammande siluer,	P	G N
MA 199	With dariells endoride / and / daynteez ynewe;	C	N A
MA 200	Thane clarett and creette, / clergyally rennen,	/	Z V
MA 201	With condethes full curious, / all of / clene siluyre,	Z P	A N
MA 202	Osay a[n]d algarde / and / other ynewe,	C	H A
MA 203	Rynisch wyne and rochell, / richere was neuer,	/	A be Z
MA 204	Vernage of Venyce / vertuouse and Crete,	/	A C N
MA 205	In faucetez of fyn golde, / fonode whoso lykes.	/	V Q V
MA 206	The Kyngez cope-borde / was / closed in siluer,	be	E P N
MA 207	In grete goblettez ouergylte, / glorious of hewe;	/	A P N
MA 208	There was a cheefe buttlere, / a / cheualere noble,	D	N A

MA 209	Sir Cayous the curtaise, / that of the / cowpe seruede:	that P D	N V
MA 210	Sexty cowpes of suyte / fore the / Kyng seluyn,	P D	N self
MA 211	Crafty and curious, / coruen full faire,	/	E Z A
MA 212	In euerilk a party pyghte / with / precyous stones,	P	A N
MA 213	That nan enpoyson sulde goo / preuely thervndyre,	/	Z Z
MA 214	Bot the bryght golde for brethe / sulde / briste al to peces,	X	V Z P N
MA 215	Or ells the venym sulde voyde / thurghe / vertue of the stones.	P	N P D N
MA 216	And the Conquerour hym seluen, / so / clenly arayede,	Z	Z E
MA 217	In colours of clene golde / cleede, wyth his knyghttys,	/	E P D N
MA 218	Drissid with his dyademe / on his / deesse ryche,	P D	N A
MA 219	Fore he was demyd the doughtyeste / that / duellyde in erthe.	that	V P N
MA 220	Thane the Conquerour kyndly / carpede to those lordes,	/	V P D N
MA 221	Rehetede the Romaynes / with / realle speche:	P	A N
MA 222	"Sirs, bez knyghtly of contenaunce, / and / comfurthes ȝour seluyn;	C	V H self
MA 223	We knowe noghte in this countre / of / curious metez,	P	A N
MA 224	In thees barayne landez, / bredes none other;	/	V Z
MA 225	Forethy, wythowttyn feynyng, / enforce ȝow the more	/	V H Z
MA 226	To feede ȝow with syche feble / as ȝe / before fynde."	C H	Z V
MA 227	"Sir," sais the Senatour, / "soo / Criste motte me helpe,	C	N X H V
MA 228	There ryngnede neuer syche realtee / within / Rome walles!	P	N N
MA 229	There ne es prelatte, ne pape, / ne / prynce in this erthe,	D	N P D N
MA 230	That he ne myghte be wele payede / of thees / pryce metes."	P D	A N
MA 231	Aftyre theyre welthe they wesche / and / went vnto chambyre,	C	V P N
MA 232	This ilke kydde Conquerour, / with / knyghtes ynewe;	P	N A
MA 233	Sir Gaywayne the worthye Dame / Waynour he ledys;	/	N H V
MA 234	Sir Owghtreth on the tother syde, / of / Turry was lorde.	P	N be N
MA 235	Thane spyces vnsparyly / thay / spendyde thereaftyre:	H	V Z
MA 236	Maluesye and muskadell, / thase / meruelyous drynkes,	D	A N
MA 237	Raykede full rathely / in / rossete cowpes,	P	A N
MA 238	Till all the riche on rawe, / Romaynes and other.	/	N C H
MA 239	Bot the soueraingne sothely, / for / solauce of hym seluen,	P	N P H self
MA 240	Assingnyde to the Senatour / certaygne lordes,	/	A N
MA 241	To lede to his leuere, / whene he / leue askes,	C H	N V
MA 242	With myrthe and with melodye / of / mynstralsy noble.	P	N A
MA 243	Thane the Conquerour to concell / cayres thereaftyre,	/	V Z
MA 244	Wyth lordes of his lygeaunce / that to hym / selfe langys;	that P H	self V
MA 245	To the geauntes toure / iolily he wendes,	/	Z H V
MA 246	Wyth justicez and iuggez / and / gentill knyghtes.	C	A N
MA 247	Sir Cador of Cornewayle / to the / Kyng carppes,	P D	N V
MA 248	Lughe on hym luffly / with / lykande lates:	P	G N
MA 249	"I thanke Gode of that thra / that vs / thus thretys!	that H	Z V
MA 250	Ȝow moste be traylede, I trowe, / bot ȝife ȝe / trett bettyre.	C C H	V Z
MA 251	The lettres of Sir Lucius / lyghttys myn herte!	/	V D N
MA 252	We hafe as losels liffyde / many / longe daye,	D	A N
MA 253	Wyth delyttes in this land / with / lordchipez many,	P	N A
MA 254	And forelytenede the loos / that / we are layttede;	that	H be E
MA 255	I was abaischite, be oure Lorde, / of oure / beste bernes,	P D	A N
MA 256	Fore gret dule of deffuse / of / dedez of armes.	P	N P N
MA 257	Now wakkenyse the were! / Wyrchipide be Cryste!	/	E be N
MA 258	And we sall wynn it ag[a]yne / be / wyghttnesse and strenghe!"	P	N C N
MA 259	"Sir Cadour," quod the Kyng, / "thy / concell es noble;	D	N be A
MA 260	Bot thou arte a meruailous man / with thi / mery wordez;	P D	A N
MA 261	For thy countez no caas, / ne / castes no forthire,	D	N Z
MA 262	Bot hurles furthe appon heuede, / as thi / herte thynkes.	C D	N V
MA 263	I moste trette of a trew / towchande thise nedes,	/	G D N
MA 264	Talke of thies tythdands / that / tenes myn herte:	that	V D N
MA 265	Thou sees that the Emperour / es / angerde a lyttill;	be	E Z
MA 266	Yt semes be his sandismen / that he es / sore greuede;	that H be	Z E
MA 267	His senatour has sommonde / me and / said what hym lykyde,	H C	V Q H V
MA 268	Hethely in my hall, / wyth / heynȝous wordes,	P	A N
MA 269	In speche disspyszede / me and / sparede me lyttill,	H C	V H Z
MA 270	I myght noghte speke for spytte, / so my / herte trymblyde!	C D	N V
MA 271	He askyde me tyrauntly / tribute of Rome,	/	N P N
MA 272	That tenufully tynt / was in / tym of myn elders.	be P	N P D N(A)
MA 273	There alyenes, in absence / of / all men of armes,	P	A N P N
MA 274	Couerd it of comons, / as / cronicles telles.	C	N V
MA 275	I have title to take / tribute of Rome;	/	N P N
MA 276	Myne ancestres ware emperours / and / aughte it them seluen,	C	V H H self
MA 277	Belyn and Brene / and / Bawdewyne the Thyrde;	C	N D H
MA 278	They ocupyede the Empyre / aughte score wynnttyrs,	/	A N N
MA 279	Ilkane ayere aftyre other, / as / awlde men telles;	C	A N V

The Alliterative Morte Arthure   245

MA 280	Thei couerde the capitoile / and / keste doun the walles,	C		V Z D N
MA 281	Hyngede of theire heddys-men / by / hundrethes at ones.	P		N Z
MA 282	Seyn Constantyne, our kynsmane, / conquerid it aftyre,	/		V H P
MA 283	That ayere was of Ynglande / and / Emperour of Rome,	C		N P N
MA 284	He that conquerid the crosse / be / craftez of armes	P		N P N
MA 285	That Criste was on crucifiede, / that / Kyng es of Heuen.	that		N be P N
MA 286	Thus hafe we euydens to aske / the / Emperour the same,	D		N D A
MA 287	That thus regnez at Rome, / whate / ryghte that he claymes."	Q		N that H V
MA 288	Than answarde Kyng Aungers / to / Arthure hym seluyn,	P		N H self
MA 289	Thow aughte to be ouerlynge / ouer all / other kynges,	P D		A N
MA 290	Fore wyseste and worthyeste / and / wyghteste of hanndes,	C		A P N
MA 291	The knyghtlyeste of counsaile / that euer / coron bare;	that Z		N V
MA 292	I dare saye fore Scottlande / that we them / schathe lympyde:	that H H		V V
MA 293	When the Romaynes regnede / thay / raunsound oure eldyrs,	H		V D N
MA 294	And rade in theire ryotte / and / rauyschett oure wyfes,	C		V D N
MA 295	Withowttyn reson or ryghte / refte vs oure gudes.	/		V H D N
MA 296	And I sall make myn avowe / deuotly to Criste,	/		Z P N
MA 297	And to the haly vernacle, / vertuus and noble,	/		A C A
MA 298	Of this grett velany / I sall be / vengede ones,	H X be		E Z
MA 299	On ȝone venemus men, / wyth / valiant knyghtes!	P		A N
MA 300	I sall the forthire of defence, / fosterde ynewe,	/		E Z
MA 301	Fifty thowsande men, / wythin / two eldes,	P		A N
MA 302	Of my wage for to wende / whare so the lykes,	/		Q H V
MA 303	To fyghte wyth thy faamen, / that vs / vnfaire ledes!	that H		Z V
MA 304	Thane the burelyche Beryn / of / Bretayne the Lyttyll	P		N D A
MA 305	Counsayles Sir Arthure, / and of / hym besekys	C P		H V
MA 306	To ansuere the alyenes / wyth / austeren wordes,	P		A N
MA 307	To entyce the Emperour / to / take ouere the mounttes.	to		V Z D N
MA 308	He said, I make myn avowe / verreilly to Cryste	/		Z P N
MA 309	And to the haly vernacle / that / voide schall I neuere,	that		V X H Z
MA 310	For radnesse of na Romayne / that / regnes in erthe,	that		V P N
MA 311	Bot aye be redye in araye / and at / areste founden.	C P		N E
MA 312	No more dowtte the dynte / of theire / derfe wapyns,	P D		A N
MA 313	Than the dewe that es dannke / when that it / doun falles:	C that H		Z V
MA 314	Ne no more schoune fore the swape / of theire / scharpe suerddes,	P D		A N
MA 315	Then fore the faireste flour / thatt on the / folde growes!	that P D		N V
MA 316	I sall to batell the brynge / of / brenyede knyghtes	P		E N
MA 317	Thyrtty thosannde be tale, / thryftye in armes,	/		A P N
MA 318	Wythin a monethe daye / into / whatte marche	P		Q N
MA 319	That thow wyll sothelye assygne, / when thy / selfe lykes.	C H		self V
MA 320	A! A! sais the Walsche kyng, / wirchipid be Criste!	/		E be N
MA 321	Now schalle we wreke full wele / the / wrethe of oure elders!	D		N P D N
MA 322	In West Walys iwysse / syche / wonndyrs thay wroghte,	D		N H V
MA 323	That all for wandrethe may wepe / that on that / were thynkes.	that P that		be V
MA 324	I sall haue the avanttwarde / wytterly my seluen,	/		Z H self
MA 325	Tyll that I haue venquiste / the / Vicounte of Rome,	D		N P N
MA 326	That wroghte me at Viterbe / a / velanye ones,	D		N Z
MA 327	As I paste in pylgremage / by the / Pounte Tremble;	P D		N N
MA 328	He was in Tuskayne that tyme / and / tuke of oure knyghttes,	C		V P D N
MA 329	Areste them vnryghttwyslye / and / raunsound tham aftyre;	C		V H P
MA 330	I sall hym surelye ensure / that / saghetyll sall we neuer,	that		V X H Z
MA 331	Are we sadlye assemble / by oure / selfen ones,	P D		self Z
MA 332	And dele dynttys of dethe / with oure / derfe wapyns!	P D		A N
MA 333	And I sall wagge to that were, / of / wyrchipfull knyghtes,	P		A N
MA 334	Of Wyghte and of Walschelande / and of the / weste marches,	C P D		A N
MA 335	Twa thosande in tale, / horsede one stedys,	/		E P N
MA 336	Of the wyghteste wyes / in all ȝone / weste landys!"	P D D		A N
MA 337	Syre Ewan fytz Vryence / thane / egerly fraynez,	Z		Z V
MA 338	Was cosyn to the Conquerour, / corageous hym selfen,	/		A H self
MA 339	"Sir, and we wyste ȝour wyll, / we walde / wirke theraftyre:	H X		V Z
MA 340	ȝif this journee sulde halde / or be / ajournede forthyre,	C be		E Z
MA 341	To ryde one ȝone Romaynes / and / ryott theire landez,	C		V D N
MA 342	We walde schape vs therefore / to / schippe whene ȝow lykys."	to		V Q H V
MA 343	"Cosyn," quod the Conquerour, / "kyndly thou asches;	/		Z H V
MA 344	ȝife my concell accorde / to / conquere ȝone landez,	to		V D N
MA 345	By the kalendez of Iuny / we schall / encountre ones,	H X		V Z
MA 346	Wyth full creuell knyghtez, / so / Cryste mot me helpe!	C		N X H V
MA 347	Thereto make I myn avowe / devottly to Cryste,	/		Z P N
MA 348	And to the holy vernacle, / vertuous and noble,	/		A C A
MA 349	I sall at Lammesse take leue / to / lenge at my large	to		V P D N
MA 350	In Lorayne or Lumberdye, / whethire me / leue thynkys;	Q H		A V

MA 351	Merke vnto Meloyne / and / myne doun the wallez,	C	V Z D N
MA 352	Bathe of Petyrsande and of Pyś / and of the / Pounte Tremble,	C P D	N N
MA 353	In the Vale of Viterbe / vetaile my knyghttes,	/	V D N
MA 354	Suggourne there sex wokes / and / solace my selfen;	C	V H self
MA 355	Send prekers to the price toun / and / plaunte there my segge,	C	V Z D N
MA 356	Bot if thay profre me the pece / be / processe of tym."	P	N P N
MA 357	"Certys," sais Sir Ewayn, / "and I / avowe aftyre,	C H	V Z
MA 358	And I that hathell may see / euer with myn eghn,	/	Z P D N
MA 359	That occupies thin heritage, / the / Empyere of Rome,	D	N P N
MA 360	I sall auntyre me anes / hys / egle to touche,	D	N to V
MA 361	That borne es in his banere / of / brighte golde ryche,	P	A N A
MA 362	And raas it from his riche men / and / ryfe it in sondyre,	C	V H Z
MA 363	Bot he be redily reschowede / with / riotous knyghtez!	P	A N
MA 364	I sall enforsse ʒowe in the felde / with / fresche men of armes,	P	A N P N
MA 365	Fyfty thosande folke / apon / faire stedys,	P	A N
MA 366	On thi foomen to foonde, / there the / faire thynkes,	Q H	Z V
MA 367	In Fraunce or in Friselande, / feghte when the lykes!	/	V C H V
MA 368	By oure Lorde, quod Sir Launcelott, / now / lyghttys myn herte!	Z	V D N
MA 369	I loue Gode of this loue / this / lordes has avowede.	D	N have E
MA 370	Nowe may lesse men haue leue / to / say whatt them lykes,	to	V Q H V
MA 371	And hafe no lettyng be lawe, / bot / lystynnys thise wordez:	C	V D N
MA 372	I sall be at journee / with / gentill knyghtes,	P	A N
MA 373	On a jamby stede, / full / jolyly graythide,	Z	Z E
MA 374	Or any journee begane / to / juste with hym selfen,	to	V P H self
MA 375	Emange all his geauntez, / Genyuers and other,	/	N C H
MA 376	Stryke hym styfflye fro his stede, / with / strenghe of myn handys,	P	N P D N
MA 377	For all tha steryn in stour / that in his / stale houys!	that P D	N V
MA 378	Be my retenu arayede, / I / rekke bott a lyttill	H	V Z Z
MA 379	To make rowtte into Rome / with / ryotous knyghtes;	P	A N
MA 380	Within a seuenyghte daye, / with / sex score helmes,	P	A A N
MA 381	I sall be seen on the see, / saile when the lykes!	/	V C H V
MA 382	Thane laughes Sir Lottez / and all on / lowde meles:	C H Z	Z V
MA 383	Me likez that Sir Lucius / lannges aftyre sorowe;	/	V P N
MA 384	Now he wylnez the were, / hys / wanedrethe begynnys!	D	N V
MA 385	It es owre weredes to wreke / the / wrethe of oure elders.	D	N P D N
MA 386	I make myn avowe to Gode / and to the / holy vernacle,	C P D	V
MA 387	And I may se the Romaynes, / that are so / ryche halden,	that be Z	A E
MA 388	Arayede in theire riotes / on a / rounde felde,	P D	A N
MA 389	I sall at the reuerence / of the / Rounde Table,	P D	A N
MA 390	Ryde thrughte all the rowtte, / rerewarde and other,	/	N C H
MA 391	Redy wayes to make / and / renkkes full rowme,	C	N Z A
MA 392	Rynnande on rede blode / as my / stede ruschez!	C D	N V
MA 393	He that folowes my fare / and / fyrste commes aftyre	C	Z V Z
MA 394	Sall fynde in my farewaye / many / fay leuyde!	D	N(A) V
MA 395	Thane the Conquerour kyndly / comforthes these knyghtes,	/	V D N
MA 396	Alowes thaim gretly / theire / lordly avowes:	/	A N
MA 397	Alweldande Gode / wyrchip ʒow all,	/	V H Z
MA 398	And latte me neuere wanntte / ʒow, whylls I in / werlde regne;	H C H P	N V
MA 399	My menske and my manhede / ʒe / mayntene in erthe,	H	V P N
MA 400	Myn honour all vtterly / in other / kyngys landes;	P D	N N
MA 401	My wele and my wyrchipe, / of all this / werlde ryche,	P D D	N A
MA 402	ʒe haue knyghtly conqueryde, / that to my / coroun langes;	that P D	N V
MA 403	Hym thare be ferde for no faees / that swylke a / folke ledes,	that D D	N V
MA 404	Bot euer fresche for to fyghte / in / felde when hym lykes;	P	N C H V
MA 405	I acounte no kynge / that vndyr / Criste lyffes;	that P	N V
MA 406	Whills I see ʒowe all sounde, / I / sette be no more."	H	E be Z
MA 407	Qwhen they tristily had tretyd, / thay / trumppede vp aftyre,	H	V Z Z
MA 408	Descendyd doune with a daunce / of / dukes and erles.	P	N C N
MA 409	Thane they semblede to sale / and / sowpped als swythe,	C	V Z Z
MA 410	All this semly sorte, / wyth / semblante full noble.	P	N Z A
MA 411	Thene the roy reall / rehetes thes knyghttys,	/	V D N
MA 412	Wyth reuerence and ryotte / of all his / Rounde Table	P D D	A N
MA 413	Till seuen dayes was gone, / the / Senatour askes	D	N V
MA 414	Answere to the Emperour / with / austeryn wordez.	P	A N
MA 415	Aftyre the Epiphanye, / when the / purpos was takyn,	C D	N be E
MA 416	Of peris of the parlement, / prelates and other,	/	N C H
MA 417	The Kyng in his concell, / curtaise and noblee,	/	A C A
MA 418	Vtters the alienes / and / ansuers hym seluen:	C	N H self
MA 419	"Gret wele Lucius, thi lorde, / and / layne noghte thise wordes,	C	V not D N
MA 420	Ife thow be lygmane lele, / late hym wiet sone		V H V Z
MA 421	I sall at Lammesse take leue / and / loge at my large	C	V P D N

MA 422	In delitte in his laundez, / wyth / lordes ynewe,	P	N A
MA 423	Regne in my realtee / and / ryste when me lykes,	C	V C H V
MA 424	By the reyuere of Reone / halde my / Rounde Table,	V D	A N
MA 425	Fannge the fermes, in faithe, / of all tha / faire rewmes,	P D D	A N
MA 426	For all the manace of hys myghte / and / mawgree hys eghne!	C	P D N
MA 427	And merke sythen ouer the mounttez / into his / mayne londez,	P D	A N
MA 428	To Meloyne the meruaylous, / and / myn doun the walles;	C	V Z D N
MA 429	In Lorrayne ne in Lumberdye / lefe schall I nowthire	/	V X H C
MA 430	Nokyn lede appon liffe / that thare his / lawes ȝemes;	that Q D	N V
MA 431	And turne into Tuschayne, / whene me / tyme thynkys,	C H	N V
MA 432	Ryde all thas rowme landes / wyth / ryotous knyghttes;	P	A N
MA 433	Byde hy[m] make reschewes, / fore / menske of hym seluen,	P	N P H self
MA 434	And mette me fore his manhede / in thase / mayne landes.	P D	A N
MA 435	I sall be foundyn in Fraunce, / fraiste when hym lykes,	/	V C H V
MA 436	The fyrste daye of Feuerȝere, / in thas / faire marches;	P D	A N
MA 437	Are I be fechyde wyth force / or / forfette my landes,	C	V D N
MA 438	The flour of his faire folke / full / fay sall be leuyde!	Z	A X be E
MA 439	I sall hym sekyrly ensure, / vndyre my / seele ryche,	P D	N A
MA 440	To seege the cetee of Rome / wythin / seuen wyntyre,	P	A N
MA 441	And that so sekerly ensege / apon / sere halfes,	P	A N
MA 442	That many a senatour sall syghe / for / sake of me one!	P	N P H Z
MA 443	My sommons er certified, / and thow arte / full seruyde	C H be	Z E
MA 444	Of cundit and credense, / kayre the lykes;	/	V H V
MA 445	I sall thi journaye engyste, / enjoynne them my seluen,	/	V H H self
MA 446	Fro this place to the porte, / there thou sall / passe ouer;	Q H X	V Z
MA 447	Seuen dayes to Sandewyche / I / sette at the large,	H	V P D N
MA 448	Sexty myle on a daye, / the / somme es bott lyttill.	D	N be Z A
MA 449	Thowe moste spede at the spurs / and / spare noghte thi fole;	C	V not D N
MA 450	Thow weyndez by Watlyng Strette / and by no / waye ells;	C P D	N A
MA 451	Thare thow nyghes on nyghte / nedez moste thou lenge;	/	Z X H V
MA 452	Be it foreste or felde, / found thou no forthire;	/	V H Z
MA 453	Bynde thy blonke by a buske / with thy / brydill euen,	P D	N Z
MA 454	Lugge thi selfe vndyre lynde, / as the / leefe thynkes;	C H	A V
MA 455	There awes none alyenes / to / ayer appon nyghttys,	to	V P N
MA 456	With syche a rebawdous rowtte / to / ryot thy seluen.	to	V H self
MA 457	Thy lycence es lemete / in / presence of lordys;	P	N P N
MA 458	Be now lathe or lette, / ryghte as the thynkes,	/	Z C H V
MA 459	For bothe thi lyffe and thi lym / lygges therappon,	/	V Z
MA 460	Thofe Sir Lucius had laide / the / lordchipe of Rome;	D	N P N
MA 461	For the thow founden a fute / withowte the / flode merkes,	P D	N N
MA 462	Aftyr the aughtende day, / when / vndroun es rungen,	C	N be E
MA 463	Thou sall be heuedede in hye / and with / horsse drawen,	C P	N E
MA 464	And seyn heyly be hangede, / houndes to gnawen!	/	N to V
MA 465	The rente ne rede golde / that vnto / Rome langes	that P	N V
MA 466	Sall noghte redily, renke, / raunson thyn one!"	/	V H H
MA 467	"Sir," sais the Senatour, / "so / Crist mot me helpe,	C	N X H V
MA 468	Might I with wirchip / wyn awaye ones,	/	V Z Z
MA 469	I sulde neuer fore emperour / that on / erthe lenges,	that P	N V
MA 470	Efte vnto Arthure / ayere on syche nedys;	/	V P D N
MA 471	Bot I am sengilly here, / with sex / sum of knyghtes;	P D	N P N
MA 472	I beseke ȝow, Sir, / that we may / sounde passe:	that H X	Z V
MA 473	In any vnlawefull lede / lette vs by the waye,	/	V H P D N
MA 474	Within thy lycence, lorde, / thy / loosse es enpeyrede."	D	N be E
MA 475	"Care noghte," quod the Kyng; / "thy / coundyte es knawen	D	N be E
MA 476	Fro Carlele to the coste, / there thy / cogge lengges;	Q D	N V
MA 477	Thoghe thy cofers ware full, / cramede with syluer,	/	E P N
MA 478	Thow myghte be sekyre of my sele / sexty myle forthire."	/	A N Z
MA 479	They enclined to the Kyng, / and / counge thay askede,	C	N H V
MA 480	Cayers owtt of Carelele, / catchez on theire horsez;	/	V P D N
MA 481	Sir Cadore the curtayes / kende them the wayes,	/	V H D N
MA 482	To Catrike them cunvayede / and to / Crist them bekennyde.	C P	N H V
MA 483	So they spede at the spoures, / they / sprangen theire horses,	H	V D N
MA 484	Hyres them hakenayes / hastyly thereaftyre;	/	Z Z
MA 485	So fore reddour they reden / and / risted them neuer,	C	V H Z
MA 486	Bot ȝif they luggede vndire lynd / whills them / lyghte failede;	C H	N V
MA 487	Bot euere the Senatour forsothe / soghte at the gayneste.	/	V P D N
MA 488	By the sevend day was gone / the / cetee thai rechide;	D	N H V
MA 489	Of all the glee vndire Gode / so / glade ware they neuere,	Z	A be H Z
MA 490	As of the sounde of the see / and / Sandwyche belles.	C	N N
MA 491	Wythowttyn more stownntyng / they / schippide theire horsez,	H	V D N
MA 492	Wery, to the wane see / they / went all att ones;	H	V Z Z

MA 493	With the men of the walle / they / weyde vp theire ankyrs,	H	V Z D N
MA 494	And fleede at the fore flude, / in / Flaundrez they lowede,	P	N H V
MA 495	And thorughe Flaundres they founde, / as them / faire thoghte,	C H	A V
MA 496	Till Akyn in Almayn, / in / Arthur landes;	P	N N
MA 497	Gosse by the Mount Goddarde, / full / greuous wayes,	Z	A N
MA 498	And so into Lumberddye, / lykande to schewe.	/	G to V
MA 499	They turne thurghe Tuskayne, / with / towres full heghe,	P	N Z A
MA 500	In Pis appairells / them in / precious wedez;	H P	A N
MA 501	The Sonondaye in Suters / thay / suggourne theire horsez,	H	V D N
MA 502	And sekes the seyntez of Rome, / be / assente of knyghtes;	P	N P N
MA 503	Sythyn prekes to the pales, / with / portes so ryche,	P	N Z A
MA 504	Thare Sir Lucius lenges, / with / lordes enowe;	P	N A
MA 505	Lowttes to hym lufly, / and / lettres hym bedes,	C	N H V
MA 506	Of credence enclosyde, / with / knyghtlyche wordez.	P	A N
MA 507	Then the Emperour was egree / and / enkerly fraynes;	C	Z V
MA 508	The answere of Arthure / he / askes hym sone,	H	V H Z
MA 509	How he arayes the rewme / and / rewlys the pople,	C	V D N
MA 510	3if he be rebell to Rome / whate / ryghte that he claymes.	Q	N that H V
MA 511	"Thow sulde his ceptre haue sesede / and / syttyn aboun,	C	E Z
MA 512	Fore reuerence and realtee / of / Rome the noble;	P	N D N(A)
MA 513	By sertes thow was my sandee, / and / senatour of Rome;	C	N P N
MA 514	He sulde, fore solempnitee, / hafe / seruede the hym seluen!"	have	E H H self
MA 515	"That will he neuer for no wye / of all this / werlde ryche,	P D D	N A
MA 516	Bot who may wynn hym of werre, / by / wyghtnesse of handes;	P	N P N
MA 517	Many fey schall be fyrste / appon the / felde leuyde,	P D	N E
MA 518	Are he appere in this place / profre when the likes.	/	V C H V
MA 519	I saye the, Sir, Arthure / es thyn / enmye fore euer,	be D	N Z
MA 520	And ettells to bee ouerlyng / of the / Empyre of Rome,	P D	N P N
MA 521	That alle his ancestres aughte, / bot / Vtere hym selfe.	P	N H self
MA 522	Thy nedes this Newe 3ere / I / notifiede my selfen,	H	V H self
MA 523	Before that noble of name / and / neynesom of kynges;	C	N P N
MA 524	In the moste reale place / of the / Rounde Table,	P D	A N
MA 525	I somounde hym solepnylye, / one-seeande his knyghtez.	/	G D N
MA 526	Sen I was formyde, in faythe, / so / ferde was I neuere,	C	E be H Z
MA 527	In all the placez ther I passede / of / pryncez in erthe.	P	N P N
MA 528	I wolde foresake all my suyte / of / segnourry of Rome,	P	N P N
MA 529	Or I efte to that soueraygne / whare / sente one suyche nedes!	Q	V Z D N
MA 530	He may be chosyn cheftayne, / cheefe of all other,	/	N P D H
MA 531	Bathe de chauncez of armes / and / cheuallrye noble,	C	N A
MA 532	For whyeseste and worthyeste / and / wyghteste of hanndez;	C	A P N
MA 533	Of all the wyes thate I watte / in this / werlde ryche,	P D	N A
MA 534	The knyghtlyeste creatoure / in / Cristyndome halden,	P	N E
MA 535	Of kyng or of conquerour / crownede in erthe;	/	E P N
MA 536	Of countenaunce, of corage, / of / crewelle lates,	P	A N
MA 537	The comlyeste of knyghtehode / that vndyre / Cryste lyffes.	that P	N V
MA 538	He maye be spoken in dyspens / despysere of syluere,	/	N P N
MA 539	That no more of golde gyffes / than of / grette stones,	C P	A N
MA 540	No more of wyne than of watyre / that of the / welle rynnys,	that P D	N V
MA 541	Ne of welthe of this werlde / bot / wyrchipe allone.	P	N Z
MA 542	Syche contenaunce was neuer knowen / in no / kythe ryche,	P D	N A
MA 543	As was with that conquerour / in his / courte halden;	P D	N V
MA 544	I countede at this Crystynmesse / of / kyngez enoynttede	P	N E
MA 545	Hole ten at his table / that / tym with hym selfen.	that	N P H self
MA 546	He wyll werraye iwysse, / he / ware 3if the lykes;	V	V C H V
MA 547	Wage many wyghtemen / and / wache thy marches,	C	A D N
MA 548	That they be redye in araye / and at / areste foundyn;	C P	N E
MA 549	For 3ife he reche vnto Rome, / he / raunsouns it for euere!	H	V H Z
MA 550	I rede thow dresce the therfore, / and / drawe no lytte langere;	C	V Z Z
MA 551	Be sekyre of thi sowdeours / and / sende to the mowntes;	C	V P D N
MA 552	Be the quartere of this 3ere, / and hym / quarte stannde,	C H	N V
MA 553	He wyll wyghtlye in a qwhyle / on his / wayes hye."	P D	N V
MA 554	"Bee estyre," sais the Emperour, / "I / ettyll my selfen	H	V H self
MA 555	To hostaye in Almayne / with / armede knyghtez;	P	E N
MA 556	Sende freklye into Fraunce, / that / flour es of rewmes,	that	N be P N
MA 557	Fande to fette that freke / and / forfette his landez;	C	V D N
MA 558	For I sall sette kepers, / full / conaunde and noble,	Z	G C A
MA 559	Many geaunte of Geen, / justers full gude,	/	N Z A
MA 560	To mete hym in the mountes / and / martyre hys knyghtes,	C	V D N
MA 561	Stryke them doun in strates / and / struye them fore euere!	C	V H Z
MA 562	There sall appon Godarde / a / garette be rerede,	D	N be E
MA 563	That schall be garneschte and kepyde / with / gude men of armes,	P	A N P N

MA 564	And a bekyn abouen / to / brynne when them lykys,	P	E C H V
MA 565	That nane enmye with hoste / sall / entre the mountes;	X	V D N
MA 566	There schall one Mounte Bernarde / be / beyldede anothere,	be	E H
MA 567	Buschede with banerettes / and / bachelers noble;	C	N A
MA 568	In at the portes of Pavye / schall no / prynce passe,	X D	N V
MA 569	Thurghe the perelous places, / for my / pris knyghttes."	P D	A N
MA 570	Thane Sir Lucius lordlyche / lettres he sendys	/	N H V
MA 571	Onone into the Oryente, / with / austeryn knyghtez,	P	A N
MA 572	Till Ambyganye and Orcage / and / Alysaundyre eke,	C	N Z
MA 573	To Inde and to Ermonye, / as / Ewfrates rynnys,	C	N V
MA 574	To Asye and to Affrike / and / Ewrope the large,	C D D	N D N(A)
MA 575	To Irritayne and Elamet / and all thase / owte ilez,	C D D	A N
MA 576	To Arraby and Egipt, / till / erles and other,	P	N C H
MA 577	That any erthe ocupyes / in thase / este marches,	P D	A N
MA 578	Of Damaske and Damyat, / and / dukes and erles,	C	N C N
MA 579	For drede of his daungere / they / dresside them sone;	H	V H Z
MA 580	Of Crete and of Capados / the / honourable kyngys	D	A N
MA 581	Come at his commandmente / clenly at ones,	/	Z Z
MA 582	To Tartary and Turky, / when / tythynngez es comen;	C	N be E
MA 583	They turne in by Thebay, / terauntez full hugge,	/	N Z A
MA 584	The flour of the faire realle / of / Amazonnes landes,	P	N N
MA 585	All thate faillez on the felde / be / forfette fore euere!	be	E Z
MA 586	Of Babyloyn and Baldake / the / burlyche knyghtes,	D	A N
MA 587	Bayous with theire baronage / bydez no langere;	/	V Z
MA 588	Of Perce and of Pamphile / and / Preter Iohne landes,	C	N N N
MA 589	Iche prynce with his powere / appertlyche graythede;	/	Z E
MA 590	The Sowdane of Surrye / assemblez his knyghtes,	/	V D N
MA 591	Fra Nylus to Nazarethe, / nommers full huge;	/	N Z A
MA 592	To Garyere and to Galele / they / gedyre all at ones,	H	V Z Z
MA 593	The sowdanes that ware sekyre / sowdeours to Rome;	/	N P N
MA 594	They gadyrede ouere the Grekkes See / with / greuous wapyns,	P	A N
MA 595	In theire grete galays, / wyth / gleterande scheldez;	P	G N
MA 596	The kynge of Cyprys on the see / the / Sowdane habydes,	D	N V
MA 597	With all the realls of Roodes / arayede with hym one.	/	E P H A
MA 598	They sailede with a syde wynde / oure the / salte strandez,	P D	A N
MA 599	Sodanly the Sarezenes, / as them / selfe lykede;	C H	self V
MA 600	Craftyly at Cornett / the / kynges are aryefede,	D	N be E
MA 601	Fra the cete of Rome / sexti myle large.	/	A N A
MA 602	Be that the Grekes ware graythede, / a full / gret nombyre,	D Z	A N
MA 603	The myghtyeste of Macedone, / with / men of tha marches;	P	N P D N
MA 604	Pulle and Pruyslande / presses with other,	/	V P H
MA 605	The legemen of Lettow / with / legyons ynewe.	P	N A
MA 606	Thus they semble in sortes, / summes full huge,	/	N Z A
MA 607	Sowdanes and Sarezenes / owt of / sere landes;	P P	A N
MA 608	The Sowdane of Surry / and / sextene kynges,	C	A N
MA 609	At the cetee of Rome / assemblede at ones.	/	V Z
MA 610	Thane yschewes the Emperour, / armede at ryghtys,	/	E Z
MA 611	Arayede with his Romaynes / appon / ryche stedys;	P	A N
MA 612	Sexty geauntes before, / engenderide with fendes,	/	E P N
MA 613	With weches and warlaws / to / wacchen his tentys,	to	V D N
MA 614	Ayware whare he wendes, / wyntres and 3eres.	/	N C N
MA 615	Myghte no blonkes them bere, / thos / bustous churlles,	D	A N
MA 616	Bot couerde camellez of tourse, / enclosyde in maylez.	/	E P N
MA 617	He ayerez oute with alyenez, / ostes full huge,	/	N Z A
MA 618	Ewyn into Almayne, / that / Arthure hade wonnyn;	that	N have E
MA 619	Rydes in by the ryuere / and / ryottez hym seluen,	C	V H self
MA 620	And ayerez with a huge wyll / all thas / hye landez.	D D	A N
MA 621	All Westwale of werre / he / wynnys as hym lykes,	H	V C H V
MA 622	Drawes in by Danuby / and / dubbez hys knyghtez;	C	V D N
MA 623	In the contre of Coloine / castells enseggez,	/	N V
MA 624	And suggeournez that seson / wyth / Sarazenes ynewe.	P	N A
MA 625	At the vtas of Hillary, / Syr / Arthure hade myselfe seluen	D	N H self
MA 626	In his kydde councell / commande the lordes:	/	V D N
MA 627	"Kayere to 3our cuntrez / and / semble 3our knyghtes,	C	V D N
MA 628	And kepys me at Constantyne / clenlyche arayede;	/	Z E
MA 629	Byddez me at Bareflete / apon tha / blythe stremes,	P D	A N
MA 630	Baldly within borde, / with 3owre / beste beryns;	P D	A N
MA 631	I schall menskfully 3owe mete / in thos / faire marches."	P D	A N
MA 632	He sendez furthe sodaynly / sergeantes of armes	/	N P N
MA 633	To all hys mariners on rawe, / to / areste hym schippys.	to	V H N
MA 634	Wythin sexten dayes / hys / fleet whas assemblede,	D	N be E

MA 635	At Sandwyche on the see, / saile when hym lykes.	/	V C H V
MA 636	In the palez of 3orke / a / parlement he haldez,	D	N H V
MA 637	With all the perez of the rewme, / prelates and other;	/	N C H
MA 638	And aftyre the prechynge, / in / presence of lordes,	P	N P N
MA 639	The Kyng in his concell / carpys thes wordes:	/	V D N
MA 640	"I am in purpos to passe / perilous wayes,	/	A N
MA 641	To kaire with my kene men / to / conquere 3one landes,	to	V D N
MA 642	To owttraye myn enmy, / 3if / auenture it schewe,	C	A H V
MA 643	That ocupyes myn heritage, / the / Empyre of Rome.	D	N P N
MA 644	I sett 3ow here a soueraynge, / ascente 3if 3owe lykys,	/	V C H V
MA 645	That es me sybb, my syster son, / Sir / Mordrede hym seluen,	D	N H self
MA 646	Sall be my leueteunaunte, / with / lordchipez ynewe,	P	N A
MA 647	Of all my lele legemen / that my / landez 3emes."	that D	N V
MA 648	He carpes till his cosyne thane, / in / counsaile hym seluen:	D	N H self
MA 649	"I make the kepare, Sir Knyghte, / of / kyngrykes manye,	P	N A
MA 650	Wardayne wyrchipfull, / to / weilde al my landes,	to	V D D N
MA 651	That I haue wonnen of werre, / in all this / werlde ryche.	P D D	N A
MA 652	I wyll that Waynour, my weife, / in / wyrchipe be holden,	P	N be E
MA 653	That hire wannte noo wele / ne / welthe that hire lykes;	D	N that H V
MA 654	Luke my kydde castells / be / clenlyche arrayede,	be	Z E
MA 655	There cho maye suggourne hire selfe / wyth / semlyche berynes;	P	A N
MA 656	Fannde my forestez be frythede / o / frenchepe for euere,	P	N Z
MA 657	That nane werreye my wylde / botte / Waynour hir seluen,	P	N H self
MA 658	And that in the seson / whene / grees es assignyde,	C	N be E
MA 659	That cho take hir solauce / in / certayne tymms.	P	A N
MA 660	Chauncelere and chambyrleyn / chaunge as the lykes;	/	V C H V
MA 661	Audytours and offycers / ordayne thy seluen,	/	V H self
MA 662	Bathe jureez and juggez / and / justicez of landes;	C	N P N
MA 663	Luke thow justifye them wele / that / injurye wyrkes.	that	N V
MA 664	If me be destaynede to dye / at / Dryghtyns wyll,	P	N N
MA 665	I charge the my sektour, / cheffe of all other,	/	A P A H
MA 666	To mynystre my mobles / fore / mede of my saule	P	N P D N
MA 667	To mendynauntez and mysese / in / myschefe fallen;	P	N V
MA 668	Take here my testament / of / tresoure full huge:	P	N Z A
MA 669	As I trayste appon the, / betraye thowe me neuer!	/	V H H Z
MA 670	As thow will answere / before the / austeryn Jugge,	P D	A N
MA 671	That all this werlde wynly / wysse as Hym lykes,	/	V C H V
MA 672	Luke that my laste wyll / be / lelely perfournede.	be	Z E
MA 673	Thow has clenly the cure / that to my / coroune langez	that P D	N V
MA 674	Of all my wer[l]dez wele, / and my / weyffe eke;	C D	N Z
MA 675	Luke thowe kepe the so clere / there be no / cause fonden	Z be D	N E
MA 676	When I to contre come, / if / Cryste will it thole;	C	N X H V
MA 677	And thow haue grace gudly / to / gouerne thy seluen,	to	V H self
MA 678	I sall coroune the, knyghte, / kyng with my handez."	/	N P D N
MA 679	Than Sir Modrede full myldly / meles hym seluen,	/	V H self
MA 680	Knelyd to the Conquerour / and / carpes thise wordez:	C	V D N
MA 681	"I beseke 3ow, Sir, / as my / sybbe lorde,	P D	A N
MA 682	That 3e will for charyte / cheese 3ow another;	/	V H H
MA 683	For if 3e putte me in this plytte, / 3owre / pople es dyssauyde;	D	N be E
MA 684	To presente a prynce astate / my / powere es symple.	D	N be A
MA 685	When othere of werre wysse / are / wyrchipide hereaftyre,	be	N Z
MA 686	Than may I forsothe / be / sette bott at lyttill.	be	E C Z
MA 687	To passe in 3our presance / my / purpos es takyn,	D	N be E
MA 688	And all my purueaunce apperte fore / my / pris knyghtez."	P	A N
MA 689	"Thowe arte my neuewe full nere, / my / nurree of olde,	D	N P N(A)
MA 690	That I haue chastyede and chosen, / a / childe of my chambyre;	D	N P D N
MA 691	For the sybredyn of me, foresake / noghte this offyce;	/	not D N
MA 692	That thow ne wyrk my will, / thow / watte whatte it menes."	H	V Q H V
MA 693	Nowe he takez hys leue / and / lengez no langere,	C	V Z
MA 694	At lordez at legemen, / that / leues hym byhynden.	that	V H Z
MA 695	And seyne that worthilyche wy / went vnto chambyre,	/	V P N
MA 696	For to comfurthe the Qwene, / that in / care lenges.	that P	N V
MA 697	Waynour, waykly / wepande, hym kyssiz,	/	G H V
MA 698	Talkez to hym tenderly / with / teres ynewe:	P	N A
MA 699	"I may wery the wye / thatt this / werre mouede,	that D	N E
MA 700	That warnes me wyrchippe / of my / wedde lorde;	P D	E N
MA 701	All my lykyng of lyfe / owte of / lande wendez,	P P	N V
MA 702	And I in langour am lefte, / leue 3e, for euere.	/	V H Z
MA 703	Whyne myghte I, dere lufe, / dye in 3our armes,	/	V P D N
MA 704	Are I this destanye of dule / sulde / drye by myne one?"	X	V P D H
MA 705	"Grefe the noghte, Gaynour, / fore / Goddes lufe of Hewen,	P	N N P N

MA 706	Ne gruche noghte my ganggyng: / it sall to / gude turne.	H X P	N V
MA 707	Thy wonrydez and thy wepyng / woundez myn herte;	/	V D N
MA 708	I may noghte wit of this woo, / for all this / werlde ryche!	P D D	N A
MA 709	I haue made a kepare, / a / knyghte of thyn awen,	D	N P D A
MA 710	Ouerlyng of Ynglande, / vndyre thy seluen,	/	P H self
MA 711	And that es Sir Mordrede, / that thow has / mekyll praysede,	that H have	Z E
MA 712	Sall be thy dictour, my dere, / to / doo whatte the lykes."	to	V Q H V
MA 713	Thane he takes hys leue / at / ladys in chambyre,	P	N P N
MA 714	Kysside them kyndlyche / and to / Criste beteches;	C P	N V
MA 715	And then cho swounes full swythe, / whe[n] he hys / swerde aschede,	C H D	N V
MA 716	Twys in a swounyng, / swelte as cho walde.	/	V C H X
MA 717	He pressed to his palfray, in presance of lordes,	P	N P N
MA 718	Prekys of the palez / with his / prys knyghtes;	P D	A N
MA 719	Wyth a reall rowte / of the / Rounde Table	P D	A N
MA 720	Soughte towarde Sandwyche, / cho / sees hym no more.	H	V H Z
MA 721	Thare the grete ware gederyde, / wyth / galyarde knyghtes,	P	A N
MA 722	Garneschit on the grene felde / and / graythelyche arayede;	C	Z E
MA 723	Dukkes and duzseperez / daynttehely rydes,	/	Z V
MA 724	Erles of Ynglande, / with / archers ynewe;	P	N A
MA 725	Schirreues scharply / schiftys the comouns,	/	V D N
MA 726	Rewlys before the ryche / of the / Rounde Table;	P D	A N
MA 727	Assingnez ilke a contree / to / certayne lordes,	P	A N
MA 728	In the southe on the see banke, / saile when them lykes.	/	V C H V
MA 729	Thane bargez them buskez / and to the / baunke rowes,	C P D	N V
MA 730	Bryngez blonkez on bourde / and / burlyche helmes;	C	A N
MA 731	Trussez in tristly / trappyde stedes,	/	E N
MA 732	Tentez and othire toylez / and / targez full ryche,	C	N Z A
MA 733	Cabanes and clathe-sekkes / and / coferez full noble,	C	N Z A
MA 734	Hekes and haknays / and / horsez of armez;	C	N P N
MA 735	Thus they stowe in the stuffe / of full / steryn knyghtez.	P Z	A N
MA 736	Qwen all was schyppede that scholde / they / schounte no lengere,	H	V Z
MA 737	Bot ventelde them tyte, / as the / tyde rynnez;	C D	N V
MA 738	Coggez and crayers / than / crossez thaire mastez,	C	V D N
MA 739	At the comandment of the Kynge / vncouerde at ones.	/	V Z
MA 740	Wyghtly on the wale / thay / wye vp thaire ankers,	H	V Z D N
MA 741	By wytt of the watyre-men / of the / wale ythez;	P D	A N
MA 742	Frekes on the forestavne / faken theire coblez,	/	V D N
MA 743	In floynes and fercostez / and / Flemesche schyppes;	C	A N
MA 744	Tytt saillez to the toppe / and / turnez the lufe,	C	V D N
MA 745	Standez appon stere-bourde, / sternly thay songen.	/	Z H V
MA 746	The pryce schippez of the porte / prouen theire depnesse,	/	V D N
MA 747	And fondez wyth full saile / ower the / fawe ythez;	P D	A N
MA 748	Holly withowttyn harme / thay / hale in bottes;	H	V P N
MA 749	Schipemen scharply / schoten thaire portez,	/	V D N
MA 750	Launchez lede apon lufe, / lacchen ther depez;	/	V D N
MA 751	Lukkez to the lade-sterne / when the / lyghte faillez,	C D	N V
MA 752	Castez coursez be crafte / when the / clowde rysez,	C D	N V
MA 753	With the nedyll and the stone / one the / nyghte tydez;	P D	N N
MA 754	For drede of the derke nyghte / thay / drecchede a lyttill,	H	V Z
MA 755	And all the steryn of the streme / strekyn at onez.	/	V Z
MA 756	The Kynge was in a gret cogge, / with / knyghtez full many,	P	N Z A
MA 757	In a cabane enclosede, / clenlyche arayede;	/	Z E
MA 758	Within on a ryche bedde / rystys a littyll,	/	V Z
MA 759	And with the swoghe of the see / in / swefnyng he fell.	P	G H V
MA 760	Hym dremyd of a dragon, / dredfull to beholde,	/	A to V
MA 761	Come dryfande ouer the depe / to / drenschen hys pople,	to	V D N
MA 762	Ewen walkande / owte of the / weste landez,	P P D	A N
MA 763	Wanderande vnworthyly / ouere the / wale ythez;	P D	A N
MA 764	Bothe his hede and hys hals / ware / halely all ouer	be	Z Z
MA 765	Oundyde of azure, / enamelde full faire;	/	E Z Z
MA 766	His scoulders ware schalyde / all in / clene syluere,	Z P	A N
MA 767	Schreede ouer all the schrympe / with / schrinkande poyntez;	P	G N
MA 768	Hys wombe and hys wenges / of / wondyrfull hewes,	P	A N
MA 769	In meruaylous maylys / he / mountede full hye;	H	V Z Z
MA 770	Whaym that he towchede / he was / tynt for euer.	H be	E Z
MA 771	Hys feete ware floreschede / all in / fyne sabyll,	Z P	A N
MA 772	And syche a vennymous flayre / flowe fro his lyppez,	/	V P D N
MA 773	That the flode of the flawez / all on / fyre semyde.	Z P	N V
MA 774	Thane come of the oryente, / ewyn hym agaynez,	/	Z H P
MA 775	A blake, bustous bere / abwen in the clowdes,	/	Z P D N
MA 776	With yche a pawe as a poste / and / paumes full huge,	C	N Z A

MA 777	With pykes full perilous, / all / plyande tham semyde;	Z	G H V
MA 778	Lothen and lodlely / lokkes and other,	/	N C H
MA 779	All with lutterde legges, / lokerde vnfaire,	/	E Z
MA 780	Filtyrde vnfrely, / with / fomaunde lyppez,	P	G N
MA 781	The foulleste of fegure / that / fourmede was euer.	that	E be Z
MA 782	He baltyrde, he bleryde, / he / braundyschte therafter;	H	V Z
MA 783	To bataile he bounnez / hym with / bustous clowez;	H P	A N
MA 784	He romede, he rarede, / that / roggede all the erthe,	that	V Z D N
MA 785	So ruydly he rappyd / at to / ryot hym seluen.	Z to	V H self
MA 786	Thane the dragon on dreghe / dressede hym aȝaynez,	/	V H P
MA 787	And with hys d[i]nttez hym drafe / on / dreghe by the walkyn;	P	N P D N
MA 788	He fares as a fawcon: / frekly he strykez;	/	Z H V
MA 789	Bothe with feete and with fyre / he / feghttys at ones.	H	V Z
MA 790	The bere in the bataile / the / bygger hym semyde,	D	A H V
MA 791	And byttes hym boldlye / wyth / balefull tuskez;	P	A N
MA 792	Syche buffetez he hym rechez / with hys / brode klokes,	P D	A N
MA 793	Hys brest and his brayell / whas / blodye all ouer.	be	A Z
MA 794	He rawmpyde so ruydly / that all the / erthe ryfez,	that Z D	N V
MA 795	Rynnande on reede blode / as / rayne of the heuen.	P	N P D N
MA 796	He hade weryede the worme / by / wyghtnesse of strenghte,	P	N P N
MA 797	Ne ware it fore the wylde fyre / that he hym / wyth defendez.	that H H	P V
MA 798	Thane wandyrs the worme / awaye to hys heghttez,	/	Z P D N
MA 799	Commes glydande fro the clowddez / and / cowpez full euen,	C	V Z Z
MA 800	Towchez hym wyth his talounez / and / terez hys rigg,	C	V D N
MA 801	Betwyx the taile and the toppe / ten fote large.	/	A N A
MA 802	Thus he brittenyd the bere / and / broghte hym o lyfe,	C	V H P N
MA 803	Lette hym fall in the flode, / fleete whare hym lykes.	/	V Q H V
MA 804	So they thryng the bolde kyng / bynne the / schippe-burde,	P D	N N
MA 805	That nere he bristez for bale, / on / bede whare he lyggez.	P	N Q H V
MA 806	Than waknez the wyese kyng, / wery foretrauaillede,	/	Z E
MA 807	Takes hym two phylozophirs / that / folowede hym euer,	that	V H Z
MA 808	In the seuyn scyence / the / suteleste fonden,	D	A E
MA 809	The cony[n]geste of clergye / vndyre / Criste knowen.	P	N E
MA 810	He tolde them of hys tourmente / that / tym that he slepede:	that	N that H V
MA 811	"Drechede with a dragon, / and syche a / derfe beste,	C D D	A N
MA 812	Has mad me full wery; / I / ȝe / tell me my swefen,	H	V H D N
MA 813	Ore I mon swelte as swythe, / as / wysse me oure Lorde!"	C	V H D N
MA 814	"Sir," saide they son thane, / thies / sagge philosopherse,	D	A N
MA 815	"The dragon that thow dremyde / of, so / dredfull to schewe,	Z Z	A to V
MA 816	That come dryfande ouer the deepe / to / drynchen thy pople,	to	V D N
MA 817	Sothely and certayne, / thy / seluen it es,	D	self H be
MA 818	That thus saillez ouer the see / with thy / sekyre knyghtez;	P D	A N
MA 819	The colurez that ware castyn / appon his / clere wengez,	P D	A N
MA 820	May be thy kyngrykez all, / that thow has / ryghte wonnyn;	that H have	Z E
MA 821	And the tatterede taile / with / tonges so huge,	P	N Z A
MA 822	Betakyns this faire folke / that in thy / fleet wendez;	that P D	N V
MA 823	The bere that bryttenede / was / abowen in the clowdez	be	Z P D N
MA 824	Betakyns the tyrauntez / that / tourmentez thy pople;	that	V D N
MA 825	Or ells with somme gyaunt / some / journee sall happyn,	D	N X V
MA 826	In syngulere batell / by ȝoure / selfe one,	P D	self Z
MA 827	And thow sall hafe the victorye, / thurghe / helpe of oure Lorde,	P	N P D N
MA 828	As thow in thy visione / was / opynly schewede.	be	Z E
MA 829	Of this dredfull dreme / ne / drede the no more;	not	V H Z
MA 830	Ne kare noghte, Sir Conquerour, / bot / comforth thy seluen;	C	V H self
MA 831	And thise that saillez ouer the see, / with thy / sekyre knyghtez."	P D	A N
MA 832	With trumppez then trystly / they / trisen vpe thaire saillez,	H	V Z D N
MA 833	And rowes ouer the ryche see, / this / rowtte all at onez;	D	N Z Z
MA 834	The comely coste of Normandye / they / cachen full euen,	H	V Z Z
MA 835	And blythely at Barflete / theis / bolde are arryfede,	D	N(A) be E
MA 836	And fyndys a flete / therof of / frendez ynewe,	Z P	N A
MA 837	The floure and the faire folke / of / fyftene rewmez;	P	A N
MA 838	Fore kyngez and capytaynez / kepyde hym fayre,	/	V H A
MA 839	As he at Carelele commaundyde / at / Cristynmesse hym seluen.	P	N H self
MA 840	Be they had taken the lande / and / tentez vpe rerede,	C	N Z E
MA 841	Comez a templere tyte / and / towchide to the Kynge:	C	V P D N
MA 842	"Here es a teraunt besyde / that / tourmentez thi pople,	that	V D N
MA 843	A grett geaunte of Geen, / engenderde of fendez;	/	E P N
MA 844	He has fretyn of folke / mo than / fyfe hondrethe,	A P	A N
MA 845	And als fele fawntekyns / of / freeborne childyre.	P	E N
MA 846	This has bene his sustynaunce / all this / seuen wynttrres,	Z D	A N
MA 847	And ȝitt es that sotte noghte sadde, / so / wele hym it lykez!	C	Z H H V

MA 848	In the contree of Constantyne / ne / kynde has he leuede,	D	N have H E
MA 849	Withowttyn kydd castells / enclosid wyth walles,	/	E P N
MA 850	That he ne has clenly dystroyede / all the / knaue childyre,	A D	N N
MA 851	And them caryede to the cragge / and / clenly deworyd!	C	Z E
MA 852	The Duchez of Bretayne / todaye has he takyn,	/	Z have H E
MA 853	Beside Reynes as scho rade / with hire / ryche knyghttes;	P D	A N
MA 854	Ledd hyre to the mountayne / thare that / lede lengez,	Q D	N V
MA 855	To lye by that lady / aye whyls hir / lyfe lastez.	Ʒ C D	N V
MA 856	We folowede o ferrom, / moo then / fyfe hundrethe	A P	A N
MA 857	Of beryns and of burgeys / and / bachelers noble,	C	N A
MA 858	Bot he couerde the cragge, / cho / cryede so lowde,	H	V Z Z
MA 859	The care of that creatoure / couer sall I neuer!	/	V X H Z
MA 860	Scho was flour of all Fraunce, / or of / fyfe rewmes,	C P	A N
MA 861	And one of the fayreste / that / fourmede was euere,	that	E be Z
MA 862	The gentileste jowell / ajuggede with lordes	/	E P N
MA 863	Fro Geen vnto Geron, / by / Ihesu of Heuen!	P	N P N
MA 864	Scho was thy wyfes cosyn, / knowe it if the lykez,	/	V H C H V
MA 865	Comen of the rycheste / that / rengnez in erthe;	that	V P N
MA 866	As thow arte ryghtwise Kyng, / rewe on thy pople,	/	V P D N
MA 867	And fande for to venge / them that / thus are rebuykyde!"	H that	Z be E
MA 868	"Allas!" sais Sir Arthure, / "so / lange haue I lyffede;	Ʒ	Z have H E
MA 869	Hade I wyten of this, / wele had me chefede;	/	Z have H V
MA 870	Me es noghte fallen faire, / bot me es / foule happynede,	C H be	Z E
MA 871	That thus this faire ladye / this / fende has dystroyede!	D	N have E
MA 872	I had leuere thane all Fraunce / this / fyftene wynter	D	A N
MA 873	I hade bene before thate freke / a / furfange of waye,	D	N P N
MA 874	When he that ladye had laghte / and / ledde to the montez;	C	E P D N
MA 875	I hadde lefte my lyfe / are cho hade / harme lymppyde.	C H have	N E
MA 876	Bot walde thow kene me to the crage / thare that / kene lengez;	Q D	N(A) V
MA 877	I walde cayre to that coste / and / carpe wythe hym seluen,	C	V P H self
MA 878	To trette with that tyraunt / fore / treson of londes,	P	N P N
MA 879	And take trewe for a tym, / till it may / tyde bettyr."	C H X	V Z
MA 880	"Sire, see ʒe ʒone farlande, / with ʒone / two fyrez?	P D	A N
MA 881	Thar filsnez that fende, / fraiste when the lykes,	/	V C H V
MA 882	Appone the creste of the cragge, / by a / colde welle,	P D	A N
MA 883	That enclosez the clyfe / with the / clere strandez;	P D	A N
MA 884	Ther may thow fynde folke / fay wythowttyn nowmer,	/	A P N
MA 885	Mo florenez, in faythe, / than / Fraunce es in aftyre;	C	N be Z Z
MA 886	And more tresour vntrewely / that / traytour has getyn	that	N have E
MA 887	Thane in Troye was, as I trowe, / that / tym that it was wonn."	that	N that H be E
MA 888	Thane romyez the ryche kynge / for / rewthe of the pople,	P	N P D N
MA 889	Raykez ryghte to a tente / and / restez no lengere;	C	V Z
MA 890	He welterys, he wristeles, / he / wryngez hys handez;	H	V D N
MA 891	Thare was no wy of this werlde / that / wyste whatt he menede.	that	V Q H V
MA 892	He calles Sir Cayous, / that of the / cowpe serfede,	that P D	N V
MA 893	And Sir Bedvere the bolde, that bare / hys / brande ryche:	D	N A
MA 894	"Luke ʒe aftyre euensang / be / armyde at ryghttez,	be	E P N
MA 895	On blonkez by ʒone buscayle, / by ʒone / blythe stremez,	P D	A N
MA 896	Fore I will passe in pilgremage / preuely hereaftyre,	/	Z Z
MA 897	In the tyme of suppere, / whene / lordez are servede,	C	N be E
MA 898	For to seken a saynte / be ʒone / salte stremes,	P D	A N
MA 899	In Seynt Mighell Mount, / there / myraclez are schewede."	Q	N be E
MA 900	Aftyre euesange, / Sir / Arthure hym se[l]fen	D	N H self
MA 901	Wente to hys wardrop / and / warp of hys wedez,	C	V Z N
MA 902	Armede hym in a acton / with / orfraeez full ryche,	P	N Z A
MA 903	Abouen on that a jeryn / of / Acres owte ouer,	P	N Z Z
MA 904	Abouen that a jesseraunt / of / jentyll maylez,	P	A N
MA 905	A jupon of Ierodyn, / jaggede in schredez;	/	E P N
MA 906	He brayedez on a bacenett, / burneschte of syluer,	/	E P N
MA 907	The beste that was in Basill, / wyth / bordurs ryche;	P	N A
MA 908	The creste and the coronall / enclosed so faire	/	E Z Z
MA 909	Wyth clasppis of clere golde, / couched wyth stones;	/	E P N
MA 910	The vesare, the aventaile, / enarmede so faire,	/	E Z Z
MA 911	Voyde withowttyn vice, / with / wyndowes of syluer;	P	N P N
MA 912	His gloues gaylyche gilte / and / grauen at the hemmez,	C	E P D N
MA 913	With graynez and gobelets, / glorious of hewe.	/	A P N
MA 914	He bracez a brade schelde / and his / brande aschez,	C D	N V
MA 915	Bounede hym a broun stede / and on the / bente houys;	C P D	N V
MA 916	He sterte till his sterep / and / stridez on lofte,	C	V Z
MA 917	Streynez hym stowttly / and / sterys hym faire,	C	V H Z
MA 918	Brochez the baye stede / and to the / buske rydez,	C P D	N V

MA 919	And there hys knyghtes hym kepede / full / clenlyche arayede.	Z	Z E
MA 920	Than they roode by that ryuer / that / rynnyd so swythe,	that	V ? ?
MA 921	Thare the ryndez ouerrechez / with / reall bowghez;	P	A N
MA 922	The roo and the raynedere / reklesse thare ronnen,	/	Z Z V
MA 923	In ranez and in rosers, / to / ryotte tham seluen;	to	V H self
MA 924	The frithez ware floreschte / with / flourez full many,	P	N Z A
MA 925	Wyth fawcouns and fesantez / of / ferlyche hewez;	P	A N
MA 926	All the feulez thare fleschez / that / flyez with wengez,	that	V P N
MA 927	Fore thare galede the gowke / one / greuez full lowde:	P	N Z Z
MA 928	Wyth alkyn gladchipe / thay / gladden them seluen;	H	V H self
MA 929	Of the nyghtgale notez / the / noisez was swette,	D	N be A
MA 930	They threpide wyth the throstills, / thre hundreth at ones;	/	A N Z
MA 931	That whate swowyng of watyr / and / syngyng of byrdez,	C	G P N
MA 932	It myghte salue hym of sore / that / sounde was neuere.	that	A be Z
MA 933	Than ferkez this folke / and on / fotte lyghttez,	C P	N V
MA 934	Festenez theire faire stedez / o / ferrom bytwene;	Z	Z Z
MA 935	And thene the Kyng kenely / comandyde hys knyghtez	/	V D N
MA 936	For to byde with theire blonkez / and / bowne no forthyre:	C	V Z
MA 937	"Fore I will seke this seynte / by my / selfe one,	P D	self A
MA 938	And mell with this mayster mane / that this / monte ȝemez;	that D	N V
MA 939	And seyn sall ȝe offyre, / aythyre aftyre other,	/	H P H
MA 940	Menskfully at Saynt Mighell / full / myghtty with Criste."	Z	A P N
MA 941	The Kyng coueris the cragge / wyth / cloughes full hye,	P	N Z A
MA 942	To the creste of the clyffe / he / clymbez on lofte;	H	V Z
MA 943	Keste vpe hys vmbrer / and / kenly he lukes,	C	Z H V
MA 944	Caughte of the colde wynde / to / comforthe hym seluen.	to	V H self
MA 945	Two fyrez fyndez, / flawmande full hye;	/	G Z Z
MA 946	The fourtedele a furlang / betwene / thus he walkes;	P	Z H V
MA 947	The waye by the welle strandez / he / wandyrde hym one,	H	V H A
MA 948	To wette of the warlawe, / whare that he lengez.	/	Q that H V
MA 949	He ferkez to the fyrste fyre, / and / euen there he fyndez	C	Z Z H V
MA 950	A wery wafull wedowe, / wryngande hire handez,	/	G D N
MA 951	And gretande on a graue / grysely teres;	/	A N
MA 952	Now merkyde on molde / sen / myddaye it semede.	P	N H V
MA 953	He saluȝede that sorowfull / with / sittande wordez,	P	G N
MA 954	And fraynez aftyre the fende / fairely thereaftyre.	/	Z Z
MA 955	Thane this wafull wyfe / vnwynly hym gretez,	/	Z H V
MA 956	Couerd vp on hire kneess / and / clappyde hire handez;	C	V D N
MA 957	Said "Carefull careman, / thow / carpez to lowde;	H	V Z Z
MA 958	May ȝone warlawe wyt, / he / worows vs all!	H	V H Z
MA 959	Weryd worthe the wyghte ay / that the thy / wytt refede,	that H D	N V
MA 960	That mase the to wayfe / here in thise / wylde lakes.	Z P D	A N
MA 961	I warne the fore wyrchipe / thou / wylnez aftyr sorowe;	H	V P N
MA 962	Whedyre buskes thow, berne? / Vnblysside thow semes.	/	E H V
MA 963	Wenez thow to britten / hym with thy / brande ryche?	H P D	N A
MA 964	Ware thow wyghttere than Wade / or / Wawayn owthire,	C	N Z
MA 965	Thow wynnys no wyrchip, / I / warne the before.	H	V H Z
MA 966	Thow saynned the vnsekyrly / to / seke to these mountez;	to	V P D N
MA 967	Siche sex ware to symple / to / semble with hym one,	to	V P H A
MA 968	For and thow see hym with syghte, / the / seruez no herte	H	V D N
MA 969	To sayne the sekerly, / so / semez hym huge!	Z	V H A
MA 970	Thow arte frely and faire / and in thy / fyrste flourez,	C P D	A N
MA 971	Bot thow arte fay, be my faythe, / and that me / forthynkkys.	C that H	V
MA 972	Ware syche fyfty on a felde / or one a / faire erthe,	C P D	A N
MA 973	The freke walde with hys fyste / fell ȝow at ones!	/	V H Z
MA 974	Loo, here the duchez dere, / todaye was cho takyn,	/	Z be H E
MA 975	Depe doluen and dede, / dyked in moldez;	/	E P N
MA 976	He hade morthirede this mylde / be / myddaye war rongen,	P	N be E
MA 977	Withowttyn mercy one molde, / I not / watte it ment.	H not	V H V
MA 978	He has forsede hir and fylede, / and cho es / fay leuede;	C H be	A E
MA 979	He slewe hir vnslely / and / slitt hir to the nauyll.	C	V H P D N
MA 980	And here haue I bawmede / hir and / beryede theraftyr;	H C	E Z
MA 981	For bale of the botelesse, / blythe be I neuer.	/	A be H Z
MA 982	Of alle the frendez cho hade, / there / folowede none aftyre,	Q	V H Z
MA 983	Bot I, hir foster modyr / of / fyftene wynter;	P	A N
MA 984	To ferke of this farlande, / fande sall I neuer.	/	V X H Z
MA 985	Bot here be founden on felde / till I be / fay leuede."	C H be	A E
MA 986	Thane answers Sir Arthure / to that / alde wyf,	P D	A N
MA 987	"I am comyn fra the Conquerour, / curtaise and gentill,	/	A C A
MA 988	As one of the hathelest / of / Arthur knyghtez,	P	N N
MA 989	Messenger to this myx, / for / mendemente of the pople,	P	N P D N

MA 990	To mele with this maister man / that here this / mounte ȝemez;	that Z D	N V
MA 991	To trete with this tyraunt / for / tresour of landez,	P	N P N
MA 992	And take trew for a tym, / to / bettyr may worthe."	P	N(A) X V
MA 993	"Ȝa, thire wordis are bot waste," / quod this / wif thane,	V D	N Z
MA 994	"For bothe landez and lythes / full / lyttill by he settes;	Z	Z Z H V
MA 995	Of rentez ne of rede golde / rekkez he neuer,	/	V H Z
MA 996	For he will lenge owt of lawe, / as hym / selfe thynkes,	C H	self V
MA 997	Withowten licence of lede, / as / lorde in his awen.	P	N P D A
MA 998	Bot he has a kyrtill one, / kepide for hym seluen,	/	V P H self
MA 999	That was sponen in Spayne / with / specyall byrdez,	P	A N
MA 1000	And sythyn garnescht in Grece / full / graythly togedirs.	Z	Z Z
MA 1001	It es hyded all with har / hally al ouere,	/	Z Z
MA 1002	And bordyrde with the berdez / of / burlyche kyngez,	P	A N
MA 1003	Crispid and kombide, / that / kempis may knawe	that	N X V
MA 1004	Iche kyng by his colour, / in / kythe there he lengez;	P	N Q H V
MA 1005	Here the fermez he fangez / of / fyftene rewmez;	P	A N
MA 1006	For ilke Esterne ewyn, / howeuer that it fall,	/	Q that H V
MA 1007	They send it hym sothely / for / saughte of the pople,	P	N P D N
MA 1008	Sekerly at that seson, / with / certayne knyghtez.	P	A N
MA 1009	And he has aschede Arthure / all this / seuen wynntter:	Z D	A N
MA 1010	Forthy hurdez he here, / to / owttraye hys pople,	to	V D N
MA 1011	Till the Bretons kyng / haue / burneschte his lyppys,	have	E D N
MA 1012	And sent his berde to that bolde / wyth his / beste berynes.	P D	A N
MA 1013	Bot thowe hafe broghte that berde, / bowne the no forthire,	/	V H Z
MA 1014	For it es buteless bale / thowe / biddez oghte ells;	H	V H Z
MA 1015	For he has more tresour / to / take when hym lykez	to	V Q H V
MA 1016	Than euere aughte Arthure / or / any of hys elders;	C	H P D N
MA 1017	If thowe hafe broghte the berde / he / bese more blythe	H	be A A
MA 1018	Thane thowe gafe hym Burgoyne / or / Bretayne the More.	C	N D N(A)
MA 1019	Bot luke nowe for charitee / thow / chasty thy lyppes,	H	V D N
MA 1020	That the no wordez eschape, / whateso betydez;	/	Q V
MA 1021	Luke thi presante be priste, / and / presse hym bott lytill.	C	V H Z Z
MA 1022	For he es at his sowper, / he will be / sone greuyde:	H X be	Z E
MA 1023	And thow my concell doo, / thow / dosse of thy clothes,	H	V P D N
MA 1024	And knele in thy kyrtyll, / and / call hym thy lorde.	C	V H D N
MA 1025	He sowppes all this seson / with / seuen knaue childre,	P	A N N
MA 1026	Choppid in a chargour / of / chalke-whytt syluer,	P	N A N
MA 1027	With pekill and powdyre / of / precious spycez,	P	A N
MA 1028	And pyment full plenteuous / of / Portyngale wynes;	P	A N
MA 1029	Thre balefull birdez / his / brochez they turne,	D	N H V
MA 1030	That byddez his bedgatt, / his / byddyng to wyrche;	D	G to V
MA 1031	Siche foure scholde be fay / within / foure hourez,	P	A N
MA 1032	Are his fylth ware filled / that his / flesch ȝernes."	that D	N V
MA 1033	"Ȝa, I haue broghte the berd," / quod he, "the / bettyr me lykez;	V H D	A H V
MA 1034	Forthi will I boun / me, and / bere it my seluen;	H C	V H H self
MA 1035	Bot, lefe, walde thow lere / me whare that / lede lengez,	H Q D	N V
MA 1036	I sall alowe the and I liffe, / oure / Lorde so me helpe."	D	N Z H V
MA 1037	"Ferke fast to the fyre," / quod cho, "that / flawmez so hye;	V H that	V Z Z
MA 1038	Thare fillis that fende / hym, / fraist when the lykez;	H	V C H V
MA 1039	Bot thowe moste seke more southe, / sydlyngs a lyttill,	/	Z Z
MA 1040	For he will hafe sent hym selfe / sex myle large."	/	A N A
MA 1041	To the sowthe of the reke / he / soghte at the gaynneste,	H	V P D A
MA 1042	Saynede hym sekerly / with / certeyne wordez,	P	A N
MA 1043	And sydlyngs of the segge / the / syghte had he rechid,	D	N have H E
MA 1044	How vnsemly that sott satt / sowpand hym one;	/	G H A
MA 1045	He lay lenand on lang, / lugand vnfaire,	/	G Z
MA 1046	The thee of a manns lymme / lyfte vp by the haunche;	/	E Z P D N
MA 1047	His bakke and his bewschers / and his / brode lendez	C D	A N
MA 1048	He bekez by the bale-fyre, / and / breklesse hym semede.	C	A H V
MA 1049	Thare ware rostez full ruyd / and / rewfull bredez,	C	A N
MA 1050	Beerynes and bestaile / brochede togeders,	/	V Z
MA 1051	Cowle full cramede / of / crysmed childyre,	P	E N
MA 1052	Sum as brede brochede, / and / bierdez tham tournede.	C	N H V
MA 1053	And than this comlyche kyng, / bycause of his pople,	/	P P D N
MA 1054	His herte bledez for bale, / one / bent ware he standez.	P	N Q H V
MA 1055	Thane he dressede one his schelde, / schuntes no lengere,	/	V Z
MA 1056	Braundesch[t]e his bryghte swerde / by the / bryghte hiltez,	P D	A N
MA 1057	Raykez towarde the renke reghte / with a / ruyd will,	P D	A N
MA 1058	And hyely hailsez that hulke / with / hawtayne wordez:	P	A N
MA 1059	"Now allweldand Gode, / that / wyrscheppez vs all,	that	V H Z
MA 1060	Giff the sorowe and syte, / sotte, there thow lygges,	/	N Q H V

MA 1061	For the fulsomeste freke / that / fourmede was euere;	that	E be Z
MA 1062	Foully thow fedys / the, the / Fende haue thi saule!	H D	N V D N
MA 1063	Here es cury vnclene, / carle, be my trowthe,	/	N P D N
MA 1064	Caffe of creatours / all, thow / curssede wriche!	Z H	V N
MA 1065	Because that thow killide / has thise / cresmede childyre,	have D	E N
MA 1066	Thow has marters made, / and / broghte oute of lyfe,	C	E P P N
MA 1067	That here are brochede on bente / and / brittened with thi handez,	C	E P D N
MA 1068	I sall merke thy mede, / as thou has / myche serfed,	C H have	Z E
MA 1069	Thurghe myghte of Seynt Mighell, / that this / monte ʒemes;	that D	N V
MA 1070	And for this faire ladye, / that thow has / fey leuyde,	that H have	A E
MA 1071	And thus forced one foulde, / for / fylth of thi selfen.	P	N P H self
MA 1072	Dresse the now, dogge-sone, / the / Deuell haue thi saule,	D	N V D N
MA 1073	For thow sall dye this day, / thurghe / dynt of my handez!"	P	N P D N
MA 1074	Than glopned the gloton / and / glored vnfaire:	C	V Z
MA 1075	He grenned as a grewhounde, / with / grysly tuskes;	P	A N
MA 1076	He gaped, he groned faste, / with / grucchand latez,	P	G N
MA 1077	For grefe of the gude kyng / that hym with / grame gretez.	that H P	N V
MA 1078	His fax and his foretoppe / was / filterede togeders,	be	E Z
MA 1079	And owte of his face come / ane / halfe fote large;	D	A N A
MA 1080	His frount and his forheued / all was it ouer,	/	Z be H Z
MA 1081	As the fell of a froske, / and / fraknede it semede;	C	A(E) H V
MA 1082	Huke-nebbyde as a hawke, / and a / hore berde,	C D	A N
MA 1083	And herede to the hole eyghn / with / hyngande browes;	P	G N
MA 1084	Harske as a hunde-fisch / hardly whoso lukez,	/	Z Q V
MA 1085	So was the hyde of that hulke / hally al ouer.	/	Z Z
MA 1086	Erne hade he full huge / and / vgly to schewe,	C	A to V
MA 1087	With eghne full horreble / and / ardauunt forsothe;	A	A Z
MA 1088	Flatt-mowthede as a fluke, / with / fleryand lyppys,	P	G N
MA 1089	And the flesche in his fortethe / fowly as a bere.	/	A P D N
MA 1090	His berde was brothy and blake, / that till his / brest rechede,	that C D	N V
MA 1091	Grassede as a mereswyne, / with / corkes full huge,	P	N Z A
MA 1092	And all falterd the flesche / in his / foule lippys,	P D	A N
MA 1093	Ilke wrethe as a wolfe-heuede, / it / wraythe owtt at ones.	H	V Z Z
MA 1094	Bulle-nekkyde was that bierne / and / brade in the scholders,	C	A P D N
MA 1095	Brok-brestede as a brawne, / with / brustils full large,	P	N Z A
MA 1096	Ruyd armes as an ake / with / rusclede sydes,	P	E N
MA 1097	Lym and leskes full lothyn, / leue ʒe forsothe.	/	V H Z
MA 1098	Schouell-foted was that schalke, / and / schaylande hyn semyde,	C	G H V
MA 1099	With schankez vnschaply, / schowand togedyrs,	/	G Z
MA 1100	Thykke theese as a thursse, / and / thikkere in the hanche,	C	A P D N
MA 1101	Greesse growen as a galte, / full / gry[s]lych he lukez.	Z	A H V
MA 1102	Who the lenghe of the lede / lelly accountes,	/	Z V
MA 1103	Fro the face to the fote / was / fyfe fadom lange.	be	A N A
MA 1104	Thane stertez he vp sturdely / on two / styffe schankez,	P D	A N
MA 1105	And sone he caughte hym a clubb / all of / clene yryn;	Z P	A N
MA 1106	He walde hafe kyllede the Kyng / with his / kene wapen,	P D	A N
MA 1107	Bot thurghe the crafte of Cryste / ʒit the / carle failede;	C D	N V
MA 1108	The creest and the coronall, / the / claspes of syluer,	D	N P N
MA 1109	Clenly with his clubb / he / crassched doune at onez.	H	V Z Z
MA 1110	The Kyng castes vp his schelde / and / couers hym faire,	C	V H Z
MA 1111	And with his burlyche brande / a / box he hym reches;	D	N H H V
MA 1112	Full butt in the frunt / the / fromonde he hittez,	D	N H V
MA 1113	That the burnyscht blade / to the / brayne rynnez.	P D	N V
MA 1114	He feyed his fysnamye / with his / foule hondez,	P D	A N
MA 1115	And frappez faste at his face / fersely theraftyre;	/	Z Z
MA 1116	The Kyng chaungez his fote, / eschewes a lyttill,	/	V Z
MA 1117	Ne had he eschapede that choppe, / cheuede had euyll;	/	E have N
MA 1118	He folowes in fersly / and / festenesse a dynte	C	V D N
MA 1119	Hye vpe on the hanche / with his / harde wapyn,	P D	A N
MA 1120	That he hillid the swerde / halfe a fote large,	/	A D N A
MA 1121	The hott blode of the hulke / vnto the / hilte rynnez;	P D	N V
MA 1122	Ewyn into inmette / the / gyaunt he hyttez,	D	N H V
MA 1123	Iust to the genitales / and / jaggede tham in sondre.	C	V H Z
MA 1124	Thane he romyed and rared, / and / ruydly he strykez	C	Z H V
MA 1125	Full egerly at Arthur, / and on the / erthe hittez;	C P D	N V
MA 1126	A swerde lenghe within the swarthe / he / swappez at ones,	H	V Z
MA 1127	That nere swounes the Kyng / for / swoughe of his dynnttez.	P	N P D N
MA 1128	Bot ʒit the Kyng sweperly / full / swythe he byswenkez,	Z	Z H V
MA 1129	Swappez in with the swerde / that it the / swange brystedd;	that H D	N V
MA 1130	Bothe the guttez and the gorr / guschez owte at ones,	/	V Z Z
MA 1131	That all englaymez the gresse / one / grounde ther he standez.	P	N Q H V

MA 1132	Thane he castez the clubb / and the / Kyng hentez:	C D	N V
MA 1133	On the creeste of the cragg / he / caughte hym in armez,	H	V H P N
MA 1134	And enclosez hym clenly, / to / cruschen hys rybbez,	to	V D N
MA 1135	So hard haldez he that hende / that nere his / herte brystez.	that Z D	N V
MA 1136	Thane the balefull bierdez / bownez to the erthe,	/	V P D N
MA 1137	Kneland and cryande, / and / clappide theire handez:	C	V D N
MA 1138	"Criste comforthe ȝone knyghte, / and / kepe hym fro sorowe,	C	V H P N
MA 1139	And latte neuer ȝone fende / fell hym o lyfe."	/	V H P N
MA 1140	Ȝitt es the warlow so wyghte, / he / welters hym vnder,	H	V H P
MA 1141	Wrothely thai wrythyn / and / wrystill togederz,	C	V Z
MA 1142	Welters and walowes / ouer / within thase buskez,	Z	P D N
MA 1143	Tumbellez and turnes faste / and / terez thaire wedez;	C	V D N
MA 1144	Vntenderly fro the toppe / thai / tiltin togederz,	H	V Z
MA 1145	Whilom Arthure ouer / and / otherwhile vndyre;	C	Z Z
MA 1146	Fro the heghe of the hyll / vnto the / harde roche,	P D	A N
MA 1147	They feyne neuer are they fall / at the / flode merkes.	P D	N N
MA 1148	Bot Arthur with ane anlace / egerly smyttez,	/	Z V
MA 1149	And hittez euer in the hulke / vp to the hiltez;	/	P P D N
MA 1150	The theefe at the dede-thrawe / so / throly hym thryngez,	Z	Z H V
MA 1151	That three rybbys in his syde / he / thrystez in sunder.	H	V Z
MA 1152	Then Sir Kayous the kene / vnto the / Kyng styrtez:	P D	N V
MA 1153	Said "Allas, we are lorne, / my / lorde es confundede;	D	N be E
MA 1154	Ouerfallen with a fende, / vs es / full hapnede!	H be	Z E
MA 1155	We mon be forfeted, in faith, / and / flemyde for euer!"	C	E Z
MA 1156	Thay hafe vp hys hawberke / than and / handilez thervndyr,	Z C	V Z
MA 1157	His hyde and his haunche eke, / on / heghte to the schuldrez,	P	N P D N
MA 1158	His flawnke and his feletez / and his / faire sydez,	C D	A N
MA 1159	Bothe his bakke and his breste / and his / bryghte armez;	C D	A N
MA 1160	Thay ware fayne that they fande / no / flesche entamed,	D	N E
MA 1161	And for that journee made joye, / thir / gentill knyghttez.	D	A N
MA 1162	"Now certez," saise Sir Bedwere, / "it / semez, be my Lorde,	H	V P D N
MA 1163	He sekez seyntez bot selden, / the / sorer he grypes,	D	Z H V
MA 1164	That thus clekys this corsaunt / owte of thir / heghe clyffez,	P P D	A N
MA 1165	To caryе forthe siche a carle / at / close hym in siluer.	P	V H P N
MA 1166	Be Myghell, of syche a makk / I hafe / myche wondyre	H V	A N
MA 1167	That euer owre soueraygne Lorde / suffers hym in Heuen;	/	V H P N
MA 1168	And all seyntez be syche / that / seruez oure Lorde,	that	V D N
MA 1169	I sall neuer no seynt bee, / be my / fadyre sawle!"	P D	N N
MA 1170	Thane bourdez the bolde kyng / at / Bedvere wordez:	P	N N
MA 1171	"This seynt haue I soghte, / so / helpe me owre Lorde!	C	V H D N
MA 1172	Forthy brayd owttе thi brande, / and / broche hym to the herte;	C	V H P D N
MA 1173	Be sekere of this sergeaunt, / he has me / sore greuede.	H have H	Z E
MA 1174	I faghte noghte wyth syche a freke / this / fyftene wyntyre;	D	A N
MA 1175	Bot in the montez of Araby / I / mett syche another:	H	V D H
MA 1176	He was the forcyer be ferre / that had I / nere funden,	that have H	Z E
MA 1177	Ne had my fortune bene faire, / fey had I leuede.	/	A have H E
MA 1178	Onone stryke of his heuede, / and / stake it thereaftyre,	C	V H Z
MA 1179	Gife it to thy sqwyere, / fore he es / wele horsede,	C H be	Z E
MA 1180	Bere it to Sir Howell, / that es in / harde bataile,	that be P	A N
MA 1181	And byd hym herte hym wele, / his / enmy es destruede.	D	N be E
MA 1182	Syne bere it to Barefleete, / and / brace it in yryne,	C	V H P N
MA 1183	And sett it on the barbycane, / biernes to schewe.	/	N to V
MA 1184	My brande and my brode schelde / apon the / bent lyggez,	P D	N V
MA 1185	On the creeste of the cragge, / thare / fyrste we encontrede,	Q	Z H V
MA 1186	And the clubb tharby, / all of / clene iren,	D D	A N
MA 1187	That many Cristen has kyllyde / in / Constantyne landez;	P	N N
MA 1188	Ferke to the farlande, / and / fetche me that wapen,	C	V H D N
MA 1189	And late founde till oure flete, / in / flode thare it lengez.	P	N Q H V
MA 1190	If thow wyll any tresour, / take whate the luye;	/	V Q H V
MA 1191	Haue I the kyrtyll and the clubb, / I / coueite noghte ellis."	H	V not A
MA 1192	Now they caire to the cragge, / thise / comlyche knyghtez,	D	A N
MA 1193	And broghte hym the brade schelde / and his / bryghte wapen,	C D	A N
MA 1194	The clubb and the cotte / alls, Syr / Kayous hym seluen,	Z D	N H self
MA 1195	And kayres with [the] Conquerour, / the / kyngez to schewe	D	N to V
MA 1196	That in couerte the Kyng / helde / closse to hym seluen,	V	Z P H self
MA 1197	Whills clene day fro the clowde / clymbyd on lofte.	/	V Z
MA 1198	Be that to courte was comen / clamour full huge;	/	N Z A
MA 1199	And before the comlyche kyng / they / knelyd all at ones:	H	V Z Z
MA 1200	"Welcom, our liege lorde, / to / lang has thow duellyde,	Z	Z have H E
MA 1201	Gouernour vndyr Gode, / graytheste and noble,	/	A C A
MA 1202	To whaт grace es graunted / and / gyffen at His will;	C	E P D N

MA 1203	Now thy comly come / has / comforthede vs all.	have	E H Z	
MA 1204	Thow has in thy realtee / reuengyde thy pople,	/	F D N	
MA 1205	Thurghe helpe of thy hande, / thyne / enmyse are struyede,	D	N be E	
MA 1206	That has thy renkes ouerronne / and / refte them theire childyre;	C	E H D N	
MA 1207	Whas neuer rewme owte of araye / so / redyly releuede!"	Z	Z E	
MA 1208	Than the Conquerour Cristenly / carpez to his pople:	/	V P D N	
MA 1209	"Thankes Gode," quod he, "of this grace, / and no / gome ells,	C D	N A	
MA 1210	For it was neuer manns dede, / bot / myghte of Hym selfen,	P	N P H self	
MA 1211	Or myracle of Hys Modyr, / that / mylde es till all."	that	A be P H	
MA 1212	He somond than the schippemen / scharpely theraftyre,	/	Z Z	
MA 1213	To schake furthe with the schyremen / to / schiffe the gudez,	to	V D N	
MA 1214	All the myche tresour / that / traytour had wonnen,	that	N have E	
MA 1215	To comouns of the contre, / clergye and other:	/	N C H	
MA 1216	"Luke it be done and delte / to my / dere pople,	P D	A N	
MA 1217	That none pleyn of theire parte, / o / peyne of ʒour lyfez."	P	N P D N	
MA 1218	He comande hys cosyn, / with / knyghtlyche wordez,	P	A N	
MA 1219	To make a kyrke on the cragg, / ther the / corse lengez,	Q D	N V	
MA 1220	And a couent therein, / Criste for to serfe,	/	N for to V	
MA 1221	In mynde of that martyre, / that in the / monte rystez.	that P D	N V	
MA 1222	Qwen Sir Arthur the Kyng / had / kylled the gyaunt,	have	E D N	
MA 1223	Than blythely fro Bareflete / he / buskes on the morne;	H	V P D N	
MA 1224	With his batell on brede, / by tha / blythe stremes,	P D	A N	
MA 1225	Towarde Castell Blanke / he / chesez hym the waye;	H	V H D N	
MA 1226	Thurghe a faire champayne, / vndyr / schalke hyllis,	P	N N	
MA 1227	The Kyng fraystez a furth / ouer the / fresche strandez,	P D	A N	
MA 1228	Foundez with his faire folke / ouer as hym lykez;	/	Z C H V	
MA 1229	Furthe stepes that steryn / and / strekez his tentis	C	V D N	
MA 1230	One a strenghe by a streme, / in thas / straytt landez.	P D	A N	
MA 1231	Onone aftyre myddaye, / in the / mene-while,	P D	N N	
MA 1232	Thare comez two messangers / of tha / fere marchez,	P D	A N	
MA 1233	Fra the Marschall of Fraunce, / and / menskfully hym gretes,	C	Z H V	
MA 1234	Besoghte hym of sucour / and / saide hym thise wordez:	C	V H D N	
MA 1235	"Sir, thi marschall, thi mynistre, / thy / mercy besekez,	D	N V	
MA 1236	Of thy mekill magestee, / fore / mendement of thi pople,	P	N P D N	
MA 1237	Of thise marchez-men, / that / thus are myskaryede,	that	Z be E	
MA 1238	And thus merred amang, / maugree theire eghne.	/	P D N	
MA 1239	I witter the the Emperour / es / entirde into Fraunce,	be	E P N	
MA 1240	With ostes of enmyse, / orrible and huge;	/	A C A	
MA 1241	Brynnez in Burgoyne / thy / burghes so ryche,	D	N Z A	
MA 1242	And brittenes thi baronage, / that / bieldez tharein;	that	V Z	
MA 1243	He encrochez kenely / by / craftez of armez,	P	N P N	
MA 1244	Countrese and castells / that to thy / coroun langez,	that P D	N V	
MA 1245	Confoundez thy comouns, / clergy and other:	/	N C H	
MA 1246	Bot thow comfurth them, Sir Kyng, / couer sall they neuer!	/	V X H Z	
MA 1247	He fellez forestez fele, / forrayse thi landez,	/	V D N	
MA 1248	Frysthez no fraunchez, / bot / fraiez the pople;	C	V D N	
MA 1249	Thus he fellez thi folke / and / fangez theire gudez:	C	V D N	
MA 1250	Fremedly the Franche tung / fey es belefede.	/	A be E	
MA 1251	He drawes into douce Fraunce, / as / Duchemen tellez,	C	N V	
MA 1252	Dresside with his dragouns, / dredfull to schewe;	/	A to V	
MA 1253	All to dede they dyghte / with / dynnttys of swerddez,	P	N P N	
MA 1254	Dukez and dusperes / that / dreches tharein.	that	V Z	
MA 1255	Forthy the lordez of the lande, / ladys and other,	/	N C H	
MA 1256	Prayes the for Petyr luffe, / the / Apostyll of Rome,	D	N P N	
MA 1257	Sen thow arte present in place, / that thow will / profyre make	that H X	N V	
MA 1258	To that perilous prynce, / be / processe of tym.	P	N P N	
MA 1259	He ayers by ʒone hilles, / ʒone / heghe holtez vndyr,	D	A N P	
MA 1260	Hufes thare with hale strenghe / of / haythen kyngez;	P	A N	
MA 1261	Helpe now for His lufe, / that / heghe in Heuen sittez,	that	A P N V	
MA 1262	And talke tristly to them / that / thus vs destroyes."	that	Z H V	
MA 1263	The Kyng biddis Sir Boice, / "Buske the belyfe;	/	V H Z	
MA 1264	Take with the Sir Berill / and / Bedwere the ryche,	C	N D N(A)	
MA 1265	Sir Gawayne and Sir Geryn, / these / galyarde knyghtez,	D	A N	
MA 1266	And graythe ʒowe to ʒone grene wode, / and / gose on ther nedes:	C	V P D N	
MA 1267	Saise to Syr Lucius, / to / vnlordly he wyrkez,	Z	Z H V	
MA 1268	Thus letherly agaynes law / to / lede my pople,	to	V D N	
MA 1269	I lette hym or opile lange, / ʒif me the / lyffe happen,	C H D	N V	
MA 1270	Or many lyghte sall lawe / that hym ouere / lande folowes.	that H P	N V	
MA 1271	Comande hym kenely / wyth / crewell wordez,	P	A N	
MA 1272	Cayre owte of my kyngryke / with his / kydd knyghtez:	P D	E N	
MA 1273	In caase that he will noghte, / that / cursede wreche,	that	E N	

The Alliterative Morte Arthure

MA 1274	Com for his curtaisie, / and / countere me ones.	C	V H Z
MA 1275	Thane sall we rekken full rathe / whatt / ryghte that he claymes,	Q	N that H V
MA 1276	Thus to ryot this rewme / and / raunsone the pople.	C	V D N
MA 1277	Thare sall it derely be delte / with / dynttez of handez,	P	N P N
MA 1278	The Dryghtten at Domesdaye / dele as Hym lykes!"	/	V C H V
MA 1279	Now thei graythe them to goo, / theis / galyarde knyghttez,	D	A N
MA 1280	All gleterande in golde, / appon / grete stedes,	P	A N
MA 1281	Towarde the grene wode, / with / grownden wapyn,	P	E N
MA 1282	To grete wele the grett lorde, / that wolde be / grefede sone.	that X be	E Z
MA 1283	Thise hende houez on a hill / by the / holte eyues,	P D	N N
MA 1284	Behelde the howsyng full hye / of / hathen kynges:	P	A N
MA 1285	They herde in theire herbergage / hundrethez full many	/	N Z A
MA 1286	Hornez of olyfantez / full / helych blawen;	Z	Z E
MA 1287	Palaisez proudliche pyghte, / that / palyd ware ryche,	that	E be Z
MA 1288	Of pall and of purpure, / with / precyous stones;	P	A N
MA 1289	Pensels and pomell / of / ryche prynce armez,	P	A N N
MA 1290	Pighte in the playn mede, / the / pople to schewe.	D	N to V
MA 1291	And than the Romayns so ryche / had / arayede their tentez,	have	E D N
MA 1292	On rawe by the ryuer, / vndyr the / round hillez,	P D	A N
MA 1293	The Emperour for honour / ewyn in the myddes,	/	Z P D N
MA 1294	Wyth egles al ouer, / ennelled so faire;	/	E Z Z
MA 1295	And saw hym and the Sowdane, / and / senatours many	C	N A
MA 1296	Seke towarde a sale / with / sextene kyngez,	P	A N
MA 1297	Syland softely / in, / swettly by them selfen,	Z	Z P H self
MA 1298	To sowpe withe that soueraygne / full / selcouthe metez.	Z	A N
MA 1299	Nowe they wende ouer the watyre, / thise / wyrchipfull knyghttez,	D	A N
MA 1300	Thurghe the wode to the wone / there the / wyese rystez;	Q D	N V
MA 1301	Reght as they weschen / and / went to the table,	C	V P D N
MA 1302	Sir Wawayne the worthy / vnwynly he spekes:	/	Z H V
MA 1303	The myghte and the maiestee / that / menskes vs all,	that	V H Z
MA 1304	That was merked and made / thurghe the / myghte of Hym seluen,	P D	N P H self
MA 1305	Gyffe ʒow sytte in ʒour sette, / Sowdane and other,	/	N C H
MA 1306	That here are semblede in sale, / vnsawghte mott ʒe worthe!	/	A X H V
MA 1307	And the fals heretyke / that / Emperour hym callez,	that	N H V
MA 1308	That ocupyes in erroure / the / Empyre of Rome,	D	N P N
MA 1309	Sir Arthure herytage, / that / honourable kyng,	that	A N
MA 1310	That all his auncestres aughte / but / Vtere hym one,	P	N H self
MA 1311	That ilke cursynge that Cayme / kaghte for his brothyre	/	V P D N
MA 1312	Cleffe on the, cukewalde, / with / croune ther thow lengez,	P	N Q H V
MA 1313	For the vnlordlyeste lede / that I on / lukede euer!	that H Z	V Z
MA 1314	My lorde meruailles hym mekyll, / man, be my trouthe,	/	N be D N
MA 1315	Why thow morthires his men, / that no / mysse serues,	that D	N V
MA 1316	Comouns of the countre, / clergye and other,	/	N C H
MA 1317	That are noghte couppable therin, / ne / knawes noght in armez.	not	N not P N
MA 1318	Forthi the comelyche kynge, / curtays and noble,	/	A C A
MA 1319	Comandez the kenely / to / kaire of his landes,	to	V P D N
MA 1320	Ore ells for thy knyghthede / encontre hym ones;	/	V H Z
MA 1321	Sen thow couettes the coroune, / latte it be declarede!	/	V H be E
MA 1322	I hafe dyschargide me here, / chalange whoo lykez,	/	V Q V
MA 1323	Before all thy cheualrye, / cheftaynes and other;	/	N C H
MA 1324	Schape vs an ansuere, / and / schunte thow no lengere,	C	V H Z
MA 1325	That we may schifte at the schorte / and / schewe to my lorde.	C	V P D N
MA 1326	The Emperour ansuerde / wyth / austeryn wordez:	P	A N
MA 1327	ʒe are with myn enmy, / Sir / Arthur hym seluen;	D	N H self
MA 1328	It es non honour to me / to / owttray hys knyghttez,	to	V D N
MA 1329	Thoghe ʒe bee irous men / that / ayres on his nedez;	that	V P D N
MA 1330	Bot say to thy soueraygne / I / send hym thes wordez,	H	V H D N
MA 1331	Ne ware it for reuerence / of my / ryche table,	P D	A N
MA 1332	Thou sulde repent full rathe / of thi / ruyde wordez,	P D	A N
MA 1333	Siche a rebawde as thowe / rebuke any lordez,	/	V D N
MA 1334	Wyth theire retenuz arrayede, / full / reall and noble,	Z	A C A
MA 1335	Here will I suggourne / whills me / lefe thynkes,	C H	A V
MA 1336	And sythen seke in by Sayne / with / solace theraftere,	P	N Z
MA 1337	Ensegge al tha cetese / be the / salte strandez,	P D	A N
MA 1338	And seyn ryde in by Rone, / that / rynnez so faire,	that	V Z Z
MA 1339	And of all his ryche castells / rusche doun the wallez;	/	V Z D N
MA 1340	I sall noghte lefe in Paresche, / by / processe of tyme,	P	N P N
MA 1341	His parte of a pechelyne, / proue when hym lykes!"	/	V C H V
MA 1342	"Now certez," sais Sir Wawayne, / "myche / wondyre haue I	D	N V H
MA 1343	That syche an alfyn as thow / dare / speke syche wordez!	V	V D N
MA 1344	I had leuer then all Fraunce, / that / heuede es of rewmes,	D	N be P N

MA 1345	Fyghte with the faythefully / on / felde be oure one."	P	N P D H
MA 1346	Thane answers Sir Gayous / full / gobbede wordes,	Z	A N
MA 1347	Was eme to the Emperour / and / erle hym selfen,	C	N H self
MA 1348	"Euere ware thes Bretouns / braggers of olde!	/	N P N(A)
MA 1349	Loo, how he brawles / hym for hys / bryghte wedes,	H P D	A N
MA 1350	As he myghte bryttyn vs all / with hys / brande ryche;	P D	N A
MA 1351	ȝitt he berkes myche boste, / ȝone / boy there he standes!"	D	N Z H V
MA 1352	Than greuyde Sir Gawayne / at his / grett wordes,	P D	A N
MA 1353	Graythes towarde the gome / with / grucchande herte;	P	G N
MA 1354	With hys stelyn brande / he / strykes of hys heuede,	H	V P D N
MA 1355	And sterttes owtte to hys stede, / and with his / stale wendes.	C P D	N V
MA 1356	Thurghe the wacches they wente, / thes / wirchipfull knyghtez,	D	A N
MA 1357	And feyndez in theire farewaye / wondyrlyche many;	/	Z A
MA 1358	Ouer the watyre they wente / by / wyghtnesse of horses,	P	N P N
MA 1359	And tuke wynde as they walde / by the / wodde hemmes.	P D	N N
MA 1360	Thane folous frekly one fote / frekkes ynewe,	/	N A
MA 1361	And of the Romayns arrayed / appon / ryche stedes,	P	A N
MA 1362	Chasede thurghe a champayne / oure / cheualrous knyghtez,	D	A N
MA 1363	Till a cheefe forest, / on / scalke-whitte horses.	P	N A N
MA 1364	Bot a freke all in fyne golde, / and / fretted in sable,	C	E P N
MA 1365	Come forthermaste on a freson, / in / flawmande wedes;	P	G N
MA 1366	A faire floreschte spere / in / fewtyre he castes,	P	N H V
MA 1367	And folowes faste on owre folke / and / freschelye ascryez.	C	Z V
MA 1368	Thane Sir Gawayne the gude, / appone / a graye stede,	P D	A N
MA 1369	He gryppes hym a grete spere / and / graythely hym hittez;	C	Z H V
MA 1370	Thurghe the guttez into the gorre / he / gyrdes hym ewyn,	H	V H Z
MA 1371	That the grounden stele / glydez to his herte;	/	V P D N
MA 1372	The gome and the grette horse / at the / grounde lyggez,	P D	N V
MA 1373	Full gryselyche gronande, / for / grefe of his woundez.	P	N P D N
MA 1374	Thane presez a preker / in, full / proudely arayede,	Z Z	Z E
MA 1375	That beres all of pourpour, / palyde with syluer;	/	E P N
MA 1376	Bryggly on a broune stede / he / profers full large,	H	V Z Z
MA 1377	He was a paynyme of Perse / that / thus hym persuede.	that	Z H V
MA 1378	Sir Boys, vnabaiste / all, he / buskes hym agaynes,	Z H	V H Z
MA 1379	With a bustous launce / he / berez hym thurghe,	H	V H Z
MA 1380	That the breme and the brade schelde / appon the / bente lyggez;	P D	N V
MA 1381	And he bryngez furthe the blade / and / bownez to his felowez.	C	V P D N
MA 1382	Thane Sir Feltemour of myghte, / a / man mekyll praysede,	D	N Z V
MA 1383	Was mouede on his manere / and / manacede full faste;	C	V Z Z
MA 1384	He graythes to Sir Gawayne / graythely to wyrche,	/	Z to V
MA 1385	For grefe of Sir Gayous, / that es on / grounde leuede.	that be P	N E
MA 1386	Than Sir Gawayne was glade: / agayne hym he rydez,	/	P H H V
MA 1387	Wyth Galuth his gude swerde / graythely hym hyttez;	C	Z H V
MA 1388	The knyghte on the coursere / he / cleuede in sondyre,	H	V Z
MA 1389	Clenlyche fro the croune / his / corse he dyuysyde,	D	N H V
MA 1390	And thus he killez the knyghte / with his / kydd wapen.	P D	E N
MA 1391	Than a ryche man of Rome / relyede to his byerns:	/	V P D N
MA 1392	"It sall repent vs full sore / and we / ryde forthire!	C H	V Z
MA 1393	ȝone are bolde bosturs / that syche / bale wyrkez;	that D	N V
MA 1394	It befell hym full foule / that tham so / fyrste namede."	that H Z	Z V
MA 1395	Thane the riche Romayns / retournes thaire brydills	/	V D N
MA 1396	To thaire tentis in tene, / telles theire lordez	/	V D N
MA 1397	How Sir Marschalle de Mowne / es on the / monte lefede,	be P D	N E
MA 1398	Forejustyde at that journee / for his / grett japez.	P D	A N
MA 1399	Bot thare chasez on oure men / cheuallrous knyghtez,	/	A N
MA 1400	Fyfe thosande folke / appon / faire stedes,	P	A N
MA 1401	Faste to a foreste / ouer a / fell watyr,	P D	A N
MA 1402	That fillez fro the falow see / fyfty myle large.	/	A N A
MA 1403	Thare ware Bretons enbuschide, / and / banarettez noble,	C	N A
MA 1404	Of the cheualrye cheefe / of the / kyngez chambyre,	P D	N N
MA 1405	Seese them chase oure men / and / changen theire horsez,	C	V D N
MA 1406	And choppe doun cheftaynes / that they / moste chargyde.	that H	Z V
MA 1407	Thane the enbuschement of Bretons / brake owte at ones,	/	V Z Z
MA 1408	Brothely at baner, / and / Bedwyne knyghtez	C	N V
MA 1409	Arrestede of the Romayns / that by the / fyrthe rydez	that P D	N V
MA 1410	All the realeste renkes / that to / Rome lengez;	that P	N V
MA 1411	Thay iche on the enmyse / and / egerly strykkys,	C	Z V
MA 1412	Erles of Ingland, / and / "Arthure!" ascryes;	C	N V
MA 1413	Thrughe brenes and bryghte scheldez / brestez they thyrle,	/	N H V
MA 1414	Bretons of the boldeste, / with theire / bryghte swerdez.	P D	A N
MA 1415	Thare was Romayns oueredyn / and / ruydly wondyde,	C	Z E

MA 1416	Arrestede as rebawdez / with / ryotous knyghttez;	P	A N
MA 1417	The Romaynes owte of araye / remoued at ones,	/	V Z
MA 1418	And rydes awaye in a rowtte, / for / reddoure it semys.	C	N H V
MA 1419	To the Senatour Petyr / a / sandesmane es commyn,	D	N be E
MA 1420	And saide "Sir, sekerly, ȝour / seggez are supprysside."	D	N be E
MA 1421	Than ten thowsande men / he / semblede at ones,	H	V Z
MA 1422	And sett sodanly on our seggez, / by the / salte strandez;	P D	A N
MA 1423	Than ware Bretons abaiste / and / greuede a lyttill,	C	V Z
MA 1424	Bot ȝit the banerettez bolde / and / bachellers noble	C	N A
MA 1425	Brekes that battailes / with / brestez of stedes;	P	N P N
MA 1426	Sir Boice and his bolde men / myche / bale wyrkes.	D	N V
MA 1427	The Romayns redyes / tham, / arrayez tham better,	H	V H Z
MA 1428	And al toruscheez oure men / withe theire / ryste horsez,	P D	A N
MA 1429	Arestede of the richeste / of the / Rounde Table,	P D	A N
MA 1430	Ouerrydez oure rerewarde / and / grette rewthe wyrkes.	C	A N V
MA 1431	Thane the Bretons on the bente / habyddez no lengere,	/	V Z
MA 1432	Bot fleede to the foreste / and the / feelde leuede;	C D	N V
MA 1433	Sir Beryll es born / down and Sir / Boice taken,	Z C D	N E
MA 1434	The beste of our bolde men / vnblythely wondyde;	/	Z E
MA 1435	Bot ȝitt our stale on a strenghe / stotais a lyttill,	/	V Z
MA 1436	All tostonayede with the stokes / of tha / steryn knyghtez;	P D	A N
MA 1437	Made sorowe fore theire soueraygne, / that / so thare was nomen,	that	C Z be E
MA 1438	Besoughte Gode of socure, / sende whene Hym lykyde.	/	V C H V
MA 1439	Than commez Sir Idrus, / armede vp at all ryghttez,	/	E Z P A N
MA 1440	Wyth fyue hundrethe men / appon / faire stedes;	P	A N
MA 1441	Fraynez faste at oure folke / freschely thareaftyre,	/	Z Z
MA 1442	ȝif ther frendez ware ferre, / that on / the felde foundide.	that P D	N V
MA 1443	Thane sais Sir Gawayne, / "So me / God helpe,	C H	N V
MA 1444	We hafe bene chased todaye / and / chullede as hares,	C	E P N
MA 1445	Rebuyked with Romaynes / appon theire / ryche stedez,	P D	A N
MA 1446	And we lurkede vndyr lee / as / lowrande wreches!	P	G N
MA 1447	I luke neuer on my lorde / the / dayes of my lyfe,	D	N P D N
MA 1448	And we so lytherly hym helpe / that hym so / wele lykede."	that H Z	Z V
MA 1449	Thane the Bretons brothely / brochez theire stedez,	/	V D N
MA 1450	And boldly in batell / appon the / bent rydes;	P D	N V
MA 1451	All the ferse men before / frekly ascryes,	/	V Z
MA 1452	Ferkand in the foreste, / to / freschen tham selfen.	to	V H self
MA 1453	The Romaynes than redyly / arrayes them bettyre,	/	V H Z
MA 1454	One rawe on a rowm felde, / reghttez theire wapyns,	/	V D N
MA 1455	By the ryche reuere, / and / rewles the pople;	C	V D N
MA 1456	And with reddour Sir Boice / es in / areste halden.	be P	N E
MA 1457	Now thei semblede vnsaughte / by the / salte strandez:	P D	A N
MA 1458	Saddly theis sekere menn / settys theire dynttez;	/	V D N
MA 1459	With lufly launcez on lofte / they / luyschten togedyres,	H	V Z
MA 1460	In lorayne so lordlye / on / leppande stedes.	P	G N
MA 1461	Thare ware gomes thurghegirde / with / grundyn wapyns,	P	E N
MA 1462	Grisely gayspand / with / grucchande lotes;	P	G N
MA 1463	Grete lordes of Greke / greffede so hye.	/	E Z Z
MA 1464	Swyftly with swerdes / they / swappen thereaftyre,	H	V Z
MA 1465	Swappez doun full sweperlye / swelltande knyghtez,	/	G N
MA 1466	That all swellttez one swarthe / that they / ouerswyngen;	that H	Z V
MA 1467	So many sweys in swoghe, / swounande att ones.	/	G Z
MA 1468	Syr Gaweayne the gracyous / full / graythelye he wyrkkes:	Z	Z H V
MA 1469	The gretteste he gretez / wyth / gryselye wondes;	P	A N
MA 1470	Wyth Galuth he gyrdez / doun full / galyard knyghtez,	Z Z	A N
MA 1471	Fore greefe of the grett lorde / so / grymlye he strykez.	Z	Z H V
MA 1472	He rydez furthe ryallye / and / redely thereaftyre,	C	Z Z
MA 1473	Thare this reall renke / was in / areste halden;	be P	N E
MA 1474	He ryfez the raunke stele, / he / ryghttez theire brenez,	H	V D N
MA 1475	And refte them the ryche man / and / rade to his strenghes.	C	V P D N
MA 1476	The Senatour Peter / thane / persewede hym aftyre,	Z	V H P
MA 1477	Thurghe the presse of the pople, / wyth his / pryce knyghttes;	P D	A N
MA 1478	Apperttly fore the prysonere / proues his strenghes,	/	V D N
MA 1479	Wyth prekers the proudeste / that to the / presse lengez.	that P D	N V
MA 1480	Wrothely on the wrange hande / Sir / Gawayne he strykkes,	D	N H V
MA 1481	Wyth a wapen of were / vnwynnly hym hittez;	/	Z H V
MA 1482	The breny one the bakhalfe / he / brystez in sondyre,	H	V Z
MA 1483	Bot ȝit he broghte forthe Sir Boyce, / for all theire / bale biernez.	P D D	A N
MA 1484	Thane the Bretons boldely / braggen theire tromppez,	/	V D N
MA 1485	And fore blysse of Sir Boyce / was / broghte owtte of bandez,	be	E P P N
MA 1486	Boldely in batell / they / bere doun knyghtes;	H	V Z N

MA 1487	With brandes of broun stele / they / brettened maylez;	H	V N
MA 1488	Thay stekede stedys in stour / with / stelen wapyns,	P	A N
MA 1489	And all stewede with strenghe / that / stode them agaynes.	that	V H P
MA 1490	Sir Idrus fitz Ewayn / than / "Arthur!" ascryeez,	Z	N V
MA 1491	Assemblez on the Senatour / wyth / sextene knyghttez,	P	A N
MA 1492	Of the sekereste men / that to oure / syde lengede.	that P D	N V
MA 1493	Sodanly in a soppe / they / sett in att ones,	H	V Z Z
MA 1494	Foynes faste att the forebreste / with / flawmande swerdez,	P	G N
MA 1495	And feghttes faste att the fronte / freschely thareaftyre,	/	Z Z
MA 1496	Felles fele on the felde / appon the / ferrere syde,	P D	A N
MA 1497	Fey on the faire felde / by tha / fresche strandez.	P D	A N
MA 1498	Bot Sir Idrus fytz Ewayn / anters hym seluen,	/	V H self
MA 1499	And enters in anly / and / egyrly strykez,	C	Z V
MA 1500	Sekez to the Senatour / and / sesez his brydill;	C	V D N
MA 1501	Vnsaughtely he saide / hym these / sittande wordez:	H D	G N
MA 1502	"3elde the, Sir, 3apely, / 3ife thou thi / lyfe 3ernez;	C H D	N V
MA 1503	Fore gyftez that thow gyffe / may thou / 3eme now the selfen.	X H	V Z H self
MA 1504	Fore dredlez dreche / thow or / droppe any wylez,	H C	V D N
MA 1505	Thow sall dy this daye / thorowe / dyntt of my handez!"	P	N P D N
MA 1506	"I ascente," quod the Senatour, / "so me / Criste helpe;	C H	N V
MA 1507	So that I be safe broghte / before the / Kyng seluen,	P D	N self
MA 1508	Raunson me resonabillye, / as I may / ouerreche	C H X	Z V
MA 1509	Aftyre my renttez in Rome / may / redyly forthire."	X	Z V
MA 1510	Thane answers Sir Idrus / with / austeryn wordez:	P	A N
MA 1511	"Thow sall hafe condycyon, / as the / Kyng lykes,	C D	N V
MA 1512	When thow comes to the kyth / there the / courte haldez,	Q H	N V
MA 1513	In caase his concell / bee to / kepe the no langere,	be to	V H Z
MA 1514	To be killyde at his commandment / his / knyghttez before."	D	N P
MA 1515	Thay ledde hym furthe in the rowte / and / lached ofe his wedes,	C	V Z D N
MA 1516	Lefte hym wyth Lyonell / and / Lowell, hys brothire.	C	N D N
MA 1517	O lawe in the launde / than, by the / lythe strandez,	Z P D	A N
MA 1518	Sir Lucius lyggemen / loste are fore euer.	/	E be Z
MA 1519	The Senatour Peter / es / prysoner takyn;	be	N E
MA 1520	Of Perce and of Porte Iaffe / full many / price knyghtez,	Z D	A N
MA 1521	And myche pople wythall / perischede tham selfen,	/	V H self
MA 1522	For presse of the passage / they / plungede at onez.	H	V Z
MA 1523	Thare myghte men see Romaynez / rewfully wondyde,	/	Z V
MA 1524	Ouerredyn with renkes / of the / Round Table.	P D	A N
MA 1525	In the raike of the furthe / they / righten theire brenys,	H	V D N
MA 1526	That rane all on reede blode / redylye all ouer.	/	Z Z
MA 1527	They raughte in the rerewarde / full / ryotous knyghtez	Z	A N
MA 1528	For raunsone of rede golde / and / reall stedys;	C	A N
MA 1529	Radly relayes / and / restez theire horsez,	C	V D N
MA 1530	In rowtte to the ryche kynge / they / rade al at onez.	H	V Z Z
MA 1531	A knyghte cayrez before / and to the / Kynge telles,	C P D	N V
MA 1532	"Sir, here commez thy messangerez / with / myrthez fro the mountez;	P	N P D N
MA 1533	Thay hafe bene machede todaye / with / men of the marchez,	P	N P D N
MA 1534	Foremaglede in tha marras / with / meruailous knyghtez.	P	A N
MA 1535	We hafe foughten, in faithe, / by 3one / fresche strandez,	P D	A N
MA 1536	With the frekkeste folke / that to thi / foo langez;	that P D	N V
MA 1537	Fyfty thosaunde on felde / of / ferse men of armez,	P	A N P N
MA 1538	Wythin a furlange of waye, / fay ere bylefede.	/	A be E
MA 1539	We hafe eschewede this chekke / thurghe / chance of oure Lorde,	P	N P D N
MA 1540	Of tha cheualrous men / that / chargede thy pople.	that	V D N
MA 1541	The cheefe chaunchelere of Rome, / a / cheftayne full noble,	D	N Z A
MA 1542	Will aske the chartyre of pesse, / for / charitee, hym selfen.	P	N H self
MA 1543	And the Senatour Petire / to / prisoner es takyn;	P	N be E
MA 1544	Of Perse and of Porte Iaffe / paynymmez ynewe	/	N A
MA 1545	Commez prekande in the presse / with thy / prysse knyghttez,	P D	A N
MA 1546	With pouerte in thi preson / theire / paynez to drye.	D	N to V
MA 1547	I beseke 3ow, Sir, / say whate 3owe lykes,	/	V Q H V
MA 1548	Whethire 3e suffyre them saughte / or / sone delyuerde.	C	Z E
MA 1549	3e may haue fore the Senatour / sextie horse chargede	/	A N E
MA 1550	Of siluer be Seterdaye, / full / sekyrly payede;	Z	Z E
MA 1551	And for the cheefe chauncelere, / the / cheualere noble,	D	N A
MA 1552	Charottez chokkefull / charegyde with golde;	/	E P N
MA 1553	The remenaunt of the Romaynez / be in / areste halden,	be P	N E
MA 1554	Till thiere renttez in Rome / be / rightewissly knawen.	be	Z E
MA 1555	I beseke 3ow, Sir, / certyfye 3one lordez,	/	V D N
MA 1556	3if 3e will send tham ouer the see / or / kepe tham 3our selfen.	C	V H H self
MA 1557	All 3our sekyre men, forsothe, / sounde are byleuyde,	/	A be E

MA 1558	Saue Sir Ewayne fytz Henry / es in the / side wonddede."	be P D	N E
MA 1559	"Crist be thankyde," quod the Kyng, / "and hys / clere Modyre,	C D	A N
MA 1560	That ʒowe comforthed and helpede / be / crafte of Hym selfen;	P	N P H self
MA 1561	Skilfull skomfyture / he / skiftez as Hym lykez;	H	V C H V
MA 1562	Is none so skathlye may skape / ne / skewe fro His handez.	not	V P D N
MA 1563	Desteny and doughtynes / of / dedys of armes,	P	N P N
MA 1564	All es demyd and delte / at / Dryghtynez will.	P	N N
MA 1565	I kwn the thanke for thy come, / it / comfortes vs all.	H	V H Z
MA 1566	Sir Knyghte," sais the Conquerour, / "so me / Criste helpe,	C H	N V
MA 1567	I ʒif the for thy thyʒandez / Tolouse the riche,	/	N D N(A)
MA 1568	The toll and the tachementez, / tauernez and other,	/	N C H
MA 1569	The town and the tenementez, / with / towrez so hye,	P	N Z A
MA 1570	That towchez to the temporaltee, / whills my / tym lastez.	C D	N V
MA 1571	Bot say to the Senatour / I / sende hym thes wordez:	H	V H D N
MA 1572	Thare sall no siluer hym saue / bot / Ewayn recouer;	C	N V
MA 1573	I had leuer see hym synke / on the / salte strandez,	P D	A N
MA 1574	Than the seegge ware seke, / that es so / sore woundede.	that be Z	Z E
MA 1575	I sall disseuere that sorte, / so me / Criste helpe,	C H	N V
MA 1576	And sett them full solytarie, / in / sere kyngez landez.	P	A N N
MA 1577	Sall he neuer sownde see / his / seynowres in Rome,	D	N P N
MA 1578	Ne sitt in the assemble / in / syghte wyth his feris;	P	N P D N
MA 1579	For it comes to no kyng / that / Conquerour es holden,	that	N be E
MA 1580	To comon with his captifis / fore / couatys of siluer.	P	N P N
MA 1581	It come neuer of knyghthede, / knawe if ʒif hym lyke,	/	V C C H V
MA 1582	To carpe of coseri / when / captyfis ere takyn;	C	N be E
MA 1583	It aughte to no presoners / to / prese no lordez,	to	V D N
MA 1584	Ne come in presens of pryncez / whene / partyes are mouede.	C	N be E
MA 1585	Comaunde ʒone constable, / the / castell that ʒemes,	D	N that V
MA 1586	That he be clenlyche kepede, / and in / close halden;	C P	N E
MA 1587	He sall haue maundement tomorne, / or / myddaye be roungen,	C	N be E
MA 1588	To what marche thay sall merke, / with / mauger to lengen."	P	N to V
MA 1589	Thay conuaye this captyfe / with / clene men of armez,	P	A N P N
MA 1590	And kend hym to the constable, / alls the / Kynge byddez;	C D	N V
MA 1591	And seyn to Arthure they ayr / and / egerly hym towchez	C	Z H V
MA 1592	The answere of the Emperour, / irows of dedez.	/	A P N
MA 1593	Thane Sir Arthur, on erthe / atheliste of othere,	/	A P H
MA 1594	At euen at his awen borde / auantid his lordez:	/	V D N
MA 1595	"Me aughte to honour them in erthe / ouer all / other thyngez	P D	A N
MA 1596	That thus in myn absens / awnters them selfen;	/	N H self
MA 1597	I sall them luffe whylez I lyffe, / so me our / Lorde helpe,	C H D	N V
MA 1598	And gyfe them landys full large / whare them / beste lykes;	Q H	Z V
MA 1599	Thay sall noghte losse on this layke, / ʒif me / lyfe happen,	C H	N V
MA 1600	That thus are lamede for my lufe / be this / lythe strandez."	P D	A N
MA 1601	Bot in the clere daweyng, / the / dere kynge hym selfen	D	A N H self
MA 1602	Comaundyd Sir Cadore, / with his / dere knyghttes,	P D	A N
MA 1603	Sir Cleremus, Sir Cleremonde, / with / clene men of armez,	P	A N P N
MA 1604	Sir Clowdmur, Sir Clegis, / to / conuaye theis lordez;	to	V D N
MA 1605	Sir Boyce and Sir Berell, / with / baners displayede,	P	N E
MA 1606	Sir Bawdwyne, Sir Bryane, / and Sir / Bedwere the ryche,	C D	N D N(A)
MA 1607	Sir Raynalde and Sir Richere, / Rawlaund childyre,	/	N N
MA 1608	To ryde with the Romaynes / in / rowtte wyth theire feres.	P	N P D N
MA 1609	"Prekez now preualye / to / Parys the ryche,	/	N D N(A)
MA 1610	Wyth Petir the pryssonere / and his / price knyghttez;	C D	A N
MA 1611	Beteche tham the prouesste, / in / presens of lordez,	P	N P N
MA 1612	O payne and o perell / that / pendes theretoo;	that	V Z
MA 1613	That they be weselye wachede / and in / warde holden,	C P	N E
MA 1614	Warded of warantizez / with / wyrchipfull knyghttez,	C	A N
MA 1615	Wagge hym wyghte men, / and / woonde for no siluyre,	C	V P D N
MA 1616	I haffe warnede that wy, / be / ware ʒif hym lykes."	be	A C H V
MA 1617	Now bownes the Bretons, / als the / Kynge byddez,	C D	N V
MA 1618	Buskez theire batells, / theire / baners displayez;	D	N E
MA 1619	Towardez Chartris they chese, / thes / cheualrous knyghttez,	D	A N
MA 1620	And in the champayne lande / full / faire thay eschewede:	Z	Z H V
MA 1621	For the Emperour of myghte / had / ordand hym selfen	have	E H self
MA 1622	Sir Vtolfe and Sir Ewandyre, / two / honourable kyngez,	D	A N
MA 1623	Erles of the Orient, / with / austeryn knyghttez,	/	A N
MA 1624	Of the awntrouseste men that / to his / oste lengede,	P D	N V
MA 1625	Sir Sextynour of Lyby / and / senatours many,	C	N A
MA 1626	The Kyng of Surrye hym selfe, / with / Sarzynes ynowe,	P	N A
MA 1627	The Senatour of Sutere, / wyth / sowmes full huge,	P	N Z A
MA 1628	Whas assygnede to that courte / be / sent of his / peres,	be	E P D N

MA 1629	Traise towarde Troys / the / treson to wyrke,	D	N to V
MA 1630	Is hare betrappede with a trayne / oure / traueland knyghttez,	D	G N
MA 1631	That hade persayfede that Peter / at / Parys sulde lenge,	P	N X V
MA 1632	In presonne with the prouoste, / his / paynez to drye.	D	N to V
MA 1633	Forthi they buskede them bownn, / with / baners displayede,	P	N E
MA 1634	In the buskayle of his waye, / on / blonkkes full hugge;	P	N Z A
MA 1635	Planttez them in the pathe / with / powere arrayede,	P	N E
MA 1636	To pyke vp the presoners / fro oure / pryse knyghttez.	P D	A N
MA 1637	Syr Cadore of Cornewalle / comaundez his peris,	/	V D N
MA 1638	Sir Clegis, Sir Cleremus, / Sir / Cleremownnde the noble,	D	N D N(A)
MA 1639	"Here es the close of Clyme, / with / clewes so hye:	P	N Z A
MA 1640	Lokez the contree be clere, / the / corners are large;	D	N be A
MA 1641	Discoueres now sekerly / skrogges and other,	/	N C H
MA 1642	That no skathell in the skroggez / skorne vs hereaftyre;	/	V H Z
MA 1643	Loke ʒe skyfte it so / that vs no / skathe lympe,	that H D	N V
MA 1644	For na skomfitoure in skoulkery / is / skomfite euer."	be	E Z
MA 1645	Now they hye to the holte, / thes / harageous knyghttez,	D	A N
MA 1646	To herken of the hye men, / to / helpen theis lordez;	to	V D N
MA 1647	Fyndez them helmede hole / and / horsyde on stedys,	C	E P N
MA 1648	Houande on the hye waye / by the / holte hemmes.	P D	N N
MA 1649	With knyghttly contenaunce / Sir / Clegis hym selfen	D	N H self
MA 1650	Kryes to the companye / and / carpes thees wordez:	C	V D N
MA 1651	"Es there any kyde knyghte, / kaysere or other,	/	N C H
MA 1652	Will kyth for his kyng lufe / craftes of armes?	/	N P N
MA 1653	We are comen fro the Kyng / of this / kythe ryche,	P D	N A
MA 1654	That knawen as for conquerour, / corownde in erthe,	/	E P N
MA 1655	His ryche retenuz / here all of his / Round Table,	Z Z P D	A N
MA 1656	To ryde with that reall rowtt / where hym lykes;	/	Q H V
MA 1657	We seke justyng of werre, / ʒif any / will happyn,	C H	X V
MA 1658	Of the jolyeste men / ajuggede be lordes,	/	E P N
MA 1659	If here be any hathell man, / erle or other,	/	N C H
MA 1660	That for the Emperour lufe / will / awntere hym selfen."	X	V H self
MA 1661	And ane erle thane in angere / answeres hym son:	/	V H Z
MA 1662	"Me angers at Arthure, / and att his / hathell bierns,	C P D	A N
MA 1663	That thus in his errour / ocupyes theis rewmes,	/	V D N
MA 1664	And owtrayes the Emperour, / his / erthely lorde.	D	A N
MA 1665	The araye and the ryalltez / of the / Rounde Table	P D	A N
MA 1666	Es wyth rankour rehersede / in / rewmes full many;	P	N Z A
MA 1667	Of oure renttez of Rome / syche / reuell he haldys,	D	N H V
MA 1668	He sall ʒife resoun full rathe, / ʒif vs / reghte happen,	C H	Z V
MA 1669	That many sall repente / that in his / rowtte rydez,	that P D	N V
MA 1670	For the reklesse roy / so / rewlez hym selfen!"	Z	V H self
MA 1671	"A!" sais Sir Clegis than, / "so me / Criste helpe,	C H	N V
MA 1672	I knawe þe thi carpyng / a / cowntere the semes!	D	N H V
MA 1673	Bot be thou auditoure or erle / or / Emperour thi selfen,	C	N H self
MA 1674	Appon Arthurez byhalue / I / answere the sone:	H	V H Z
MA 1675	The renke so reall / that / rewllez vs all,	that	V H Z
MA 1676	The ryotous men and the ryche / of the / Rounde Table,	P D	A N
MA 1677	He has araysede his accownte / and / redde all his rollez,	C	E D D N
MA 1678	For he wyll gyfe a rekenyng / that / rewe sall aftyre,	that	V X Z
MA 1679	That all the ryche sall repente / that to / Rome langez,	that P	N V
MA 1680	Or the rereage be requit / of / rentez that he claymez.	P	N that H V
MA 1681	We crafe of ʒour curtaisie / three / coursez of werre,	D	N P N
MA 1682	And claymez of knyghthode, / take / kepe to ʒour selfen!	V	N P H self
MA 1683	ʒe do bott trayne vs todaye / wyth / trofeland wordez;	P	G N
MA 1684	Of syche trauaylande men / trecherye me thnykes.	/	N H V
MA 1685	Sende owte sadly / certayne knyghttez,	/	A N
MA 1686	Or say me sekerly sothe, / forsake ʒif ʒowe lykes."	/	V C H V
MA 1687	Thane sais the Kynge of Surry, / "Alls / saue me oure Lorde,	C	V H D N
MA 1688	ʒif thow hufe all the daye, / thou bees / noghte delyuerede,	H be	not E
MA 1689	Bot thow sekerly ensure / with / certeyne knyghtez,	P	A N
MA 1690	That thi cote and thi breste / be / knawen with lordez,	be	E P N
MA 1691	Of armes of ancestrye / entyrde with londez."	/	V P N
MA 1692	"Sir Kyng," sais Sir Clegys, / "full / knyghttly thow askez;	Z	Z H V
MA 1693	I trowe it be for cowardys / thow / carpes thes wordez.	H	V D N
MA 1694	Myn armez are of ancestrye / enueryd with lordez,	/	E P N
MA 1695	And has in banere bene borne / sen Sir / Brut tyme;	P D	N N
MA 1696	At the cite of Troye / that / tymme was ensegede,	that	N be E
MA 1697	Ofte seen in asawtte / with / certayne knyghttez,	P	A N
MA 1698	Fro the Borghte broghte / vs and all oure / bolde elders	H C D D	A N
MA 1699	To Bretayne the Braddere, / within / chippe-burdez."	P	N N

MA 1700	"Sir," sais Sir Sextenour, / "saye what the lykez,	/	V Q H V
MA 1701	And we sall suffyre / the, als vs / beste semes;	H C H	A V
MA 1702	Luke thi troumppez be trussede, / and / trofull no lengere,	C	V Z
MA 1703	For thoghe thou tarye all the daye, / the / tyddes no bettyr.	H	V Z
MA 1704	For there sall neuer Romayne / that in my / rowtt rydez	that P D	N V
MA 1705	Be with rebawdez rebuykyde / whills I in / werlde regne!"	C H P	N V
MA 1706	Thane Sir Clegis to the Kyng / a / lyttill enclinede,	Z	Z V
MA 1707	Kayres to Sir Cadore / and / knyghtly hym tellez,	C	Z H V
MA 1708	"We hafe founden in ȝone firthe, / floresched with leues,	/	E P N
MA 1709	The flour of the faireste folke / that to thi / foo langez:	that P D	N V
MA 1710	Fifty thosandez of folke / of / ferse men of armez,	P	A N P N
MA 1711	That faire are fewteride on frounte / vndyr ȝone / fre bowes;	P D	A N
MA 1712	They are enbuschede on blonkkes, / with / baners displayede,	P	N E
MA 1713	In ȝone bechen wode / appon the / waye sydes.	P D	N N
MA 1714	Thay hafe the furthe forsette / all of the / faire watyre,	H P D	A N
MA 1715	That fayfully of force / feghte vs byhowys;	/	V H V
MA 1716	For thus vs schappes todaye, / shortly to tell,	/	Z to V
MA 1717	Whedyre we schone or schewe, / schyft as the lykes."	/	V C H V
MA 1718	"Nay," quod Cador, / "so me / Criste helpe,	C H	N V
MA 1719	It ware schame that we scholde / schone for so lytyll.	/	V P Z A
MA 1720	Sir Lancelott sall neuer laughe, / that with the / Kyng lengez,	that P D	N V
MA 1721	That I sulde lette my waye / for / lede appon erthe;	P	N P N
MA 1722	I sall be dede and vndone / ar I / here dreche,	C H	Z V
MA 1723	For drede of any doggeson / in ȝone / dym schawes!"	P D	A N
MA 1724	Syr Cador thane knyghtly / comforthes his pople,	/	V D N
MA 1725	And with corage kene / he / karpes thes wordes:	H	V D N
MA 1726	"Thynk on the valyaunt prynce / that / vesettez vs euer	that	V H Z
MA 1727	With landez and lordcheppez, / whare vs / beste lykes;	Q H	Z V
MA 1728	That has vs ducheres delte / and / dubbyde vs knyghttez,	C	V H N
MA 1729	Gifen vs gersoms and golde / and / gardwynes many,	C	N A
MA 1730	Grewhoundez and grett horse / and / alkyn gamnes,	C	A N
MA 1731	That gaynez till any gome / that vndyre / God leuez.	that P	N V
MA 1732	Thynke on riche renoun / of the / Rounde Table,	P D	A N
MA 1733	And late it neuer be refte / vs fore / Romayne in erthe;	H P	N P N
MA 1734	Feyne ȝow noghte feyntly, / ne / frythes no wapyns,	not	V D N
MA 1735	Bot luke ȝe fyghte faythefully, / frekes, ȝour selfen;	/	N H self
MA 1736	I walde be wellyde all qwyke / and / quarterde in sondre,	C	E Z
MA 1737	Bot I wyrke my dede, / whils I in / wrethe lenge."	C H P	N V
MA 1738	Than this doughtty duke / buddyd his knyghttez,	/	V D N
MA 1739	Ioneke and Askanere, / Aladuke and other,	/	N C H
MA 1740	That ayerez were of Esex / and all thase / este marchez,	C D D	A N
MA 1741	Howell and Hardelfe, / happy in armez,	/	A P N
MA 1742	Sir Heryll and Sir Herygall, / thise / harageouse knyghttez.	D	A N
MA 1743	Than the souerayn assignede / certayne lordez,	/	A N
MA 1744	Sir Wawayne, Sir Vryell, / Sir / Bedwere the ryche,	D	N D N(A)
MA 1745	Raynallde and Richeere / and / Rowlandez childyre:	C	N N
MA 1746	"Takez kepe on this prynce / with ȝoure / price knyghtez,	P D	A N
MA 1747	And ȝife we in the stour / withstonden the better,	/	V D N(A)
MA 1748	Standez here in this stede, / and / stirrez no forthire;	C	V Z
MA 1749	And ȝif the chaunce falle / that we bee / ouerchargged,	that H be	E
MA 1750	Eschewes to som castell, / and / chewyse ȝour selfen,	C	V H self
MA 1751	Or ryde to the riche Kyng, / ȝif ȝow / roo happyn,	C H	N V
MA 1752	And bidde hym com redily / to / rescewe hys biernez."	to	V D N
MA 1753	And than the Bretons brothely / enbrassez theire scheldez,	/	V D N
MA 1754	Braydez one bacenetez / and / buskes theire launcez;	C	V D N
MA 1755	Thus he fittez his folke / and to the / felde rydez,	C P D	N V
MA 1756	Fif hundreth on a frounte / fewtrede at onez.	/	V Z
MA 1757	With trompes thay trine, / and / trappede stedes,	C	E N
MA 1758	With cornettes and clarions / and / clergiall notes;	C	A N
MA 1759	Schokkes in with a schakke / and / schontez no langere,	C	V Z
MA 1760	There schawes ware scheen / vndyr the / schire eyuez.	P D	A N
MA 1761	And thane the Romaynez rowtte / remowes a lyttill,	C	V Z
MA 1762	Raykes with a rerewarde / thas / reall knyghttez;	D	A N
MA 1763	So raply thay ryde thare / that all the / rowte ryngez	that D D	N V
MA 1764	Of ryues and raunke stele / and / ryche golde maylez.	C	A N N
MA 1765	Thane schotte owtte of the Kynge / schiltrounis many,	/	N A
MA 1766	With sharpe wapynns of were / schotand at ones;	/	G Z
MA 1767	The Kyng of Lebe / before the / wawarde he ledez,	P D	N H V
MA 1768	And all his lele ligemen / o / laundon ascriez.	P	N V
MA 1769	Thane this cruell kyng / castis in fewtire,	/	V P N
MA 1770	Kaghte hym a couerde horse / and his / course haldez,	C D	N V

MA 1771	Beris to Sir Berill / and / brathely hym hittes,	C	Z H V
MA 1772	Throwghe golet and gorger / he / hittez hym ewyne,	H	V H Z
MA 1773	The gome and the grette horse / at the / ground liggez,	P D	N V
MA 1774	And gretez graythely to Gode / and / gyffes Hym the saule.	C	V H D N
MA 1775	Thus es Berell the bolde / broghte owtte of lyue,	/	V P P N
MA 1776	And byddez aftyre beryell / that hym / beste lykez.	that H	Z V
MA 1777	And thane Sir Cador of Cornewayle / es / carefull in herte,	be	A P N
MA 1778	Because of his kynysemane, / that / thus es myscaryede;	that	Z be E
MA 1779	Vmbeclappes the cors / and / kyssez hym ofte,	C	V H Z
MA 1780	Gerte kepe hym couerte / with his / clere knyghttez.	P D	A N
MA 1781	Thane laughes the Lebe Kyng / and all on / lowde meles,	C Z Z	Z V
MA 1782	"ʒone lorde es lyghttede, / me / lykes the bettyre;	H	V D N(A)
MA 1783	He sall noghte dere vs todaye, / the / Deuyll haue [his] bones!"	D	N V D N
MA 1784	"ʒone kyng," said Cador, / "karpes full large,	/	V Z Z
MA 1785	Because he killyd this kene, / Criste hafe thi saule:	C	N V D N
MA 1786	He sall hafe corne-bote, / so me / Criste helpe;	C H	N V
MA 1787	Or I kaire of this coste, / we sall / encontre ones.	H X	V Z
MA 1788	So may the wynde weile turnne, / I / quytte hym or ewyn,	H	V H C Z
MA 1789	Sothely hym selfen / or / summ of his ferez."	C	H P D N
MA 1790	Thane Sir Cador the kene / knyghttly he wyrkez,	/	Z H V
MA 1791	Cryez "A Cornewale!" / and / castez in fewtere,	C	V P N
MA 1792	Girdez streke thourghe the stour / on a / stede ryche;	P D	N A
MA 1793	Many steryn mane he steride / by / strenghe of hym one.	P	N P H H
MA 1794	Whene his spere was sprongen, / he / spede hym full ʒerne,	H	V H Z Z
MA 1795	Swappede owtte with a swerde / that / swykede hym neuer,	that	V H Z
MA 1796	Wroghte wayes full wyde / and / wounded knyghttez,	C	E N
MA 1797	Wyrkez in his wayfare / full / werkand sydez,	Z	G N
MA 1798	And hewes of the hardieste / halsez in sondyre,	/	N Z
MA 1799	That all blendez with blode / thare his / blanke rynnez.	Z D	N V
MA 1800	So many biernez the bolde / broughte owt of lyfe,	/	V P P N
MA 1801	Tittez tirauntez doun / and / temez theire sadills,	C	V D N
MA 1802	And turnez owte of the toile / when hym / tyme thynkkez.	C H	N V
MA 1803	Thane the Lebe Kynge / criez full lowde	/	V Z Z
MA 1804	One Sir Cador the kene, / with / cruell wordez,	P	A N
MA 1805	"Thowe hase wyrchipe wonne / and / wondyde knyghttez;	C	E N
MA 1806	Thowe wenes for thi wightenez / the / werlde es thy nowen.	D	N be D A
MA 1807	I sall wayte at thyne honnde, / wy, be my trowthe;	/	N P D N
MA 1808	I haue warnede the wele, / be / ware ʒif the lykez!"	be	A C H V
MA 1809	With cornuse and clariones / theis / newe-made knyghttez	D	Z E N
MA 1810	Lythes vnto the crye / and / castez in fewtire;	C	V P N
MA 1811	Ferkes in on a frounte / one / feraunte stedez,	P	A N
MA 1812	Fellede at the fyrste / come / fyfty att ones.	V	N Z
MA 1813	Schotte thorowe the schiltrouns / and / scheuerede launcez,	C	V N
MA 1814	Laid doun in the lumppe / lordly biernez.	/	A N
MA 1815	And thus nobilly oure newe men / notez theire strenghez,	/	V D N
MA 1816	Bot new notte es onon / that / noyes me sore.	that	V H Z
MA 1817	The Kyng of Lebe has laughte / a / stede that hym lykede,	D	N that H V
MA 1818	And comes in lordely / in / lyonez of siluere,	P	N P N
MA 1819	Vmbelappez the lumpe / and / lattes in sondre,	C	V Z
MA 1820	Many lede with his launce / the / liffe has he refede.	D	N have H E
MA 1821	Thus he chaces the childire / of the / Kyngez chambire,	P D	N N
MA 1822	And killez in the champanyse / cheualrous knyghttez;	/	A N
MA 1823	With a chasyng spere / he / choppes doun many.	H	V Z H
MA 1824	Thare was Sir Alyduke slayne / and / Achinour wondyde,	C	N E
MA 1825	Sir Origg and Sir Ermyngall / hewen al to pecez.	/	E Z P N
MA 1826	And ther was Lewlyn laughte / and / Lewlyns brothire,	C	N N
MA 1827	With lordez of Lebe, / and / lede to theire strenghez,	C	E P D N
MA 1828	Ne hade Sir Clegis comen / and / Clemente the noble,	C	N D N(A)
MA 1829	Oure newe men hade gone to noghte / and / many ma other.	C	A A H
MA 1830	Thane Sir Cador the kene / castez in fewtire	/	V P N
MA 1831	A cruell launce and a kene / and to the / Kynge rydez,	C P D	N V
MA 1832	Hittez hym heghe on the helme / with his / harde wapen,	P D	A N
MA 1833	That all the hotte blode / of hym to his / hande rynnez.	P H P D	N V
MA 1834	The hethen harageous kynge / appon the / hethe lyggez,	P D	N V
MA 1835	And of his hertly hurte / helyde he neuer.	/	V H Z
MA 1836	Thane Sir Cador the kene / cryez full lowde,	/	V Z Z
MA 1837	"Thow has corne-botte, Sir Kyng, / thare / God gyfe the sorowe;	Z	N V H N
MA 1838	Thow killyde my cosyn, / my / kare es the lesse.	D	N be D A
MA 1839	Kele the nowe in the claye, / and / comforthe thi selfen!	C	V H self
MA 1840	Thow skornede vs lang ere / with thi / skornefull wordez,	P D	A N
MA 1841	And nowe has thow cheuede / soo, it es thyn / awen skathe.	Z H be D	A N

MA 1842	Holde at thow hente has, / it / harmez bot lyttill,	H	V Z Z
MA 1843	For hethynge es hame-holde, / vse it who-so will."	/	V H Q X
MA 1844	The Kyng of Surry / than es / sorowfull in herte,	Z be	A P N
MA 1845	For sake of this soueraygne, / that / thus was suppressede;	that	Z be E
MA 1846	Semblede his Sarazenes / and / senatours manye:	C	N A
MA 1847	Vnsaughtyly they sette / thane appon oure / sere knyghttez.	Z P D	A N
MA 1848	Sir Cador of Cornewaile / he / cownterez them sone,	H	V H Z
MA 1849	With his kydde companye / clenlyche arraayede;	/	Z E
MA 1850	In the frount of the fyrthe, / as the / waye forthis,	C H	N V
MA 1851	Fyfty thosande of folke / was / fellide at ones.	be	E Z
MA 1852	Thare was at the assemble / certayne knyghttez	/	A N
MA 1853	Sore wondede sone / appone / sere halfes;	P	A N
MA 1854	The sekereste Sarzanez / that to that / sorte lengede,	that P D	N V
MA 1855	Behynde the sadylls ware sette / sex fotte large.	/	A N A
MA 1856	They scherde in the schiltrone / scheldyde knyghttez,	/	E N
MA 1857	Schalkes they schotte / thrughe / schrenkande maylez,	P	G N
MA 1858	Thurghe brenys browden / brestez they thirllede,	/	N H V
MA 1859	Brasers burnyste / bristez in sondyre,	/	V Z
MA 1860	Blasons blode / and / blankes they hewen,	C	N H V
MA 1861	With brandez of browne stele / brankkand stedez.	/	A N
MA 1862	The Bretons brothely / brittenez so many,	/	V Z A
MA 1863	The bente and the brode felde / all on / blode rynnys.	Z P	N V
MA 1864	Be thane Sir Cayous the kene / a / capitayne has wonnen,	D	N have E
MA 1865	Sir Clegis clynges / in and / clekes another,	Z C	V H
MA 1866	The capitayne of Cordewa, / vndire the / Kynge selfen,	P D	N self
MA 1867	That was keye of the kythe / of all that / coste ryche;	P D D	N A
MA 1868	Vtolfe and Ewandre / Ioneke had nommen,	/	N have E
MA 1869	With the Erle of Affryke / and / other grette lordes;	C	A A N
MA 1870	The Kyng of Surry the kene / to Sir / Cador es ʒelden,	P D	N be E
MA 1871	The Synechall of Soter / to / Segramoure hym selfen.	P	N H self
MA 1872	When the cheualrye saw / theire / cheftaynes were nommen,	D	N be E
MA 1873	To a cheefe foreste / they / chesen theire wayes,	H	V D N
MA 1874	And felede them so feynte, / they / fall in the greues,	H	V P D N
MA 1875	In the ferynne of the fyrthe, / fore / ferde of oure pople.	P	N P D N
MA 1876	Thare myght men see the ryche / ryde in the schawes,	/	V P D N
MA 1877	To rype vpe the Romaynez / ruydlyche wondyde;	/	Z E
MA 1878	Schowttes aftyre men, / harageous knyghttez,	/	A N
MA 1879	Be hunndrethez they hewede / doun be the / holte eyuys.	Z P D	N N
MA 1880	Thus oure cheualrous men / chasez the pople;	/	V D N
MA 1881	To a castell they eschewede, / a / fewe that eschappede.	D	H that V
MA 1882	Thane relyez the renkez / of the / Rounde Table,	P D	A N
MA 1883	For to ryotte the wode / ther the / duke restez;	Q D	N V
MA 1884	Ransakes the ryndez / all, / raughte vp theire feres	Z	V Z D N
MA 1885	That in the fightyng before / fay ware byleuyde.	/	A be E
MA 1886	Sir Cador garte chare / theym and / couere them faire,	H C	V H Z
MA 1887	Kariede them to the Kyng / with his / beste knyghttez;	P D	A N
MA 1888	And passez vnto Paresche / with / presoners hym selfen,	P	N H self
MA 1889	Betoke theym the prouste, / pryncez and other;	/	N C H
MA 1890	Tase a sope in the toure / and / taryez no langere,	C	V Z
MA 1891	Bot tournes tytte to the Kynge / and hym wyth / tunge telles.	C H P	N V
MA 1892	"Syr," sais Sir Cador, / a / caas es befallen;	D	N be E
MA 1893	We hafe cowntered today, / in ʒone / coste ryche	P D	N A
MA 1894	With kyngez and kayseres, / krouell and noble,	/	A C A
MA 1895	And knyghtes and kene men, / clenlych arayede.	/	Z E
MA 1896	They hade at ʒone foreste / forsette vs the wayes,	/	E H D N
MA 1897	At the furthe in the fyrthe, / with / ferse men of armes;	P	A N P N
MA 1898	Thare faughtte we, in faythe, / and / foynede with sperys,	C	V P N
MA 1899	One felde with thy foomen / and / fellyd them on lyfe.	C	V H P N
MA 1900	The Kyng of Lebe es laide / and in the / felde leuyde,	C P D	N V
MA 1901	And manye of his legemen / that / thare to hym langede.	that	Q P H V
MA 1902	Other lordez are laughte / of / vncouthe ledes;	P	A N
MA 1903	We hafe lede them at lenge, / to / lyf whilles the lykez.	to	V C H V
MA 1904	Sir Vtolfe and Sir Ewaynedyr, / theis / honourable knyghttez,	D	A N
MA 1905	Be a nawntere of armes / Ioneke has nommen,	/	N have E
MA 1906	With erlez of the Oryentte / and / austeren knyghttez,	C	A N
MA 1907	Of awncestrye the beste men / that to the / oste langede;	that P D	N V
MA 1908	The Senatour Carous / es / kaughte with a knyghtte,	be	E P D N
MA 1909	The Capitayne of Cornette, / that / crewell es halden,	that	A be E
MA 1910	The Syneschall of Suter / vnsaughte wyth thes other,	/	A P D H
MA 1911	The Kyng of Surry hym selfen / and / Sarazenes [ynowe].	C	N A
MA 1912	Bot fay of ours in the felde / a / fourtene knyghttez,	D	A N

MA 1913	I will noghte feyne ne forbere, / bot / faythfully tellen;	C	Z V
MA 1914	Sir Dereft es one, / a / baneretre noble,	D	N A
MA 1915	Was killyde at the fyrste come / with a / kyng ryche;	P D	N A
MA 1916	Sir Alidoyke of Towell, / with his / tende knyghtez,	P D	A N
MA 1917	Emange the Turkys was tynte / and in / tym fonden;	C P	N V
MA 1918	Gude Sir Mawrell of Mauncez / and / Mawren his brother,	C	N D N
MA 1919	Sir Meneduke of Mentoche, / with / meruailous knyghttez."	P	A N
MA 1920	Thane the worthy Kyng wrythes / and / wepede with his eughne,	C	V P D N
MA 1921	Karpes to his cosyn / Sir / Cador theis wordez:	D	N D N
MA 1922	"Sir Cador, thi corage / confundez vs all!		V H Z
MA 1923	Kowardely thow castez / owtte all my / beste knyghttez.	Z D D	A N
MA 1924	To putte men in perille, / it es no / pryce holden,	H be D	N E
MA 1925	Bot the partyes ware puruayede / and / powere arayede;	C	N E
MA 1926	When they ware stade on a strenghe, / thou / sulde hafe withstonden,	H	X have E
MA 1927	Bot ȝif thowe wolde all my steryn / stroye for the nonys!"	/	V P D N
MA 1928	"Sir," sais Sir Cador, / "ȝe / knowe wele ȝour selfen	H	V Z H self
MA 1929	ȝe are kyng in this kythe, / karpe whatte ȝow lykys;	/	V Q H V
MA 1930	Sall neuer vpbrayde / me, that to thi / burde langes,	H that P D	N V
MA 1931	That I sulde blyn fore theire boste / thi / byddyng to wyrche;	D	G to V
MA 1932	When any stirttez to stale, / stuffe tham the bettere,	/	V H D Z
MA 1933	Ore thei will be stonayede and stroyede / in ȝone / strayte londez.	P D	A N
MA 1934	I dide my delygens todaye, / I / doo me one lordez,	H	V H P N
MA 1935	And in daungere of dede / fore / dyuerse knyghttez;	P	A N
MA 1936	I hafe no grace to thi gree, / bot syche / grett wordez,	P D	A N
MA 1937	ȝif I heuen my herte, / my / hape es no bettyre."	D	N be Z
MA 1938	Thofe Sir Arthure ware angerde, / he / ansuers faire;	H	V Z
MA 1939	"Thow has doughttily donn, / Sir / Duke, with thi handez,	D	N P D N
MA 1940	And has donn thy deuer / with my / dere knyghttez;	P D	A N
MA 1941	Forthy thow arte demyde, / with / dukes and erlez,	P	N C N
MA 1942	For one of the doughtyeste / that / dubbede was euer.	that	E be Z
MA 1943	Thare es non ischewe of vs / on this / erthe sprongen;	P D	N E
MA 1944	Thow arte apparant to be ayere, / are / one of thi childyre,	be	H P D N
MA 1945	Thow arte my sister sone, / forsake sall I neuer."	/	V X H Z
MA 1946	Thane gerte he in his awen tente / a / table be sette,	D	N be E
MA 1947	And tryede in with tromppez / trauaillede biernez;	/	E N
MA 1948	Serfede them solempnely / with / selkouthe metez,	P	A N
MA 1949	Swythe semly in syghte / with / syluerendischees.	P	A N
MA 1950	Whene the senatours harde saye / that it / so happenede,	that H	Z V
MA 1951	They saide to the Emperour, / "Thi / seggez are supprysede;	D	N be E
MA 1952	Sir Arthure, thyn enmy, / has / owterayede thi lordez,	have	E D N
MA 1953	That rode for the rescowe / of ȝone / riche knyghttez.	P D	A N
MA 1954	Thow dosse bot tynnez thi tym / and / turmenttez thi pople;	C	V D N
MA 1955	Thow arte betrayede of thi men / that / moste thow on traystede,	that	Z H Z V
MA 1956	That schall turne the to tene / and / torfere for euer."	C	N Z
MA 1957	Than the Emperour irus / was / angerde at his herte,	be	E P D N
MA 1958	For oure valyant biernez / siche / prowesche had wonnen.	D	N have E
MA 1959	With kyng and with kaysere / to / consayle they wende,	P	N H V
MA 1960	Soueryngez of Sarazenez / and / senatours manye;	C	N A
MA 1961	Thus he semblez full sone / certayne lordez,	/	A N
MA 1962	And in the assemble thane / he / sais them theis wordez:	H	V H D N
MA 1963	"My herte sothely es sette, / assente ȝif ȝowe lykes,	/	V C H V
MA 1964	To seke into Sexon, / with my / sekyre knyghttez,	P D	A N
MA 1965	To fyghte with my foemen, / if / fortune me happen,	C	N H V
MA 1966	ȝif I may fynde the freke / within the / four haluez;	P D	A N
MA 1967	Or entir into Awguste, / awnters to seke,	/	N to V
MA 1968	And byde with my balde men / within the / burghe ryche;	P D	N A
MA 1969	Riste vs and reuell / and / ryotte oure selfen,	C	V H self
MA 1970	Lende thare in delytte / in / lordechippez ynewe,	P	N A
MA 1971	To Sir Leo be comen / with all his / lele knyghtez,	P D D	A N
MA 1972	With lordez of Lumberdye, / to / lette hym the wayes."	to	V H D N
MA 1973	Bot owre wyese Kyng es warre / to / waytten his renkes,	to	V D N
MA 1974	And wysely by the woddez / voydez his oste;	/	V D N
MA 1975	Gerte felschen his fyrez, / flawmande full heghe,	/	G Z Z
MA 1976	Trussen full traystely / and / treunt thereaftyre.	C	V Z
MA 1977	Sethen into Sessoyne / he / soughte at the gayneste,	H	V P D N(A)
MA 1978	And at the surs of the sonne / disseuerez his knyghttez;	/	V D N
MA 1979	Forsette them the cite / appon / sere halfez,	P	A N
MA 1980	Sodaynly on iche halfe, / with / seuen grett stales.	P	A A N
MA 1981	Anely in the vale / a / vawewarde enbusches;	D	N V
MA 1982	Sir Valyant of Vyleris, / with / valyant knyghttez,	P	A N
MA 1983	Before the Kyngez visage / made siche avowez	/	V D N

MA 1984	To venquyse by victorie / the / Vescownte of Rome;	D	N P N
MA 1985	Forthi the Kyng chargez / hym, what / chaunce so befall,	H Q	N Z V
MA 1986	Cheftayne of the cheekke, / with / cheualrous knyghttez.	P	A N
MA 1987	And sythyn meles with mouthe, / that he / moste traistez;	that H	Z V
MA 1988	Demenys the medylwarde / menskfully hym selfen:	/	Z H self
MA 1989	Fittes his fotemen / alls hym / faire thynkkes,	C H	A V
MA 1990	On frounte in the forebreste / the / flour of his knyghtez;	D	N P D N
MA 1991	His archers on aythere halfe / he / ordaynede theraftyre	H	V Z
MA 1992	To schake in a sheltrone, / to / schotte when tham lykez.	to	V C H V

The Wars of Alexander

A	1	When folk ere festid and fed, / fayn wald thai here	/	Z X H V
A	2	Sum farand thing efter fode, / to / fayn thare her[t],	to	V D N
A	3	Or thai ware fourmed on fold, / or thaire / fadirs other.	C D	N A
A	4	Sum is leue to lythe, / the / lesing of Sayntis,	D	N P N
A	5	That lete ther lifis be lorne, / for oure / lordis sake;	P D	N N
A	6	And sum has langing of lufe, / lays to herken,	/	V to V
A	7	How ledis for thaire lemmans, / has / langor endured.	have	N E
A	8	Sum couettis and has comforth, / to / carpe and to lestyn	P	G C P G
A	9	Of curtaissy of kny3thode, / of / craftis of armys,	P	N P N
A	10	Of kyngis at has conquirid, / and ouer-/ comyn landis.	C Z	E N
A	11	Sum of wirschip I-wis, / slike as tham / wyse lattis,	D P D	A N
A	12	And sum of wanton werkis, / tha that ere / wild-hedid;	H that be	A E
A	13	Bot if thai wald on many wyse, / a / wondire ware it els;	D	N be H Z
A	14	For as thaire wittis ere with-in, / so ther / will folowis.	C D	N V
A	15	And I forwith 3ow all, / ettillis to schewe	/	N to V
A	16	Of ane Emperoure the a3efullest, / that euer / armys hauntid,	that Z	N V
A	17	That was the athill Alexsandire, / as the / buke tellis,	C D	N V
A	18	That a3te euyn as his awyn, / all the werd ouire.	/	Z D N D
A	19	For he recouerd quills he regnyd, / the / regions all clene,	D	N Z A
A	20	And all rialme and the riches, / into the / rede est.	P D	A N
A	21	I sall rehers, and 3e will, renkis, / rekyn 3our tongis,	/	V D N
A	22	A remnant of his rialte, / and / rist quen vs likis.	C	V C H V
A	23	Oute in the erth of Egipt, / enhabet vmquile	/	V Z
A	24	The wysest wees of the werd, / as I in / writt fynd.	C H P	N V
A	25	For thai the mesure and the mett, / of all the / mulde couthe,	P D D	N V
A	26	The sise of all the grete see, / and of the / grym wawys;	C P D	N V
A	27	Of the ordere of that odde home, / that ouer the / aire hingis	that P D	N V
A	28	Knew the kynd, and the curses, / of the / clere sternys,	P D	A N
A	29	Of Articus the aghill, / tre / airis and othire	H	V C Z
A	30	Of the fold and of the firmament, / wele the / fete cuthe;	Z D	N V
A	31	And Antarticus also, / that / all apon turnys,	that	H Z V
A	32	The pasage of the planettis, / the / poyntis and the sygnes.	D	N C D N
A	33	Thai ware the kiddest of that craft, / knawyn in thaire tyme,	/	E P D N
A	34	And the sotellest vndere son, / segis in thaire lyfe.	/	N P D N
A	35	Thus ware thai breued for the best, / as the / buke tellis;	C D	N V
A	36	All thai lerid of that lare, / that it / lerne wald.	that H	V X
A	37	As wide as the werd / was, / went worde of thaire teching,	be	V N P D N
A	38	Of sorsery and slike werkis, / sle3tis enogh.	/	N A
A	39	And the kyng of that contre, / was a / clerke noble,	be D	N A
A	40	The athelest ane of the werd, / and / Anec was hatten.	C	N be E
A	41	He was wyse eno3e, / wirdis to reken,	/	N to V
A	42	When he the heuyn beheld, / of / lede[s] opon lyfe;	P	N P N
A	43	The iapis of all gemetri, / gentilli he couth,	/	Z H V
A	44	And wele as Aristotill, / the / artis all seuyn.	D	N D A
A	45	Ther preued neuer nane his prik, / for / passing of witt,	P	G P N
A	46	Plato nor Piktagaras, / ne / Prektane him seluen.	not	N H self
A	47	Emang his duykis on a day, / as he on / dese syttis,	C H P	N V
A	48	Than was him bodword vnblyth, / bro3t to the sale,	/	E P D N
A	49	That Artaxenses was armed, / with the / men of his rewme,	P D	N P D N
A	50	The proude kinge of Persy, / to / pase him agayn.	to	V H Z
A	51	Tho3e he tha sawis herd say, / 3it / samyd he na princis,	C	V H D N
A	52	Ne ost ordand he nane, / of / na kyd kny3tis,	P	D A N
A	53	Bot airis euen furth him ane, / and / entirs his chambre,	C	V D N
A	54	To knaw by his clergi, / the / come of his faa.	D	N P D N
A	55	He takis a Boll of bras, / burneschid full clene,	/	E Z Z
A	56	And full he fillis it of the flode, / at / fell fra the heuen.	that	V P D N
A	57	On hi3t in his a hand, / haldis a wand	/	V D N
A	58	And kenely be coniurisons, / callis to him spritis.	/	V P H N
A	59	In-to this water as he waitis, / was he / ware sone	be H	A Z
A	60	Of his enmys in that Element, / ane / endles nombre;	D	A N
A	61	He sa3e them in the hi3e see, / sailand to-gedire,	/	G Z
A	62	Was neuer sene slike a some, / vnder the / son bemys.	P D	N N
A	63	Carrygis comand he knew, / keruand the ithis,	/	G D N
A	64	Dromonds dryfes ouer the depe / with / dukis and Erles,	P	N C N
A	65	Gales and grete schipis, / full of / grym wapens,	A P	A N
A	66	And full of breneid bernes, / bargis a hundreth,	/	N D A

The Wars of Alexander

A	67	Of slik a naue is noy, / to / here or to tell.	to	V C to V
A	68	For all the largenes of lenth, / at he / luke myȝt,	Z H	V X
A	69	Slik was the multitude of mast, / so / mekil and so thike,	Z	A C Z A
A	70	That all him thoȝt bot he treis, / a / hare wod it semyd.	D	A N H V
A	71	At the enteris of Egipt, / as / Anec had beden,	C	N have E
A	72	Ware peris of his prouynce, / and / princes of his cytes,	C	N P D N
A	73	Was comandid of thaire kyng, / to / kepe tha landis,	to	V D N
A	74	That nane aproche it to paire, / of / Persy ne othire.	P	N Z
A	75	Than was a wardan ware, / oute in the / wale stremys	P P D	A N
A	76	Of all the naue and the note, / I / neuenyd be-fore;	H	V Z
A	77	Laȝt liȝtly his ledis, / and / leuys his warde,	C	V D N
A	78	Comes to courte to the kyng, / and on / kneys fallis,	C P	N V
A	79	Anec bi his awyn name, / he / onane gretis,	H	Z V
A	80	Sais, "ȝare the now ȝapely, / or / ȝild vp thi rewme;	C	V Z D N
A	81	Artaxenses is at hand, / and has ane / ost reryd,	C have D	N E
A	82	And resyn vp with all his rewme, / to / ride vs agayn;	to	V H Z
A	83	For he him-self is on the se, / with siche a / somme armed,	P D D	N E
A	84	That any hathill vnder heuen, / ware / hardy to rekyn.	be	A to V
A	85	For ther is comyn with him knyȝt[es], / of / landis dyuerse,	P	N A
A	86	Segis of many syde, / oute of / sere remys,	P P	A N
A	87	The perseyns and a pupill, / that / panthy is callid,	that	N be E
A	88	Men of Mesepotayme, / and of / Mede bathe,	C P	N Z
A	89	Of Syre and of Sychim, / and / selle nounbre,	D	A N
A	90	Of Capidos and Caldec, / kene men of armes,	/	A N P N
A	91	Fell feȝtand folke, / that / Faire we call,	that	N H V
A	92	The Arrabiens and all tha, / [of] that / origyne,	P D	N
A	93	Bernys out of Batary, / batails arayed,	/	N V
A	94	And othire out of the orient, / many / od hundrethe."	D	A N
A	95	Then Anec onane / riȝt, / efter thire wordis,	Z	P D N
A	96	A lowde laȝter he loȝe, / and to the / lede said,	C P D	N V
A	97	"Haue thou na care," quod the kyng, / "bot / kepe to the marche,	C	V P D N
A	98	As I haue demyd the to do, / and / dred thou na ferryre;	C	V H Z
A	99	For soth it is vnsemely, / slike / sawis of a prynce.	D	N P D N
A	100	I kan noȝt knaw at thou carpis, / as a / knyȝt suld,	C D	N X
A	101	Bot as a frek at ware ferid, / and / feynes riȝt nowe.	C	V Z Z
A	102	Ert thou noȝt hurtles and hale?, / lat noȝt thi / hert faile.	V not D	N V
A	103	For vertu vailes / noȝt all, if thou / avaied worthe,	not Z C H	E V
A	104	Emang the multitude of men, / quare / mane ere togeder,	Q	N be Z
A	105	Bot ther aboute as thai ere blend, / with / bignes of will.	P	N P N
A	106	If thai be folke bot a fa, / oft / tydis tham the better.	Z	V H D A
A	107	Or elis wate thou noȝt wele, / the / witles berne,	D	A N
A	108	How it is comonly carped, / in / contries a-boute,	P	N Z
A	109	That anelepy leon, / that ouer the / land rynnys,	that P D	N V
A	110	Will make to fange to the fliȝt, / and / flay many hertis?"	C	V D N
A	111	With that the segge all him selfe, / silis to his chambre,	/	V P D N
A	112	And in the brasen boll, / full [of] / blak watere	A P	A N
A	113	He shapis him of shire wax, / litill / schipis many,	A	N A
A	114	And ȝapely ȝarkid in his hand, / a / ȝerd of a palme.	D	N P D N
A	115	Then con he chater and enchant, / with all his / chefe miȝtis,	P D D	A N
A	116	A-vysid him in the vessell, / and was / avaied sone,	C be	E Z
A	117	How the powere out of Persy, / pellid doune his knyȝtis,	/	V Z D N
A	118	And how his land suld be lost, / withouten / lett mare.	P	N A
A	119	When he was ware of this wathe, / how it / worthe suld,	Q H	V X
A	120	Than wendis he wiȝtly / furth, and his / wede changis,	Z C D	N V
A	121	Clede him all as a clerke, / and his / croune shauys,	C D	N V
A	122	And with a bytand blade, / he his / bered voydis.	H D	N V
A	123	Then takis to him tresour, / and / trusses in baggis,	C	V P N
A	124	As many Besandis on his bake, / as he / bere miȝt,	C H	V X
A	125	And othire necessari notis, / as / nedis to his craftis,	C	V P D N
A	126	To sike salmary dangell, / as him / self vyses.	C H	self V
A	127	He toke traimmes / him with, to / tute in the sternes,	H P to	V P D N
A	128	Astralabus algate, / as his / arte wald,	C D	N V
A	129	Quadrentis coruen all of quyte, / siluyre full quaynte,	/	N Z A
A	130	Mustours and mekil quat, / mare then a littill.	/	A C D A
A	131	When he was grathed with his gere, / a / gladen he waytis,	D	N H V
A	132	And passis furthe at a Posterne, / preualy alane,	/	Z Z
A	133	Furthe on his fete withouten fole, / he / passis his way,	H	V D N
A	134	Vn-wetandly to any wee, / that / wont he his wanes.	that	V P D N
A	135	Thus airis he out of Egipte, / and his / erde leuys,	C D	N V
A	136	Fled for ferd of his fais, / fere fra his kythis,	/	N P D N
A	137	It was na bote him to bide, / ne / batill to ȝelde;	not	N to V

A	138	For all his kyngdome he knew, / suld be / kast vnder.	X be	E Z	
A	139	Fra the paitis of Persy, / he / past bot a litill,	H	V Z Z	
A	140	And euyn so thurȝe Ethyope, / and thar him / eft clethis,	C Z H	Z N	
A	141	All his liche in lyn clathe, / for / ledis suld trowe	C	N X V	
A	142	And all the puple persayue, / a / prophete he were.	D	N H be	
A	143	Then metis he furthe to Messadon, / full / vn-mete gatis,	Z	A N	
A	144	And quen he come to that kith, / as the / chance tellis,	C D	N V	
A	145	Oft with his instrumentis / out, he / openly deuynes,	Z H	Z V	
A	146	And nother hild he it ne hid, / bot / here qua sa likid.	C	V Q Z V	
A	147	Bot than was methe for to mele, / thurȝe / men of his burȝ,	P	N P D N	
A	148	That he by-hind him at hame, / withoute / hede leuyd.	P	N V	
A	149	Slik care kindils in his curte, / quen thai ther / kyng myssid,	Q H D	N V	
A	150	That it ware tere any tonge, / of thar / tene to reken;	P D	N to V	
A	151	Princes of his palas, / preses in-to chambre,	/	V P N	
A	152	To laite thar lord at was lost, / with / latis vn-blythe;	P	N A	
A	153	Kairis in-to closettis, / knyȝtis and Erlis,	/	N C N	
A	154	Sekand thar souerayn, / with many / salt terys;	P D	A N	
A	155	Barons and bachelers, / balefully gretis,	/	Z V	
A	156	Swiers swemyle, / swouned ladys,	/	E N	
A	157	And many was the bald berne, / at / banned thar quile,	that	V D N	
A	158	That euer he dured that day, / vndede opon erthe.	/	A P N	
A	159	Bot quen thai wist he was went, / and / wald noȝt be foun,	C	X not be E	
A	160	Couth thai na bote tham ebland, / how / best for to wirke,	Q	Z for to V	
A	161	Bot silis to ser Sirraphis, / at / sittis in his trone,	that	V P D N	
A	162	That was thar god althire-graythist, / on the / ground samen.	P D	N Z	
A	163	Him thai supplyed and soȝt, / and him / ensence castis,	C H	N V	
A	164	Honourd him with offyrings, / and / elkend him fayre.	C	V H Z	
A	165	That he suld say tham the sothe, / and / sorely tham teche	C	Z H V	
A	166	Queder thaire kyng was becomen, / at thar / care kyndils	that D	N V	
A	167	Than sayd Syraphis him selfe, / he / sayd tham thir wordis:	H	V H D N	
A	168	"Anec, ȝour athill kyng, / is out of his / awyn land,	be P P D	A N	
A	169	For Artaxenses aȝe, / is all him / ane foundid,	be Z H	A E	
A	170	The proude kyng of Persee, / that / passes vs a-gaynes.	that	V H P	
A	171	Full wele he wist, or he went, / quat suld / worthe efter,	Q X	V Z	
A	172	And all the fourme of the fare, / that / fall ȝow be-houys.	that	V H V	
A	173	For all the erth of Egipt, / fra / rond vn-to othire	P	N P H	
A	174	Bees conquirid and ouercomyn, / clene alto-gedre.	/	Z Z	
A	175	The puple out of Perse, / is / purvaid all samen;	be	E Z Z	
A	176	The kyng is comand full kene / with his / kene ostis,	P D	A N	
A	177	That sall oure renkis all rayme, / and oure / rewme bathe,	C D	N A	
A	178	And we be all at thare will, / thus is / wirdis schapen.	C be	N E	
A	179	Sen it is sett to be soo, / and / slipe it ne may,	C	V H not X	
A	180	Ne schewid to be na nothire schap, / ne we to / schount nouthire,	not H P	G Z	
A	181	Bot gefe thaim vp the girdill, / vs / gaynes noȝt ellis.	H	V not Z	
A	182	Bot seses, seris, of ȝour syte, / and / soruȝes na mare;	C	N Z	
A	183	For certayn," quod Syraphis, / "my- / selfe I it knawe,	H	self H H V	
A	184	Ȝour king sall in a nothire kithe, / kast out his elde,	/	E Z D N	
A	185	And come a-gayn eft ȝonge man, / ȝit to his rewme.	/	C P D N	
A	186	Than said that victoure ȝow venge, / on ȝour / vile fais,	P D	A N	
A	187	And the province of Persee, / purely distruye,	/	Z V	
A	188	And gett agayn his avyn gronde, / at he / forgais nowe,	that H	V Z	
A	189	And ane of the oddist Emperours, / of the / werde worthe."	P D	N V	
A	190	When he this talis had tald, / then / tuke thai be-lyfe,	C	V H Z	
A	191	And efter Anec on-ane, / ane / ymage gert make;	D	N E V	
A	192	The buke sais, of blake stane, / all the / bode ouyre,	D D	N P	
A	193	With corone and with conyschantis, / as it a / kynge were.	C H D	N be	
A	194	Quen it was perfite and piȝt, / a / place thai it wayted,	D	N that H V	
A	195	And stallid him in a stoute stede, / and / stiȝthed him faire.	C	V H Z	
A	196	Lordis lift him on loft, / and / lawe to him bowid,	C	Z P H V	
A	197	In reuerence of the riche kyng, / at had ther / rewme gydid.	that have D	N E	
A	198	Quen he was semely vp set, / with / septour in hand,	P	N P N	
A	199	Then ledis at ware lettird, / on / lawe at his feet	Z	Z P D N	
A	200	All the sawis of thaire Syre, / as / Siraphis tald,	C	N V	
A	201	Thare gan thai graithly tham graue, / in / golden lettirs,	P	A N	
A	202	All the wordis at he thaim werpid, / of thaire / ware kynge.	P D	A N	
A	203	Thare he wrate tham I-wis, / as the / buke tellis,	C D	N V	
A	204	Supposand thaim in sum tyme, / for / sothe to be knawen,	P	N to be E	
A	205	And men to make of tham mynd, / euer-mare efter.	/	Z Z	
A	206	Be that thaire enmes thar erde, / was / entird with-in,	be	E Z	
A	207	The powere oute of Persee, / with many / proude ostes;	P D	A N	
A	208	Bot of thar batails to brefe, / it / botis me na ferrire.	H	V H Z	

A	209	For all thai conquirid clene, / this / cithe at thaire will,	D	N P D N
A	210	And Anec is all his ane, / ferre of his awyn landis,	/	A P D A N
A	211	With-in the merris of Messedoyn, / thar na / man him knewe.	Q D	N H V
A	212	Bot will ȝe herken hende, / now sall ȝe here	/	Z X H V
A	213	How he kide him in the courete, / and / quayntid him with ladis.	C	V H P N
A	214	Syre, it be-tid on a tyme, / the / text me recordis,	D	N H V
A	215	That the mode kynge of Messedone, / with / mekill nounbre,	P	A N
A	216	That was sire Philip the fers, / farne out of toune,	/	E P P N
A	217	For to feȝt with his fais, / out of / fere landis.	P P	A N
A	218	Quen he was boune oute of burȝe, / and his / bake turned,	C D	N V
A	219	As tite as Anec him amed, / out of his / awyn kythe,	P P D	A N
A	220	He paste vp to the Palais, / and / preualy entirs,	C	Z V
A	221	That he miȝt lend thare on loft, / and / luke on the qwene.	C	V P D N
A	222	Sone as him selfe was in the sale, / and / saȝe hire with eȝe,	C	V H P N
A	223	He beheld Olympadas, / that / honourable lady;	D	A N
A	224	Hire bewte bitis in his brest, / and his / bodi thrillis,	C D	N V
A	225	And drifes thurȝe his depe hert, / as he ware / dart-wondid.	C H be	N E
A	226	The lede lawid in hire lofe, / as / leme dose of gledis,	C	N V P N
A	227	Put vp his hand to his hare, / and / heldid it bot littill.	C	V H Z Z
A	228	"Haile, modi qwene of Messidoyne" , / he / maister-like said;	H	Z V
A	229	Thare deyned him na daynte, / 'madame' hire to call,	/	N H to V
A	230	Be-cause he knew him a kyng, / he / carpid on this wyse.	H	V P D N
A	231	For if he come as A clerke, / with a / croune schauyn,	P D	N E
A	232	And diȝt as a Doctour, / in / drabland wedis,	P	G N
A	233	ȝit all the erth of Egipt, / had he bene / aire ouire.	have H been	N P
A	234	Than answars him the qwene, / with full / myld speche,	P Z	A N
A	235	"Haile, maister," quod that myld, / and / made hire to sytt	C	V H to V
A	236	On a sege hire be-syde, / of / silkyn clathis,	P	A N
A	237	And thar hire spakid with his speche, / and / spird of him wordis.	C	V P H V
A	238	Quen he was sete in his sete, / that / semely qwene	D	A N
A	239	Ai of Egipt erd, / enquirid if he were,	/	V C H be
A	240	Thoȝt him like of that lede, / be / langage and othire;	P	N C H
A	241	For-thi scho wetis if he wald, / wete hire to say.	/	V H to V
A	242	"A! athel qwene," quod Anec, / "ai be thou ioyed!	/	Z be H E
A	243	If thou a wirschipfull worde, / has / werpid and spoken,	have	E C E
A	244	A riall roune thou me redis, / a / reson of blis,	D	N P N
A	245	Quen thou mynnys of that marche, / and with thi / mouth tellis.	C P D	N V
A	246	For thare enhabetis in that erd, / that thou / are sayd.	that H	Z V
A	247	The wisest wees in this werd, / the / welken vndire.	D	N P
A	248	For thai can swyth of a sweuyn, / all the / swepe tell,	D D	N V
A	249	Whethire it be sele or soroȝe, / in a / sete quile,	P D	A N
A	250	And thai can certifi and se, / by / sygnes of the heuyn,	P	N P D N
A	251	Quat sall be-fall a-pon fold, / with-inen a / fewe ȝerys.	P D	A N
A	252	Sum vndirstandis in a stounde, / the / steuen of the briddis,	D	N P D N
A	253	To say the by thar sapience, / quat thar / sange menys;	Q D	N V
A	254	Sum can thi consaile declare, / thofe thou it / carpid neuire,	C H H	V Z
A	255	The poyntis of all thi preuates, / pertly can schewe.	/	Z X V
A	256	Sum can the brefe be-life, / the / birth of thine childire,	D	N P D N
A	257	Be it hee, be [it] scho, / haly thare werdes.	/	Z D N
A	258	And if I say it my-selfe, / slik / sotellte I haue,	D	N H V
A	259	Sa clere a witt and sa clene, / my / creatoure I lofe,	D	N H V
A	260	That all the notis at I neuyn, / nobly I can,	/	Z H X
A	261	As any prophet a-perte, / to / proue ȝow the sothe."	to	V H D N
A	262	Quen he thire sawis had sayd, / he in his / sege lened,	H P D	N V
A	263	In stody still as a stane, / and / starid in hire face,	C	V P D N
A	264	Beheld haterly that hend, / that had his / hert percid,	that had D	N E
A	265	With depe desire of delite, / ay on that / dere waytis.	Z P D	N(A) V
A	266	Sone as hire selfe it sawe, / at he hire / sa behaldis,	that H H	Z V
A	267	Then scho talkis him to, / and / titely him fraynes:	C	Z H V
A	268	"Quare-on muse ȝe sa mekill, / maister?" scho sayd;	/	N H V
A	269	"ȝe behald me sa hogely, / quare-on is ȝour mynd?"	/	Q be D N
A	270	"My frely fode," / quod the / freke, "noȝt bot the werdes	V D	N not P D N
A	271	Of my gracious goddis, / the / grettest on erde.	D	N(A) P N
A	272	Thai haue told me be-for this tyme, / that now I / trew fynd,	that Z H	A V
A	273	How I suld lenge in a land, / and / loke on a qwene."	C	V P D N
A	274	Than out of his bosom he brayd, / a / blesand table	D	G N
A	275	Of Euour and of othire thingis, / odly fourmed,	/	Z E
A	276	Of bras and of brynt gold, / and o[f] / briȝt siluer,	C P	A N
A	277	That thre serclis sere, / in it / selfe had.	P H	self V
A	278	In the first compas I ken, / as me the / claus tellis,	C H D	N V
A	279	Stude the xij vndirstandings, / stoutly engrauen.	/	Z E

A	280	In this othir draʒt ware deuysid, / a / dusan of bestis,	D	N P N
A	281	And semely sett was in the thrid, / the / son and the mone.	D	N C D N
A	282	Sethen he clekis out of a cas, / vij / clere sternes	D	A N
A	283	To tell him takens of the tymes, / and / talis of our werdis;	C	N P D N
A	284	And vij stele-grauyn stanys, / and / stoute othire tway,	C	A A N
A	285	That wald for hurte or for harme, / any / hathill kepe.	D	N V
A	286	Thus as he tuke furth his toylis, / and his / trammys schewis,	C D	N V
A	287	"If I sall lefe on thi lare" , / , / quod the / leue qwene,	V D	A N
A	288	"Say me the day and the same ʒere, / and the / selfe tyme	C D	A N
A	289	Of the birth of the bald kyng, / that I / best lufe."	that H	Z V
A	290	Than answars Anec onane, / sayd, "is thar / oʒt ellis	V be Z	H Z
A	291	At ʒe wald, hend, of me here, / or at ʒoure / hert willis?	C P D	N V
A	292	For any cas that is to com, / to / knaw if the likis,	to	V C H V
A	293	I sall as namely ʒow neuyn, / as it ware / nowe done."	C H be	Z E
A	294	"Than will I," quod the wale qwene, / / ʒe / wete me to say,	H	V H to V
A	295	Quat me and Philip, / sall / fall vs be-twene.	X	V H P
A	296	For, bow he fra the bataill, / bernys me tell,	/	N H V
A	297	Then will he wed anothire wife, / and / wayfe me for euer."	C	V H Z
A	298	"Nay, noʒt for ay," quod the freke, / "thar haue thai / fals spoken;	Z have H	Z E
A	299	Neuer the latter, or oʒt lange, / sall / lymp as thou sayd.	X	V C H V
A	300	Bot ʒit I fynd, for all his fare, / fleme he sall the tothire,	/	V H X D H
A	301	And wild ʒour self to will, / nyll he so / will he."	X H Z	V H
A	302	Than was a-wondird of his wordis, / the / worthe lady,	D	A N
A	303	Be-soʒt sekirly this sire, / if he / safe vouchid,	C H	A V
A	304	That scho myʒt weterly wete, / the / will of all thingis,	D	N P D N
A	305	Quatkyn poynt or plyte, / predestend hire were.	/	E H be
A	306	"Athill qwene," quod Anec, / "as / I am enfourmed,	C	H be E
A	307	Ane of the grettist of oure godis, / of / grace and of miʒt,	P	N C P N
A	308	I fynd, or it be fere, / to / fleschely the knaw,	Z	Z H V
A	309	And efter in all aduersites, / is / amed the to help."	be	E H to V
A	310	Than sayd Olympadas, "now, / honourable maister,	/	A N
A	311	I be-seke the, my sire, / if thou me / say wald,	C H H	V X
A	312	Quatkyn fygour on fold, / or / fourme at he beris,	C	N P H V
A	313	That demyd is or destaned, / this / dede for to worche."	D	N for to V
A	314	"That will I wele," quod the wee, / "and noʒt a / word leʒe.	C not D	N V
A	315	This myʒty god at I me[ne], / is of a / medill age,	be P D	A N
A	316	Noʒt of ʒouth nor of eld, / nor / ʒerris to many,	C	N Z A
A	317	Bot euyn so be-twene twa, / and / to [mekyll] of nouthire.	C	Z A P H
A	318	How he is merkid and made, / is / mervaile to neuyn;	be	N to V
A	319	With – tachid in his for-top –, / twa / tufe hornes;	D	A N
A	320	A berd as a besom, / with thyn / bred haris,	P A	E N
A	321	A mouthe as a mastif hunde, / vn-metely to shaw.	/	A to V
A	322	Bot, dame, if he be thus diʒt, / drede the neuer the more,	/	V H Z Z
A	323	Bot ʒe be buxsom and bayne, / and / boune to his will.	C	V P D N
A	324	Be nyʒter-tale he sall the neʒe, / this / note to begyn,	D	N to V
A	325	And ʒe be merryd neuer the mare, / bot / mete him in sweuyn."	C	V H P N
A	326	"Now certayn, sire," sayd the qwene, / "selly me thinke.	/	A H V
A	327	Bot may I se this be sothe, / at ʒe me / say here,	that H H	V V
A	328	Noʒt as a prophet ne a prest, / I / prays sall thi selfe,	H	V X H self
A	329	Bot rehers as the hieʒe gode, / and / hie the for euire."	C	V H Z
A	330	With that rysis of the renke, / and his / rowme lefys,	C D	N V
A	331	Laʒt leue at the qwene, / for a / litill quile,	P D	A N
A	332	Gase him doune be the grecis, / a-gayn fra the sale,	/	Z P D N
A	333	Furthe to make his maistryse, / and / mose in his arte.	C	N P D N
A	334	Thus passis he fra the place, / to / proue his sleʒtis,	to	V D N
A	335	Silis furth all him selfe, / the / cyte with-outen,	D	N P
A	336	Drafe in-to a depe dissert, / and / drewe vp herbis,	C	V Z N
A	337	The chosest for inchantement, / at he / chese couthe.	that H	V X
A	338	Quen he had gedird his grese, / and / grune thaim esundire,	C	E H Z
A	339	For lapis of his gemetry, / the / ious out he wrengis,	D	N Z H V
A	340	Erne till exorʒise, / and / ethis euer elike,	C	V Z Z
A	341	That it suld worthe as he wald, / and on na / way faile.	C P D	N V
A	342	He clatird on coniurisons, / and / calid to him deuyls,	C	V P N N
A	343	And all the incheson of his charme, / with that the / chefe qwene	P D D	A N
A	344	The same nyʒt in hire slep, / suld / se with hire eʒen	X	V P D N
A	345	Amon hire awyn god, / in hire / armes ligge,	P D	N V
A	346	And dreme at he didd / hire swa, and quen he / done hadd,	H Z C C H	E have
A	347	Than suld he say to hire-selfe, / sadly thire wordis,	/	Z D N
A	348	"Now has thou, woman, I-wys, / with-in thi twa sydis	/	P D D N
A	349	Consayued him at in all thi care, / thi / cors sall defend."	D	N X V
A	350	This ilk euyn ouer-ʒede, / and / arly on the morne,	C	Z P D N

A	351	As arly as the riche qwene, / was / resyn fra slepe,	be	E P N
A	352	Than efter Anec on-ane, / scho / al aboute sendis,	H	Z V
A	353	Takis him betwene tham twa, / tald him hire sweuyn.	/	V H D N
A	354	"ȝa," quod he, "comly qwene, / I / couthe, and thou wald	H	V C H V
A	355	Preualy in thi palais, / lat me a / place haue,	V H D	N V
A	356	Make the to se the same gode, / and / thi-selfe wakand,	C	H self G
A	357	Face to face all his fourme, / and his / effecte clene.	C D	N A
A	358	This grete god full of grace, / sall / glide to thi chambre,	X	V P D N
A	359	In a dredfull deuys, / a / dragons fourme,	D	N N
A	360	And than the figour of a freke, / he sall / take eftire,	H X	V Z
A	361	And preualy in that part, / a-pere ȝowe be-forne."	/	V H P
A	362	Than answars him the swete quene, / and / sone him it grantis,	C	Z H H V
A	363	"Sire, chese the a chambre, / quare the / chefe thinkis,	Q H	Z V
A	364	Nowthire myne awen ne na nothire, / god lat the / noȝt spare,	N V H	not V
A	365	Or any place at ȝow plece, / my / palas with-in.	D	N P
A	366	For may thou hald me this hest, / as thou / here tellis,	C H	Z V
A	367	And profe thus in my presens, / as a / propire sothe,"	P D	A N
A	368	Then sall I cherische the with chere, / as thou my / child were,"	C H D	N be
A	369	Loute the louely and loue, / all my / lyfe days."	D D	N N
A	370	"Graunt mercy," quod the grete clerke, / to the / gude lady,	P D	A N
A	371	Thankis hire full thraly, / and / then forth wendis	C	Z Z V
A	372	To loke and layte him a loge, / quare he / lenge myȝte,	Q H	V X
A	373	And buske him a bedsted, / quare him / best likid.	Q H	Z V
A	374	Qwen it was metyn to the merke, / that / men ware to ryst,	that	N be P N
A	375	And folke was on thaire firste slepe, / and it was / furth euyns,	C H be	Z Z
A	376	Than Anec on ane, / his / artis he fandis,	D	N H V
A	377	And changid by enchantmentis, / his / chere all to-gedire.	D	N Z Z
A	378	Ther worthid he by his wiche-craft, / in-to a / wild dragon,	P D	A N
A	379	And to the ladi lere, / he / lendid in haste,	H	V P N
A	380	Fliȝand in his fethire-hames, / and / ferly fast sletis,	C	Z Z V
A	381	And in a braide, or he blan, / he the / bed entris.	H D	N V
A	382	Quen he was laide be-lyfe, / his / liknes he changis,	D	N H V
A	383	Worthis agayn to a wee, / fra a / worme turnys.	P D	N V
A	384	Then kisses kenely the quene, / and / clappis in armes,	C	V P N
A	385	Langis sare to the layke, / and / on-loft worthis.	C	Z V
A	386	Quen he had wroȝt all his will, / hire / wame then he touches,	D	N Z H V
A	387	And with a renyst reryd, / this / reson he said,	D	N H V
A	388	"This concepcion with kyngis, / sal be / callid here-efter	X be	E Z
A	389	A verra victor a-vansid, / with all the / vayne werde."	P D D	A N
A	390	Thus be-gylid he this gude wyfe, / and / makis hire to wene	C	V H to V
A	391	It ware na gett of na gome, / bot of / god ane.	P P	N H
A	392	Qwen the day-raw rase, / he / rysis be-lyfe,	H	V Z
A	393	Lendis a-lande fra the loft, / and / left hire with child.	C	V H P N
A	394	Sone as hire bele gun bolne, / all hire / blee changis,	D D	N V
A	395	So was scho ferd and a-friȝt, / a / ferly ware ellis.	D	N be Z
A	396	To be bonden with barne, / mekill / bale to hire neȝehis,	D	N P H V
A	397	For it and Philip hire fere, / o-ferrom was sybb.	/	Z be N
A	398	Than Anec hire awyn clerke, / scho / on-ane callis,	H	Z V
A	399	"Lo, maister, slike a myschefe!" , / and / maynly hire pleynes.	C	Z D N
A	400	"I dred that I nere dee, / bot ȝe me / deme sone	C H H	V Z
A	401	Quat me is beste of this case, / if euer the / kyng turne."	C Z D	N V
A	402	"Be noȝt a-bayste," quod the berne, / "ne / a-bleyd nothire,	not	E Z
A	403	Thare sall na chanche the chefe, / the / charge of a pese.	D	N P D N
A	404	For Amon oure athill gode, / sall / all-way the helpe,	X	Z H V
A	405	And kepe the full careles, / if any / cas falliss."	C D	N V
A	406	Quat dose now this diuinour, / bot to / desert wendis,	C P	N V
A	407	Airis on all him ane, / out of the / cite,	/	P P D N
A	408	ȝede him furthe eftirsons, / herbis to seche,	/	N to V
A	409	Reft tham vp be the rotis, / and / radly tham stampis.	C	Z H V
A	410	The Iuse for his gemetry, / that / Iogloure takis,	that	N V
A	411	A[nd] sythen a brid of the see, / him / seluyn him fangis,	H	self H V
A	412	Clatirs to hyre coynte thingis, / kenely enchantis,	/	Z V
A	413	And [with] the wose of the wede, / hire / wengis anoyntis;	D	N V
A	414	And all this demerlayke he did, / bot be the / deuyllis craftis,	P P D	N N
A	415	How he myȝt compas and kast, / the / kynge to begyle.	D	N to V
A	416	He wroȝt a wondirfull wile, / and / will ȝe now here	C	X H Z V
A	417	How he be-glouird this gome, / and / gilid him in sweuyn?	C	V H P N
A	418	This ilk Philip the fyrs, / that in the / fiȝt lenges,	that P D	N V
A	419	The same nyȝt in his slepe, / he / saȝe, as him thoȝt,	H	V C H V
A	420	Amon his awen god, / in / armes with his qwene,	P	N P D N
A	421	And make with hire market, / as [he] a / man were.	C H D	N be

A	422	And quen he wroȝt had his will, / then / witrely him metis,	Z	Z H V
A	423	That he bowes to hire belechiste, / and / bigly it sewys,	C	Z H V
A	424	And sethen asselis it him selfe, / semely and faire	/	Z C Z
A	425	With a rede golde rynge, / on this / aray grayuyn;	P D	N E
A	426	A lyons heuyd was on-loft, / louely coruyn;	/	Z E
A	427	The bounde of a briȝt son, / and a / brande kene.	C D	N A
A	428	And then he went furth his way, / sayd, / "woman, thou hauys	V	N H V
A	429	Thi full defendoure on fold, / now / frely consa[u]yd."	Z	Z E
A	430	Als radly as the riche kyng, / rase on the morne,	/	V P D N
A	431	Riȝt in the dawynge of day, / a / diuinour he callis,	D	N H V
A	432	And as him dremyd ilke a dele, / that / doctour he tellis,	that	N H V
A	433	And fraynes him fast on this fare, / how it / be-fall suld.	Q H	V X
A	434	"Phylyp," quod the phylysofyre, / "thi / fere is with childe,	D	N be P N
A	435	And with no gett of na gome, / bot of / god selfe.	C P	A self
A	436	And, gudman, [on] the gold rynge, / the thre / grauen thyngis,	D D	E N
A	437	Thai ere thus mekill to mene, / as me my / mynd tellis.	C H D	N V
A	438	To the lyon hede," quod the lede, / "then / licken I, on first,	Z	V H Z
A	439	The birth that scho bere sall, / als / best it be-semys,	C	A H V
A	440	That chefe sall to a chiftan, / and slike a / chefe maister,	C D D	A N
A	441	As to be halden heuydman, / of all the / hale werde.	P D D	A N
A	442	Now sall I clerily declare, / the / course on the sonne;	D	N P D N
A	443	That sygnyfys the same man, / that / sett is, be, wird,	that	E be P N
A	444	So many prouynce to pas, / thurȝe / prowis of armys,	P	N P N
A	445	That he sall hit with his hede, / in-to the / heghe est.	P D	A N
A	446	Now of this bytand brand, / berne, will ȝe here;	/	N X H V
A	447	And all is bot this hathill man, / as / I are sayd,	C	H Z E
A	448	That sall sa fele men afray, / with / fauchon in hande,	P	N P N
A	449	And out of nounbre to neuyn, / of / nacions wynn."	P	N V
A	450	Than foundis Philip to the fyȝt, / and the / fild entres,	C D	N V
A	451	And sone in delingis of dyntis, / a / dragon aperis,	D	N V
A	452	That streȝt be-for him in the stoure, / strikis doune his faas,	/	V Z D N
A	453	And all his enmys in that erd, / he / endid in a stounde.	H	V P D N
A	454	When Phylyp with his faire folke, / had the / fild won,	have D	N E
A	455	Than metis he him to Messadone, / thar / metis him the qwene,	Q	V H D N
A	456	Kyssis comly hire king, / and of his / come ioys,	C P D	N V
A	457	And how he fore scho him fraynes, / ferly ȝerne.	/	Z Z
A	458	"Wele, graunt mercy," quod the kyng, / "my / god, I him loue;	D	N H H V
A	459	Bot how that ȝe ga sa grete, / gud dame?" he sayd.	/	A N H V
A	460	Thou has ragid," quod the renge, / "with / vnryd gestis,	P	A N
A	461	Now hafe I, lede, all to lange, / lengid fra hame."	/	V P N
A	462	Thus to bre neire o bourde, / he / breuys thire wordis;	H	V D N
A	463	"To quam has thou the tane / till, / tell m[e] the sothe?	P	V H D N
A	464	Outhire mete has mendid the full mekill, / as / may I noȝt trowe,	C	X H not V
A	465	Or ane has stollen in my stede, / sen I was / stad thare."	C H be	E Z
A	466	Thus bayst he the briȝt qwene, / that all hire / ble changid,	that D D	N V
A	467	To skyre skarlet hewe, / skyftis hire face,	/	V D N
A	468	Hire chere at was chalke-quyte, / as any / chaffe worthis;	C D	N V
A	469	So was scho schamed of the schont, / that hire the / schalk made.	that H D	N E
A	470	"Nay, quod the comly kyng, / "cache vp thine hert,	/	V Z D N
A	471	Thofe thou haue forfet, na force, / so has / fele othire.	C V	A H
A	472	Thou has giltid, bot noȝt gretly, / it / greuys me the les;	H	V H Z
A	473	For god has geten the this gett, / a-gaynes thi will;	/	P D N
A	474	All that was done the bedene, / was me be / dreme schewyd,	be H P	N E
A	475	I saȝe it surely as my-selfe, / slepe in my tentis,	/	G P D N
A	476	And oure god all-to-gedire, / is / ground of the cause;	be	E P D N
A	477	Of me worthis the the wite, / ne of na / wee ellis."	not P D	N Z
A	478	Then tyd it anes on a tym, / a lytill / terme efter,	D A	N P
A	479	This dere kyng on a day, / on his / dese syttis,	P D	N V
A	480	Had parreld him a proude feste, / of / princes and dukis,	P	N C N
A	481	With maisterlingis of Messadone, / and / many othire noble[s].	C	A D N(A)
A	482	Thus as he sat in his sete, / softly by his qwene,	/	Z P D N
A	483	In schene schemerand schroude, / all of / schire stanes,	D D	A N
A	484	He kest vp his contenance, / and / knyȝtly he lokes,	C	Z H V
A	485	And gladis gudly his gestis, / as his / degre wald.	C D	N X
A	486	Than Anec[t]anabus on-ane, / in / althire-mast ioy	P	A N
A	487	Did on him his dragon-hame, / and / drafe thurȝe the sale,	C	V P D N
A	488	With slike a rowste and rerid, / the / romance it wittnes,	D	N H V
A	489	That nere had bernes for that bere, / bene / broȝt out of witt.	be	E P P N
A	490	He was sa hatter and sa hoge, / quen he the / hall entirid,	C H D	N V
A	491	Lete sa lathely a late, / and sa / loude cried,	C Z	Z V
A	492	That all the fest was a-ferd, / and othire / folke bathe.	C D	N Z

A	493	To the chefe chaiare of the qwene, / he / chese him be-lyue,	H	V H Z
A	494	And laide as hendly as a hunde, / his / hede in hire arme,	D	N P D N
A	495	Sethin kyssis he hire clene mouthe, / enclynes hire lawe,	/	V H Z
A	496	And braydis furth with a brym bere, / out at the / brade ȝatis.	P P D	A N
A	497	Then sayd Philip to his fere, / and all his / fre gestis,	C D D	A N
A	498	"ȝone selfe dragon forsothe, / I / saȝe with myne eȝen;	H	V P D N
A	499	Quen I was stad in the stoure, / he / strenthid all myne oste,	H	V D D N
A	500	And thar the floure in the filde, / I / fangid thurȝe him selfe."	H	V P H self
A	501	Anothire ferly thar fell, / within / fewe days,	P	A N
A	502	The king was sett in his sale, / with / septer in hand;	P	N P N
A	503	Then come thar-in a litill brid, / in-to his / arme floȝe,	P D	N V
A	504	And thar hurkils and hydis, / as scho were / hand-tame;	C H be	N E
A	505	Fast scho flekirs about his fete, / and / fleȝtirs aboute,	C	V Z
A	506	And thar it nestild in a noke, / as it a / nest were,	C H D	N be
A	507	Qwill scho had layd in his lape, / a / litill tyne egg,	D	A A N
A	508	And than scho fangis hire fliȝt, / and / floȝe away swyth.	C	V Z Z
A	509	This egg, or the kyng wyst, / to the / erth fallis,	P D	N V
A	510	Brak, and so it wele burde, / and / brast all e-soundir;	C	V Z Z
A	511	Than wendis thar-out a litill worm, / and / wald it eft enter,	C	X H Z V
A	512	And or scho hit in hire hede, / a / hard deth suffirs.	D	A N V
A	513	Than was ser Philip of that fare, / ferly mekill sturbid,	/	Z Z E
A	514	Callis to him a kid clerke, / declaris to him this wonder,	/	V P H D N
A	515	Besoȝt him quat it sygnified, / to / tell him the treuthe.	to	V H D N
A	516	"That graunt I gudly," quod the gome, / and / thus-gate he spekis:	C	C H V
A	517	"Sire, there sall borne be a barne, / of thi / blithe lady,	P D	A N
A	518	That driȝtyn efter thi day, / has / destaned to regne,	have	E to V
A	519	The quilke sall walke all the werd, / and / wyn it him selfe,	C	V H H self
A	520	And hent sall a full hetire deth, / or he may / hame couer."	C H X	Z V
A	521	Thus he vndid him ilka dele, / and him the / dome reched,	C H D	N V
A	522	Said it was sett to be so, / he / saȝe by his artis.	H	V P D N
A	523	And if ȝow likis of this lare, / to / lesten any forthire,	to	V Z
A	524	Sone sall I tell ȝow a text, / how it / be-tid efter.	Q H	V Z
A	525	Now it teȝt the tyme, / at / trauald that qwene,	P	V D N
A	526	Quen scho suld bryng furth, / hire / birth to the werd.	D	N P D N
A	527	Scho bidis many hard brayde, / baret enduris,	/	N V
A	528	What of wandreth and wa, / as / wemen dose all.	C	N V Z
A	529	Thik schouris hire thrat, / tholid mekill soroȝe,	/	V D N
A	530	Many peralus pull, / grete payne suffirs,	/	A N V
A	531	Sa sare werkis hire the wame, / and slik / vn-wyn dreis,	C D	N V
A	532	That all scho dredis hire dede, / and / doute for the werst.	C	V P D N(A)
A	533	Than efter Anectanabus, / scho / on-ane clepis,	H	Z V
A	534	And he was boune at hire bode, / and / bowes to hire chambre,	C	V P D N
A	535	Gais him vp at the grece, / and / gretis him faire,	D	V H Z
A	536	Fand hire sett in a sege, / and / soroȝe ay elike.	C	N Z Z
A	537	"A! Anec!" quod the qwene, / "me / arȝes of my-selfe;	H	V P H self
A	538	I am all in aunter, / sa / akis me the wame,	Z	V H D N
A	539	Of werke well ne I wede, / and / slike / wa tholis,	C D	N V
A	540	That me ware dere to be dede, / and / dure thus on lyfe."	C	V C P N
A	541	"ȝa, wynnes ȝow vp," quod the we, / "and / walkis a littill,	C	V Z
A	542	For the aire nowe and the elementis, / ere / evyn in this tyme	be	Z P D N
A	543	So trauailid out of temperoure, / and / troubild of that sone,	C	V P D N
A	544	That makis thi grippis and thi gridis, / a / grete dele the kenere."	D	A N D A
A	545	Than faris scho vp and farkis furth, / a / fute or tway,	D	N C N
A	546	And sone sesis all hire syte, / in a / sete quyle.	P D	A N
A	547	"Now bow the doune," quod the berne, / and scho his / bone fillis,	C H D	N V
A	548	And syttand so in hire sege, / was / softly delyuerd.	be	Z E
A	549	Bot now is meruaill, / to / me of this wondire,	P	H P D N
A	550	Quen this man fra his modire wambe, / on the / mold fell;	P D	N V
A	551	For all the erd euyn ouer, / sa / egirly schakis,	Z	Z V
A	552	That teldis, templis, and touris, / tomble on hepis.	/	V P N
A	553	The liȝt lemand late, / laschis fra the heuyn,	/	V P D N
A	554	Thonere thrastis ware thra, / thristid the welkyn,	/	V D N
A	555	Cloudis clenely to-clefe, / clatird vn-faire,	/	V Z
A	556	All blakenid a-boute, / and / boris the son.	C	V D N
A	557	Wild wedirs vp werpe, / and the / wynd ryse,	C D	N V
A	558	And all flames the flode, / as it / fire were,	C H	N be
A	559	Nowe briȝt, nowe blaa, / nowe on / blase efter,	Z P	N Z
A	560	And than ouer-qwelmys in a qwirre, / and / qwatis euer e-like.	C	V Z Z
A	561	Than slike a derknes thar drafe, / and / demyd the skewys,	C	V D N
A	562	As blesenand as bale fyre, / and / blake as the hell,	C	A P D N
A	563	That it was neuer bot as nyȝt, / fra the / none tyme	P D	A N

A	564	Till it to mydday was meten, / on the / morne efter.	P D	N Z
A	565	Gife this ware mervale to myn, / 3et / emang othire	C	P H
A	566	Then rekils it vnruydly, / and / raynes doune stanys,	C	V Z N
A	567	Fell fra the fyrmament, / as a / hand lyftyng,	C D	N G
A	568	And some as hoge as thi hede, / fra the / heuyn fallis.	P D	N V
A	569	Sa ferd was Philip of that fare, / in his / flesche trymblid,	that D	N V
A	570	For sere sygnes at he sa3e, / as / selly ware ellis.	C	A be Z
A	571	As wyde as all the werd / was thur3e, / warnyng thai hadd,	be Z	N H V
A	572	That houre that Olympadas, / was of hire / son li3ter.	be P D	N A
A	573	Than lendis him vp the leue kyng, / his / lady to vysite,	D	N to V
A	574	Quod the man to his make, / "I am / in many tho3tis,	H be P	A N
A	575	That this frute sall haue na fostring, / ne be / fed nouthire;	not be	E Z
A	576	I ges it be no3t of my gett, / bot of / god fourmed;	C P	N E
A	577	Be many cause at I ken, / I / kan no3t supose	H	X not V
A	578	It be consayued of my kynde, / ne / come of my-selfe.	not	E P H self
A	579	I sa3e so, in the same tyme, / he / seuyrd fra thi wambe,	H	V P D N
A	580	The erd and all the elementis, / so / egirly schoutid.	Z	Z V
A	581	And quether 3it, for any quat, / a / quyle latt him kepe,	Z	Z V H V
A	582	And norisch him as namely, / as he myne / awyn warre,	C H D	A be
A	583	3it will thare make of him mynde, / and / myn it here-eftire	C	H H Z
A	584	Hathils, swilke a haly son, / I / hade in my tyme.	H	V P D N
A	585	Another barne," quod the berne, / "I of my / blode haue,	H P D	N V
A	586	Ane of my sede, I supose, / and / sibbire of the twa,	C	A P D H
A	587	That I wan on myne othire wyfe, / that I / wedd first.	that H	V Z
A	588	Lat him as ayre, quen I am erthed, / enherit my landis,	/	V D N
A	589	And stall we him in stede / of this, to / sti3till my rewme,	P H to	V D N
A	590	For he is borne of my blode, / and / a-bore nerre,	C	E Z
A	591	And fede we this othire, that folke, / quen we ere / fay worthid,	C H be	A E
A	592	May sitt and carpe, slike a knaue, / thaire last / kyng hade."	D D	N V
A	593	Thai did all as he demed, / and his / domes plesed,	C D	N V
A	594	Cherest thai this 3onge child, / and / chosely him kepid;	C	Z H V
A	595	Thai ware as besy him a-boute, / birdis and ladis,	/	N C N
A	596	As he had bene thar hi3e god, / for sa thai / hopid all,	C Z H	V Z
A	597	This barne, quen he borne was, / as me the / boke tellis,	C H D	N V
A	598	Mi3t wele a-prefe for his a-port, / to any / prince oute.	P D	N Z
A	599	Bot of the lyfe the li3t / off, he / like was to nane,	Z H	A be P H
A	600	Nouther of fetour ne of face, / to / fadire ne to modyre;	P	N not P N
A	601	The fax on his faire hede, / was / ferly to schawe,	be	A to V
A	602	Large lyons lockis, / that / lange ere and scharpe;	that	A N C A
A	603	With grete glesenand e3en, / grymly he lokis,	/	Z H V
A	604	That ware as blyckenand bri3t, / as / blesand sternes,	P	G N
A	605	3it ware thai sett vn-samen, / of / serelypy hewys;	P	A N
A	606	The tane to brene at a blisch, / as / blak as a cole,	C	A C D N
A	607	As any 3are 3eten gold, / 3alow was the tothire.	/	A be D H
A	608	And he wald-e3ed was, / as the / writt schewys,	C D	N V
A	609	3it it tellis me this tale, / the / tethe in his hede	D	N P D N
A	610	Was as bitand breme, / as any / bare tuskis.	C D	N N
A	611	His steuyn stiffe was [and] steryn, / that / stonayd many,	that	V H
A	612	And as a lyon he lete, / quen he / loude romys.	C H	Z V
A	613	His fell fygoure and his fourme, / fully be-takend	/	Z E
A	614	The prowis and the grete pryse, / that he / a-preuyd eftire,	that H	V Z
A	615	His hardynes, his hyndelaike, / and his / hetter my3tis,	C D	A N
A	616	The wirschip that he wan, / quen he / wex eldire.	C H	V A
A	617	Than sembled his syb men, / be / sent of tham all,	be	E P H Z
A	618	To consaile of this kyng son, / how thai him / call suld,	Q H H	V X
A	619	And so him neuyned was the name, / of his / next frendis	P D	A N
A	620	Alexsandire the athill, / be / allirs a-corde.	P	A N
A	621	Than was he lede furthe be-lyfe, / to / lere at the scole,	to	V P D N
A	622	As sone as to that sapient, / him-self was of elde,	/	H self be P N
A	623	On-ane vn-to Arystotill, / that was his / awen maister,	that be D	A N
A	624	And one of the coronest clerkis, / that euer / knew letter.	that Z	V N
A	625	Than was he bro3t to a benke, / a / boke in his hand,	D	N P D N
A	626	And faste by his enfourme, / was / fettild his place;	be	E D N
A	627	For it come no3t a kyng son, / 3e / knaw wele, to sytt	H	V Z to V
A	628	Doune in margon and molle, / emange othire schrewis.	/	P D N
A	629	Sone wex he witter and wyse, / and / wonder wele leres,	C	N Z V
A	630	Sped him in a schort space, / to / spell and to rede,	to	V C to V
A	631	And sethen to gramere he gase, / as the / gyse wald,	C D	N X
A	632	And that he all hale, / in a / hand-quyle.	P D	N N
A	633	In foure or in fyfe 3ere, / he / ferre was in lare	H	Z be P N
A	634	Than othire at had bene thare, / seuynte wynter;	/	A N

A	635	That he suld passe him in that plite, / vnpussible semed,	/	A V
A	636	Bot at god will at gaa furth, / qua may / agayn stande?	Q X	Z V
A	637	In absens of Arystotill, / if / any of his feris	C	H P D N
A	638	Raged with him vnridly, / or / rofe him with harme,	C	V H P N
A	639	Him wald he kenely on the croune, / knok with his tablis,	/	V P D N
A	640	That al to-brest wald the bordis, / and the / blode folowe.	C D	N V
A	641	If any scolere in the scole, / his / skorne at him makis,	D	N P H V
A	642	He skapis him full skathely, / bot if he / skyp better.	C C H	V Z
A	643	Thus with his feris he faʒt, / as I / fynd wreten,	C H	V E
A	644	As wele in letter and in lare, / as any / laike ellis.	P D	N Z
A	645	Thus skilfull lange he scolaid, / and the / scole vsed,	C D	N V
A	646	Tille he was euyn of eld, / elleuyn wynter.	/	A N
A	647	He had na pere in na place, / that / proued so his tyme,	that	V Z D N
A	648	For the principalte of all the pake, / he of / a-prefe wynnys.	H Z	N V
A	649	And qwen it teʒt to the tyme, / of / ten ʒere of age,	P	A N P N
A	650	Then was him kend of the kynde, / and / craft of bataile,	C	N P N
A	651	Wele and wiʒtly in were, / to / welden a spere,	to	V D N
A	652	A[nd] preke on a proude stede, / proudly enarmed.	/	Z E
A	653	That lare was him lefe / to, and / lerid in a qwile	Z C	V P D N
A	654	Was thar na lede to him like, / with-in a / fewe ʒeris.	P D	A N
A	655	So cheualus a chiftan, / he / cheuys in a stonde,	H	V P D N
A	656	That in anters of armes, / all men he passes.	/	A N H V
A	657	Quen Philip see him sa fers, / in his / first elde,	P D	A N
A	658	His hert and his hardynes, / hiʒely he lofed,	/	Z H V
A	659	Comendid mekill his knyʒt-hede, / and him / callid on a day	C H	V P D N
A	660	Be-twene tham selfe on a tyme, / and / talkis thire wordis:	C	V D N
A	661	"Alexander," quod the kyng, / "I / augirly prayse	H	Z V
A	662	Thi wirschip, thi worthines, / thi / wit and thi strenth.	D	N C D N
A	663	Es nane so teche of thi tyme, / to / tryi now o lyfe.	to	V Z P N
A	664	How suld I, lede, for thi lofe, / bot / lufe the in hert?	C	V H P N
A	665	Bot I am sary for sothe, / my / son, at thi fourme	D	N P D N
A	666	Is lickenand on na lym, / ne / like to my selfe;	not	A P H self
A	667	Oft storbis me thi statour, / and / stingis me ʒerne,	C	V H Z
A	668	That thi personale proporcion, / sa / party is to myne."	C	A be P H
A	669	This herd hire the hend quene, / and / heterly scho dredis,	H	Z H V
A	670	Sent efter Anec, / and / askis him be-lyue,	C	V H Z
A	671	Be-knew him clene all the case, / how the / kyng sayd,	Q D	N V
A	672	And frayns him fast quat the freke, / of hire / fare thingis.	P D	A N
A	673	Then con he calke and a-conte, / and / kest on his fyngirs,	C	V P D N
A	674	Lokis him vp to the lifte, / and the / lady swares:	C D	N V
A	675	"Be noʒt a-friʒt, / quod the freke, / "ne / a-frayd nouthire,	not	A Z
A	676	It sall the noy noʒt a neg, / nane of his thoʒtis."	/	H P D N
A	677	With that he heuys vp [his] hede, / and to the / heuyn lokis,	C P D	N V
A	678	Hedis heterly on hiʒe, / behald on a sterne,	/	V P D N
A	679	Of the quilke he hopid in his hert, / sumquat to knawe,	/	Q to V
A	680	Quat euire he wald wete, / of his / will all-to-gedire.	P D	N Z
A	681	Quod Alexander to this athill, / as he his / arte fandis,	C H D	N V
A	682	"Quat is the planet or the poynt, / ʒe / purpose to seme?	H	V to V
A	683	Quat sterne is it at ʒe stody / on, quare / stekis it in heuyn?	Z Q	V H P N
A	684	May ʒe oʒt me in any maner, / to that / sterne schewe?"	P D	N V
A	685	"That can I wele," quod the clerke, / "ellis / couthe I littill;	Z	V H Z
A	686	Noʒt bot sewe me, son, / quen the / son is to reste,	Q D	N be to V
A	687	Quen it [is] dreuyn to the derke, / and the / day fynyst,	C D	N V
A	688	And thou sall sothely se, / the / same with thine eʒen.	D	N(A) P D N
A	689	"Is oʒt thi werid to the wissid?" , / quod the / wee than;	V D	N Z
A	690	"For that I couet to ken, / if thou me / kythe wald."	C H H	V X
A	691	"Sire, sothely of myne awen son, / slayne mon I worth,	/	E X H V
A	692	So was me destaned to dye, / gane many winter."	/	E D N
A	693	As tyte as Anec[tanabus], / this / aunter had tald,	D	N have E
A	694	Then [he] treyned doune fra the toure, / to / tute in the sternes.	to	V P D N
A	695	Than airis ser Alexander, / eftire his fadire,	/	P D N
A	696	That euer he kyndild of his kynde, / kend he bot litill.	/	V H Z Z
A	697	Thus led he furthe his leue child, / late on ane euen,	/	Z P D N
A	698	Sylis softely him selfe, / the / cite with-outen,	D	N P
A	699	Boʒes him vp to a brenke, / as the / buke tellis,	C D	N V
A	700	To the hiʒt of the depe dike, / and to the / heuyn waytis.	C P D	N V
A	701	"Alexander, athil son" , / quod / Anec his syre,	V	N D N
A	702	"Loo! ʒonder behald ouer thi hede, / and se my / hatter werdis;	C V D	A N
A	703	The euyll sterne of Ercules, / how / egirly it soroʒes,	Q	Z H V
A	704	And how the mode Marcure, / makis sa mekill ioy;	/	V D D N
A	705	Loo! ʒonder the gentill Iubiter, / how / Iolyle he schynes	Q	Z H V

A	706	The domes of my destany, / drawis to me swythe.	/	V P H Z
A	707	Thik and thrathly am I thret, / and / thole mon I sone	C	V X H Z
A	708	The slaʒter of myne awen son, / as me was / sett euer."	C H be	E Z
A	709	Vnethis werped he that worde, / the / writt me recordis,	D	N H V
A	710	That ne Alexander as sone, / was at / him be-hind,	be that	H P
A	711	And on the bake with slike a bire, / he / bare with his handis	H	V P D N
A	712	That doune he drafe to the depest, / of the / dike bothom,	P D	N N
A	713	Sayd, "lo! vnhappeiste vndire heuyn, / that thus on / hand takis	that C P	N V
A	714	As be the welken to wete, / quat suld / come efter!	Q X	V Z
A	715	Thou has feynd the for wyse, / and / fals all-to-gedire,	C	V Z
A	716	Wele semys slike a sacchell, / to / syeʒe thus of lyfe!"	to	V C P N
A	717	Than Anec, as him aʒt, / wele / augirly granys,	Z	Z V
A	718	Dryues vp a dede voyce, / and / dymly he spekis,	C	Z H V
A	719	"Wele was this cas to me knawen, / and / kyd many wynter,	C	E D N
A	720	That I suld dee slike a dethe, / be / dome of my werdis.	P	N P D N
A	721	Sayd I the noʒt so, / my / selfe here be-fore,	H	self Z Z
A	722	I suld be slayn of my son / as now / sothe worthis?"	C Z	A V
A	723	Thof I this wirschip the wayfe, / as / wald thine astate,	C	V D N
A	724	Lat thou thi hert neuer the hiʒere, / hale in-to pride.	/	V P N
A	725	For it was wont," quod the wee, / "as / wyse men tellis,	C	A N V
A	726	Full hiʒe thingis ouer-heldis, / to / held other-quile.	to	V Z
A	727	Slike as ere now broʒt a-bofe, / nowe the / bothum askis,	Z D	N V
A	728	And slike at left ere on lawe, / ere / lift to the sternes."	be	E P D N
A	729	"Sa ma aydeus," quod that othire man, / "thou / tellis me treuthe,	H	V H N
A	730	Son this ensample of thi-selfe, / thou / sais me, I trowe.	H	V H H V
A	731	Vn-behalde the wele on ilk halfe, / and / haue a gud eʒe,	C	V D A N
A	732	Les on thine ane here-efterward, / thine / ossyngis liʒt.	D	N V
A	733	Than Alexander all in ire, / angrile spekis:	/	Z V
A	734	"Hy the hethen-ward, thou hathill, / and / houe thou na langire.	C	V H Z
A	735	For na-thing as a-nente / me, thou has / noʒt to mell,	H H have	not to V
A	736	Ne with thi domes me to dele, / dole vndire sonne."	/	N P N
A	737	Now is ser Nicollas anoyed, / and / nettild with ire,	C	E P N
A	738	As wrath as [a] waspe, / and / wode of his mynde,	C	A P D N
A	739	Reviles he this othire renke, / with / vnrid speche:	P	A N
A	740	"Behald," quod he hedirward, / "and / herken how I say;	C	V Q H V
A	741	Now be the hert and the hele, / of my / hathill fadire,	P D	A N
A	742	And be the god," quod the gome, / "that / gafe me the saule,	that	V H D N
A	743	A[ls] sprent [of] my spittyng, / a / specke on thi chere,	D	N P D N
A	744	Thou sall be diʒt to the deth, / and / drepid of my handis."	C	E P D N
A	745	Quen he had spokin so, for spyte, / he / spittis in his face,	H	V P D N
A	746	Dispises him despetously, / dispersons him foule.	/	V H Z
A	747	"Hent the thare," quod the hatill, / "as the to / haue semes,	C H to	V V
A	748	Cure, for thi kene carpe, / chache nowe a schame!"	/	V Z D N
A	749	Than went him furthe Alexander, / and his / ande takis,	C D	N V
A	750	Lete a-swage or he sware, / the / swelme of his angirs,	D	N P D N
A	751	Be-seʒis him how he say wold, / or he his / saʒe ʒeld,	C H D	N V
A	752	And turnes him then to the tulke, / and / talkis thire wordis:	C	V D N
A	753	"For thou has noʒtid me now, / Nicollas," he sayd,	/	N H V
A	754	I swere the, be my syre saule, / and by his / selfe pite,	C P D	self N
A	755	And be the worthe wombe, / of my / wale modre	P D	A N
A	756	That I was geten in of gode, / and / graithely consayued,	C	Z E
A	757	Thou seis me, lede, or oʒt lange, / in thi / lande armed,	P D	N E
A	758	And othire recouyre me thi rewme, / or / reche vp the girdill."	C	V Z D N
A	759	Than set thai tham slike a day, / to / semble and to fiʒt,	to	V C to V
A	760	And thar-to tuke vp thaire trouthis, / and / twyned esondre.	C	V Z
A	761	Then ʒode him furthe thi[s] ʒong man, / ʒapeli and swythe	/	Z C Z
A	762	In-to the marche of Messedone, / and / manly a-semblis	C	Z V
A	763	Of saudiours and sekir men, / a / soume out of nounbre,	D	N P P N
A	764	That was the baldest and the best, / breueyd in armes.	/	V P N
A	765	He parrails him a proude ost, / of / princes and othire,	P	N C H
A	766	Farkis to ser Philip, / and / fangis his leue,	C	V D N
A	767	And than Bocifilas his blonke, / he / bremely ascendis,	H	Z V
A	768	And bounes on with his bataill, / out at the / brade ʒatis.	P P D	A N
A	769	The same day at was sett, / the / sembling of bathe,	D	N P H
A	770	Aithire with a firs flote, / in the / fild metis.	P D	N V
A	771	The nounbre of ser Nicollas, / it / noyes me to reken,	H	V H to V
A	772	And Alexander was ane oste, / of / augird many.	P	Z A
A	773	With that thai tuke vp thaire trompes, / a-pon / the / twa sidis,	P D	A N
A	774	Braidis banars a-brade, / buskis to mete.	/	V to V
A	775	So kinlid the clarons, / that all the / cliffe ryngs,	that D D	N V
A	776	The holtis and the haire heere, / and the / hillis scheuyn.	C D	N V

A	777	Ilk a hathill to hors, / hiȝis him be-lyue,	/	V H Z	
A	778	Stridis into stele-bowe, / stertis apon loft,	/	V Z	
A	779	Has a helme on his hede, / and / honge on his swyre	C	V P D N	
A	780	A schene schondirhand schild, / and a / schaft hentis.	C D	N V	
A	781	Quat of stamping of stedis, / and / stering of bernes,	C	G P N	
A	782	All dymed the dale, / and the / dust ryses.	C D	N V	
A	783	With slik a bront and a brusche, / the / bataill a-sembild,	D	N V	
A	784	As the erth and all the el[e]mentis, / at / anes had wrestild.	Z	Z have E	
A	785	Now aithire stoure on thar stedis, / strikis to-gedire,	/	V Z	
A	786	Spurnes out spakly, / with / speris in hand,	P	N P N	
A	787	Brekis in-to blasons, / bordren shildis,	/	V N	
A	788	Beris in-to briȝt stele, / bitand lances,	/	A N	
A	789	Sone in scheuerand schidis, / schaftis ere brosten,	/	N be E	
A	790	Al to-spryngis in sprotis, / speris of syris,	/	N P N	
A	791	Dryfuys doune duchepers, / and / doykis of thar horses,	C	N P D N	
A	792	Fellis fay to the fold, / many / fresch knyȝtis.	D	A N	
A	793	Quat dose now this Nichollas, / but / nymes him a spere,	C	V H D N	
A	794	Kest him on this ȝong knyȝt, / to / couire him a name;	to	V H D N	
A	795	And Alexander with anothire, / airis him agayne,	/	V H Z	
A	796	Girdis grymly to-gedire, / greuosly metis.	/	Z V	
A	797	Sa sare was the semble, / thire / seggis be-twene,	D	N P	
A	798	That al to-wraiste thai thar wode, / and / werpis in-sondire,	C	V Z	
A	799	Al to-clatirs in-to cauels, / clene to thaire handis,	/	Z P D N	
A	800	Thar left nouthire in thar hand, / the / lengthe of an ellyn.	D	N P D N	
A	801	Then littid thai na langer, / bot / laschid out swerdis,	C	V Z N	
A	802	Aithire a blesynand brand, / brait out of schethe,	/	V P P N	
A	803	Hewis on hattirly, / had thurgh mailes,	/	V P N	
A	804	Many starand stanes, / strikis of thaire helmes.	/	V P D N	
A	805	Then Alexander in ane ire, / his / arme vp-liftis,	D	N V	
A	806	Swythe swyngis out his swerde, / and his / swayfe feches.	C D	N V	
A	807	The noll of Nicollas the kyng, / he fra the / nebb partis,	H P D	N V	
A	808	That doun he fell fra his fole, / and / fynyst for euir.	C	V Z	
A	809	Thus was him destand that day, / as / driȝten had shapid,	C	N have E	
A	810	To hent him the hiȝere hande, / of his / athill fais.	P D	A N	
A	811	Thare slike wirschip he wan, / ware / wonder to tell;	be	A to V	
A	812	Had of that hiȝe kyng, / the / hede fra the shuldirs.	D	N P D N	
A	813	Then was him geuyn vp the ȝerde, / and / ȝolden the rewme,	C	E D N	
A	814	And all at left was o lyfe, / lordis and othire,	/	N C H	
A	815	Come to that conquerour, / and on / knese fallis,	C P	N V	
A	816	And in his mercy and meth, / mekely thaim put.	/	Z H V	
A	817	This renke and his rounsy, / thar / reche vp a croune,	H	V Z H V	
A	818	As gome at has the garland, / and all the / gre wonn.	C D D	N V	
A	819	Thus with the floure in the fild, / he / fangid his enmy,	H	V D N	
A	820	And haldis on with hale here, / hame to his fadire.	/	N P D N	
A	821	Than fyndis he Philip on his flett, / with a / fest huge	P D	N A	
A	822	Had wed him another wyfe, / and / wayfid his quene;	C	E D N	
A	823	Ane Cleopatras caled, / a / grete kyngis doȝter,	D	A N N	
A	824	And [laft] had Olympadas, / and / openly for-saken.	C	Z E	
A	825	"Fadire," quad this fell knyȝt, / quen he this / fest entirs,	C H D	N V	
A	826	"The palme here of my first price, / I / pray the resayfe,	H	V H V	
A	827	Forthe to the weding or I winde, / of my / wale modire,	P D	A N	
A	828	And kaire me to a-nothire kyng, / to / couple hire to wyfe.	to	V H P N	
A	829	For the to felsen ne to foloȝe, / fallis me na mare,	/	V H Z	
A	830	Ne here to duell with thi douce, / deynes me na langer,	/	V H Z	
A	831	Now thou mas the slike a mangery, / and / macchis changis,	C	N V	
A	832	And I to consaile vn-callid, / I / can noȝt thar-on."	H	V not Z	
A	833	With that thar carpis to the kyng, / a / knyȝt at the table,	D	N P D N	
A	834	Ane lesias, a lede, / and on / loude speches:	C P	A N	
A	835	"Cleopatras a knafe child, / consayue sall and bere,	/	V X C V	
A	836	That demed is eftir thi deth, / duly to regne."	/	Z to V	
A	837	Than Alexander at this knyȝt, / angirs vnfaire,	/	V Z	
A	838	Wynnes him vp a wardrere, / he / walt in his handis,	H	V P D N	
A	839	So hard him hittis on the hede, / his / hernes out weltid,	D	N Z V	
A	840	And sa he lost has the lyfe, / for his / lether wordis.	P D	A N	
A	841	Than was the wale kyng wrath, / as / wonder ware ellis,	C	A be Z	
A	842	Braydis him vp fra the borde, / and a / brand clekis,	C D	N V	
A	843	Airid toward Alexander, / and / ames him to strike.	C	V H to V	
A	844	Bot than him failis the feete, / or he / first wenys,	C H	Z V	
A	845	He stakirs, he stumbils, / and / stande he ne miȝt,	C	V H not X	
A	846	Bot ay fundirs and fallis, / as he / ferde ware.	C H	A be	
A	847	The faster forward him he faris, / the / faster he snapirs;	D	Z H V	

A	848	Quat was the cause of the case, / that / knawis oure lorde.	that	V D N
A	849	"Quat now," quad athill Alexander, / "quat / ailis the to fall?	Q	V H to V
A	850	Has thou na force in thi fete, / ne / fele of thi-selfe?	not	N P H self
A	851	For a freke to be ferd, / or / a-fraid outhire,	C	A Z
A	852	And thou the gouernere of grece, / that ware / grete wondire!"	that be	A N
A	853	Then tittis he doune in that tene, / the / tablis ilkane,	D	N H
A	854	Out of the hall be [the] hare, / halis he the bride,	/	V H D N
A	855	And so the wee in his wreth, / wrekis his modire,	/	V D N
A	856	And Philip falne [was] sare seke, / and all the / fest strubled.	C D D	N E
A	857	As sone as Alexander, / of / angire he slakis,	P	N H V
A	858	He lendis o-loft to the lede, / a / litlll days eftir,	Z	Z N P
A	859	Cairis vp with comfurth, / the / kyng for to vysite,	D	N for to V
A	860	He comes to the curten, / and / carpis this wordis:	C	V D N
A	861	"Philip," quod this ilke freke, / and / forwith him standis,	C	P H V
A	862	"Thof it vn-semely me sytt, / the / so for to call,	H	Z for to V
A	863	Noȝt as thi suget and thi son, / my / sawe I the ȝeld,	D	N H H V
A	864	Bot as a felaw or a frynde, / fallis to a-nothire.	/	V P H
A	865	Sire, latt thi wreth a-wai wende, / and with thi / wyfe saȝtill,	C P D	N V
A	866	And the los of Lesias, / litill thou charge.	/	Z H V
A	867	I did bot my deuire, / to / drepe him, me thinke;	to	V H H V
A	868	For it awe him noȝt sa openly, / slike / ossing to make.	D	N to V
A	869	And ser, vnwortheley thou wroȝt, / and that thou / wele knawis,	C that H	Z V
A	870	Quen thou was boune with a brand, / my / bodi to schende."	D	N to V
A	871	Then rewis the riche kyng, / of / vnride werkis,	P	A N
A	872	Blischis vp to the berne, / and / braste out at grete.	C	V Z to V
A	873	Then airis him on Alexander, / to his / awen modire;	P D	A N
A	874	"Bees not a-glopened, madame, / ne / greued at my fadire;	not	E P D N
A	875	If all ȝe synned him be-syde, / as ȝour / selfe knawis,	C H	self V
A	876	Thar-of na we may the wite, / it was / godis will."	H be	N N
A	877	With that he fanges hire furthe, / to / Philip hire ledis,	P	N D N
A	878	And he comly hire kist, / and / cordis with hire faire,	C	V P N Z
A	879	Anes with Olympadas, / and the / tothire woydis,	C D	H V
A	880	And lofes hire lely, / to his / lyfes ende.	P D	N N
A	881	Sone eftir in a seson, / as the / duke sais,	C D	N V
A	882	Come driuand fra Darius, / the / deyne Empereure,	D	A N
A	883	Heraudis on heȝe hors, / hendly a-rayed,	/	Z E
A	884	To ser Philip the fers, / to / feche thar trouage.	to	V D N
A	885	Litill kyngis thar come, / as the / clause tellis,	C D	N V
A	886	Liȝt doune at the loge, / and thar / blonkis leues:	C D	N V
A	887	Caires in-to the curte, / to / craue him thar dettis,	to	V H D N
A	888	Touchis titly thar tale, / and / tribute him askis.	C	N H V
A	889	"Ȝa, caires hame," quod Alexander, / "a-gayn to ȝour kithes,	/	Z P D N
A	890	And sais ȝour maister, he make, / na / ma sandis;	D	A N
A	891	For sen Philip had a fresche son, / that / fast now encressis,	that	Z Z V
A	892	That bees noȝt suffird, I suppose, / nane / slike him to ȝeld.	H	A H to V
A	893	For sais ȝour lord, the lefe hen, / that / laide hir first egg,	that	V D D N
A	894	Hire bodi nowe with barante, / is / barely consumed,	be	Z E
A	895	And is Darius so of his dett, / duly depryued;	/	Z E
A	896	And be this titill, him tellis, / na / tribute him fallis."	D	N H V
A	897	Then merualid tham the messangirs, / mekill of his speche,	/	Z P D N
A	898	His witt and his wisdome, / wonderly praysed.	/	Z E
A	899	Faire at ser Ph[ilip] the fers, / fang thai thar leue,	/	V H D N
A	900	And syne clene of all the curte, / and / cairis to thar landis.	C	V P D N
A	901	To the palais of the proude kyng, / to / persie thai went,	P	N H V
A	902	Dose tham in to Darius, / thar he on / dese syttis,	Q H P	N V
A	903	And telles him how his trouage, / is / tynt al-to-gedire,	be	E Z
A	904	As Alexander awyn mouth, / had tham / all enfourmed.	have H	Z E
A	905	Then messangirs to Messedoyne, come / in the / mene qwile	P D	A N
A	906	To Ph[ilip] the fell kyng, / and / freschly him tald,	C	Z H V
A	907	That all the erthe of Ermony, / Erles and princes,	/	N C N
A	908	That sulde suget to him-selfe, / wald / seke him with armes.	X	V H P N
A	909	And Alexander belyfe, / as / athil man suld,	C	A N X
A	910	Vndirfangid to feȝt, / for / Ph[ilip] to wende,	P	N to V
A	911	Gedirs him a grete ost, / graithes him in plates,	/	V H P N
A	912	And aires toward Ermony, / that / erd to distroy.	D	N to V
A	913	Than was a man in Messadone, / in the / marche duellid,	P D	N V
A	914	A proued prince and a proude, / Pausanna was hatten,	/	N be E
A	915	A big berne and a bald, / in / brenys to ryde,	P	N to V
A	916	The son of ane Cerastis, / as the / buke witnes.	C D	N V
A	917	This freke all his franche, / of / Ph[ilip] he haldis,	P	N H V
A	918	And was a suget to him-selfe, / and / serues him aȝt;	C	N H V

A	919	Bot than he depely many day, / disired to haue the quene,	/	V to V D N
A	920	And lyes vmlapped with hire lufe, / many / lange wynter.	D	A N
A	921	And by that cause to the kyng, / he / kest slik a hate,	H	V D D N
A	922	That he desiris his deth, / and / diʒtis [him] thare-fore.	C	V H Z
A	923	All the folke of his affinite, / he / freschly a-semblis,	H	Z V
A	924	And sekis furth with a hoge some, / a-saile him to ʒeld.	/	N H to V
A	925	Quen Ph[ilip] heris of that fare, / gret ferly him thinke[s],	/	A N H V
A	926	Ferkis furth with a fewe folk, / him in the / fild metis,	H P D	N V
A	927	Seis the multitude sa mekill, / of / men at he bringes,	P	N that H V
A	928	Braidis on his blonke toward the burʒe, / and thaim the / bak shewis.	C H D	N V
A	929	Then schrikis schilli all the schalkis, / and / schoutis him at anes,	C	V H Z
A	930	And Pausanna the prince, / a-pon a / proude stede	P D	A N
A	931	Sprengis out with a spere, / and / spedis him eftir,	C	V H P
A	932	And thurgh the bac in-to the brest, / him / beris to the erd;	H	V P D N
A	933	All ware he wondirly wondid, / he / wendis noʒt be-lyfe.	H	V not Z
A	934	His men and all the Messadones, / full / mavnly ware stourbed,	Z	Z be E
A	935	Quat of doloure and dyn, / quen thai him / dede hopid.	C H H	A V
A	936	Pausanna than for the prowis, / slike a / pride hentis,	D D	N V
A	937	Vnethes wist he for welth, / wirke quat he miʒt.	/	V Q H X
A	938	He prekis in-to the palais, / to / pull out the quene,	to	V Z D N
A	939	Wenys to wild hire at will, / and / away lede.	C	Z V
A	940	Than comes Alexander in that cas, / the / cronaclis tellis,	D	N V
A	941	With a riall ost, / of many / able princes,	P D	A N
A	942	Airand out of Ermony, / and had all the / erth won;	C have D D	N E
A	943	Sees slike a rottillyng in the rewme, / and / ridis al the faster.	C	V Z D Z
A	944	Than past vp the proud quene, / in-to / preue chambre,	P	A N
A	945	Wayues out at wyndou, / and / waytis a-boute,	C	V Z
A	946	Saʒe be the sygnes and be sike, / as with hire / son comys,	C P D	N V
A	947	And be the alyens armes, / at he was / all maister.	Q H be	A N
A	948	With that scho haldis out hire hede, / and / heʒe to him callis,	C	Z P H V
A	949	"Quare is thi werdes, my wale son, / thou / wan of thi godis,	H	V P D N
A	950	Thou sald be victour and venge, / and / vencust neuire?	C	V Z
A	951	If thou haue any hert here, / help now thi modire."	/	V Z D N
A	952	Sone as Pausanna the prince, / with-in the / palais heris	P D	N V
A	953	The comyng of the kene knyʒt, / he / caires him agaynes,	H	V H P
A	954	Presis out of the palais, / with a / pake armed,	P D	N E
A	955	And metes him in the myd-fild, / with a / mekill nounbre.	P D	A N
A	956	And Alexander be-lyue, / quen / he on him waites,	C	H P N V
A	957	He swyngis out with a swerd, / and / swappis him to dethe;	C	V H P N
A	958	And the renkis, all the route, / reches vp thaire wapen	/	V Z D N
A	959	Vn-to this kid conquirour, / and / cried eftir socure.	C	V Z N
A	960	Than was thar ane in the ost, / on / Alexander callis,	P	N V
A	961	Sayd, "Ph[ilip] thi fadire, / is in the / fild drepid."	be P D	N V
A	962	And he halis furth on hede, / and / halfe-dede him fyndis,	C	A H V
A	963	Brusches doune by the berne, / and / bitterly wepis.	C	Z V
A	964	"A! Alexander!" quod the kyng, / "now am / I at ane ende;"	Z be	H P D N
A	965	A litill liftis vp his liddis, / and / lokis in his face;	C	V P D N
A	966	"Bot ʒit it gladis me," quod the gome, / "to / ga thus to deth,	to	V C P N
A	967	To se my slaare in my siʒt, / be sa / sone ʒolden,	be Z	Z E
A	968	A! wele be the, my wale son" , / and / waged with his hede;	C	V P D N
A	969	"Thou has baldly on my bane, / and / bremely me vengid."	C	Z H V
A	970	With that the blothirs in the brest, / and the / breth stoppis,	C D	N V
A	971	And in a spedfull space, / so the / sprete ʒeldis.	C D	N V
A	972	And Alexander ay on-ane, / augirly he wepis,	/	Z H V
A	973	And gretis for him as greuously, / as he him / geten hade.	C H H	E have
A	974	With barons and bachelers, / him / broʒt to the cite,	H	V P D N
A	975	And erdis him in his awen erd, / as / Emperoure fallis.	C	N V
A	976	The day efter his deth, / drerely him wendis	/	Z H V
A	977	Alexander his aire, / and / syttis in his trone,	C	V P D N
A	978	A clene croune on his hede, / clustird with gemmes,	/	E P N
A	979	To se how him seme wald, / the / sete of his fadire.	D	N P D N
A	980	He seis doune in the sete, / with / septer in hande,	P	N P N
A	981	Makis a crie that all the curte, / kniʒtis and erles,	/	N C N
A	982	Suld put thaim in-to presens, / his / precep to here.	D	N to V
A	983	And all comyn at a kall, / and on / kneis heldis;	C P	N V
A	984	Than blisches he to his baronage, / and / breues thir wordis:	C	V D N
A	985	"Lo! maistirs of Messedone, / sa / miʒty men and noble,	Z	A N C A
A	986	ʒe Traces and of Tessaloyne, / and ʒe the / trewe Grekis,	C H D	A N
A	987	How likis ʒow nowe ʒour lege lord?, / on my fourme,	/	V P D N
A	988	And letis all ferdschip at flee, / and / fange vp ʒour hertis,	C	V Z D N
A	989	And aires for nane alyens, / quils / Alexander lastis.	C	N V

A	990	For with the graunt of my god, / I / gesse, or I dye,	H	V C H V
A	991	That all the Barbare blode, / sall / bowe to my-selfe.	A	V P H self
A	992	Thare is na region ne rewme, / ne / renke vnder heuen,	D	N P N
A	993	Ne nouthire-quare na nacion, / bot it sall my / name loute.	C H X D	N V
A	994	For we of grece sall haue the gree, / with / grace ay to wild,	P	N Z to V
A	995	And anely the ouer the werd, / honourd and praysed.	/	E C E
A	996	And quilk of all myne athill men, / that any / armes wantis,	that D	N V
A	997	Lat pas in-to my palais, / and / plates him delyuire,	C	N H V
A	998	And he at of his awen has, / harnas him swythe,	/	V H Z
A	999	And make him boune ilka berne, / to / bataill to ride."	P	N to V
A	1000	Than answard him with [a] voice, / all his / proud princes,	D D	A N
A	1001	And Erles in his Empire, / that ware in / eld striken,	that be P	N E
A	1002	Hathils of hiʒe age, / Auncient kniʒtis,	/	A N
A	1003	Barons and bacheleris, / and / bryssid ware in Armes:	C	E be P N
A	1004	"Sire, we hafe farne to the fiʒt, / and bene in / fild preued	C be P	N E
A	1005	With ser Ph[ilip] ʒour fadire, / mony / fele wynter,	D	A N
A	1006	And now vs failis all oure force, / and oure / flesch waykis;	C D	N V
A	1007	For be the floure neuer sa fresche, / it / fadis at the last.	H	V Z
A	1008	Sire, all the ʒeris of oure ʒouthe, / es / ʒare syne passid,	be	Z C E
A	1009	And we for-trauailid and terid, / that now oure / topp haris,	that Z D	N N
A	1010	Al to heuy to be hildid, / in any / here wedis,	P D	N N
A	1011	Or any angwische of armes, / any / mare suffire.	Z	Z V
A	1012	For-thi, lord, with ʒoure leue, / we / lawe ʒow be-sechis	H	Z H V
A	1013	We may noʒt stand now in stede, / oure / strenth is [to] febill.	D	N be Z A
A	1014	Wale ʒow other werriouris, / that / wiʒt ere and ʒonger,	that	A be C A
A	1015	Slike as ere stife in a stoure, / strakis to thole."	/	N to V
A	1016	"Nay, be my croune," quod the king, / "my / couatyng is elder	D	N be A
A	1017	The sadnes of slike men, / than / swyftnes of childir;	C	N P N
A	1018	For barnes in thar bignes, / it / baldis tham mekill,	H	V H Z
A	1019	Oft with vnprouednes in presse, / to / pas out of lyfe;	to	V P P N
A	1020	For-thi, ouer-siʒt of alde men, / I / anely me chese;	H	Z H V
A	1021	Be connynge and be consaile, / thai / kyth ai thar werkis."	H	V Z D N
A	1022	The sleʒt of hys sapience, / thai / selcuthely prayse,	H	Z V
A	1023	And clene a-cordis to his carpe, / kniʒtis and othire.	/	N C H
A	1024	Then dose him furthe this dere kyng, / a litill / dais eftir,	Z	N P
A	1025	Alexander with ane ost, / of many / athill dukis,	P D	A N
A	1026	Samed a vnsene somme, / to / saile he begynnes	to	V H V
A	1027	Ouer in-to ytaile, / tha / yles to distruye.	D	N to V
A	1028	In-to the coste of Calodone, / he / comes him ouer first,	H	V H P Z
A	1029	And thar a cite he asailes, / and in / sege lengis.	C P	N V
A	1030	Bot wees wiʒtly / with-in, the / wallis ascendid,	Z D	N V
A	1031	Freschly fendid / of, and / fersly with-stude.	Z C	Z V
A	1032	"ʒe Calodoyns," quod the kyng, / he / callis fra with-oute,	H	V Z Z
A	1033	"Outhire macches ʒow maynly / therto, or / namely dies,	Z C	Z V
A	1034	And fiʒtis fast with ʒour fais, / to ʒe / fey worthe,	P H	A V
A	1035	Or ʒefes ʒarely vp the ʒerde, / and / ʒeld me the cite."	C	V H D N
A	1036	So chaunses it this chiftan, / or he / a-cheued thine,	C H	V H
A	1037	That fele he brenes of tha bernes, / and the / burʒe wynnes,	C D	N V
A	1038	And caires so out of Calodone, / quen he it / couerid had,	C H H	E have
A	1039	Ouer the ythes in-to Italee, / and that / Ile entirs.	C D	N V
A	1040	Then ware that [redles of] rede, / all / redd of his come,	Z	A P D N
A	1041	Prays him all of the pees, / and / presandis him faire,	C	V H Z
A	1042	Sexti thousand thai him send, / of / sekire besandis,	P	A N
A	1043	Of clere gold of thaire kist, / and / coruns a hundrethe.	C	N D N
A	1044	Thare tuke he tribute that tyme, / the / titill recordis,	D	N V
A	1045	Out euyn in-to the occident, / of / all at thare duellid,	P	Z that Z V
A	1046	Of qwilke the erde and the erthe, / Europe was callid,	/	N be E
A	1047	And ames than to Affrike, / and all at / esse leues.	C Z P	N V
A	1048	Than raʒt he fra tha regions, / and / removed his ost,	C	V D N
A	1049	Cachis in-to anothire kythe, / and / crossis ouer the stremes,	C	V P D N
A	1050	Aires in-to Affrike, / with many / athill prince[s],	P D	A N
A	1051	Another wing of the werd, / and / wynnes it be-lyfe,	C	V H Z
A	1052	That syde sodanly and sone, / that / ser he a-cheues.	D	N H V
A	1053	For that he fande bot fewe, / that / felly withstude,	that	Z V
A	1054	Na ridars in tha regions, / ne / rebell bot littill;	not	A C A
A	1055	He laches it the liʒtlyere, / as was the / les wonder.	C be D	A N
A	1056	Than kaires he fra tho contres, / and / kerue[s] ouer the stremes,	C	V P D N
A	1057	Furthe to Frantites he ferd, / slike a / ferre Ile,	D D	A N
A	1058	Seches flat to a synagoge, / him- / selfe and his princes,	H	self N C D N
A	1059	Amon thar awen god, / at thai / honoure myʒt.	Q H	V X
A	1060	And so to the temple as he tiʒt, / with his / tid Erles,	P D	A N

A	1061	Than metis him myddis the way, / was / meruale to sene,	be	N to V
A	1062	A hert with a huge hede, / the / hareest on erthe,	D	A P N
A	1063	Was to be-hald as a harow, / for-helid ouer the tyndis;	/	E P D N
A	1064	And than comande him the kyng, / kenely to schote,	/	Z to V
A	1065	Bot thar was na man so nemyll, / that / him hit couthe.	that	H H X
A	1066	"A! hilla, haile," quod Alexander, / and him a / narawe hent,	C H D	N V
A	1067	Droʒe, and at the first draʒte, / him / dreped for euire.	H	V Z
A	1068	Fra thethen to this ilk day, / than is that / ilke place,	C be D	A N
A	1069	The stede thar this stith man, / strikis this hert,	/	V D N
A	1070	Sagittarius forsoth, / men gafe it to name,	/	N V H to V
A	1071	And will do for that ilke werk, / ay qwen the / werd turnes.	Z C D	N V
A	1072	Then aires him on ser Alexander, / till / Amon temple,	P	N N
A	1073	Offirs to his awen gode, / and / honours him faire,	C	V H Z
A	1074	Geuys him garsons of gold, / and of / gud stanes,	C P	A N
A	1075	And hald hestes him to hete, / him / hettirly besekis.	H	Z V
A	1076	Than passes he thethen with his princes, / to sich a / place wendis,	P D D	N V
A	1077	Capho Resey we rede, / the / romaunce it callis;	D	N H V
A	1078	And thar-in fyndis him the freke, / fyftene Burghes,	/	A N
A	1079	And glidand to the grete see, / xij / grym waters.	D	A N
A	1080	Of ilka bild, sais the buke, / barred was the ʒatis,	/	E be D N
A	1081	Stoken stifly / with-out, with / staplis and cheynes.	Z P	N C N
A	1082	Thare lengis him lefe the kynge, / and / logis all a neuen,	C	V Z Z
A	1083	And sacrifyce thar efsones, / to many / sere godis.	P D	A N
A	1084	The same niʒt in his slepe, / Seraphis aperis,	/	N V
A	1085	Anothire of his grete godis, / in a / grym fourme,	P D	A N
A	1086	Cled in a comly clathe, / of / castans hewes,	P	N N
A	1087	And silis euyn to him-selfe, / and / said him thir wordis:	C	V H D N
A	1088	"Alexander, athill kyng", / and / asperly spekis,	C	Z V
A	1089	Toward a miʒti montayne, / him / myntis with his fynger,	H	V P D N
A	1090	"May thou oʒt, lede, the ʒonder lawe, / lyft on thi schulder,	/	V P D N
A	1091	And stire it oute of the stede, / and / stable in a-nothire?"	C	V P H
A	1092	"Nay, qua miʒt that," quod the man, / "for / mede vndire heuen?"	P	N P N
A	1093	"Sire, as ʒone ʒondire hiʒe hill, / sall / hald his place,	X	V D N
A	1094	So sall thi name fra now / furth, be / mynnde in mynde,	Z be	E P N
A	1095	And ay to the day of dome, / thi / dedis be remenbrid."	D	N be E
A	1096	Than Alexander belyue, / him / askis a demaunde,	H	V D N
A	1097	"I be-seche the now, Syraphas, / if thou me / say wald	C H H	V X
A	1098	(missing)		
A	1099	The prophecy, or thou pas, / of all my / playn werdis,	P D D	A N
A	1100	How me is destayned to dye, / and quen my / day fallis?"	C C D	N V
A	1101	"Sire, certayne," quod Seraphis, / "as to / my-selfe thinkis,	C P	H self V
A	1102	For any hathill vnder heuen, / I / hald for the better,	H	V P D N(A)
A	1103	Withouten wa noʒt at wete, / the / wathe of his ende	D	N P D N
A	1104	Then know the cas or it come, / and ay in / care lenge.	C Z P	N V
A	1105	Bot neuer-the-les I sall the neuen, / sen thou me / now prays,	C H H	Z V
A	1106	Thou sall be drechid of a drinke, / a / draʒte of vnsele,	D	N P N
A	1107	And all thi ʒeris ere ʒeten ʒare, / and thi / ʒouthe fenyst,	C D	N V
A	1108	Lange or thou haue meten the merke, / of thi / mydill age.	P D	A N
A	1109	Bot quen ne in quat time, / sal / qwaite the aunter,	X	V H D N
A	1110	Enquire me noʒt that question, / for I / queth the it neuer.	C H	V H H Z
A	1111	For outhire out of the orient, / sall / openly here-efter	X	Z Z
A	1112	Vndo the dreʒt of thi days, / and thi / ded tell."	C D	N V
A	1113	Than waynest him this vayne god, / and / voidis fra the chambre.	C	V P D N
A	1114	The modi kyng on the morne, / all / monand he ryses;	Z	G H V
A	1115	The mast parti of his princes, / and of his / proud ost	C P D	A N
A	1116	Hastis tham in-to Ascoiloym, / and to thar / rewme lede.	C Z H	H V
A	1117	Than callis he to him carpentaris, / and / comandis thaim swythe	C	V H Z
A	1118	In mynde and in memory / of him, to / make a cite,	P H to	V D N
A	1119	And neuens it his awen name, / that / neuer syne changid,	that	Z Z V
A	1120	Bot Alexsander ay / furth, efter him-seluen.	Z	P H self
A	1121	Now airis he furthe with his ost, / to / Egist he thinkes;	P	N H V
A	1122	And clene all the contre, / quen thai his / come herd,	C H D	N V
A	1123	As he had bene a hiʒe gode, / thai / ʒode him a-gayn,	H	V H P
A	1124	Resaued him with reuerence, / and to thar / rewme lokis,	C P D	N V
A	1125	There entirs him that Emperoure, / and in that / erd findis	C P D	N V
A	1126	Of Anec his awen sire, / ane / ymage of sable,	D	N P N
A	1127	A berne was of blake stane, / all the / body hewen	D D	N E
A	1128	With conyschance of a kynge, / with / coron and septere.	P	N C N
A	1129	Than askis of tham Alexander, / as he / thar-on lokis,	C H	Z V
A	1130	Quat maner of man apon mold, / it was / made efter?	H be	E Z
A	1131	"Sire, Anectabus", / quod / all with a steuen,	V	H P D N

A	1132	"That all the erth of Egipte, / enerid vmquile."	/	E Z
A	1133	With that the flammand flode, / fell in his eзen,	/	V P D N
A	1134	"That Anec," quod this athil kyng, / "was myne / awen fadire."	be D	A N
A	1135	Than fallis he flat on the fold, / and the / fete kyssis;	C D	N V
A	1136	On the stane quare it stode, / stilly he mournes.	/	Z H V
A	1137	Syne in-to Sirie with his seggis, / he / soзt at the gaynest,	H	V P D N(A)
A	1138	And thai as baratours bald, / him / bigly with-standis,	H	Z V
A	1139	Set on him sadly, / and / sloзe of his kniзtis;	C	V P D N
A	1140	Bot зet зarely are he зode, / thai / зald him the regne.	H	V H D N
A	1141	Than drafe he sa to Damac, / with / dukis and princes,	P	N C N
A	1142	And sone he sesyd all that syde, / and / Sydoyne he takis,	C	N H V
A	1143	And then trussis him to Tyre, / and thare his / tentis settis	C Z D	N V
A	1144	Be-syde the cite with a some, / and in a / sege lengys.	C P D	N V
A	1145	Thare he lies with his ledis, / lang or he foundes,	/	Z C H V
A	1146	Before the burзe with his bernes, / and mekill / bale suffirs.	C D	N V
A	1147	Quat of ane, quat of othire, / oft his / oste pleynes,	Z D	N V
A	1148	For wele wist thai tham nane, / to / wyn the cite,	to	V P D N
A	1149	It was sa stiffe and sa strang, / and / stalworthly wallid,	C	Z E
A	1150	And so hedously hiзe, / it was a / huge wondire,	H be D	A N
A	1151	Tildid full of turestis, / and / toures of defence,	C	N P N
A	1152	Batailid and bretagid, / a-boute as a castell.	/	Z P D N
A	1153	The wawis of the wild see, / apon the / wallis betis,	P D	N V
A	1154	The pure populande hurle, / passis it vmby,	/	V H Z
A	1155	It was enforced with sa fele, / fludis and othire,	/	N C H
A	1156	It semed neuer sege vnder son, / be / saute it to wyn.	P	N H to V
A	1157	Than etils him sir Alexander, / and / belyue makis	C	Z V
A	1158	Be-side the cite in the See, / to / sett vp a loge,	to	V Z D N
A	1159	A hiзe tilde as a toure, / teldid on schippis,	/	E P N
A	1160	That miзt na Naue for that note, / neзe to the cite.	/	V P D N
A	1161	Quen he this baistell had bild, / vp to the / burзe wallis,	P P D	N N
A	1162	And tiзt him as tyme / was, the / toune to assaill,	be D	N to V
A	1163	Slik mischife in the mene quile, / emang his / men fallis,	P D	N V
A	1164	For megire and for meteles, / ware / mervaile to here.	be	N to V
A	1165	Thar was Princes in poynt, / to / perisch for euire,	to	V Z
A	1166	Alle in doute to be dede, / dukis and erlis,	/	N C N
A	1167	In fere to be famyschist, / many / fers kniзtis,	D	A N
A	1168	For thar is na wa in the werd, / to the / wode hunger.	P D	A N
A	1169	Than pleynis with the proud kyng, / the / pete of his men,	D	N P D N
A	1170	And sendis out his sandis-men, / with / selid lettirs,	P	E N
A	1171	To ierusalem to Iaudis, / at the / iewes teches,	that D	N V
A	1172	That was the bischop in that burзe, / breuyd in the dais;	/	E P D N
A	1173	Him moneste as a maister, / him / maynly to send	H	Z to V
A	1174	Fresch folke for the fiзt, / and / fode for his oste,	C	N P N
A	1175	And all the trouage thare / to him, / tittly to wayne,	P H	Z to V
A	1176	That he to Darius of dewe, / was / dangird to paye.	be	E to V
A	1177	And зit comand he this clerke, / for / kyng in his writtes,	D	N P D N
A	1178	For any richas him redis, / rathere to thole	/	Z to V
A	1179	The mayntenance of the Messedoyns, / and of the / meri Grekis,	C P D	A N
A	1180	Than thaim of Persy to pay, / or to / plese authere.	C to	V Z
A	1181	Than takis the bischop the breue, / and / buзes to a chambre,	C	V P D N
A	1182	Resayued it with reuerence, / and / redis it oiure,	C	V H P
A	1183	Gase him doun be degrece, / a-gayne to the sale,	/	P P D N
A	1184	Swiftly to the swiars, / and tham his / sware зeldis:	C H D	N V
A	1185	"Sirs, airis a-gayn to Alexander, / and / all thus him tellis,	C	H C H V
A	1186	That me was done many day, / depely to swere,	/	Z to V
A	1187	Neuer Persy to paire, / to / pas with myne armes	to	V P D N
A	1188	In damaging of Darius, / durand his lyfe."	/	P D N
A	1189	Sone as the wale kyng wist, / he / writhis him vnfaire,	H	V H Z
A	1190	"Now be that god," quod the gome, / "that / gatt me on erthe,	that	V H P N
A	1191	I sall anes on the iewis, / enioyne or I die,	/	V C H V
A	1192	Sall ken tham quas comandment, / to / kepe at tham fall."	to	V Q H V
A	1193	зit for na torfar him tid, / Tyre wald he noзt leue,	/	N X H not V
A	1194	Bot chese him out a chiftane, / and / charge[s] him belyue,	C	V H Z
A	1195	A mody man, ser Meliager, / a / maister of his oste,	D	N P D N
A	1196	To fande him furth with a flote, / of / fyue hundreth kniзtis;	P	A A N
A	1197	A[nd] Ioynes him to Iosaphat, / his / iournay to take,	D	N to V
A	1198	And all the pastours and the playnes, / prestly to driue,	/	Z to V
A	1199	And bring in all the bestaill, / barayn and othire,	/	N C H
A	1200	That he miзt se on any syde, / the / cite of Gadirs.	D	N P N
A	1201	Than mouys he on, ser Meliager, / this / miзtfull prince	D	A N
A	1202	With a soume of sekir men, / and / Sampson tham ledis,	C	N H V

A	1203	A renke at in tha regions, / had / redyn oft sythis,	have	E Z
A	1204	And knew the costis and the kitthis, / clene all-to-gedire.	/	Z Z
A	1205	Thus ȝede thai furthe egirly, / and / entirs the vaile,	C	V D N
A	1206	And slike a prai tham apreued, / as / pyne were to reken,	C	N be to V
A	1207	Bryngis furthe, sayd the boke, / bestis out of nounbre,	/	N P P N
A	1208	And trottes on toward Tyre, / with / taite at thaire hertis.	P	N P D N
A	1209	Bot or thai meten ware a myle, / the / meris with-outen,	D	N P
A	1210	Thar metis thaim with a mekill flote, / the / maistir of the playnes,	D	N P D N
A	1211	He that was duke of the droues, / and of the / derfe hillis,	C P D	A N
A	1212	Ane Theosellus, a tulke, / that / tened tham vnfaire.	that	V H Z
A	1213	He girdis in with a ging, / armed in plates,	/	E P N
A	1214	Alto-bruntes oure bernes, / and / brathly woundid,	C	Z E
A	1215	Fellis fele at a frusch, / fey to the gronde,	/	A P D N
A	1216	And many renke at he roue, / rase neuer efter.	/	V Z Z
A	1217	Than was ser Meliager moued, / and / maynly debatis,	C	Z V
A	1218	Flingis out on a fole, / with a / fell spere,	P D	A N
A	1219	Gers many grete syre grane, / and / girdis thurȝe maillis,	C	N P N
A	1220	And many bernes at a braide, / in his / brath endis.	P D	N V
A	1221	And Sampson on anothire side, / setis out belyue,	/	V Z Z
A	1222	Bruschis furth on a blonk, / brymly he smytis,	/	Z H V
A	1223	Betis on with a brande, / broken was his lance,	/	E be D N
A	1224	Hewis doun of tha hirdis, / hurtis tham vn-faire.	/	V H Z
A	1225	Arystes, ane athill man, / ai / elike fiȝtis,	Z	Z V
A	1226	Spirris out with a spere, / and / spedis his miȝtis,	C	V D N
A	1227	And noyed of thare note-men, / at the / nete kepid,	P D	A N
A	1228	And many bald, or he blan, / broȝt out o-lyue.	/	V P P N
A	1229	Caulus, anothire kniȝt, / on a / kene stede,	P D	A N
A	1230	On Theosellus in twa, / his / tymbre he brekis;	D	N H V
A	1231	And than he dryfes to the duke, / as / demys the textis,	C	V D N
A	1232	And with a swyng of a swerd, / swappis of hes hede.	/	V Z D N
A	1233	When he was drepid and dede, / at the / droues ȝemyd,	P D	N V
A	1234	The prekars of the pastors, / and of the / proude landis,	C P D	A N
A	1235	All the folke of his affinite, / at / fresch ware vn-wondid,	that	A be E
A	1236	That outhire fote had or fole, / to the / fliȝt foundid.	P D	N E
A	1237	Thus Meliager with his men, / the / menske has a-chevyd,	D	N have E
A	1238	For the fairere of thar faes, / and the / fild wonn;	C D	N E
A	1239	Raschis with rethere, / and / rydis bot a quyle,	C	V Z Z
A	1240	That ne neȝis tham a-nothire note, / as / new as the first.	C	A C D H
A	1241	Thare was a maister of the marches, / miȝtist of othire	/	A P H
A	1242	Ane Beritinus, a berne, / as the / buke tellis,	C D	N V
A	1243	Come girdand out of Gadirs, / out of the / grete cite,	P P D	A N
A	1244	With the selcuthest soume, / that / semblid was euire.	that	E be Z
A	1245	Slik a mynd vn-to me, / ware / meruaill to reken,	be	N to V
A	1246	Thretti thousand in thede, / of / thra men of armes,	P	A N P N
A	1247	Slike as was buskest on blonkes, / in / brenys and platis,	P	N C N
A	1248	And othire folawand on fote, / fele with-outen nounbre,	/	A P N
A	1249	The multitude was sa mekill, / as / mynes vs the writtis,	C	V H D N
A	1250	Of wees and of wild horsis, / and / wapened prenys,	C	A N
A	1251	Sa stithe a steuyn in the stoure, / of / stedis and ellis,	P	N C Z
A	1252	As it was semand to siȝt, / as all the / soyle trymblid.	C D D	N V
A	1253	Than ware the Messedones amayd, / quen tha / see sa many,	C H	V Z H
A	1254	Sire Meliager [was] in gret mynd, / a / man out to sende	D	N Z to V
A	1255	To ser Alexander belyue, / thaire / allire maister,	D	A N
A	1256	To come and help with his here, / or thai to / hande ȝode.	C H P	N V
A	1257	Thare was nane that was glad, / that / message to gange,	D	N to V
A	1258	Bot ilka lathire and othire, / to / leue thaire frynde,	to	V D N
A	1259	Fest thar forward in-fere, / that / fewe at thai ware,	that	A Q H be
A	1260	To do as driȝten wald deme, / and / dyi all to-gedire;	C	V Z Z
A	1261	To telle thaire torfere entyre, / it / taryed me swythe.	H	V H Z
A	1262	Bot so the mode Meliager, / and his / men feȝtis,	C D	N V
A	1263	That ser Beritinus the bald, / thai / bretned to dethe,	H	V P N
A	1264	And Sampson on this side, / was / slay thar-agaynys.	be	E Z
A	1265	Then mournes all the Messedones, / and / maynten him ȝerne,	C	V H Z
A	1266	Makis thar mane for that man, / and / many othire noble,	C	A A N(A)
A	1267	For maistris and mynistris, / menere and grettir,	/	Z C Z
A	1268	That was in morsels magged, / and / martrid a hundreth.	C	V D N
A	1269	And that left ware on lyfe, / bot a / litill meȝne,	P D	A N
A	1270	Ware als malstrid and mased, / and / matid of thaire strenthes,	C	E P D N
A	1271	Sa waike and so wyndles, / and / wery for-foȝten,	C	A E
A	1272	That thai were will in this werd, / qwat thai / worthe suld.	Q H	V X
A	1273	Sire Meliager and othire maa, / mayned were sare,	/	E be Z

A	1274	All be-bled and to-brissid, / that neȝe thar / breth failes,	that Z D	N V
A	1275	Thai were sa feble and sa faynt, / and / full of thaim-selfe,	C	A P H self
A	1276	That all in fere was in fourme, / the / fild for to ȝeld.	D	N for to V
A	1277	Than aires him forth Arestes, / was / augrily wondid,	be	Z E
A	1278	To Alexander onone, / thas / auntirs him tellis,	D	N H V
A	1279	The morth of all the Messedone[s], / and of the / many grekis,	C P D	A N
A	1280	Rekens him thar resons, / that / reuthe was to here.	D	N be to V
A	1281	With that the semely kyng, / chacches his bernes,	/	V D N
A	1282	Semblis him a huge soume, / and fra the / sege wendis,	C P D	N V
A	1283	The toure of Tire and the toune, / titly he leues,	/	Z H V
A	1284	And Ioynes him to Iosaphat, / full / ioyles he rydes.	Z	Z H V
A	1285	Ay he gretis as he gase, / for / grefe of his knyȝtis,	P	N P D N
A	1286	Ay he pleynys as he passes, / the / pite of his erlis,	D	N P D N
A	1287	Ay he wepis as he wendis, / for his / wale princes,	P D	A N
A	1288	And soueraynly for Sampson, / he / sorowis ay elike.	H	V Z Z
A	1289	When he was tane fraward Tyre, / toward the vaile,	/	P D N
A	1290	The werke at he wroȝt had, / that / water whyt-in,	D	N P
A	1291	That he had sett in the see, / the / cite with-out,	D	N P
A	1292	Thar-in he lefte had a lede, / the / loge for to kepe.	D	N for to V
A	1293	Bot than ser Balaan, a berne, / at in the / burȝe lengis,	that P D	N V
A	1294	Ane of the terands of Tyre, / atyres him belyue,	/	V H Z
A	1295	Buskes him in breneis, / with / big men of armes,	P	A N P N
A	1296	With traumes and with tribochetis, / the / tild to asaile.	D	N to V
A	1297	He bekirs out at the bild, / within the / burȝe-wallis,	P D	N N
A	1298	And thai without in the werke, / wiȝtly defendis,	/	Z V
A	1299	Schot scharply / betwene, / schomes of dartis;	Z	N P N
A	1300	Weris wondirly wele, / werpis out stanes.	/	V Z N
A	1301	Bot Balaa[n] in the barmeken, / sa / bitterly fiȝtis,	Z	Z V
A	1302	All to-combirs tham clene, / with / cast of engynes.	P	N P N
A	1303	Sone the top of the toure, / he / tiltis in-to the watir,	H	V P D N
A	1304	And all the tulkis in the tild, / he / termens o lyue;	H	V P N
A	1305	And than in batis and in bargis, / he / bownes him swyth,	H	V H Z
A	1306	To the bothum of the baistell, / he / buskis him with-out,	H	V H P
A	1307	Bretens doun all the bild, / and the / bernys quellis,	C D	N V
A	1308	Drenches hire in the hiȝe see, / and / drawis hire on hepis.	C	V H P N
A	1309	Quen it was smeten in small, / with the / smert waȝes,	P D	A N
A	1310	Ilka gobet his gate, / glidis fra othire.	/	V P H
A	1311	Thus the strenth ilk stike, / was in a / stounde wasted,	be P D	N E
A	1312	And Balaa[n] bowis in-to the burȝe, / and / barris to the ȝatis.	C	V P D N
A	1313	Be this oure kyng with his kniȝt[is], / is / comen in-to the vaile,	be	E P D N
A	1314	Alexander with ane ost, / his / kniȝtis to help,	D	N to V
A	1315	Fyndis a fewe of his folke, / feȝtand ȝerne,	/	G Z
A	1316	And ay a segge be him-selfe, / sett all a hundreth.	/	E D D N
A	1317	With that Bucifalon his blonke, / he / brased in the side,	H	V P D N
A	1318	Springis out with a spere, / spillis at the gaynest,	/	V P D N(A)
A	1319	Ridis euen thurȝe the route, / thar / rankest thai were,	Q	A H be
A	1320	Be rawe of thar rabetis, / he / ruschid to the erthe,	H	V P D N
A	1321	He strikis all fra thar stedis, / streȝt him be-forne.	/	Z H P
A	1322	Was nane sa stiffe in that stoure, / miȝt / stand him agayn;	X	V H P
A	1323	Quare althire-thickest was the thrange, / thurȝe thaim he rynnes,	/	P H H V
A	1324	And makis a wai wyde / enoȝe, / waynes to mete.	Z	N to V
A	1325	He laschis out a lange swerde, / quen his / launce failes,	C D	N V
A	1326	Threschis doun in a thrawe, / many / threuyn dukis,	D	E N
A	1327	Stirs him sa in a stonde, / and his / stithe erlis	C D	A N
A	1328	That thar was [na] berne on bent, / bott / bretened or ȝolden.	C	E C E
A	1329	The seggis on hew awen side, / that he / slayn fyndis,	that H	E V
A	1330	He mas to graue sum in grete, / and sum in / gray marble.	C H P	A N
A	1331	And tha that laft ware o-lyue, / he / lokis thar woundis,	H	V D N
A	1332	And faire fangis his folke, / and fra the / fild wendis.	C P D	N V
A	1333	Than bowes he to the baistall, / and / brymly it semblis,	C	Z H V
A	1334	Gedirs of ilk glode, / grettir and smallire,	/	A C A
A	1335	And prekis furth with his pray, / and / passes fraward Gadirs,	C	V Z N
A	1336	And tiȝt agayne toward Tyre, / to / termen his sege.	to	V D N
A	1337	Quen he was dreuyn ouer the dales, / and / drewe to the cite,	C	V P D N
A	1338	With that he blisches to the burȝe, / and sees his / bild voidid,	C V D	N E
A	1339	Als bare as a bast, / his / baistell a-way,	D	N Z
A	1340	But outhire burde or bate, / bot the / brade wattir,	P D	A N
A	1341	Than mournes all the Messadones, / and / maynly was sturb[i]d.	C	Z be E
A	1342	And Alexander also, / was / augrely greuyd,	be	Z E
A	1343	So ware thai troubild out of tone, / quen thai thaire / tild miste,	C H D	N V
A	1344	That of the taking of Tire, / trest thai na langire.	/	V H Z

A	1345	And so him-selfe in his slepe, / the / same niȝt eftir,	D	A N P
A	1346	Him thoȝt he had in his hand, / and / held of a vyne	C	V P D N
A	1347	A growen grape of a grype, / a / grete and a rype,	D	N(A) C D N(A)
A	1348	The quilke he flange on the flore, / and with his / fete tredis.	C P D	N V
A	1349	And quen he broken had the bery, / als the / berne semes,	C D	N V
A	1350	Thar folowis out of fresche wyne, / feetles to mete;	/	N to V
A	1351	So largely and so delauyly, / of / licoure, him thinkis,	P	N H V
A	1352	Of ane rasyn to ryn, / it was a / ryfe wondire.	H be D	A N
A	1353	The kyng callis him a clerke, / kenely on the morne,	/	Z P D N
A	1354	Als radly as he rase, / to / reche him his sweuyn.	to	V H D N
A	1355	"Sire, bees a-dred neuir a dele" , / the / diuinour said,	D	N V
A	1356	"I vndire-take on my trouthe, / Tire is thine awen;	/	N be D A(N)
A	1357	For the bery at ȝe brake / sa, is the / burȝe euen.	Z be D	N Z
A	1358	Thai sall be sesid the full sone, / and to / thi-selfe ȝolden,	C P	H self V
A	1359	For thou sall eft all on ernest, / entire on the wallis,	/	V P D N
A	1360	And foulire vndir thi feete, / with-in a / fewe days.	P D	A N
A	1361	Now compas kenely this kyng, / and / castis in his mynd	C	V P D N
A	1362	How he miȝt couir in any cas, / to / come to the cite,	to	V P D N
A	1363	Deuynes depely on dais, / dropis many wiles,	/	V D N
A	1364	If he cuthe seke any sleȝt, / that him / serue wald;	that H	V X
A	1365	And makis to sett in the see, / riȝt in the / same place,	Z P D	A N
A	1366	Thar as the bild at he bi[l]did, / biggid wasse first,	/	E be Z
A	1367	To stable vp a grete strenthe, / all on / store schipis,	Z P	A N
A	1368	Hugir be the halfe dele, / and / hiȝere than the tothire;	C	A C D H
A	1369	And that he fiches and firmes, / sa / fast to the wall,	Z	Z P D N
A	1370	So nere vnethes at ane eld, / miȝt / narowly betwene,	X	Z Z
A	1371	And band hire, as the buke / sais, / bigly to-gedire,	V	Z Z
A	1372	With that scho flisch nother fayle, / fyue score aunkirs.	/	A A N
A	1373	Quen he had tiȝt vp this tram, / and this / tild rerid,	C D	N V
A	1374	Hit had of bradnes abofe, / to / breue out of mesure;	to	V P P N
A	1375	And to hede be a huge thing, / hiȝere it semed	/	A H V
A	1376	Than was the wallis, sais the writt, / of the / wale touris.	P D	A N
A	1377	Than Alexander all his ane, / an-ane he ascendis,	/	Z H V
A	1378	Closid all in clere stele, / and in / clene plates.	C P	A N
A	1379	And monestis ilk modire son, / maynly and swyth,	/	Z C Z
A	1380	That all be bowne at a brayd, / the / burȝe to assaile.	D	N to V
A	1381	And all the ost euyn ouir, / he / openly comandis	H	Z V
A	1382	To be radly all arayd, / and / redy to fiȝt;	C	A to V
A	1383	And quen thai saȝe that him-selfe, / the / cite was entrid,	D	N be E
A	1384	Wan vp wiȝtly on the wallis, / ilk / wee him eftir.	D	N H P
A	1385	Now tenelis vp taburs, / and all the / toun rengis,	C D D	N V
A	1386	Steryn steuyn vp strake, / strakid thar trumpis,	/	V D N
A	1387	Blewe bemys of bras, / bernes assemblis,	/	N V
A	1388	Seȝes to on ilk syde, / and a / saute ȝeldis.	C D	N V
A	1389	Thare presis to with paues, / peple withouten;	/	N P
A	1390	Archars with arows, / of / atter envemonde	P	N E
A	1391	Schotis vp scharply, / at / shalkis on the wallis,	P	N P D N
A	1392	Lasch at tham of loft, / many / lede floȝen,	D	N V
A	1393	And thai ȝapely a-ȝayne, / and / ȝildis tham swythe,	C	V H Z
A	1394	Bekire out of the burȝe, / bald men many,	/	A N A
A	1395	Kenely thai kast / of, with / kastis of stanys,	Z P	N P N
A	1396	Driues dartis at oure dukis, / dedly tham woundid.	/	Z H Z
A	1397	Than passe vp oure princes, / prestly enarmed,	/	Z E
A	1398	In-to the baistell a-bofe, / bremely ascendid,	/	Z V
A	1399	Sum with lances on-loft, / and with / lange swerdis,	C P	A N
A	1400	With ax and with alblaster, / and / alkens wapen.	/	A N
A	1401	Alexander ai elike, / augrily feȝtis,	/	Z V
A	1402	Now a schaft, now a schild, / nowe a / scheue hentis,	Z D	N V
A	1403	Now a sparth, now a spere, / and / sped so his miȝtis,	C	V Z D N
A	1404	That it ware tere any tonge, / to of his / turnes rekyn.	to Z D	N V
A	1405	And thai with-in on the wall, / worthili with-stude,	/	Z V
A	1406	Fersly defend of, / and / fellid of his knyȝtis,	C	V P D N
A	1407	Thristis ouir thikefald, / many / threuyn berne[s],	D	E N
A	1408	And doun bakward tham bare, / in-to the / brad wattir.	P D	A N
A	1409	With that oure wees without, / writhis tham vnfare,	/	V H Z
A	1410	Went wode of thaire witt, / and / wrekis tham swyth;	C	V H Z
A	1411	For na wounde ne na wathe, / wand thai na langir,	/	V H Z
A	1412	Bot all wirkis him the wa, / and / wrake at he cuthe.	C	N that H X
A	1413	Sum braidis to thar bowis, / bremely thai schut,	/	Z H V
A	1414	Quethirs out quarels, / quikly be-twene;	/	Z Z
A	1415	Strykis vp of the stoure, / stanes of engynes,	/	N P N

A	1416	That the bretage a-boue, / brast all in soundire,	/	V Z Z
A	1417	Girdis ouir garettis, / with / gomes to the erthe,	P	N P D N
A	1418	Tilt torettis / doun, / toures on hepis,	Z	N P N
A	1419	Spedely with sprygaldis, / spilt thaire braynes,	/	V D N
A	1420	Many miȝtfull man, / marris on the wallis.	/	E P D N
A	1421	And be the kirnells ware kast, / and / kutt doun before,	C	E Z Z
A	1422	Be that the baistell and the burȝe, / ware / bathe elike hiȝe,	be	Z Z A
A	1423	And all oure werke without the wallis, / weterly semed,	/	Z V
A	1424	The sidis of the cite, / to / se to o fernes,	to	V P P N
A	1425	Than Alexander belyf, / on tham / all entris,	P H	Z V
A	1426	Bruschis in with a brand, / on / bernes a hundreth,	P	N D N
A	1427	Thrang thurȝe a thousand, / thare / thikest thai were,	Q	A H be
A	1428	Wynnes worthly ouer the wallis, / with-in to the cite.	/	P P D N
A	1429	The first modire son he mett, / othire / man outhire,	D	N Z
A	1430	Was Balaan the bald berne, / as the / boke tellis,	C D	N V
A	1431	And him he settis on a saute, / and / sloȝe him belyue,	C	V H Z
A	1432	And werpid him out ouir the wall, / in-to the / wild streme.	P D	A N
A	1433	Sone as oure athils be-hind, / saȝe thar he entred,	/	V Q H V
A	1434	His men and all the Messedones, / maynly ascendis,	/	Z V
A	1435	And thai of Grece gredely, / girdis vp eftire,	/	V Z Z
A	1436	Thringis vp on a thraw, / thousandis many.	/	N A
A	1437	Sum stepis vp on sties, / to the / stane wallis,	P D	N N
A	1438	On ilka staffe of a staire, / stike wald a cluster;	/	V X D N
A	1439	And qua sa leddirs had nane, / as the / lyne tellis,	C D	N V
A	1440	Wald gett tham hald with thar hend, / and / on-loft clyme.	C	Z V
A	1441	Sa freȝt ware thar othire, / that / feȝtis within,	that	V Z
A	1442	For Balaan thar bald duke, / that / broȝt was of lyue,	that	E be P N
A	1443	That all failis tham the force, / and so / ferd worthe,	C Z	A V
A	1444	That nothire with stafe ne with stane, / withstand thai na langir.	/	V H Z
A	1445	Sire Alexander with his athils, / and his / awen sleȝtis	C D	A N
A	1446	The toune of Tire thus he tuke, / and othire / twa burȝes,	C D	A N
A	1447	In the quilke the siriens of this sire, / so many / soroȝes had,	D D	N V
A	1448	As wald bot tary all oure tale, / thaire / tourment to reken.	D	N to V
A	1449	Sone as this cite was sesid, / and / slayne vp and ȝolden,	C	E Z C E
A	1450	Then ridis furth the riche kyng, / and / removed his ost,	C	V D N
A	1451	Gais him furth to Gasa, / a-nothire / grete cite,	D	A N
A	1452	And that he settis on a saute, / and / sesis it be-lyue;	C	V H Z
A	1453	And quen this Gasa was geten, / he / graythis him swyth,	H	V H Z
A	1454	And Ioynes him toward Ierusalem, / the / iewis to distroy;	D	N to V
A	1455	And ȝe that kepis of this carpe, / to / knaw any ferre,	to	V Z
A	1456	Sone sall I neuen ȝow the note, / that is / next eftir.	that be	A Z
A	1457	Als hastily as thai herd / of, in the / haly cite,	Z P D	A N
A	1458	And bodword to the bischop, / broȝt of his come,	/	V Z D N
A	1459	For Alexander aȝe, / almast he euen deis,	/	Z H Z V
A	1460	For he had nite him a nerand, / noȝt bot o / new time.	not P P	A N
A	1461	And now him thinke in his thoȝt, / him / thurt noȝt haue carid	H	V not have E
A	1462	In all his mast mystir, / nad he that / man faylid,	X H D	N V
A	1463	When he for socure to the cite, / sent him his lettir;	/	V H D N
A	1464	And he soyned him to his sorement, / that / sare him forthinkis.	that	Z H V
A	1465	"For me had leuer," quod the lede, / "be / lethirely forsworn	be	Z E
A	1466	On as many halidoms, / as / opens and speris,	C	V C V
A	1467	Than anys haue greuyd that gome, / or / warned him his erand!	C	E H D N
A	1468	That euer I warned him his will, / wa is me that stonde!"	/	N be H D N
A	1469	Thus was Iaudes of ioy, / and / iolite depryued;	C	N E
A	1470	And all the iewis of ierusalem, / he / Ioyntly a-sembles.	H	Z V
A	1471	He said, "Alexander is at hand, / and will vs / all cumbre,	C X H	Z V
A	1472	And we ere dredles vndone, / bot / driȝten vs help."	C	N H V
A	1473	Than bedis the bischop all the burȝe, / barnes and othire,	/	N C H
A	1474	Athils of all age, / eldire and ȝongire,	/	A C A
A	1475	Comandis to ilka creatour, / to / crie thurȝe the stretis,	to	V P D N
A	1476	To thre dais on a thrawe, / be / threpild to-gedire,	be	E Z
A	1477	Ilk frek and ilka fante, / to / fast and to pray,	to	V C to V
A	1478	To ocupy thar oures and orisons, / and / offire in thar temple,	C	V P D N
A	1479	And call vp with a clene voice, / to the / kyng of heuyn,	P D	N P N
A	1480	To kepe tham, at this conquiroure, / encumbrid thaim neuir.	/	V H Z
A	1481	Now seȝen thai to thar Sinagogis, / all the / cite ouire,	Z D	N P
A	1482	Ilka bodi thar bedis, / that in the / burȝe lengis,	that P D	N V
A	1483	Putt tham to prayris, / and / penaunce enduris,	C	N V
A	1484	The vengance of this victoure, / to / voide if thai miȝt.	to	V C H X
A	1485	The niȝt eftire the note, / as / tellis me the writtes,	C	V H D N
A	1486	Quen all the cite was on-slepe, / and / sacrifis endid,	C	N V

The Wars of Alexander 291

A	1487	In ane abite of the aire, / ane / Aungell aperis	D	N V
A	1488	To Iaudas of ierusalem, / and him with / ioy gretis:	C H P	N V
A	1489	"I bringe the bodword of blis, / ser / bischop," he said,	D	N H V
A	1490	"With salutis of solas, / I am / sent fra the trone,	H be	E P D N
A	1491	Fra the maister of man, / the / miȝtfull fadere,	D	A N
A	1492	That bedis the noȝt be a-baist, / he has thi / bone herd;	H have D	N E
A	1493	And I amonest the to-morne, / as / I am enIoyned,	C	H be E
A	1494	That thou as radly as thou rise, / aray all the cite,	/	V D D N
A	1495	The stretis and in all stedis, / stoutly and faire,	/	Z C Z
A	1496	That it be onest all ouire, / and / open vp the ȝatis.	C	V Z D N
A	1497	Lett than the pupill ilka poll, / apareld be clene,	/	E be A
A	1498	And al manere of men, / in / mylk-quyte clathis.	P	A N
A	1499	And pas, thou and thi prelatis, / and / prestis of the temple,	C	N P D N
A	1500	Raueste all on a raw, / as ȝoure / rewill askis.	C D	N V
A	1501	And quen this conquirour comes, / caire him agaynes;	/	V H P
A	1502	For he mon ride thus and regne, / ouire all the / ronde werde	P D D	A N
A	1503	Be lordship in ilka lede, / in-to his / laste days,	P D	A N
A	1504	And then be diȝt to the deth, / of / driȝtins ire."	P	N N
A	1505	Sone the derke ouire-drafe, / and the / day springis,	C D	N V
A	1506	Oure bischop bounes him of bed, / and / buskis on his wedis,	C	V P D N
A	1507	And then iogis, all the iewis, / and / generall callis,	C	A N
A	1508	A-vaies thaim his vision, / how the / voice bedis;	Q D	N V
A	1509	Than consals him the clergy, / clene all-to-gedire,	/	Z Z
A	1510	And all the cite asentis, / sarazens and othir,	/	N C H
A	1511	To buwne furth with all the burȝe, / and / buske tham belyue,	C	V H Z
A	1512	As him was said in his slepe, / this / souerayn to mete.	D	N to V
A	1513	Than rynnes he furth in a rase, / and / arais all the cite,	C	V D D N
A	1514	Braidis ouire with bawdkyns, / all the / brade stretis,	D D	A N
A	1515	With tars and with tafeta, / thar he / trede sulde,	Q H	V X
A	1516	For the erth to slike ane Emperoure, / ware / ouire feble.	be	Z A
A	1517	He plyes ouire the pauement, / with / pallen webis,	P	A N
A	1518	Mas on hiȝt ouire his hede, / for / hete of the sone,	P	N P D N
A	1519	Sylours of sendale, / to / sele ouire the gatis,	to	V P D N
A	1520	And sammes thaim on aithire side, / with / silken rapis,	P	A N
A	1521	And then he caggis vp on cordis, / as / curteyns it were,	C	N H be
A	1522	Euen as the esyngis ȝede, / ouire be the costes,	/	P P D N
A	1523	All the wawis with-oute, / in / webis of ynde,	P	N P N
A	1524	Of briȝt blasand blewe, / browden with sternes.	/	E P N
A	1525	Thus atired he the toune, / and / titely thar-eftir	C	Z Z
A	1526	On ilka way wid open, / werped he the ȝatis;	/	V H D N
A	1527	And qua so lukis fra with-out, / and / with-in haldis,	C	P N
A	1528	It semyd as the cite to se, / ane of the / seuyn heuyns.	H P D	A N
A	1529	Now passis furth this prelate, / with / prestis of the temple,	P	N P D N
A	1530	Reueschid him rially, / and that in / riche wedis,	C that P	A N
A	1531	With erst and abite vndire all, / as / I am in-fourmede,	C	H be E
A	1532	Fulle of bridis and of bestis, / of / bise and of purpre;	P	N C P N
A	1533	And that was garnest full gay, / with / golden skirtis,	P	A N
A	1534	Store starand stanes, / strekilland all ouire,	/	G Z Z
A	1535	Saudid full of safirs, / and othire / sere gemmes,	C D	A N
A	1536	And poudird with perry, / was / perrour and othire.	be	A C H
A	1537	And sithen he castis on a Cape, / of / kastand hewes,	P	N N
A	1538	With riche rabies of gold, / railed hi the hemmes,	/	E P D N
A	1539	A vestoure to vise on, / of / violet floures,	P	A N
A	1540	Wroȝt full of wodwose, / and other / wild bestis;	C D	A N
A	1541	And than him hiȝtild his hede, / and / had on a Mitre,	C	V P D N
A	1542	Was forgid all of fyne gold, / and / fret full of perrils,	C	E Z P N
A	1543	Stiȝt staffull of stanes, / that / straȝt out bemes,	that	V Z N
A	1544	As it ware shemerand shaftis, / of the / shire son.	P D	A N
A	1545	Doctours and diuinours, / and othire / dere maistris,	C D	A N
A	1546	Iustis of iewry, / and / iogis of the lawe,	C	N P D N
A	1547	Ware tired all in tonacles, / of / tarrayn webbis;	P	A N
A	1548	Thai were bret-full of bees, / all the / body ouire,	D D	N P
A	1549	And other clientis and clerkis, / as to the / kirke fallis,	P P D	N V
A	1550	Ware all samen of a soyte, / in / surples of raynes,	P	N P N
A	1551	That slike a siȝt, I suppose, / was neuer / sene eftire,	be Z	E Z
A	1552	So parailed a procession, / a / person a-gaynes.	D	N P
A	1553	Now bowis furth the bischop, / at the / burȝe ȝatis,	P D	N N
A	1554	With prestis and with prelatis, / a / pake out of nombre;	D	N P P N
A	1555	And all the cite in sorte, / felowis him eftir,	/	V H P
A	1556	Quirris furth all in quite, / of / qualite as aungels;	P	N P N
A	1557	Maistirs, marchands, and Maire, / mynystris and othire,	/	N C H

A	1558 Worthi wedous and wenchis, / and / wynes of the cite;	C	N P D N
A	1559 Be ilka barne in the burgh, / as / blaȝt ere thaire wedis	C	E be D N
A	1560 As any snyppand snawe, / that in the / snape liȝtis.	that P D	N N
A	1561 Thar passis the procession, / a / piple be-forne,	D	N P
A	1562 Of childire all in chalk quyte, / chosen out a hundreth,	/	E P D N
A	1563 With bellis and with baners, / and / blasand torchis,	C	G N
A	1564 Instrumentis and ymagis, / with-in of the Mynstire;	/	P P D N
A	1565 Sum with sensours and so[m], / with / siluery cheynes,	P	A N
A	1566 Quare-of the reke aromatike, / rase to the welken;	/	V P D N
A	1567 Sum with, of the saynt-ware, / many / sere thingis,	D	A N
A	1568 With tablis and topoures, / and / tretice of the lawe;	C	N P D N
A	1569 Sum bolstirs of burnet, / en-brouden with perill,	/	E P N
A	1570 Bare before the bischop, / his / buke on to lig;	D	N Z to V
A	1571 Sum candilstickis of clere gold, / and of / clene siluer,	P D	A N
A	1572 With releckis full rially, / the / richest on the auutere.	D	N(A) P D N
A	1573 Thus seyis all the semle, / the / cite with-oute,	D	N P
A	1574 Vn-to a stonen stede, / streȝt on the temple,	/	A P D N
A	1575 Scopulus, by sum skill, / the / scripture it callis,	D	N H V
A	1576 And thare the come of the kynge, / this / couent abidis.	D	N V
A	1577 Sone Alexander with ane ost, / of many / athille dukis,	P D	A N
A	1578 Come prekand toward the place, / with / princes and erlis,	P	N C N
A	1579 Sees slike a multitude of men, / in / milke-quite clathis,	P	A N
A	1580 And ilk seg in a soyte, / at / selly him thinkis.	that	A H V
A	1581 Than fyndis he in this othire flote, / fanons and stolis,	/	N C N
A	1582 Practisirs and prematis, / and / prestis of the lawe,	C	N P D N
A	1583 Of dialiticus and decre, / doctours of aythir,	/	N P Z
A	1584 Bathe chambirlayn and chaplayne, / in / chalke-quite wedis.	P	A N
A	1585 And as he waytis in a wra, / than was he / ware sone	than be H	A Z
A	1586 Of the maister of that meneyhe, / in-myddis the puple,	/	P D N
A	1587 That was the bald bischop, / a-bofe alle th[e] iewis,	/	P D D N
A	1588 Was grathid in a garment, / of / gold and of pu[r]pree.	P	N C P N
A	1589 And than he heues vp his eȝe, / be-haldis on his myter,	/	V P D N
A	1590 Be-fore he saȝe of fyne gold, / forgid a plate,	/	V D N
A	1591 Thar-in grauen the grettest, / of all / gods names,	P D	N N
A	1592 This title, Tetragramaton, / for so the / text tellis.	C Z D	N V
A	1593 With that comandis the kyng, / his / knyȝtis ouire ilkane,	D	N P H
A	1594 Bathe beron and bachelere, / and / bald men of armes,	C	A N P N
A	1595 Na nere that place to aproche, / a / payn of thar lyuys,	D	N P D N
A	1596 Bot all to hald tham be-hynd, / heraud and othire.	/	N C H
A	1597 Than airis he furth all him ane, / to this / athill meneȝe,	P D	A N
A	1598 Bowis him doun of his blonke, / the / bischop be-forne,	D	N P
A	1599 And kneland on the cald erth, / he / knockis on his brest,	H	V P D N
A	1600 And reuerencez this haly name, / at he / seis wreten.	that H	V E
A	1601 Than the iewis of ierusalem, / Iustis and othire,	/	N C H
A	1602 Lordis and ladis, / be the / litill childere,	P D	A N
A	1603 Enclynes tham to the conquirour, / and him on / kneis gretis,	C H P	N V
A	1604 Kest vp a kene crie, / and / carpis thir wordis.	C	V D N
A	1605 "Ay moȝt he lefe, ay moȝt he lefe", / quod ilka / man twyse,	V D	N Z
A	1606 "Alexander, the athill aire, / vndire the heuyn,	/	P D N
A	1607 Ay moȝt he lefe, ay moȝt he leue, / the / lege Emperoure,	D	A N
A	1608 The wildire of all the werde, / and / worthist on erthe,	C	A P N
A	1609 Ay moȝt he lef, ay moȝt he leue", / quod / loude all at anys,	V	Z Z Z
A	1610 "Ouircomere clene of ilka coste, / and / ouircomyn neuir,	C	E Z
A	1611 The gretest and the gloriosest, / that euir / god formed,	that Z	N V
A	1612 Erle or Emperoure, / and any / erdly prince."	C D	A N
A	1613 Thare was comen with him kyngis, / as the / clause tellis,	C D	N V
A	1614 Seneiours out of Sireland, / was to / him-selfe ȝolden,	be P	H self E
A	1615 And thai meruailed tham mekill, / as the / buke tellis,	C D	N V
A	1616 When thai it herd so be-heryd, / and / held it in wondire.	C	V H P N
A	1617 Than Permeon, a proude kniȝt, / a / prince of thai oste,	C	N P D N
A	1618 Aires to sir Alexander, / and / askis at him swythe,	C	V P H Z
A	1619 Syn him adoured all men, / eldire and ȝongir,	/	A C A
A	1620 Qui he obeschid so lawe and bende, / the / bischop of iewis?	D	N P N
A	1621 "Nay," quad the comly kynge, / and the / knyȝt swaris,	C D	N V
A	1622 "Nouthire haylsid I him, ne / hildid him nouthire,	H H not	V H Z
A	1623 Bot it was gode at I grete, / the / gouernoure of all,	D	N P H
A	1624 Of quam in the abite and the armes, / he was / all clethid.	H be	Z E
A	1625 For in the marche of Messedone, / me / mynes on a tyme,	H	V P D N
A	1626 That slike a segg in my slepe, / me / sodanly aperid,	H	Z V
A	1627 Euyn in slike a similitude, / and this / same wedis,	C D	A N
A	1628 For all the werd as this wee, / wendis now atired.	/	V Z E

A	1629	And then I mused in my mynde, / how at I / my3t wyn	Q that H	X V
A	1630	Anothire anell of the erth, / that / Aysy we call it,	that	N H V H
A	1631	And me thret to be thra, / and for na / thing turne,	C P D	N V
A	1632	Bot tire me titely tharto, / and / tristly to wende.	C	Z to V
A	1633	And syne sa3e I na segg, / that / sa was arayd;	that	Z be E
A	1634	And sekirly yone semys, / the / same to se to within,	D	N(A) to V P P
A	1635	The same gode at I in my slepe, / sa3e in my days;	/	V P D N
A	1636	And now I hope me, thur3e the helpe, / of the / haly fadire,	P D	A N
A	1637	Of quam the hered haly name, / is 3ondire on / hi3e wreten,	be P Z	Z E
A	1638	To do with Darius or I dyi, / how so me / dere thinke,	Q Z H	A V
A	1639	And the pride of all the Persens, / purely distroy.	/	Z V
A	1640	And 3it I sothely suppose, / quat so my / sale hopis,	Q Z D	N V
A	1641	That sall fall apon fold, / slik / fyaunce I haue	D	N H V
A	1642	In the grace of grete god, / at / gyes all the sternes,	that	V Z D N
A	1643	That it sall be in my will, / and on na / way faile."	C P D	N V
A	1644	Now tas the bischop the berne, / and to the / bur3e wendis,	C P D	N V
A	1645	With sange and solempnite, / him to the / cite ledis,	H P D	N V
A	1646	He was resayued, as I rede, / with / reuerence and Ioye,	P	N C N
A	1647	As he ware duke of ilk douth, / and / dreuyn doun fra heuen.	C	E Z P N
A	1648	Than gas he furth with his gingis, / to / godis awen temple,	P	N A N
A	1649	That of sir Salamon the sage, / sett was and foundid,	/	E be C E
A	1650	And thare he lythis of thare lare, / as the / law wald;	C D	N X
A	1651	He offird in that oratori, / and / honourd oure lorde.	C	V D N
A	1652	And Iaudas of ierusalem, / and all the / iewis eftir	C D D	N P
A	1653	Bringis out a brade buke, / and to the / berne reches,	C P D	N V
A	1654	Was plant full of prophasys, / playnely all ouire,	/	Z Z Z
A	1655	Of the doctrine of Daniell, / and of his / dere sawis.	C P D	A N
A	1656	The lord lokis on the lyne, / and on a / lefe fyndis	C P D	N V
A	1657	How the gomes out of grece, / suld with thaire / grete mi3tis	X P D	A N
A	1658	The pupill out of Persye, / purely distroy;	/	Z V
A	1659	And that he hopis sall be he, / and / hertly he ioyes.	C	Z H V
A	1660	Than partis he to tha prelatis, / many / proude giftis,	D	A N
A	1661	Was nane sa pore in that place, / bot he his / purse fillis,	C H D	N V
A	1662	Geues tham garsons of gold, / and of / gud stanes,	C P	A N
A	1663	Rife riches / eno3e, / robies and perles,	Z	N C N
A	1664	Besands to the bischop, / he / bed out of nounbre,	H	V P P N
A	1665	Reches him of rede gold, / ransons many,	/	N A
A	1666	Tas him to his tresory, / talent him to shewe,	/	N H to V
A	1667	Bad him wale quat he wald, / and / wild him the tothir.	C	V H D H
A	1668	3it bedis he him, the bald kyng, / as the / buke tellis:	C D	N V
A	1669	"Sire, quat thou will in this werd, / to / wild and to haue,	to	V C to V
A	1670	No3t bot aske it at Alexander, / quat thou will / apon reson,	Q H X	P N
A	1671	And I sall grant, or I ga, / with a / gud will."	P D	A N
A	1672	Than bowis doun the bischop, / and him a / bone askis,	C H D	N V
A	1673	"Sire, this I depely disire, / durst I it neuyn,	/	V H H V
A	1674	That it be leuefull vs oure lare, / and oure / law vse,	C D	N V
A	1675	As oure fadirs has folowid, / forwith this tyme;	/	P D N
A	1676	As 3oure grete gudnes, / at 3e / grant wald	that H	V X
A	1677	To lat vs sitt be safe, / bot for this / seuyn wyntir,	P P D	A N
A	1678	But tribute or trouag, / quils the / terme lastis,	C D	N V
A	1679	Than were we halden all the hepe, / to / hi3e the for euir.	to	V H Z
A	1680	And 3it I will, be 3oure leue, / a / worde and na mare,	D	N C Z
A	1681	That the men of Medi, / man, be 3oure leue,	/	N P D N
A	1682	Lang all in oure lawe, / lely to-gedire,	/	Z Z
A	1683	And thai of Babilon bathe, / and / bede I na nothire."	C	V H Z
A	1684	Quod Alexander belyue, / "all this I graunt,	/	Z H H V
A	1685	And els any othire thing, / aske and be serued."	/	V C be E
A	1686	"Nay, now na mare," quod the man, / and / mekly him thankid,	C	Z H V
A	1687	"Bot ay thi lordschip and thi loue, / quils my / lyfe dures."	C D	N V
A	1688	Now kastis this conquirour, / to / caire fra the cite,	to	V P D N
A	1689	And mas to bide in the bur3e, / a / berne of his awyn,	D	N P D N(A)
A	1690	A messagere to myn, / on quat / men of him said,	P Q	N P H V
A	1691	Ane Ardromacius, a gome, / as the / buke tellis.	C D	N V
A	1692	Than bowis to the bischop, / his / benyson to fang,	D	N to V
A	1693	Takis lufly his leue, / and / lendis on forthere.	C	V Z Z
A	1694	To Sere cites thar be-syde, / he / so3t with his hostis,	H	V P D N
A	1695	And thai frendly and faire, / frely resayued him.	/	Z V H
A	1696	Than of the Siriens summe, / in the / same tyme	P D	A N
A	1697	Folow fra the fell kyng, / as / fals men suld,	C	A N X
A	1698	Did tham to sir Darius, / and / depely tham playnt,	C	Z H V
A	1699	Quat erroure of this Emperoure, / and / euill thai suffrid.	C	N H V

A	1700	And he tham faire vndir-fong, / and / fraynes tham ȝerne,	C	V H Z
A	1701	Askis tham of sir Alexander, / all at the cuthe,	/	H that H X
A	1702	Bathe of his statoure and his strenth, / if he ware / store ben,	C H be	A E
A	1703	His qualite, his quantite, / he / quirys all-to-gedire;	H	V Z
A	1704	And thai in parchement him payntid, / his / person him shewid,	D	N H V
A	1705	Ane amlaȝe, ane asaleny, / ane / ape of all othire,	D	N P D H
A	1706	A wirling, a wayryngle, / a / wawil-eȝid shrewe,	D	E N
A	1707	The cait[if]este creatour, / that / cried was euire.	that	E be Z
A	1708	And than, as he lenes, / and / lokis on his fourme,	C	V P D N
A	1709	His litillaike and his licknes, / he / laythly dispiced,	H	Z V
A	1710	And thre thingis of his thede, / he / thoȝt him sa feble,	H	V H Z A
A	1711	He dressis to him in dedeyne, / and in / dispite sendis:	C P	N V
A	1712	First a ball, says the buke, / the / barne with to play,	D	N P to V
A	1713	A herne-pan es of a berne, / of / brend gold yeuen,	P	E N E
A	1714	For hottre and for hething, / a / Hatt made of twyggis;	D	N E P N
A	1715	Sayd that was benere him to bere, / than a / briȝt helme.	C D	A N
A	1716	Slike presandis out of Persy, / he to the / prince sendis,	H P D	N V
A	1717	His brefe with a brade sele, / and / biddis hum ga swythe.	C	V H V Z
A	1718	And qua sa will has to wete, / howe it / worthis eftir,	Q H	V Z
A	1719	Now sall I neuen vs here next, / the / note of his lettir.	D	N P D N
A	1720	"Sire dere Darius on dese, / the / digne Emperoure,		A N
A	1721	The kyng without comparrison, / of / kyngis all othire,	P	N A A
A	1722	Of all lordis the lord, / that / leues in erthe,	that	V P N
A	1723	Predicessour of princes, / and / peree to the sonn,	C	A P D N
A	1724	The souerayne sire of my soyle, / that / sittis in my trone,	that	V P D N
A	1725	In fang with my faire godis, / that I / affie maste,	that H	V Z
A	1726	To Alexander, that of all, / so / augrily him letes,	Z	Z H V
A	1727	Oure subiet and oure seruand, / thus we / oure-selfe write.	C H	H self V
A	1728	For it is wayued vs to wete, / that / wickidly thou haues,	that	Z H V
A	1729	Thurȝe enmyte and enuy, / elacion of pride,	/	N P N
A	1730	Be vanyte and vayne glori, / that in thi / wayns kindlis,	that P D	N V
A	1731	Puruayd the pletours, / oure / partis to ride.	D	N to V
A	1732	For thou has samed, as men he sais, / a / selly nounbre	D	A N
A	1733	Of wrichis and wirlingis, / out of the / west endis,	P P D	N N
A	1734	Of laddis and of losengers, / and of / litill theuys,	C P	A N
A	1735	Slike sary soroȝis as thi-selfe, / to / seke vs agaynes,	to	V H P
A	1736	And wenes to wild all thi will, / and that / worthis ful late,	C that	V Z Z
A	1737	The prouynce and principalte, / of / Persye la graunt.	P	N D N(A)
A	1738	For thou ert fere al to faynt, / oure / force to ministere;	D	N to V
A	1739	Thof thou had gedird all the gomes, / that euire / god fourmed,	that Z	N V
A	1740	So, man, riued is oure rewme, / that thou may / reȝt lycken	that H X	Z V
A	1741	The store strenthe of oure stoure, / to / sternes of the heuen.	P	N P D N
A	1742	And slike a nekard as thi-selfe, / a / noȝt of all othire,	D	N P D H
A	1743	Is bot a madding to mell, / with / mare than him-seluen.	P	A C H self
A	1744	Forthi is bettir vnbynd, / and of the / brathe leue,	C P D	N V
A	1745	And feyne all with fairnes, / and / fayne at thou may.	C	V Z H X
A	1746	For mare menseke is a man, / to / meke him be tyme,	to	V N P N
A	1747	Than eftir made to be meke, / malegreue his chekis.	/	P D N
A	1748	For all the gracious godis, / and / gudnes on erthe,	C	N P N
A	1749	That sanys sete and soile, / and / sustaynes the erth,	C	V D N
A	1750	Prayses ay the Persyns, / passing all othire,	/	G D H
A	1751	And for the oddiste of ilka ost, / honoures oure name.	/	V D N
A	1752	And slike a dwinyng, a dwaȝe, / and a / dwerȝe as thi-selfe,	C D	N P H self
A	1753	A grub, a grege out of grace, / ane / erd-growyn sorowe,	D	N E N
A	1754	Will couet ȝit as a king, / with / caytefes to lyte,	P	N Z A
A	1755	To couir at combrid all the kyngis, / vndire the / cape of heuen!	P D	N P N
A	1756	Riȝt as a flaw of fell snawe, / ware / fallyn of a ryft,	be	E P D N
A	1757	Of a wysti wonn waghe, / with the / wynd blawen,	P D	N E
A	1758	So with a flote of Fresons, / folowand thi helis,	/	G D N
A	1759	Thou sekis fraward Sichim, / thi-selfe wrothir-haile,	/	H self N N
A	1760	And leuys as a lorell, / thus oure / lande to entire,	C D	N to V
A	1761	And maa thi lepis and thi laikis, / and quat the / liste ellis,	C Q H	V Z
A	1762	As ratons or ruȝe myse, / in a / rowme chambre,	P D	A N
A	1763	Aboute in beddis or in bernys, / thare / baddis ere nane.	Q	N be H
A	1764	Bot I haue wilily waited, / thi / wiles and thi castis,	D	N C D N
A	1765	And quen thou hopis all-thir hiest, / to / haue all thar will,	to	V D D N
A	1766	I sall the sett on a saute, / and / sla the [with] my handis.	C	V H P D N
A	1767	For-thi for pompe or for pride, / thi / purpose a-vise,	D	N V
A	1768	Turne thee, trechoure, be-time, / that thou na / treson haue,	that H D	N V
A	1769	And drawe a-gayn to thi den, / vndire thi / dam wyngis.	P D	N N
A	1770	Se quat I send to the, son, / thi-selfe with to laike,	/	H self P to V

The Wars of Alexander

A	1771	A hatt and a hand-ball, / and a / herne-panne;	C D	N N
A	1772	Slike presandis to play / with, as / pertines to babbis.	P C	V P N
A	1773	For ai a child mot him chese, / to / childire geris;	P	N N
A	1774	For mestire and miserie, / vnneth / may thou forthe	Z	X H V
A	1775	Thine awen caitefe cors, / to / clethe and to fede,	to	V C to V
A	1776	And supposis as a sott, / to / sese oure landis,	to	V D N
A	1777	And outhire darius to drepe, / or / dryfe fra his kythis!	C	V P D N
A	1778	Bot by the grace and the gude, / that / god gaue my fadire,	that	N V D N
A	1779	So riued is the rede gold, / oure / regions with-in,	D	N P
A	1780	That qua sa had it on a hepe, / haly to-gedire,	/	Z Z
A	1781	It wald vs let, as I leue, / the / liȝt of the son!	D	N P D N
A	1782	For-thi bid I the badrich, / on / bathe twa thine eȝen,	P	Z D D N
A	1783	And on the plegg and the payn, / and / perill as folowis,	C	N C V
A	1784	All thi vanyte to voide, / and thi / vayne pride,	C D	A N
A	1785	And mew agayn to Messedone, / or any / mare fall.	C Z	Z V
A	1786	For be the saule of my sire, / bot if thou / sone turne,	C C H	Z V
A	1787	We sall the send sike a soume, / of / segis en-armed,	P	N E
A	1788	Noȝt as Philips fant, / salle / fare with thi-selfe,	X	V P H self
A	1789	Bot as a prince of proued theues, / pyne the to dede."	/	V H P N
A	1790	Als sone as his sandismen, / to this / sire come,	P D	N V
A	1791	Thai present him the playntis, / the / pistill him rechis,	D	N H V
A	1792	And Alexander belyue, / be-fore/ all his princes,	P	Z D N
A	1793	To all his ost euyn / on, he / openly declaris.	Z H	Z V
A	1794	And quen his kniȝtis of this clause, / the / carpe vndirstode,	D	N V
A	1795	Then ware thai frekly a-frayd, / of the / fell saȝes;	P D	N(A) V
A	1796	And as sone as with him-selfe saȝe, / his / seggis amoued,	D	N V
A	1797	In bilding of his bachelers, / he / breuys thire wordis:	H	V D N
A	1798	"Quat now? my worthi werriouris, / sa / wiȝt and sa noble,	Z	A C Z A
A	1799	Mi bernes and my baratours, / the / best vndire heuen;	D	A P N
A	1800	Lettis neuire it broȝt be on brade, / for / vpbraide of schame,	P	N P N
A	1801	3e doute for the indityngs, / of / Darius pistils.	P	N N
A	1802	I sett ȝowe ane ensample, / ȝe / se it all daye,	H	V H Z
A	1803	In thorps and in many thede, / thar ȝe / thurȝe ride,	Q H	Z V
A	1804	At ilka cote a kene curre, / of the / chache wald;	C H H	V X
A	1805	Bot as bremely as he baies, / he / bitis neuir the fastir.	H	V Z D Z
A	1806	Bot in sum, wite wele, / that / sothe is the lettir,	that	A be D N
A	1807	Thare as he tellis quyche a tunne, / of / tresoure he hauys.	P	N H V
A	1808	For-thi vs buse to be bigg, / and / bataill him ȝeld,	C	N H V
A	1809	The grete garisons of gold, / sall / gedire vp oure hertis."	X	V Z D N
A	1810	With that comands the kyng, / his / knyȝtis be-lyue,	D	N Z
A	1811	The donesmen that fra Darius come, / with the / derfe lettir,	P D	A N
A	1812	That thai suld titly tham take, / and by the / toȝe throtis,	C P D	A N
A	1813	And for thaire souerayne sake, / tham / send to the galawis.	H	V P D N
A	1814	Than was tha messangers a-maied, / as / mervale ware ellis,	C	N be Z
A	1815	With kene carefull crie, / this / conquirour thai said:	D	N H V
A	1816	"Allas! quat lake lyse / in vs / lord, if it be ȝoure will,	P H	N C H be D N
A	1817	Thus causeles for oure kynge, / encumbird to worthe?"	/	E to V
A	1818	"The saȝes of ȝour souerayn" , / said the kynge then,	/	V D N Z
A	1819	"Nedis me to slike notis, / as I had / neuer etlid,	C H have	Z E
A	1820	That has ȝow sent to my-selfe, / noȝt / sa as him aȝe;	not	Z C H X
A	1821	Loo, 'litill thefe' in ilka lyne, / his / lettir me callis.	D	N H V
A	1822	'3a,' quod thai, "comly kyng" , / and on / knes fallis,	C P	N V
A	1823	"Thase ditis endited / to ȝowe, sir / Darius him-seluyn,	P H D	N H self
A	1824	For he knew noȝt of ȝour kniȝthede, / ne of ȝour / kid strenth;	not P D	E N
A	1825	Ne wist noȝt of ȝour worthenes, / and / wrate all the baldire.	C	V Z D Z
A	1826	Bot wald ȝe grant vs to gaa, / and / gefe vs ȝour lefe,	C	V H D N
A	1827	Then suld we bremely ȝour bill, / to the / berne shewe."	P D	N A
A	1828	Then lete the lord tham allane, / and / went till his fest,	C	V P D N
A	1829	Takis tham with him to his tent, / and tham at / ese makis.	C H P	N V
A	1830	Sone as thai in his sale, / were / sett at the table,	be	E P D N
A	1831	"Sire Alexander, athill kyng" , / quod / all with a steuyn,	V	H P D N
A	1832	"Comands with vs to caire, / kniȝtis a thousand,	/	N D N
A	1833	And we sall surely oure sire, / the / send in thaire handis."	H	V P D N
A	1834	"3a, make we blis," quod the kyng, / "blithe mote ȝe worthe,	/	A X H V
A	1835	For as takynge of ȝour lord, / sall na / lede wynde.	X not	N V
A	1836	To Darius anothir day, / enditis he a pistill,	/	V H D N
A	1837	A crest clenly inclosid, / that / consayued this wordis.	that	V D N
A	1838	Alexander, the aire, / and / eldest childe bathe	C	A N Z
A	1839	Of kyng Philip the fers, / the / fendere of grece,	D	N P N
A	1840	And als of Olimpades, / that / honourable lady,	D	A N
A	1841	To the, Darius, on dese, / thus / dite I my lettir.	C	V H D N

A	1842	Thou prince of all the Persyns, / that / peres to the sonne,	that	V P H N
A	1843	The conqurirour of ilka cost, / callid of thi-selfe,	/	V P H self
A	1844	With all thi gracious godis, / graithid in thi trone,		V P D N
A	1845	All thus I send to ȝowe I my sawe, / vndir my / sele wreten.	P D	N E
A	1846	Sire, if we se with a suth, / surely me thinke,	/	Z H V
A	1847	Oure facultes, oure faire fees, / oure / fermes and our landis,	D	N C D N
A	1848	We may noȝt chalang tham ne clayme, / ne / call thaim oure awen,	not	V H D N(A)
A	1849	Bot all I deme it as det, / and to a / day borowid.	C P D	N V
A	1850	For sen we riden on the rime, / and on the / ringe seten	C P D	N V
A	1851	Of the qwele of Fortoun, the quene, / that / swiftly changis,	that	Z V
A	1852	Ofte pas we in pouert, / fra / plente of gudis,	P	N P N
A	1853	Fra mirthe in-to mournyng, / fra / mournyng in-to Ioye.	P	N P N
A	1854	For now vs wantis in a qwirre, / as the / quele turnes;	C D	N V
A	1855	Quen we suppose in oure sele, / to / sit althir heist,	to	V H A
A	1856	Than fondis furth dame Fortoun, / to the / flode-ȝatis,	P D	N N
A	1857	Draȝes vp the damme-borde, / and / drenchis vs euire.	C	V H Z
A	1858	For-thi a we that has wit, / thofe he / wele suffir,	C H	Z V
A	1859	So sadly in soueraynete, / he / set neuire his hope	H	V Z D N
A	1860	For pride of na pro[s]perite, / ne / prise at him folewis,	not	N P H V
A	1861	To olle ay on his vndireling, / for / ouer-laike a quyle.	P	N Z
A	1862	For any sele vndire son, / a / sott I him hald,	D	N H H V
A	1863	That ay has deyne and dispite, / at / dedis of litill,	P	N P N(A)
A	1864	Sen oft the hauenlest here, / is / houen to the sternes,	be	E P D N
A	1865	And he that graithist is of gudis, / gird all to poudire.	/	E Z P N
A	1866	For-thi a depe dishonoure, / ȝe / do to ȝoure name,	H	V P D N
A	1867	Ane emperoure that on erth, / is / euyn to ȝoure-selfe,	be	A P H self
A	1868	To me sa litill and sa lawe, / slike / lettirs to sende,	D	N to V
A	1869	And presand out of Persy, / bot for a / pure hethyng.	P P D	A N
A	1870	For thou enherestis all this erth, / and / euens to the son,	C	A P D N
A	1871	And callis the kyng of ilka kithe, / vndir the / cape of heuen,	P D	N P N
A	1872	And tharto sittis, as thou sais, / in / sege as ane Aungell,	P	N P D N
A	1873	To-gedire with thi grete gods, / and on a / gilt trone.	C P D	E N
A	1874	Bot syn gostid godesses and gods, / ere / graythid neuir to dye,	be	E Z to V
A	1875	Bot ai fall last furth elike, / on-lyue ouire mare,	/	A Z Z
A	1876	Thai naue no will, to my notis, / ne wilnyng to haue,	/	A N to V
A	1877	No dole ne no daliance, / of / dedely bernes.	P	A N
A	1878	Bot I knaw I am coruptible, / and / caire ȝow agaynes,	C	V H P
A	1879	Als with a dedly duke, / to / do my bataill;	to	V D N
A	1880	Bot thof thou the victor a-vaile, / na / vaunte sall arise,	D	N X V
A	1881	Ne lose, bot as a litill thefe, / ȝow / limpid to encumbre.	H	V to V
A	1882	Bot chance it me, that am a childe, / the / cheuer to worthe,	D	N(A) to V
A	1883	So that be geuyn me the gree, / grete glorie is myn awen.	/	A N be D N(A)
A	1884	For than sall spring vp the speche, / and / sprede out of mynd,	C	V P P N
A	1885	How I haue conquered a kyng, / the / kidest of the werd.	D	A P D N
A	1886	Bot a tale ȝe me tald, / I / trow be na faile,	H	V P D N
A	1887	Of the ryfenes of the rede gold, / ȝour / region with-in,	D	N P
A	1888	Quilke plente is in Persy, / of / perell and of ellis,	P	N C P H
A	1889	The somme of siluer and of siche, / and of / sere stanes,	C P	A N
A	1890	Thare-oure oure wittes has thou wele, / and oure / will sharpid,	C D	N E
A	1891	And blid with thi besands, / the / bataill to ȝeld;	D	N to V
A	1892	Made vs corageous and kene, / ȝoure / clere gold to wyn,	D	A N to V
A	1893	And put a-way oure pouert, / ȝe / plede vs to hald.	H	V H to V
A	1894	Bot as touchand the trufils, / that ȝe / to me sent,	that H	P H V
A	1895	The herne-pan, the hand-ball, / the / hatt made of twiggis,	D	N E P N
A	1896	Thare has thou prophesid apert, / and / playnely vs schewid,	C	Z H E
A	1897	And faire affirmed vs before, / that sall / fall eftir.	that X	V Z
A	1898	For by the ball, sir, I breue, / all the / brode werd,	D D	A N
A	1899	The erthe at to myne empire, / enterely bees ȝolden.	/	Z be E
A	1900	And be the hat, that is holewe, / be-for the / heued bowed,	P D	N V
A	1901	I constru that ilka kyng, / sall / clyne to my-selfe.	X	V P H self
A	1902	Than hope I by the hernepan, / that the / hede couirs,	that D	N V
A	1903	Ouir-comers to be callid, / and / ouire-comen neuire.	C	E Z
A	1904	Now thou, the grettest vndir god, / graithis me trouage,	/	V H N
A	1905	With all this dignites he ordane, / that I / diuined haue.	that H	E have
A	1906	This brefe bedis thaim him bere, / and / besands tham rechis;	C	N H V
A	1907	And eftir armes all his ost, / and / airis on eftir forthire.	C	V Z Z Z
A	1908	Sire Darius for the ditis, / nere / died he for angire,	Z	V H P N
A	1909	To twa of the derrest of his dukis, / ditis he this pistill:	/	V H D N
A	1910	"I, the corounnest kyng, / of / kyngis all othire,	P	N A A
A	1911	To the, sir primus, a prince, / of / Persye the grettest,	P	N D N(A)
A	1912	And als to ser Antagoyne, / myn awen / athill dukis,	D D	A N

A	1913	The soueraynest of my seniourie, / my / saroparis hatten,	D	N V
A	1914	Se here I send ȝow my seele, / with / salutis of ioye.	P	N P N
A	1915	Fra Alexander the kyng, / as / I am in-fourmed,	C	H be E
A	1916	Is entrid with oure enmys, / an / endles nounbre,	D	A N
A	1917	The Anglies of Asie, / and has tham / all stroyed,	C have H	Z E
A	1918	For-thi of life and o lym, / my / lege men I charge	D	N N H V
A	1919	To prestli ȝow apparaill, / and / pas tham agaynes,	C	V H P
A	1920	With all the hathils and the heris, / and the / hiȝe maistris	C D	A N
A	1921	That ȝe may semble in the sidis, / saudiours and othire.	/	N C H
A	1922	Then chese ȝow furth my chiftanes, / and me the / child take,	C H D	N V
A	1923	Laches me this losengere, / and / ledis me him hedire,	C	V H H Z
A	1924	That I may him skelp with a skorge, / and then of / skire porpure	C Z P	A N
A	1925	A side slauyn him sewe, / and / send him to his modire;	C	V H P D N
A	1926	For now he proches for pride, / and / propurly he wedis,	C	Z H V
A	1927	For-thi him bose to be bett, / as a / barne fallis.	C D	N V
A	1928	For it aȝe noȝt slik ane Asald, / nane / abletus to off werres,	D	N P P N
A	1929	Bot at the bowlis as a brode, / or with a / ball playe."	C P D	N V
A	1930	Thire princes, sone as the pistill, / was / put tham in hand,	be	E H P N
A	1931	Than part thai the proud sele, / the / printe thai adhoured,	D	N H V
A	1932	Vn-lappis liȝtly the lefe, / and the / line redes,	C D	N V
A	1933	And thus-gate agynward, / thai / graithid him anothire.	H	V H H
A	1934	"To the kiddest kyng to a-count, / of / kyngis all othire,	P	N A A
A	1935	Sire Dari, with the dere godis, / drised on thi trone,	/	E P D N
A	1936	Gouernoure of ilk a gome, / and / god all thi-selfe,	C	N Z H self
A	1937	Thi satrapairs, thi seniours, / with / seruage obseschen:	P	N V
A	1938	Sire, wetis it wele, ȝoure worthines, / and / wenys it na langire,	C	V H Z
A	1939	That this child, with his chiftans, / that ȝe / charge vs to take,	that H	V H to V
A	1940	Has reden all oure regions, / raymed oure landis,	/	E D N
A	1941	Departid all oure prouynce, / and / purely it wastid.	C	Z H V
A	1942	And we than lift vp a lite, / and / lent him a-gayne,	C	V H P
A	1943	Ferd furth with a flote, / and mett him in the / fyld metis;	C H P D	N V
A	1944	Bot sone we bed him the bake, / and / besely we shapid	C	Z H V
A	1945	Out of the handis vn-hewyn, / of oure / hatill fais.	P D	A N
A	1946	And now haly all the hepe, / at ȝe ȝoure / help callis,	that H D	N V
A	1947	Vn-to ȝoure mekill maieste, / we / mekely beseke,	H	Z V
A	1948	That vs ȝour lege and ȝoure lele men, / it / likid ȝow to forthire,	H	V H to V
A	1949	Or than oure wirschip at-wynde, / and / wastid be the regme."	C	E P D N
A	1950	As radly as the riche kyng, / had / red ouir this pistill,	have	E P D N
A	1951	Be that mevis in A Messangere, / and / maynly him tellis,	C	Z H V
A	1952	That Alexander was at hand, / and had his / ost loygid	C have D	N E
A	1953	A-pon the streme of Struma, / that / strekis thurȝe his landis.	that	V P D N
A	1954	Sire Darius for tha ditis, / was / depely a-greuyed,	be	Z E
A	1955	Callis him his consail, / a / clause he him enditis,	D	N N H V
A	1956	Mas a brefe at a braide, / and it in / brathe sendis,	C H P	N V
A	1957	To Alexander as be-lyue, / and / all thus him gretes.	C	H C H V
A	1958	"I, sir Dari, the deyne, / and / derfe Emperoure,	C	A N
A	1959	The kyng of kyngis I am callid, / and / conquirour bathe,	C	N Z
A	1960	Of all lordis the lord, / a-lose thurȝe the werd,	/	E P D N
A	1961	And ane of the soueraynest sires, / vndir the / vij sternes,	P D	A N
A	1962	To the, my seruand, I send, / and / suthely thou knawes,	C	Z H V
A	1963	And wete thou wele thurȝe all the werde, / is / wirschip oure name.	be	E D N
A	1964	For all the gracious gods, / at the / ground visitis,	P D	N V
A	1965	All ere done me to doute, / ducsses and othire,	/	N C H
A	1966	How burde the than be sa bald, / for / blod in thi heued,	P	N P D N
A	1967	To moue thus ouir the mountey[n]s, / and ouir the / many watirs	C P D	A N
A	1968	With slike a soumme ouir the see, / a / saute vs to ȝeld,	D	N H to V
A	1969	Or any maistrie to make, / my / maieste a-gayne?	D	N P
A	1970	For wella wide ware the wele, / wete thou na nothire,	/	V H Z
A	1971	Bathe thi glorie and thi grace, / thi / gladnes in erthe,	D	N P N
A	1972	Miȝt thou the marches of Messedoyne, / mayntene thi-selfe,	/	V H self
A	1973	And gouerne bot thine awen gronde, / agaynes oure will.	/	P D N
A	1974	For-thi ware bettir vnbynde, / or thou / bale suffire,	C H	N V
A	1975	Remowe agayne to thi rewme, / and / rew of thi werkis.	C	V P D N
A	1976	For certayne, nyf my seniourie, / ne I / my-selfe nouthire,	not H	H self Z
A	1977	All the werd myȝt a wedowe, / wele than be callid.	/	Z Z be E
A	1978	For-thi turne the be-time, / or ay / tene worthe,	C D	N V
A	1979	Or at the hate of my hert, / a-pon thi / hede kindill.	P D	N V
A	1980	Lend agayn to thi lande, / nowe quen thou / leue hauys,	Z C H	N V
A	1981	That I mete thi in my malicoly, / my / meth be to littill.	D	N be Z A
A	1982	For-thi to ken the to knaw, / my / kyndes here-eftir,	D	N Z
A	1983	Bath my grace and my glori, / and my / grete strenthe,	C D	A N

A	1984	Loo here a gloue full of graynes, / I / graythe the to take,	H		V H to V
A	1985	Of the chesses of a chesboll, / chosen for the nanys.	/		E P D N
A	1986	For may thou sowme me thire sedis, / surely thou trowe,			Z H V
A	1987	Thou miȝt a-count all oure kniȝtis, / and oure / kyd ostis;	C D		A N
A	1988	And thou truches thaim to tell, / then / tidis the na nothir,	C		V H Z
A	1989	Bot move a-gayn to Messedone, / and / meve the na forthire.	C		V H Z
A	1990	Fyne, fole, of thi fare, / and / fange to thi kythis;	C		V P D N
A	1991	Fot this sede I the send, / vnsowmyd bees neuire.	/		E N Z
A	1992	So ere we of all folke, / folke to be nombrid,	/		N to be E
A	1993	Or any wee to a-counte, / vndire the / clere sternys."	P D		A N
A	1994	Now aires furth his athill men, / to / Alexander wendis,	P		N V
A	1995	Vn-to the streme of struma, / streȝt with tha lettirs,	/		A P D N
A	1996	And he tham redis in a rese, / and / reches to the sedis,	C		V P D N
A	1997	Tastis tham vndire his tuthe, / and / talkis thir wordis:	C		V D N
A	1998	"Here I se", quod this sire, / "be thire / ilke cornes,	P D		A N
A	1999	That the pupill out of Persy, / ere / passandly many,	be		Z A
A	2000	Bot tham semes to be softe, / as thir / sedis prouys;	C D		N V
A	2001	For-thi how fele be all the flote, / it / forces bot littill."	H		V Z Z
A	2002	Be this was men of Messedone, / fra his / modire comen,	P D		N V
A	2003	And said that semely was seke, / and / semed to die;	C		V to V
A	2004	And he the waest of the werd, / wald / worth hire to visite,	X		V H to V
A	2005	Bot ȝit Dary, or he went, / he / diȝt thus a lettir.	H		V C D N

あとがき

　夫の留学に伴って住むことになったアメリカ中西部の町の州立大学大学院で学ぶ機会を得、修士と博士を修めることができた。約７年に亘って、言語学、文学、修辞学、文法等を学び、アメリカの研究者のフレンドリーだが厳しい指導や院生同士の切磋琢磨する緊張感等いいことも悪いことも様々に経験した。博士課程の最後に履修したのが、700番台の英詩韻律のコースで、学部基礎科目が100番台、大学院基礎科目が400番台であるから、700番台はコース数も少なく、博士課程の学生のみが履修を許される最後の挑戦であった。担当教授は「このコースはオリエンタルの君には難しすぎるのではないか」と危惧したが、博士論文を中英語の韻律とリズムで書きたいと考えていた私には、この分野の専門知識が必要だった。ドイツ語の響きに近い古英語から現代英語のリズムに至るには中英語期に起こった変化を知ることが不可欠であり、英語の音と響きの本質を究めたいという気持ちが博士論文の計画を練るにつれ募っていた。それを聞いた教授は、「これから何年生きるつもりなの？」と静かに尋ねられた。そのコースでは、音韻論、韻律理論、さまざまな時代、地域の詩の分析で予習をしエッセイやレポートを書き、24時間開いている図書館で夜が白むまで勉強した。授業ではアメリカ人院生が交わす活発な議論に参加し、彼らの言葉へのこだわりや批判的考え方に学んだ。また、母語だからといって、韻律や言葉のリズム、ましてそれが芸術的か陳腐か等がすぐに分かるのではないこと、韻律の理解には言語のレベルに加え意味や文法が絡んだ複雑な芸術的センスを要するこ

と、解釈や読み方に著しい個人差があることも見聞した。そのコースが終わる頃には皆が私の予習ノートを覗くようになり、教授も大変奨励下さって博士論文の主査にと願い出たところ、快諾下さった。

それ以来中英語頭韻詩を1行づつ読み進め分析データを蓄積し、国内外の学会で発表し、学術誌等に論文として発表して来た。何年かかっても成し遂げたいと思ったことが少しづつ形を成して来たが、中英語頭韻詩全体を多面的に総合的に分析して検索しやすいデータとして編集し、繰返し登場する同一あるいは酷似した連語の成り立ちが、韻律の枠組みの中でどのように機能しているかを解明するためには、1冊の本の紙幅では到底収まらない、ということも判明した。まず第一段階として基本部分を世に問うことにした。中英語頭韻詩全体のテンプレートを解明し、連語によって特に後半行にどのような繰返しの技巧が用いられているか、この後の amalgamation に心逸る。そうして得られた中英語頭韻詩全体の韻律ルールと連語タイプを基に、これまでの研究の集大成として、中英語頭韻詩について研究書をまとめることで、何十年もかかるだろうと教授に言われた問いに答えが出る。その時を待ち望みつつ、中英語頭韻詩との対峙は続く。

出版にあたり、南雲堂の原信雄氏に大変お世話になった。原氏のこぢんまりした scriptorium には特別な仕掛けはないように見えたが、どんな煩雑なことも細かいことも秀でたプロ職人のスタッフの支えで迅速精緻に進めて下さった。表紙には大英図書館の許可を得て本文に引用した The Blacksmiths の元の写本と同時代に描かれた鍛冶屋の絵を使うことができた。また国際基督教大学研究助成基金補助金が得られたことも幸いであった。深く感謝の意を表する。

英文学会のシンポジウムにお招き戴いて以来さまざまな学問の場でご一緒した敬愛する田島松二先生が編まれた『ことばの楽しみ―東西の文化を超えて―』に寄稿するという栄誉に浴したが、同じ南雲堂から出版できることは喜ばしく光栄なことであった。田島先生主催のシンポジウムは Oakden の中英語頭韻詩についての著作を読み直す、というテーマであったが、70年以上前に出版された研究書を日本人研究者が読み直し再解釈を試みる、という意義深いものであった。Oakden には到底及

ばないが、ここに示した中英語頭韻詩への取組みが数十年後にも、少数であっても中英語研究者に意味を持つことを願う。

2009年9月

大英図書館西洋写本閲覧室にて
著者

執筆者について

守屋靖代（もりや・やすよ）

国際基督教大学教養学部卒（教養学士1976）、同大学院（文学修士1978）、オハイオ州立シンシナティ大学大学院（MA in Linguistics 1986、PhD in English 1994）修了。現在、国際基督教大学教授（教養学部及び大学院で英語史、英語学担当）。1996-97年ノッティンガム大学客員研究員、2003-04年オックスフォード大学客員研究員。*Studies in Medieval English Language and Literature* (1996; 1999), *English Language Notes* (2000), *Poetica* (2000), *Neuphilologische Mitteilungen* (2000), *English Studies* (Routledge, 2004), *NOWELE* (2006) などに中英語頭韻詩韻律に関する英文研究論文。和文研究論文として、「中英語頭韻詩にみる繰り返しとリズム」（田島松二編『ことばの楽しみ—東西の文化を越えて』）南雲堂　2006。

中英語頭韻詩の繰返し技巧と連語　　　　　　　　［1G-74］

2010年3月31日　第1刷発行　　　　定価（本体6500円＋税）

著　　者　守屋靖代　Yasuyo Moriya
発行者　　南雲一範　Kazunori Nagumo
装幀者　　岡　孝治　Koji Oka
発行所　　株式会社　南雲堂
　　　　　〒162-0801　東京都新宿区山吹町361
　　　　　NAN'UN-DO Publishing Co.Ltd.
　　　　　361 Yamabuki-cho, shinjuku-ku, Tokyo162-0801, Japan
　　　　　振替口座　00160-0-46863

　　　　　［書店関係・営業部］☎03-3268-2384　FAX03-3260-5425
　　　　　［一般書・編集部］☎03-3268-2387　FAX03-3268-2650
　　　　　［学校関係・営業部］☎03-3268-2311　FAX03-3269-2486

製版所　　日本ハイコム株式会社
製本所　　長山製本所
コード　　ISBN978-4-523-30074-8 C3082

〈検印省略〉　　　　　　　　　　　　　　　　　　　　Printed in Japan

南雲堂 / 好評既刊書

ことばの楽しみ　東西の文化を越えて　田島松二編　A5判上製　8,400円

歴史の中の英語　小野茂　A5判上製　3,150円

辞書とアメリカ　英語辞典の200年　本吉侃　A5判上製　4,725円

わが国における英語学研究文献書誌 1900-1996　田島松二責任編集　A5判上製　35,000円

わが国の英語学100年　回顧と展望　田島松二　46判上製　2,500円

中世の心象　それぞれの「受難」　二村宏江　A5判上製　15,000円

フィロロジーの愉しみ　小野茂　46判上製　3,900円

言語・思考・実在　ウォーフ論文選集　B. L. ウォーフ／有馬道子訳　A5判上製　7,087円

日本語の意味 英語の意味　小島義郎　46判上製　1,942円

英語再入門　読む・書く・聞く・話す〈対談〉　柴田徹士・藤井治彦　46判上製　1,748円

＊定価は本体価格です